BUG BOYS

Adventures and Daydreams

Also by Laura Knetzger

Sea Urchin (Retrofit Comics)

Bug Boys series
Bug Boys
Bug Boys: Outside and Beyond

BUG BOYS

Adventures and Daydreams

By Laura Knetzger

RH GRAPHIC

NEW YORK

Bug Boys: Adventures and Daydreams was drawn and colored digitally in Photoshop.

This is a work of fiction. Names, characters, places, and incidents either are the product of the author's imagination or are used fictitiously. Any resemblance to actual persons, living or dead, events, or locales is entirely coincidental.

 Published in the United States by RH Graphic, an imprint of Random House Children's Books, a division of Penguin Random House LLC, New York

RH Graphic with the book design is a trademark of Penguin Random House LLC.

Visit us on the Web and sign up for our newsletter!
RHKidsGraphic.com • @RHKidsGraphic

Educators and librarians, for a variety of teaching tools, visit us at RHTeachersLibrarians.com

Library of Congress Cataloging-in-Publication Data is available upon request.
ISBN 978-0-593-30952-0 (hardcover) — ISBN 978-0-593-30953-7 (lib. bdg.)
ISBN 978-0-593-30954-4 (ebook)

Designed and lettered by Patrick Crotty

MANUFACTURED IN CHINA
10 9 8 7 6 5 4 3 2 1
First Edition

RH GRAPHIC
A comic on every bookshelf.

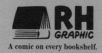

To Bob and Deb

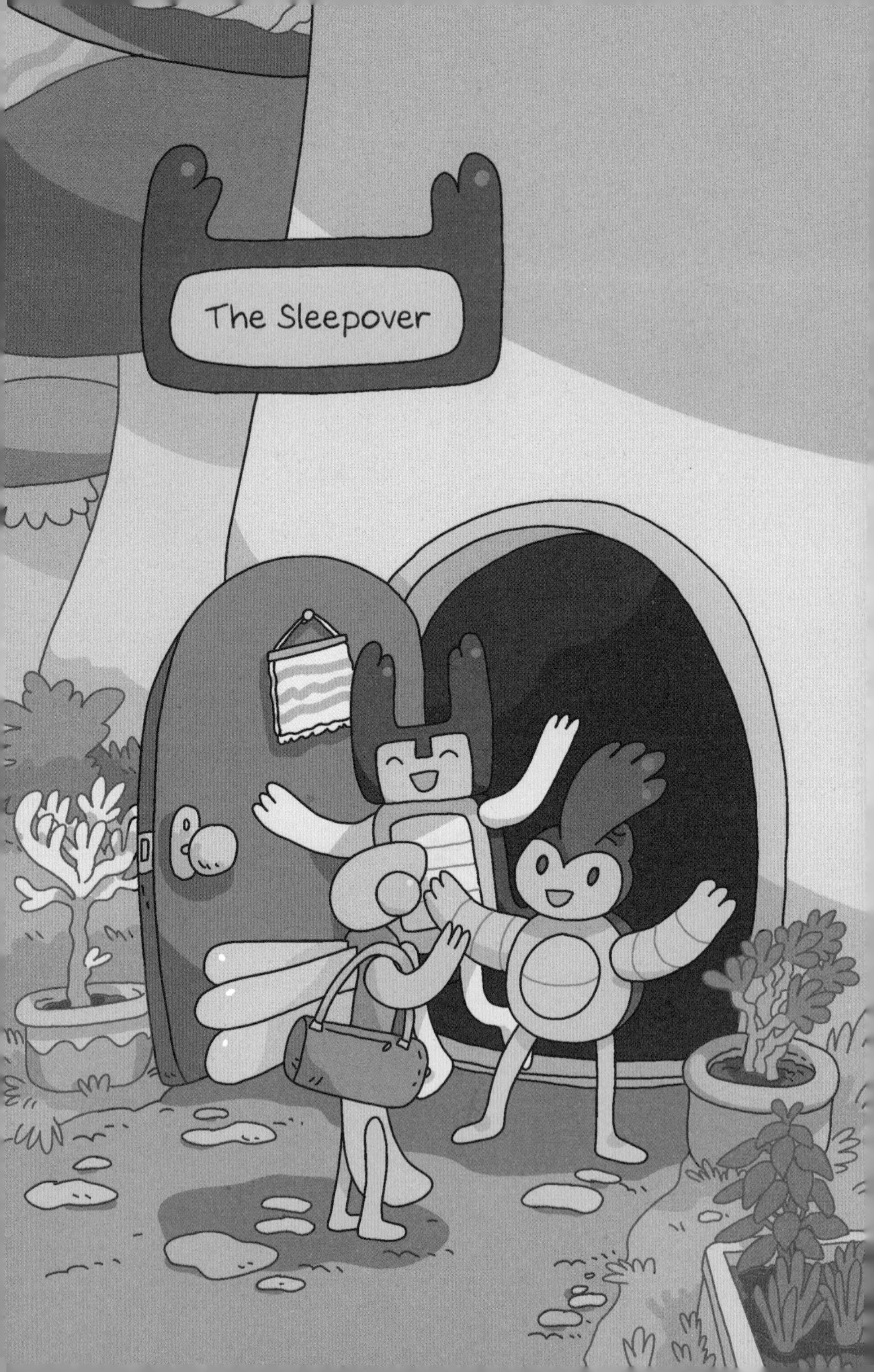
The Sleepover

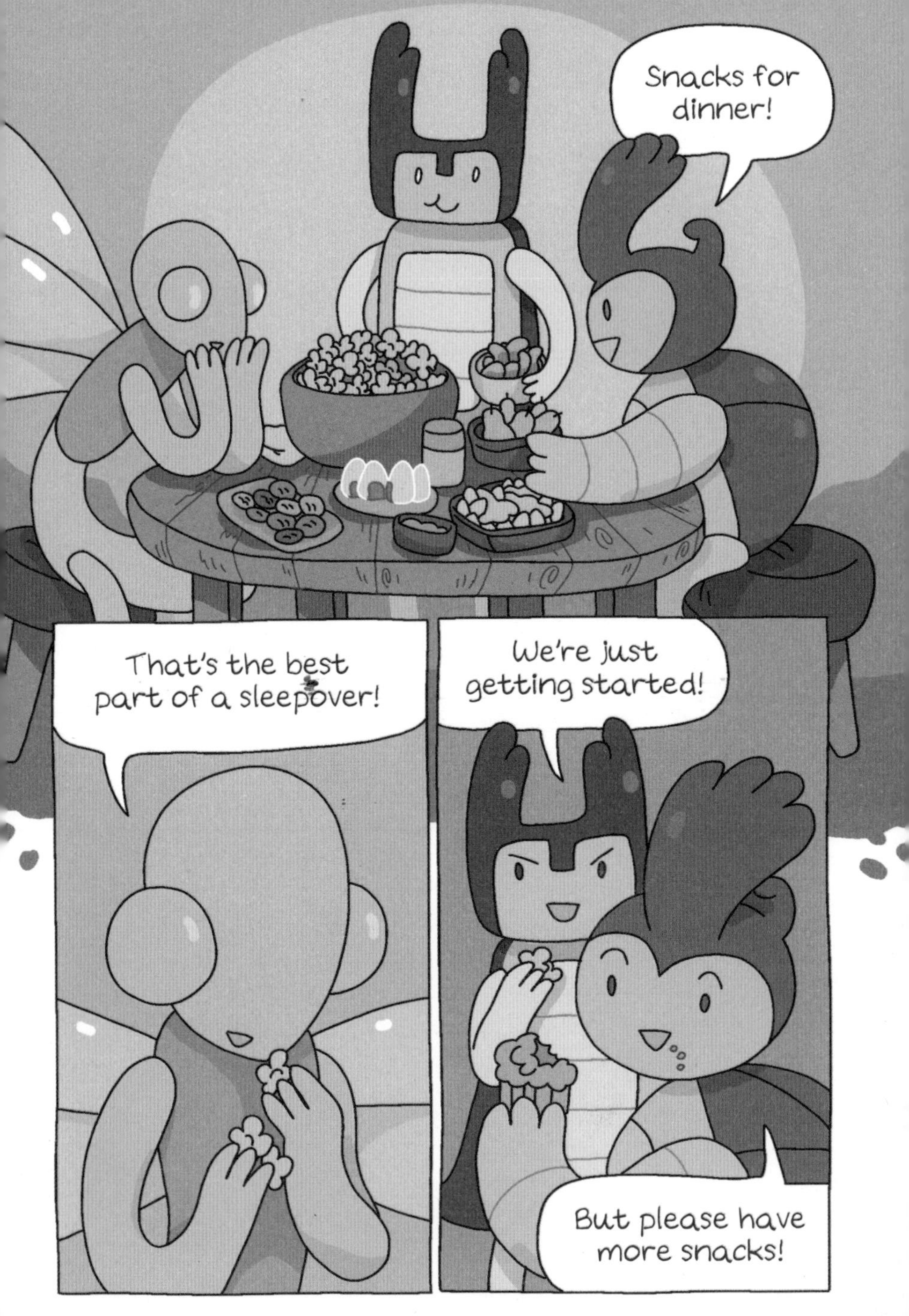
Snacks for dinner!
That's the best part of a sleepover!
We're just getting started!
But please have more snacks!

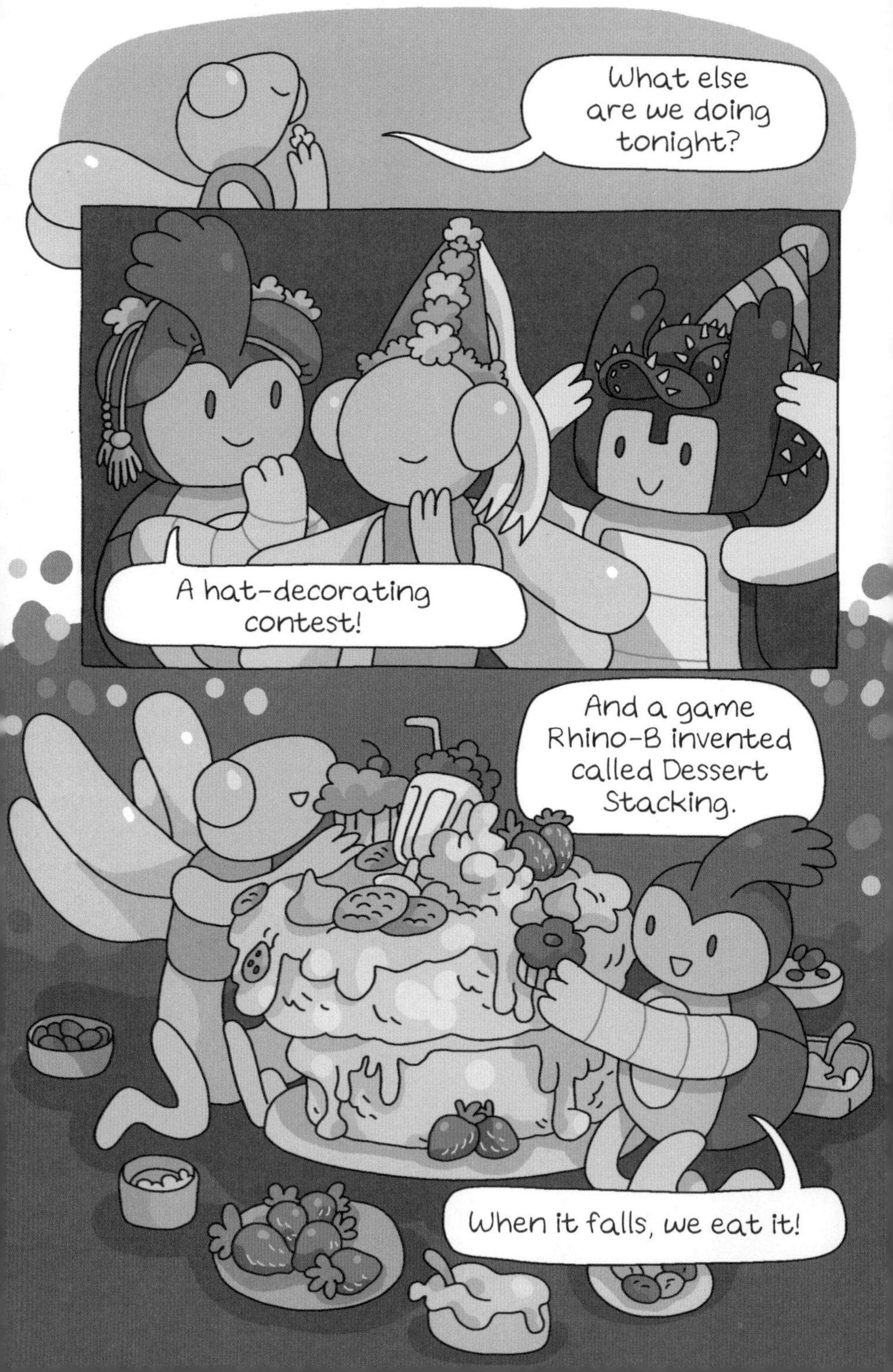

What else are we doing tonight?
A hat-decorating contest!
And a game Rhino-B invented called Dessert Stacking.
When it falls, we eat it!

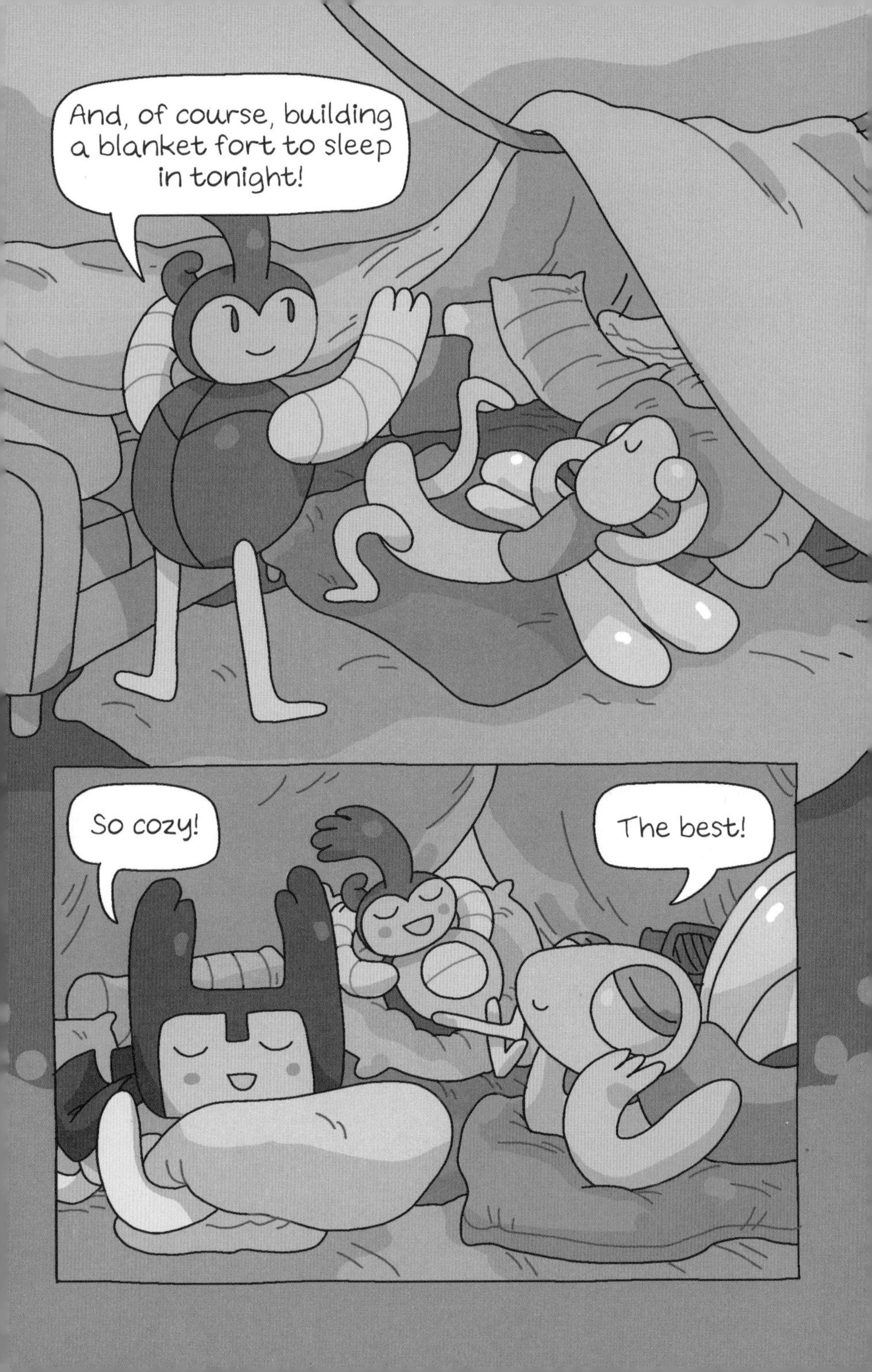
And, of course, building a blanket fort to sleep in tonight!
So cozy!
The best!

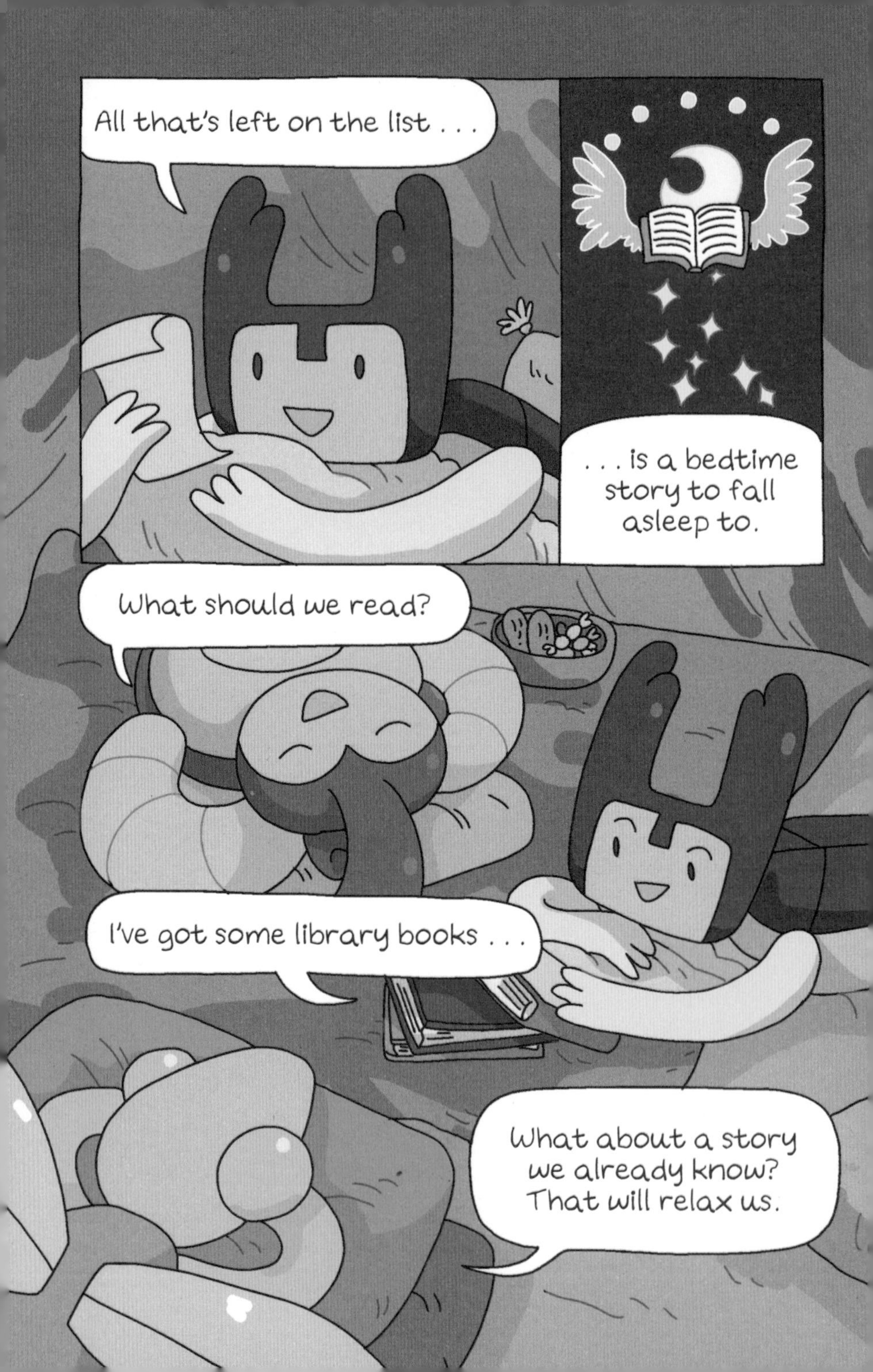
All that's left on the list . . .
. . . is a bedtime story to fall asleep to.
What should we read?
I've got some library books . . .
What about a story we already know? That will relax us.

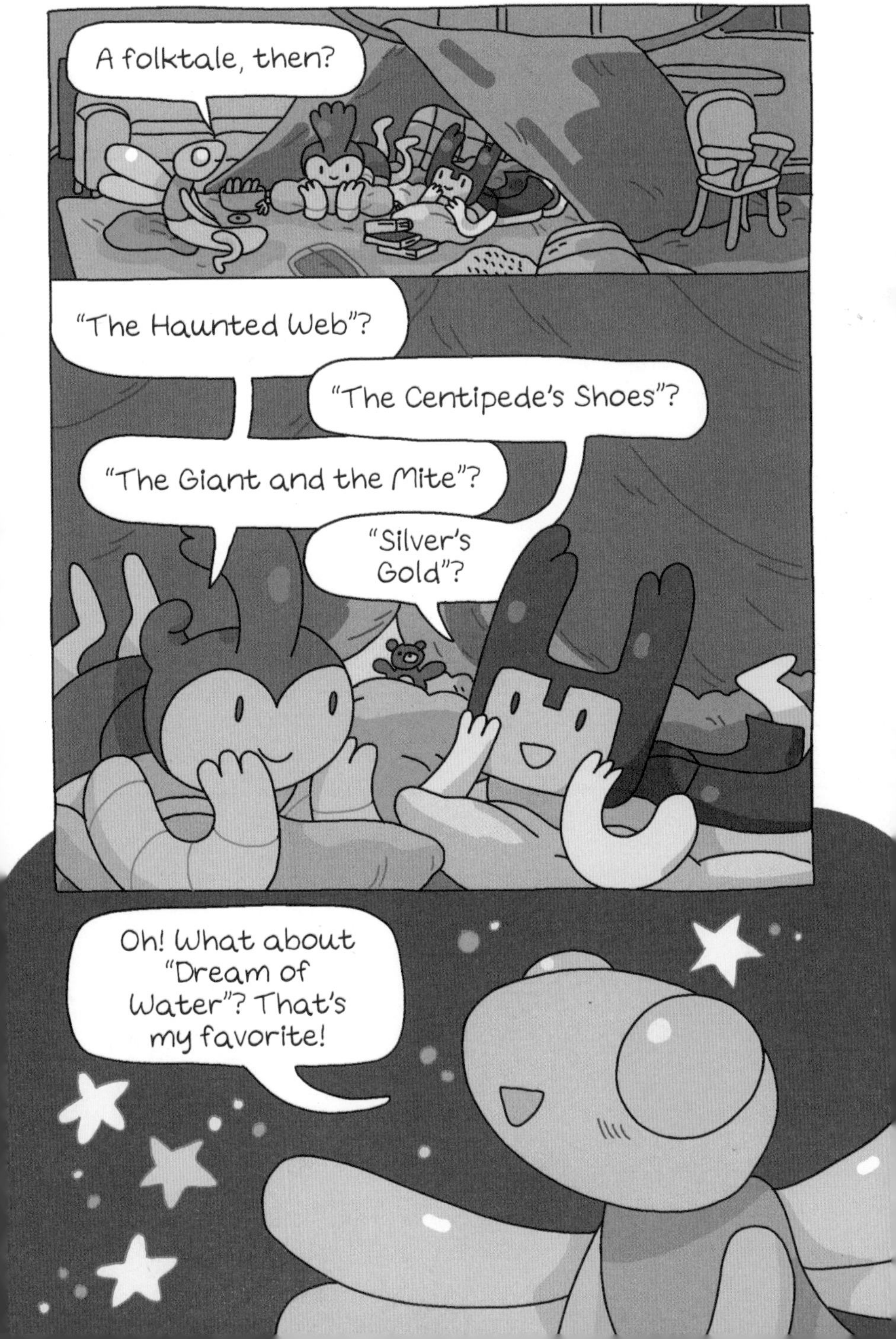
A folktale, then?
"The Haunted Web"?
"The Centipede's Shoes"?
"The Giant and the Mite"?
"Silver's Gold"?
Oh! What about "Dream of Water"? That's my favorite!

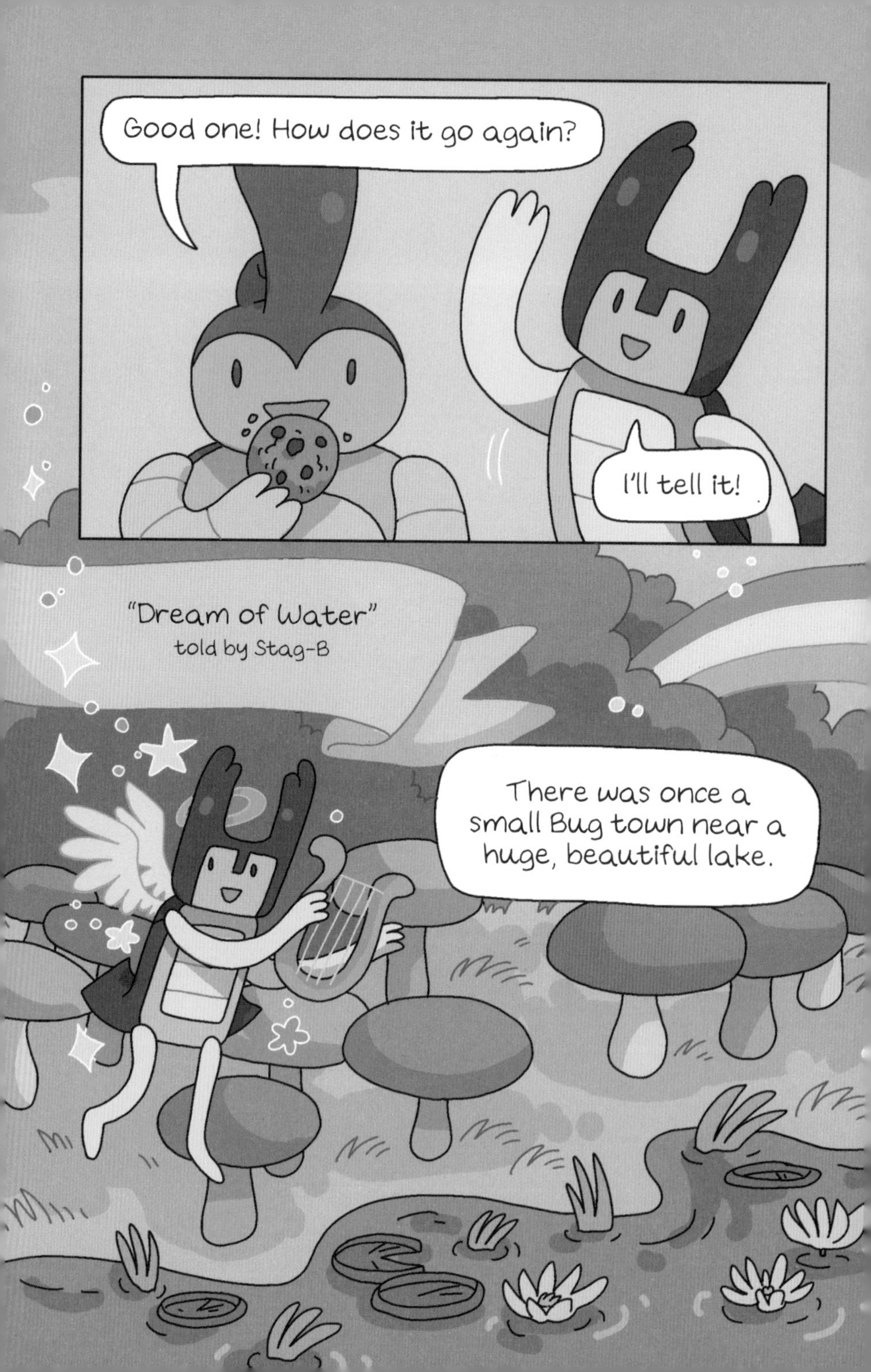
Good one! How does it go again?
I'll tell it!
"Dream of Water"
told by Stag-B
There was once a small Bug town near a huge, beautiful lake.

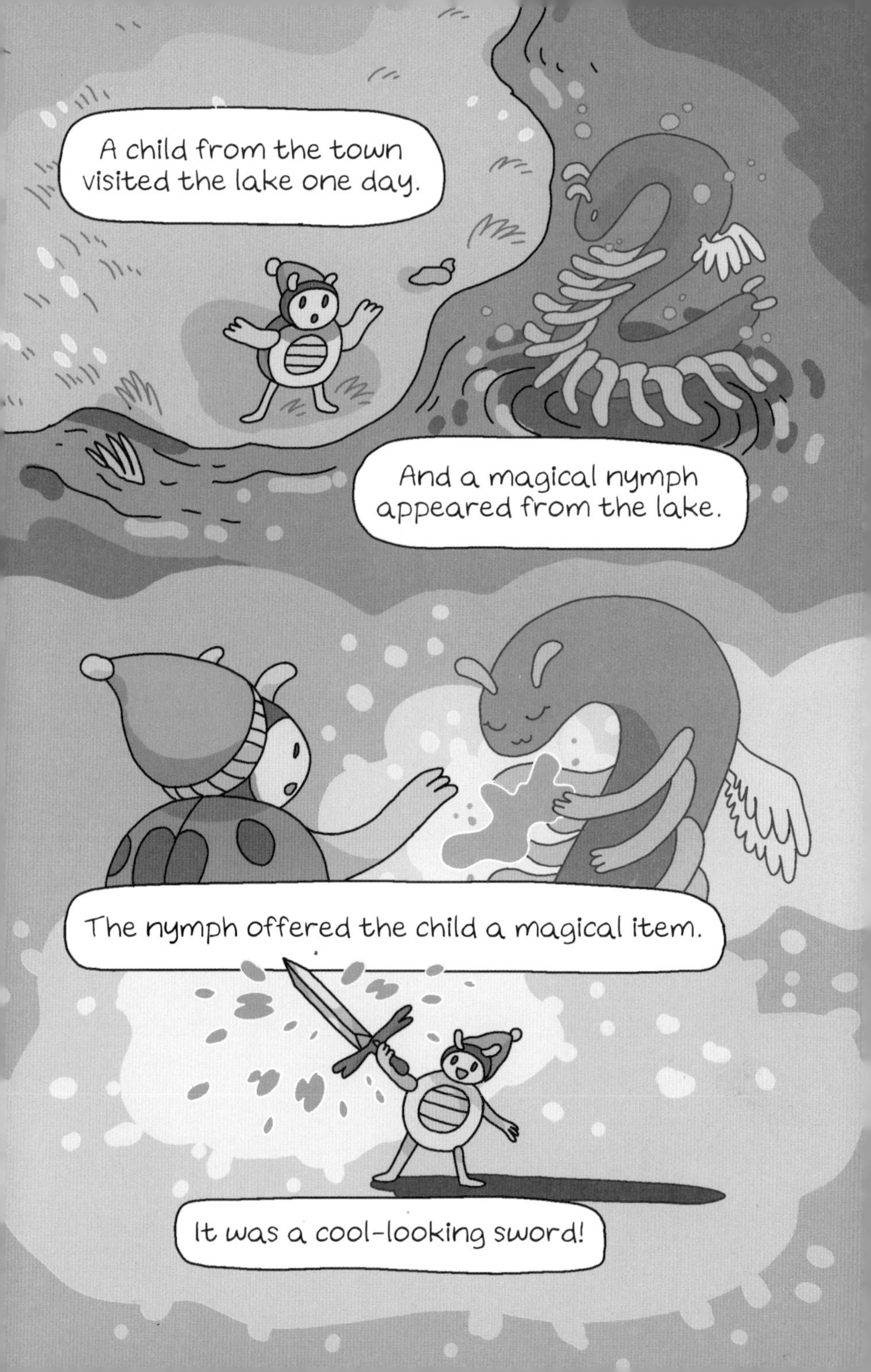
A child from the town visited the lake one day.
And a magical nymph appeared from the lake.
The nymph offered the child a magical item.
It was a cool-looking sword!

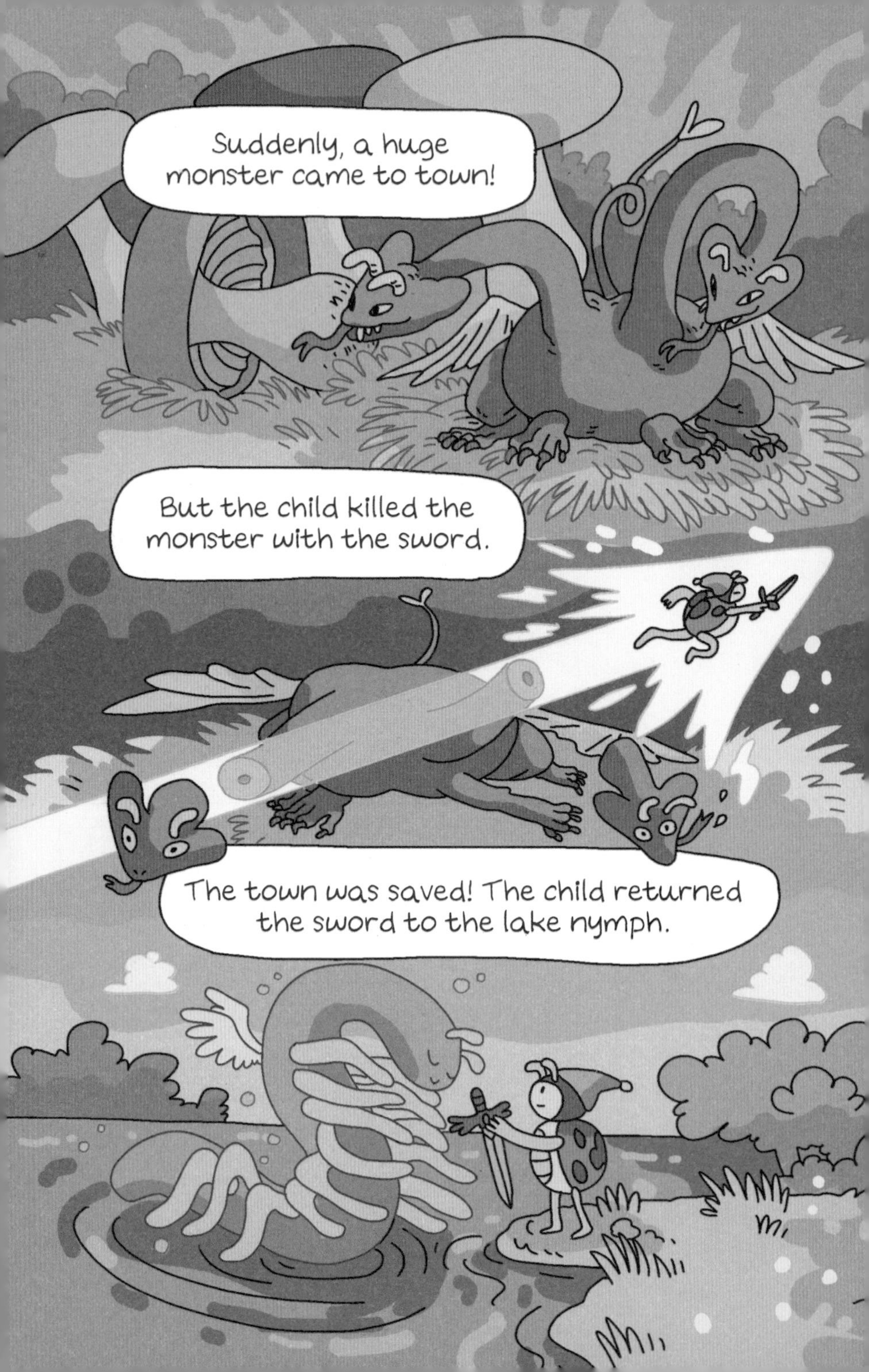
Suddenly, a huge monster came to town!
But the child killed the monster with the sword.
The town was saved! The child returned the sword to the lake nymph.

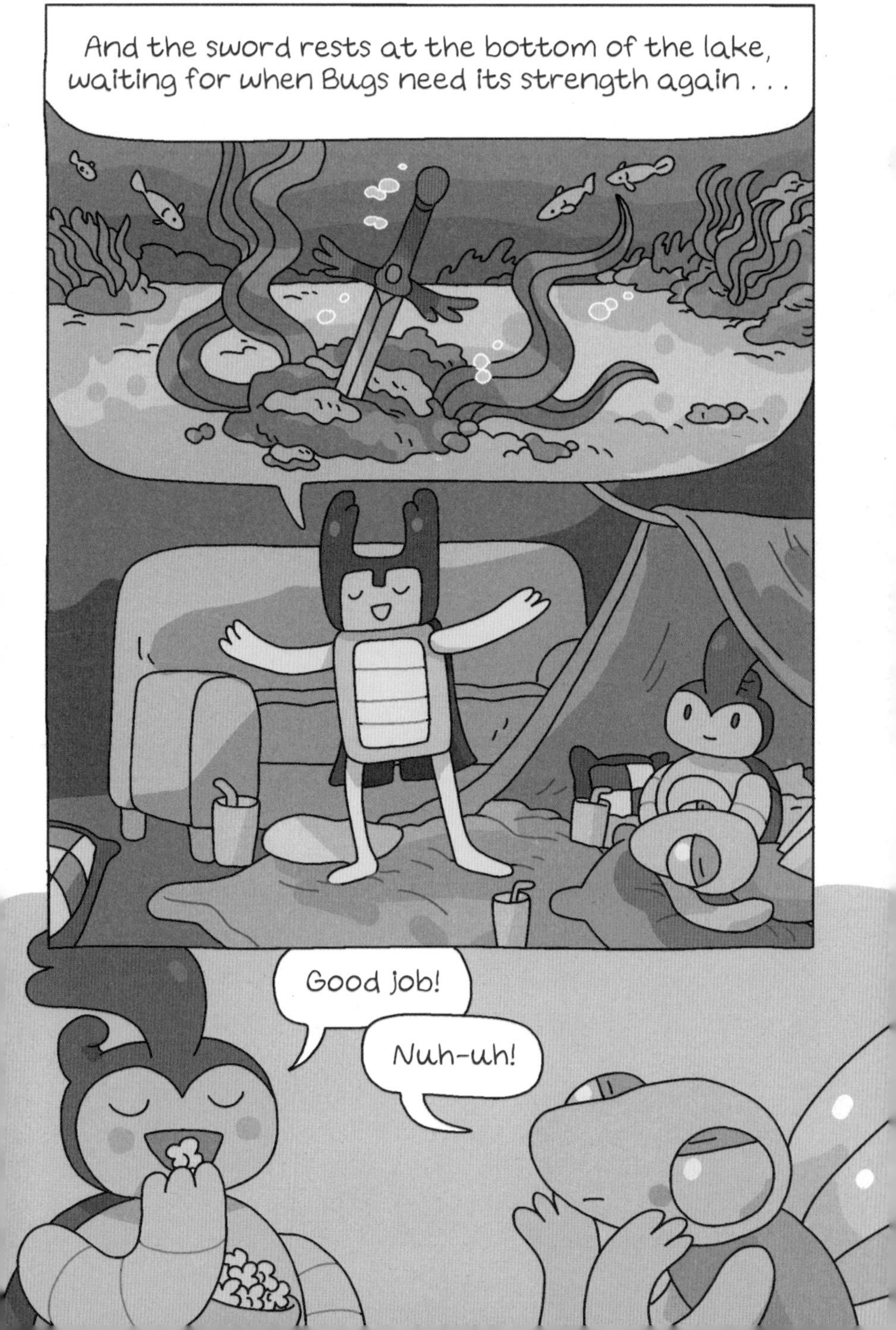
And the sword rests at the bottom of the lake, waiting for when Bugs need its strength again . . .
Good job!
Nuh-uh!

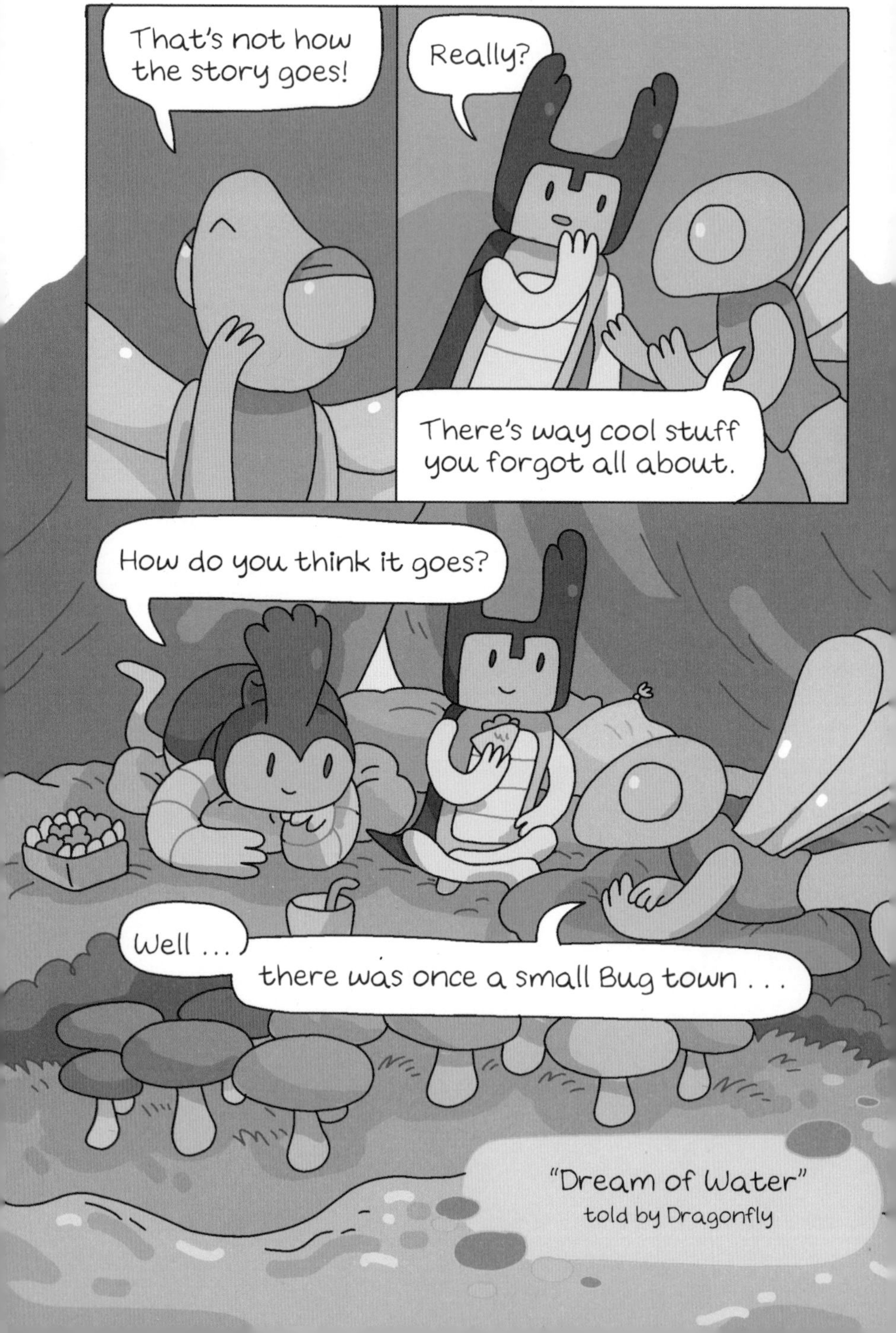
That's not how the story goes!
Really?
There's way cool stuff you forgot all about.
How do you think it goes?
Well . . .
there was once a small Bug town . . .
"Dream of Water"
told by Dragonfly

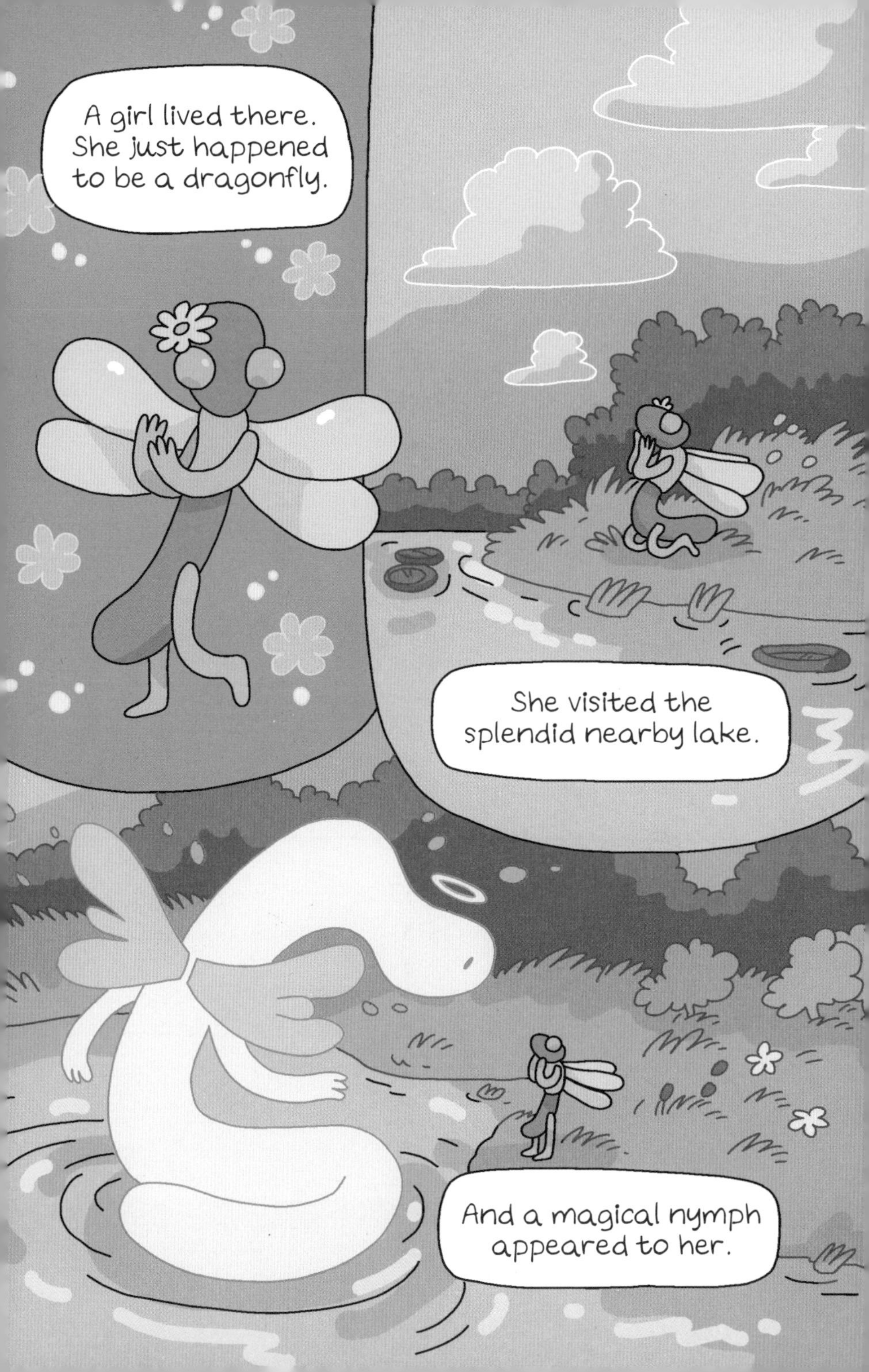
A girl lived there. She just happened to be a dragonfly.
She visited the splendid nearby lake.
And a magical nymph appeared to her.

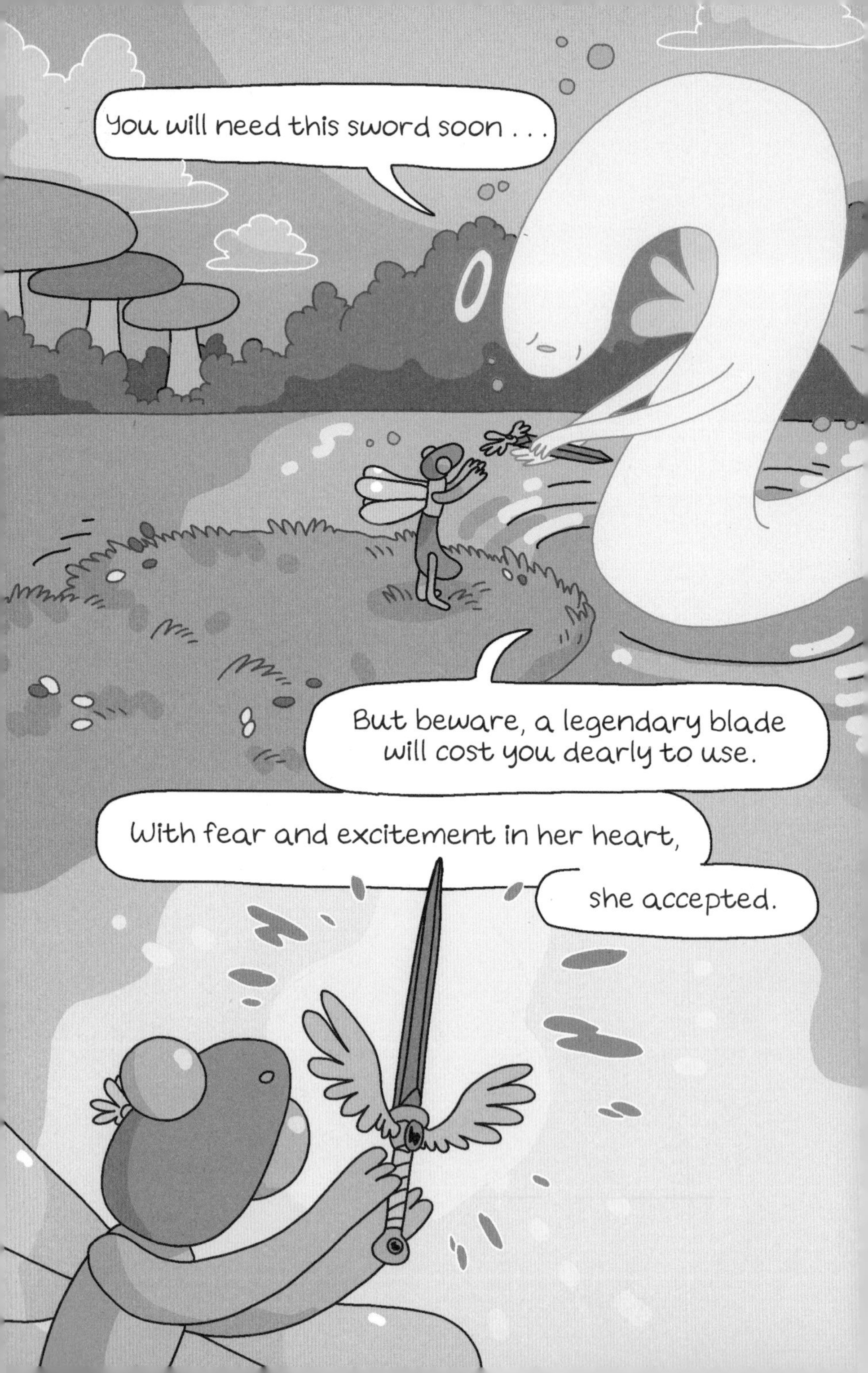
You will need this sword soon . . .
But beware, a legendary blade will cost you dearly to use.
With fear and excitement in her heart,
she accepted.

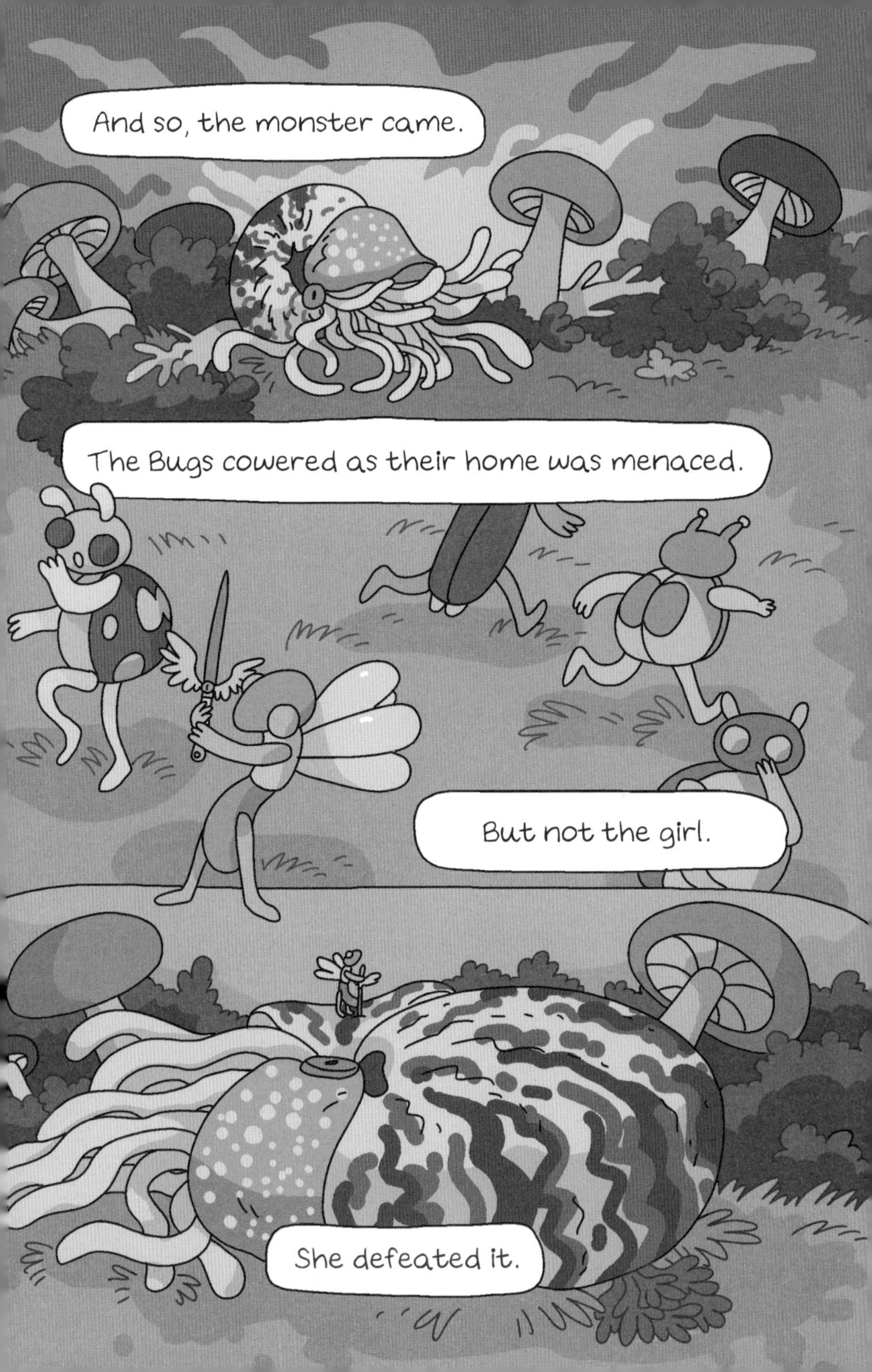
And so, the monster came.
The Bugs cowered as their home was menaced.
But not the girl.
She defeated it.

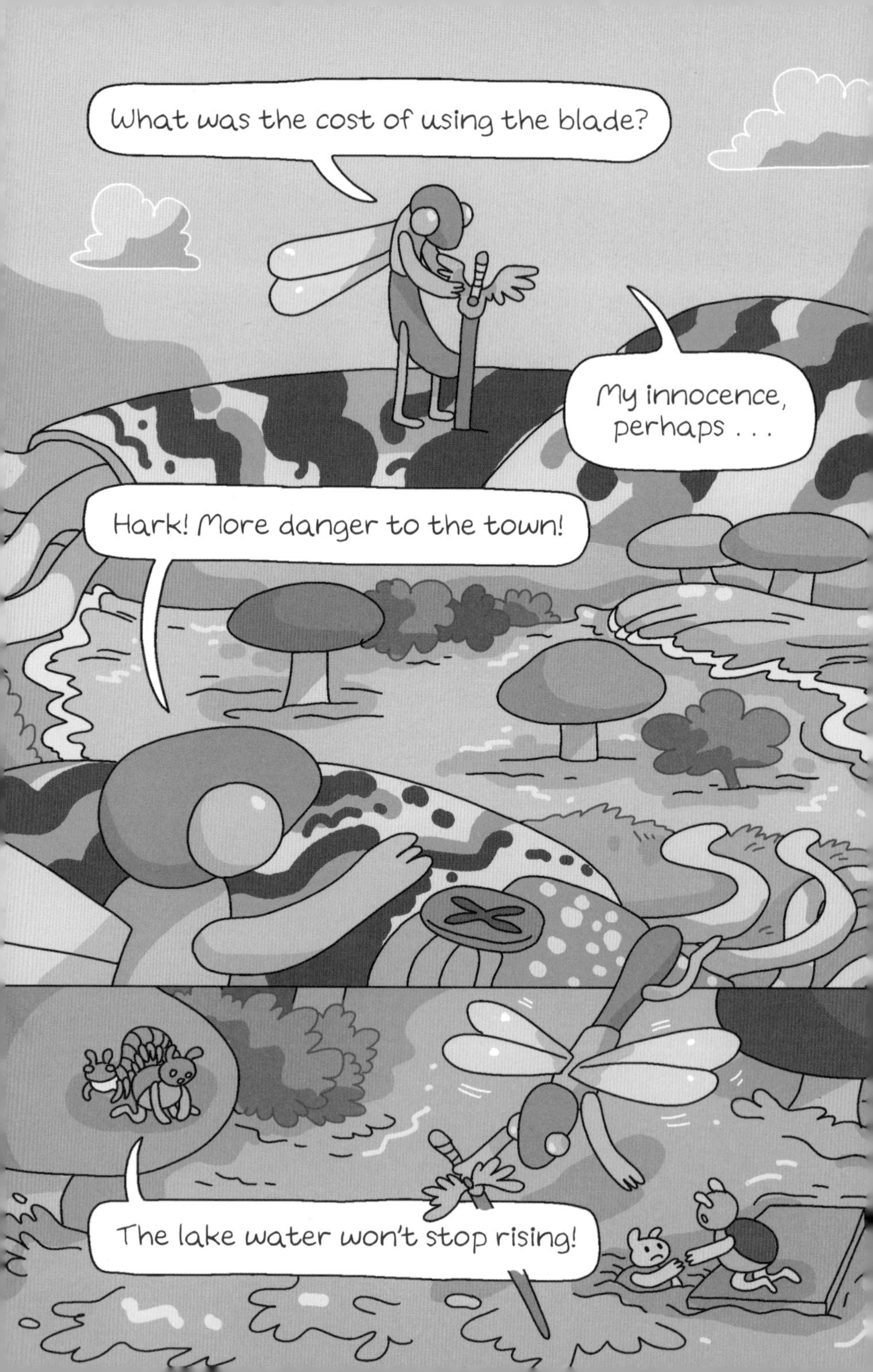
What was the cost of using the blade?
My innocence, perhaps . . .
Hark! More danger to the town!
The lake water won't stop rising!

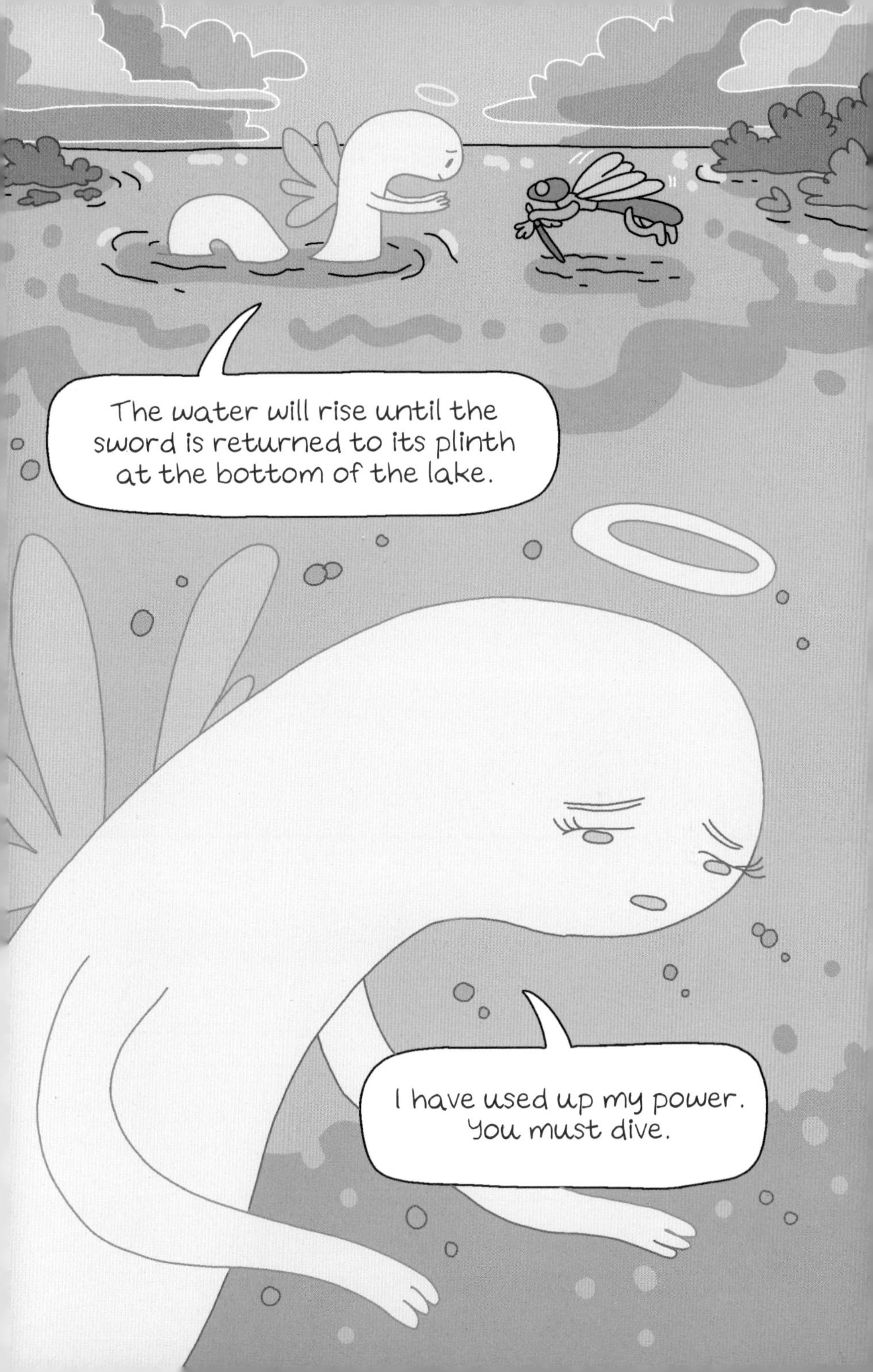
The water will rise until the sword is returned to its plinth at the bottom of the lake.
I have used up my power. You must dive.

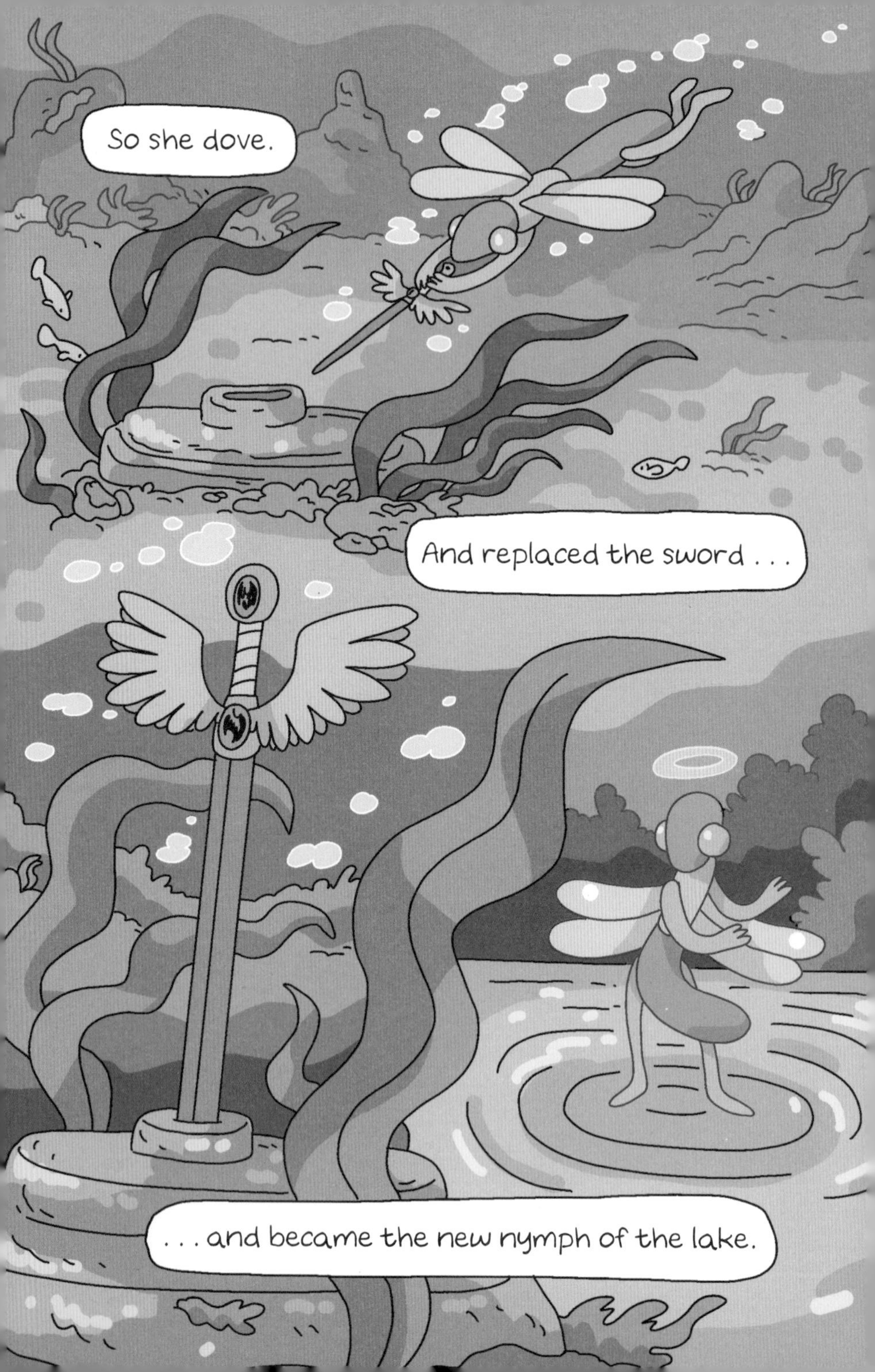
So she dove.
And replaced the sword . . .
. . . and became the new nymph of the lake.

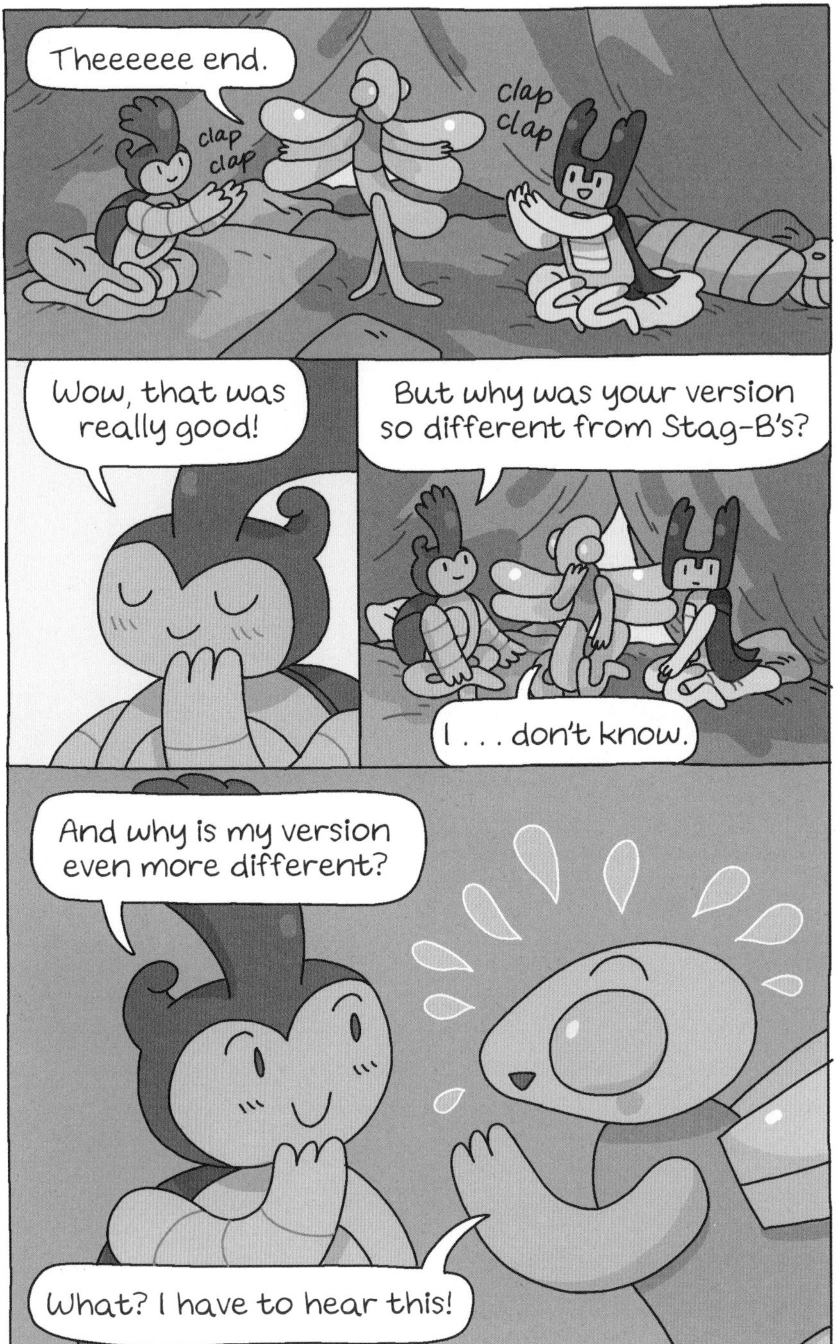
Theeeeee end.
clap clap
clap clap
Wow, that was really good!
But why was your version so different from Stag-B's?
I . . . don't know.
And why is my version even more different?
What? I have to hear this!

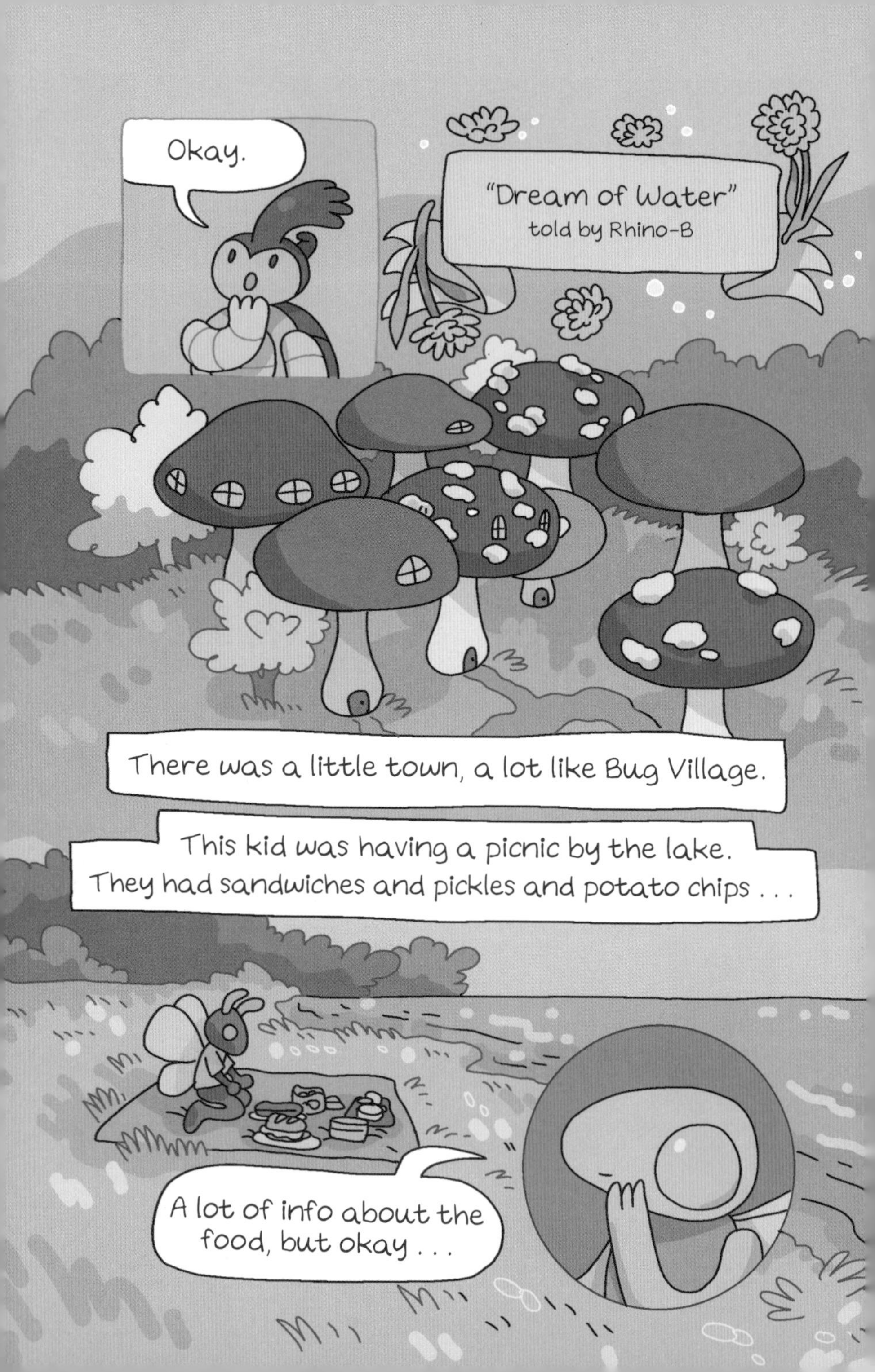
Okay.
"Dream of Water"
told by Rhino-B
There was a little town, a lot like Bug Village.
This kid was having a picnic by the lake.
They had sandwiches and pickles and potato chips . . .
A lot of info about the food, but okay . . .

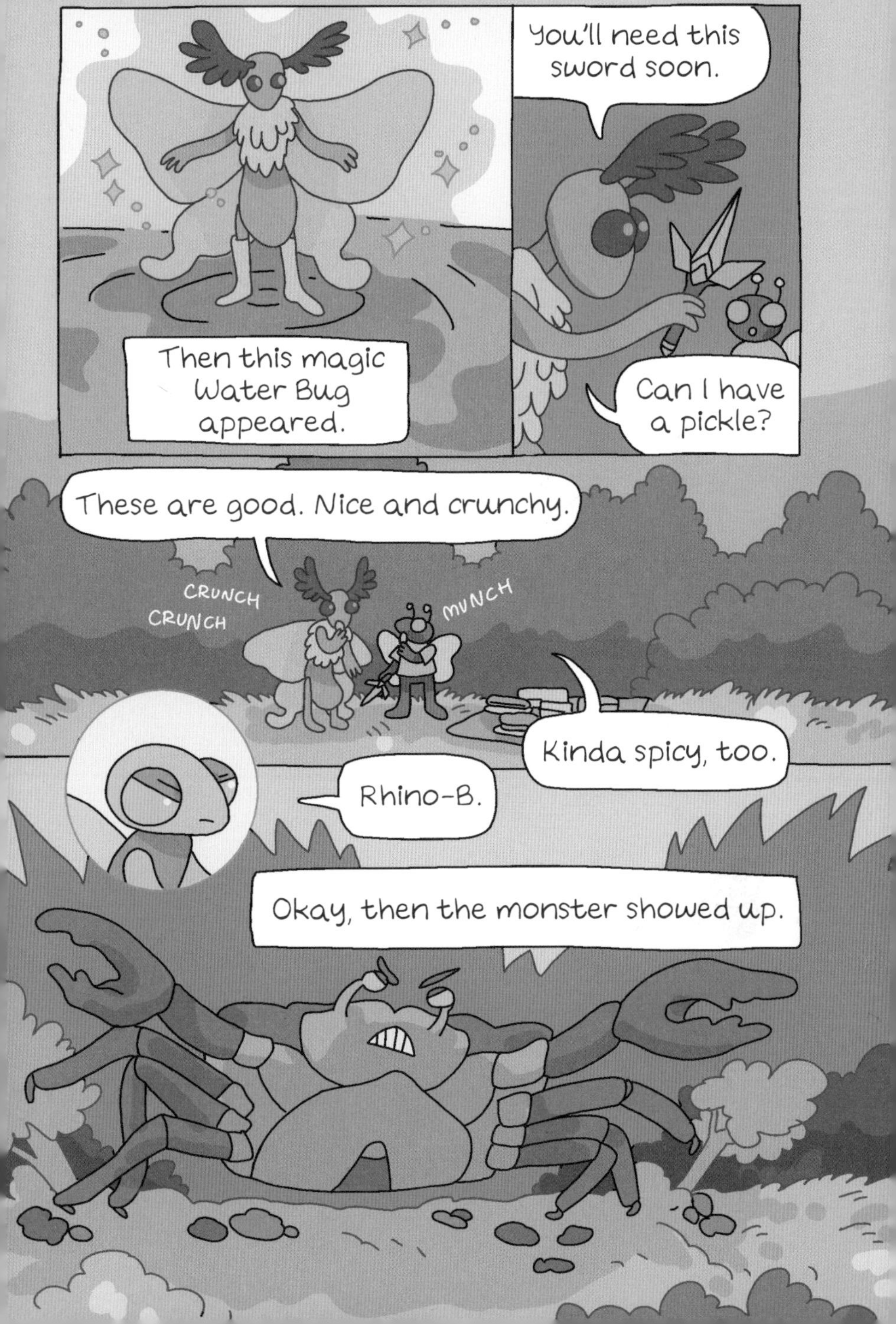

Then this magic Water Bug appeared.
You'll need this sword soon.
Can I have a pickle?
These are good. Nice and crunchy.
CRUNCH
CRUNCH
MUNCH
Kinda spicy, too.
Rhino-B.
Okay, then the monster showed up.

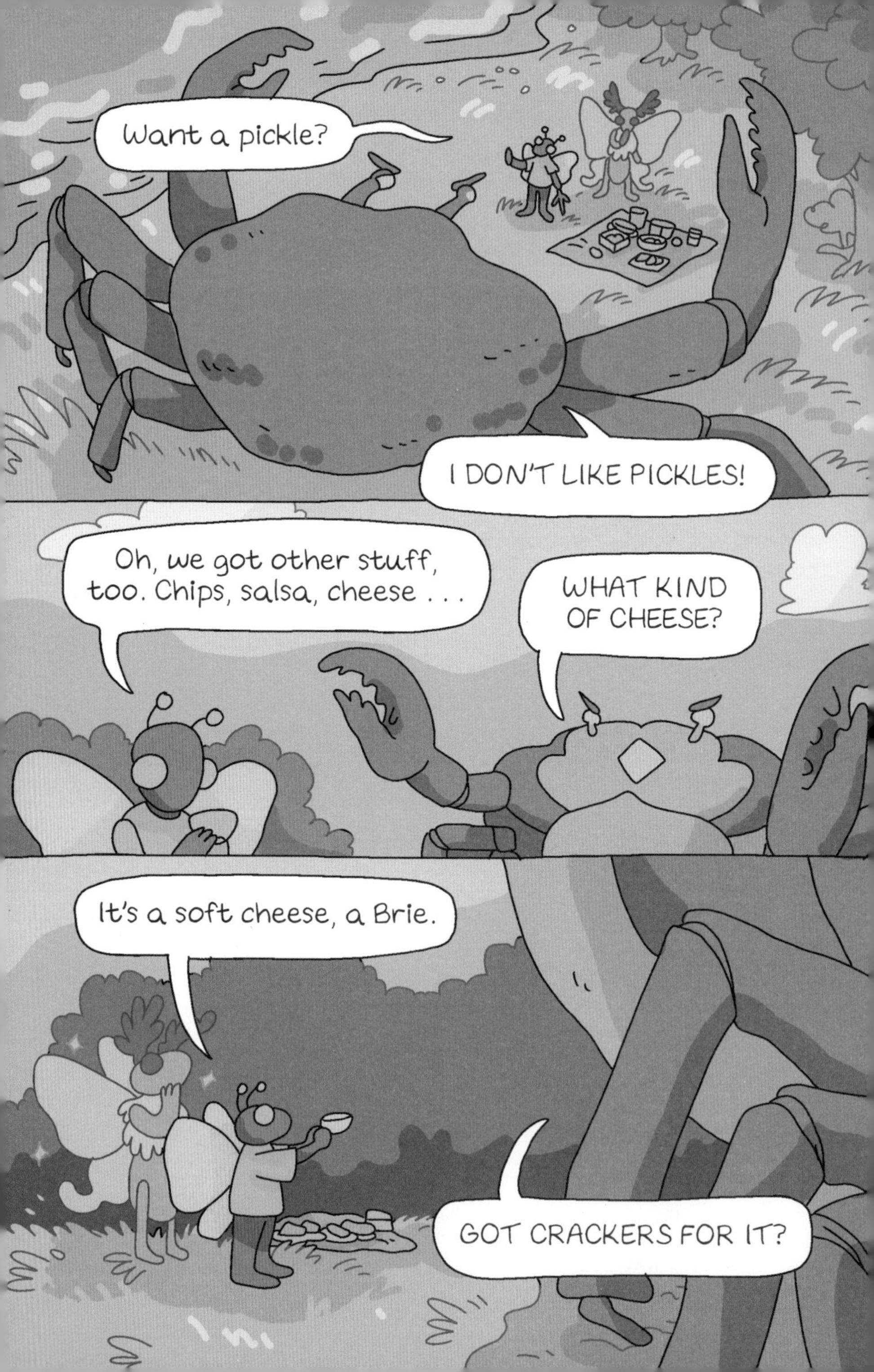
Want a pickle?
I DON'T LIKE PICKLES!
Oh, we got other stuff, too. Chips, salsa, cheese . . .
WHAT KIND OF CHEESE?
It's a soft cheese, a Brie.
GOT CRACKERS FOR IT?

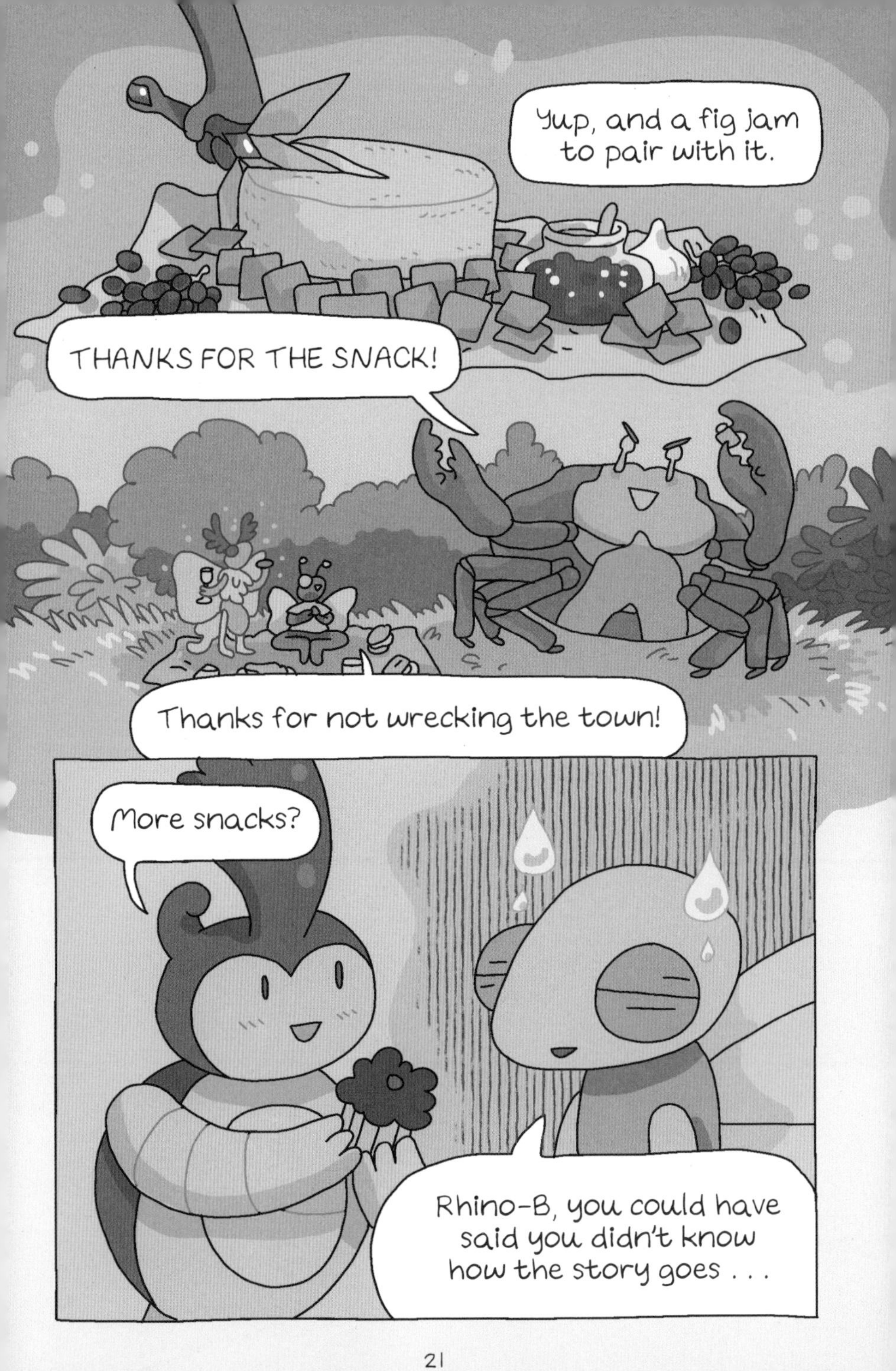
Yup, and a fig jam to pair with it.
THANKS FOR THE SNACK!
Thanks for not wrecking the town!
More snacks?
Rhino-B, you could have said you didn't know how the story goes . . .

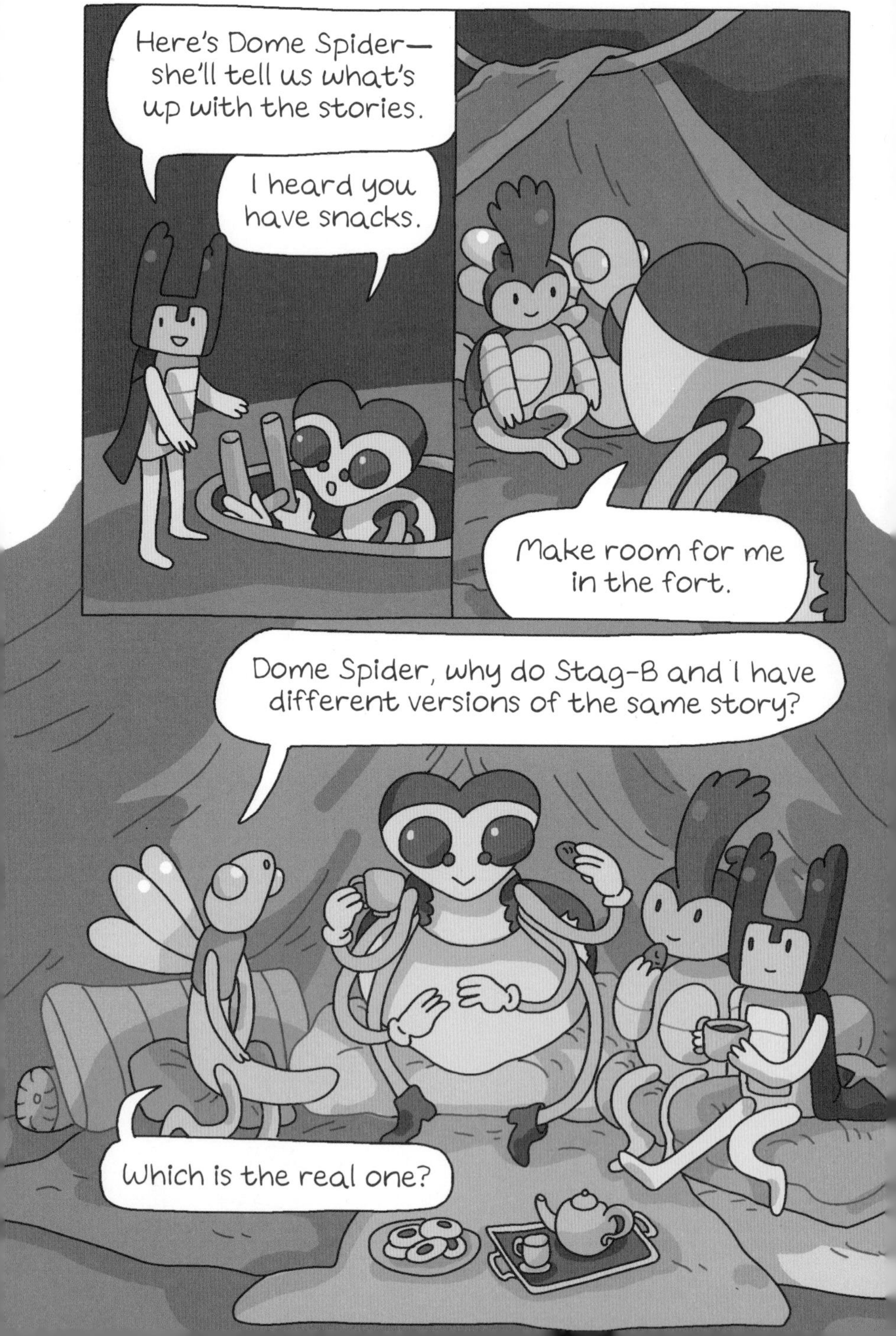
Here's Dome Spider—she'll tell us what's up with the stories.
I heard you have snacks.
Make room for me in the fort.
Dome Spider, why do Stag-B and I have different versions of the same story?
Which is the real one?

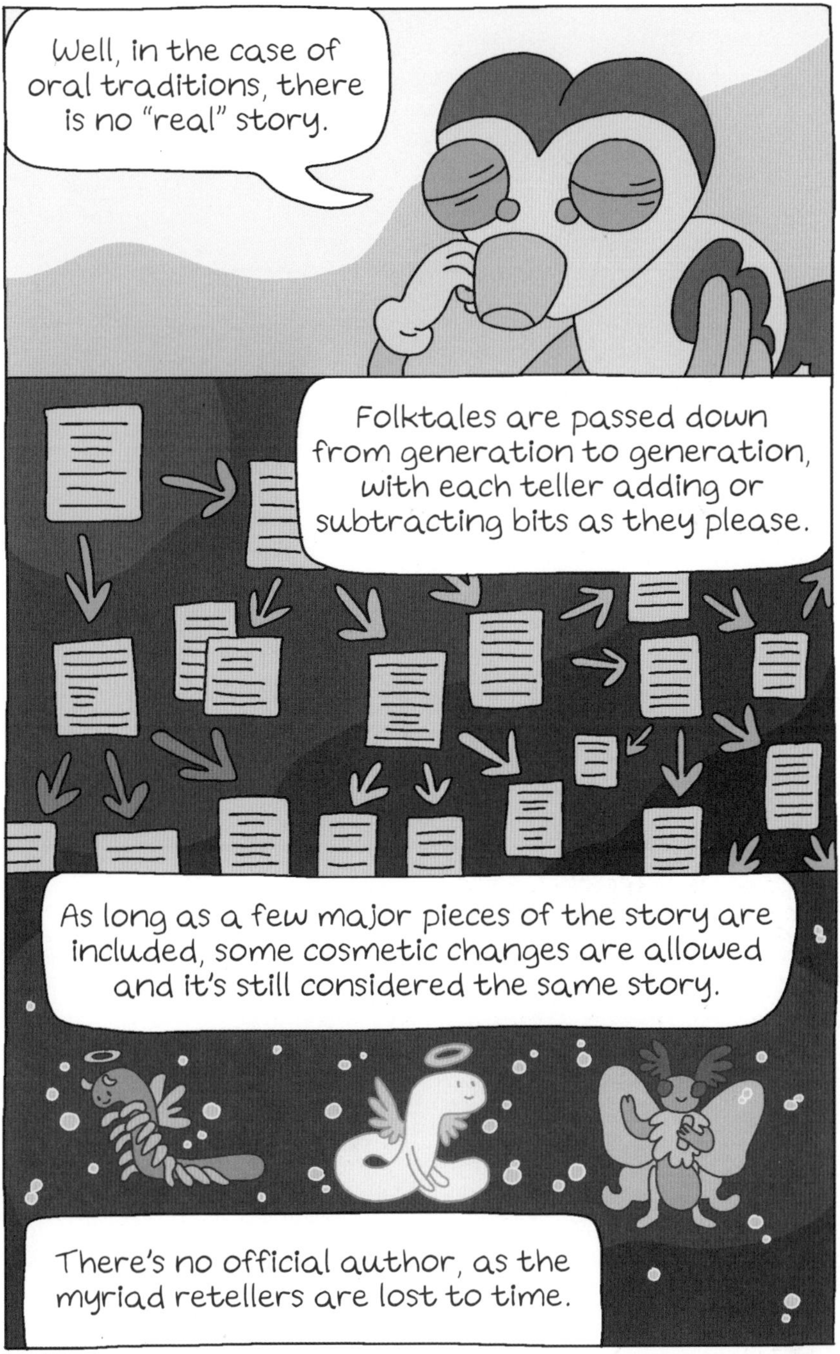
Well, in the case of oral traditions, there is no "real" story.
Folktales are passed down from generation to generation, with each teller adding or subtracting bits as they please.
As long as a few major pieces of the story are included, some cosmetic changes are allowed and it's still considered the same story.
There's no official author, as the myriad retellers are lost to time.

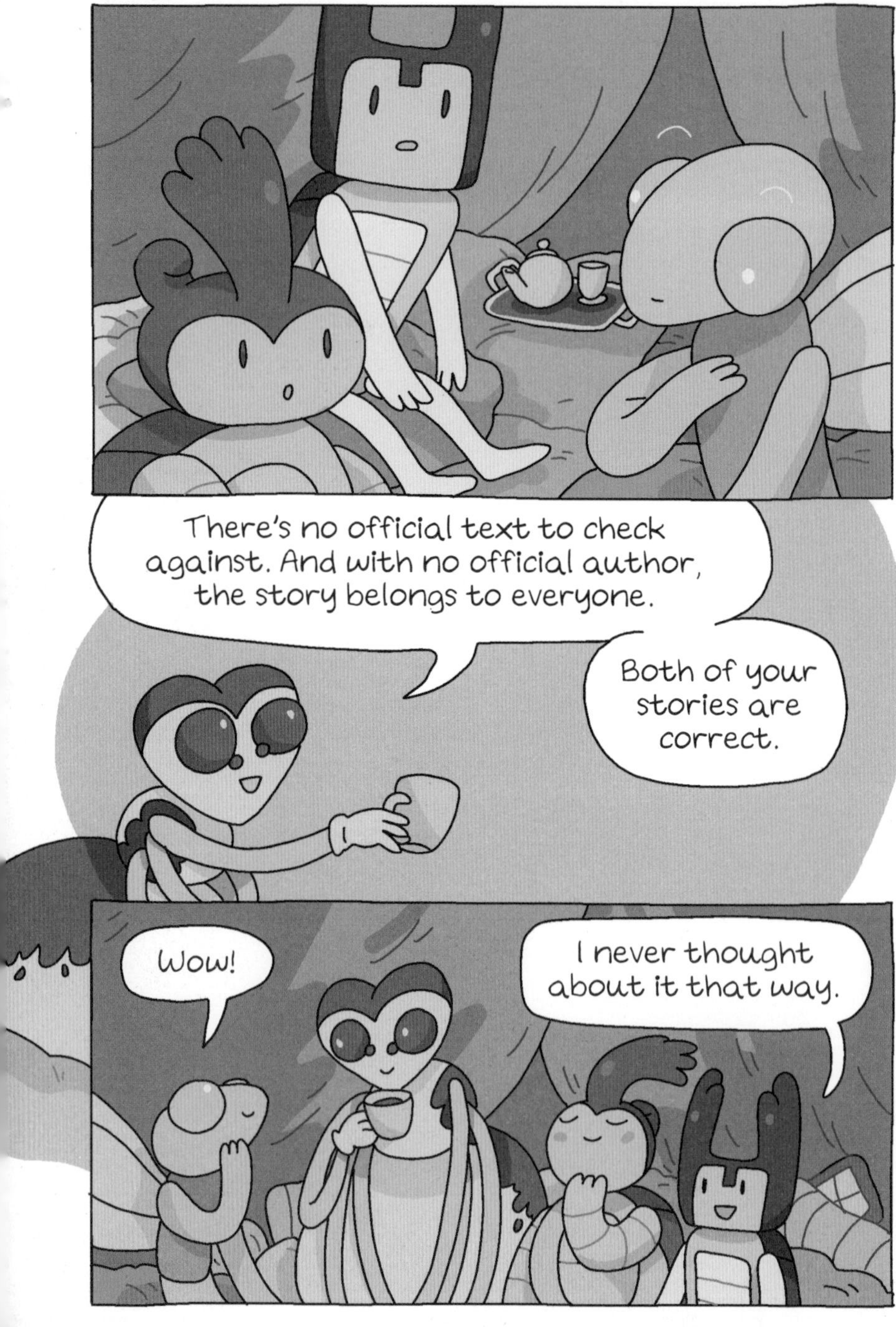
There's no official text to check against. And with no official author, the story belongs to everyone.
Both of your stories are correct.
Wow!
I never thought about it that way.

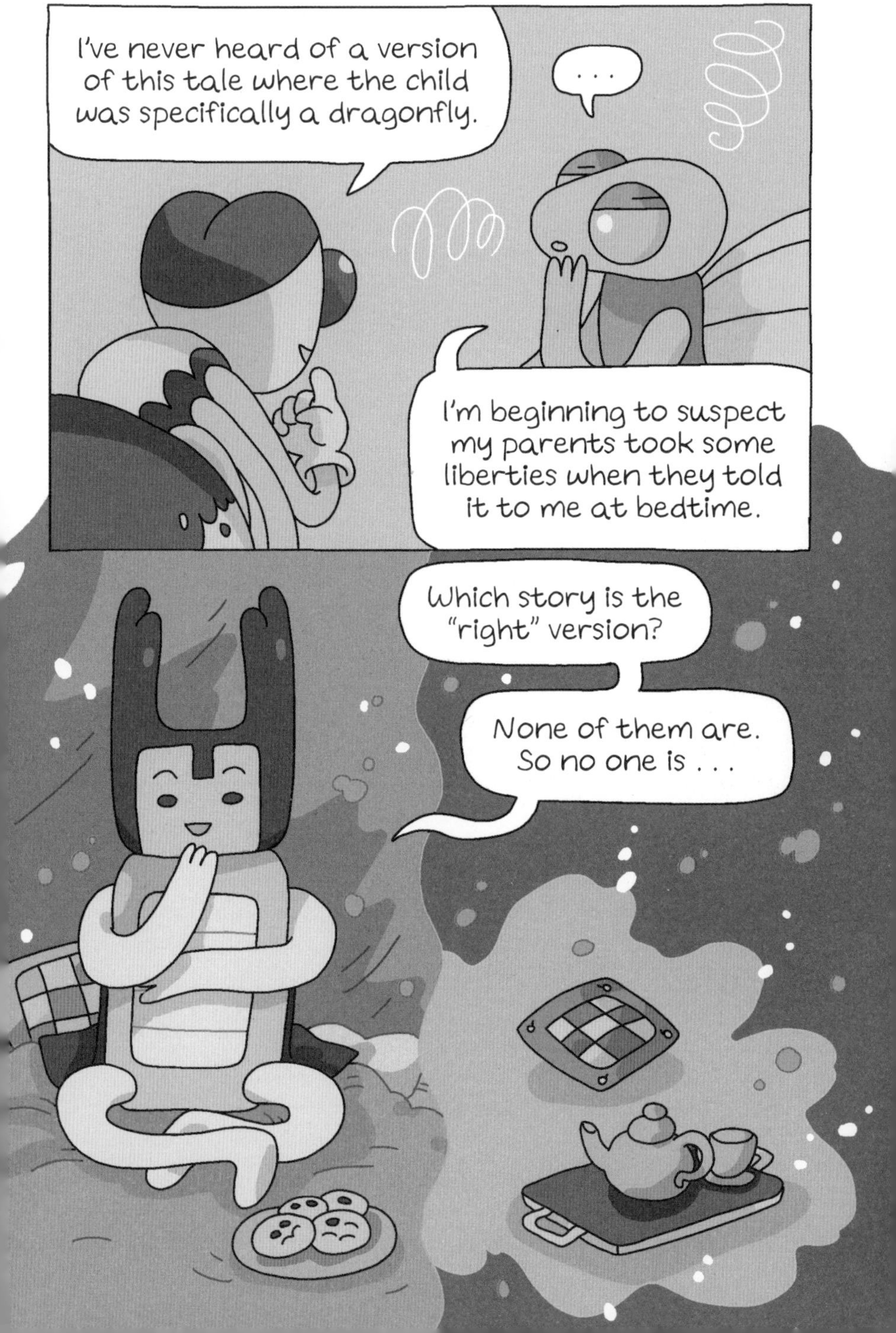
I've never heard of a version of this tale where the child was specifically a dragonfly.
. . .
I'm beginning to suspect my parents took some liberties when they told it to me at bedtime.
Which story is the "right" version?
None of them are. So no one is . . .

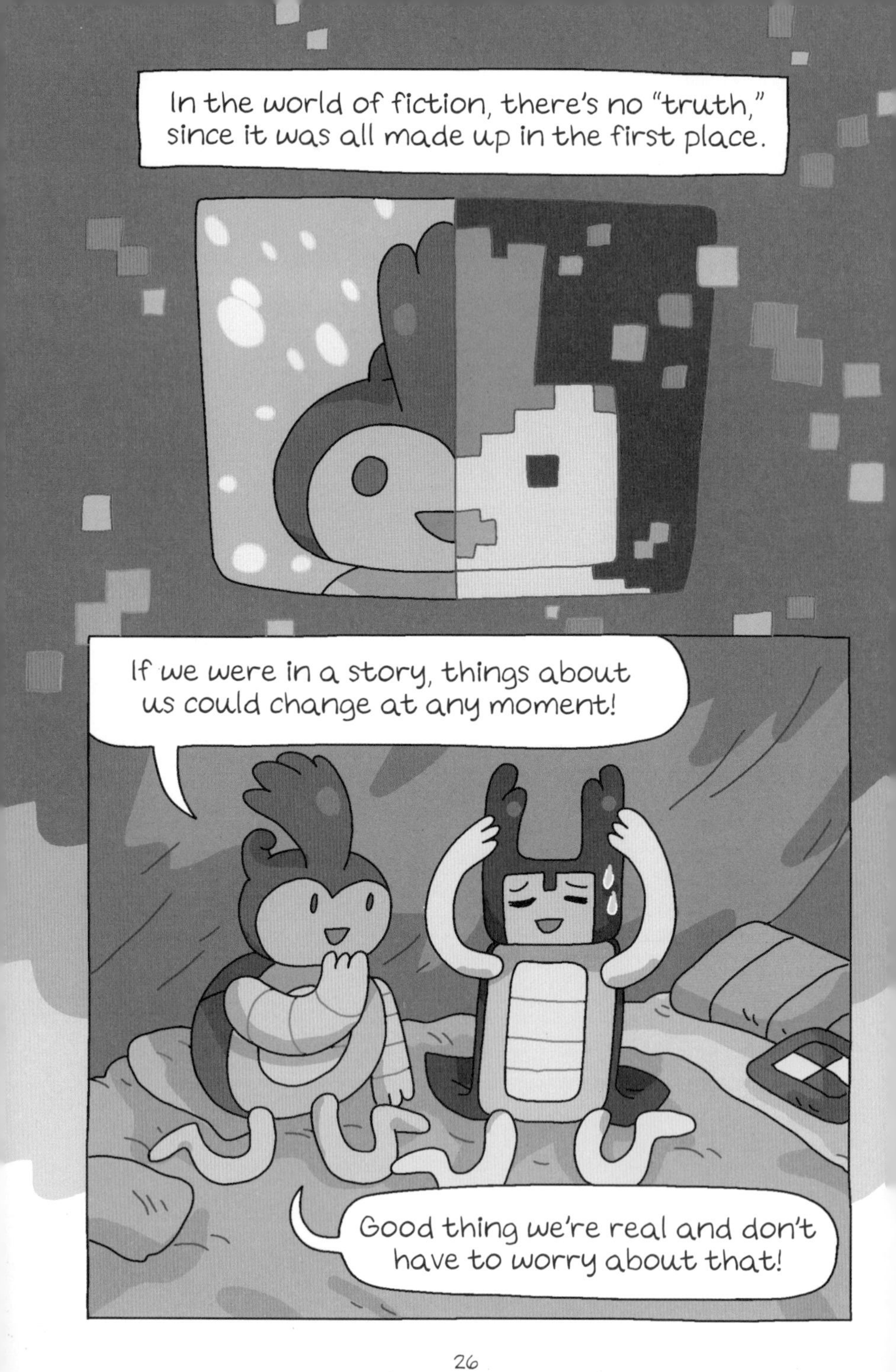
In the world of fiction, there's no "truth," since it was all made up in the first place.
If we were in a story, things about us could change at any moment!
Good thing we're real and don't have to worry about that!

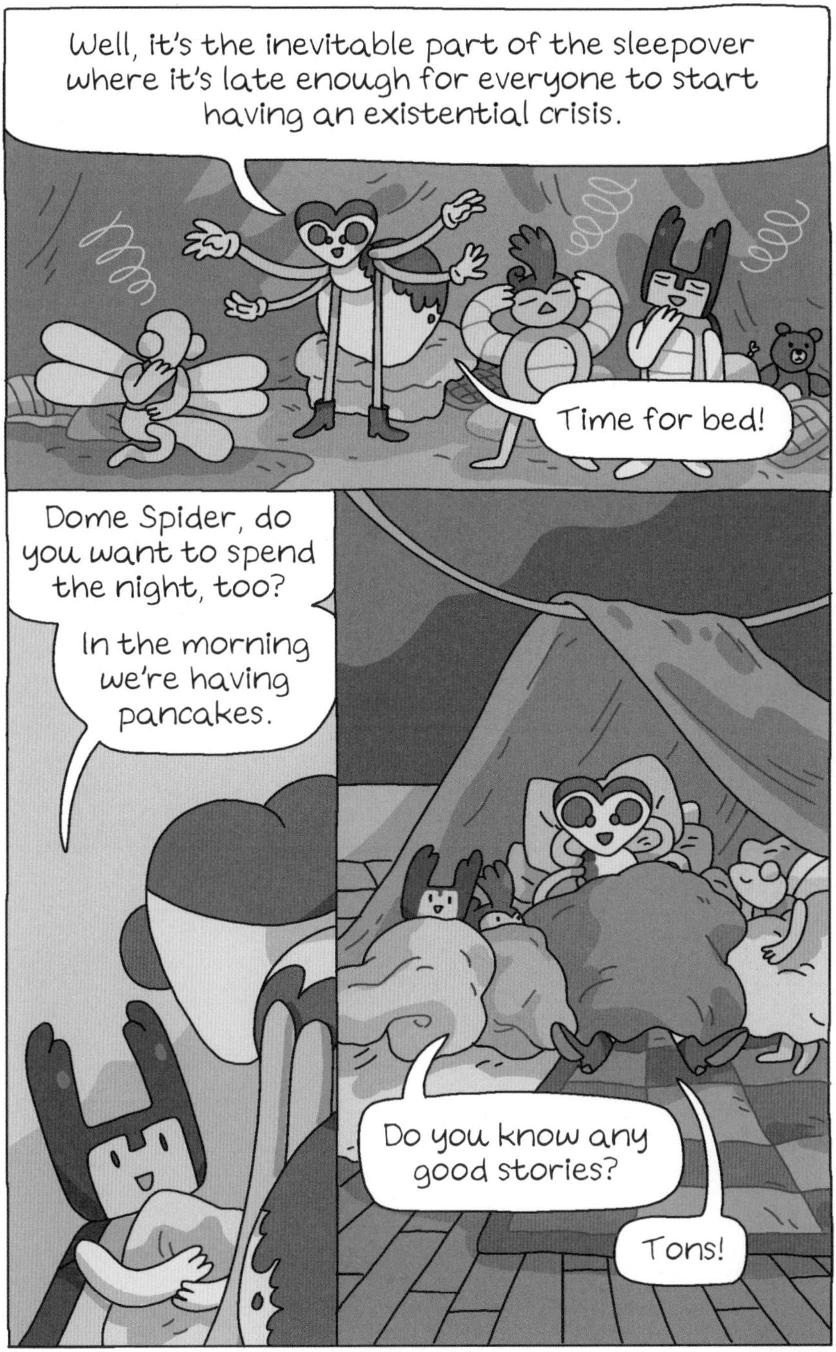
Well, it's the inevitable part of the sleepover where it's late enough for everyone to start having an existential crisis.
Time for bed!
Dome Spider, do you want to spend the night, too?
In the morning we're having pancakes.
Do you know any good stories?
Tons!

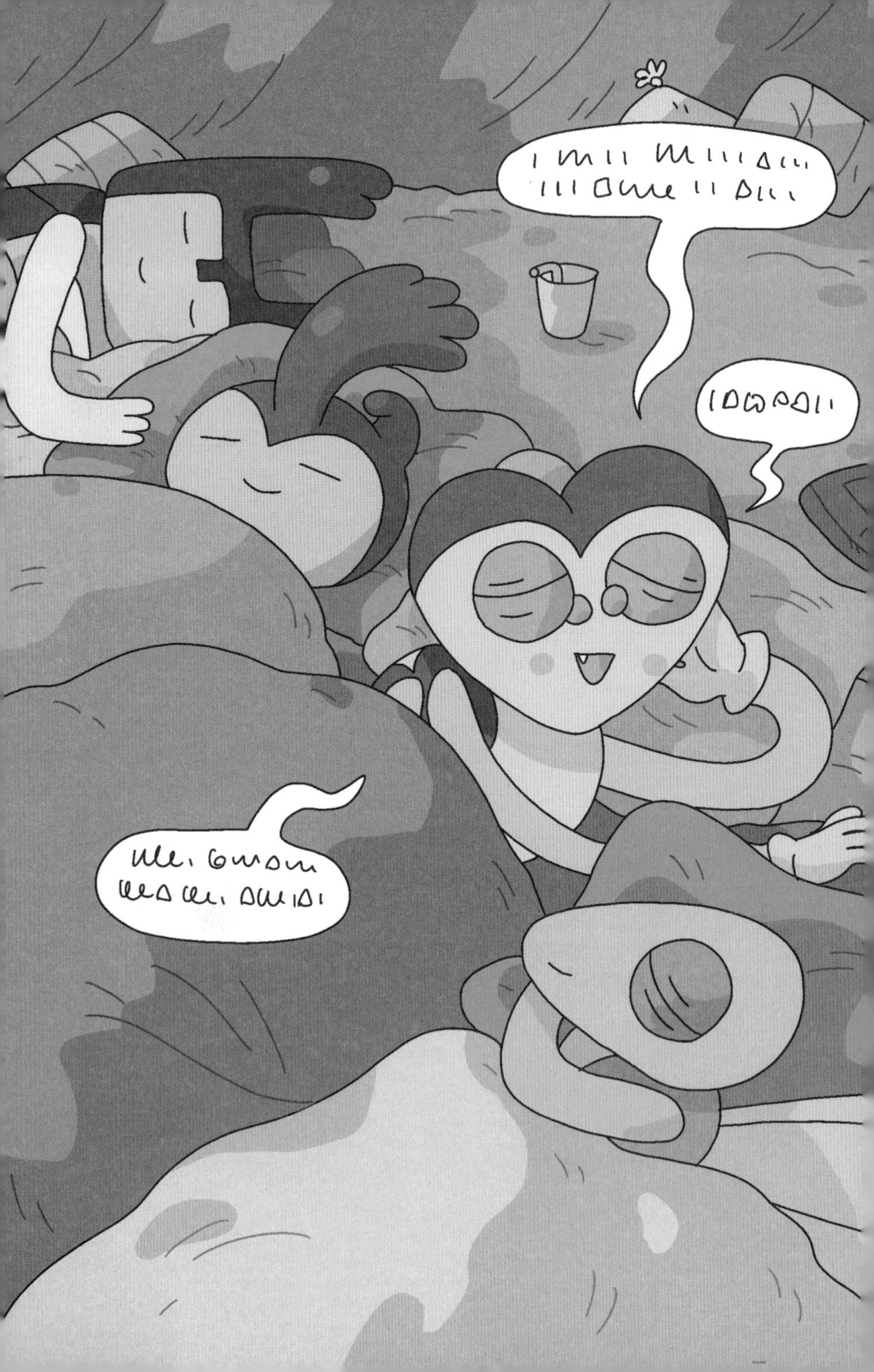

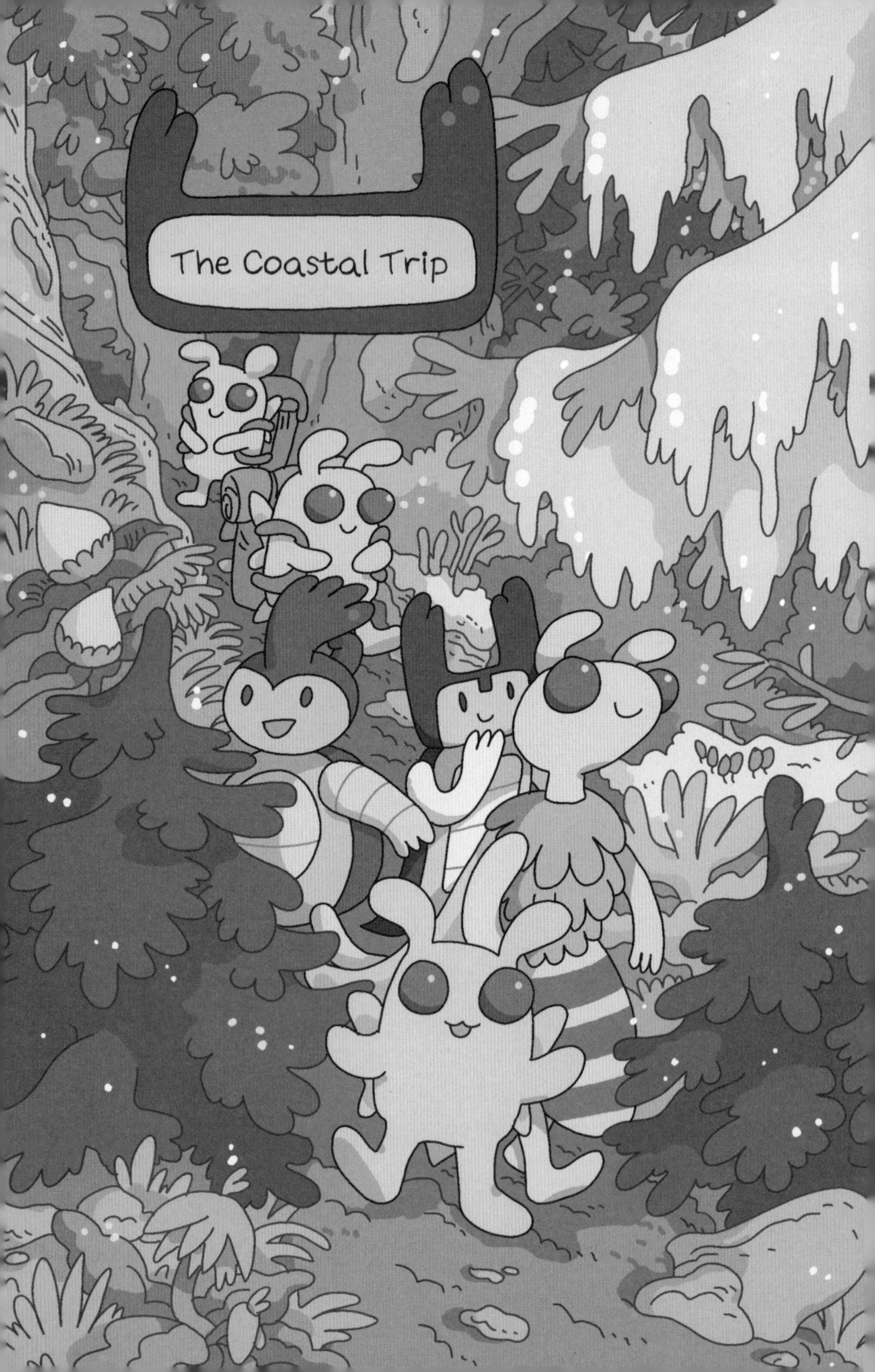
The Coastal Trip

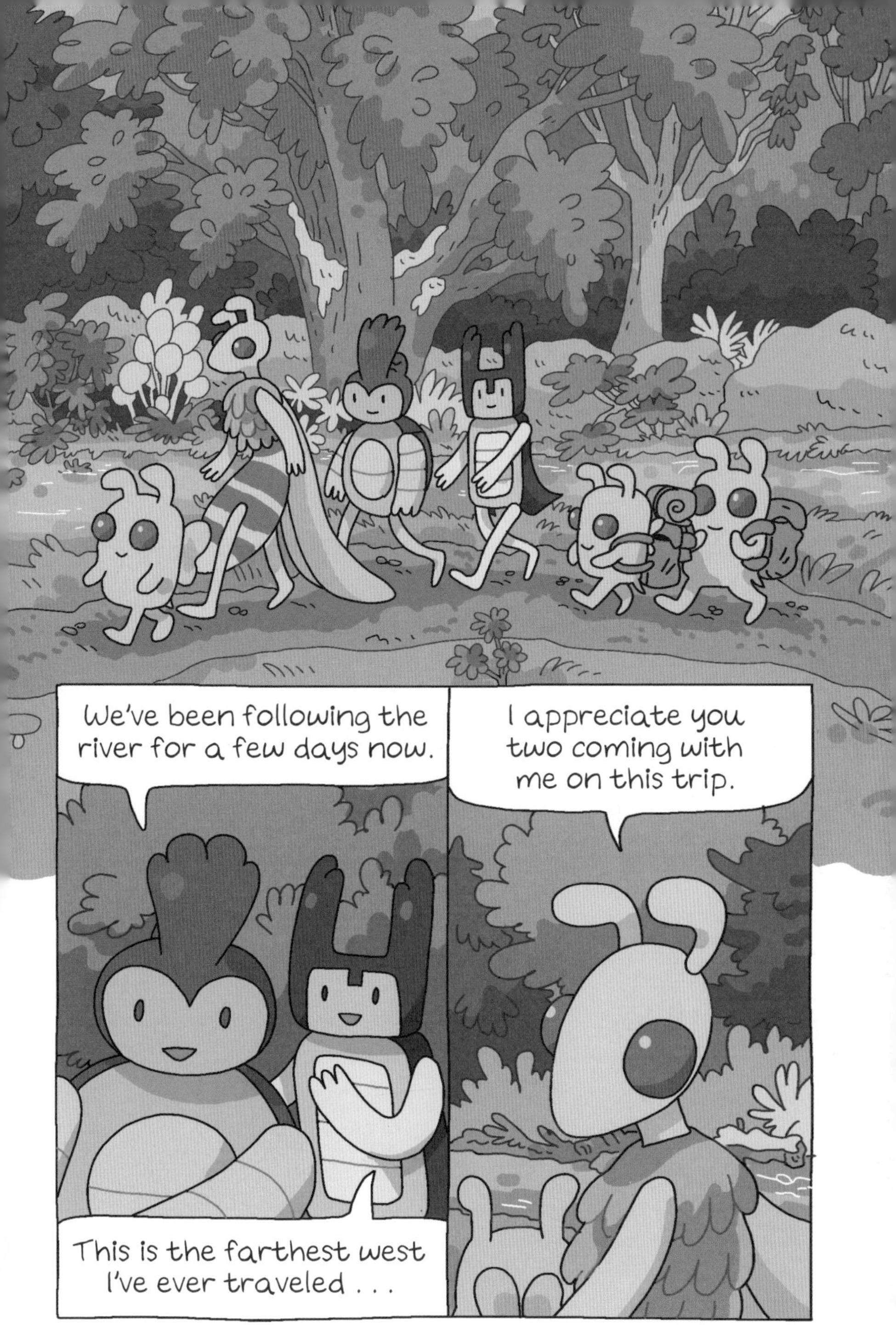
We've been following the river for a few days now.
This is the farthest west I've ever traveled . . .
I appreciate you two coming with me on this trip.

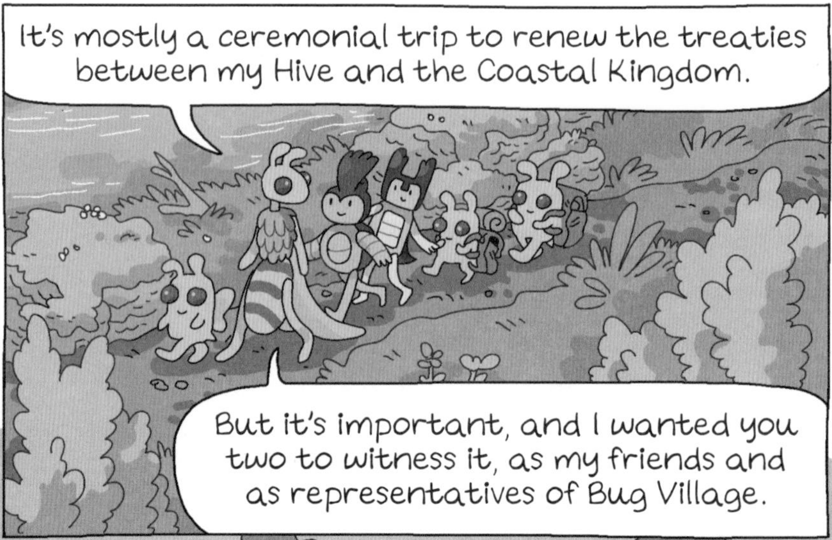
It's mostly a ceremonial trip to renew the treaties between my Hive and the Coastal Kingdom.
But it's important, and I wanted you two to witness it, as my friends and as representatives of Bug Village.
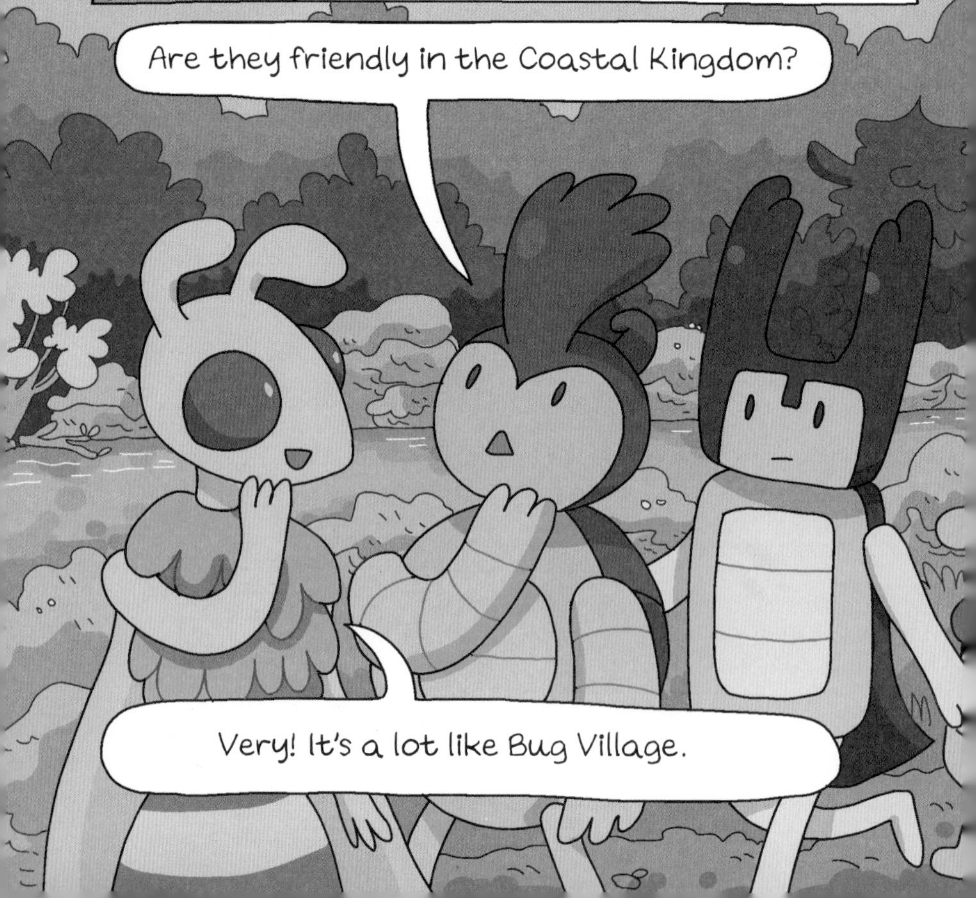
Are they friendly in the Coastal Kingdom?
Very! It's a lot like Bug Village.

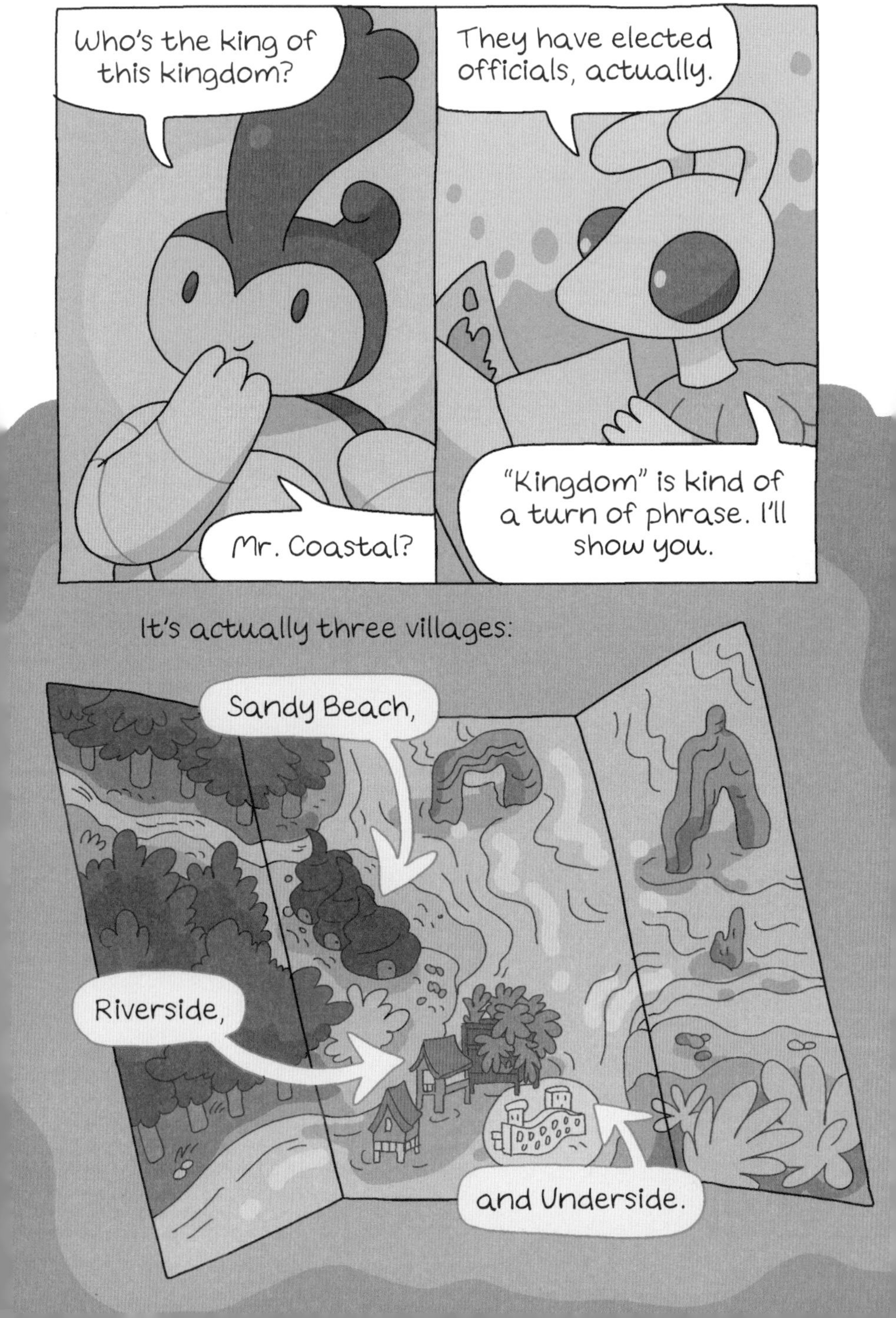
Who's the king of this kingdom?
Mr. Coastal?
They have elected officials, actually.
"Kingdom" is kind of a turn of phrase. I'll show you.
It's actually three villages:
Sandy Beach,
Riverside,
and Underside.

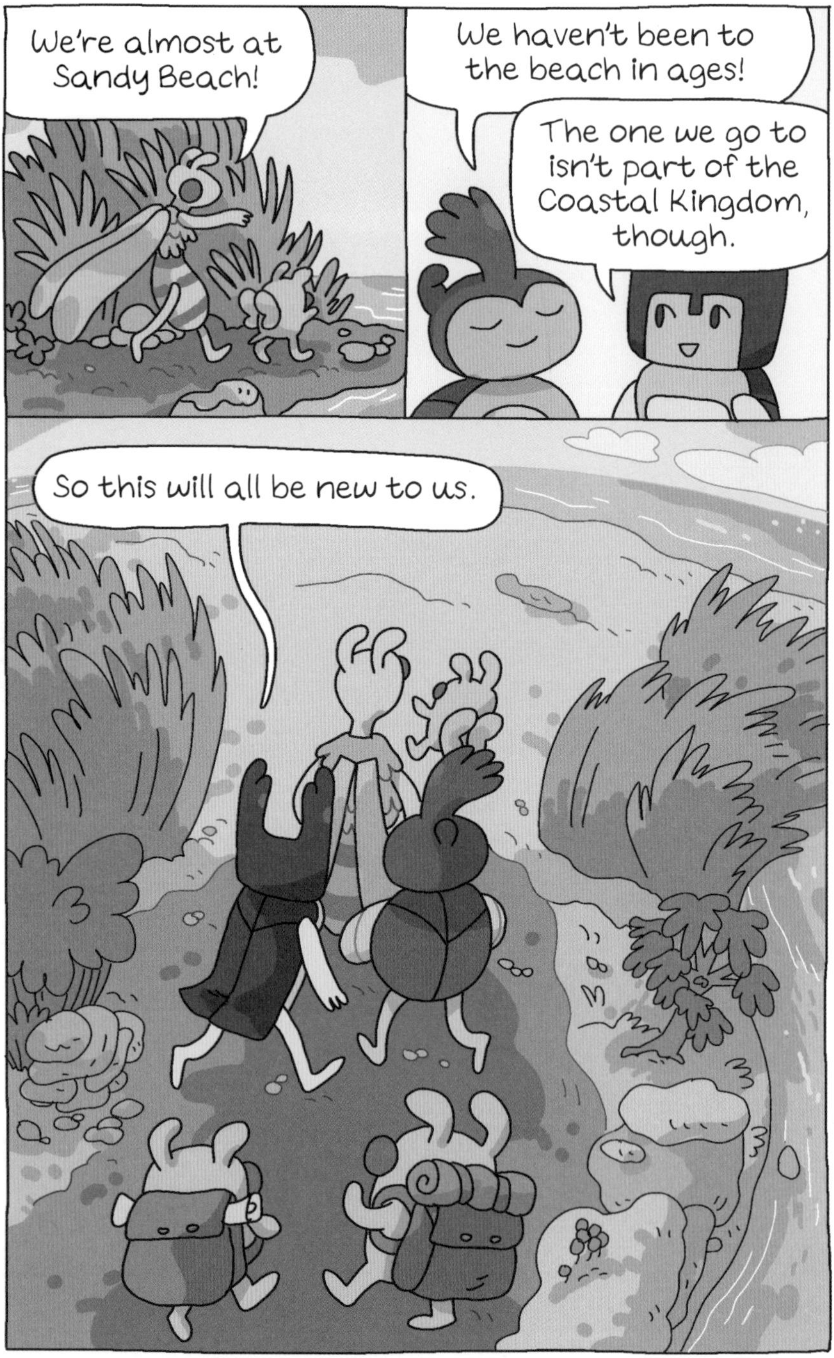
We're almost at Sandy Beach!
We haven't been to the beach in ages!
The one we go to isn't part of the Coastal Kingdom, though.
So this will all be new to us.

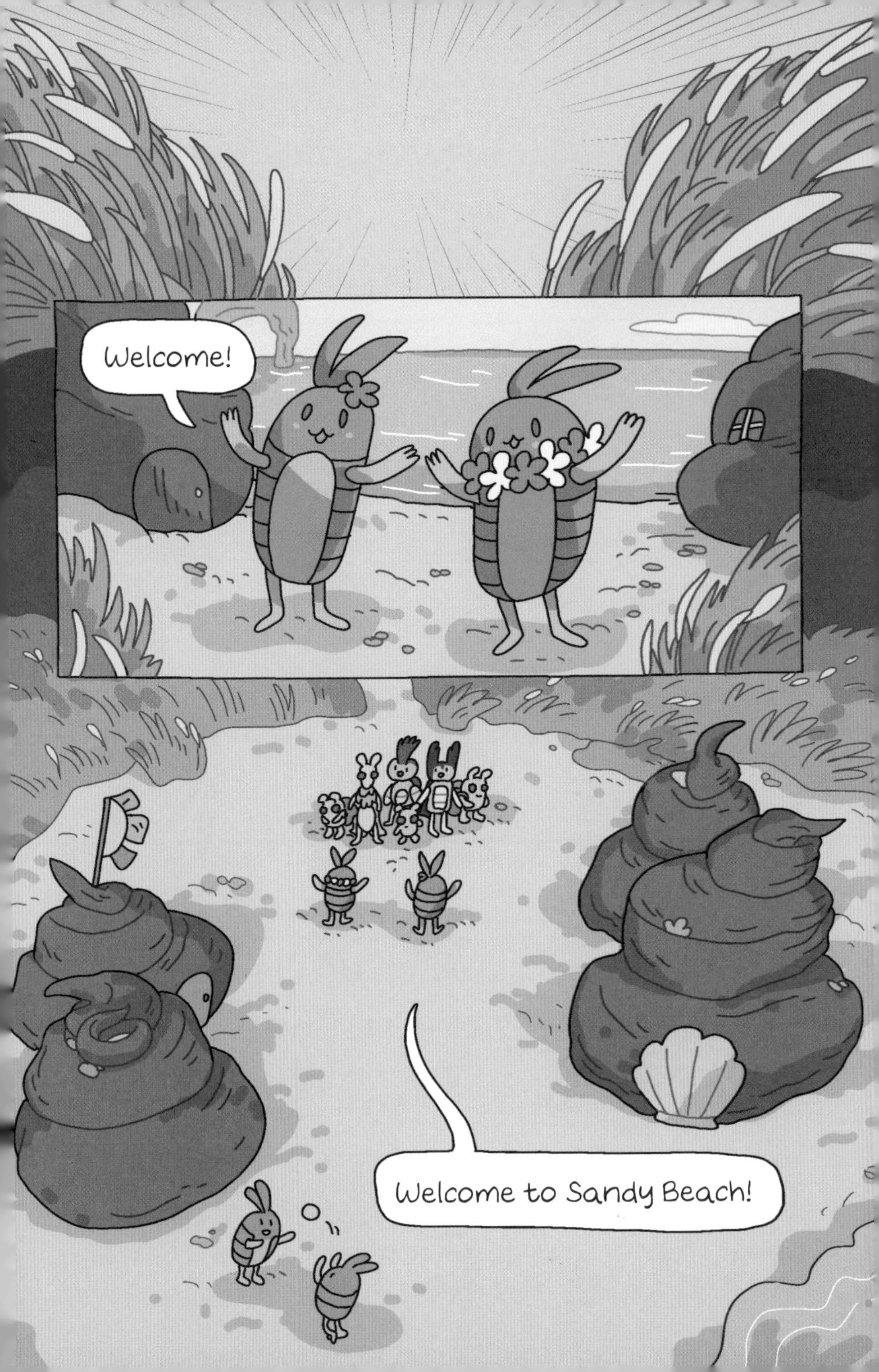
Welcome!
Welcome to Sandy Beach!

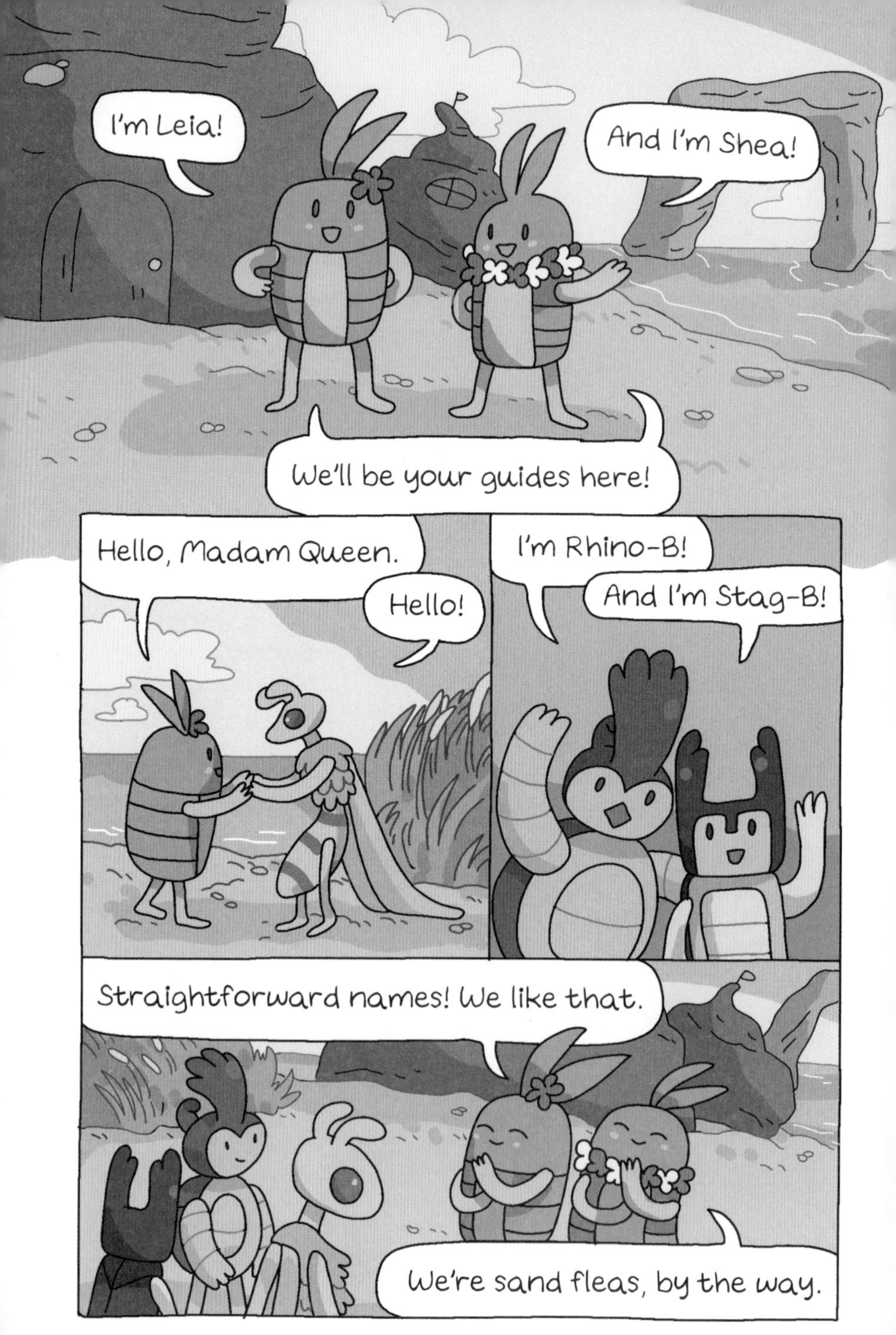
I'm Leia!
And I'm Shea!
We'll be your guides here!
Hello, Madam Queen.
Hello!
I'm Rhino-B!
And I'm Stag-B!
Straightforward names! We like that.
We're sand fleas, by the way.

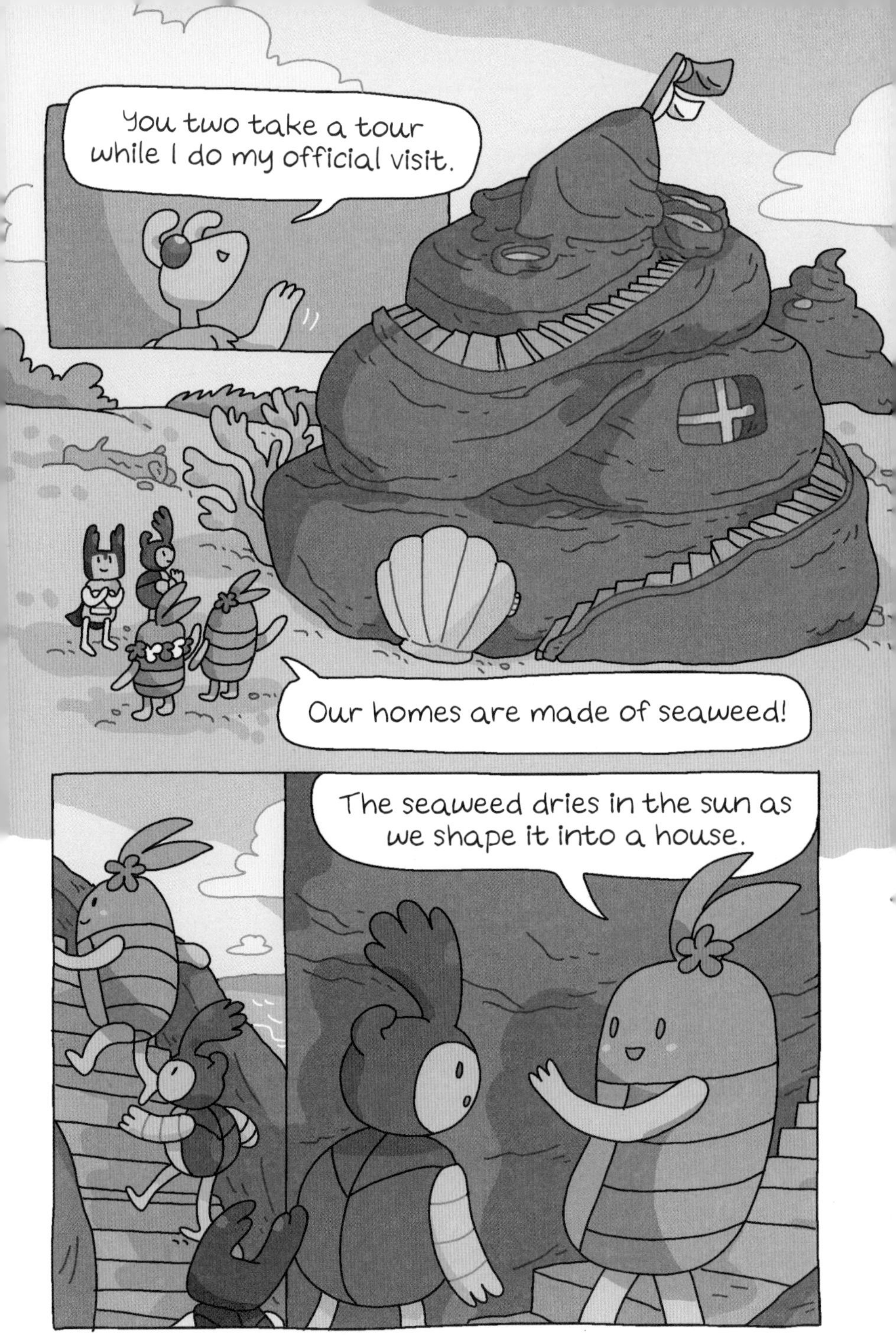
You two take a tour while I do my official visit.
Our homes are made of seaweed!
The seaweed dries in the sun as we shape it into a house.

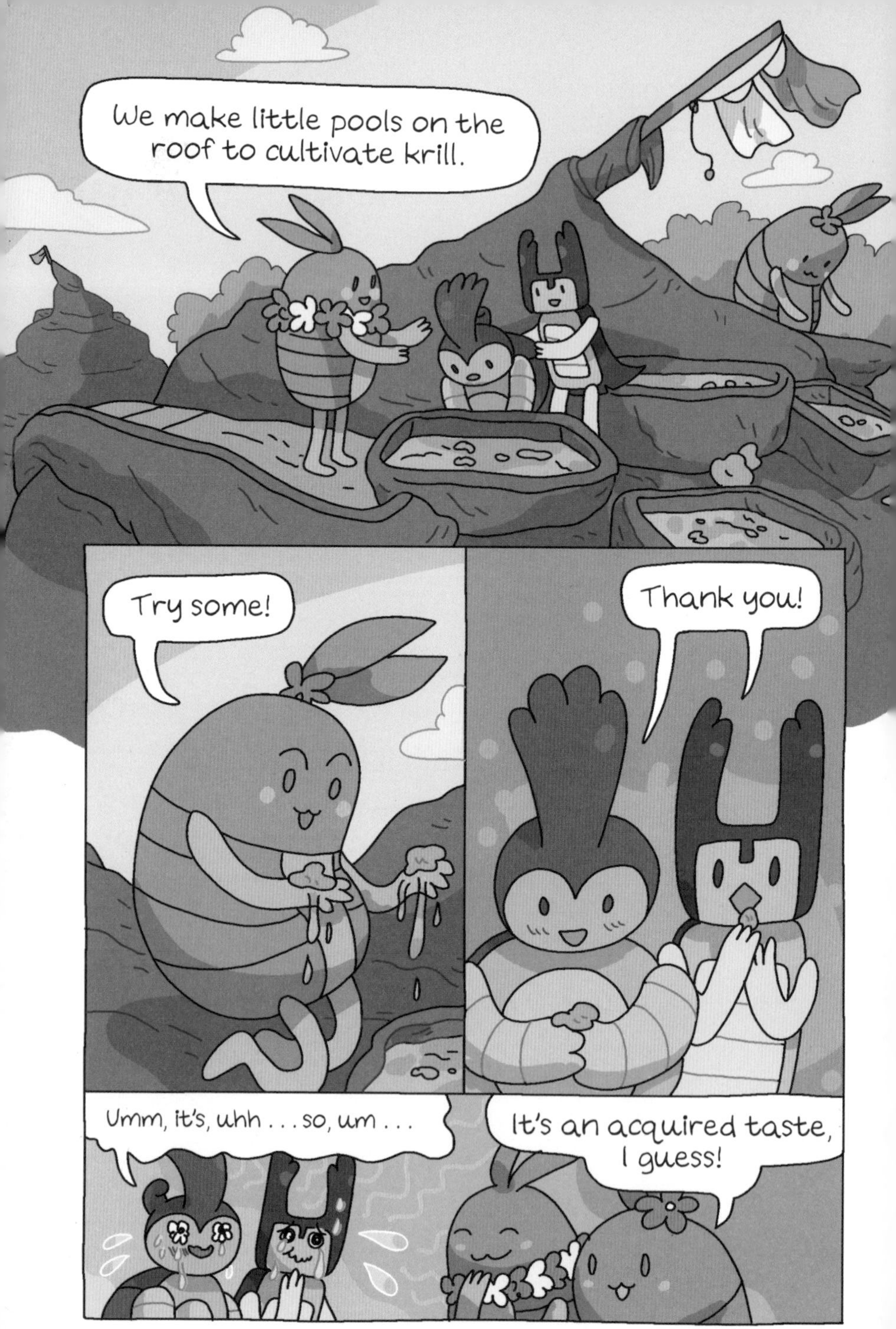
We make little pools on the roof to cultivate krill.
Try some!
Thank you!
Umm, it's, uhh . . . so, um . . .
It's an acquired taste, I guess!

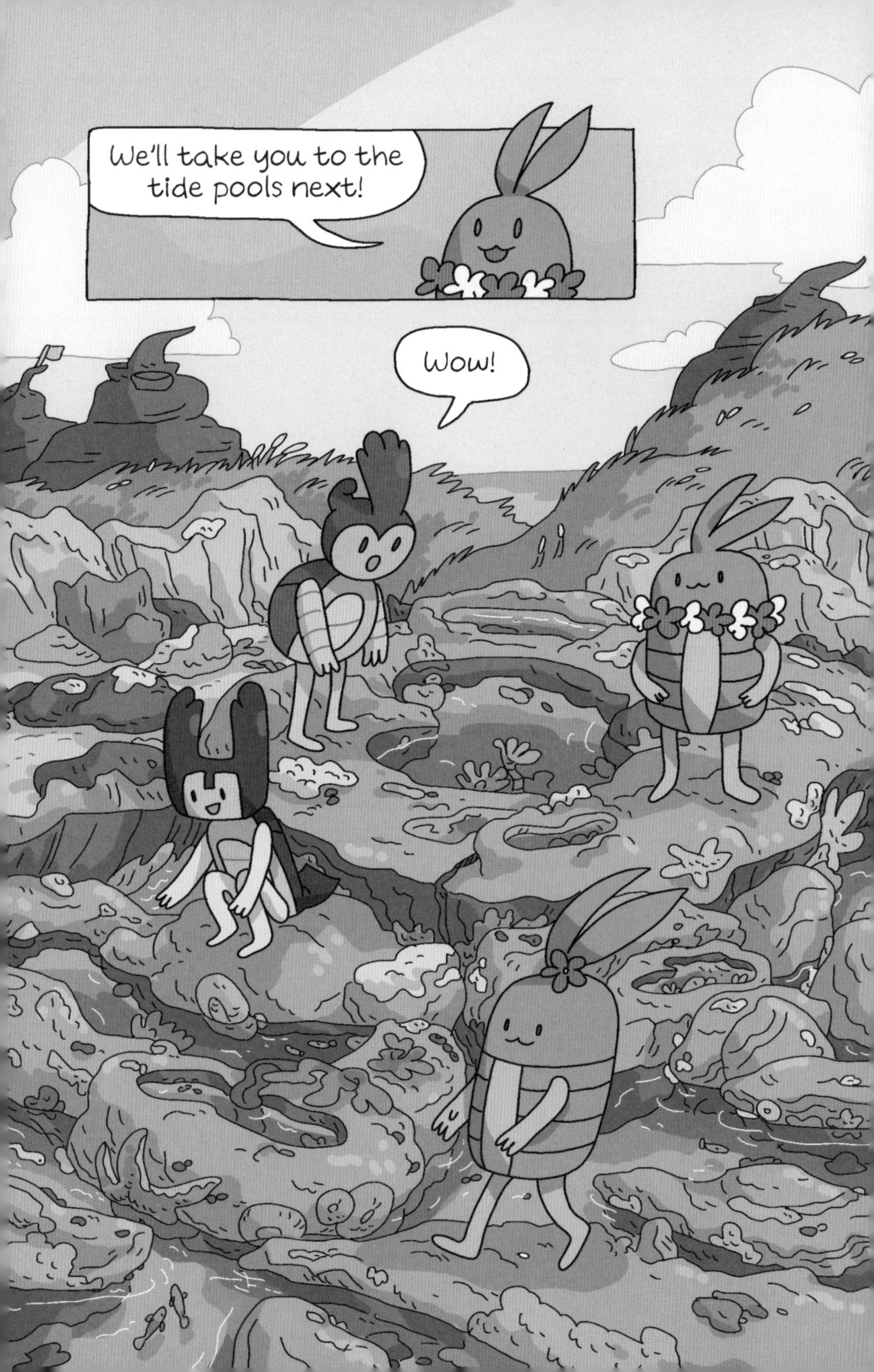
We'll take you to the tide pools next!
Wow!

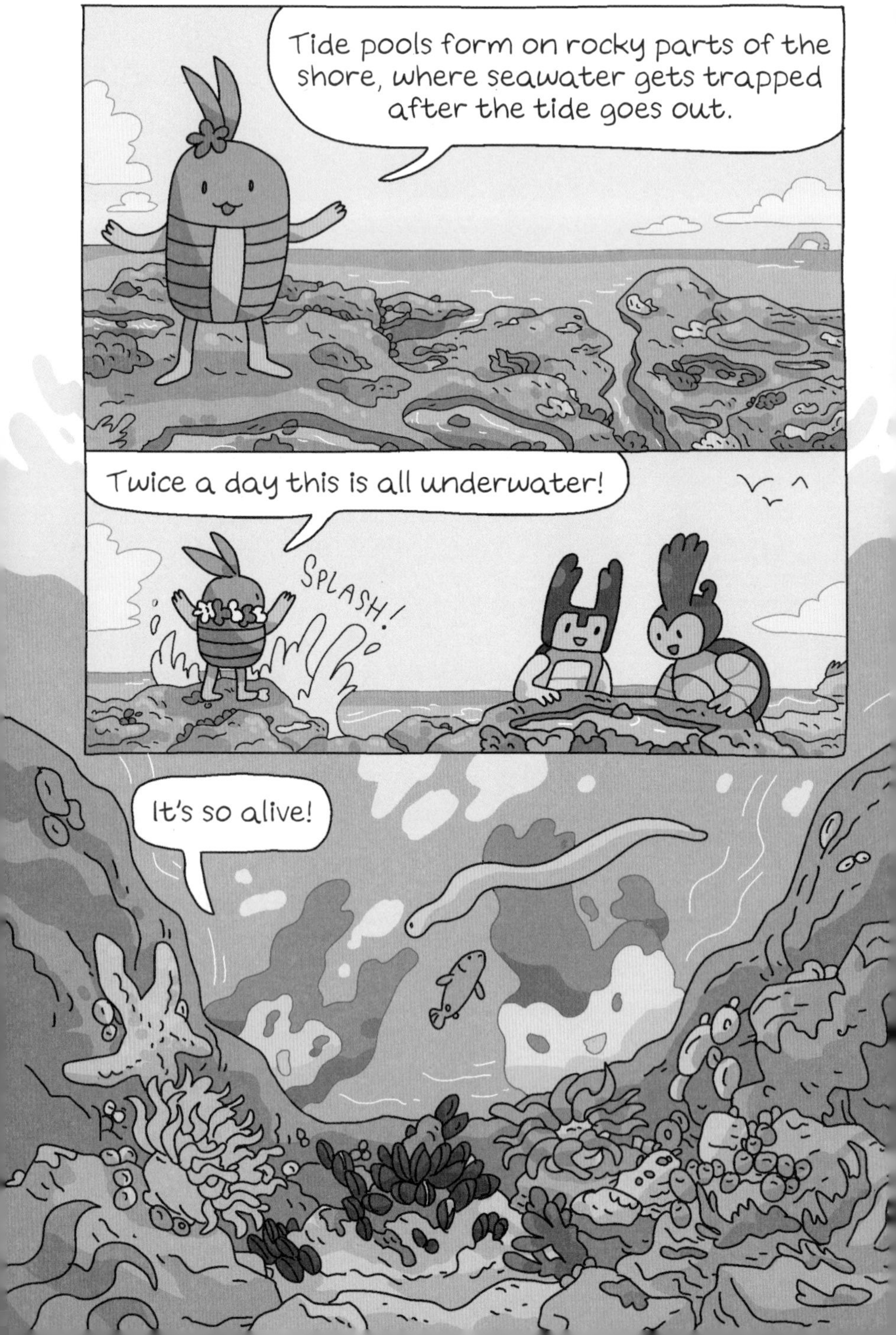
Tide pools form on rocky parts of the shore, where seawater gets trapped after the tide goes out.
Twice a day this is all underwater!
SPLASH!
It's so alive!

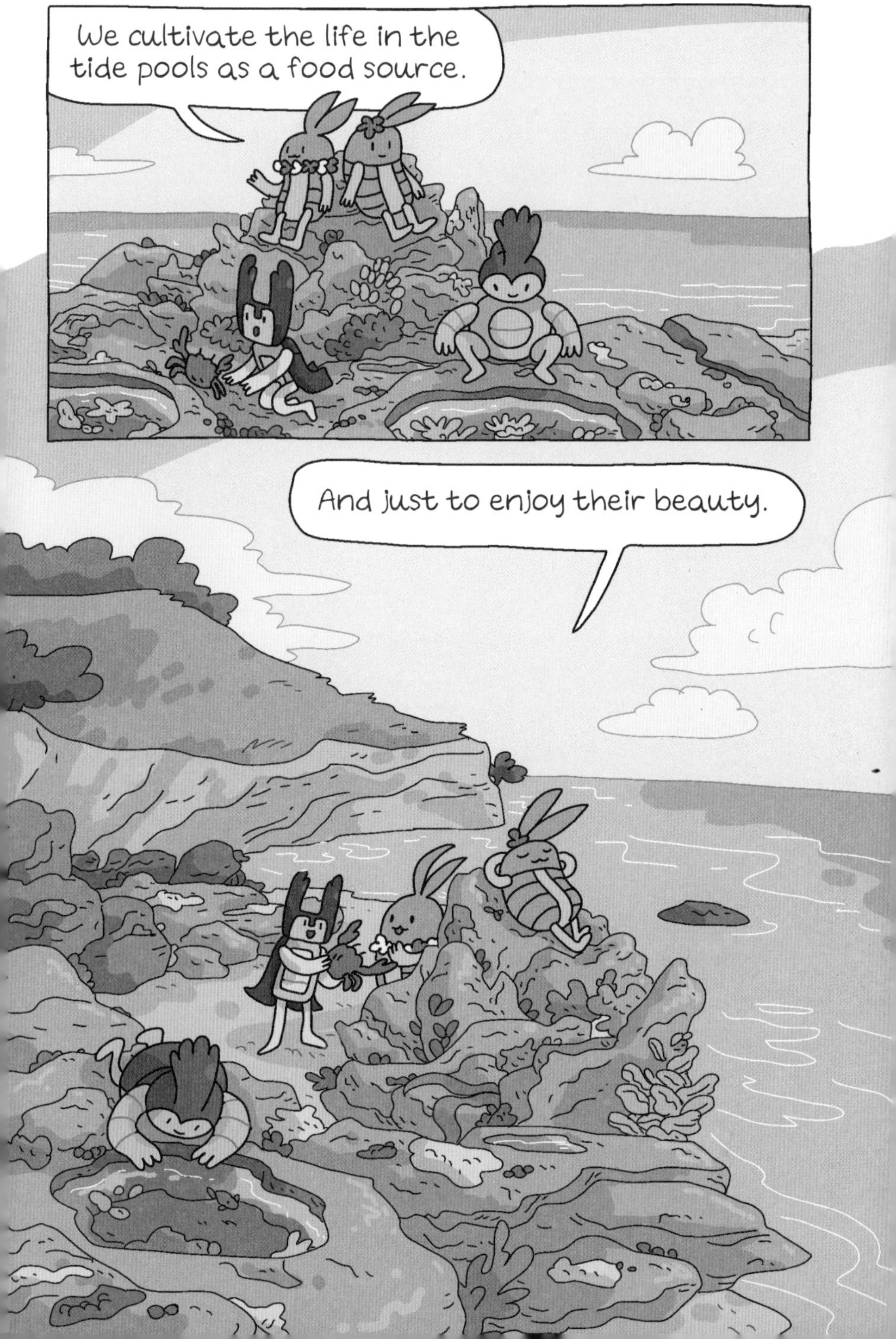
We cultivate the life in the tide pools as a food source.
And just to enjoy their beauty.

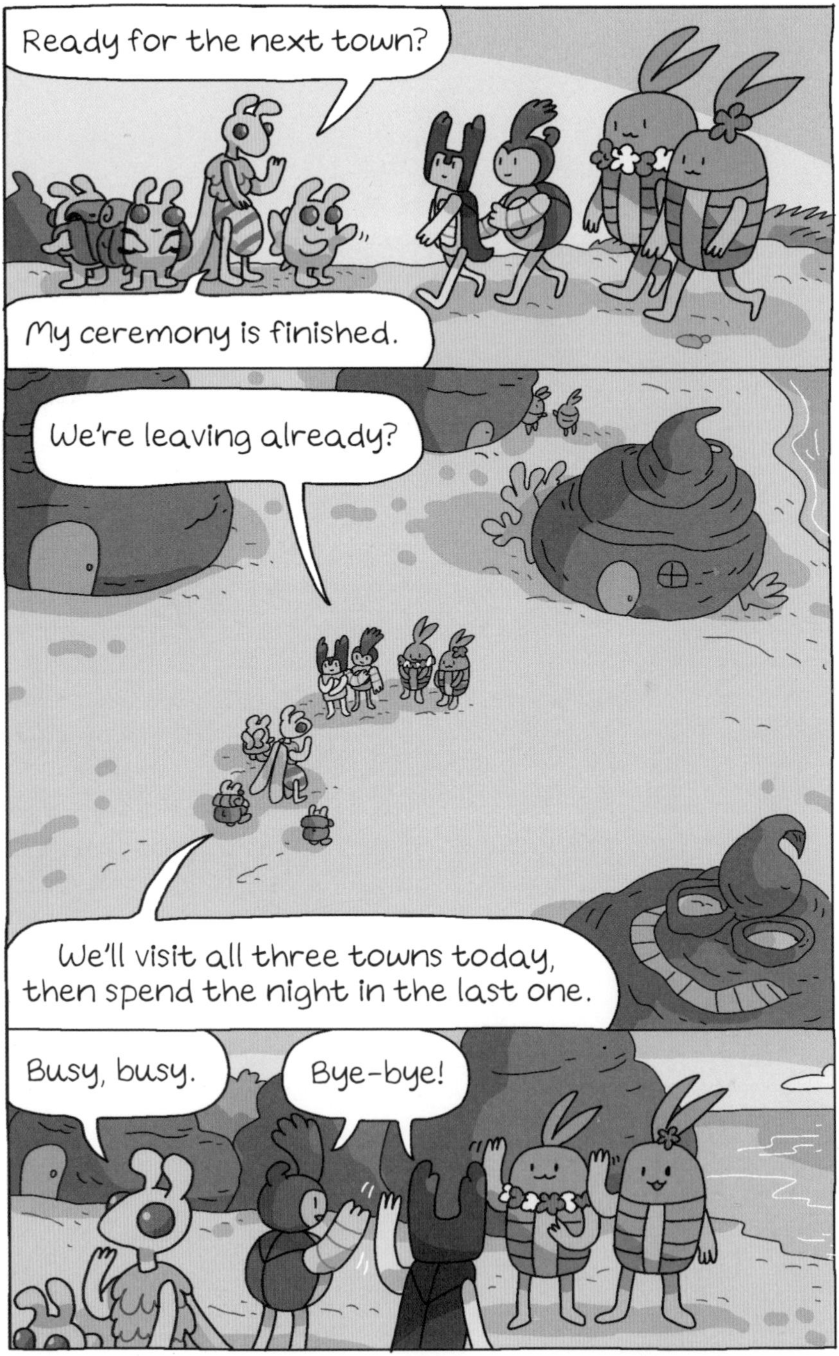

Ready for the next town?
My ceremony is finished.
We're leaving already?
We'll visit all three towns today, then spend the night in the last one.
Busy, busy.
Bye-bye!

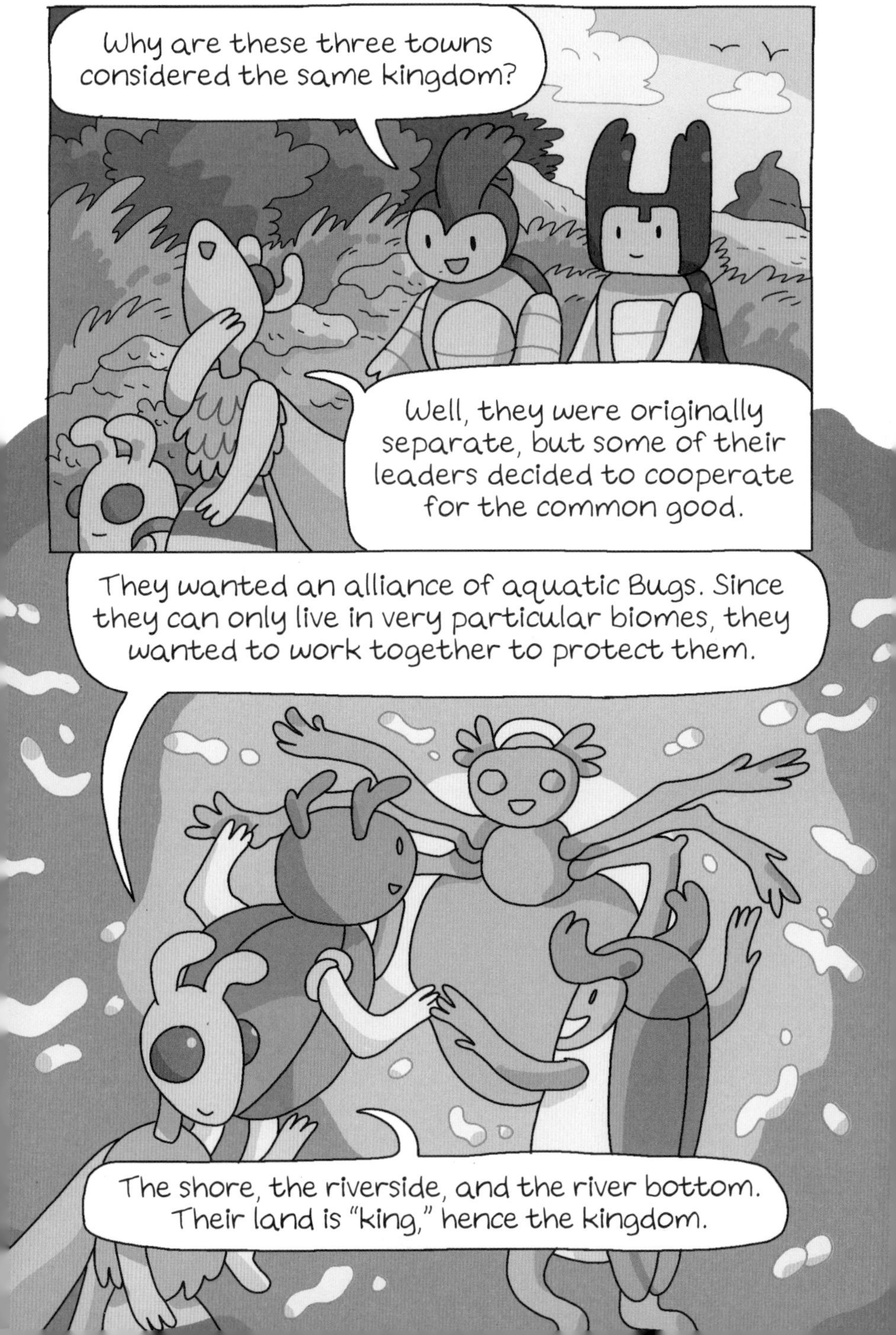
Why are these three towns considered the same kingdom?
Well, they were originally separate, but some of their leaders decided to cooperate for the common good.
They wanted an alliance of aquatic Bugs. Since they can only live in very particular biomes, they wanted to work together to protect them.
The shore, the riverside, and the river bottom. Their land is "king," hence the kingdom.

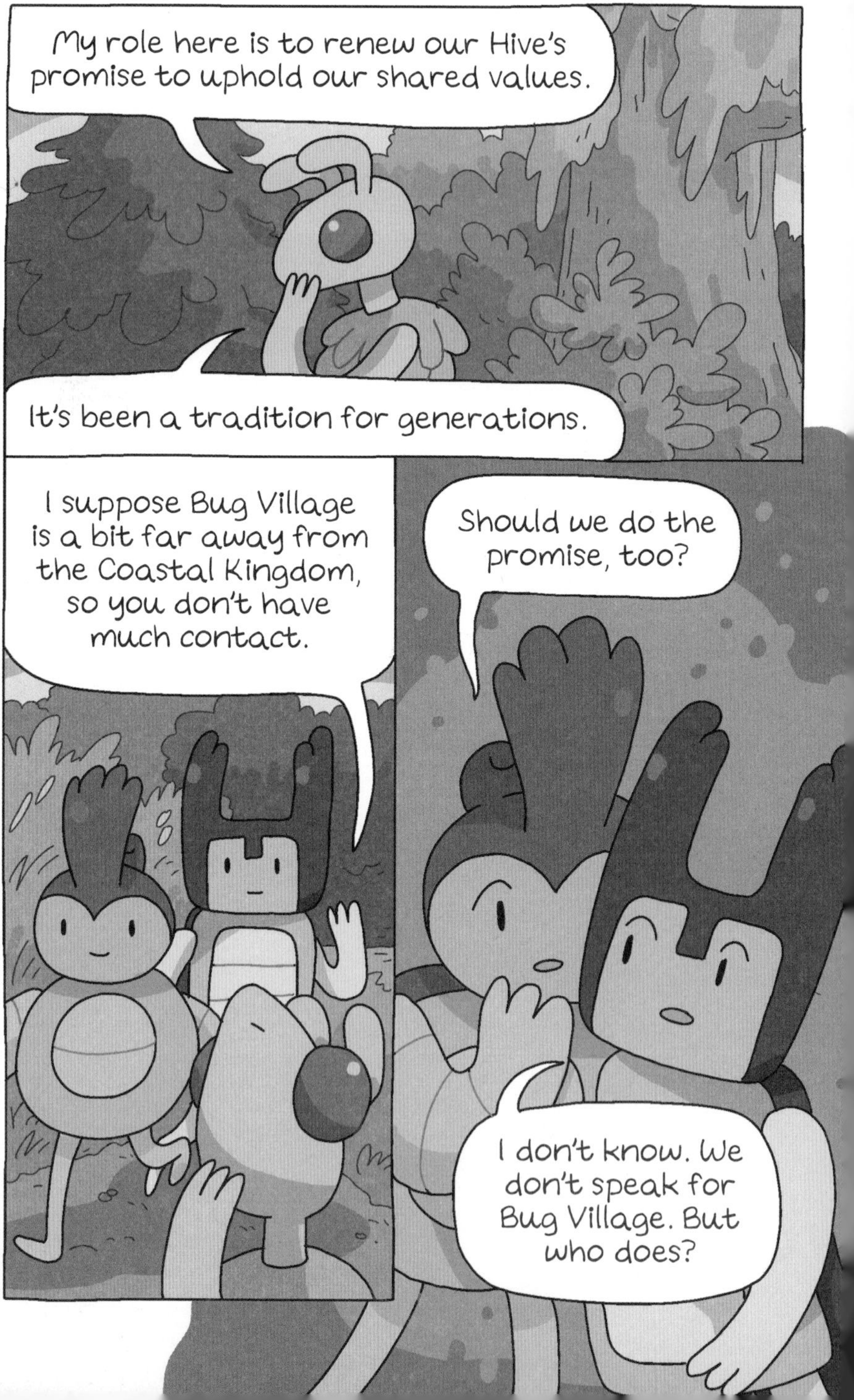
My role here is to renew our Hive's promise to uphold our shared values.
It's been a tradition for generations.
I suppose Bug Village is a bit far away from the Coastal Kingdom, so you don't have much contact.
Should we do the promise, too?
I don't know. We don't speak for Bug Village. But who does?

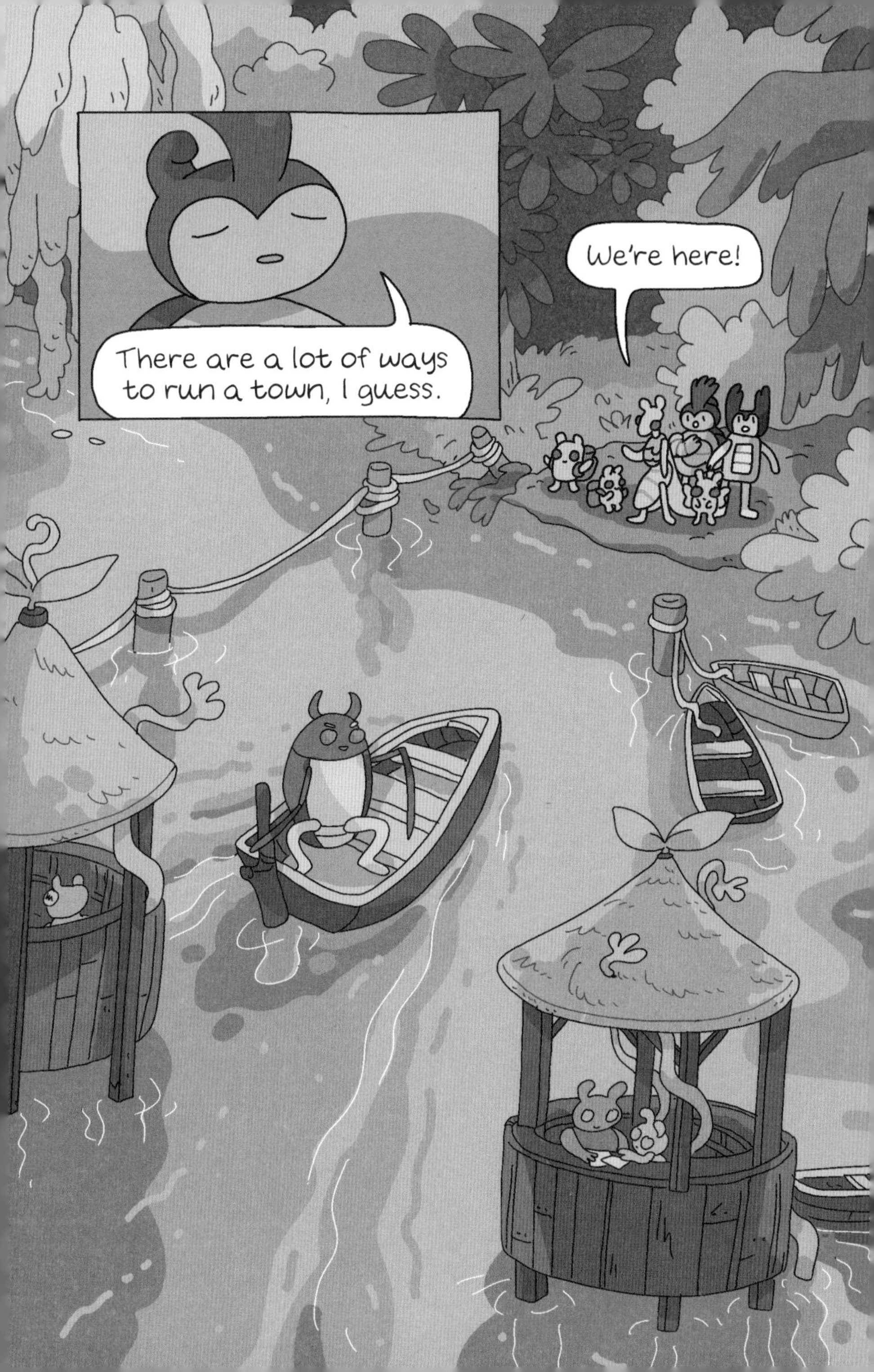
There are a lot of ways to run a town, I guess.
We're here!

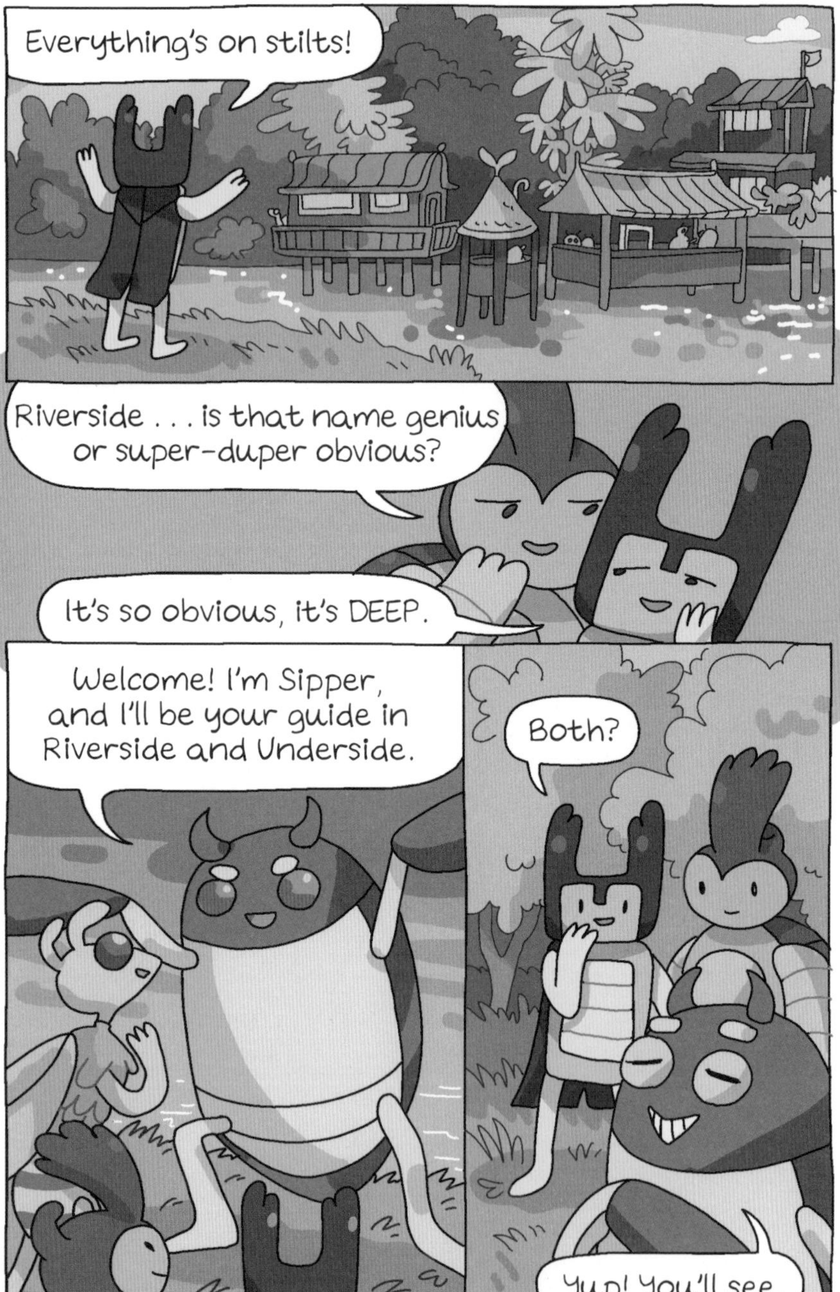
Everything's on stilts!
Riverside . . . is that name genius or super-duper obvious?
It's so obvious, it's DEEP.
Welcome! I'm Sipper, and I'll be your guide in Riverside and Underside.
Both?
Yup! You'll see.

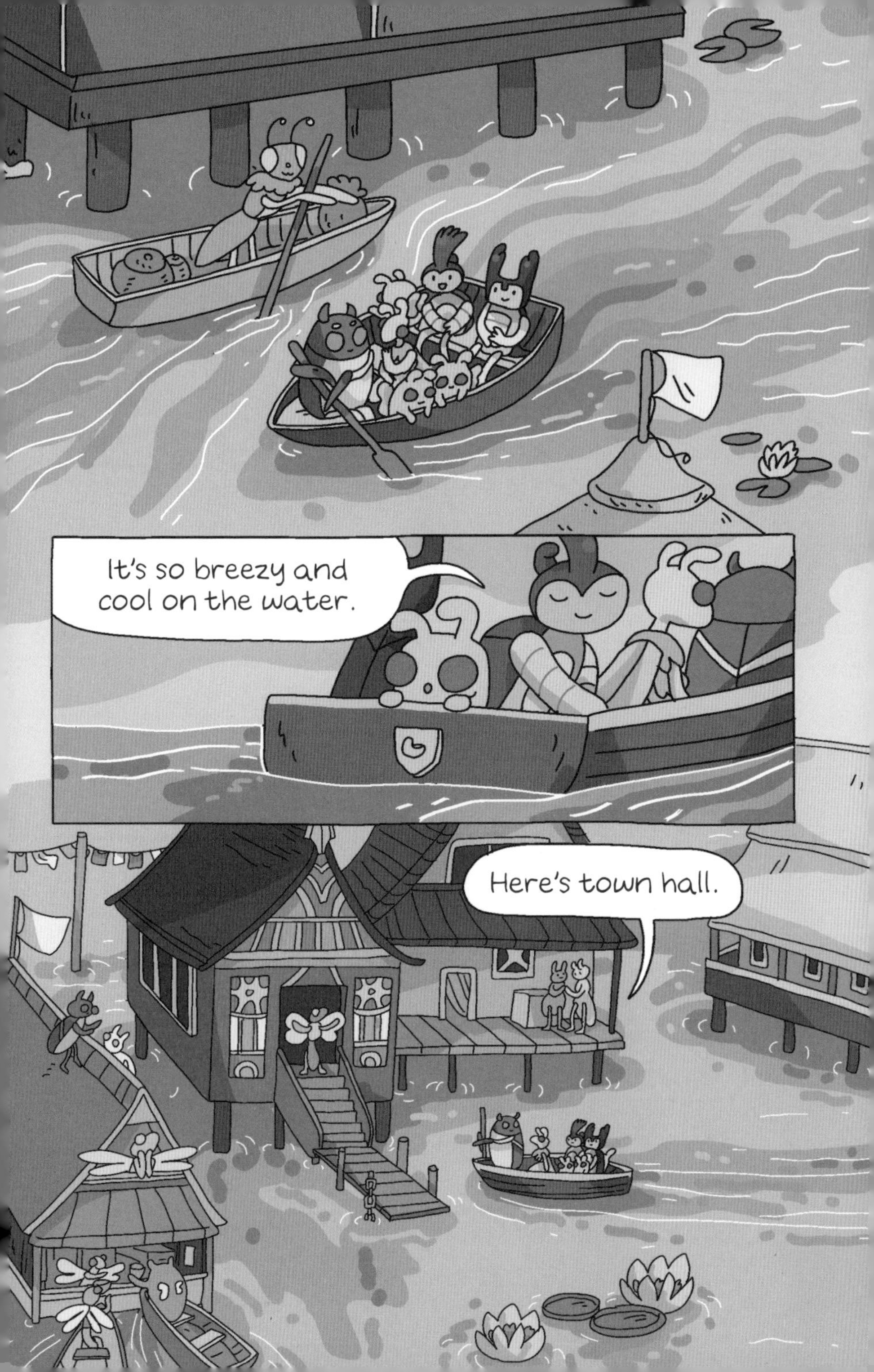
It's so breezy and cool on the water.
Here's town hall.

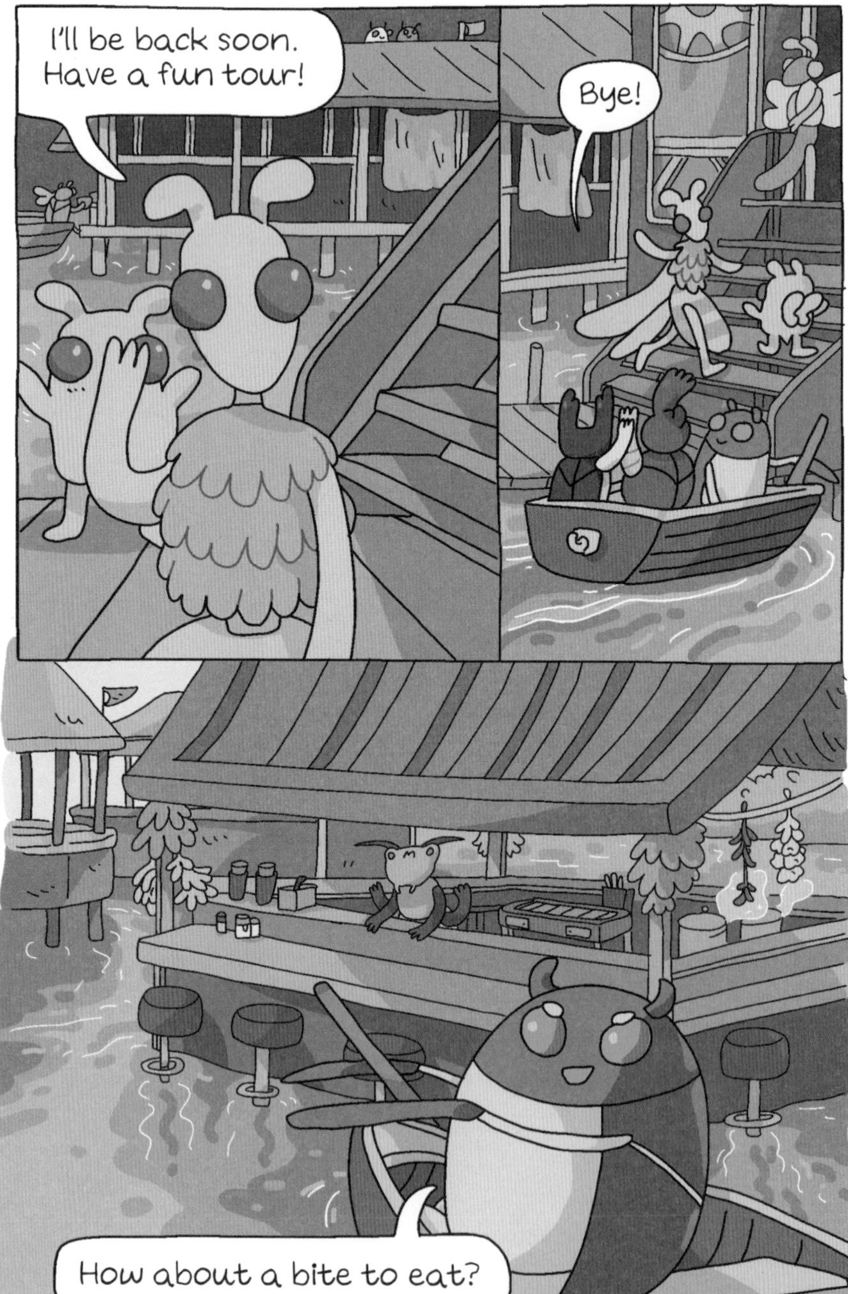
I'll be back soon.
Have a fun tour!
Bye!
How about a bite to eat?

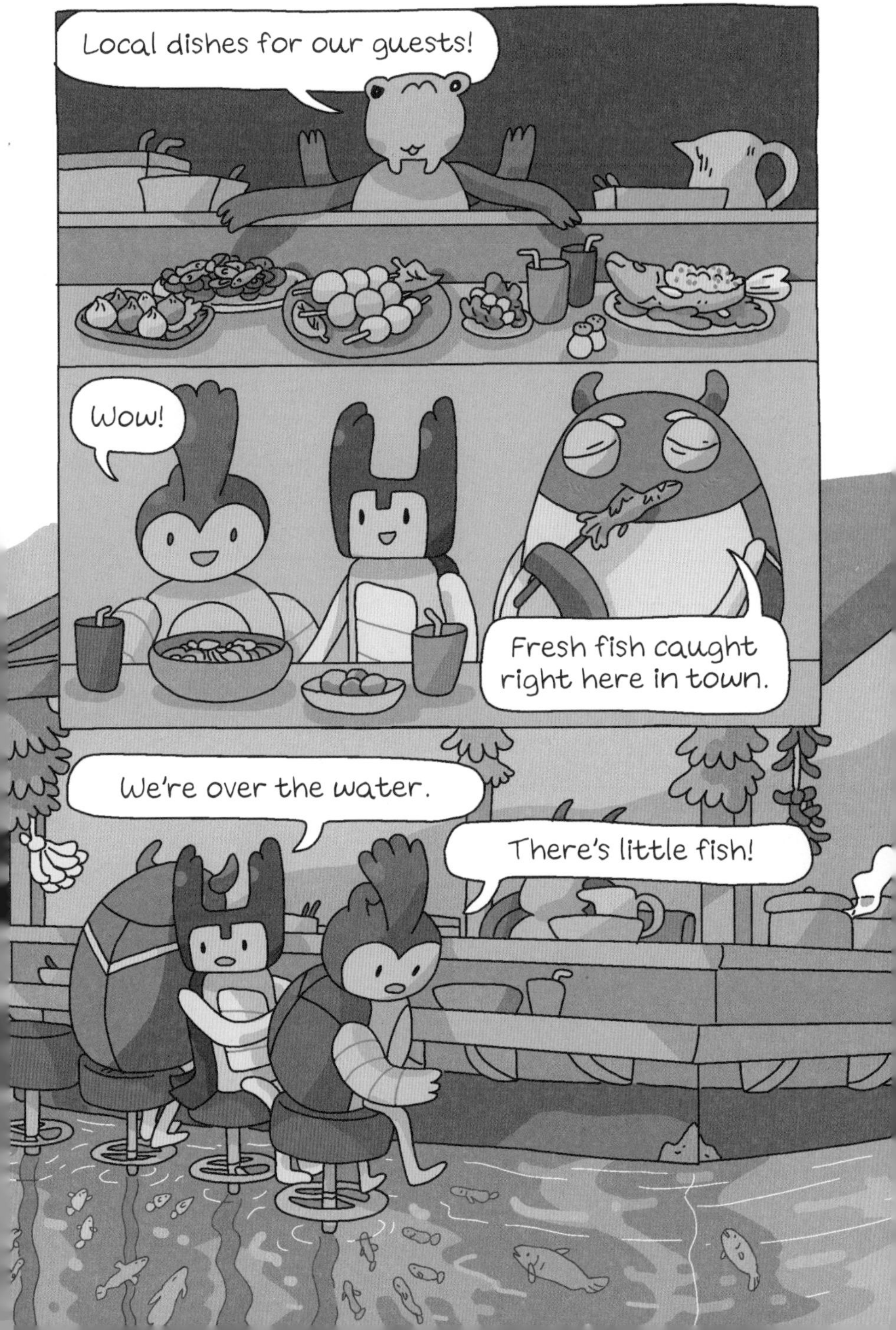
Local dishes for our guests!
Wow!
Fresh fish caught right here in town.
We're over the water.
There's little fish!

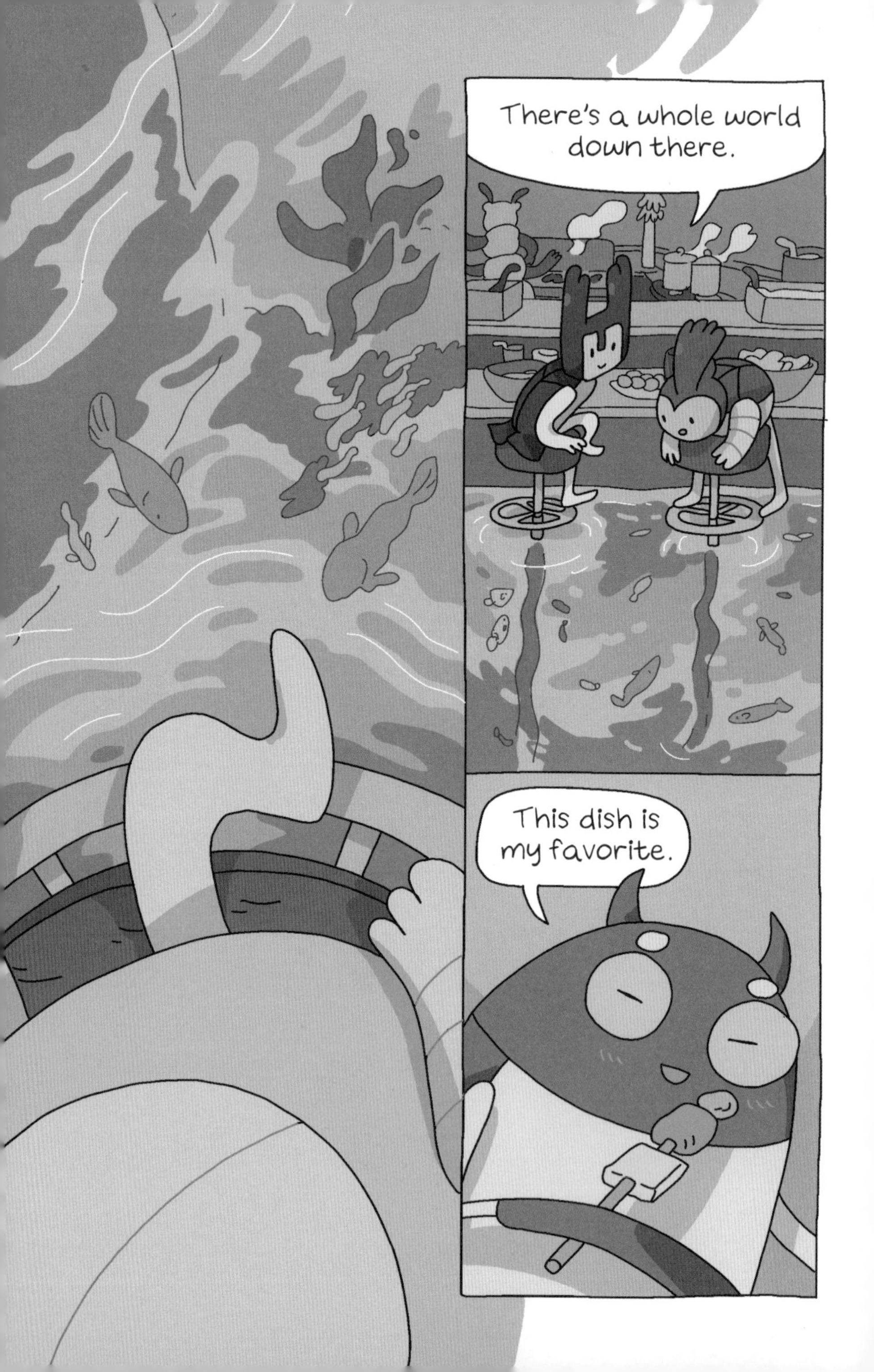
There's a whole world down there.
This dish is my favorite.

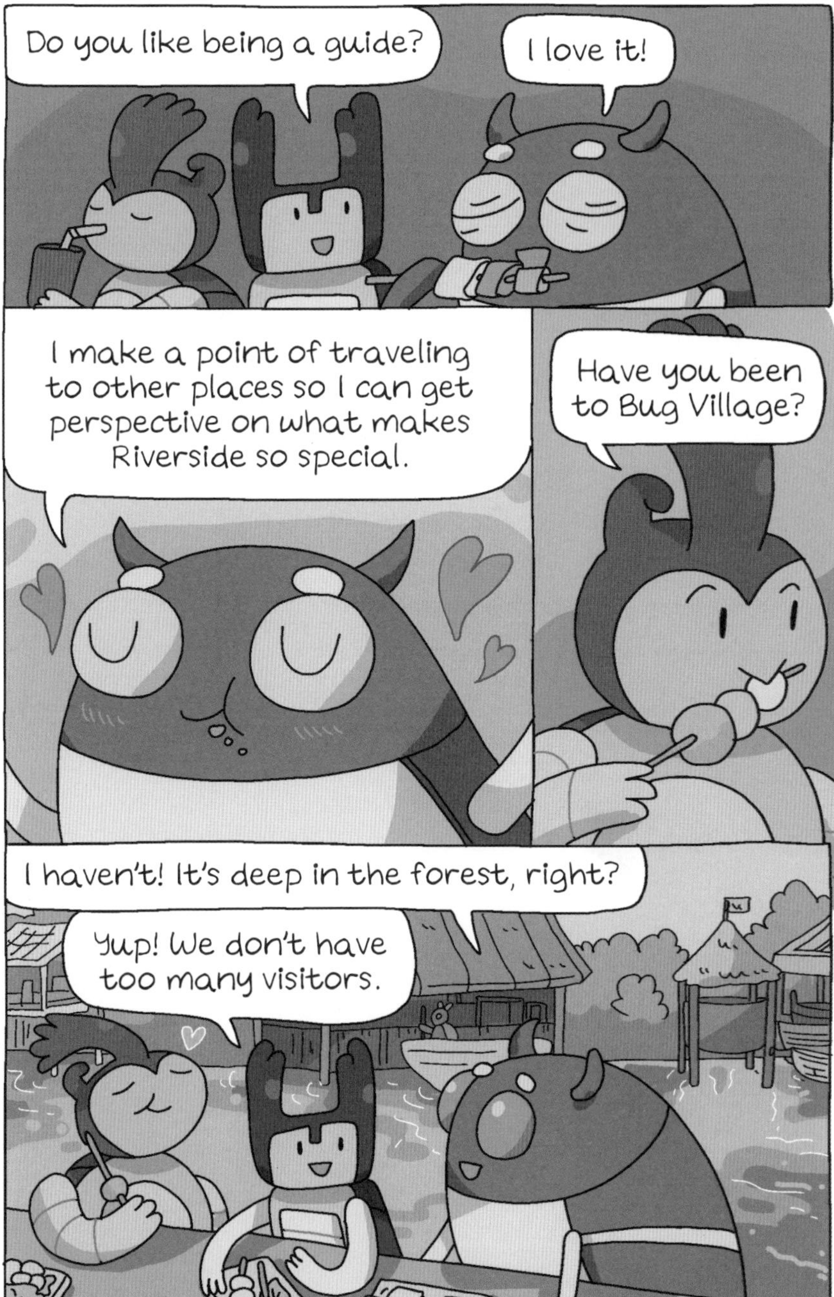
Do you like being a guide?
I love it!
I make a point of traveling to other places so I can get perspective on what makes Riverside so special.
Have you been to Bug Village?
I haven't! It's deep in the forest, right?
Yup! We don't have too many visitors.

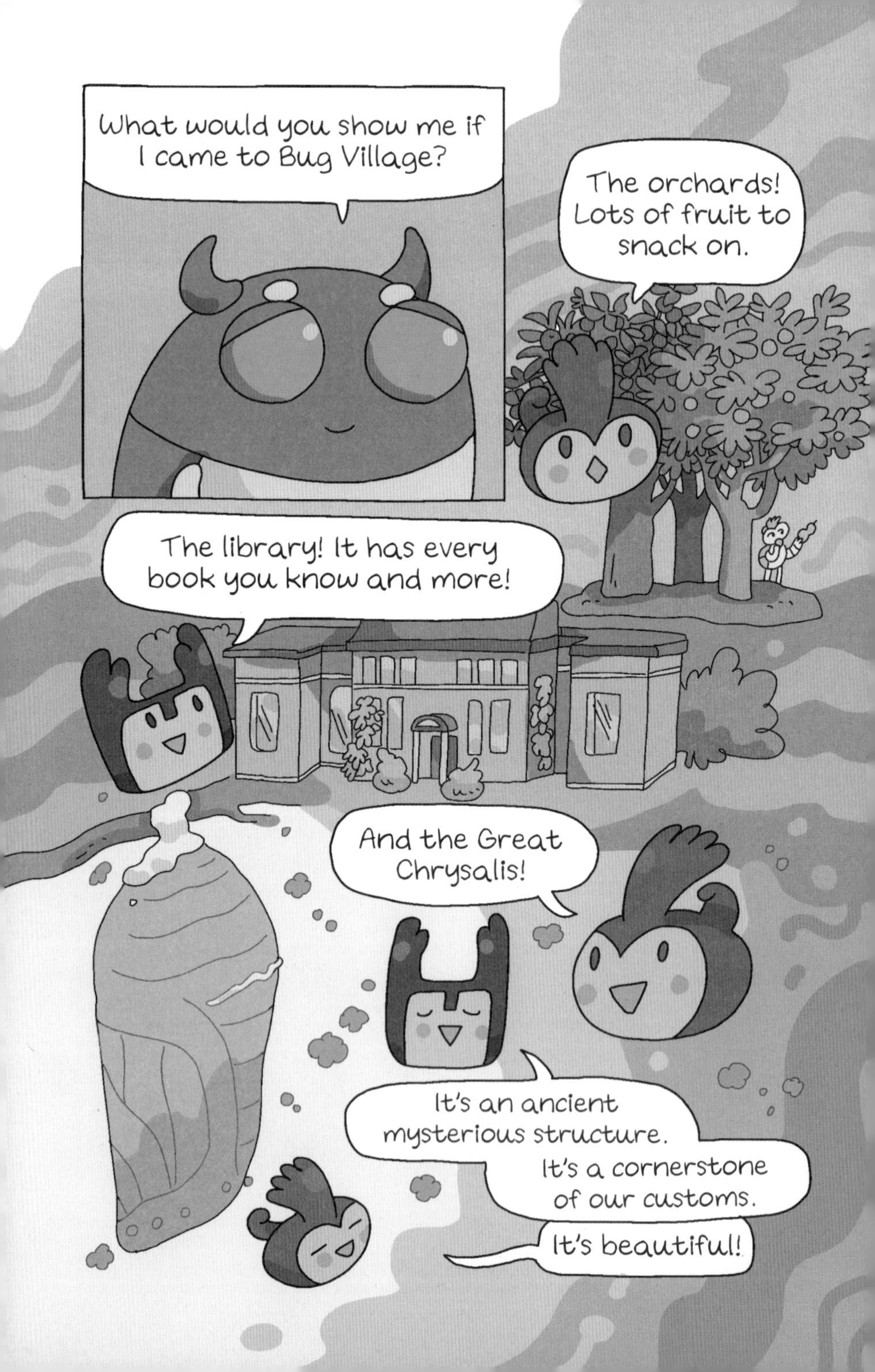
What would you show me if I came to Bug Village?
The orchards! Lots of fruit to snack on.
The library! It has every book you know and more!
And the Great Chrysalis!
It's an ancient mysterious structure.
It's a cornerstone of our customs.
It's beautiful!

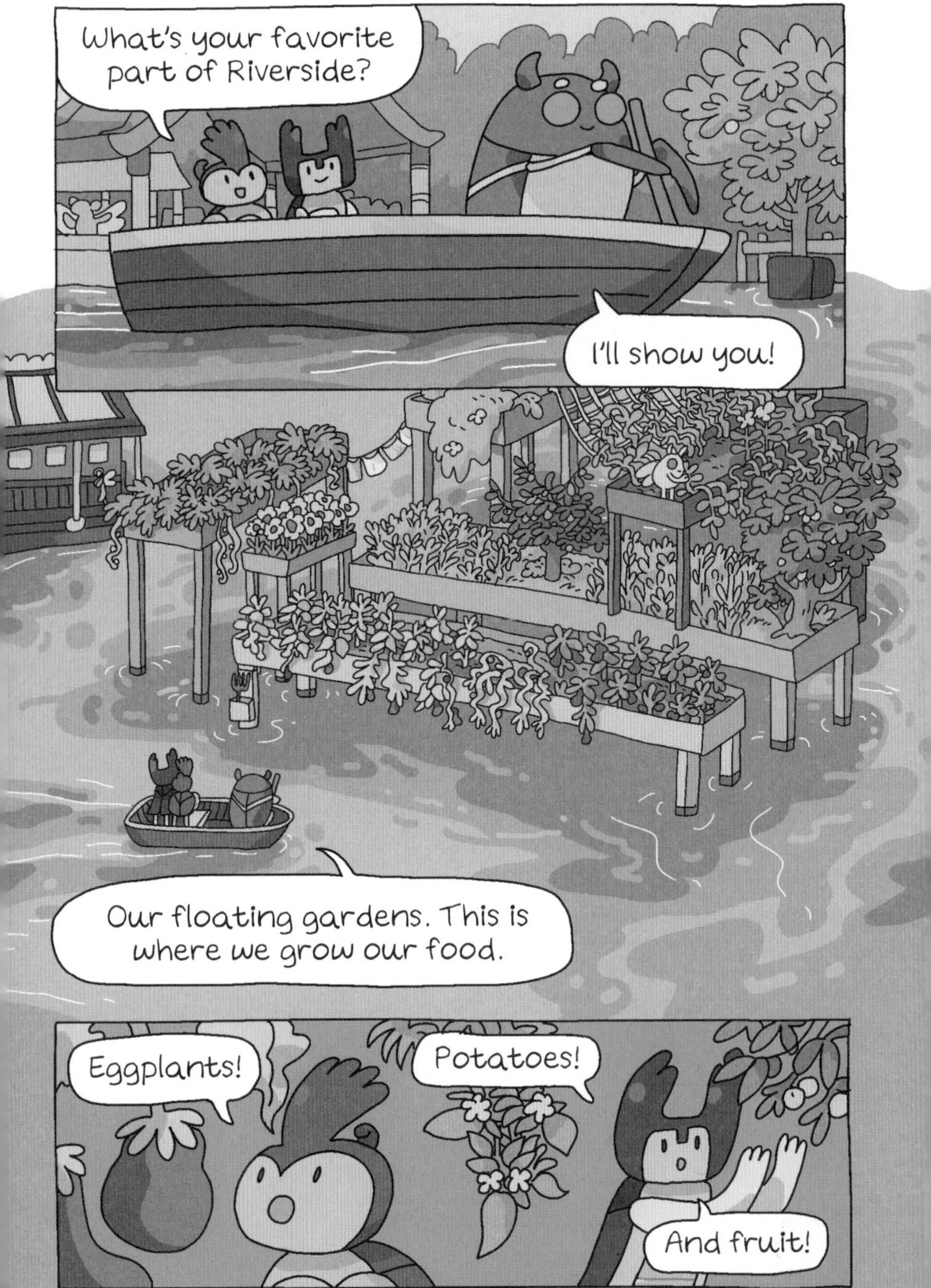
What's your favorite part of Riverside?
I'll show you!
Our floating gardens. This is where we grow our food.
Eggplants!
Potatoes!
And fruit!

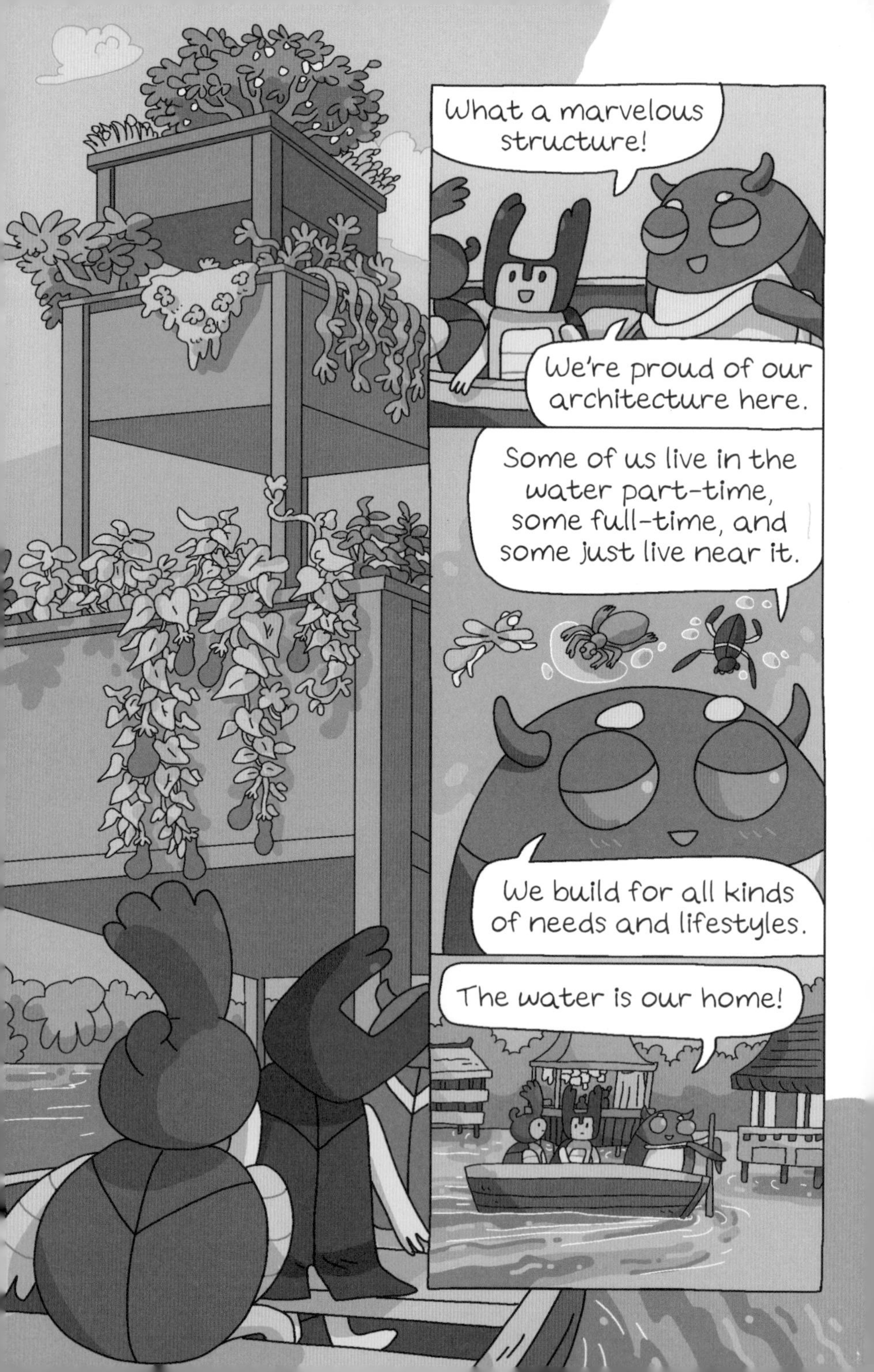
What a marvelous structure!
We're proud of our architecture here.
Some of us live in the water part-time, some full-time, and some just live near it.
We build for all kinds of needs and lifestyles.
The water is our home!

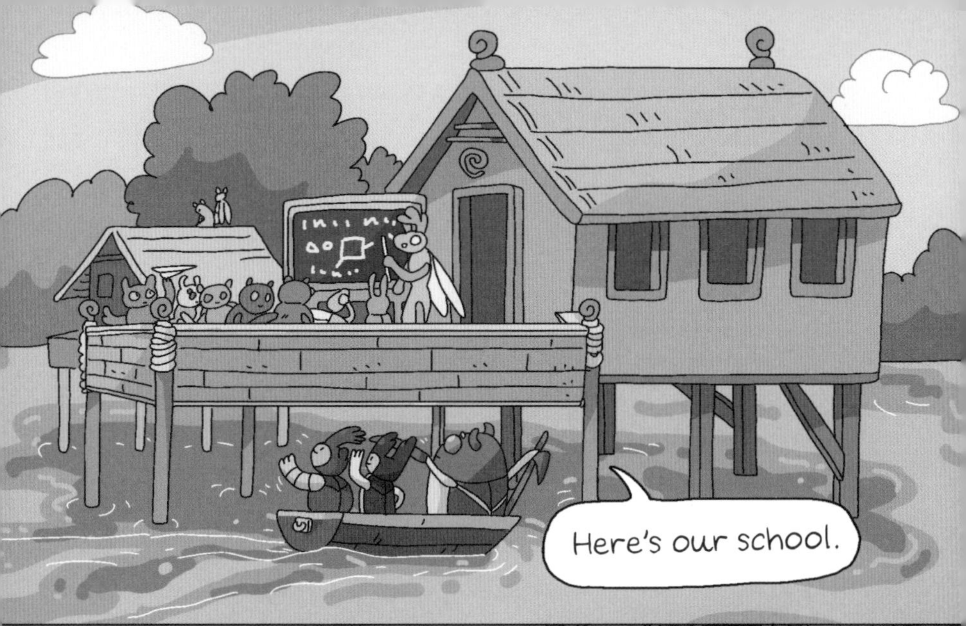
Here's our school.

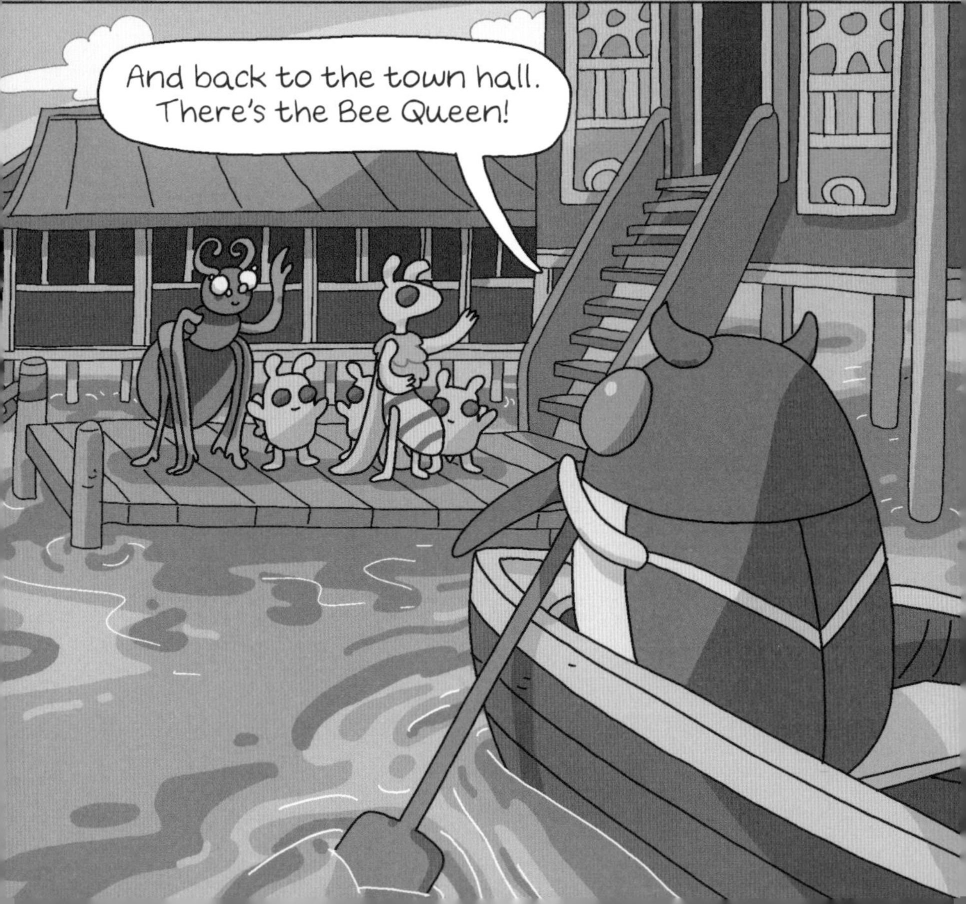
And back to the town hall.
There's the Bee Queen!

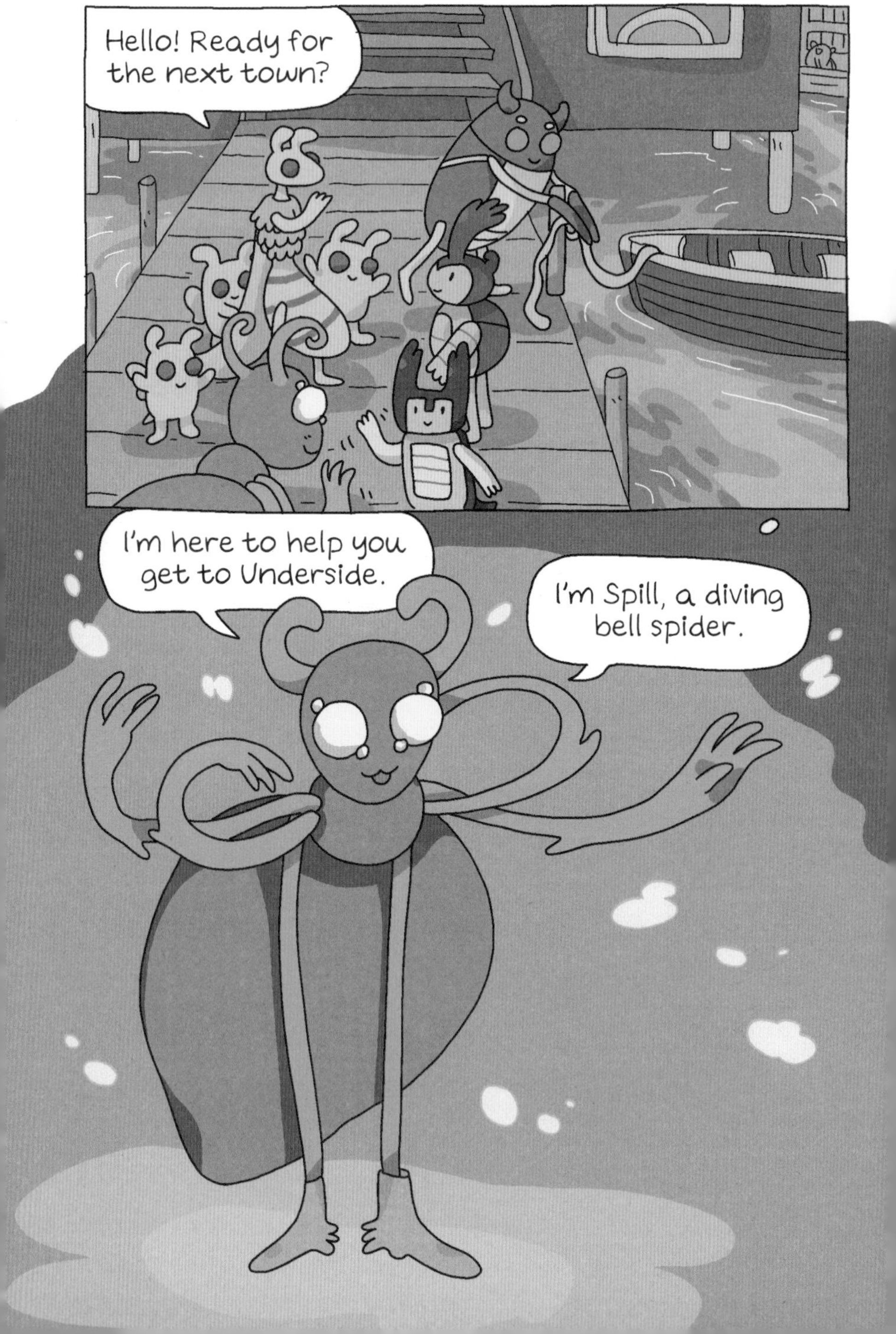
Hello! Ready for the next town?
I'm here to help you get to Underside.
I'm Spill, a diving bell spider.

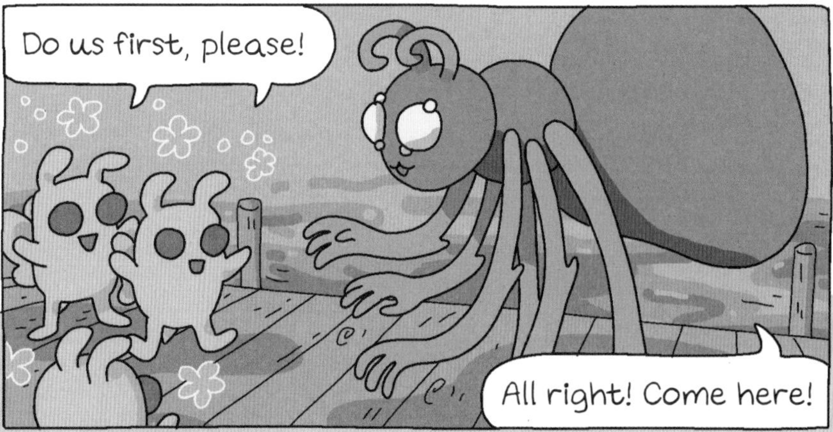
Do us first, please!
All right! Come here!

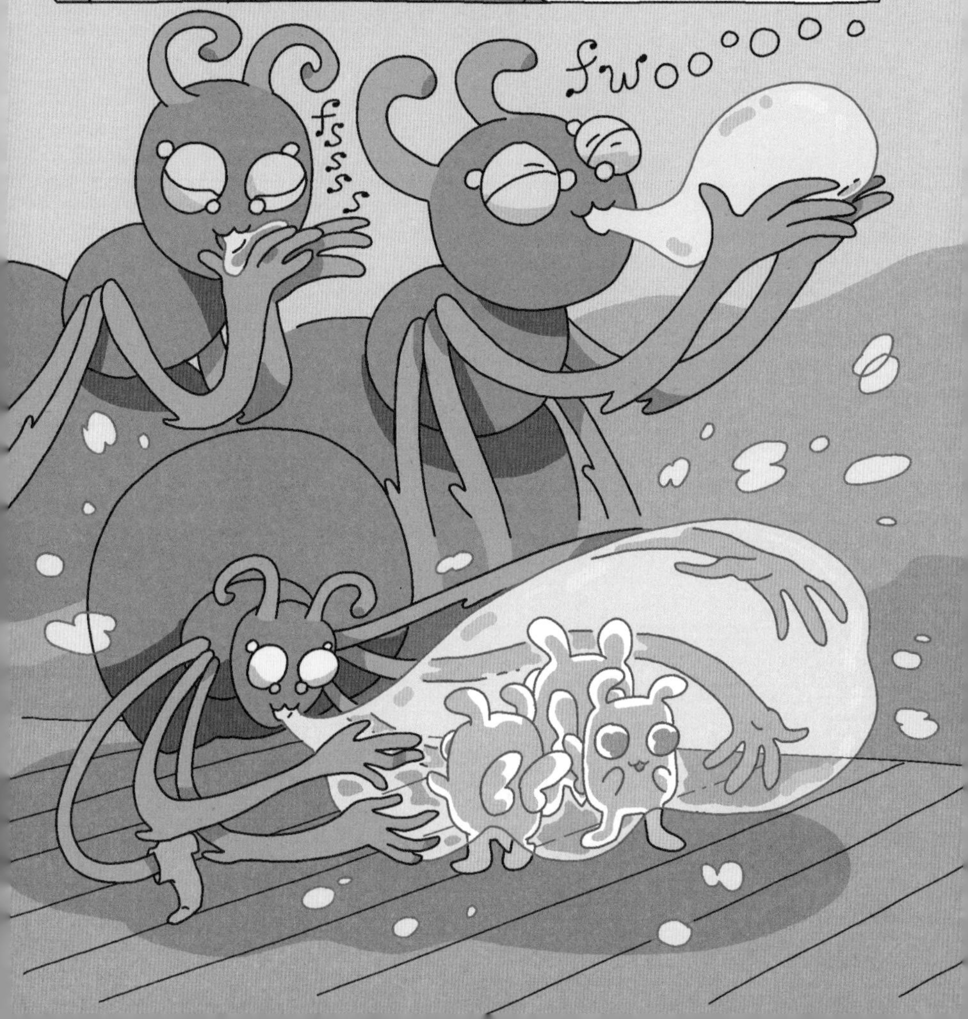
fssss
fwoooooo

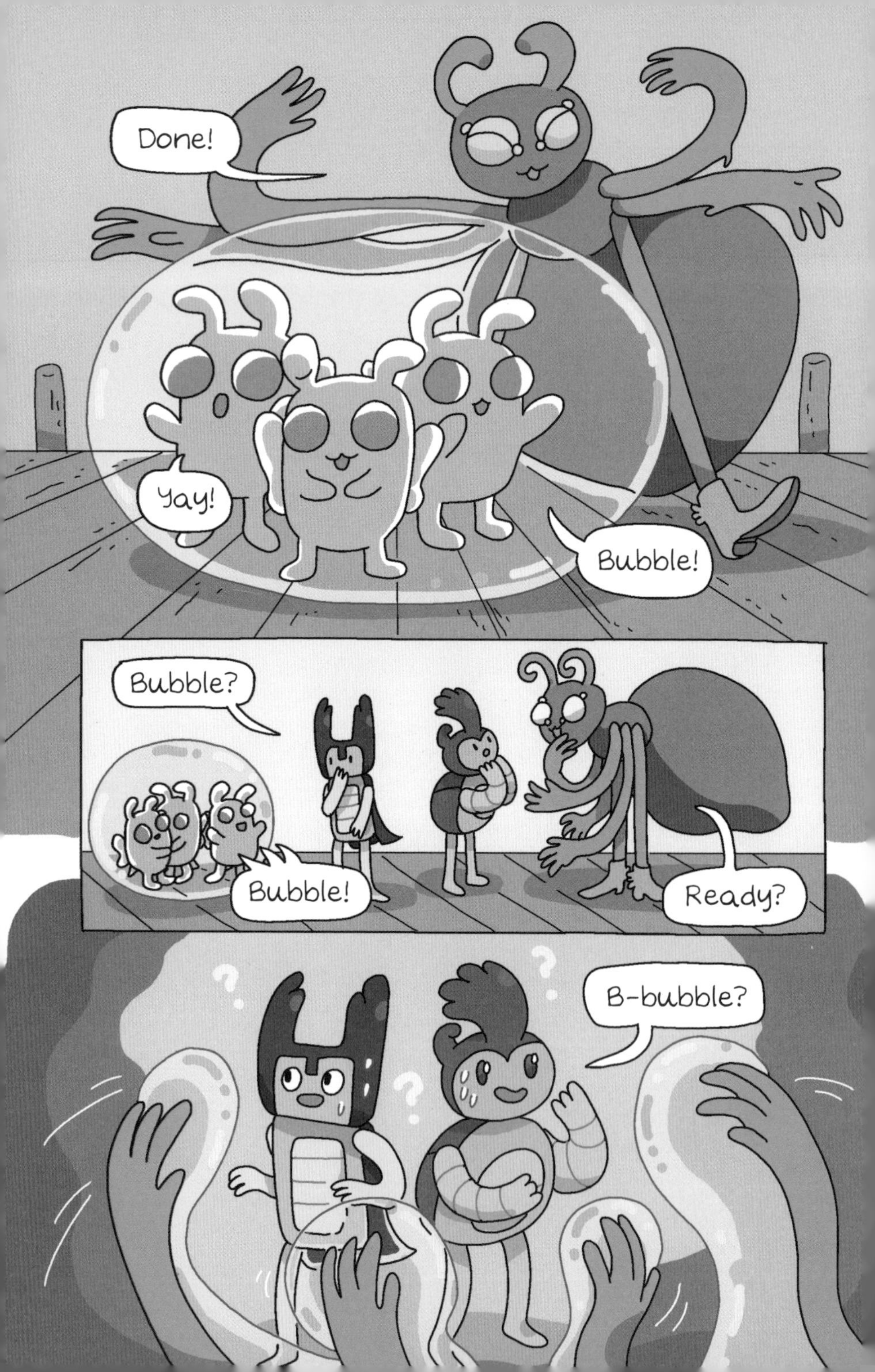
Done!
Yay!
Bubble!
Bubble?
Bubble!
Ready?
B-bubble?

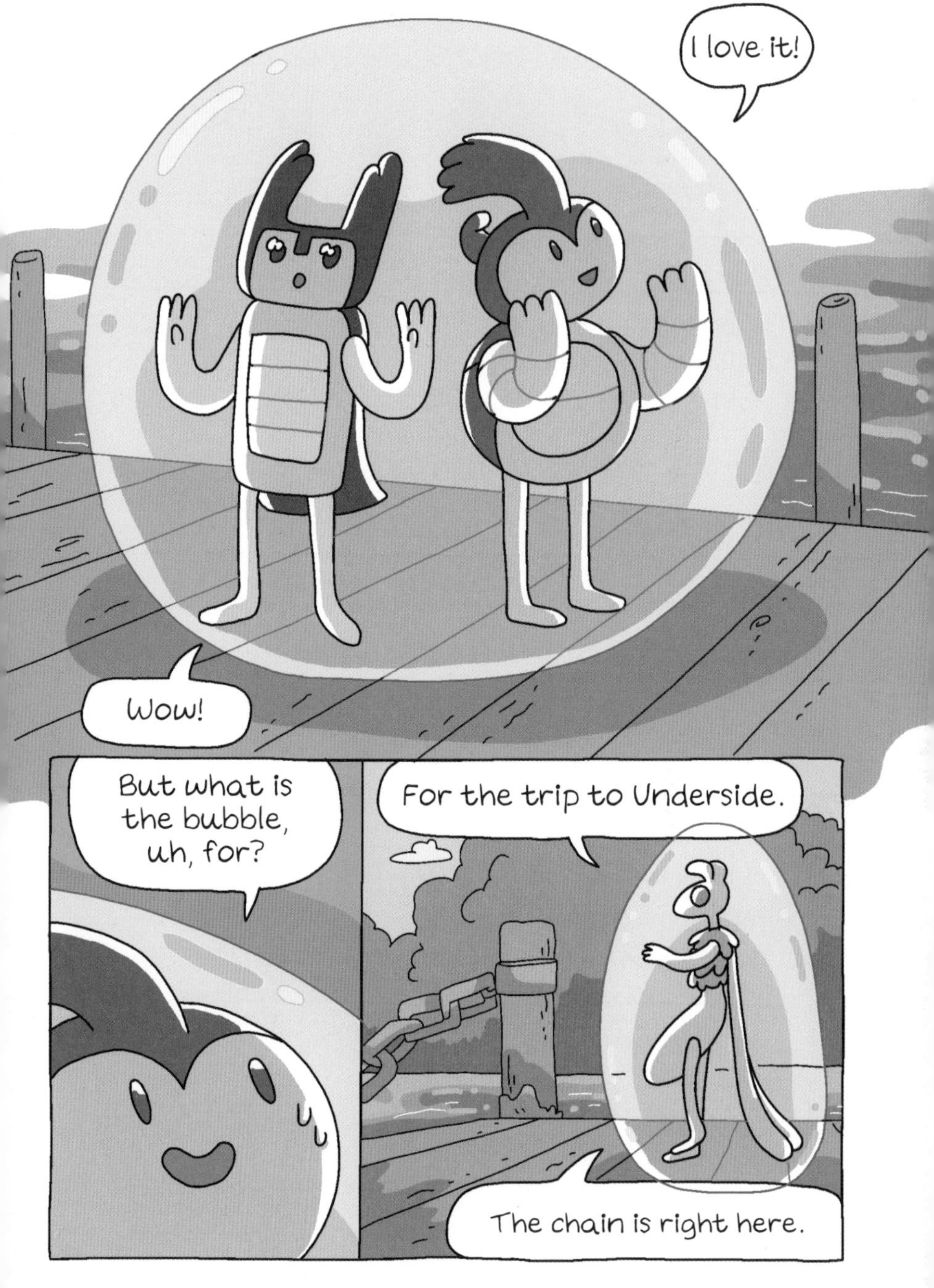
I love it!
Wow!
But what is the bubble, uh, for?
For the trip to Underside.
The chain is right here.

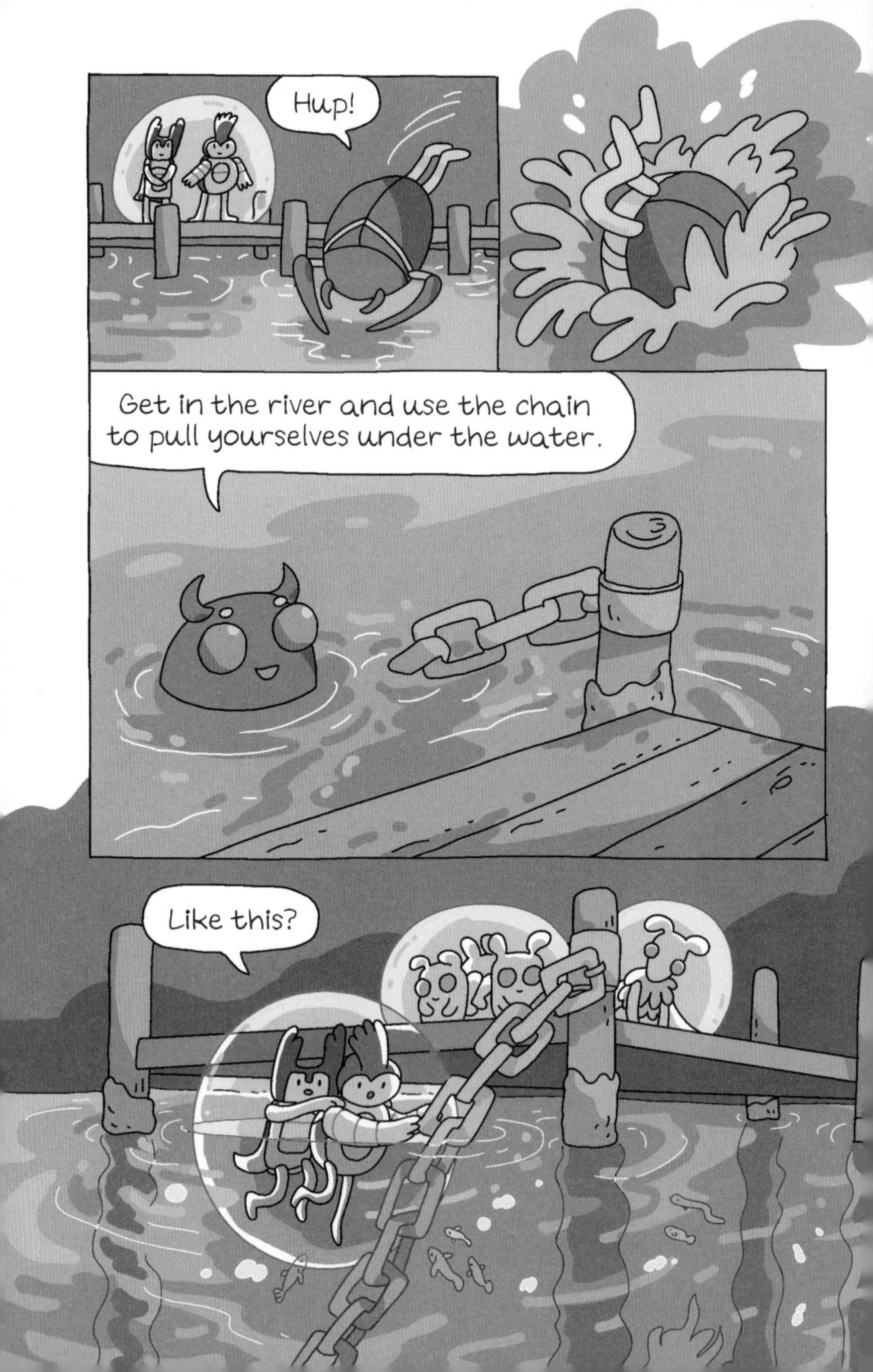
Hup!
Get in the river and use the chain to pull yourselves under the water.
Like this?

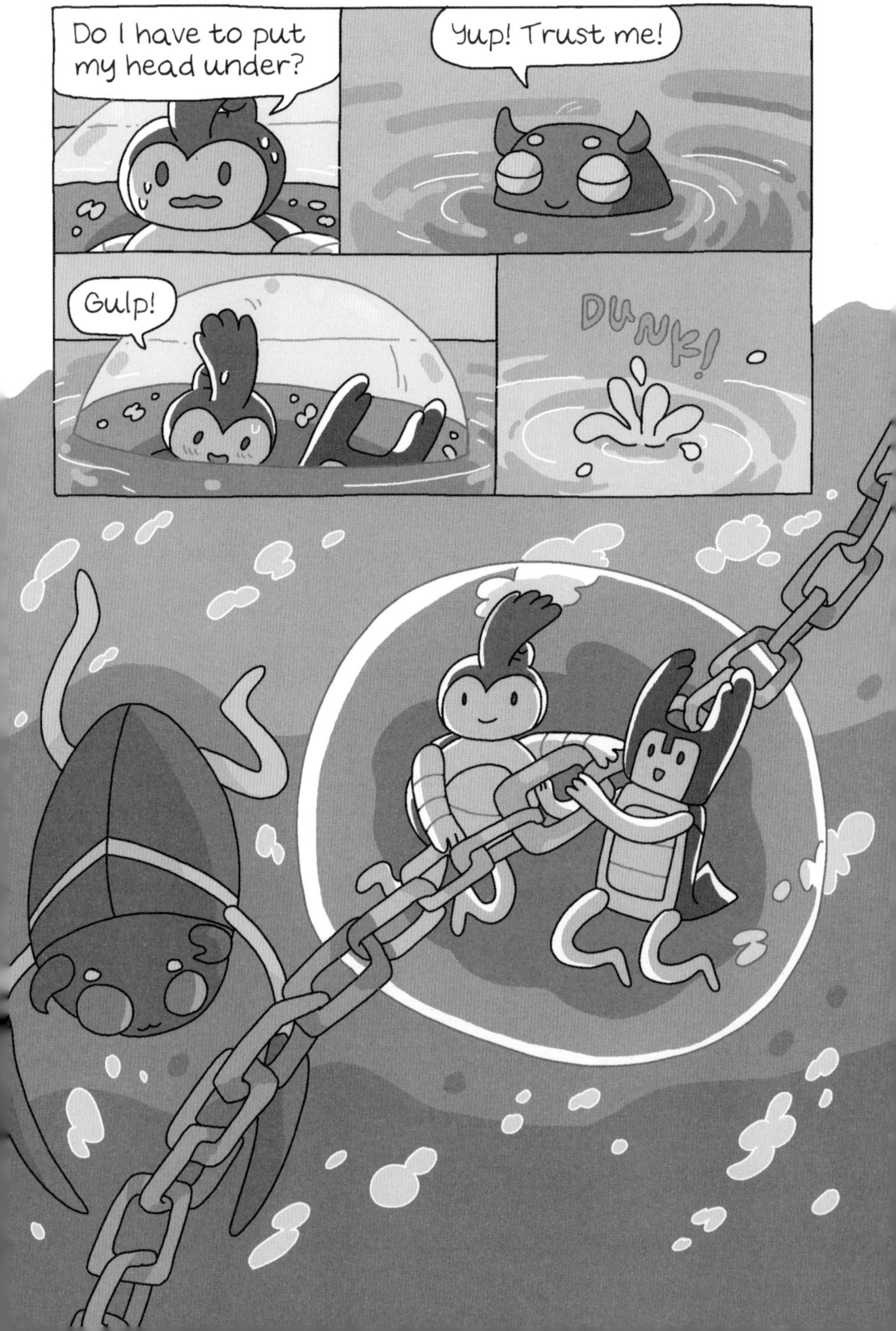
Do I have to put my head under?
Yup! Trust me!
Gulp!
DUNK!

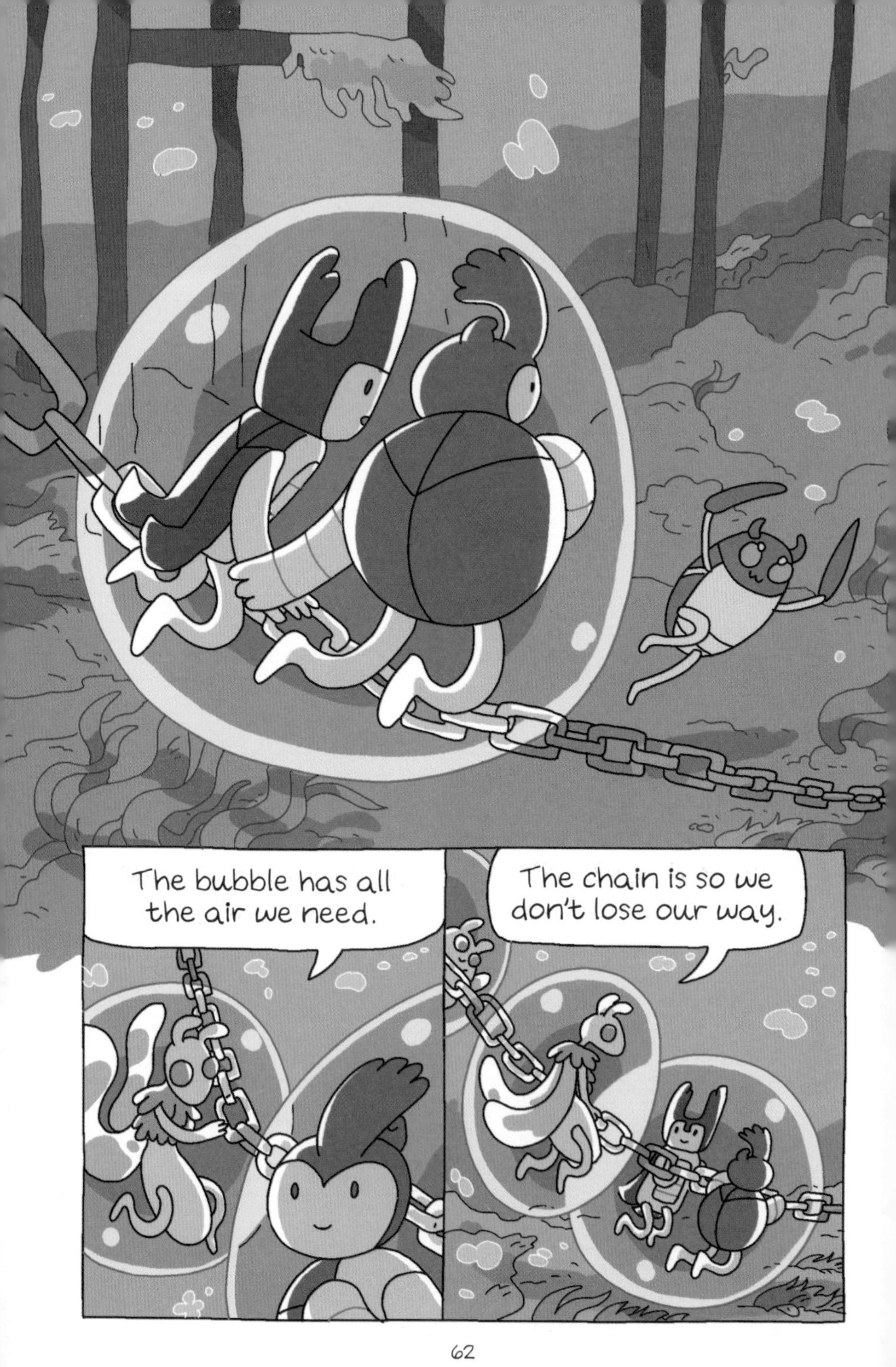
The bubble has all the air we need.
The chain is so we don't lose our way.

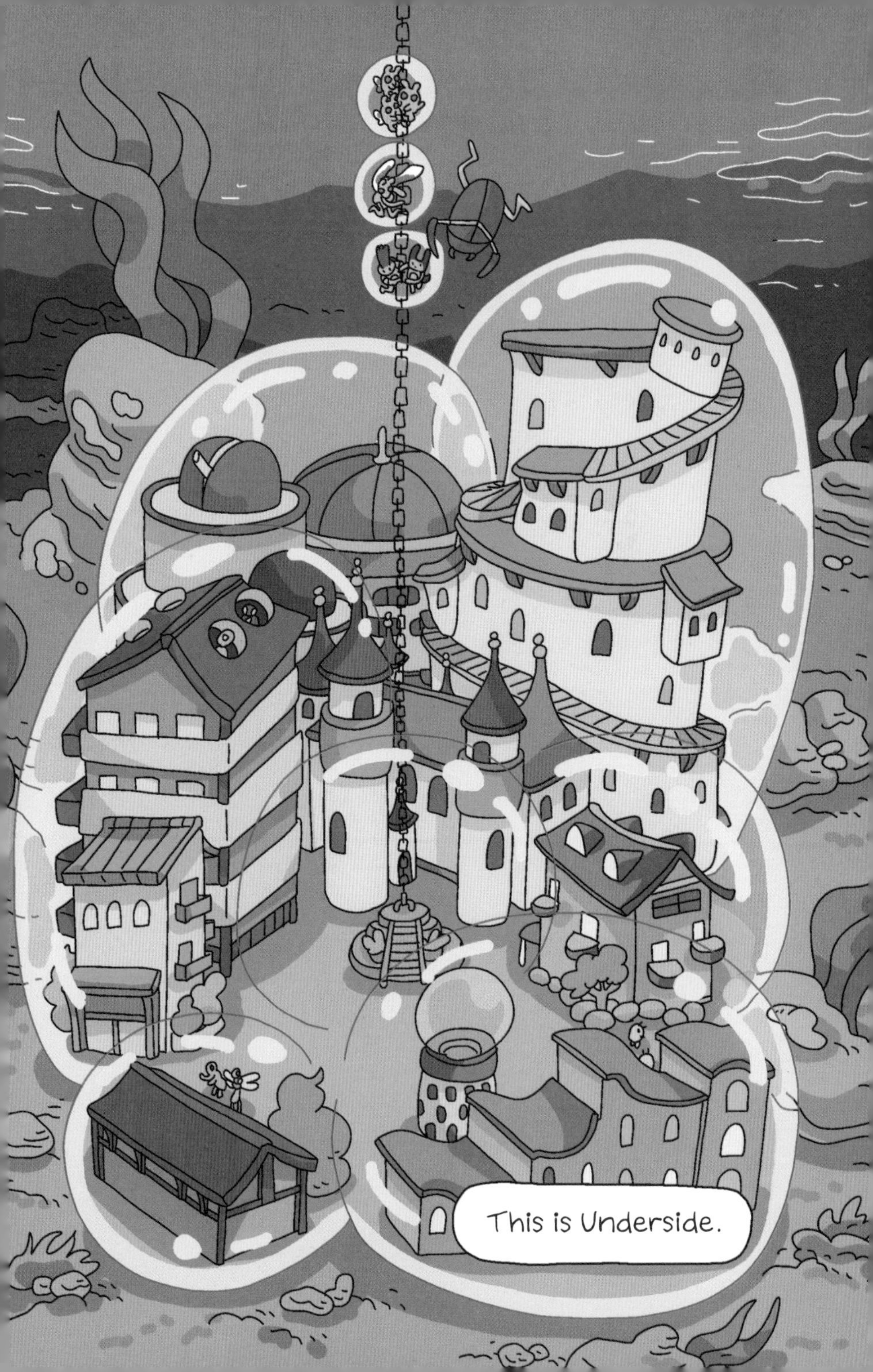
This is Underside.

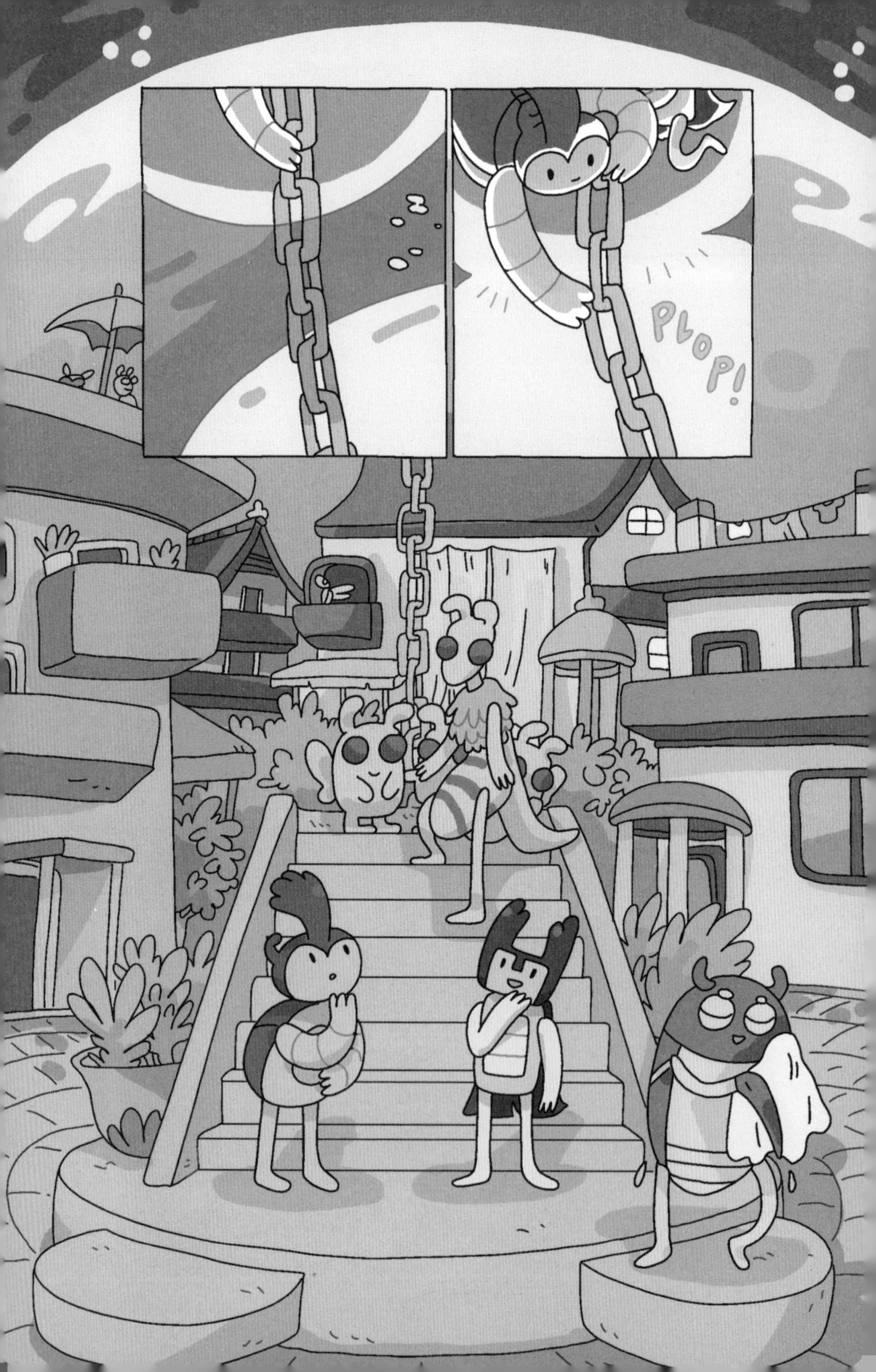
PLOP!

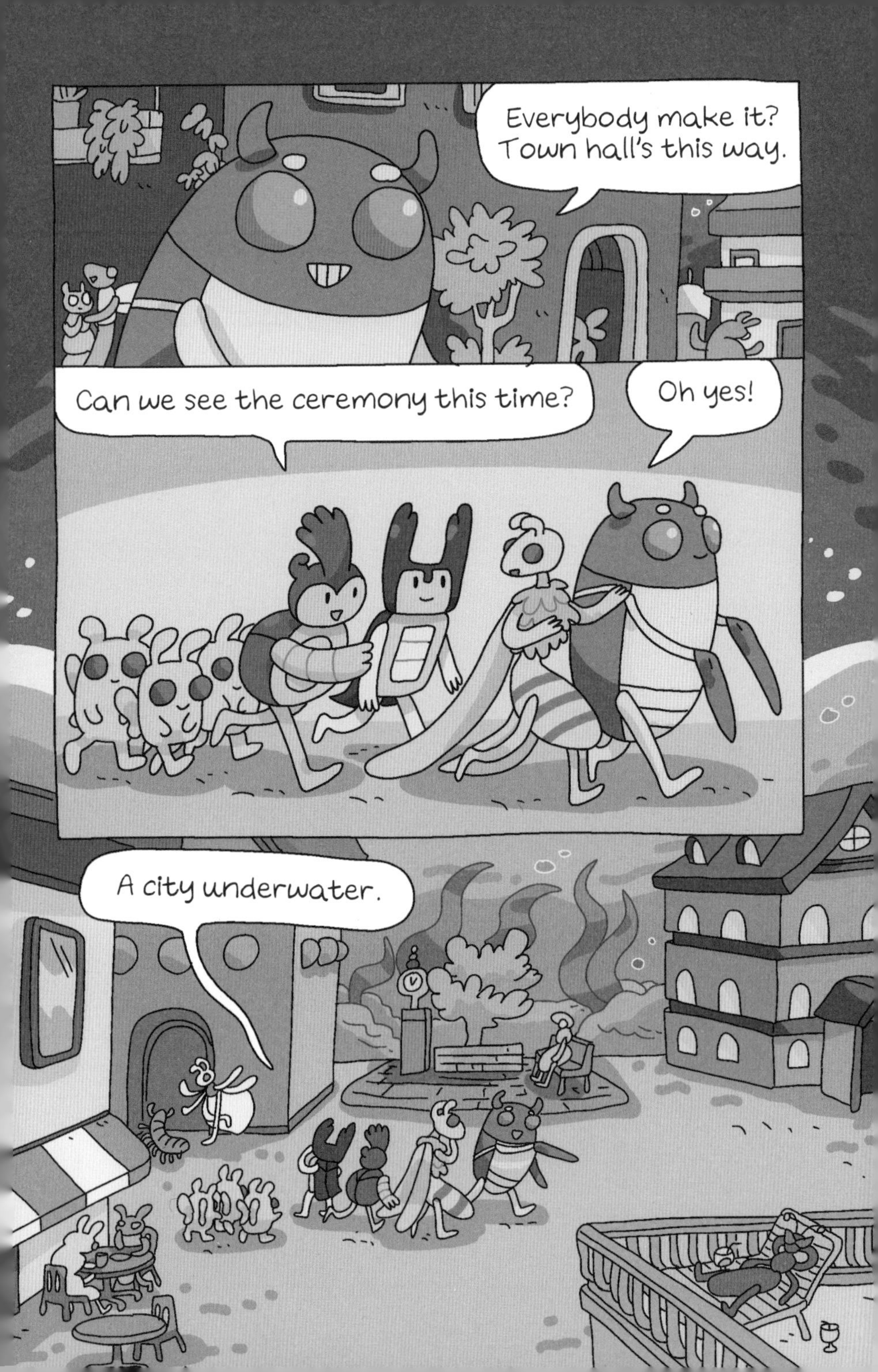
Everybody make it? Town hall's this way.
Can we see the ceremony this time?
Oh yes!
A city underwater.

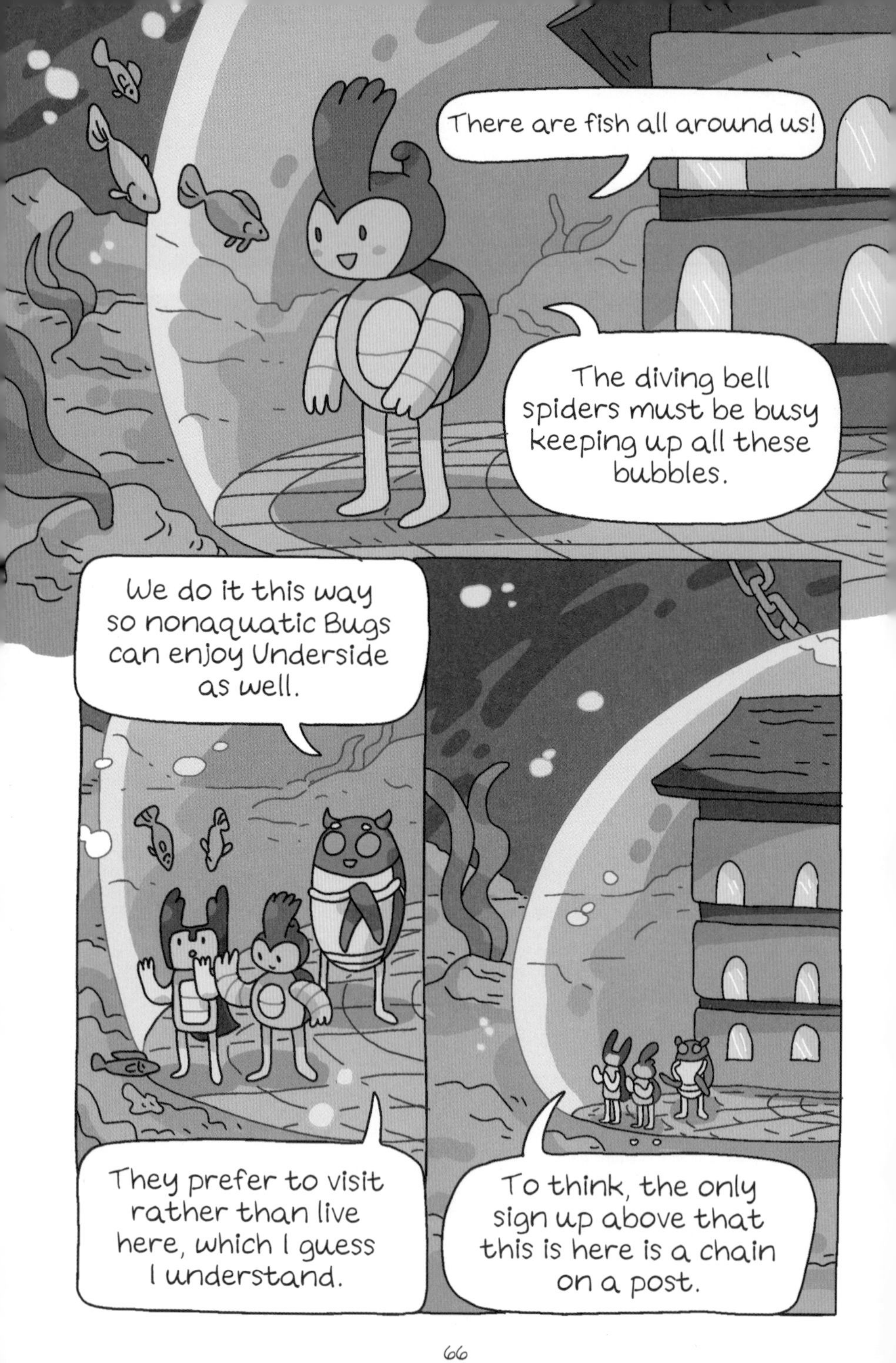
There are fish all around us!
The diving bell spiders must be busy keeping up all these bubbles.
We do it this way so nonaquatic Bugs can enjoy Underside as well.
They prefer to visit rather than live here, which I guess I understand.
To think, the only sign up above that this is here is a chain on a post.

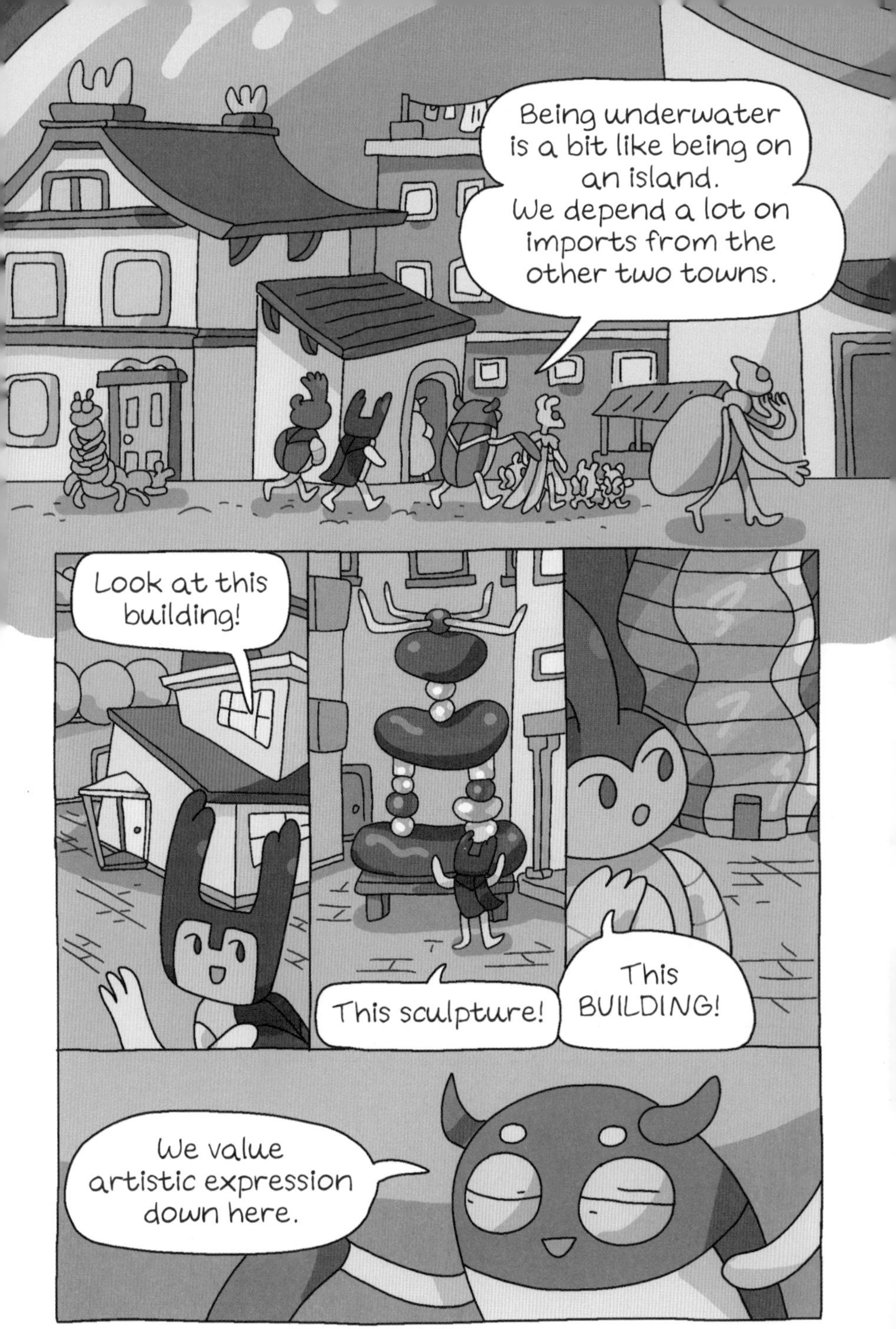
Being underwater is a bit like being on an island.
We depend a lot on imports from the other two towns.
Look at this building!
This sculpture!
This BUILDING!
We value artistic expression down here.

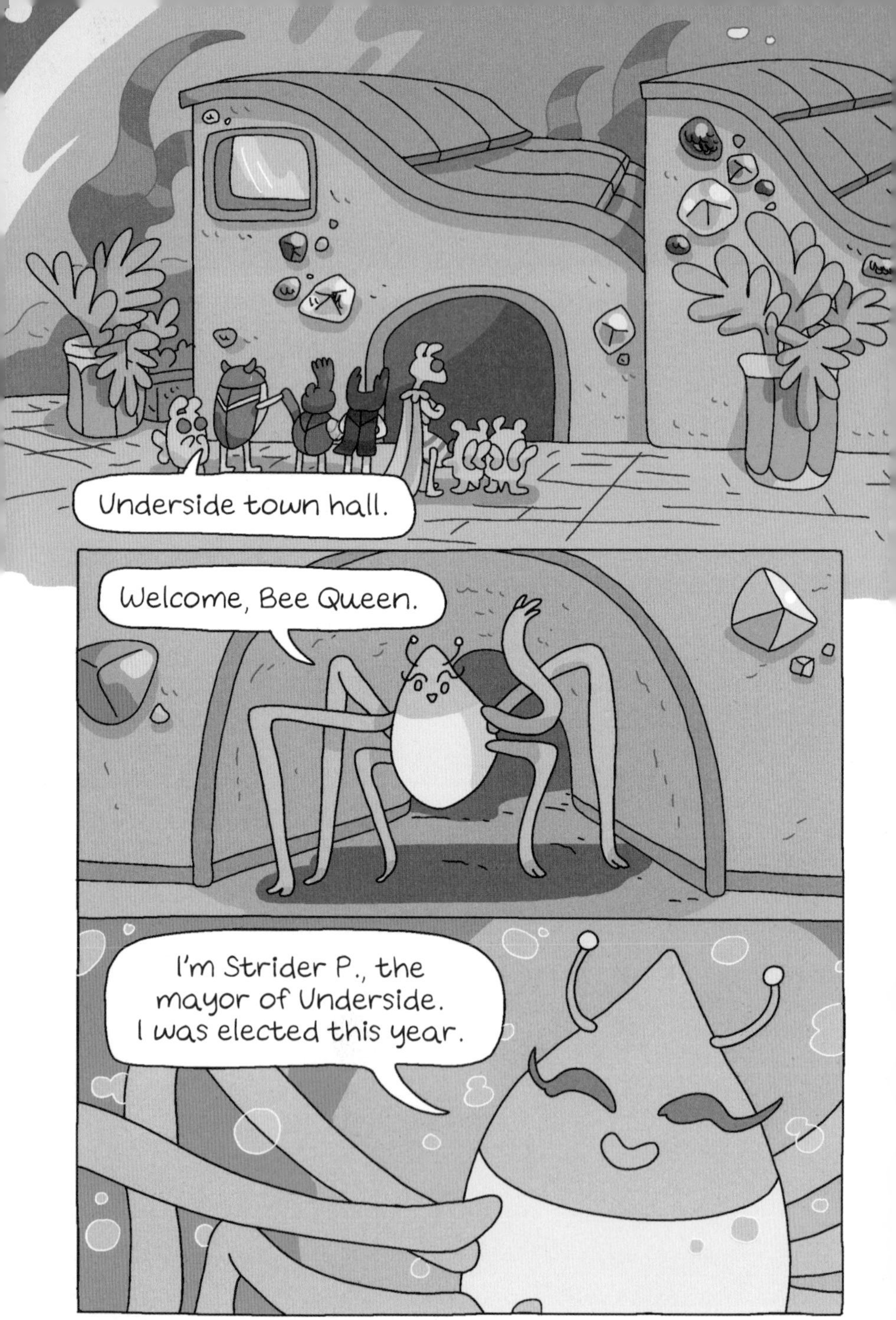
Underside town hall.
Welcome, Bee Queen.
I'm Strider P., the mayor of Underside. I was elected this year.

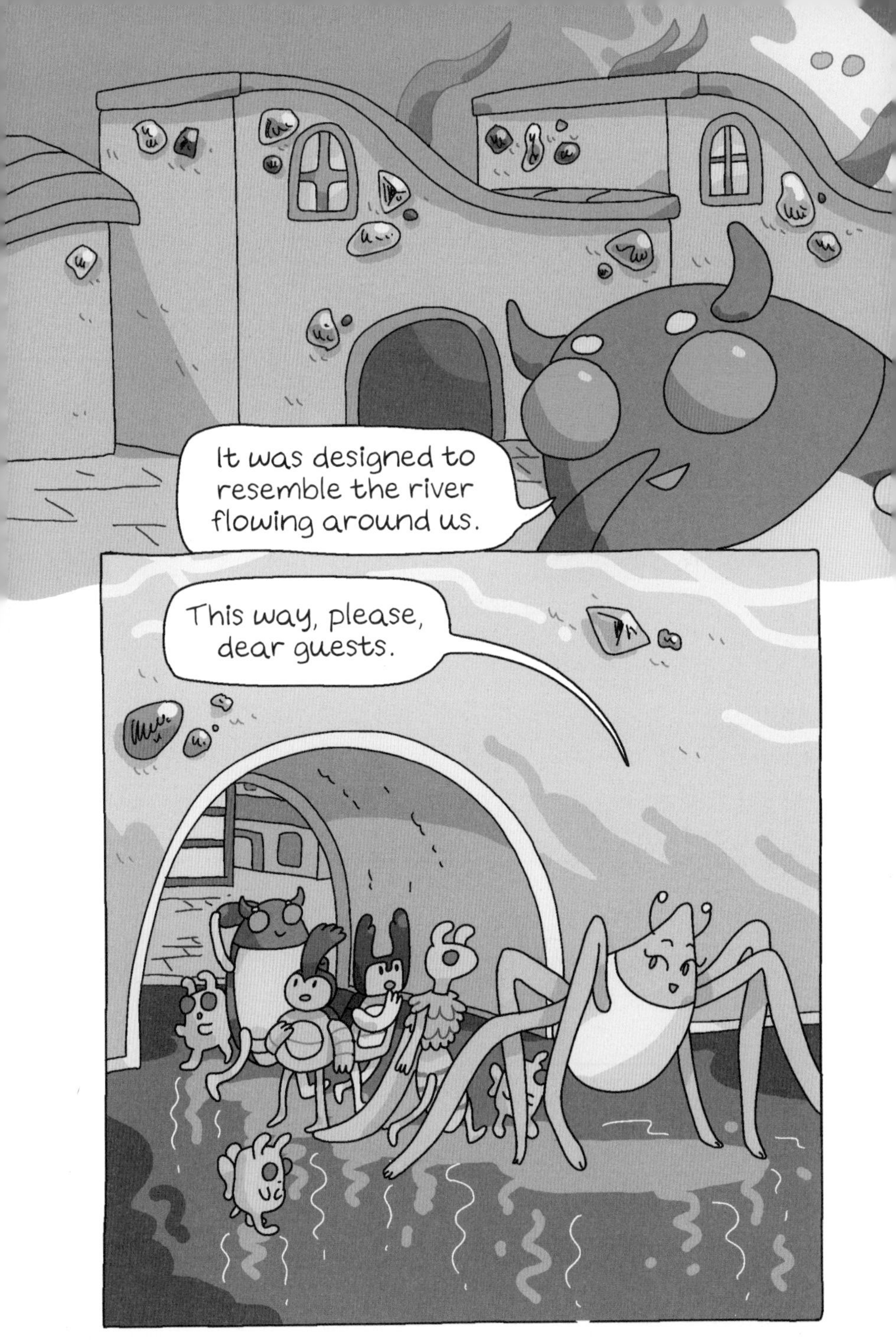
It was designed to resemble the river flowing around us.
This way, please, dear guests.

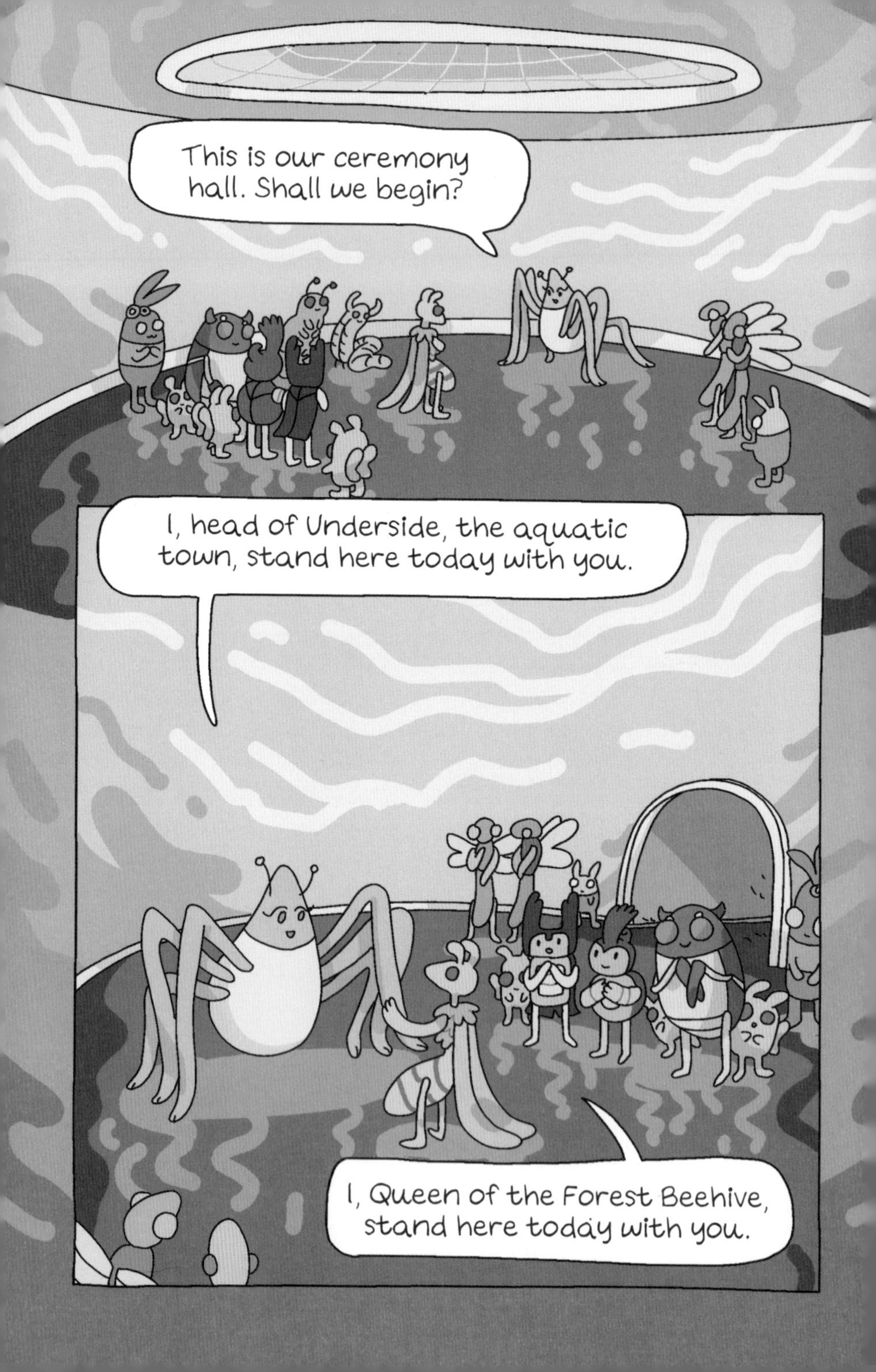
This is our ceremony hall. Shall we begin?
I, head of Underside, the aquatic town, stand here today with you.
I, Queen of the Forest Beehive, stand here today with you.

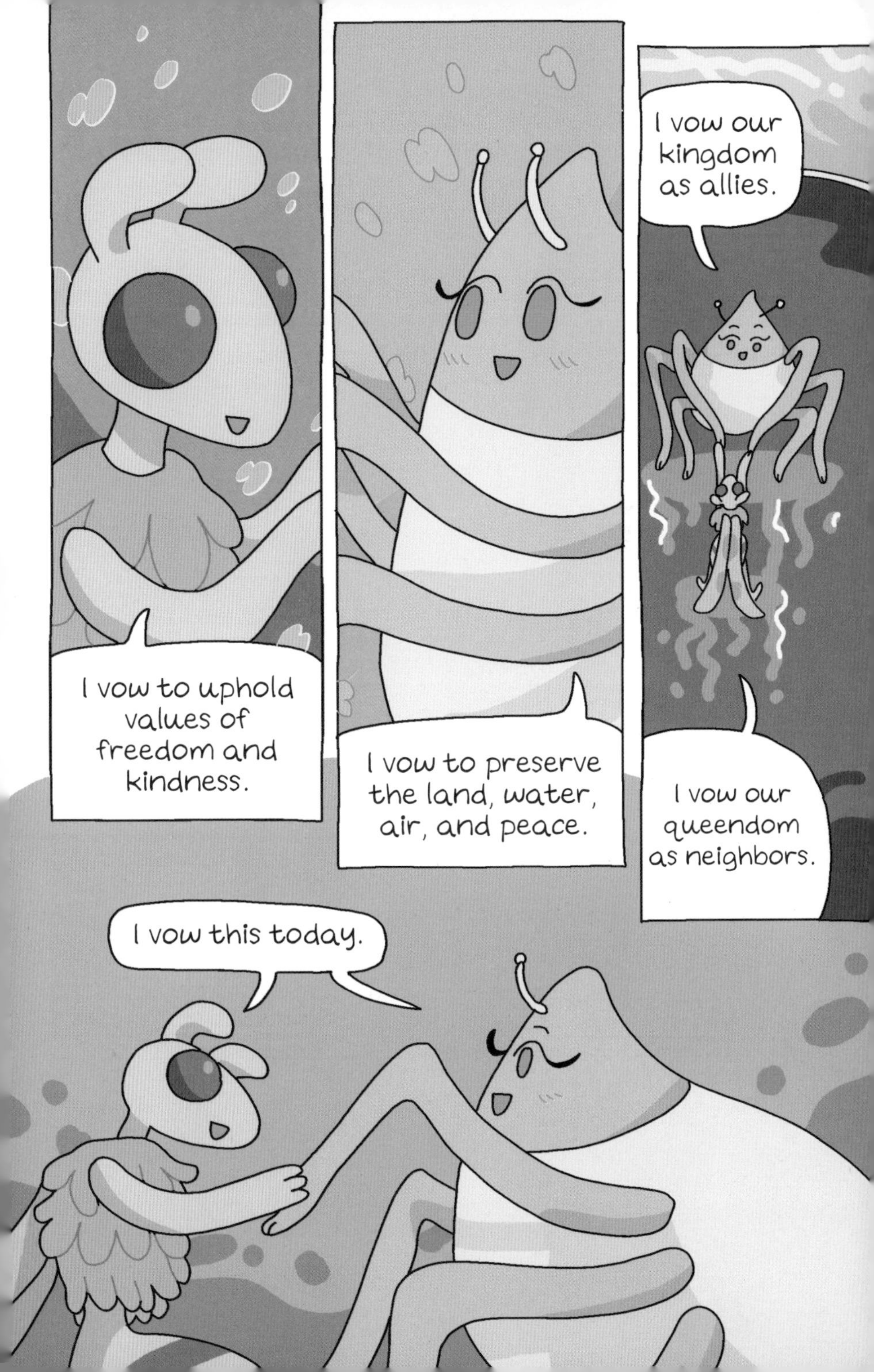
I vow to uphold values of freedom and kindness.
I vow to preserve the land, water, air, and peace.
I vow our kingdom as allies.
I vow our queendom as neighbors.
I vow this today.

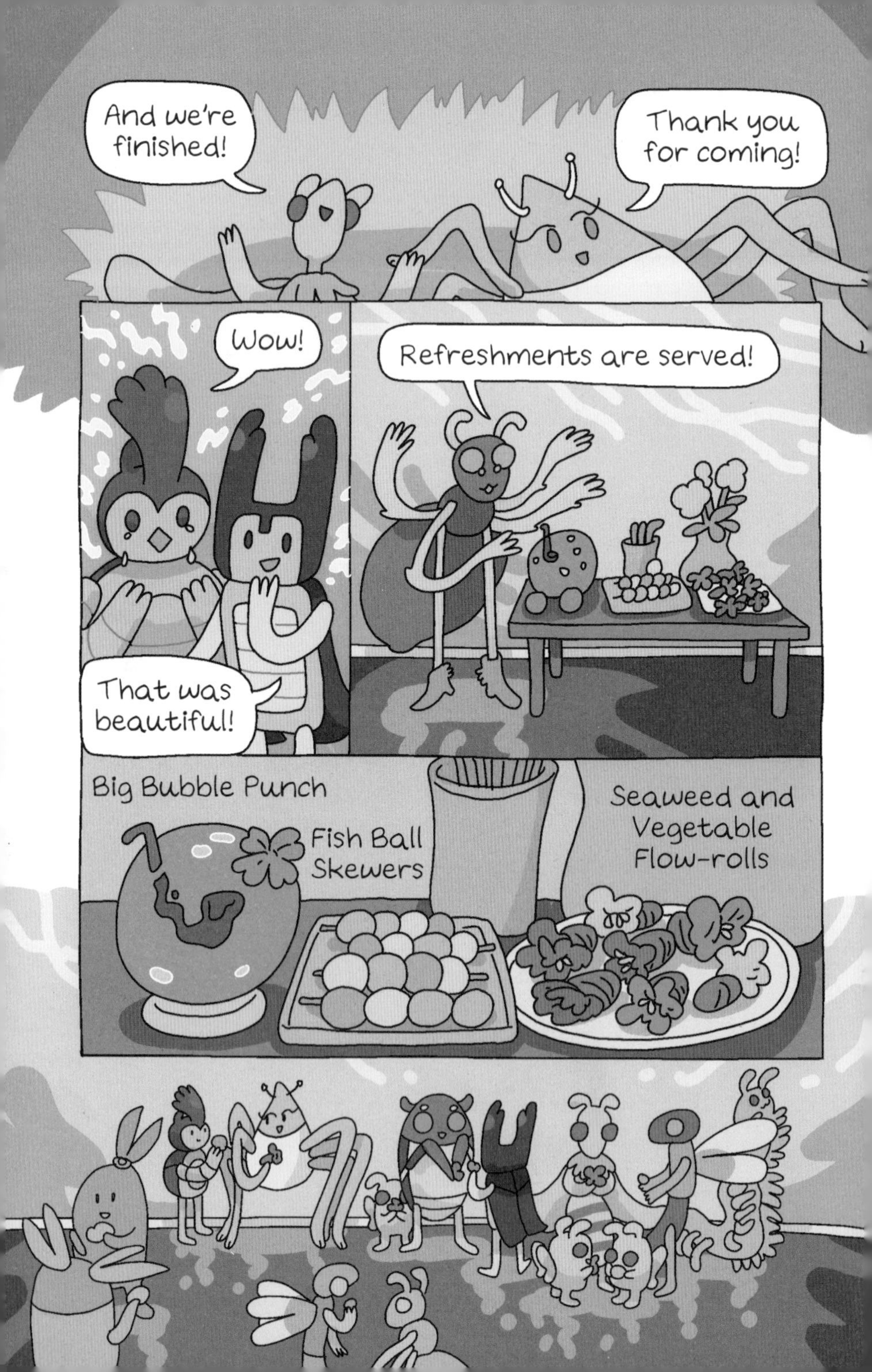
And we're finished!
Thank you for coming!
Wow!
That was beautiful!
Refreshments are served!
Big Bubble Punch
Fish Ball Skewers
Seaweed and Vegetable Flow-rolls

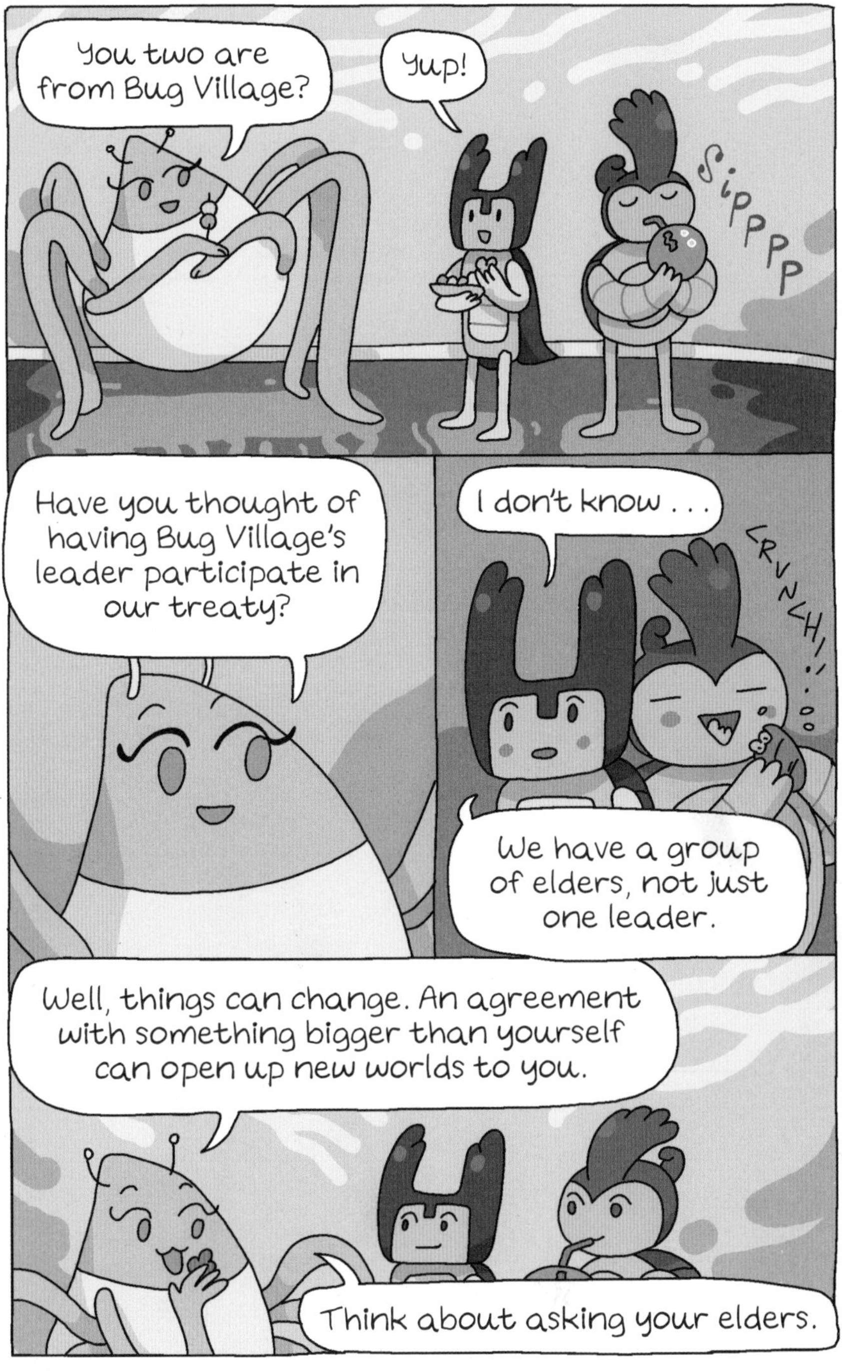
You two are from Bug Village?
Yup!
SIPPPP
Have you thought of having Bug Village's leader participate in our treaty?
I don't know . . .
CRUNCH!!
We have a group of elders, not just one leader.
Well, things can change. An agreement with something bigger than yourself can open up new worlds to you.
Think about asking your elders.

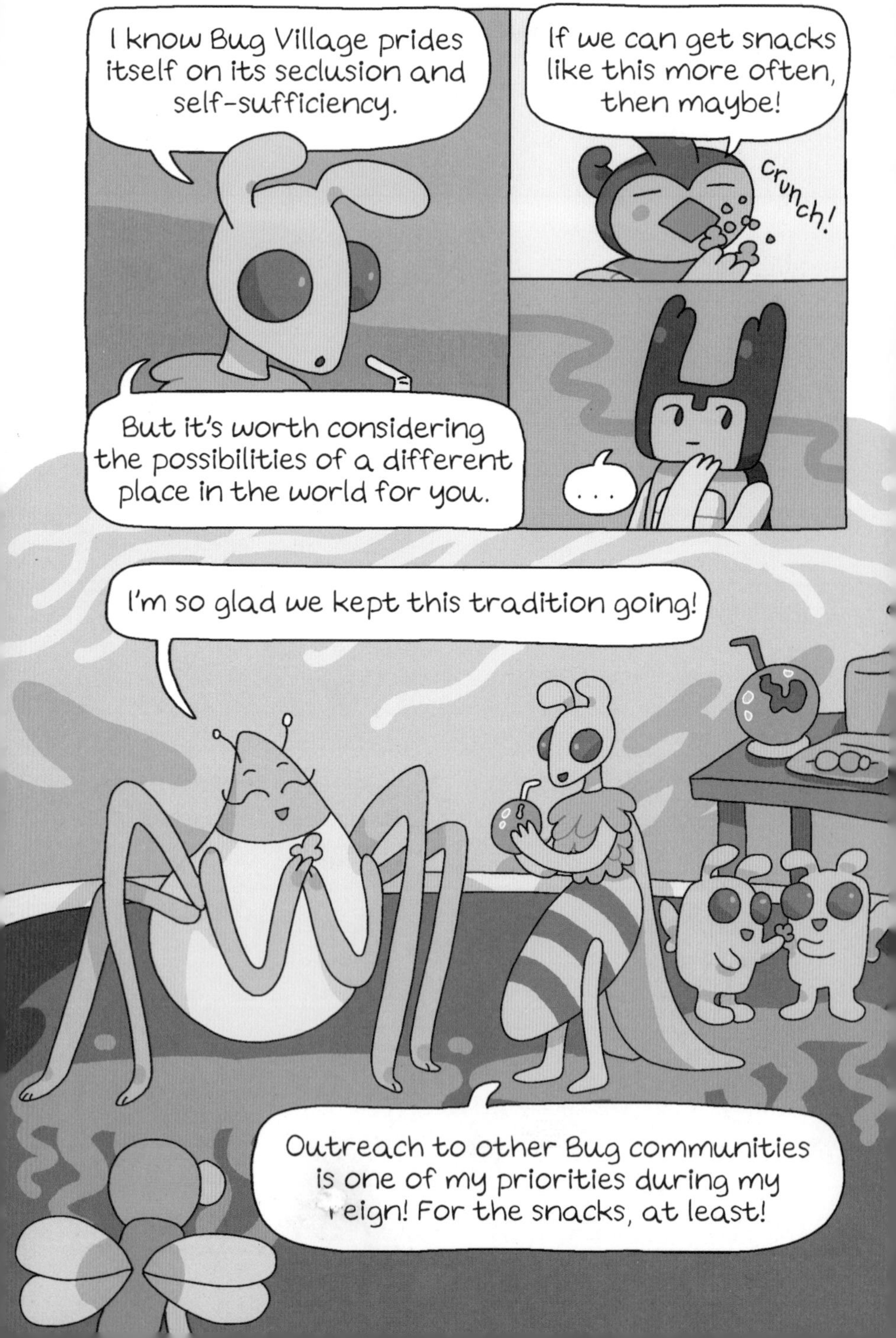
I know Bug Village prides itself on its seclusion and self-sufficiency.
But it's worth considering the possibilities of a different place in the world for you.
If we can get snacks like this more often, then maybe!
Crunch!
. . .
I'm so glad we kept this tradition going!
Outreach to other Bug communities is one of my priorities during my reign! For the snacks, at least!

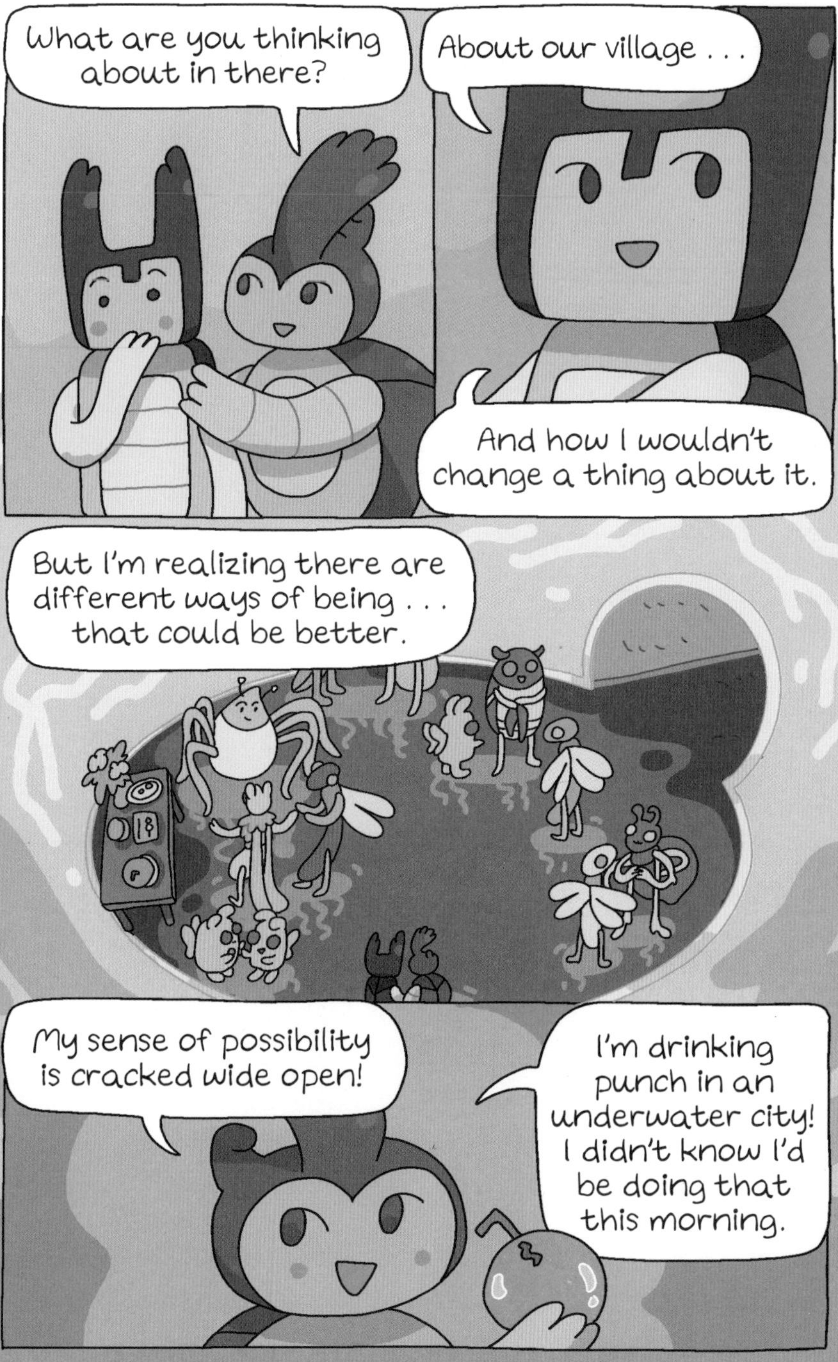
What are you thinking about in there?
About our village . . .
And how I wouldn't change a thing about it.
But I'm realizing there are different ways of being . . . that could be better.
My sense of possibility is cracked wide open!
I'm drinking punch in an underwater city! I didn't know I'd be doing that this morning.

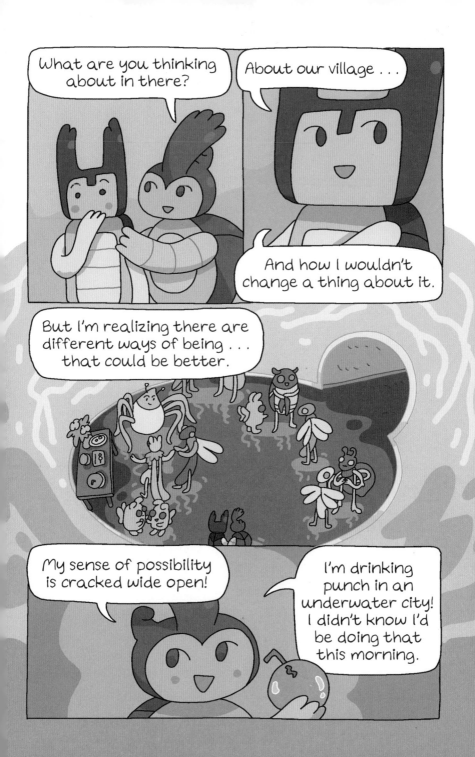

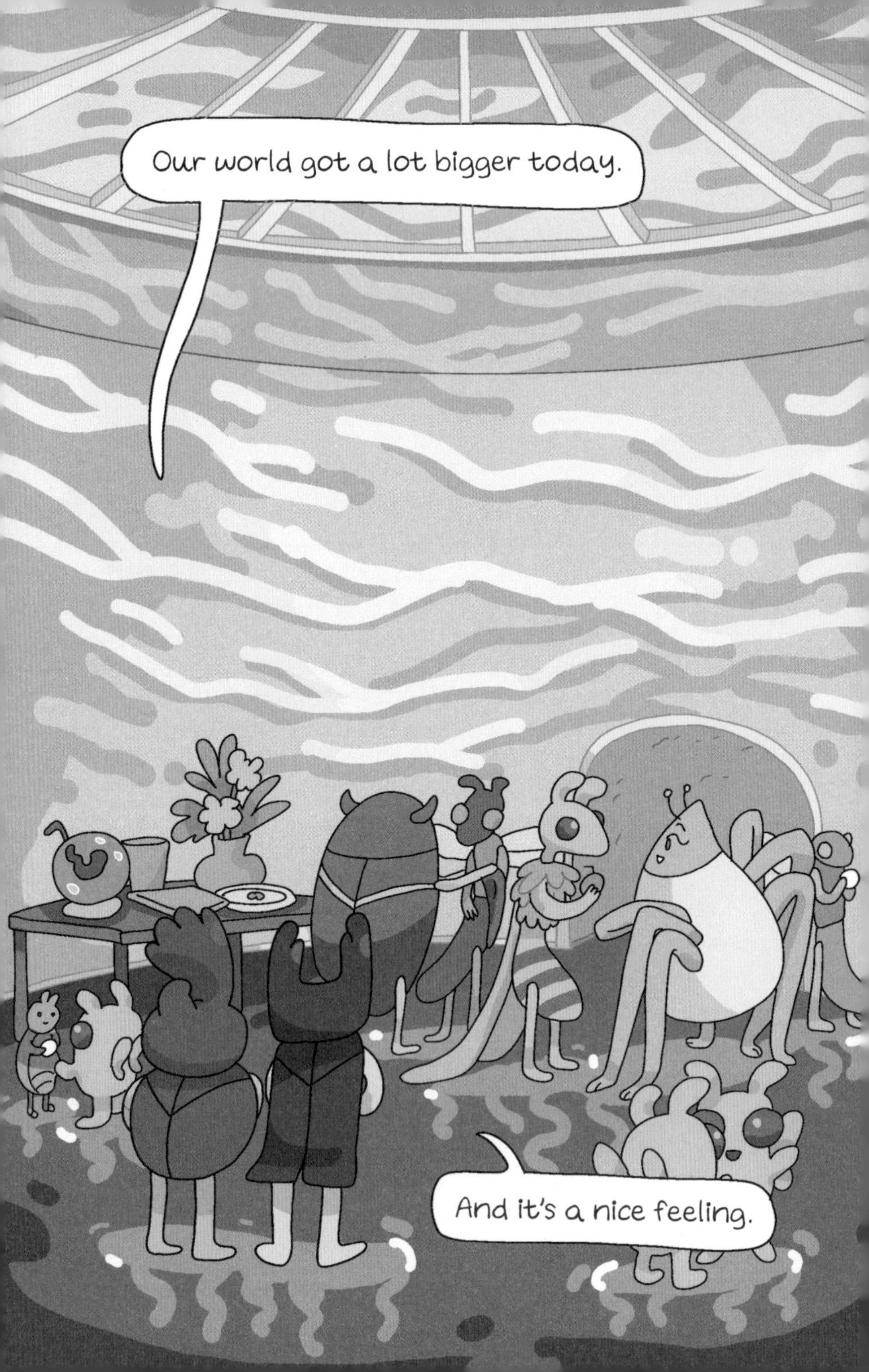
Our world got a lot bigger today.
And it's a nice feeling.

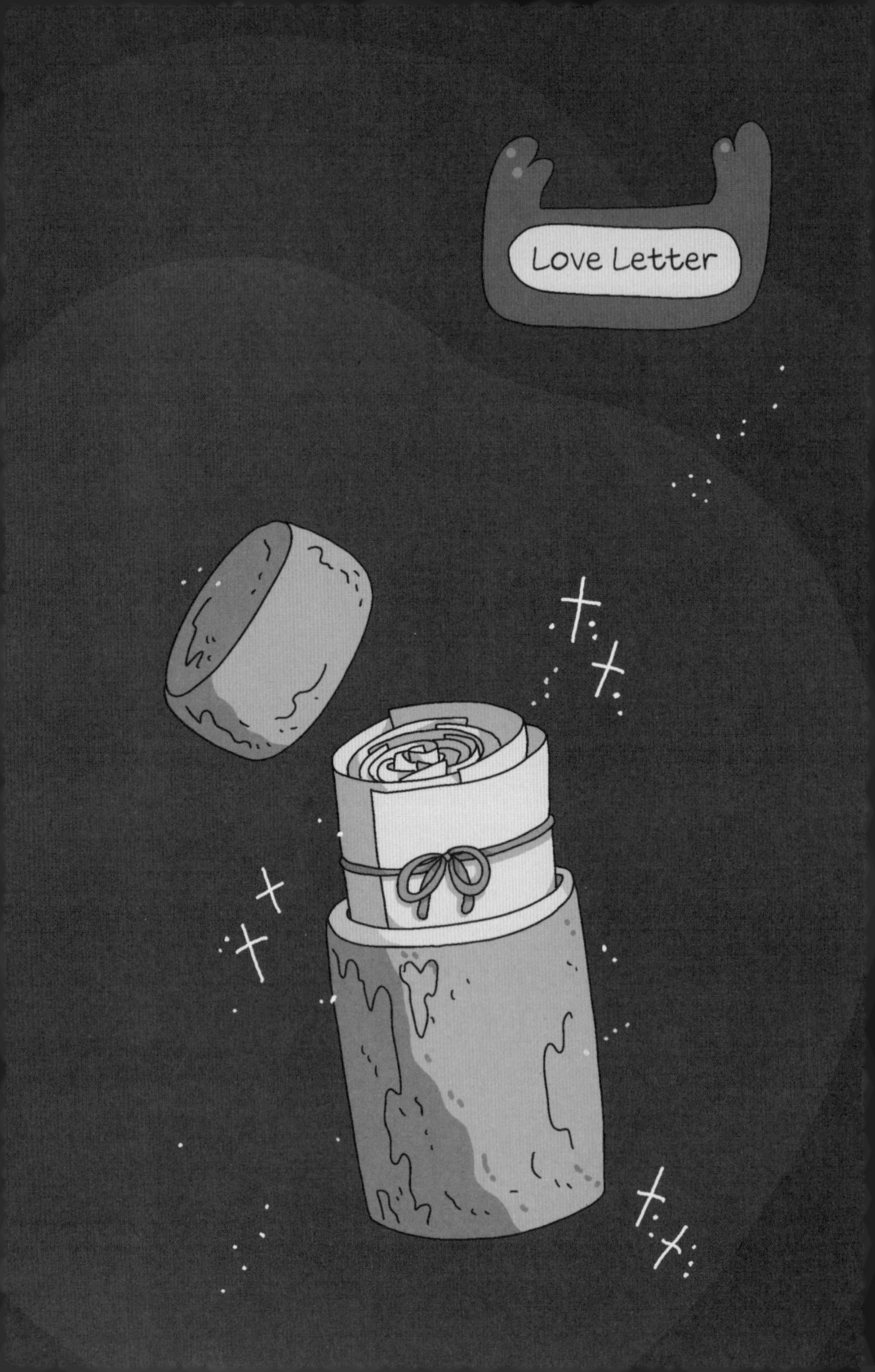
Love Letter

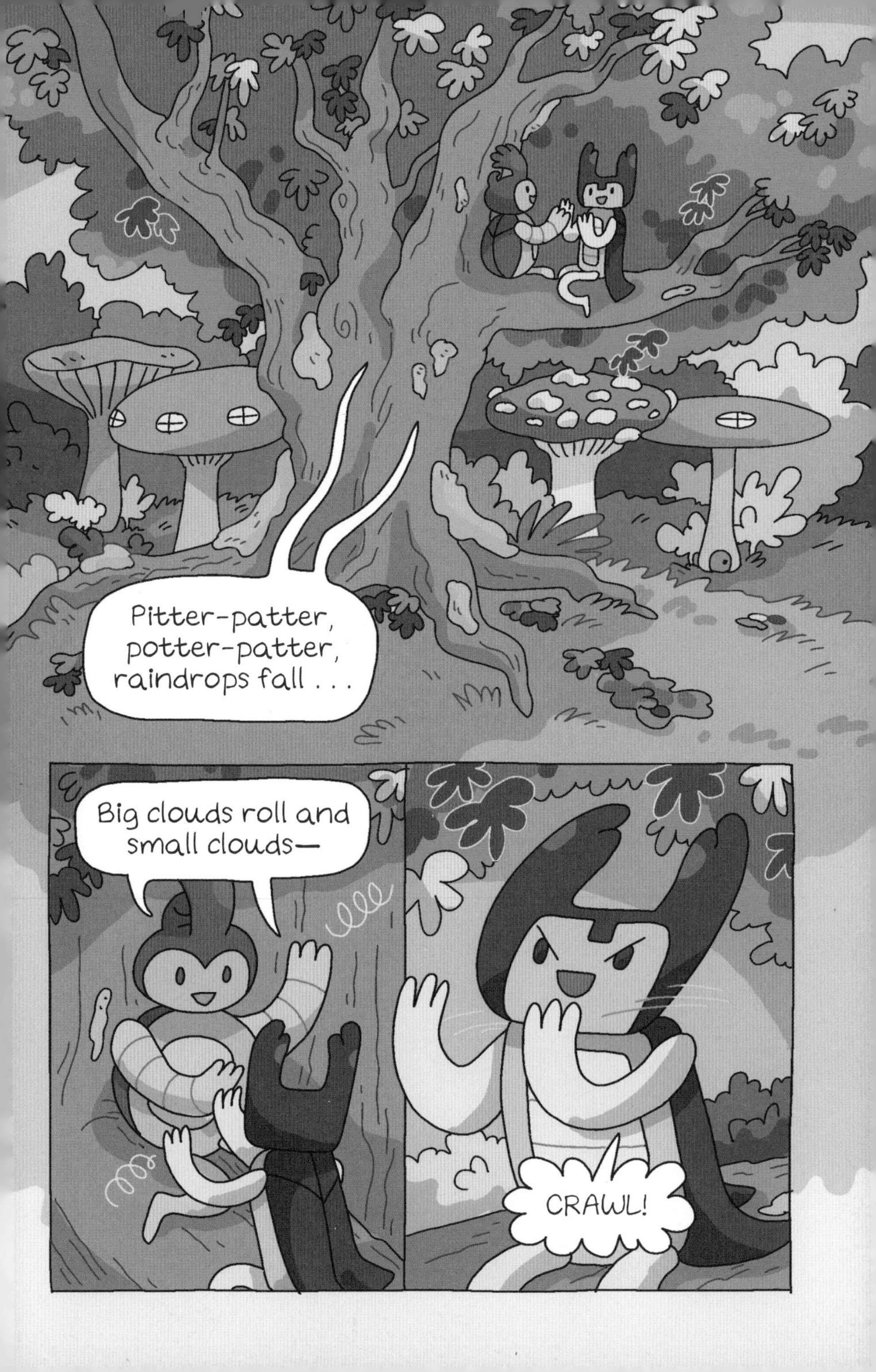

Pitter-patter, potter-patter, raindrops fall . . .
Big clouds roll and small clouds—
CRAWL!

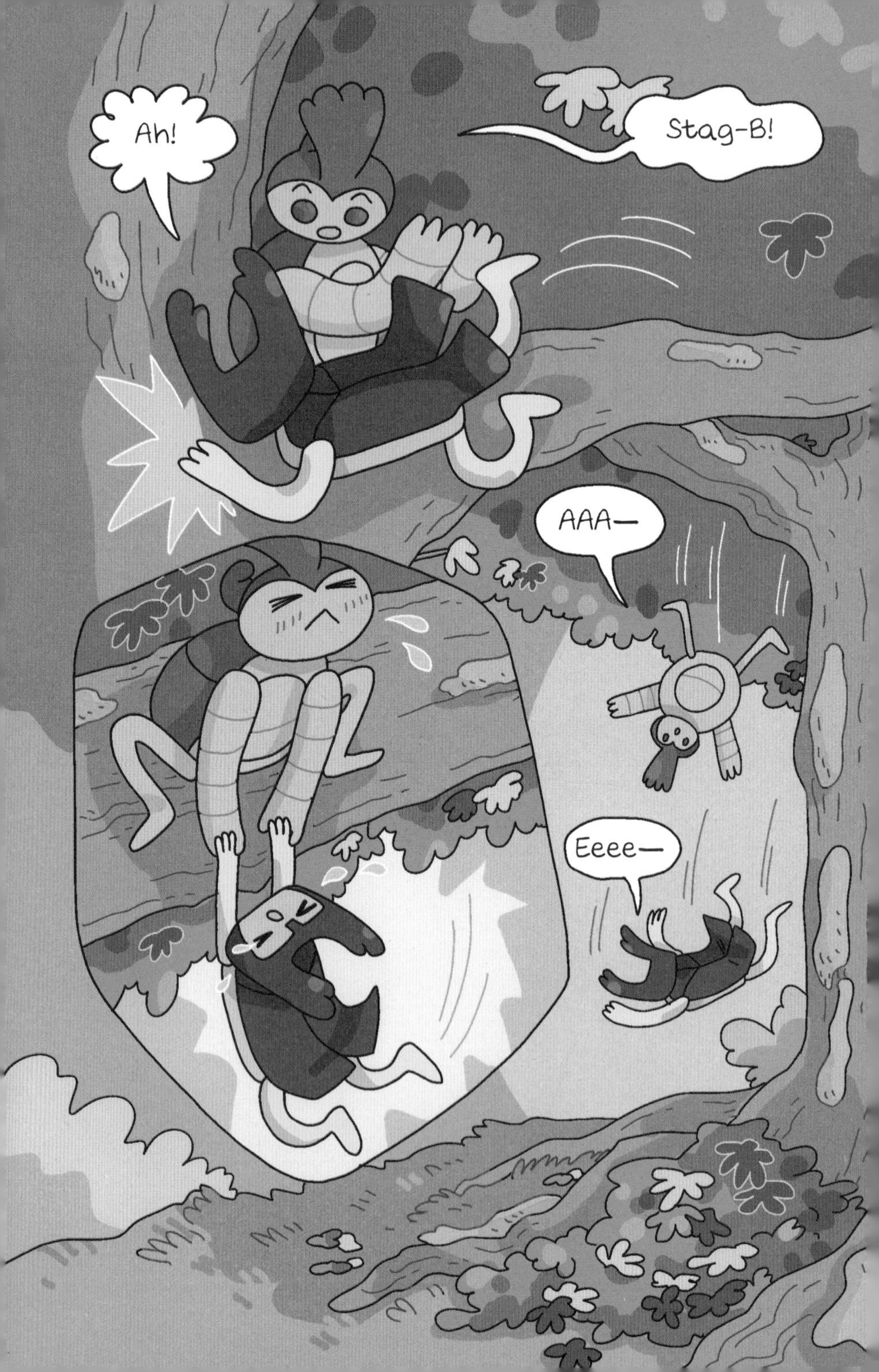
Ah!
Stag-B!
AAA—
Eeee—

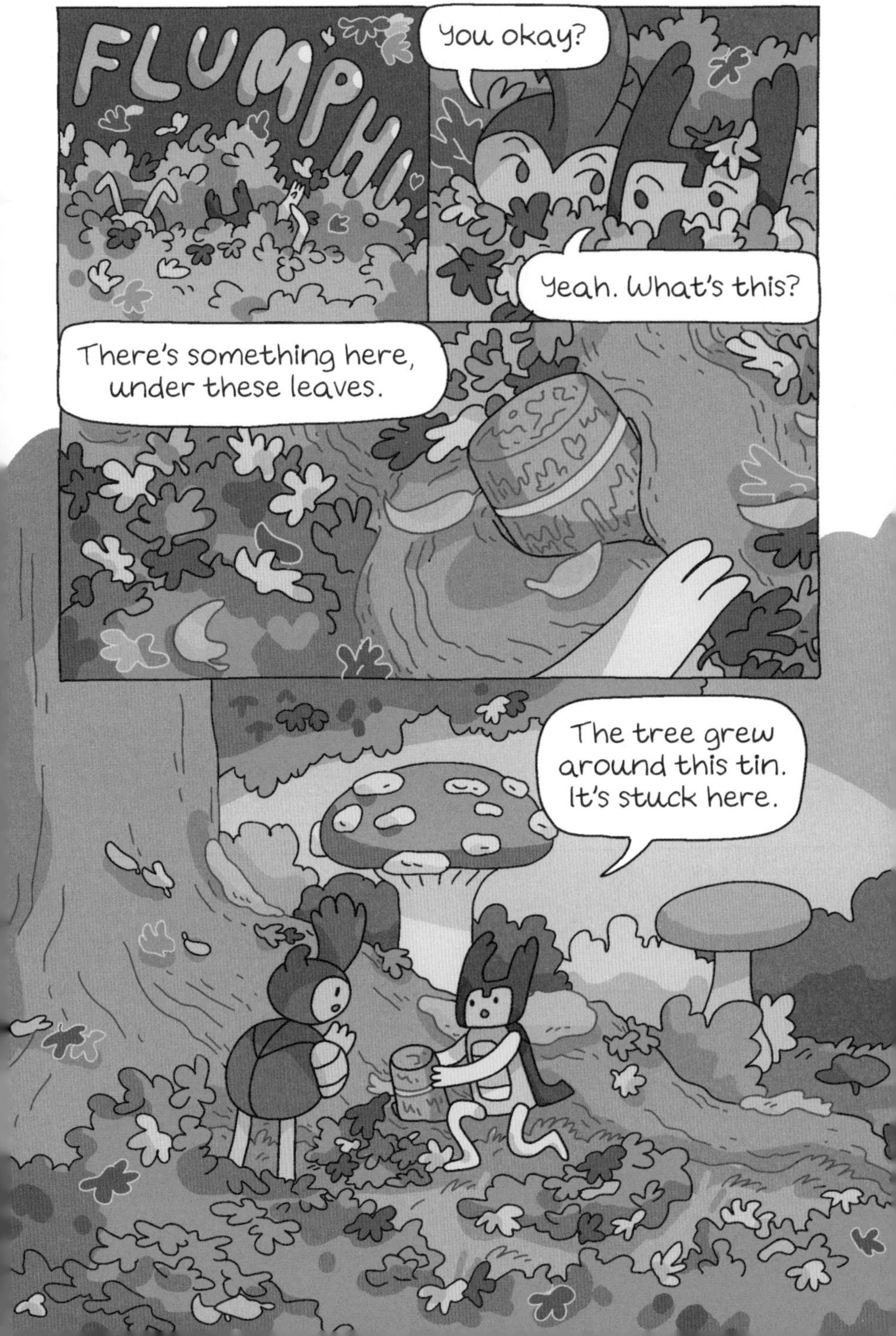
FLUMPH!
You okay?
Yeah. What's this?
There's something here, under these leaves.
The tree grew around this tin. It's stuck here.

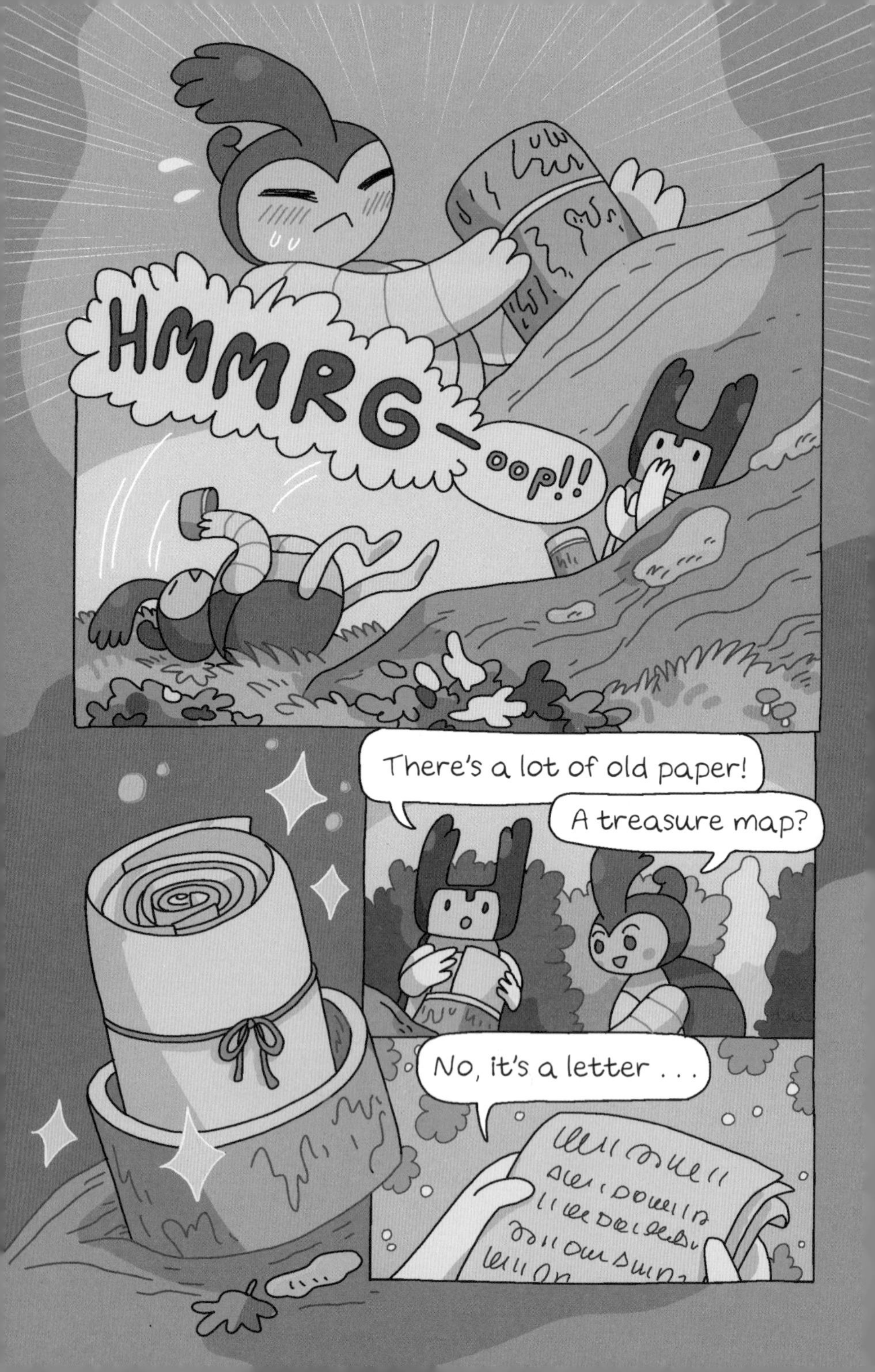

HMMRG—
oop!!
There's a lot of old paper!
A treasure map?
No, it's a letter . . .

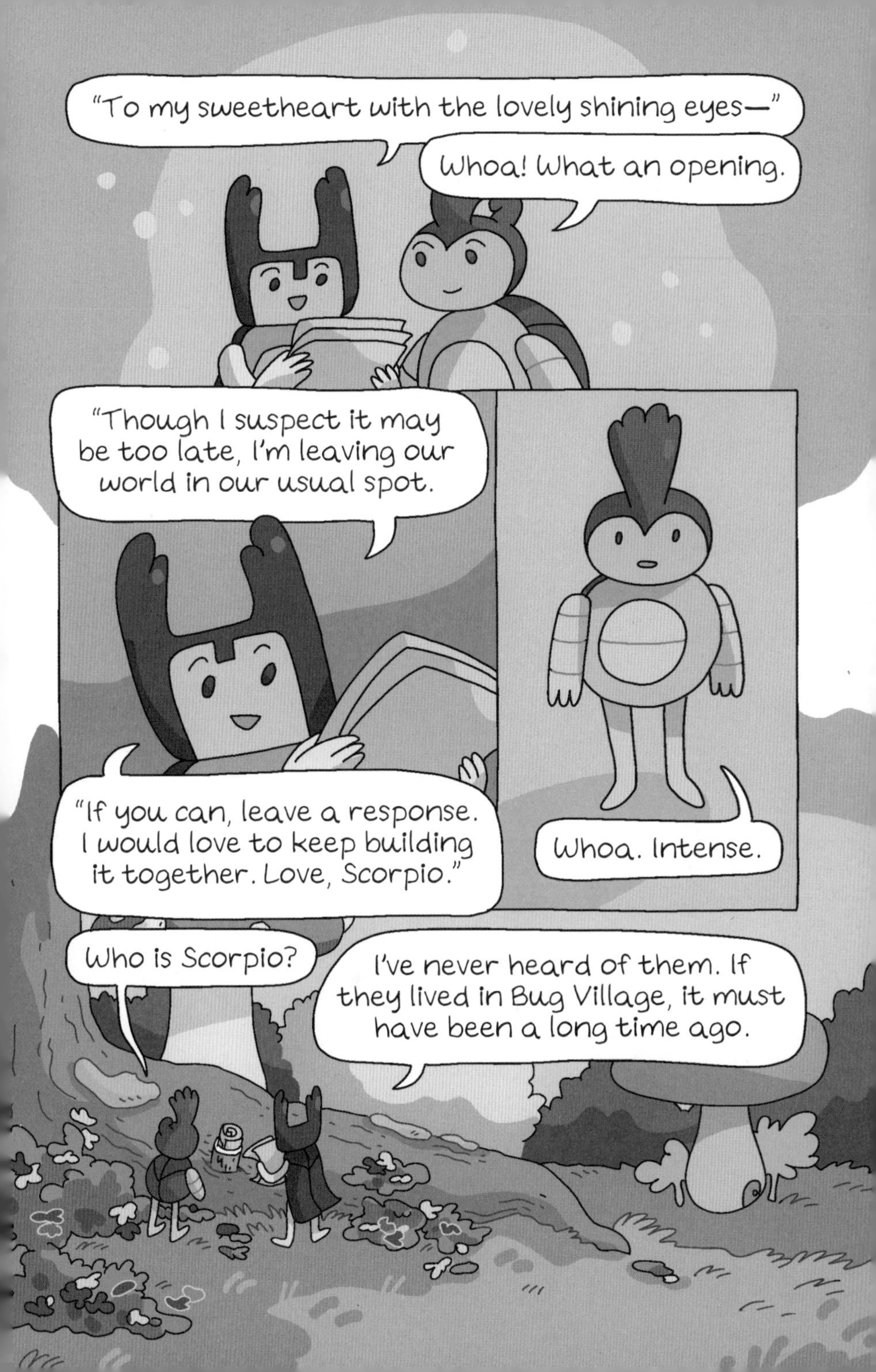
"To my sweetheart with the lovely shining eyes—"
Whoa! What an opening.
"Though I suspect it may be too late, I'm leaving our world in our usual spot.
"If you can, leave a response. I would love to keep building it together. Love, Scorpio."
Whoa. Intense.
Who is Scorpio?
I've never heard of them. If they lived in Bug Village, it must have been a long time ago.

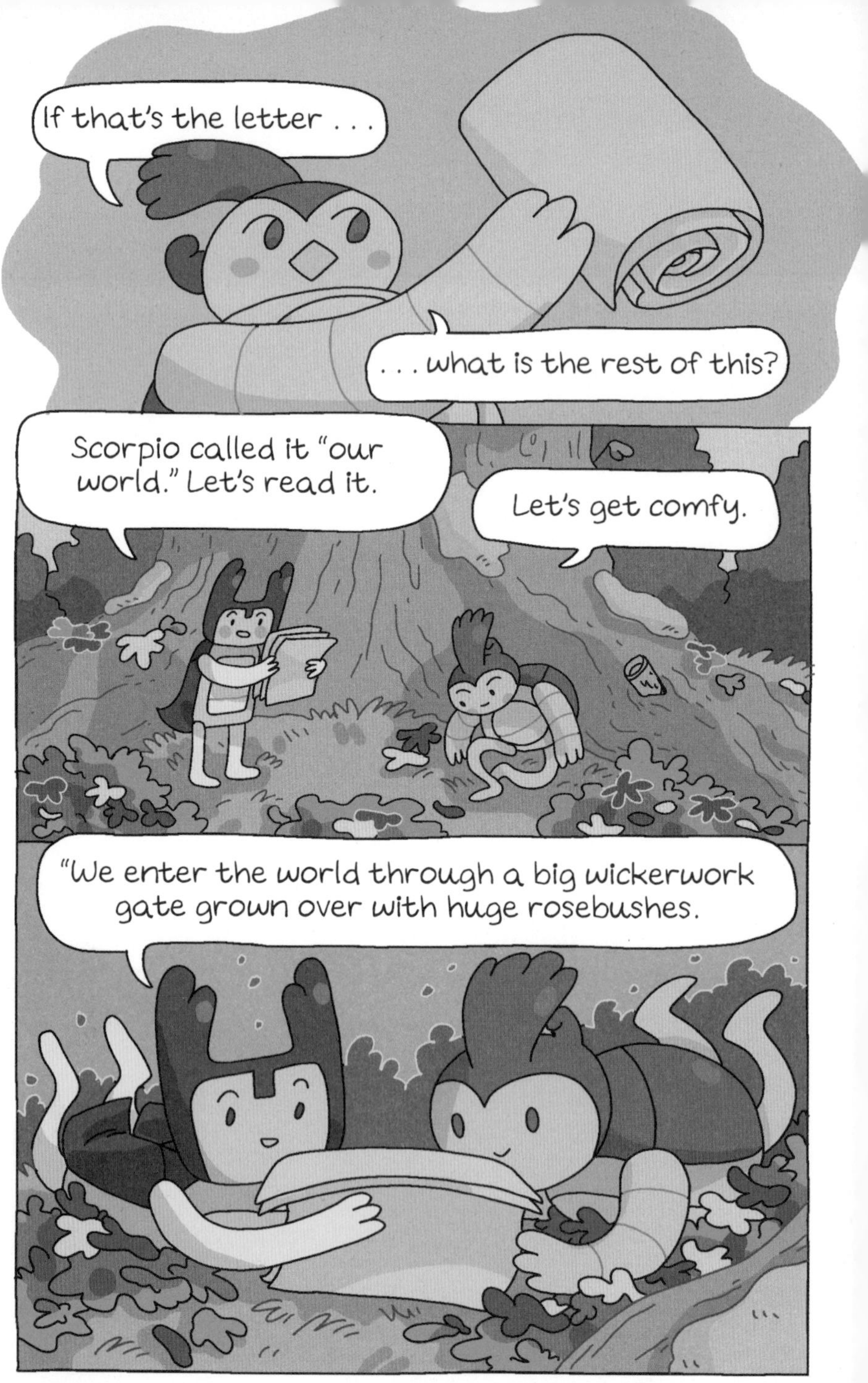
If that's the letter . . .
. . . what is the rest of this?
Scorpio called it "our world." Let's read it.
Let's get comfy.
"We enter the world through a big wickerwork gate grown over with huge rosebushes.

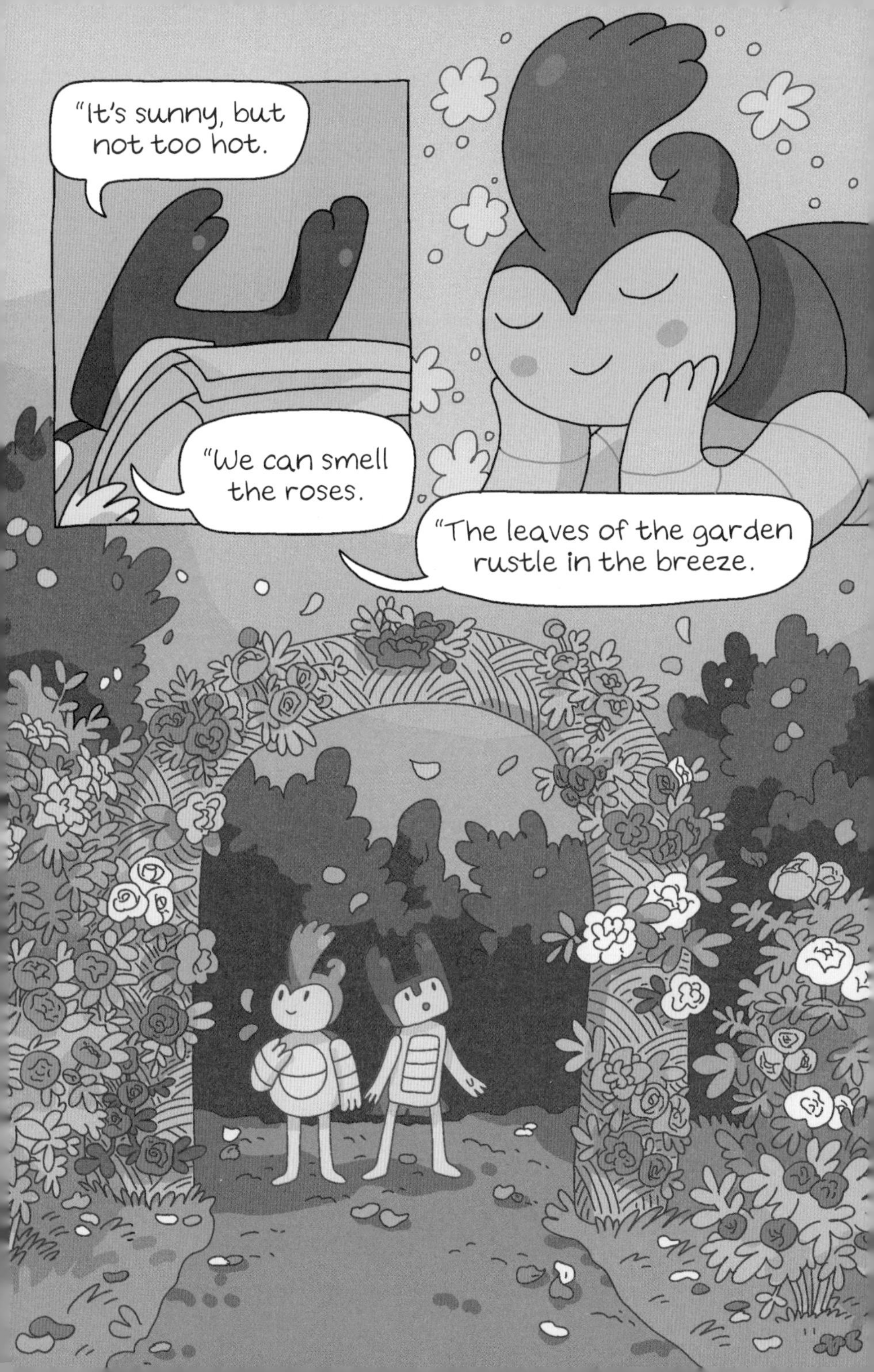
"It's sunny, but not too hot.
"We can smell the roses.
"The leaves of the garden rustle in the breeze.

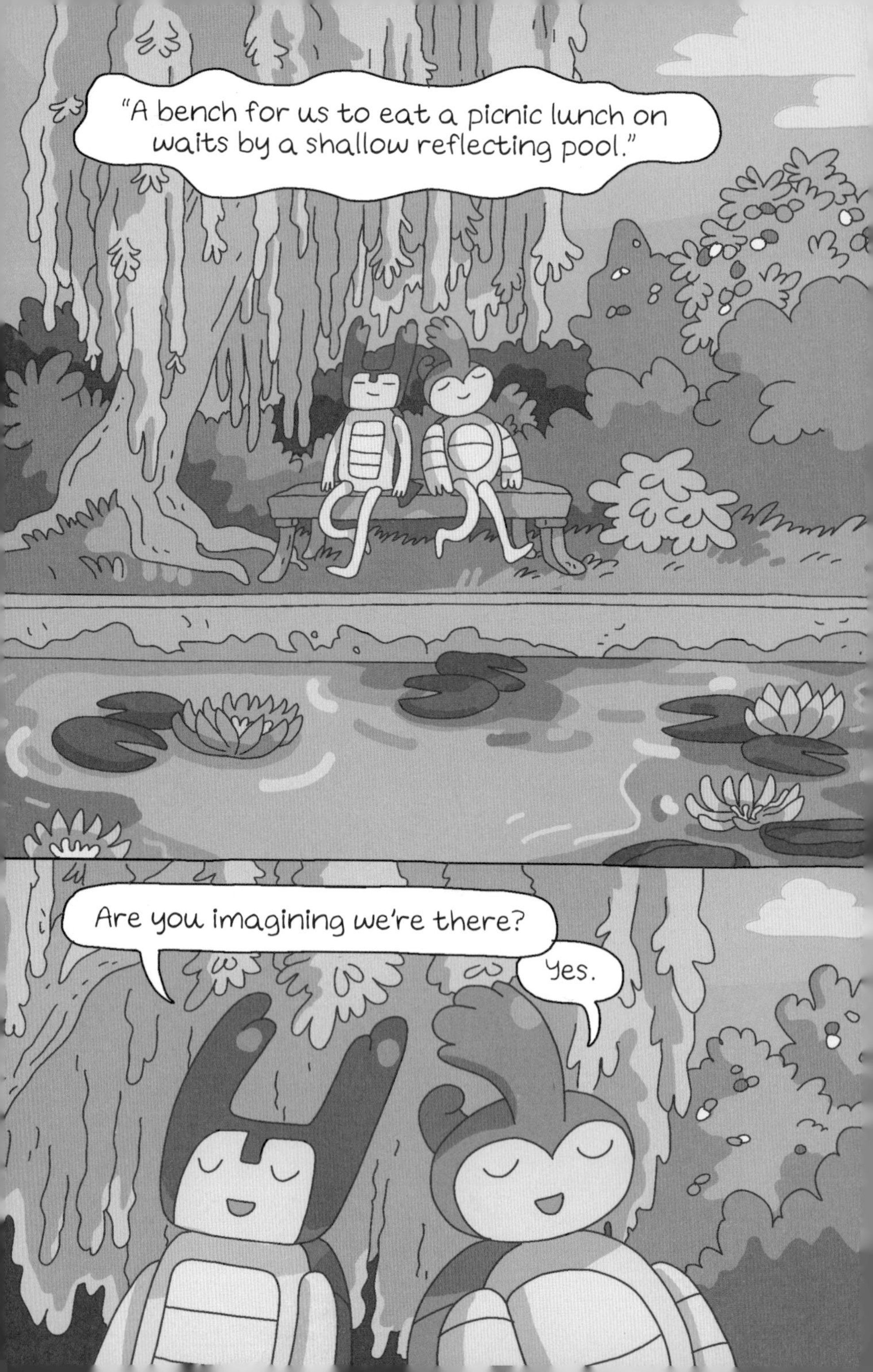
"A bench for us to eat a picnic lunch on waits by a shallow reflecting pool."
Are you imagining we're there?
Yes.

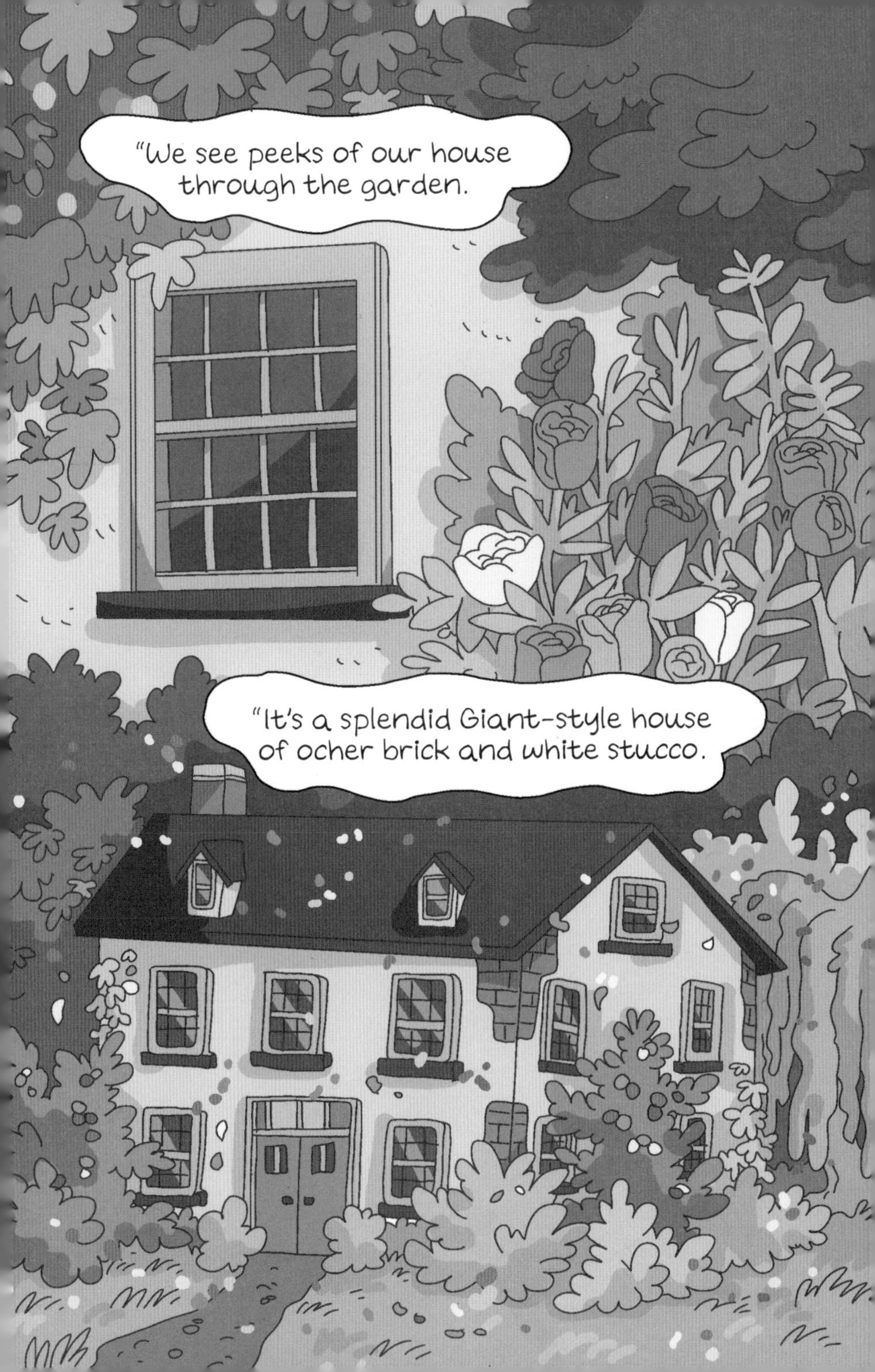
"We see peeks of our house through the garden.
"It's a splendid Giant-style house of ocher brick and white stucco.

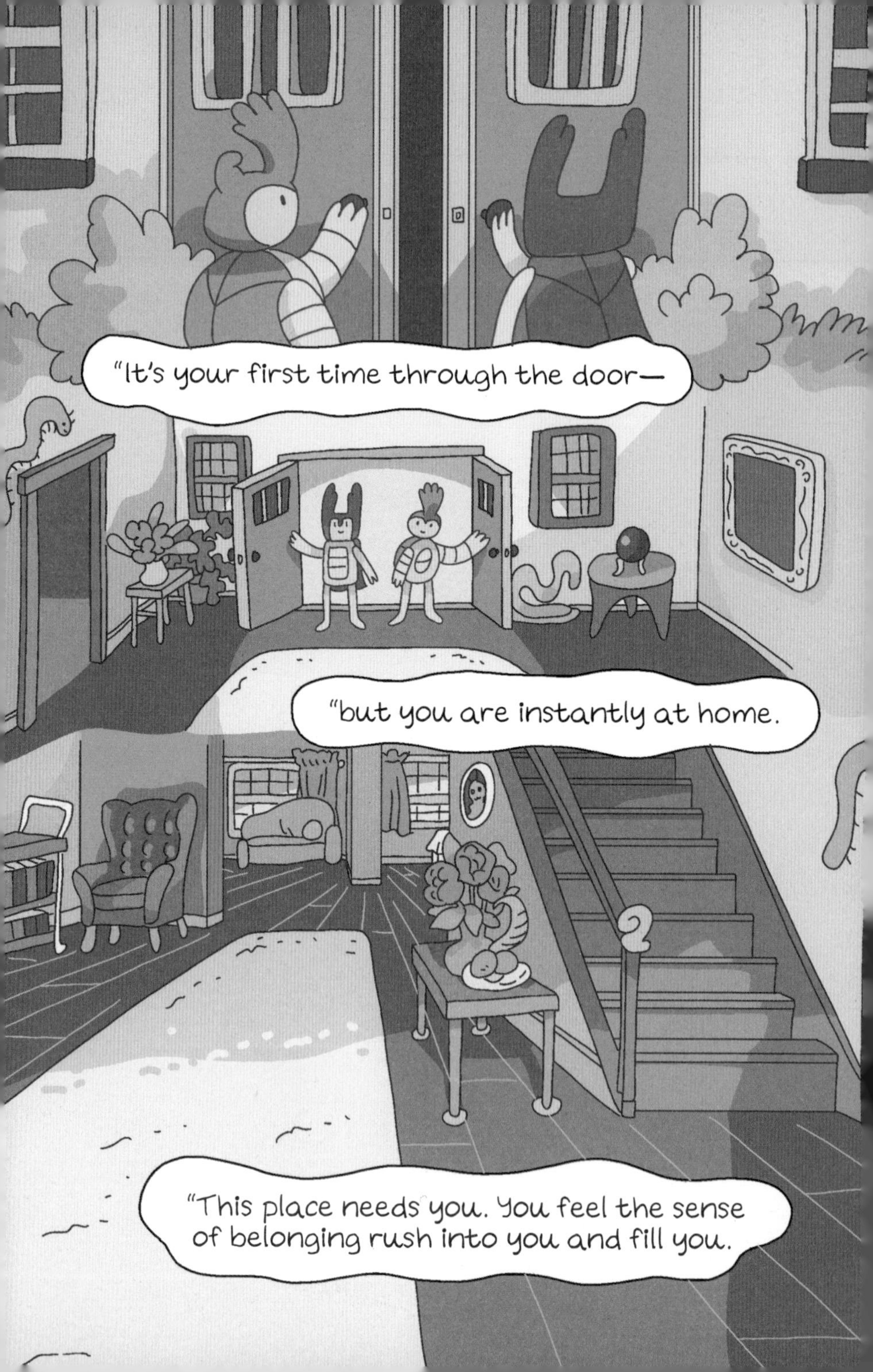
"It's your first time through the door—
"but you are instantly at home.
"This place needs you. You feel the sense of belonging rush into you and fill you.

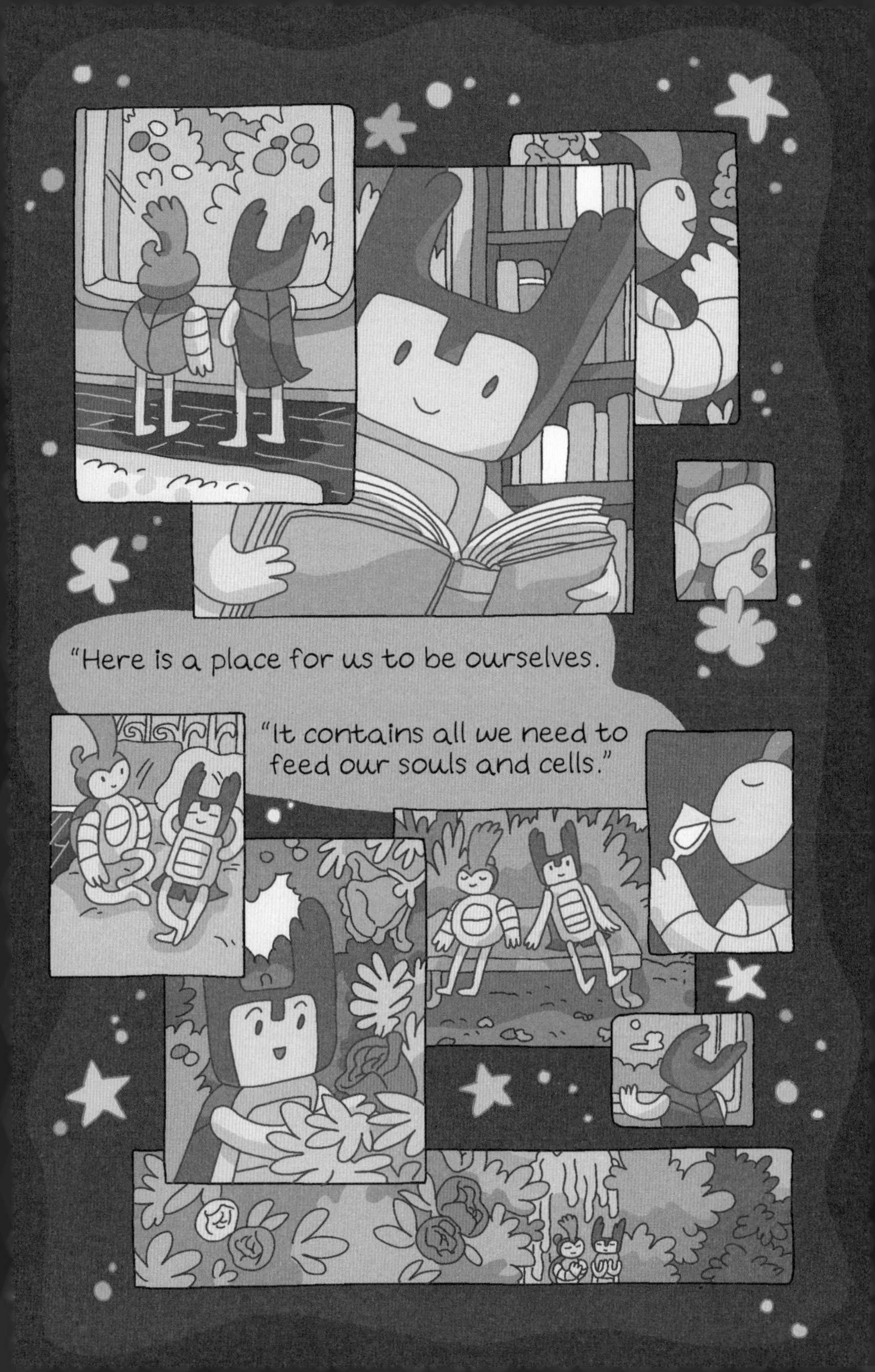
"Here is a place for us to be ourselves.
"It contains all we need to feed our souls and cells."

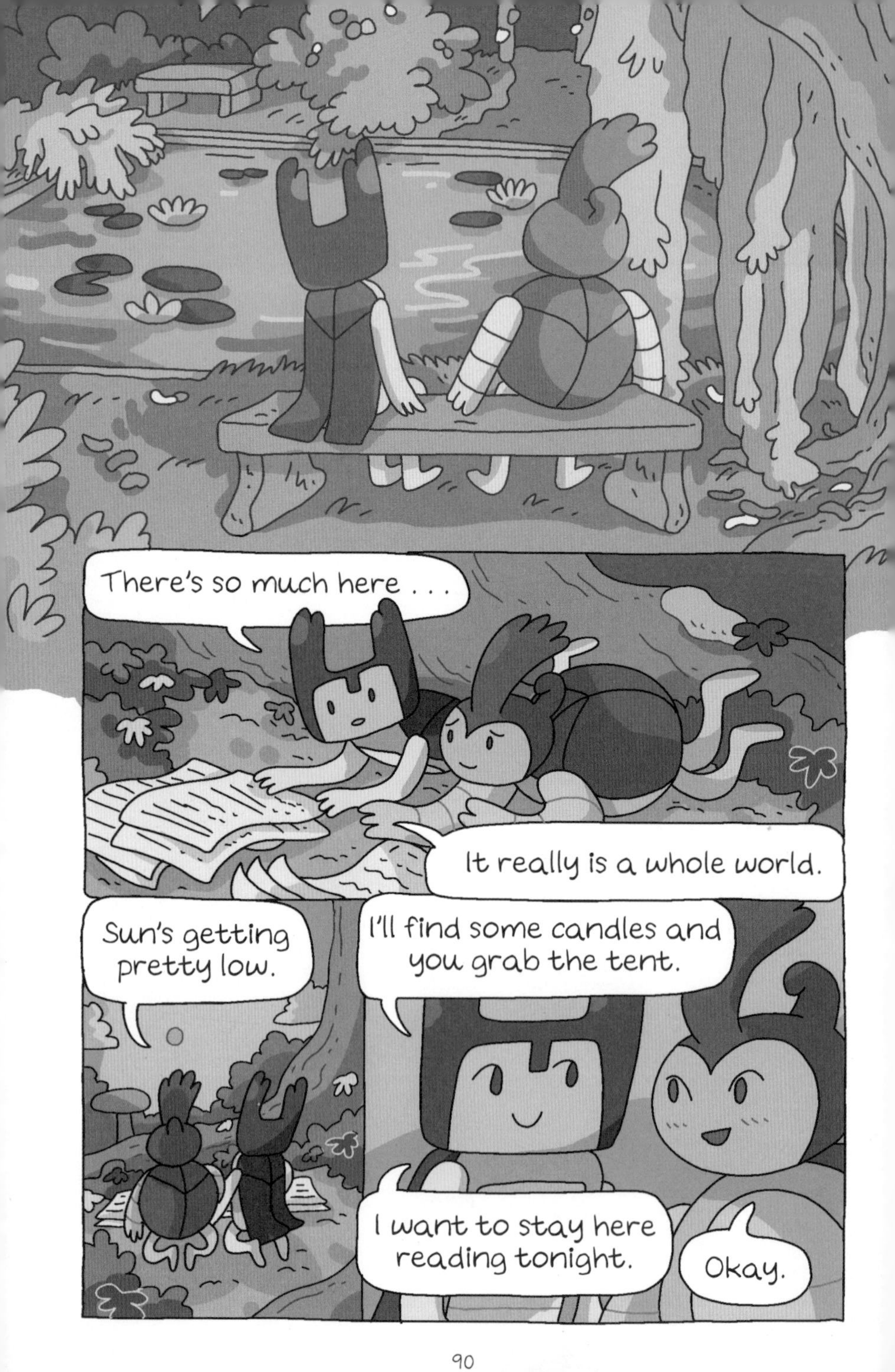
There's so much here . . .
It really is a whole world.
Sun's getting pretty low.
I'll find some candles and you grab the tent.
I want to stay here reading tonight.
Okay.

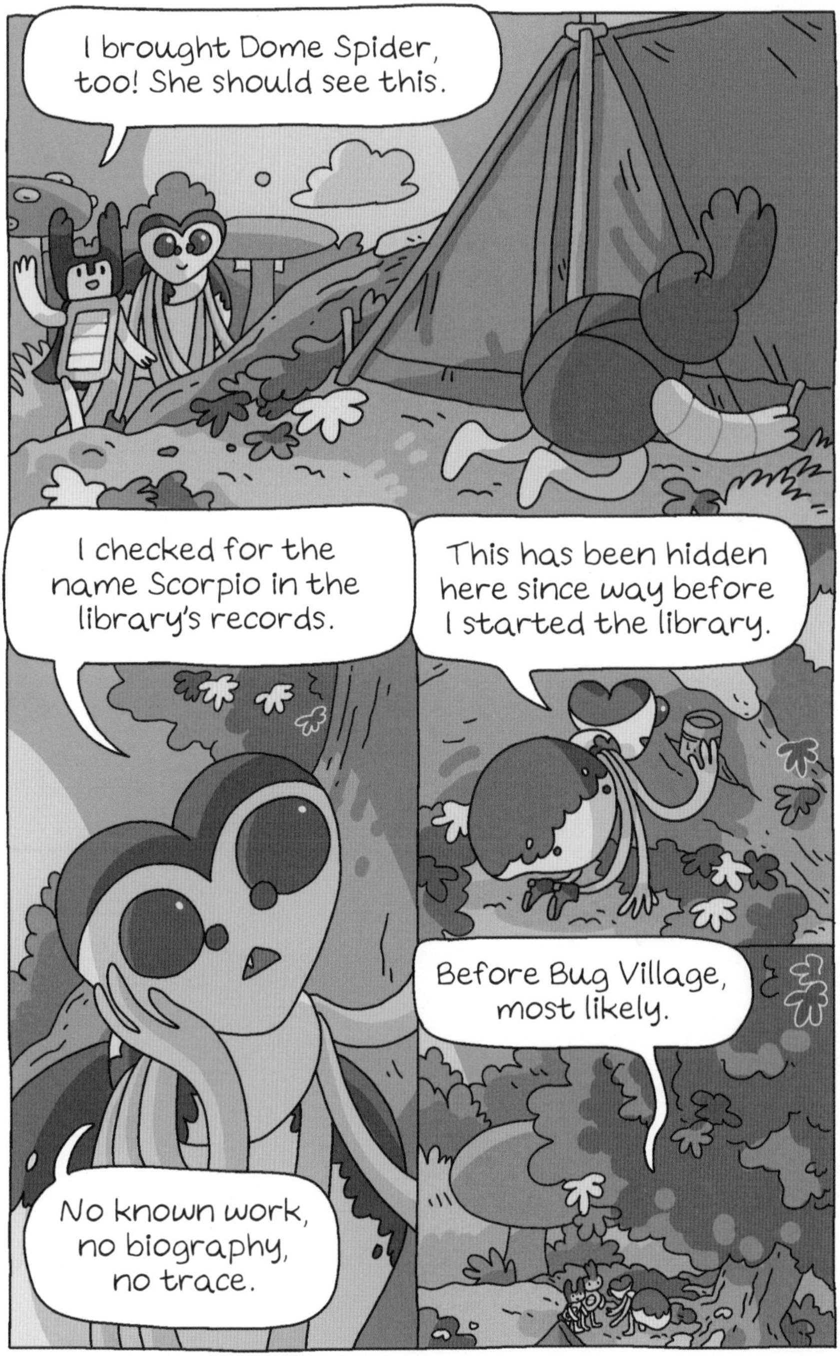
I brought Dome Spider, too! She should see this.
I checked for the name Scorpio in the library's records.
No known work, no biography, no trace.
This has been hidden here since way before I started the library.
Before Bug Village, most likely.

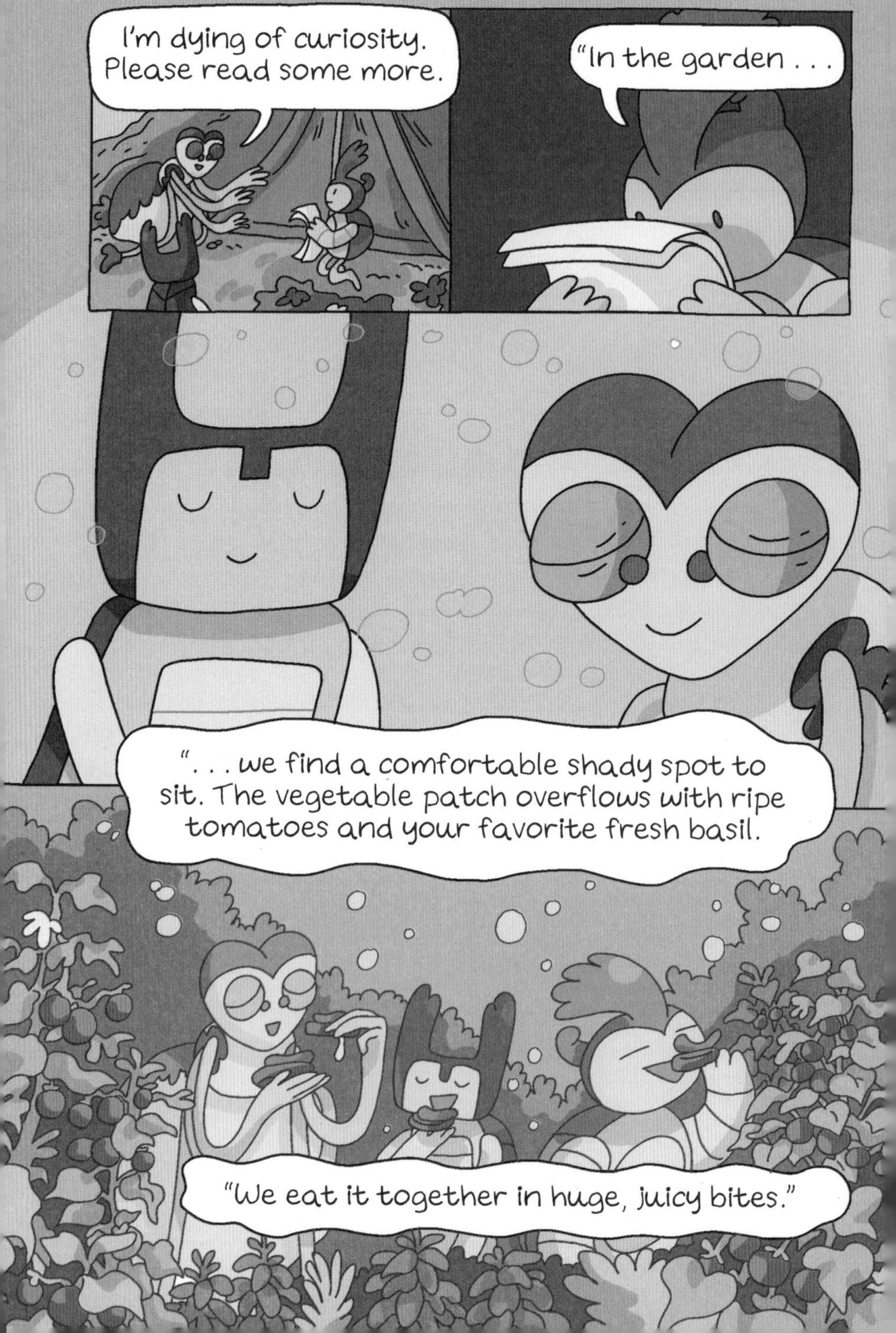
I'm dying of curiosity. Please read some more.
"In the garden . . .
". . . we find a comfortable shady spot to sit. The vegetable patch overflows with ripe tomatoes and your favorite fresh basil.
"We eat it together in huge, juicy bites."

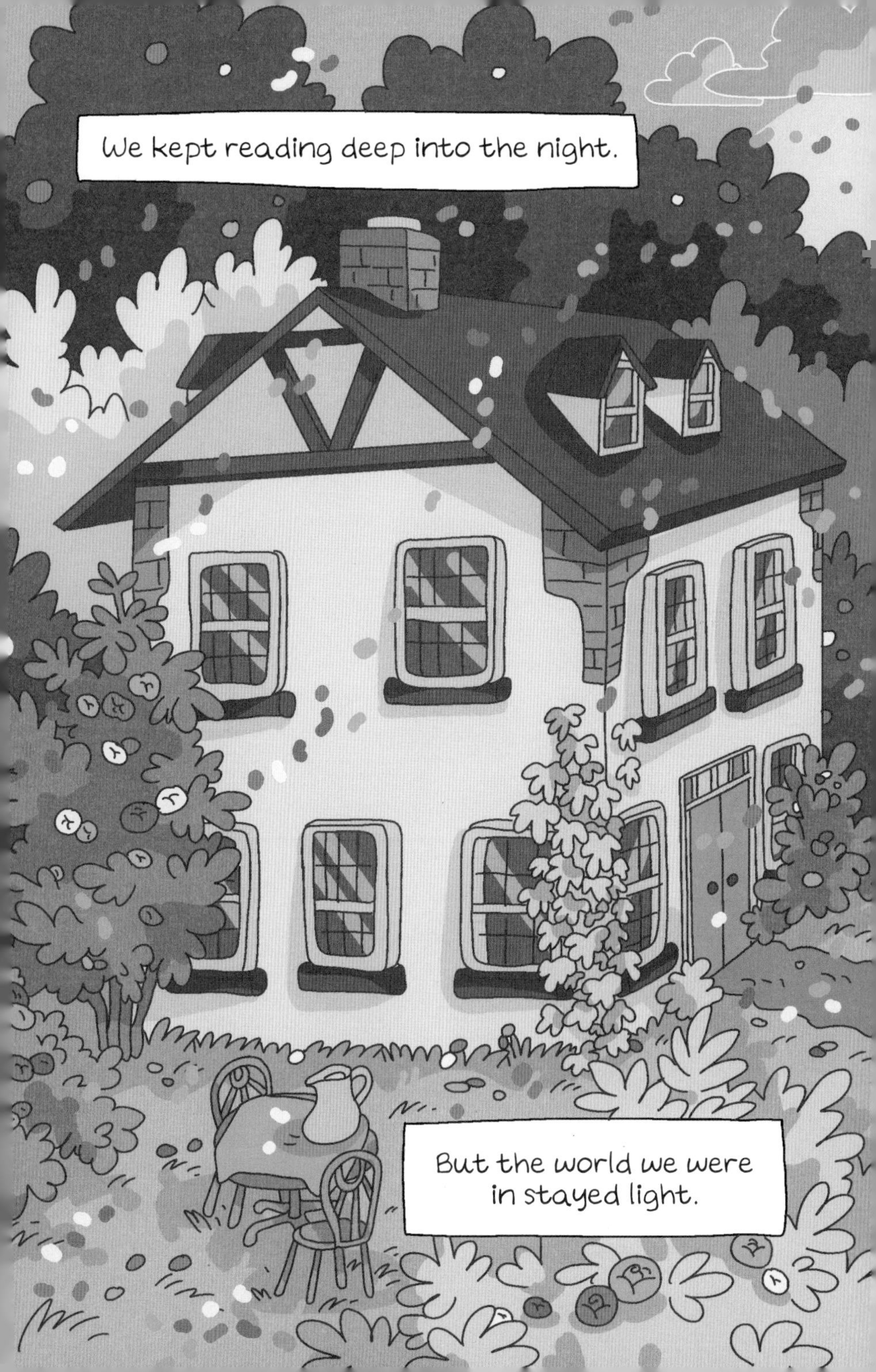
We kept reading deep into the night.
But the world we were in stayed light.

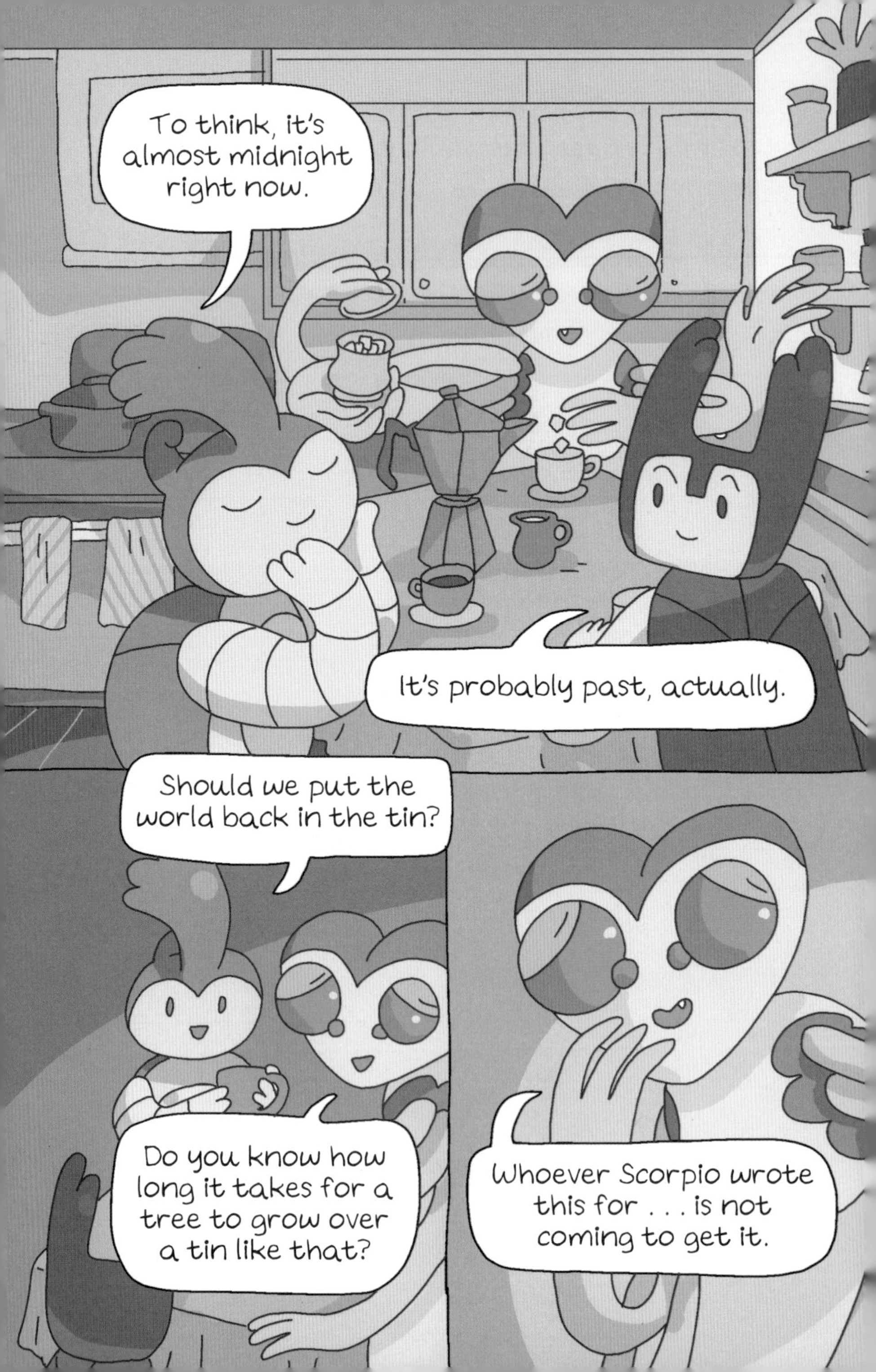
To think, it's almost midnight right now.
It's probably past, actually.
Should we put the world back in the tin?
Do you know how long it takes for a tree to grow over a tin like that?
Whoever Scorpio wrote this for . . . is not coming to get it.

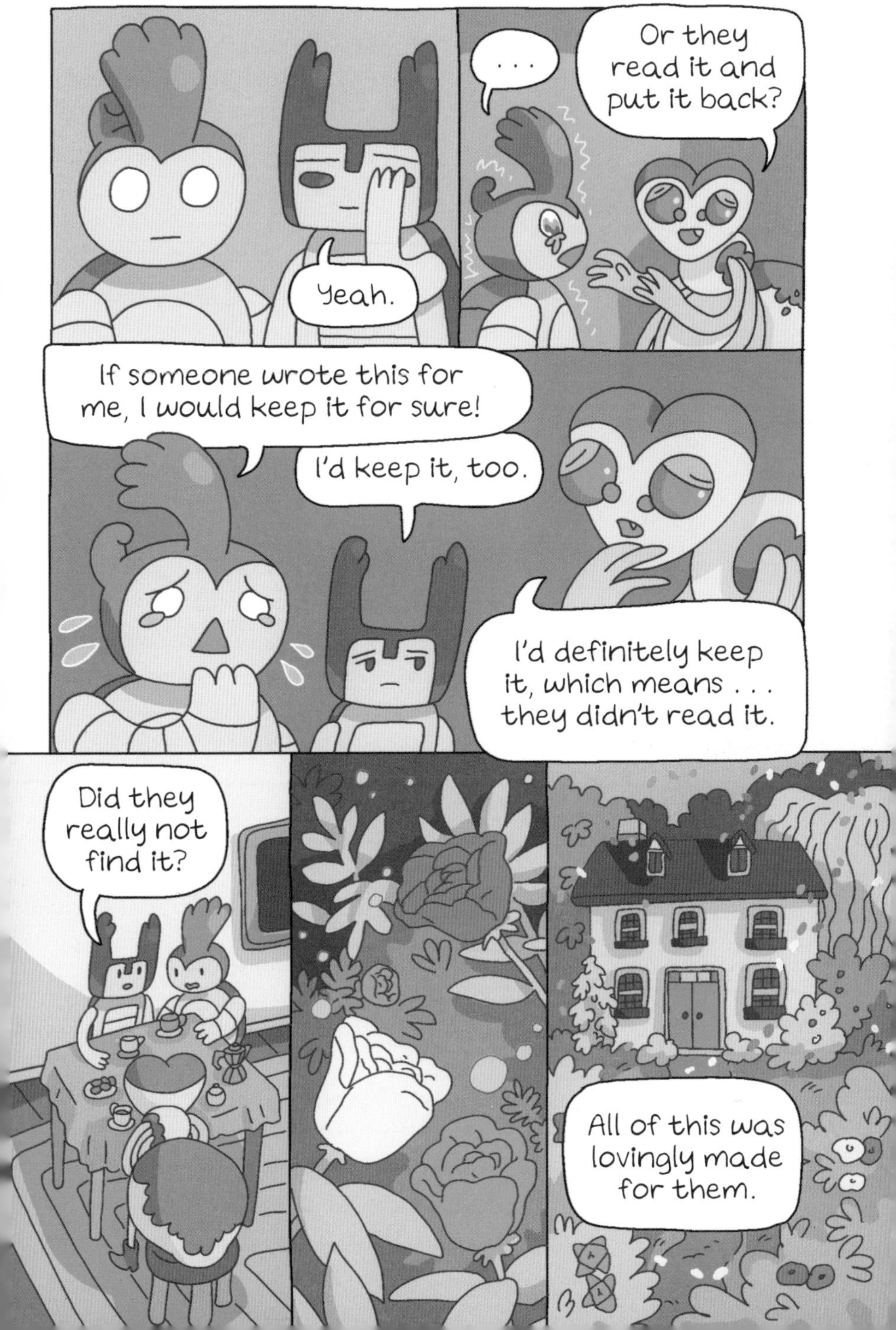
Yeah.
. . .
Or they read it and put it back?
If someone wrote this for me, I would keep it for sure!
I'd keep it, too.
I'd definitely keep it, which means . . . they didn't read it.
Did they really not find it?
All of this was lovingly made for them.

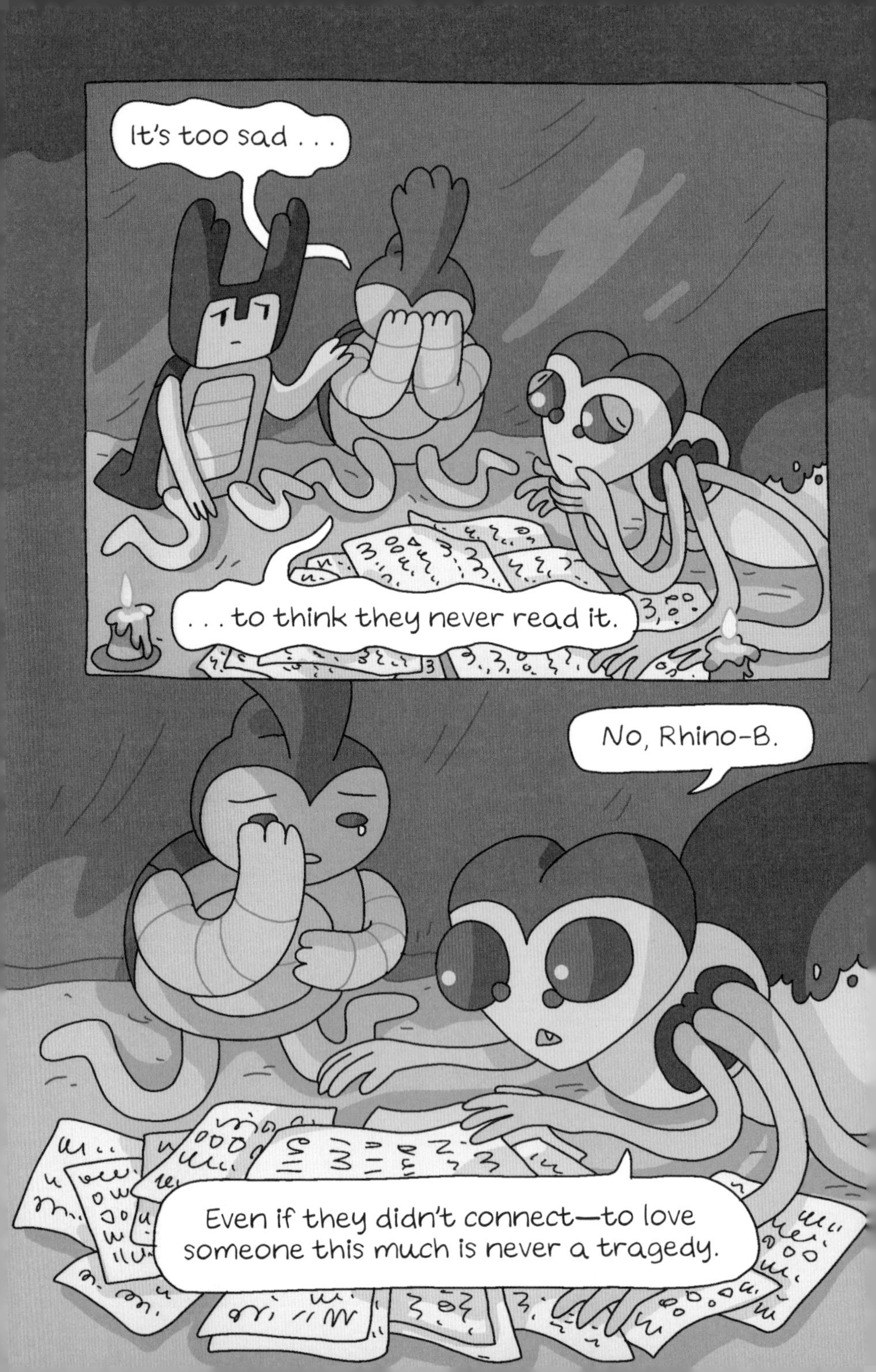
It's too sad . . .
. . . to think they never read it.
No, Rhino-B.
Even if they didn't connect—to love someone this much is never a tragedy.

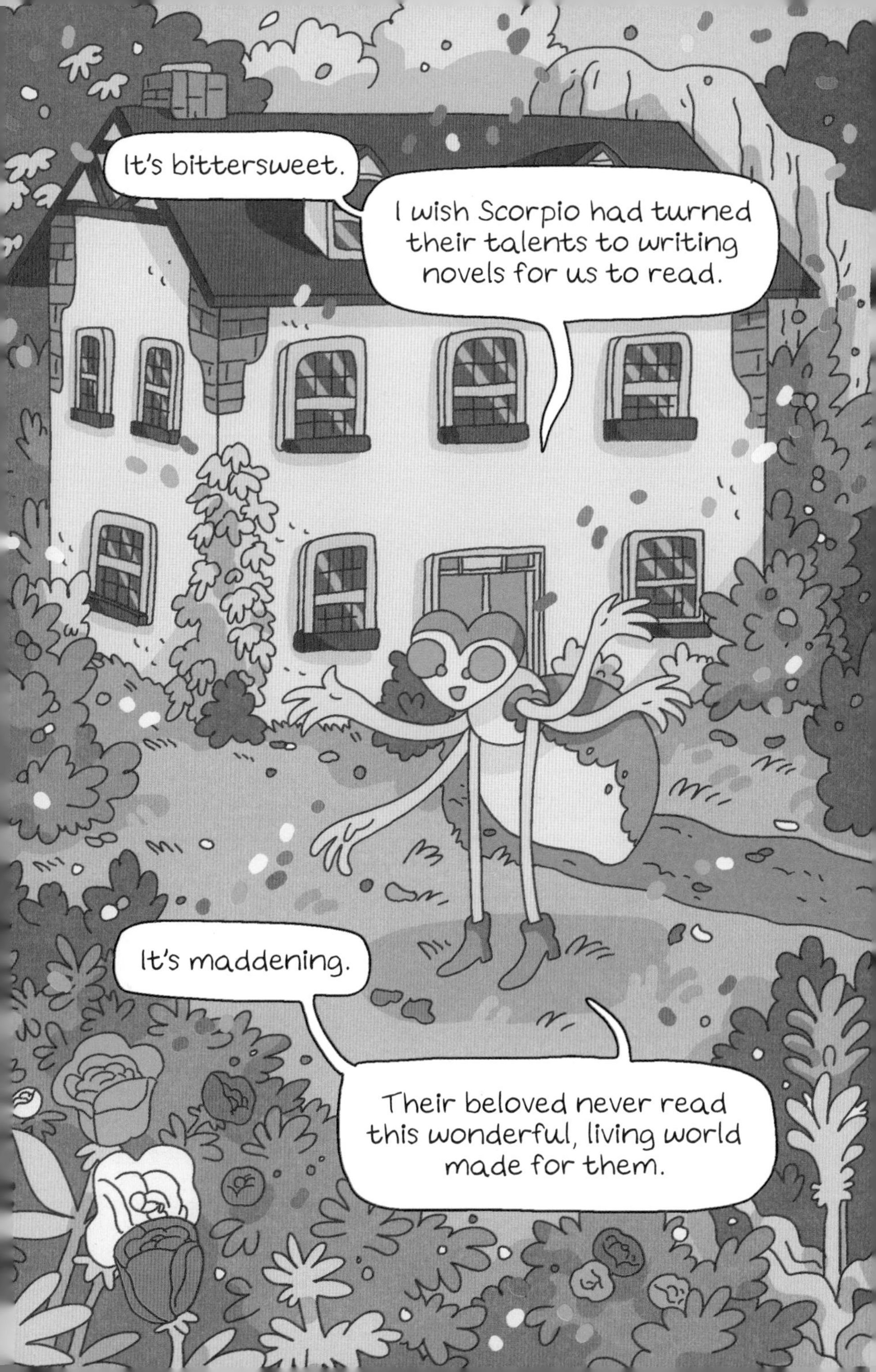
It's bittersweet.
I wish Scorpio had turned their talents to writing novels for us to read.
It's maddening.
Their beloved never read this wonderful, living world made for them.

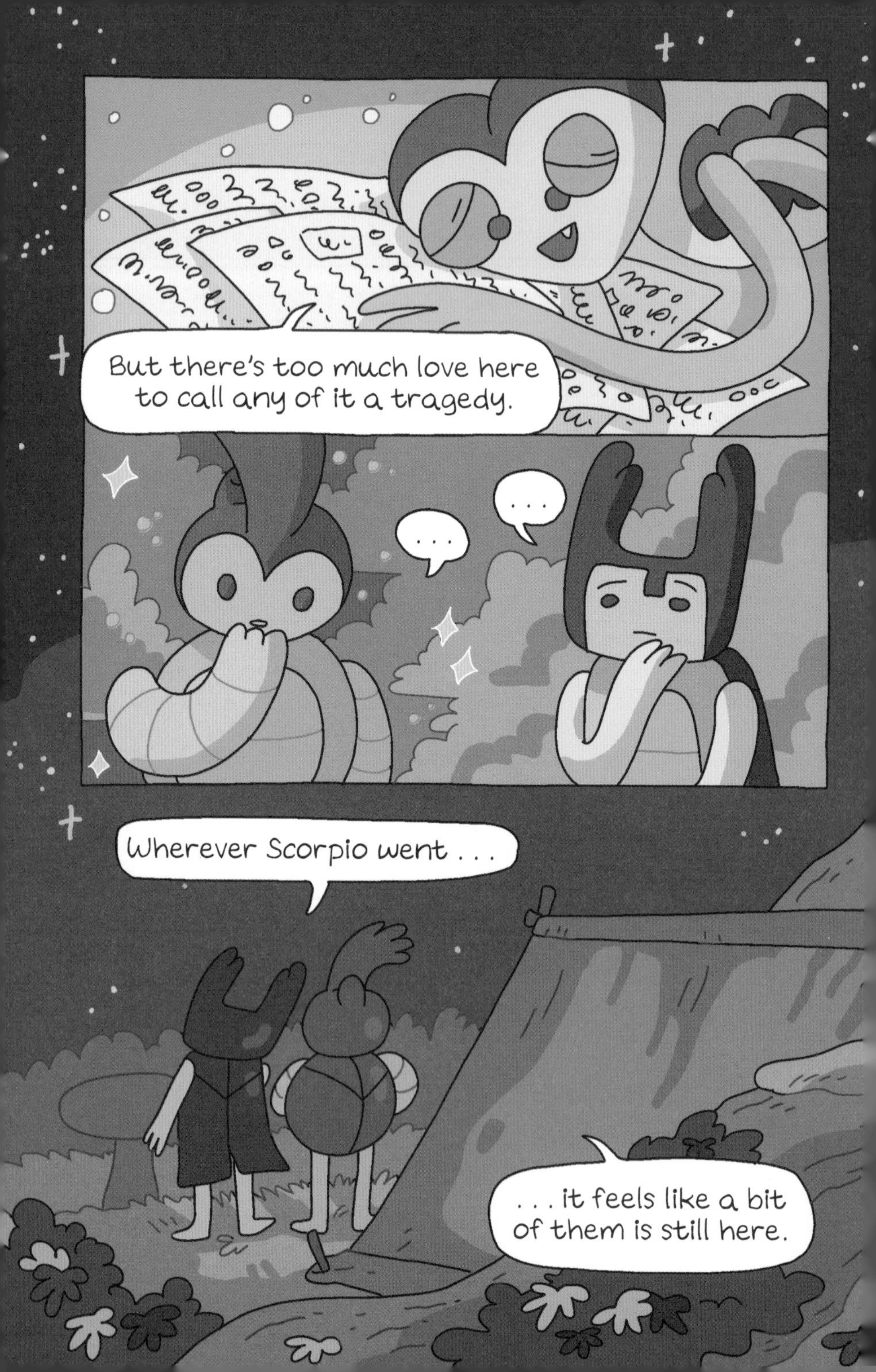
But there's too much love here to call any of it a tragedy.
. . .
. . .
Wherever Scorpio went . . .
. . . it feels like a bit of them is still here.

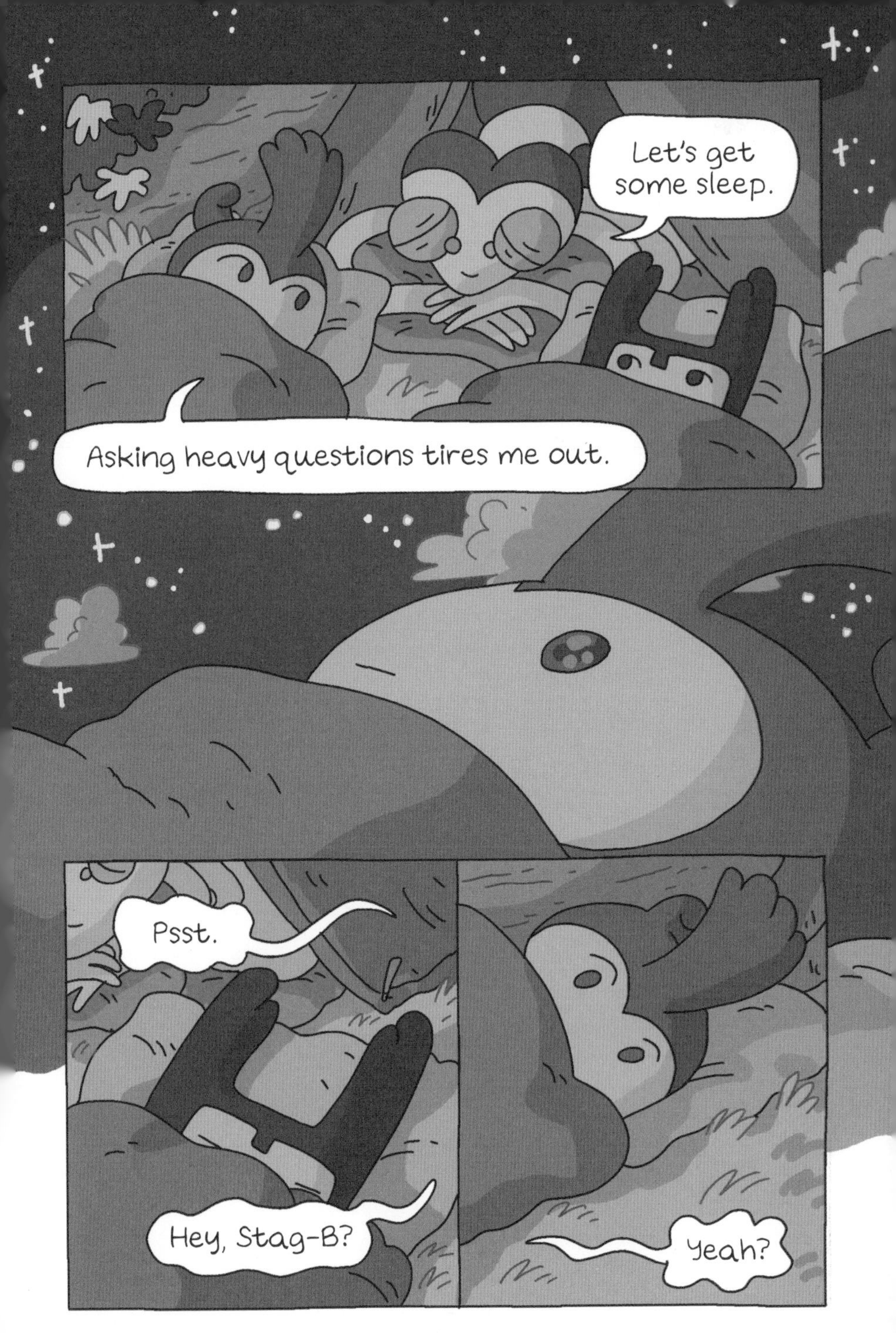
Let's get some sleep.
Asking heavy questions tires me out.
Psst.
Hey, Stag-B?
Yeah?

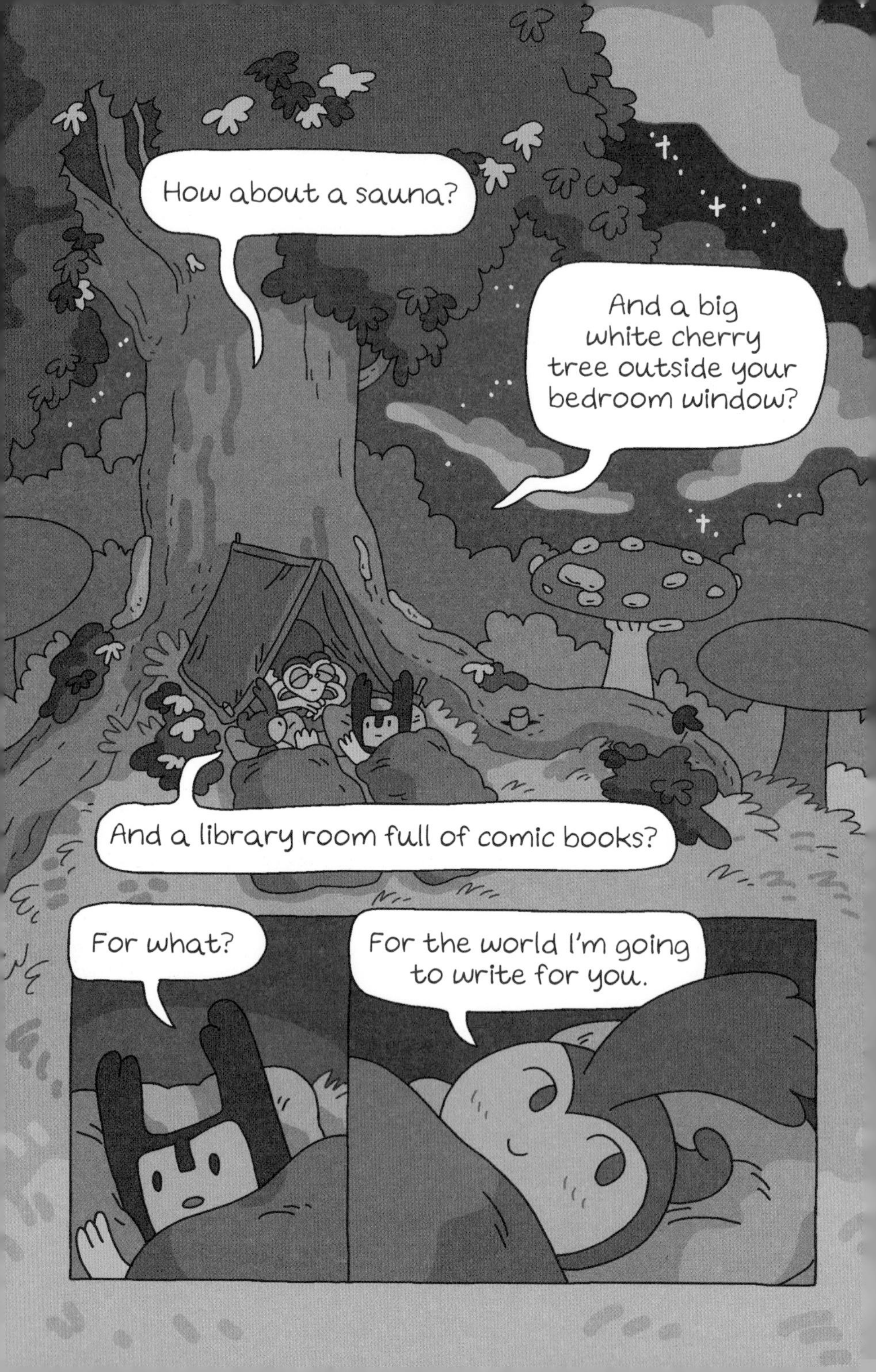
How about a sauna?
And a big white cherry tree outside your bedroom window?
And a library room full of comic books?
For what?
For the world I'm going to write for you.

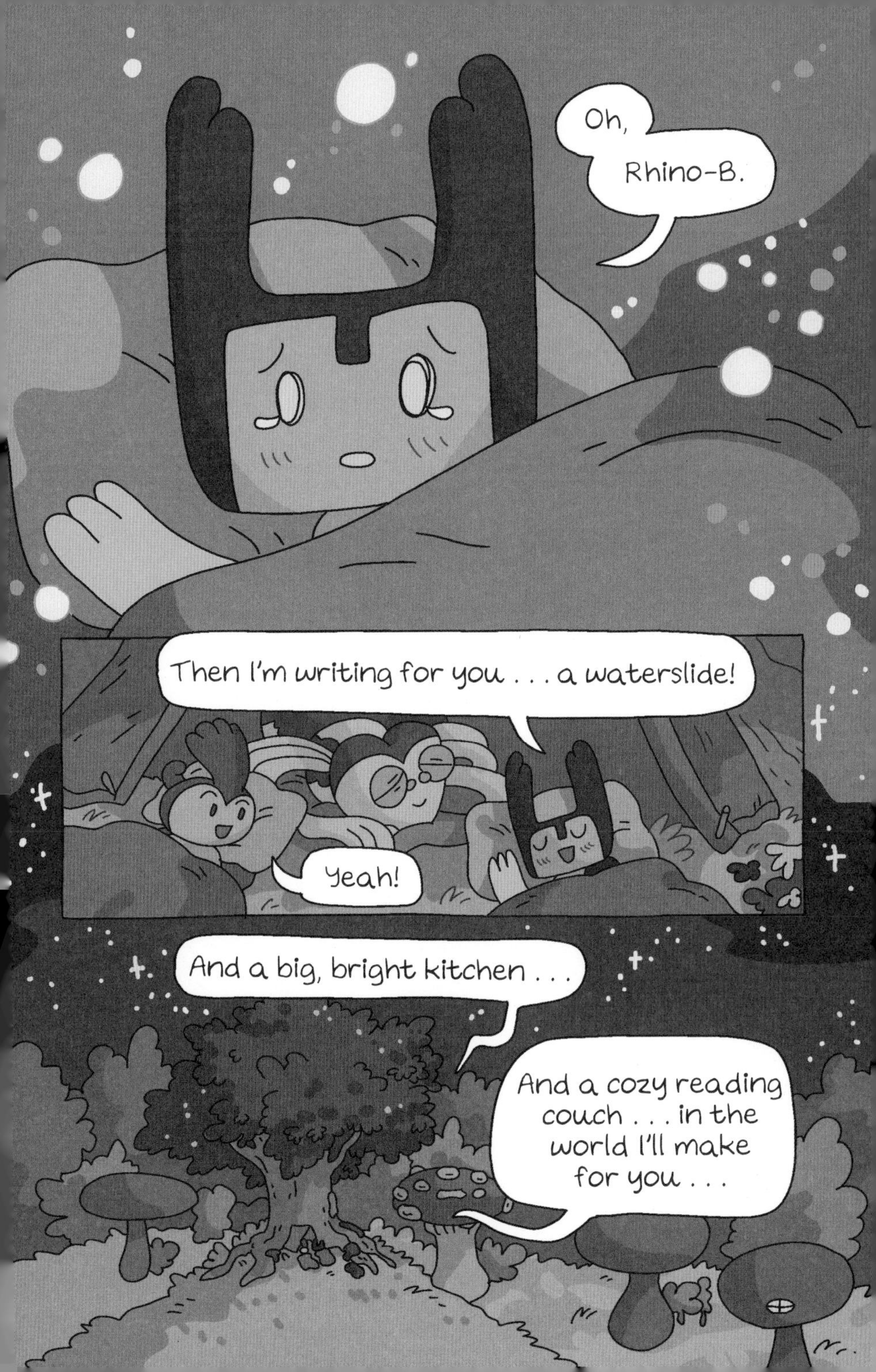
Oh,
Rhino-B.
Then I'm writing for you . . . a waterslide!
Yeah!
And a big, bright kitchen . . .
And a cozy reading couch . . . in the world I'll make for you . . .

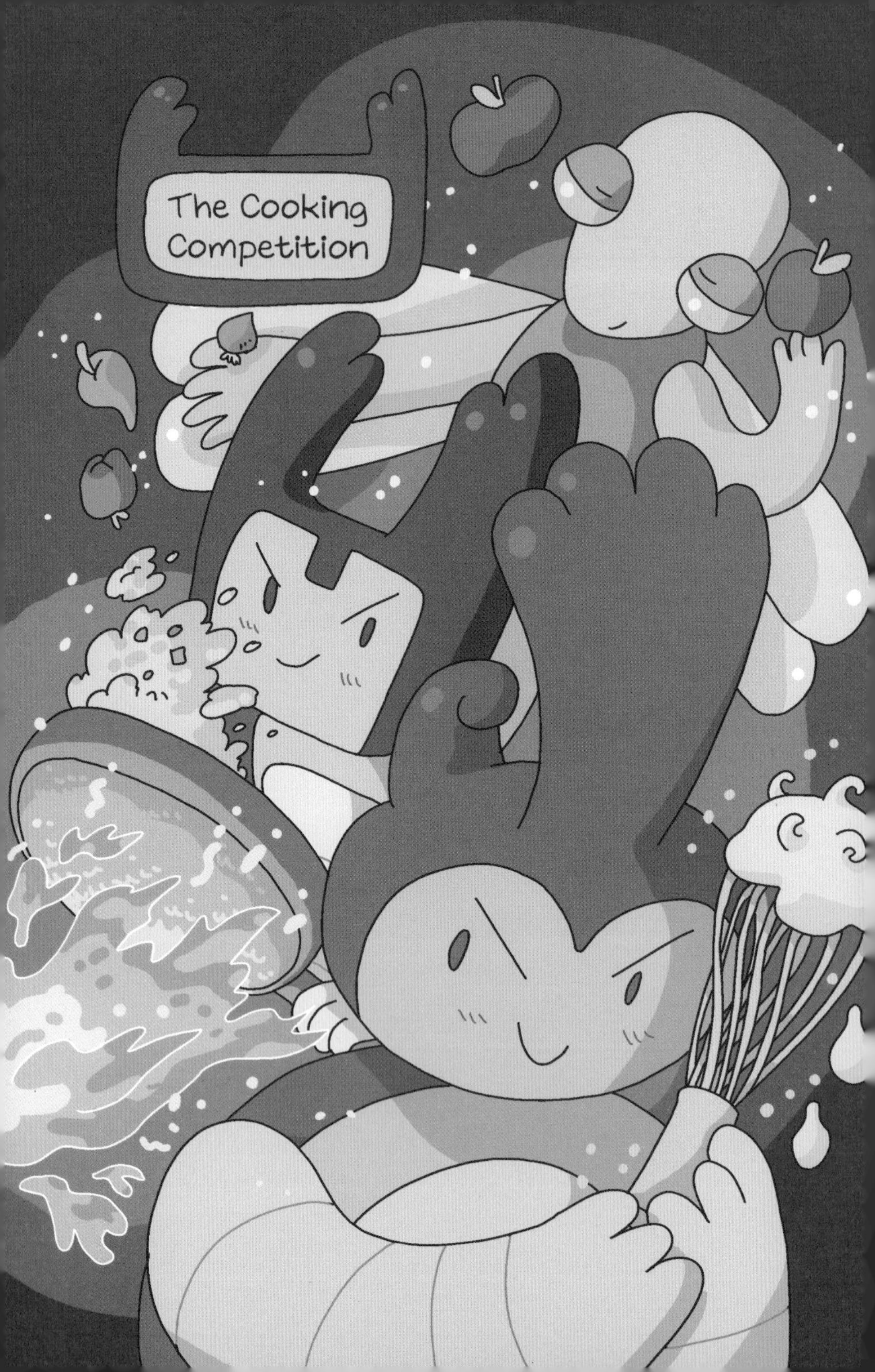
The Cooking Competition

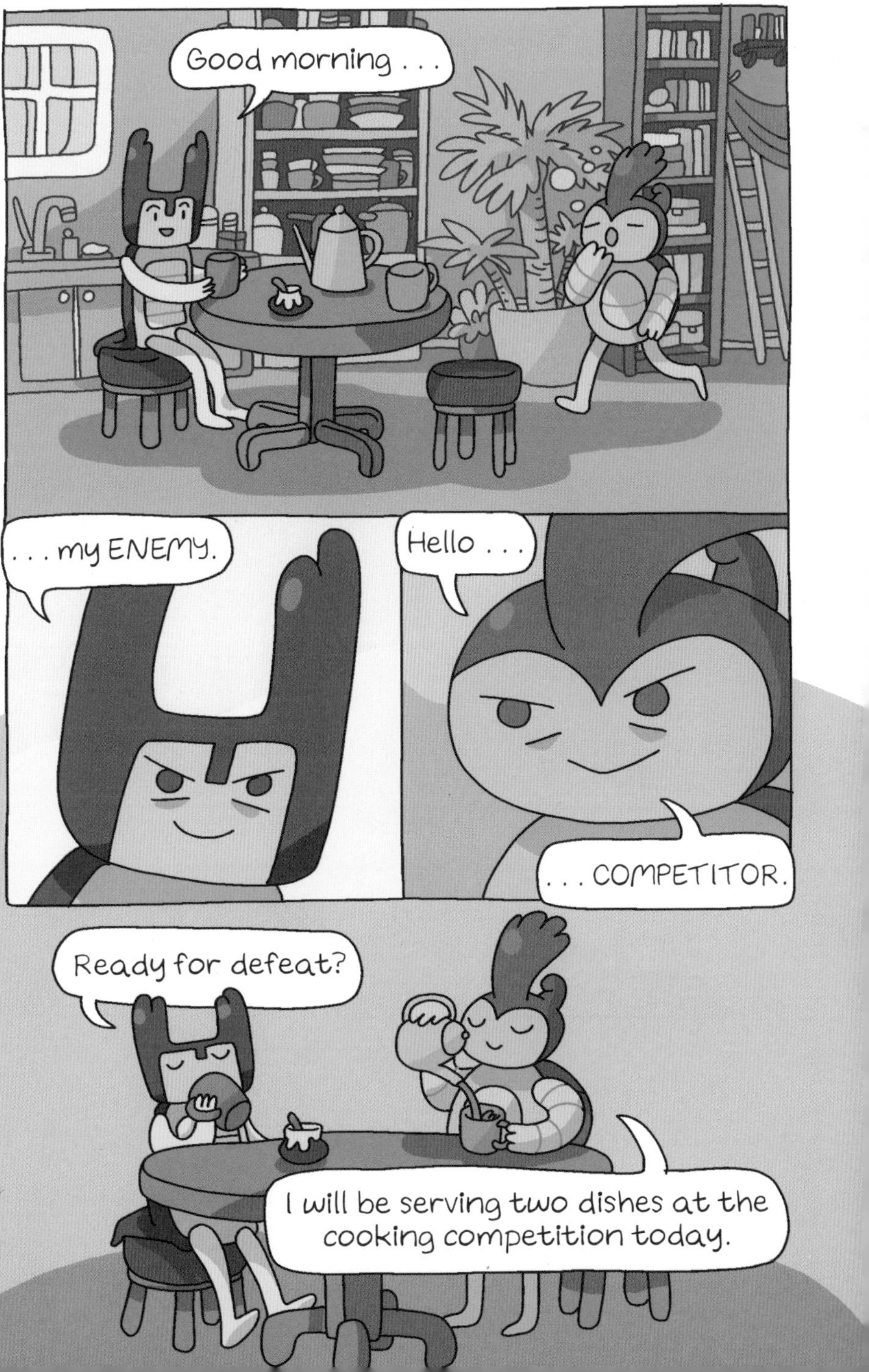
Good morning . . .
. . . my ENEMY.
Hello . . .
. . . COMPETITOR.
Ready for defeat?
I will be serving two dishes at the cooking competition today.

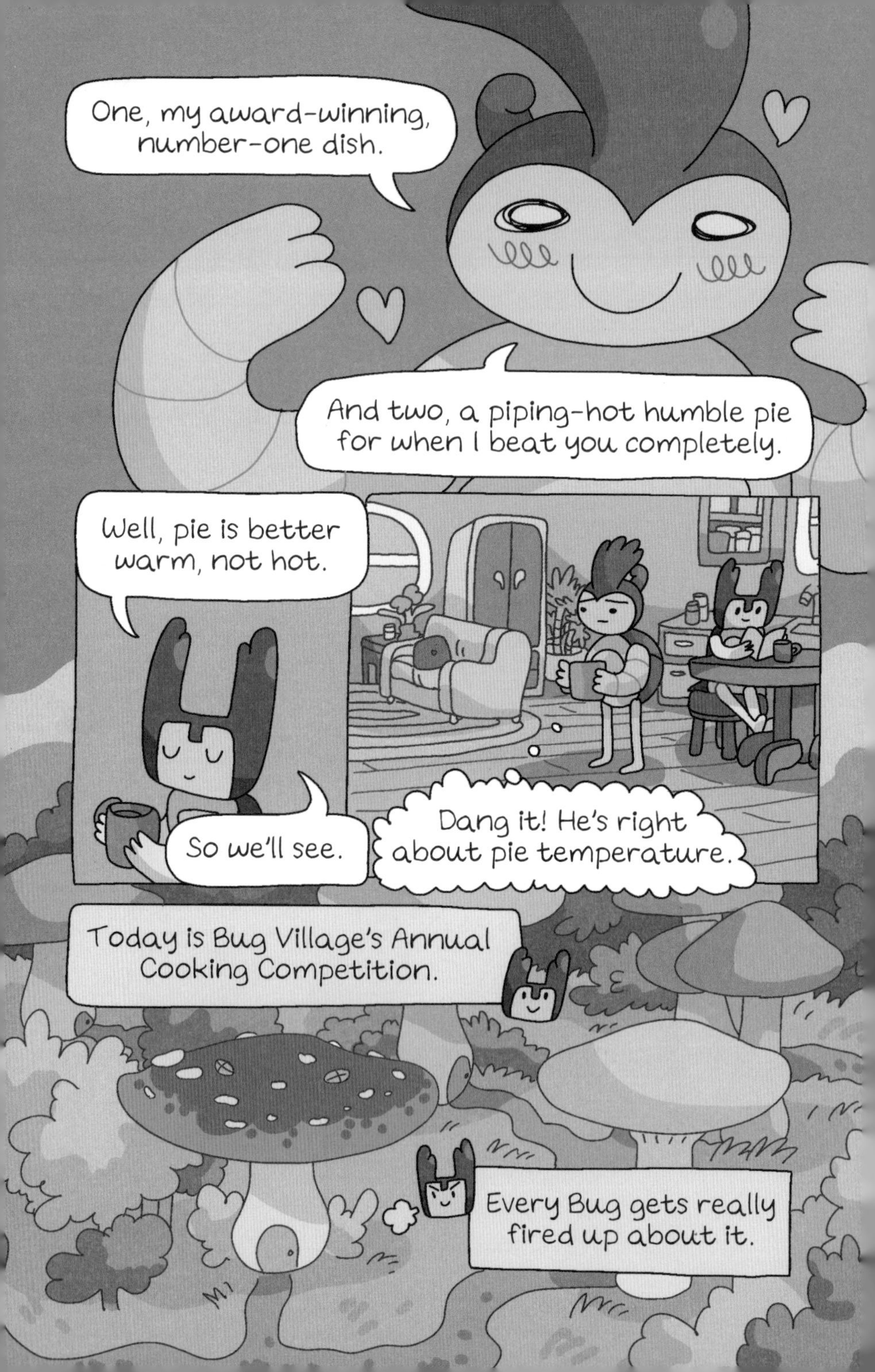
One, my award-winning, number-one dish.
And two, a piping-hot humble pie for when I beat you completely.
Well, pie is better warm, not hot.
So we'll see.
Dang it! He's right about pie temperature.
Today is Bug Village's Annual Cooking Competition.
Every Bug gets really fired up about it.

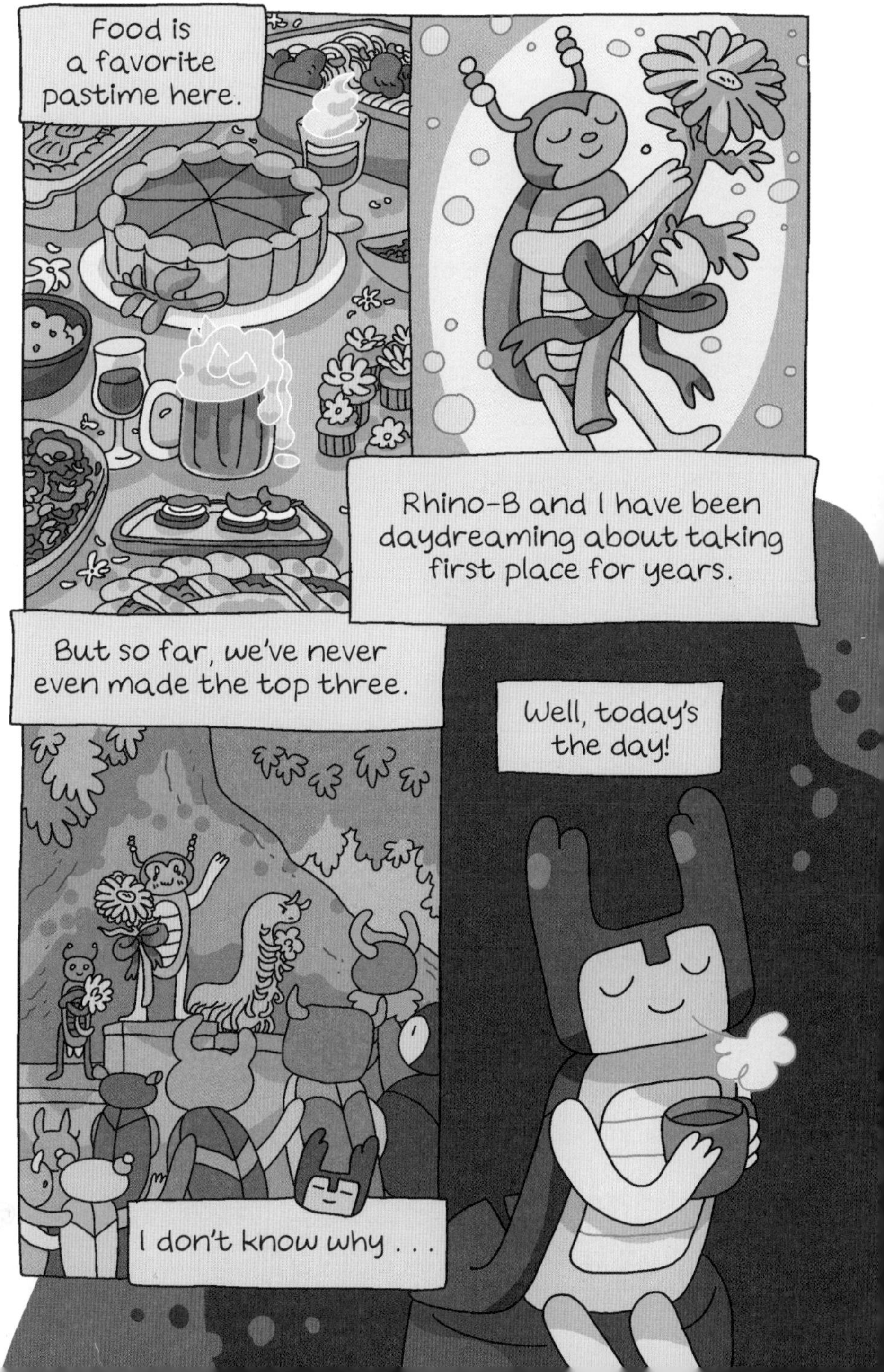
Food is a favorite pastime here.
Rhino-B and I have been daydreaming about taking first place for years.
But so far, we've never even made the top three.
Well, today's the day!
I don't know why . . .

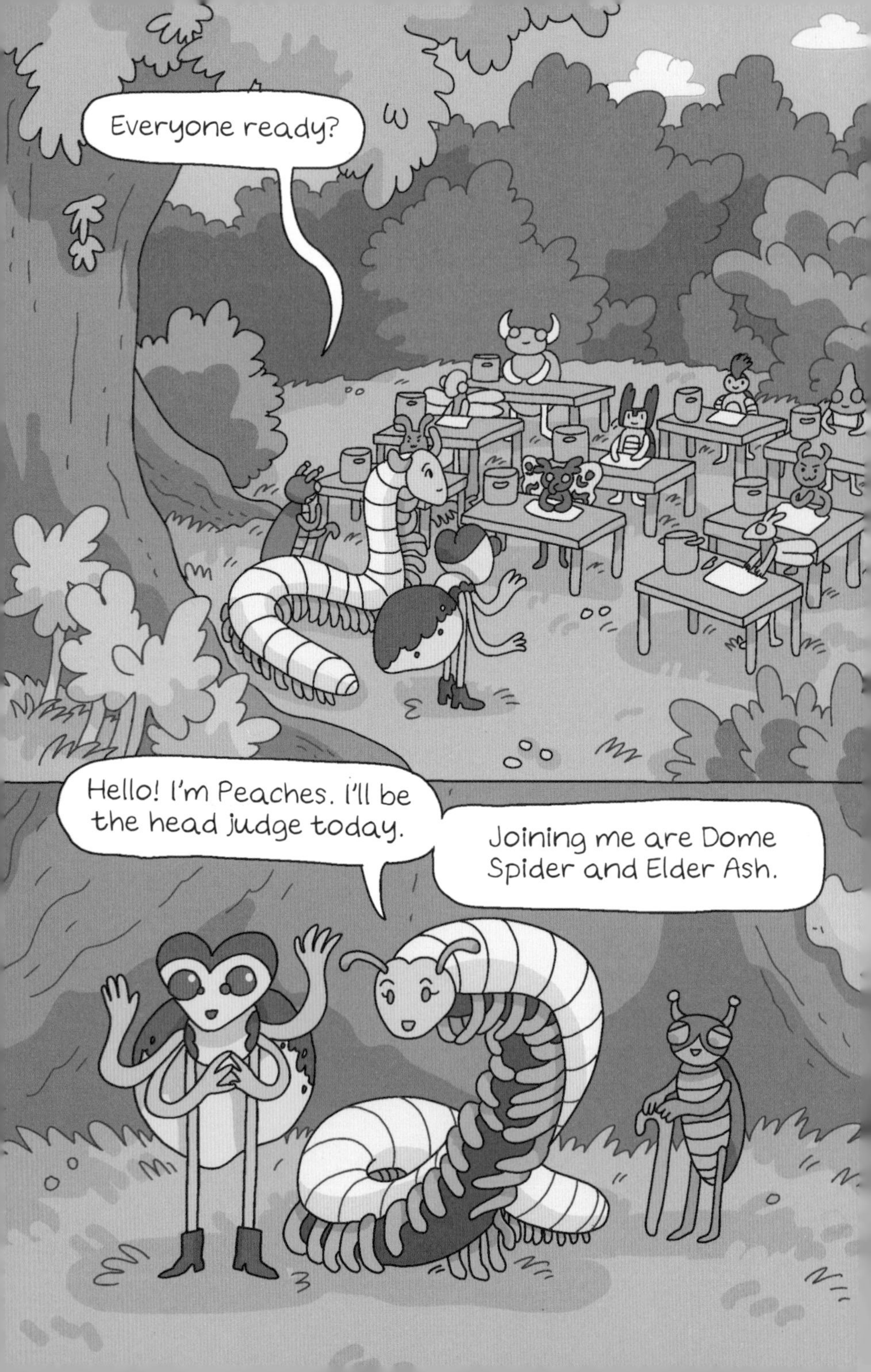
Everyone ready?
Hello! I'm Peaches. I'll be the head judge today.
Joining me are Dome Spider and Elder Ash.

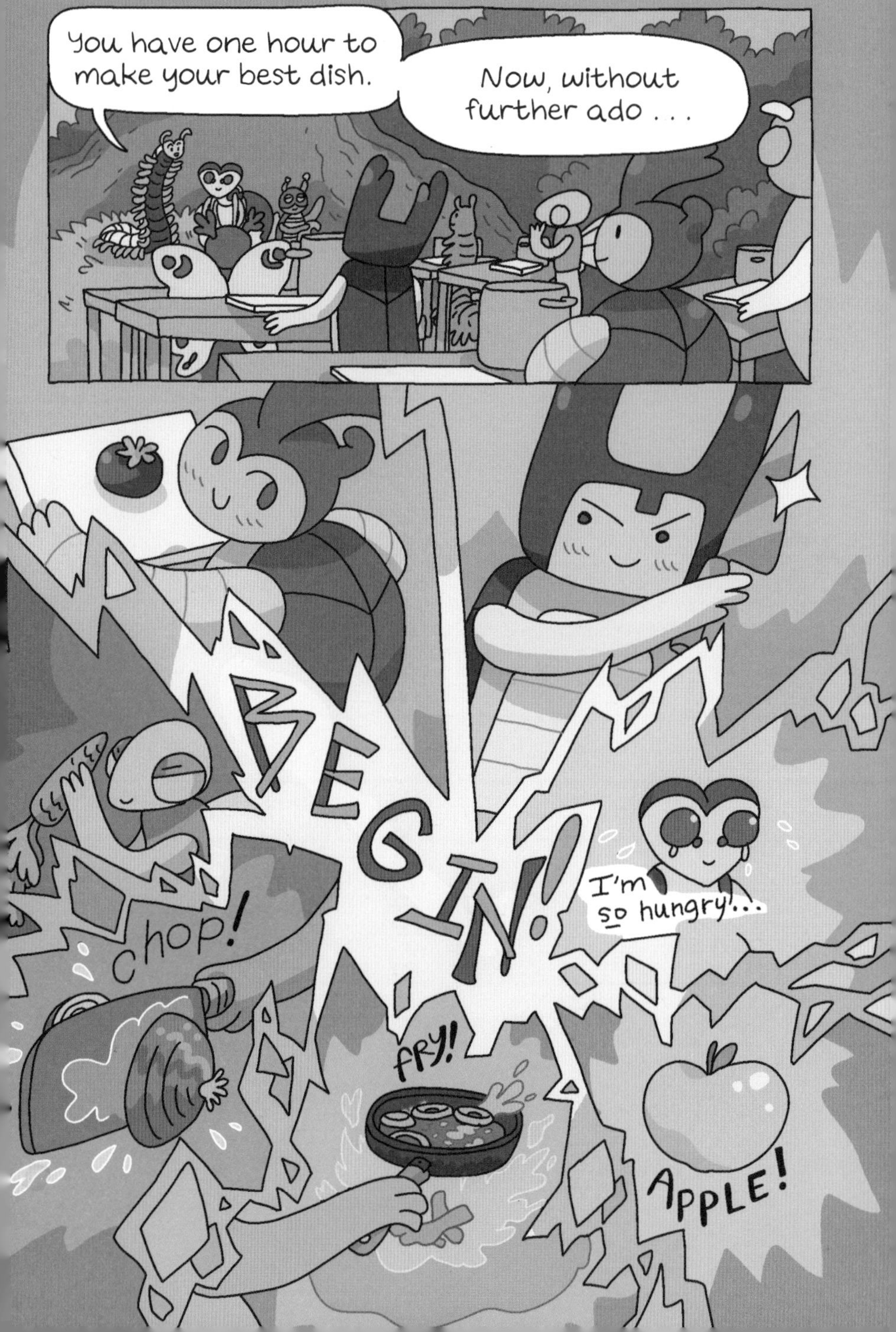
You have one hour to make your best dish.
Now, without further ado . . .
BEGIN!
I'm so hungry! . . .
chop!
FRY!
APPLE!

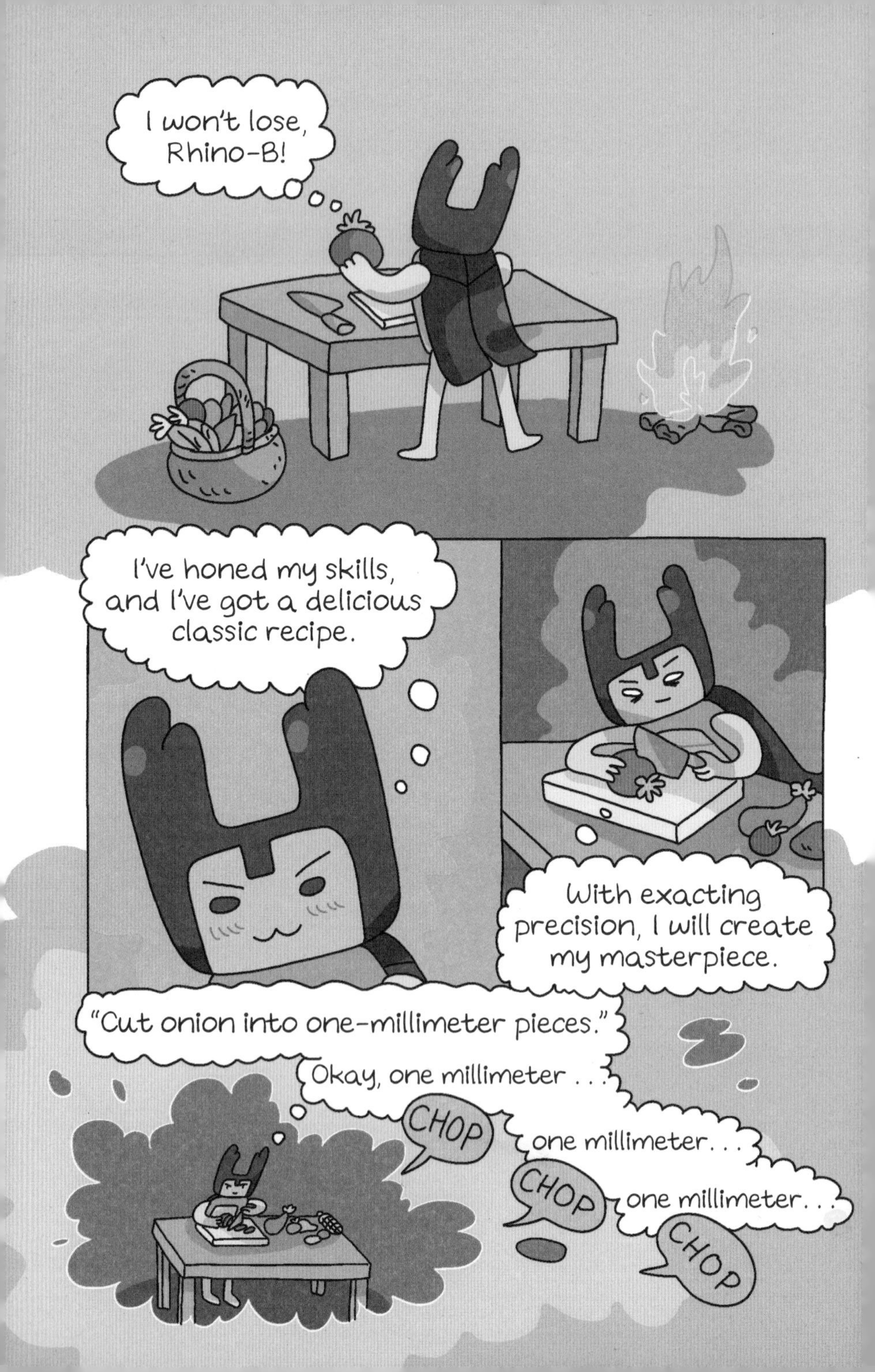
I won't lose, Rhino-B!
I've honed my skills, and I've got a delicious classic recipe.
With exacting precision, I will create my masterpiece.
"Cut onion into one-millimeter pieces."
Okay, one millimeter . . .
CHOP
one millimeter. . .
CHOP
one millimeter. . .
CHOP

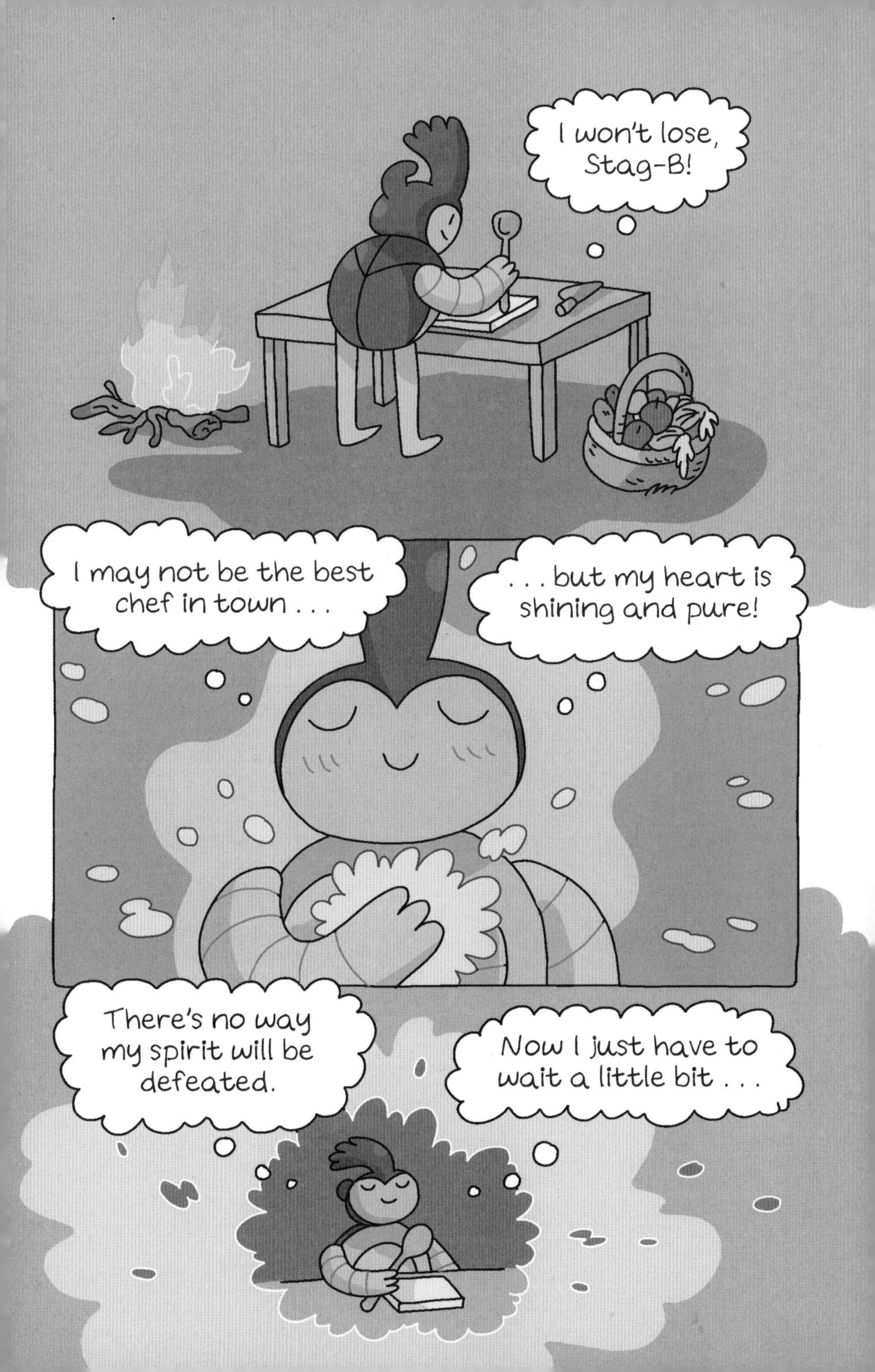
I won't lose, Stag-B!
I may not be the best chef in town . . .
. . . but my heart is shining and pure!
There's no way my spirit will be defeated.
Now I just have to wait a little bit . . .

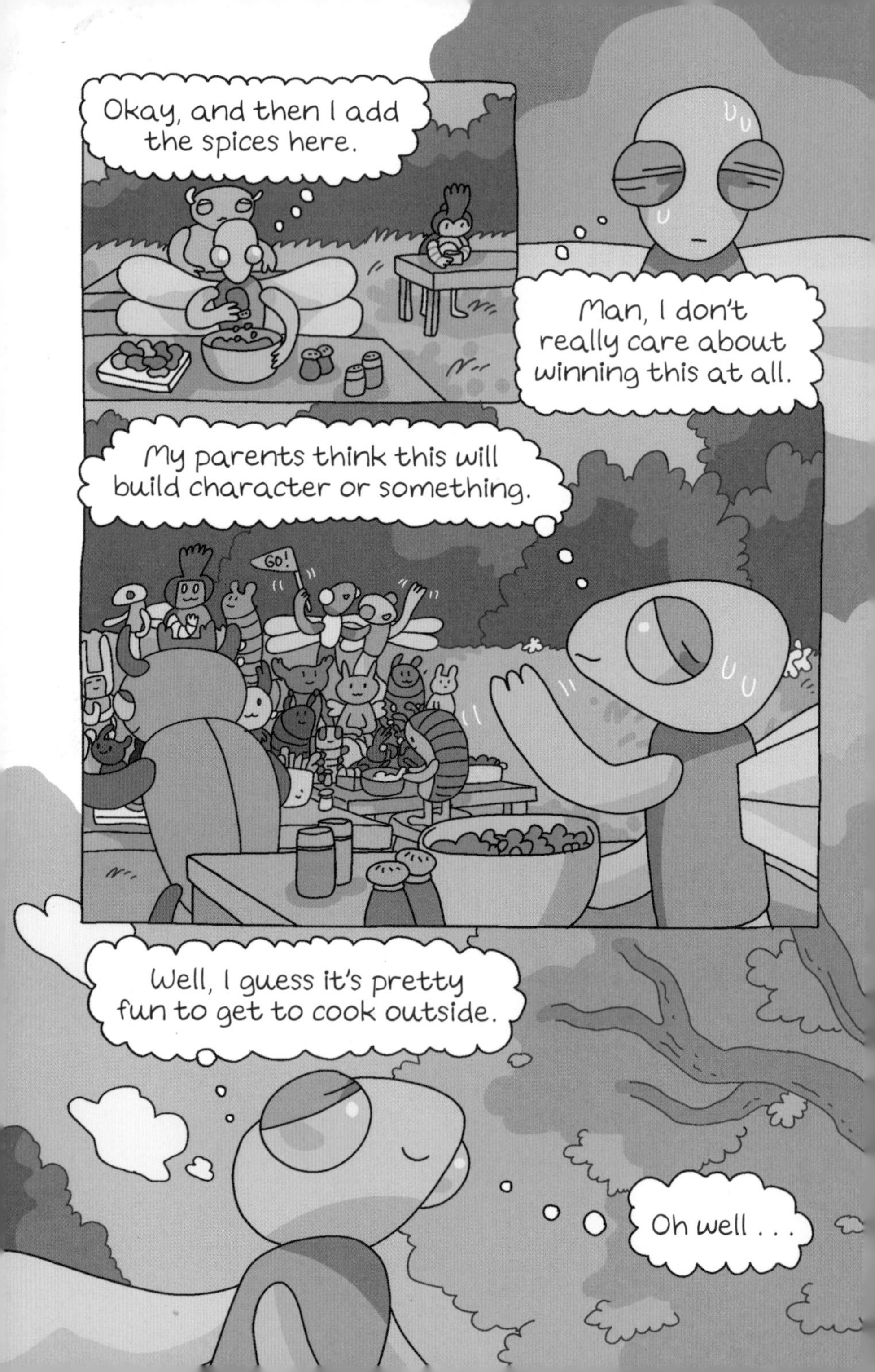
Okay, and then I add the spices here.
Man, I don't really care about winning this at all.
My parents think this will build character or something.
GO!
Well, I guess it's pretty fun to get to cook outside.
Oh well . . .

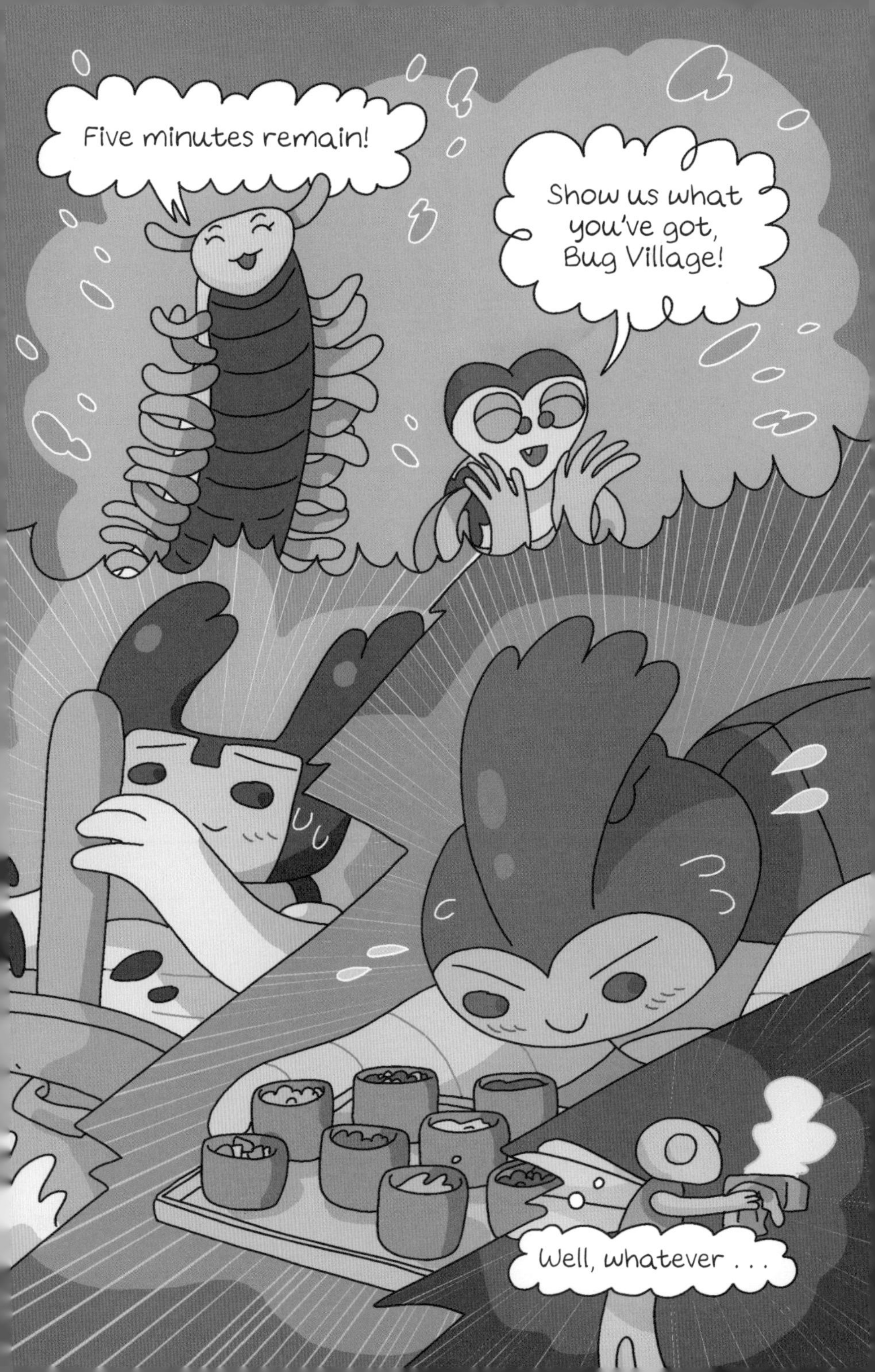
Five minutes remain!
Show us what you've got, Bug Village!
Well, whatever . . .

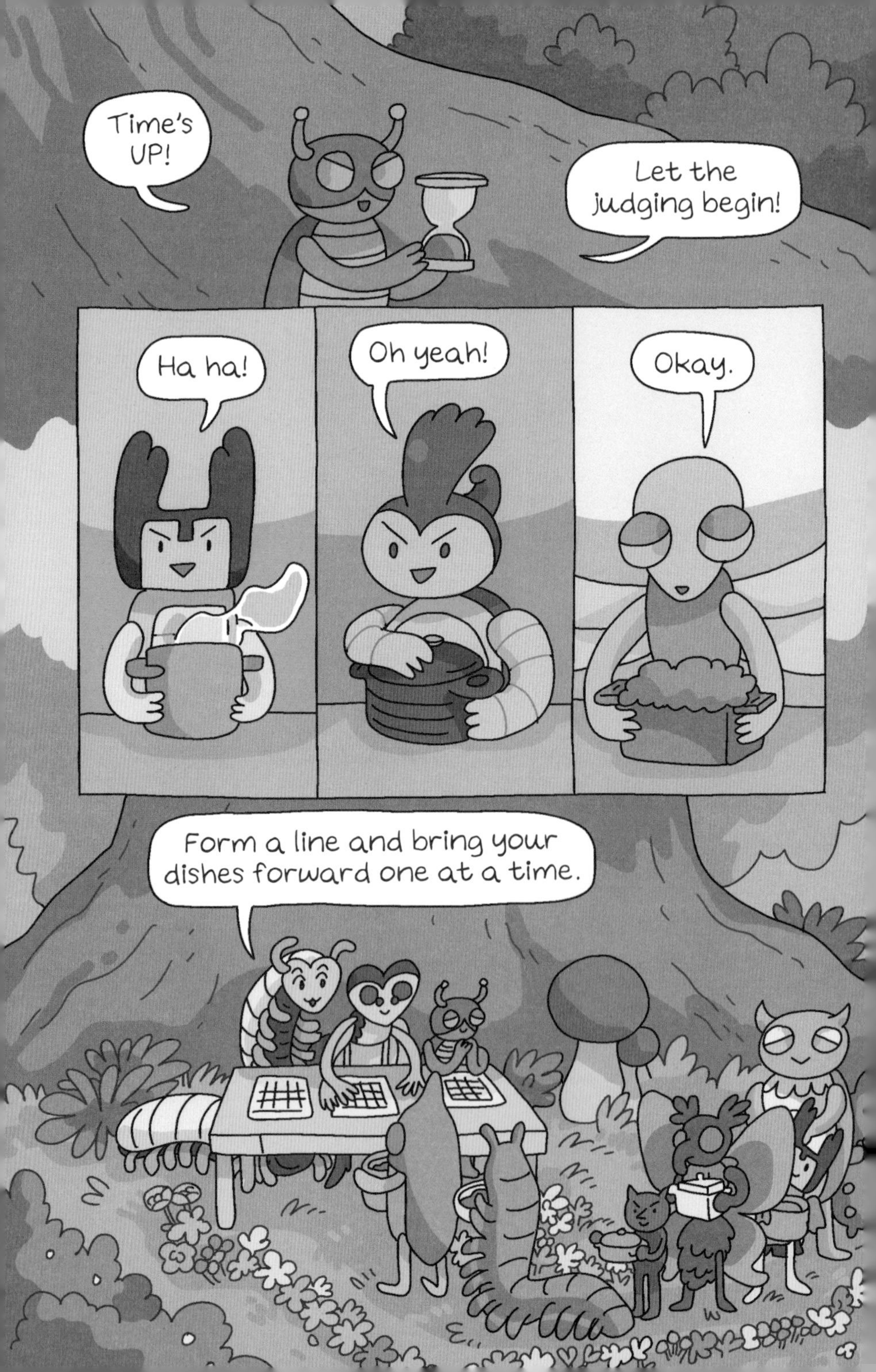
Time's UP!
Let the judging begin!
Ha ha!
Oh yeah!
Okay.
Form a line and bring your dishes forward one at a time.

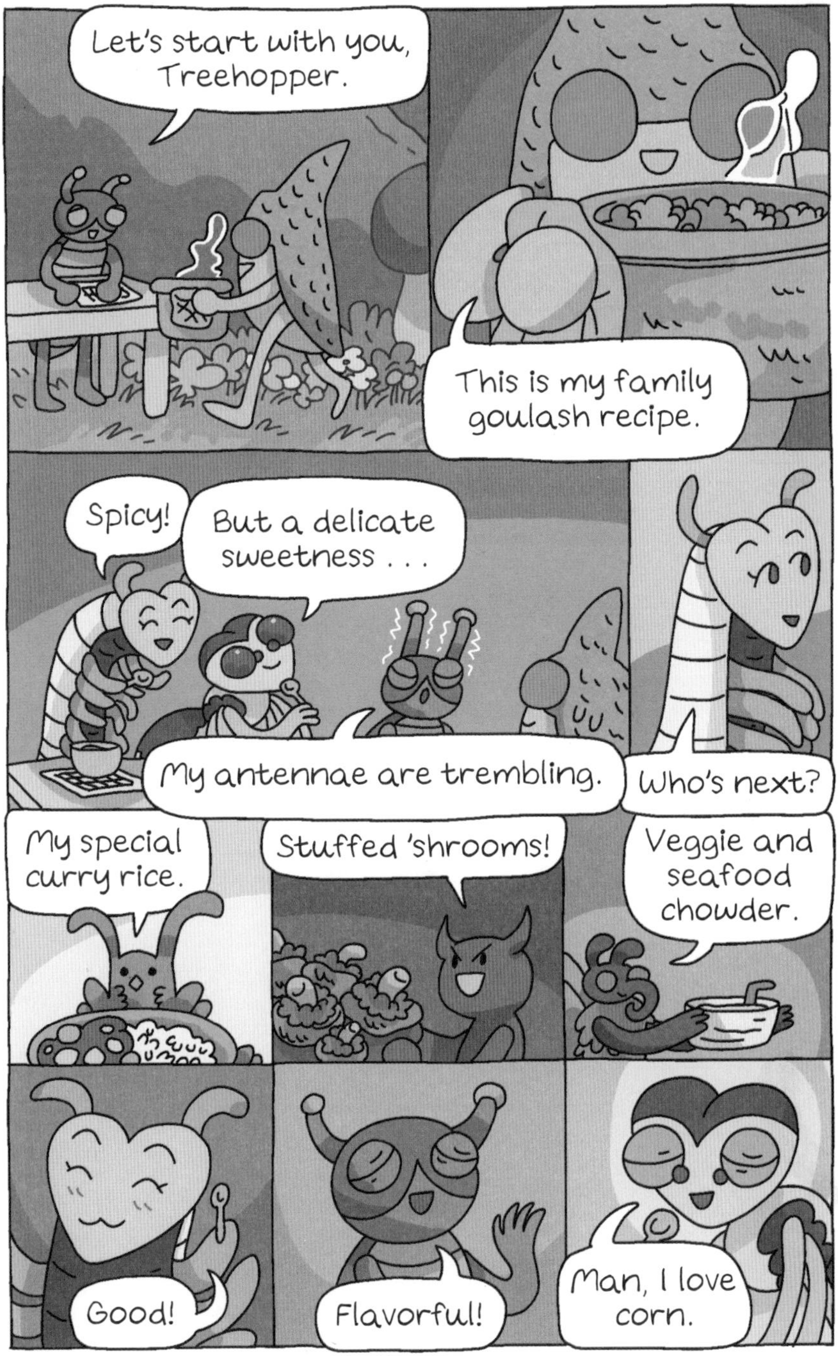
Let's start with you, Treehopper.
This is my family goulash recipe.
Spicy!
But a delicate sweetness . . .
My antennae are trembling.
Who's next?
My special curry rice.
Stuffed 'shrooms!
Veggie and seafood chowder.
Good!
Flavorful!
Man, I love corn.

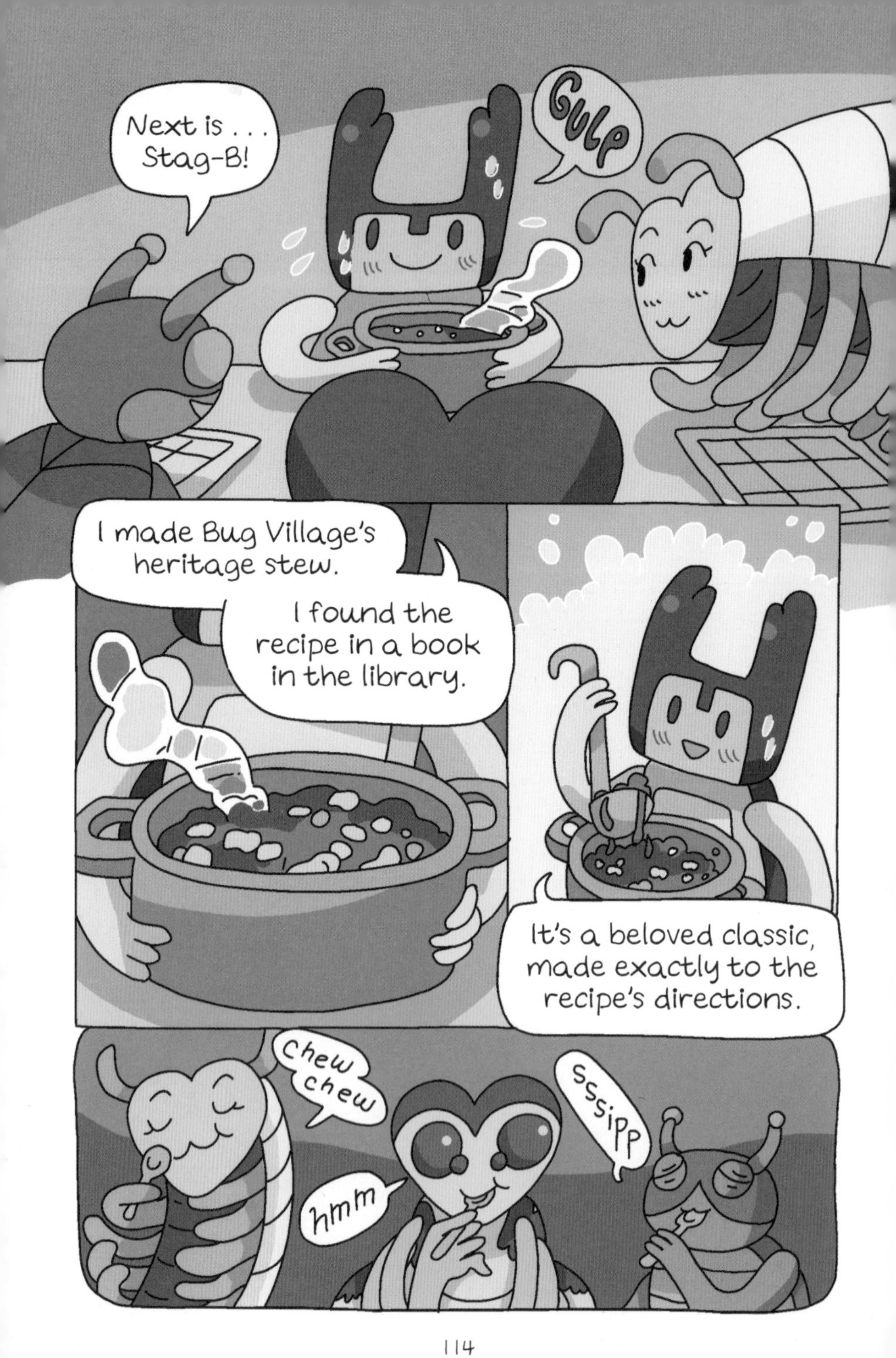
Next is . . .
Stag-B!
GULP
I made Bug Village's heritage stew.
I found the recipe in a book in the library.
It's a beloved classic, made exactly to the recipe's directions.
Chew chew
hmm
Sssipp

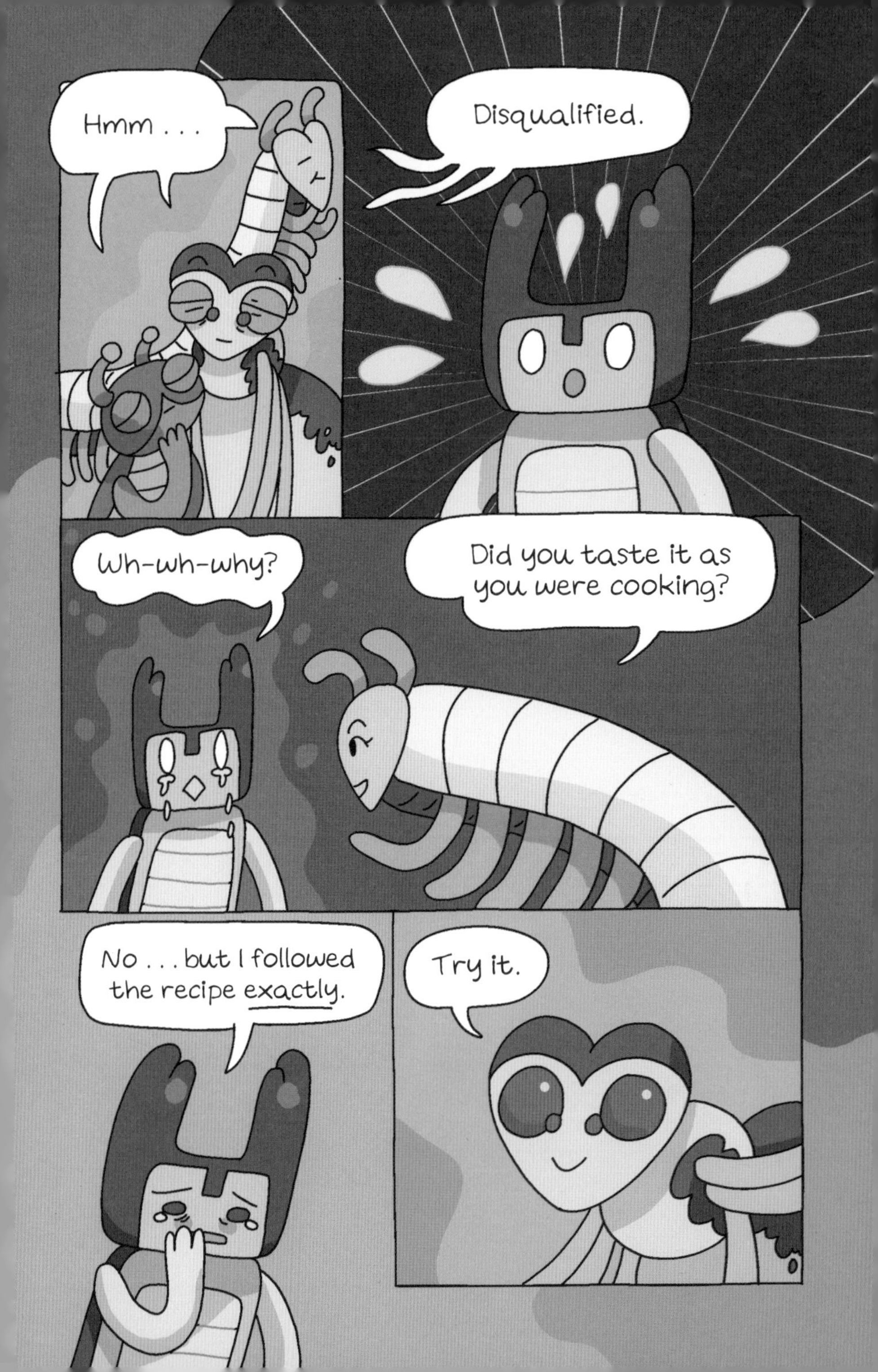
Hmm . . .
Disqualified.
Wh-wh-why?
Did you taste it as you were cooking?
No . . . but I followed the recipe exactly.
Try it.

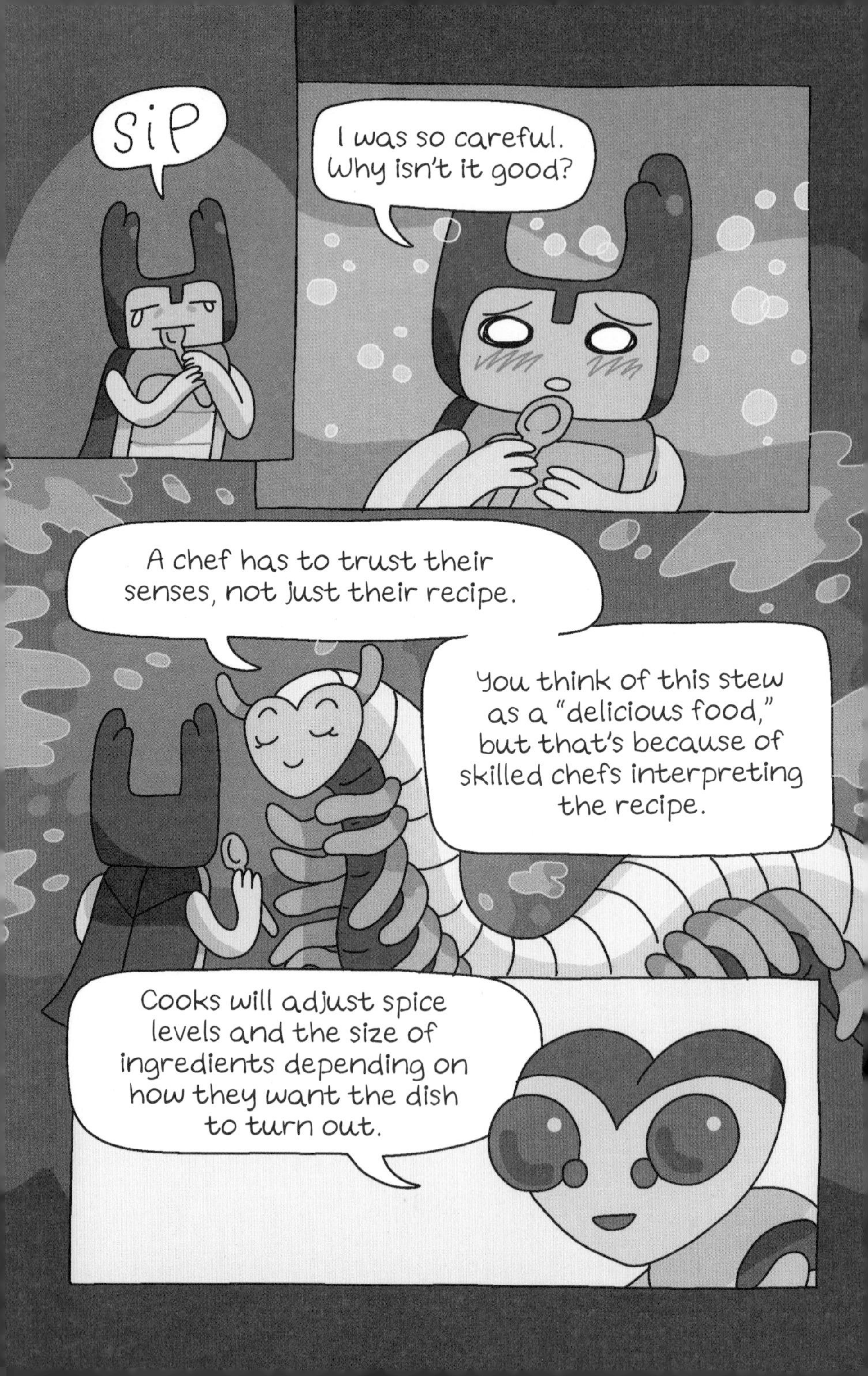
SIP
I was so careful. Why isn't it good?
A chef has to trust their senses, not just their recipe.
You think of this stew as a "delicious food," but that's because of skilled chefs interpreting the recipe.
Cooks will adjust spice levels and the size of ingredients depending on how they want the dish to turn out.

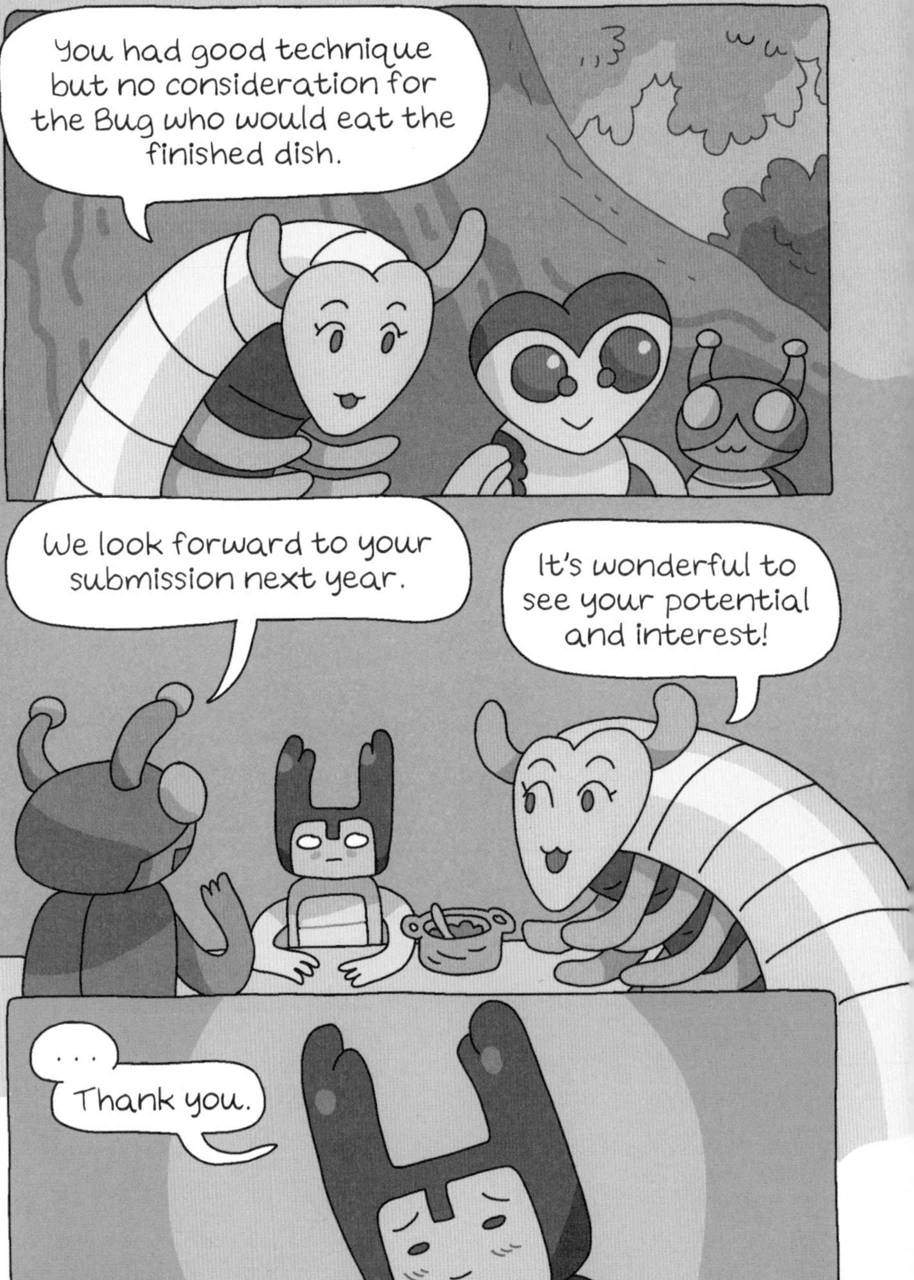
You had good technique but no consideration for the Bug who would eat the finished dish.
We look forward to your submission next year.
It's wonderful to see your potential and interest!
. . .
Thank you.

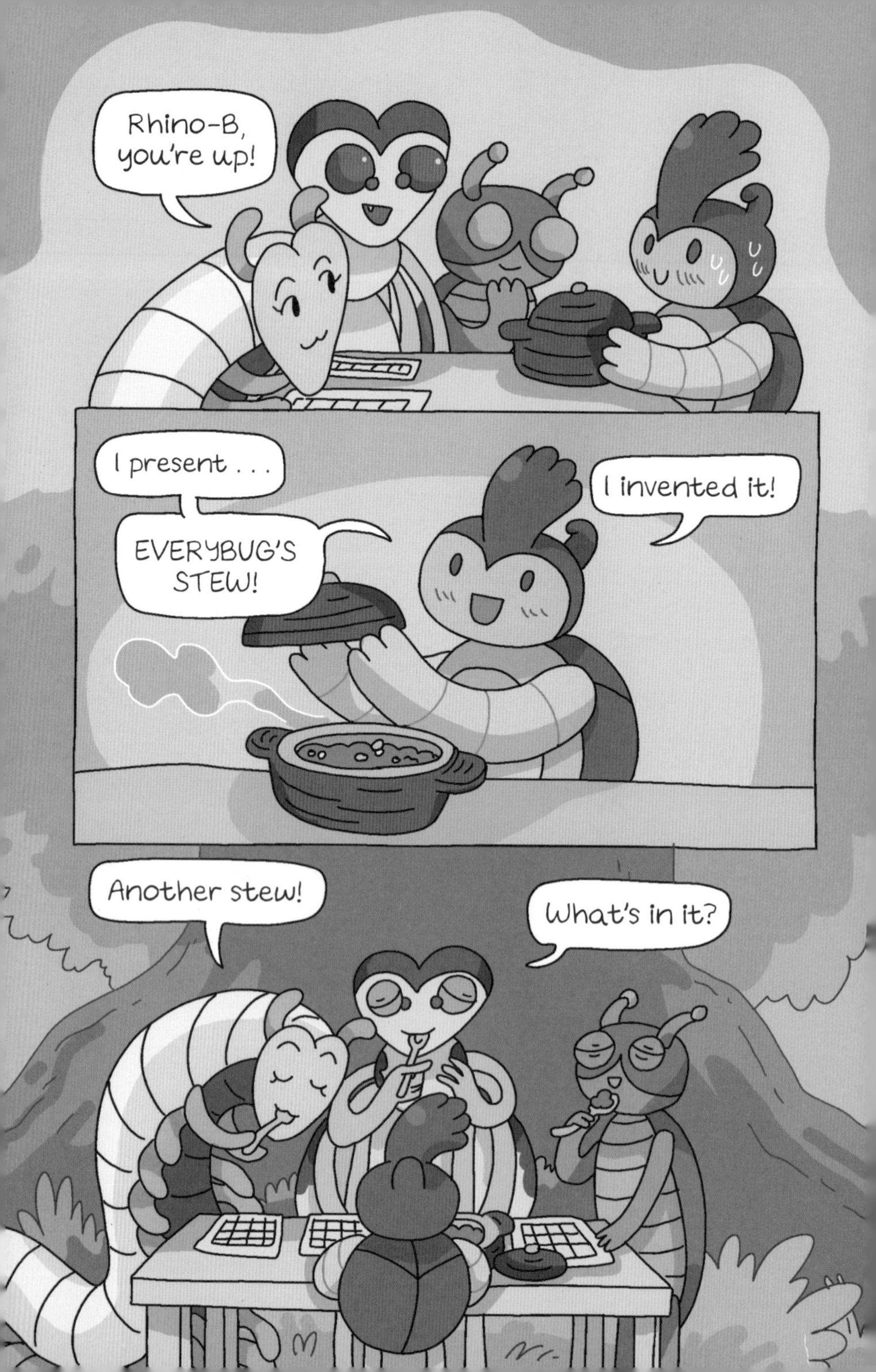
Rhino-B, you're up!
I present . . .
EVERYBUG'S STEW!
I invented it!
Another stew!
What's in it?

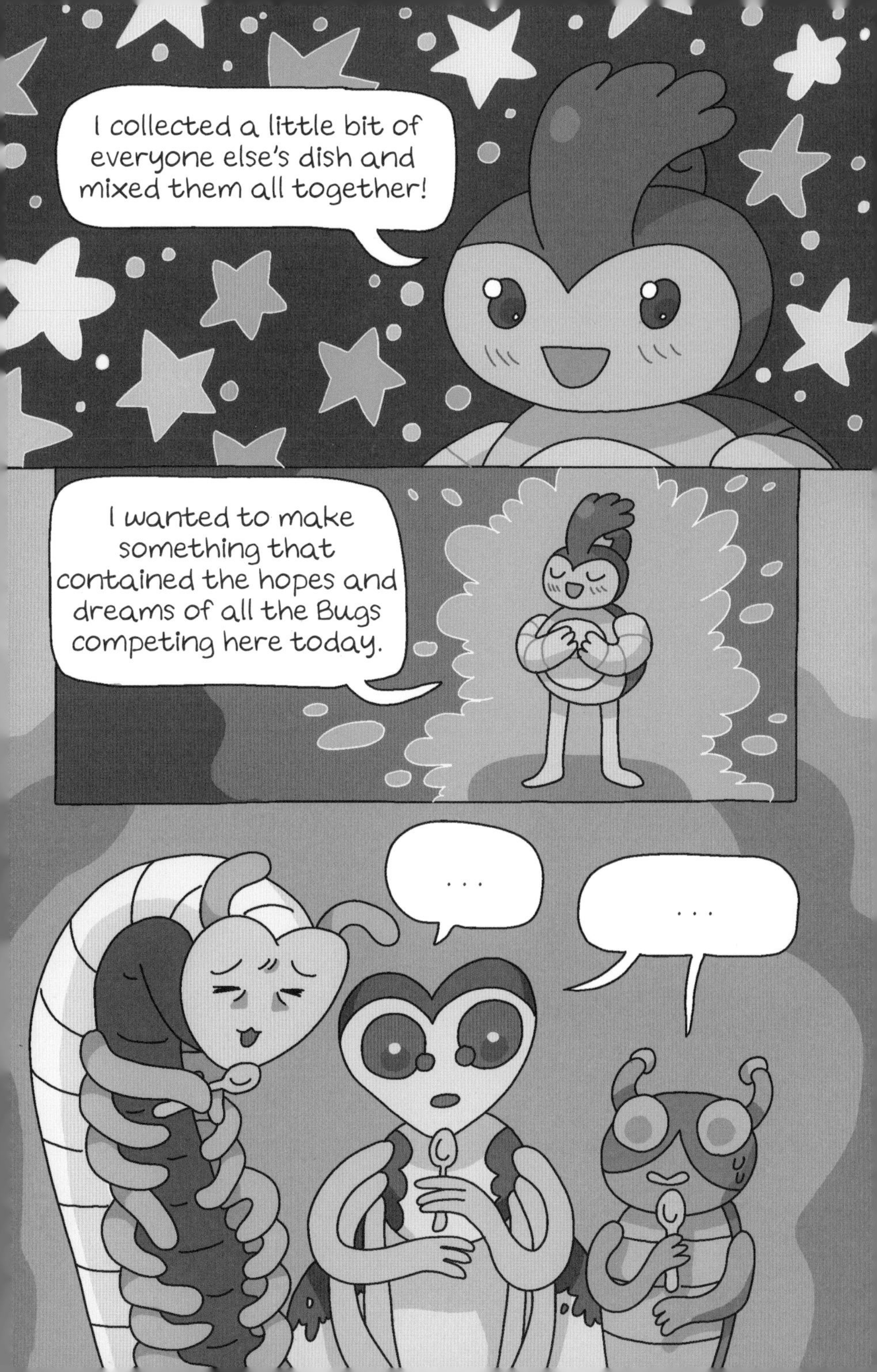
I collected a little bit of everyone else's dish and mixed them all together!
I wanted to make something that contained the hopes and dreams of all the Bugs competing here today.
. . .
. . .

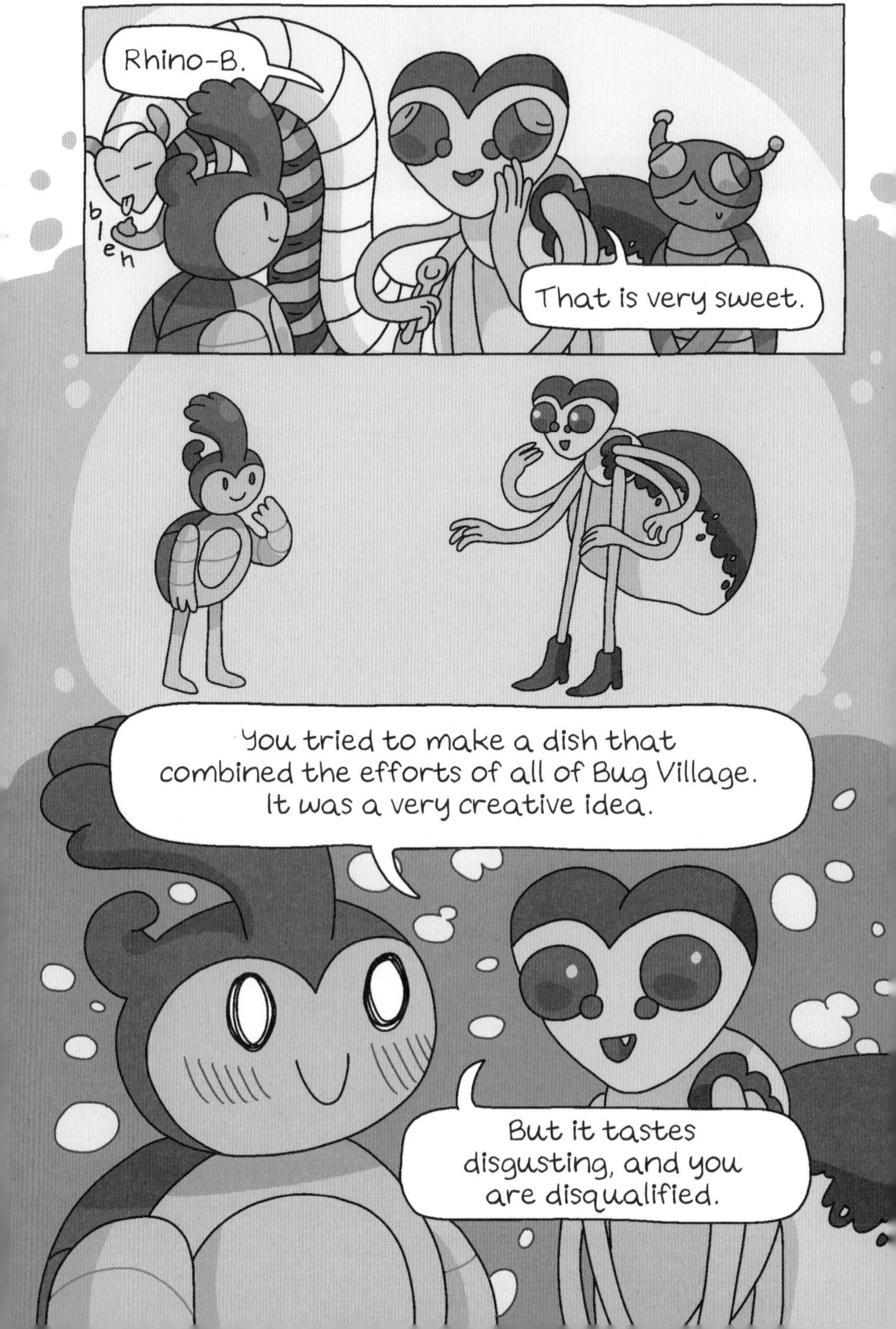
Rhino-B.
bleh
That is very sweet.
You tried to make a dish that combined the efforts of all of Bug Village. It was a very creative idea.
But it tastes disgusting, and you are disqualified.

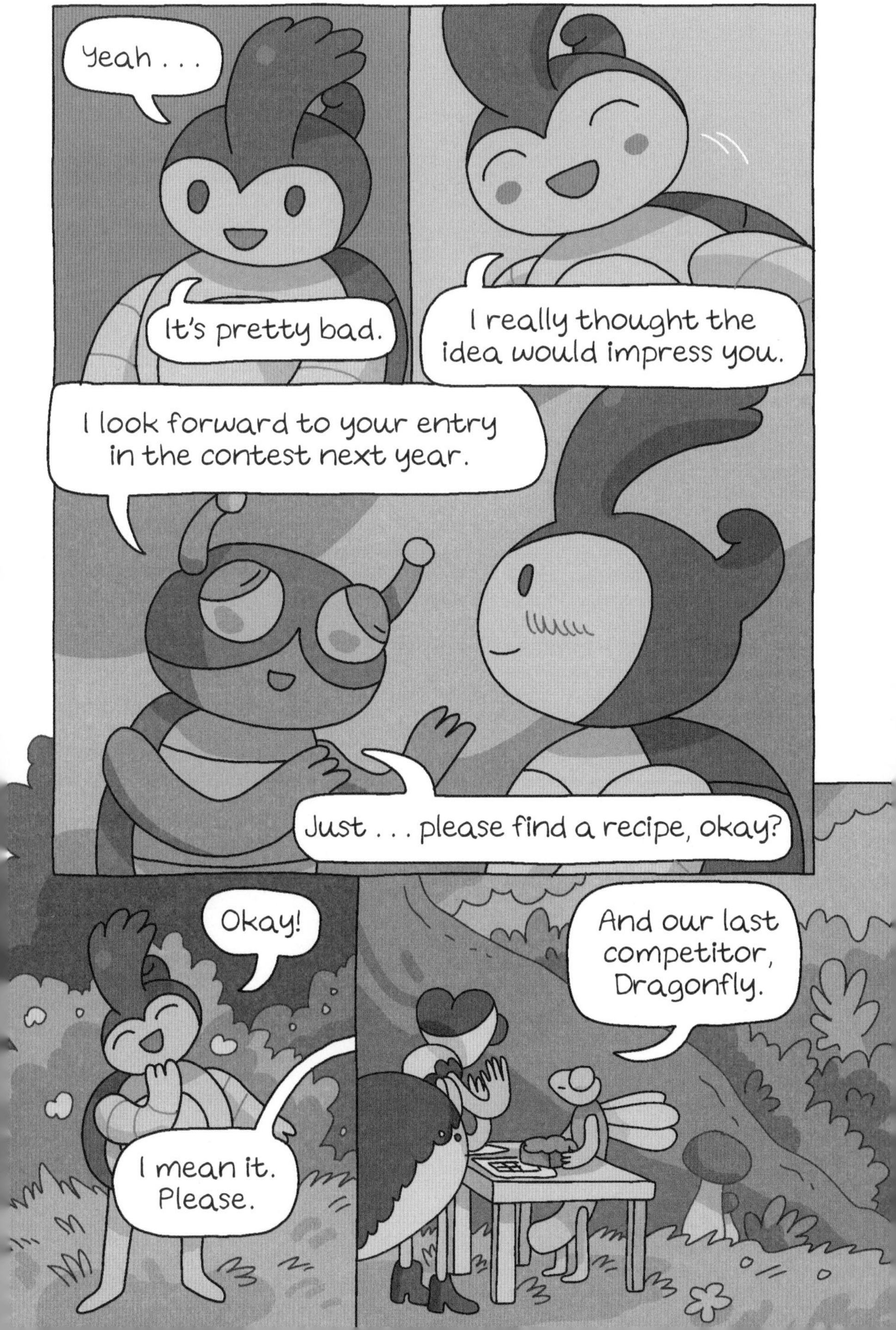
Yeah . . .
It's pretty bad.
I really thought the idea would impress you.
I look forward to your entry in the contest next year.
Just . . . please find a recipe, okay?
Okay!
I mean it. Please.
And our last competitor, Dragonfly.

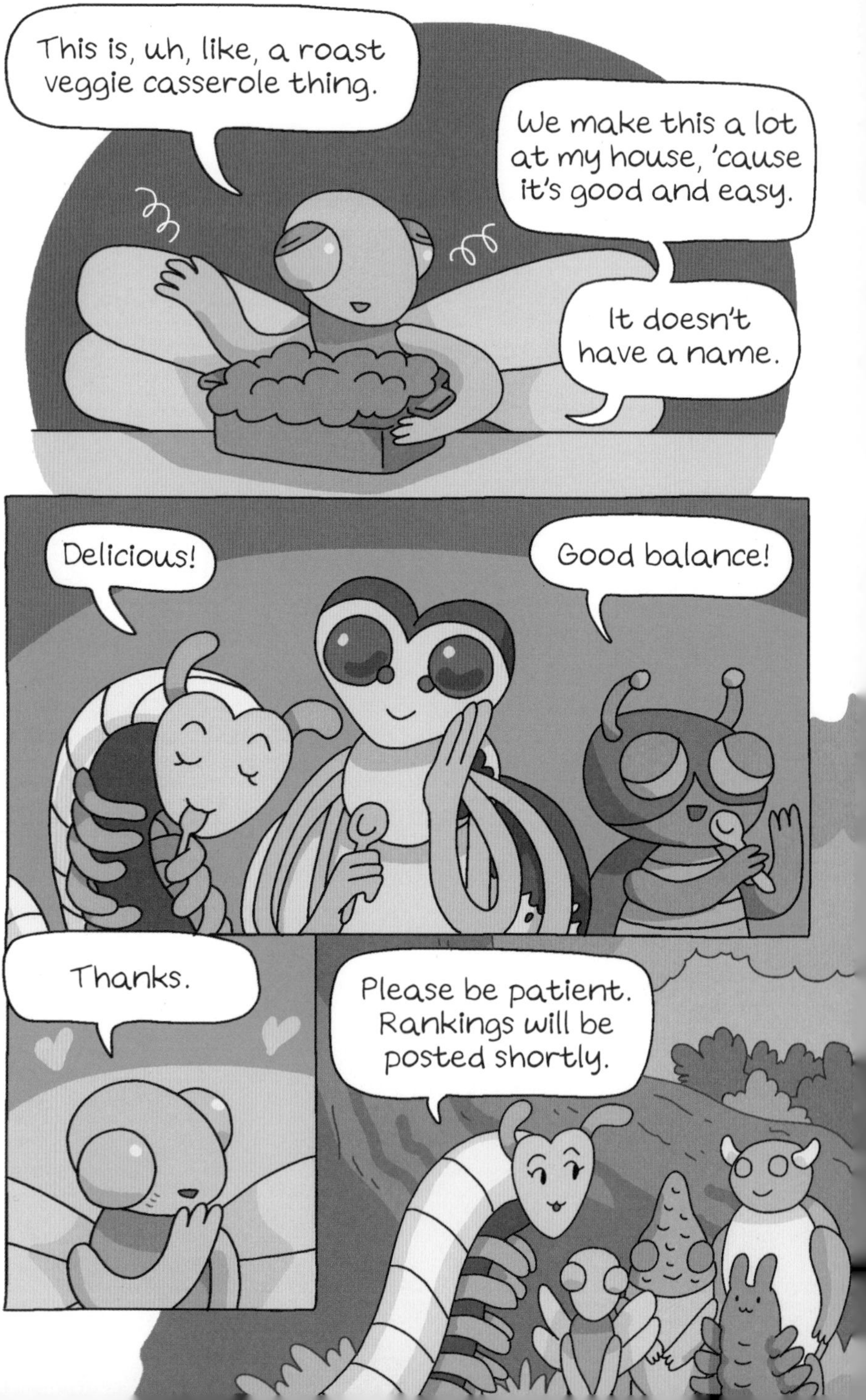
This is, uh, like, a roast veggie casserole thing.
We make this a lot at my house, 'cause it's good and easy.
It doesn't have a name.
Delicious!
Good balance!
Thanks.
Please be patient. Rankings will be posted shortly.

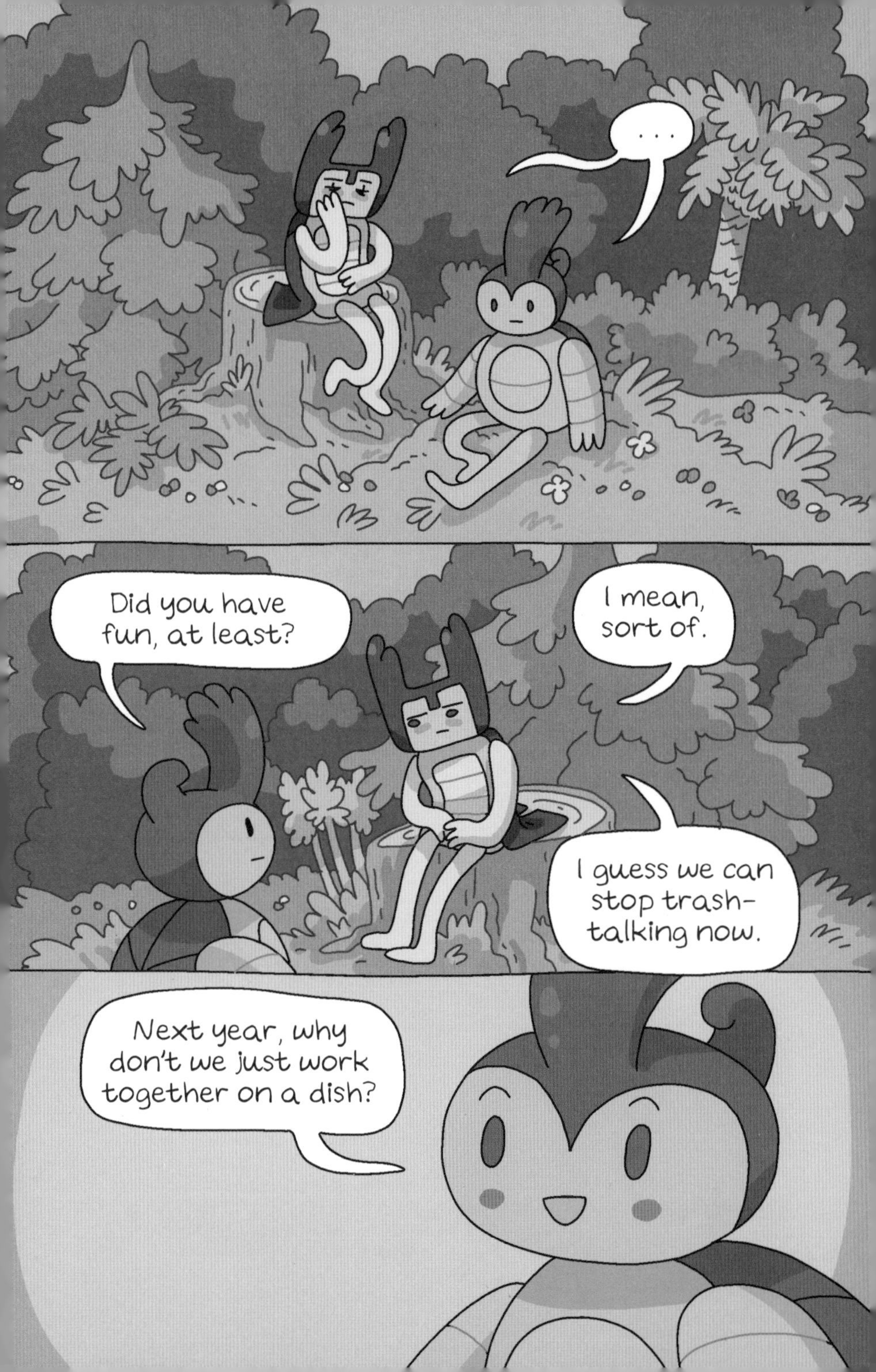
. . .
Did you have fun, at least?
I mean, sort of.
I guess we can stop trash-talking now.
Next year, why don't we just work together on a dish?

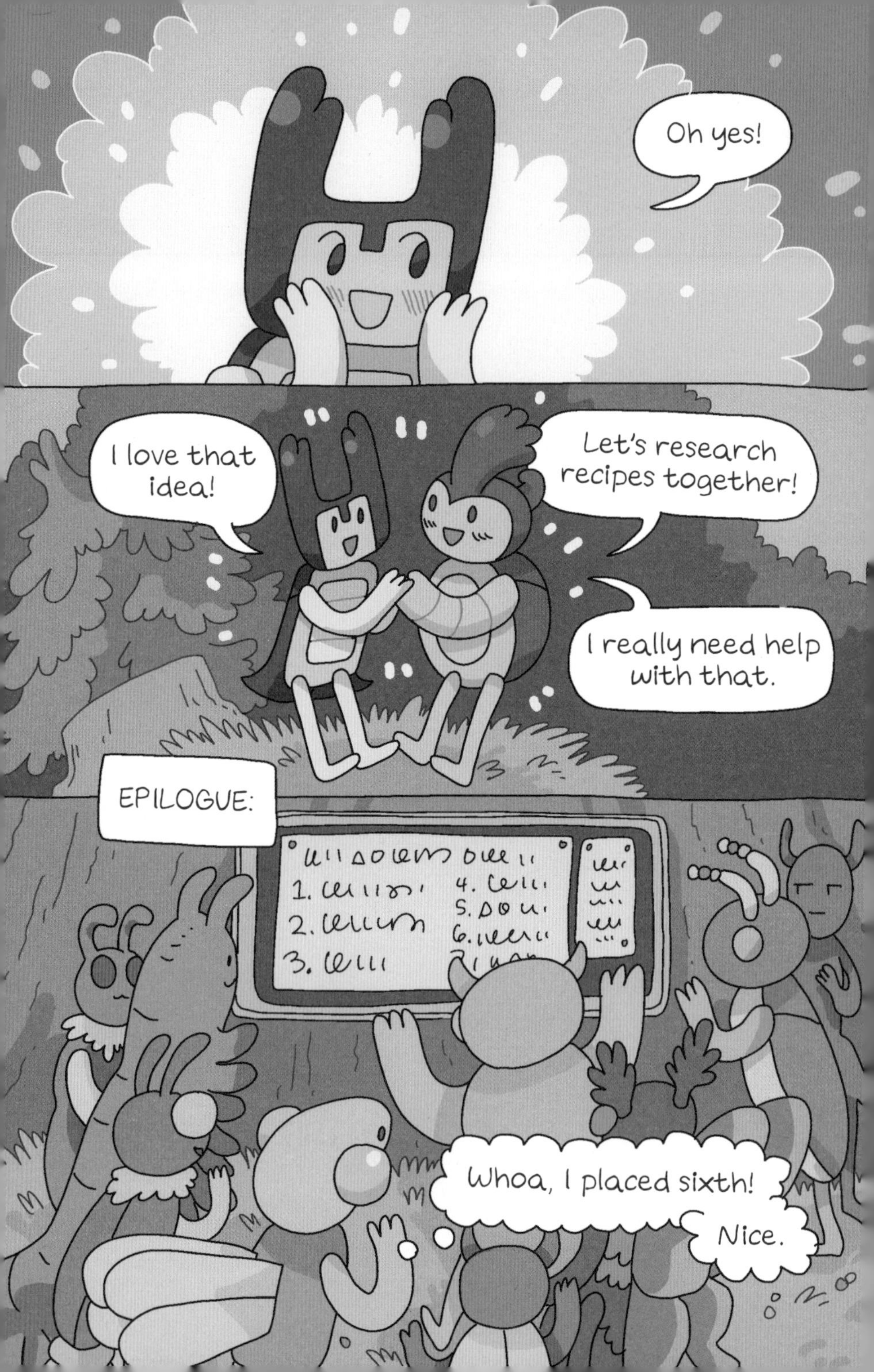
Oh yes!
I love that idea!
Let's research recipes together!
I really need help with that.
EPILOGUE:
Whoa, I placed sixth!
Nice.

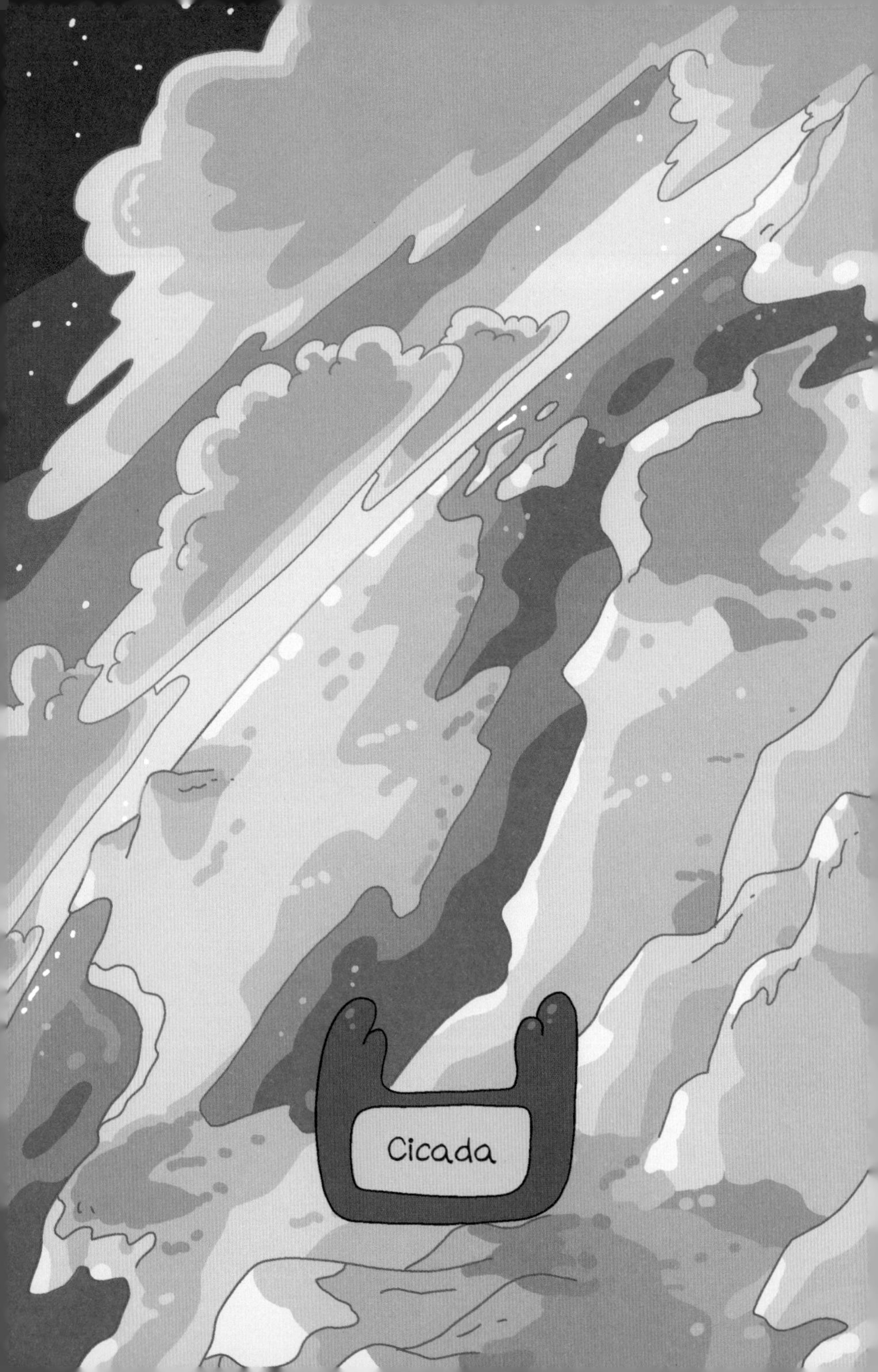
Cicada

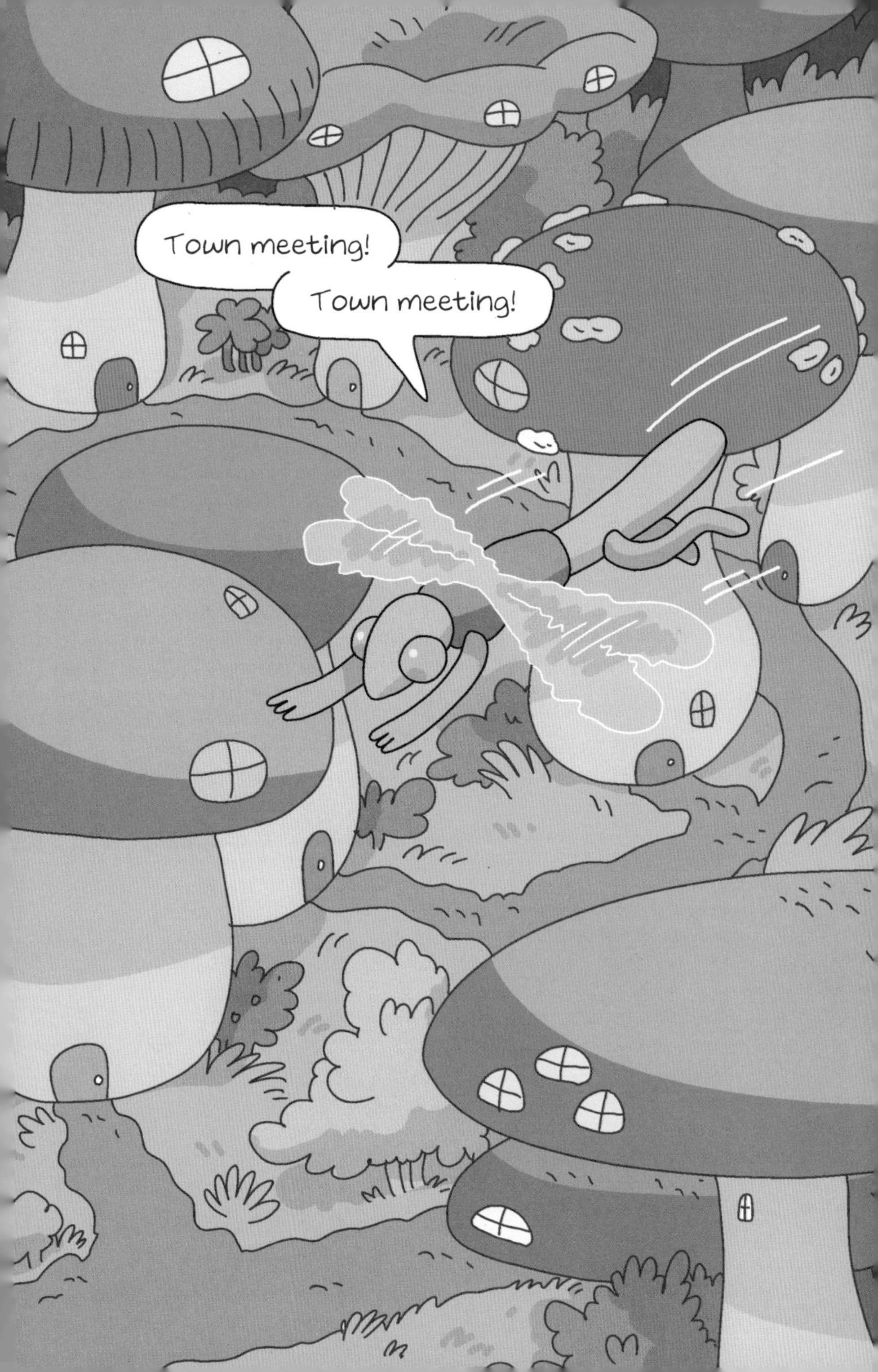
Town meeting!
Town meeting!

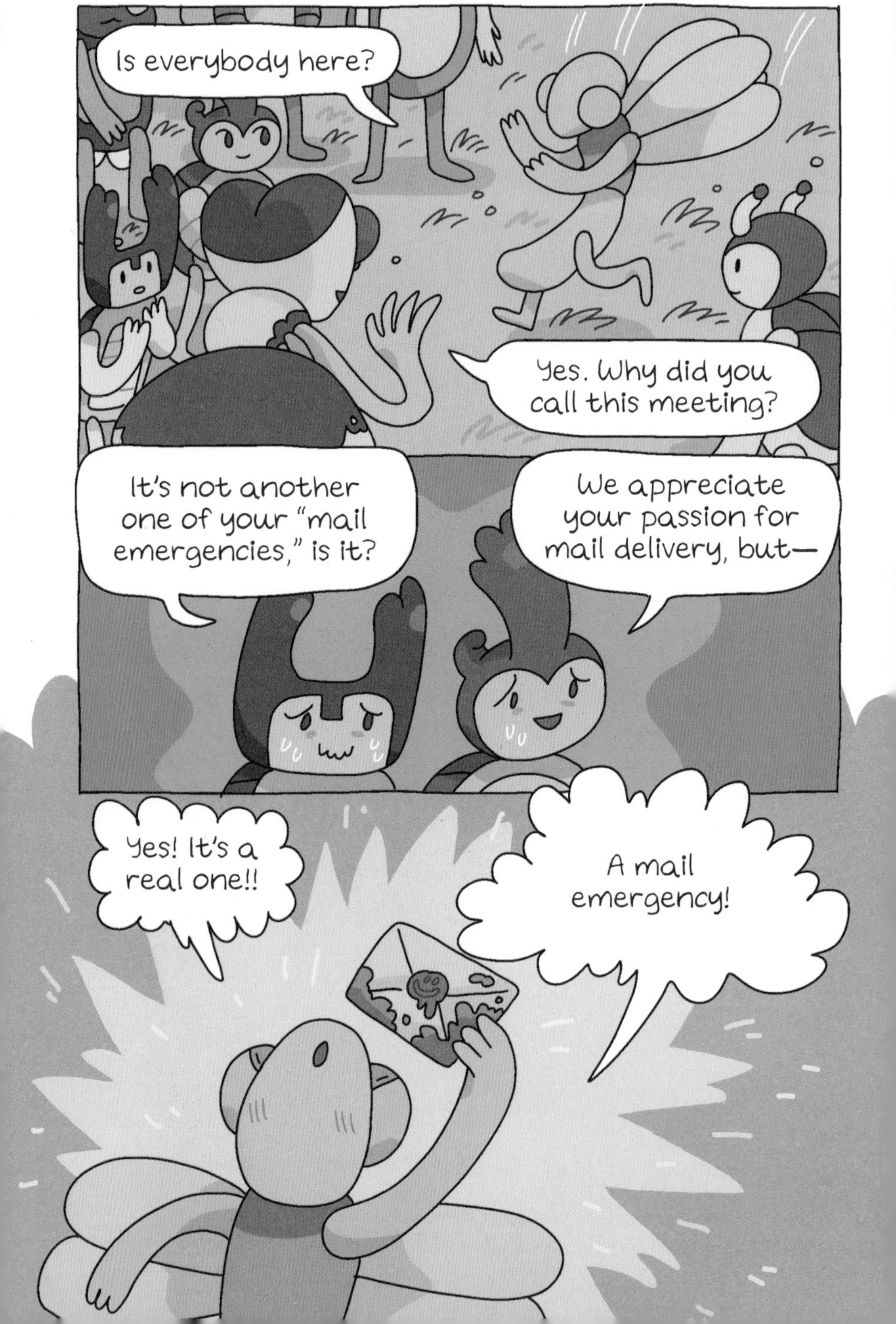
Is everybody here?
Yes. Why did you call this meeting?
It's not another one of your "mail emergencies," is it?
We appreciate your passion for mail delivery, but—
Yes! It's a real one!!
A mail emergency!

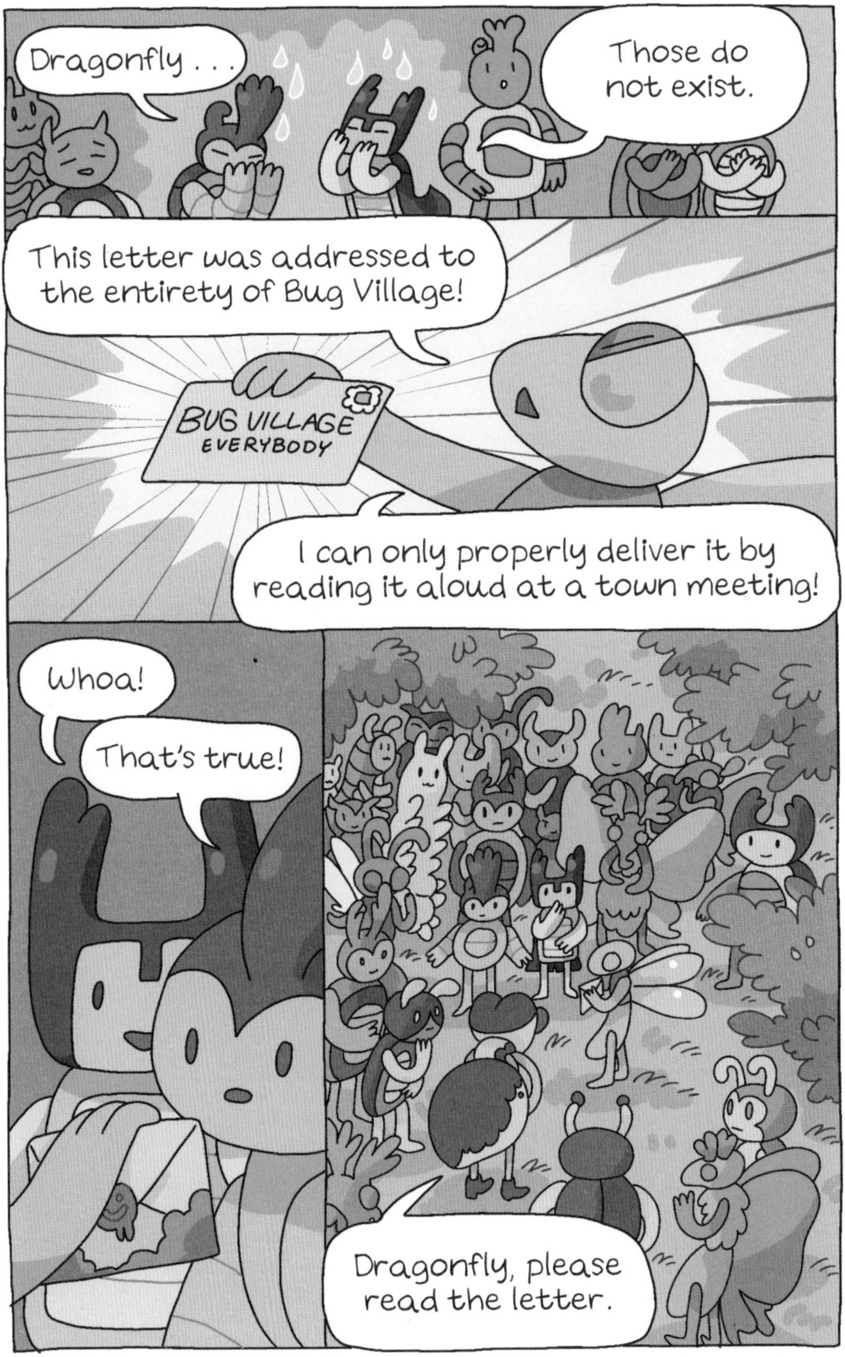
Dragonfly . . .
Those do not exist.
This letter was addressed to the entirety of Bug Village!
BUG VILLAGE
EVERYBODY
I can only properly deliver it by reading it aloud at a town meeting!
Whoa!
That's true!
Dragonfly, please read the letter.

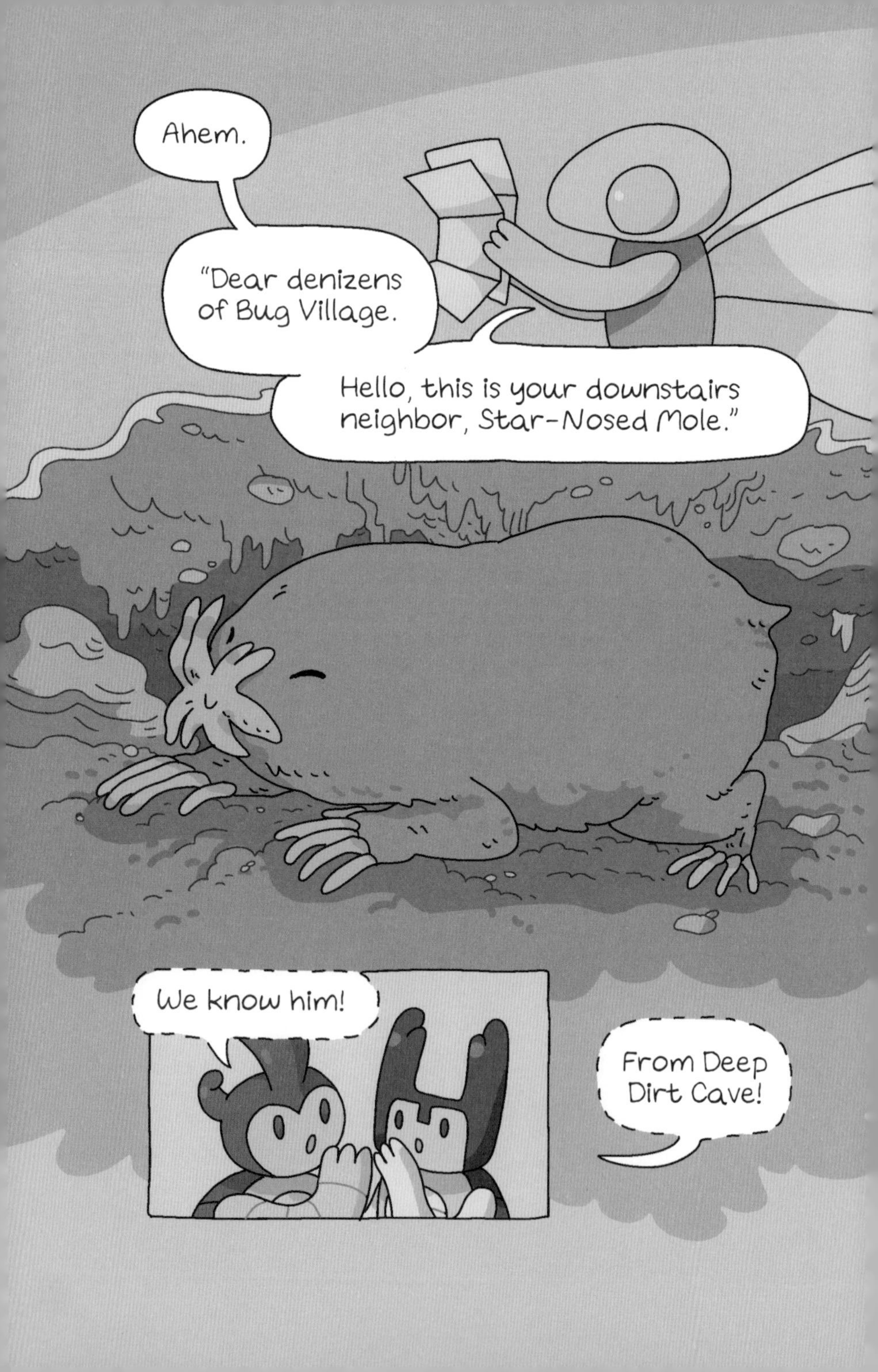
Ahem.
"Dear denizens of Bug Village.
Hello, this is your downstairs neighbor, Star-Nosed Mole."
We know him!
From Deep Dirt Cave!

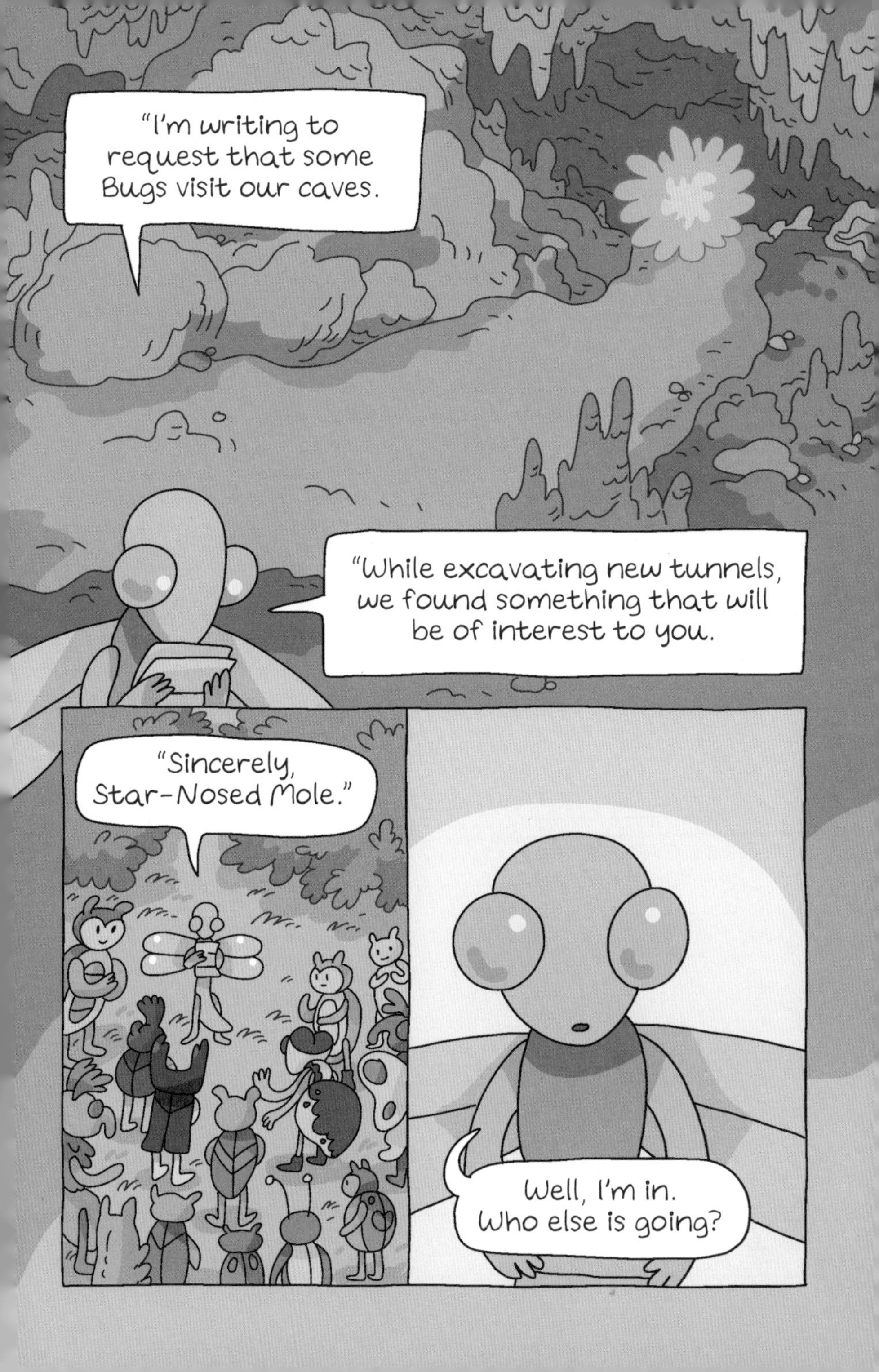
"I'm writing to request that some Bugs visit our caves.
"While excavating new tunnels, we found something that will be of interest to you.
"Sincerely, Star-Nosed Mole."
Well, I'm in. Who else is going?

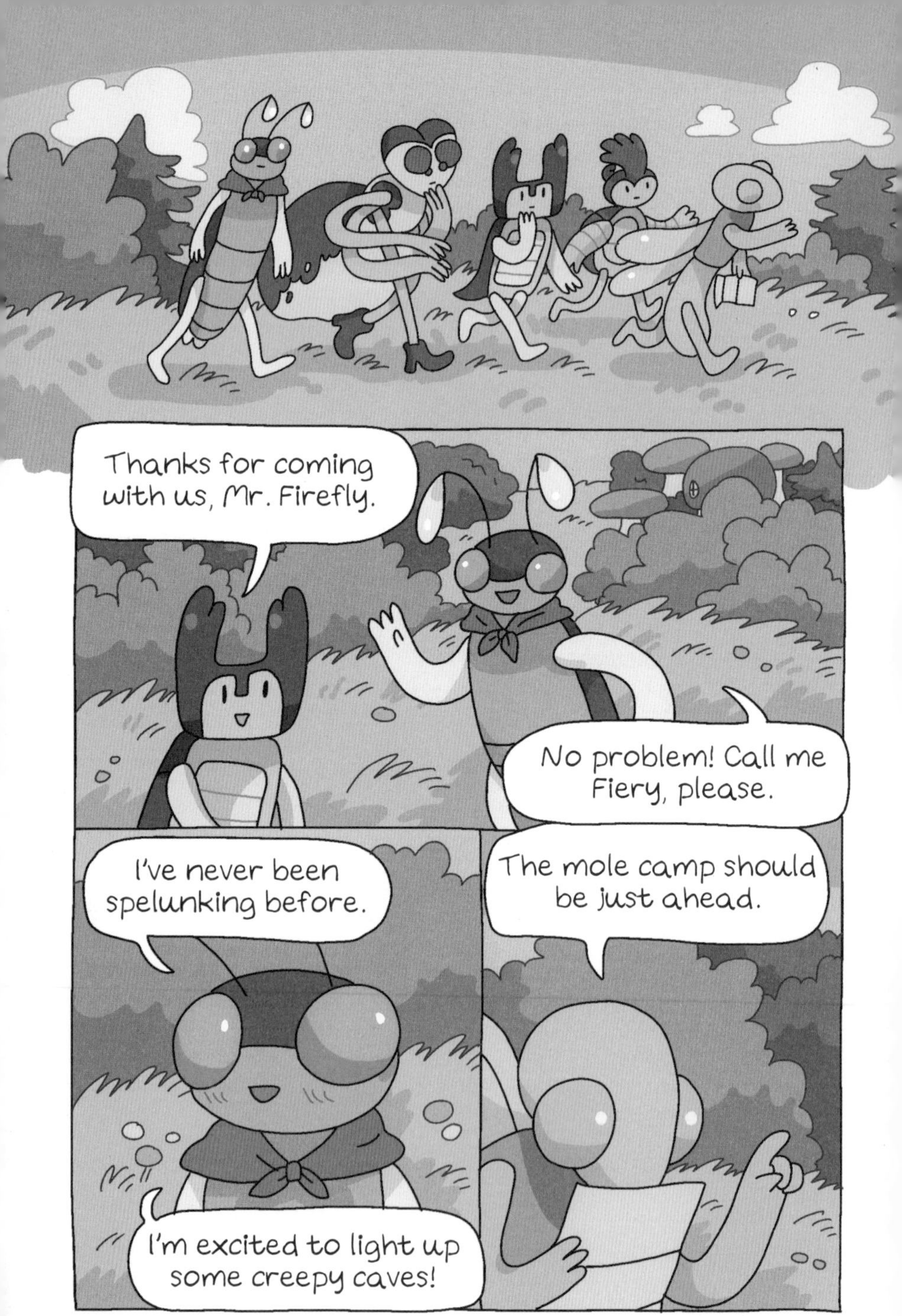
Thanks for coming with us, Mr. Firefly.
No problem! Call me Fiery, please.
I've never been spelunking before.
I'm excited to light up some creepy caves!
The mole camp should be just ahead.

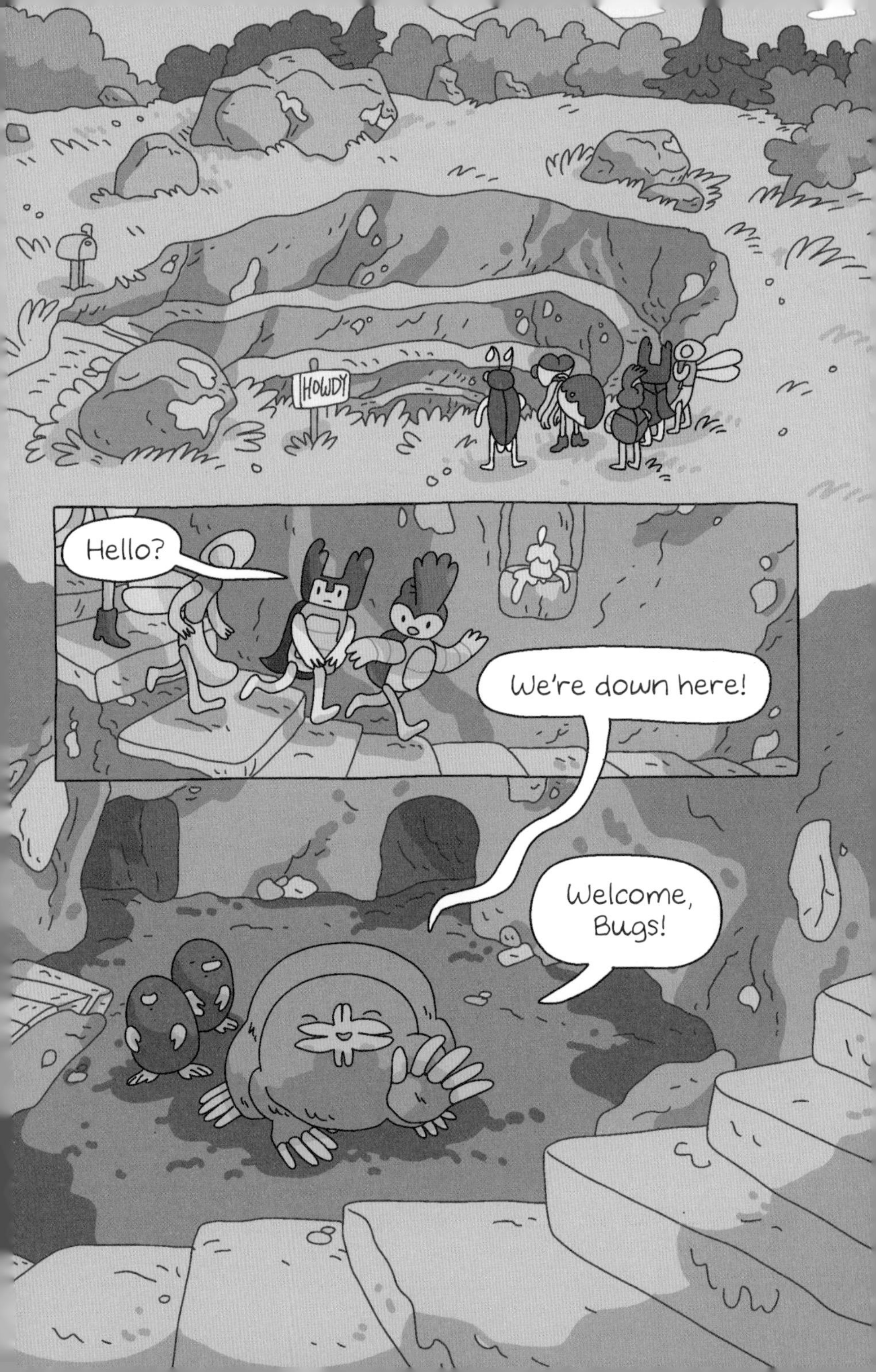
HOWDY
Hello?
We're down here!
Welcome, Bugs!

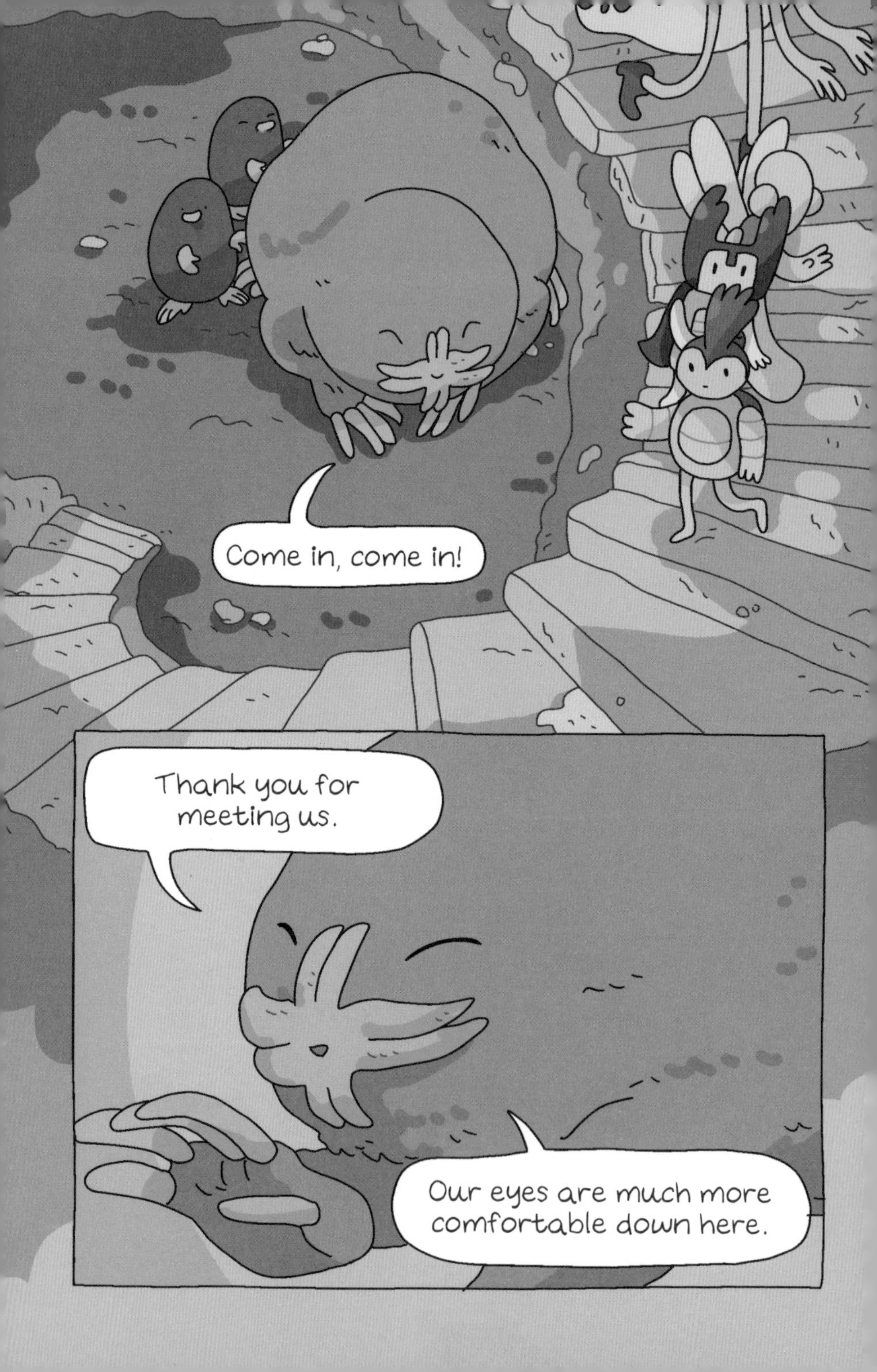
Come in, come in!
Thank you for meeting us.
Our eyes are much more comfortable down here.

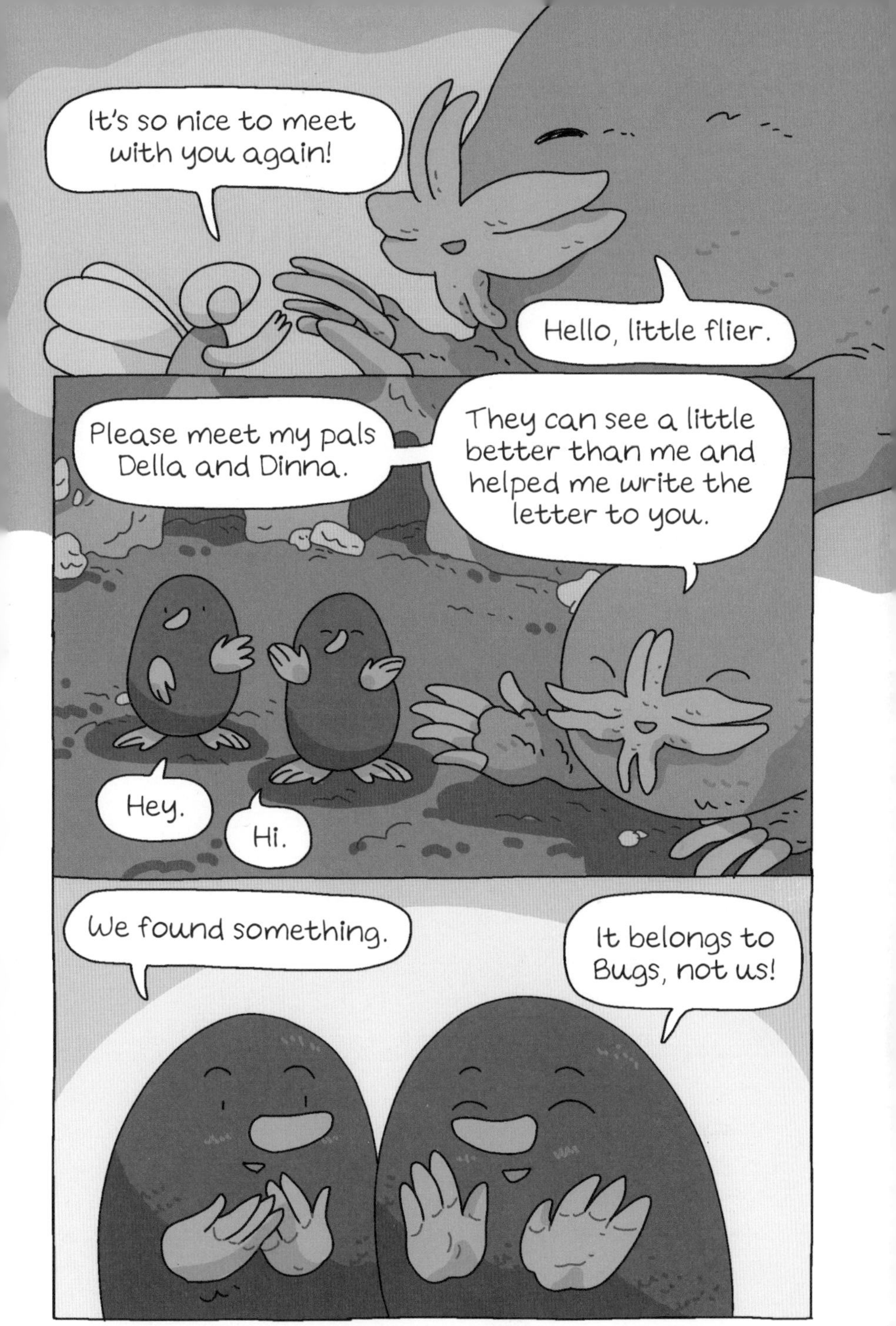
It's so nice to meet with you again!
Hello, little flier.
Please meet my pals Della and Dinna.
They can see a little better than me and helped me write the letter to you.
Hey.
Hi.
We found something.
It belongs to Bugs, not us!

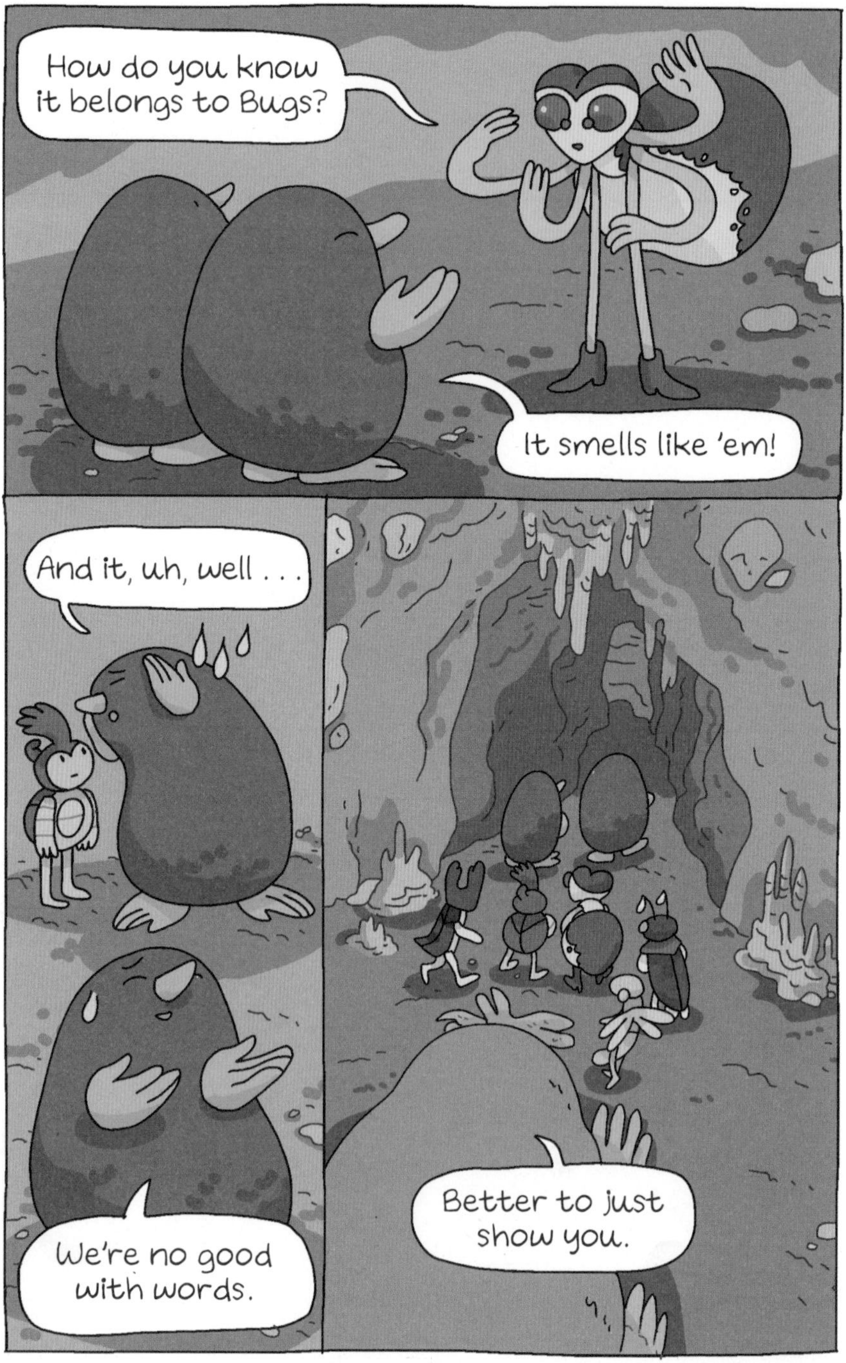
How do you know it belongs to Bugs?
It smells like 'em!
And it, uh, well . . .
We're no good with words.
Better to just show you.

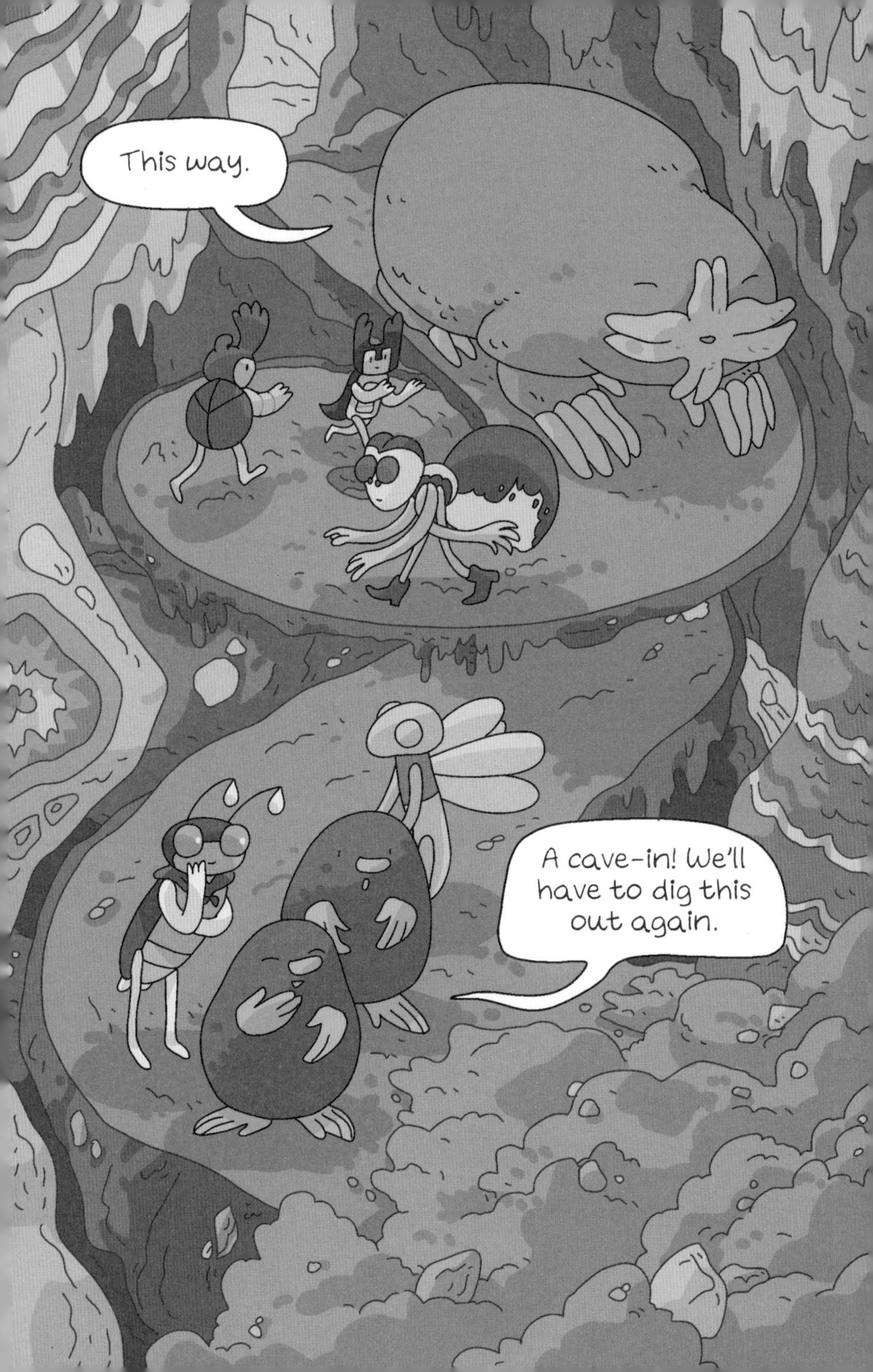
This way.
A cave-in! We'll have to dig this out again.

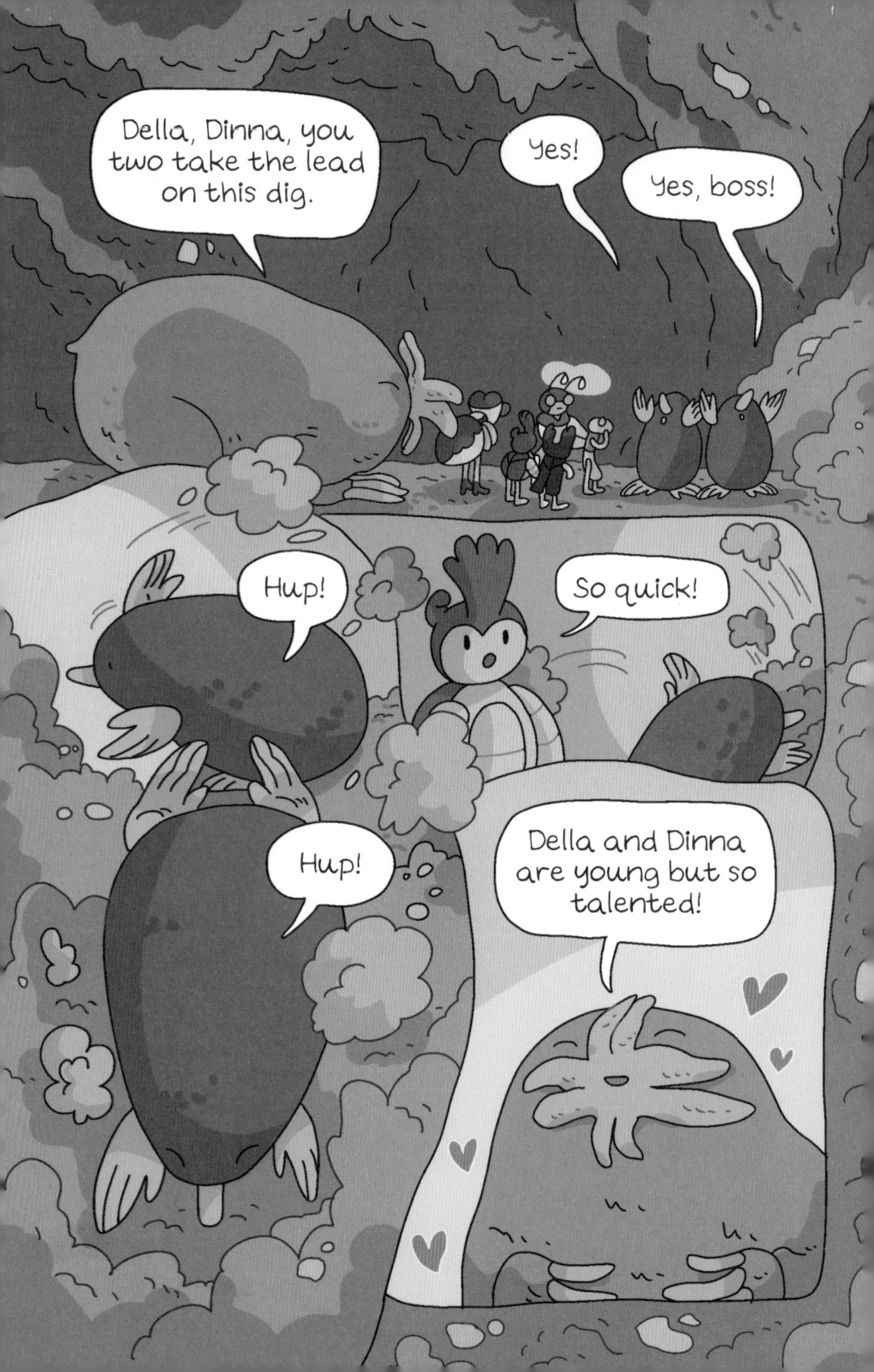
Della, Dinna, you two take the lead on this dig.
Yes!
Yes, boss!
Hup!
So quick!
Hup!
Della and Dinna are young but so talented!

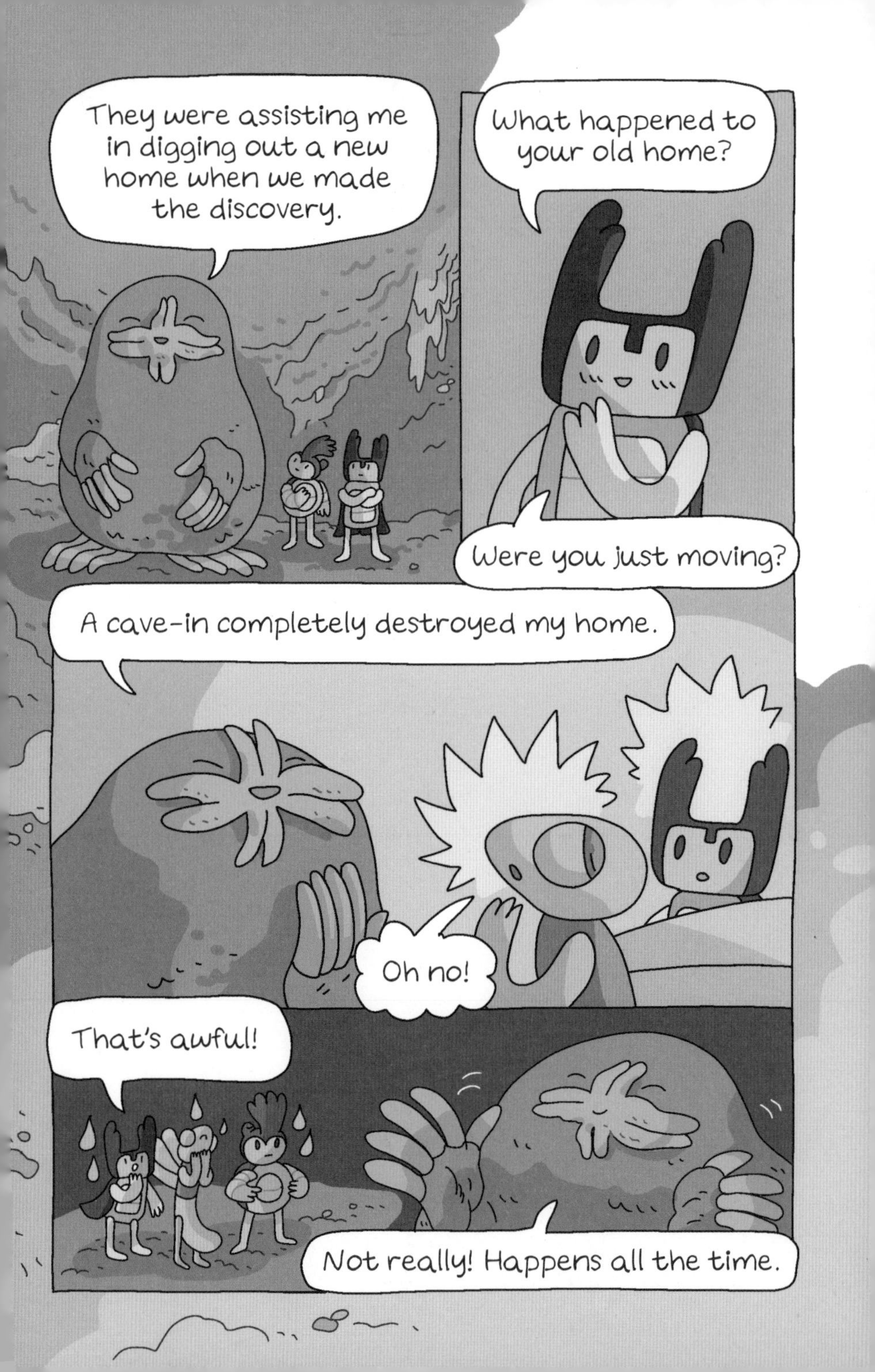
They were assisting me in digging out a new home when we made the discovery.
What happened to your old home?
Were you just moving?
A cave-in completely destroyed my home.
Oh no!
That's awful!
Not really! Happens all the time.

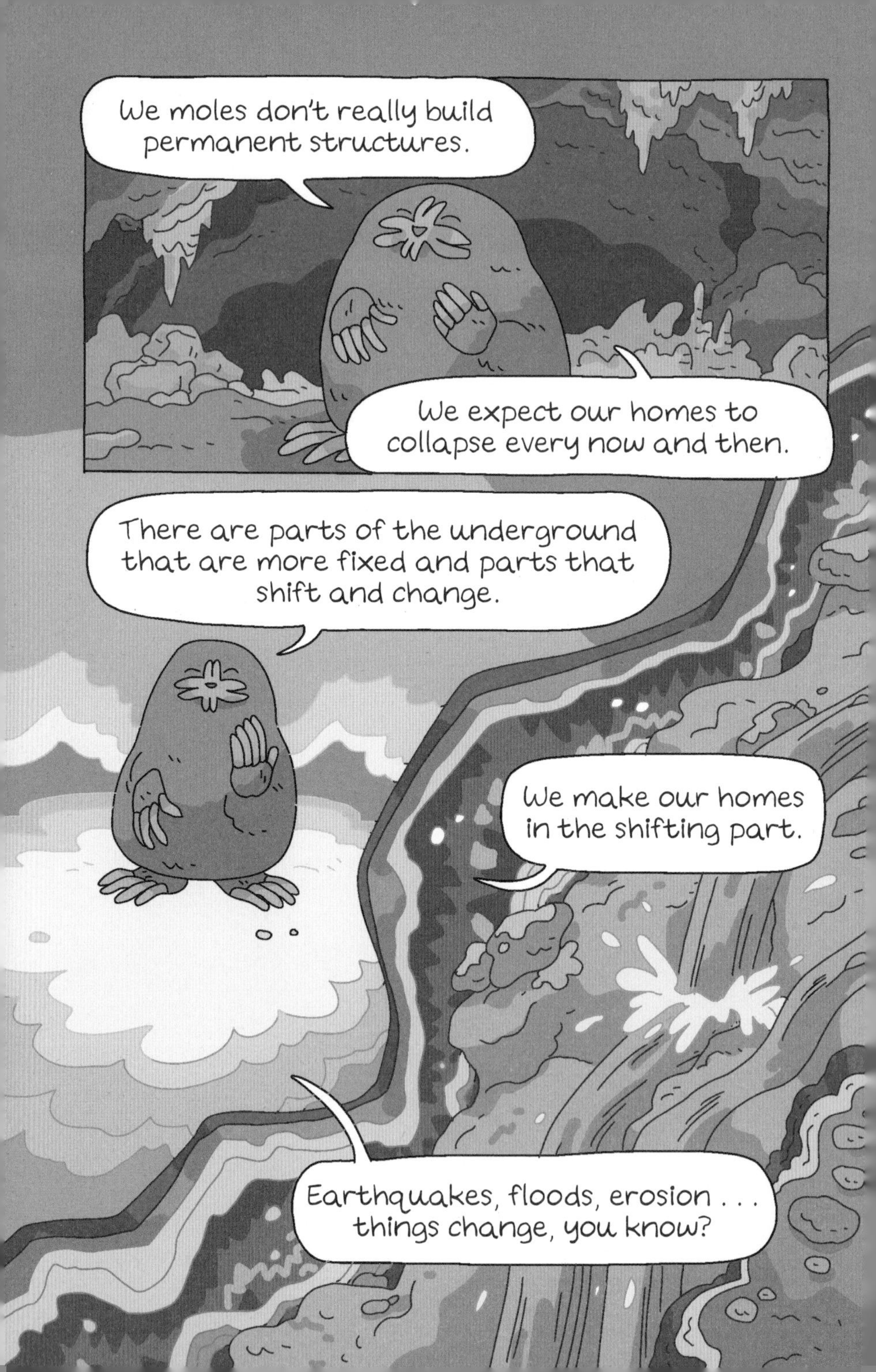
We moles don't really build permanent structures.
We expect our homes to collapse every now and then.
There are parts of the underground that are more fixed and parts that shift and change.
We make our homes in the shifting part.
Earthquakes, floods, erosion . . . things change, you know?

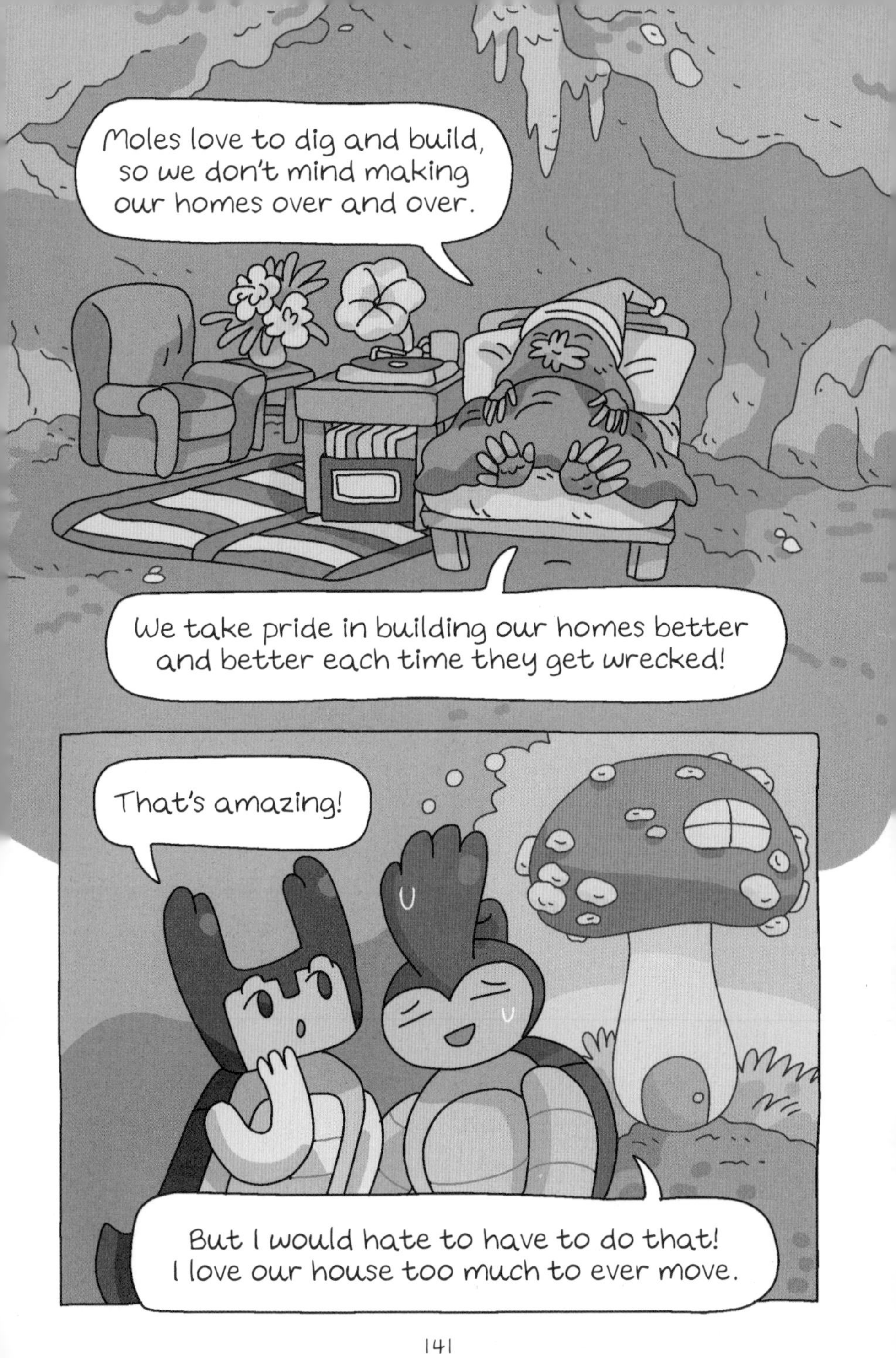
Moles love to dig and build, so we don't mind making our homes over and over.
We take pride in building our homes better and better each time they get wrecked!
That's amazing!
But I would hate to have to do that! I love our house too much to ever move.

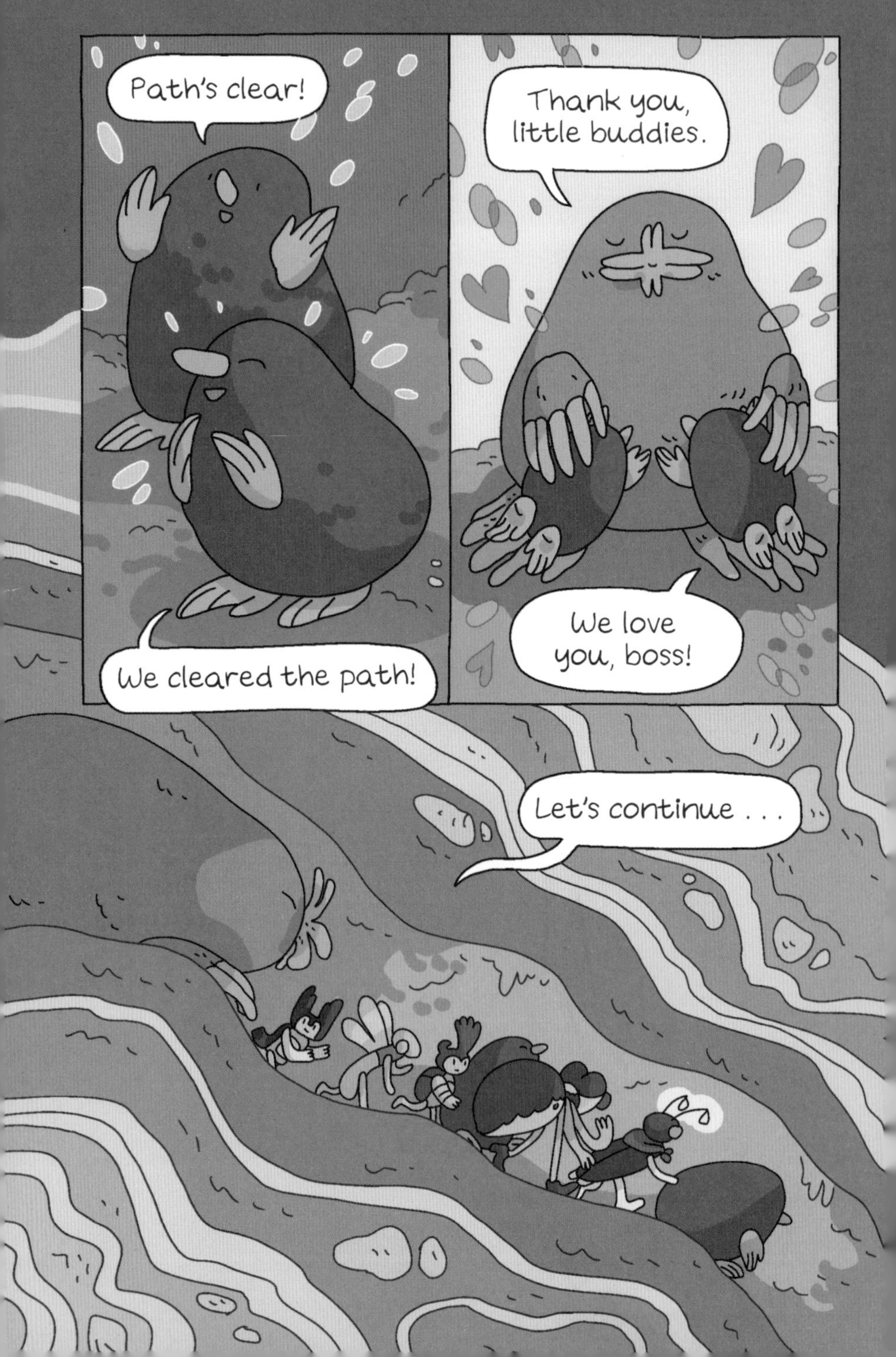
Path's clear!
We cleared the path!
Thank you, little buddies.
We love you, boss!
Let's continue . . .

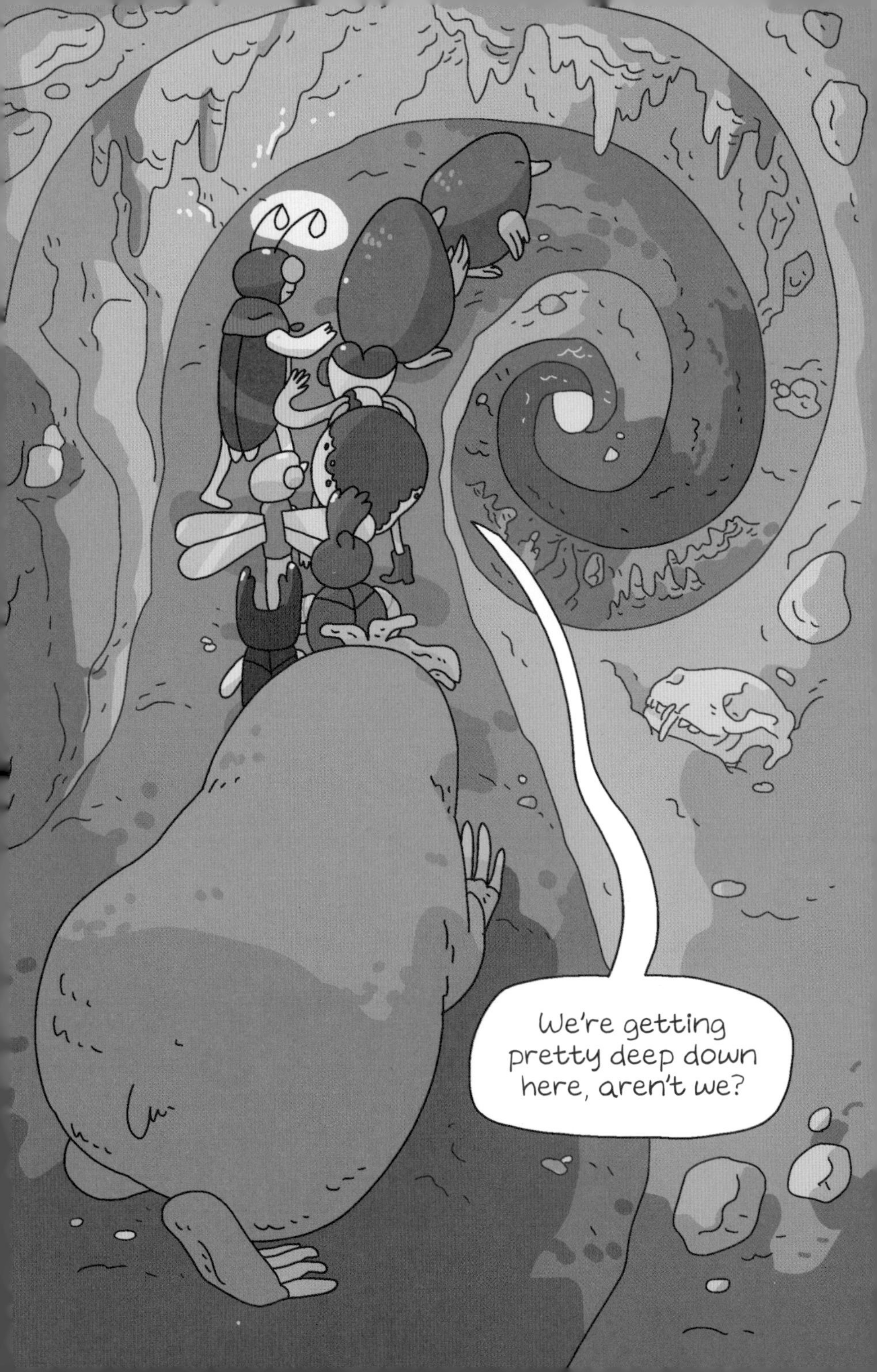
We're getting pretty deep down here, aren't we?

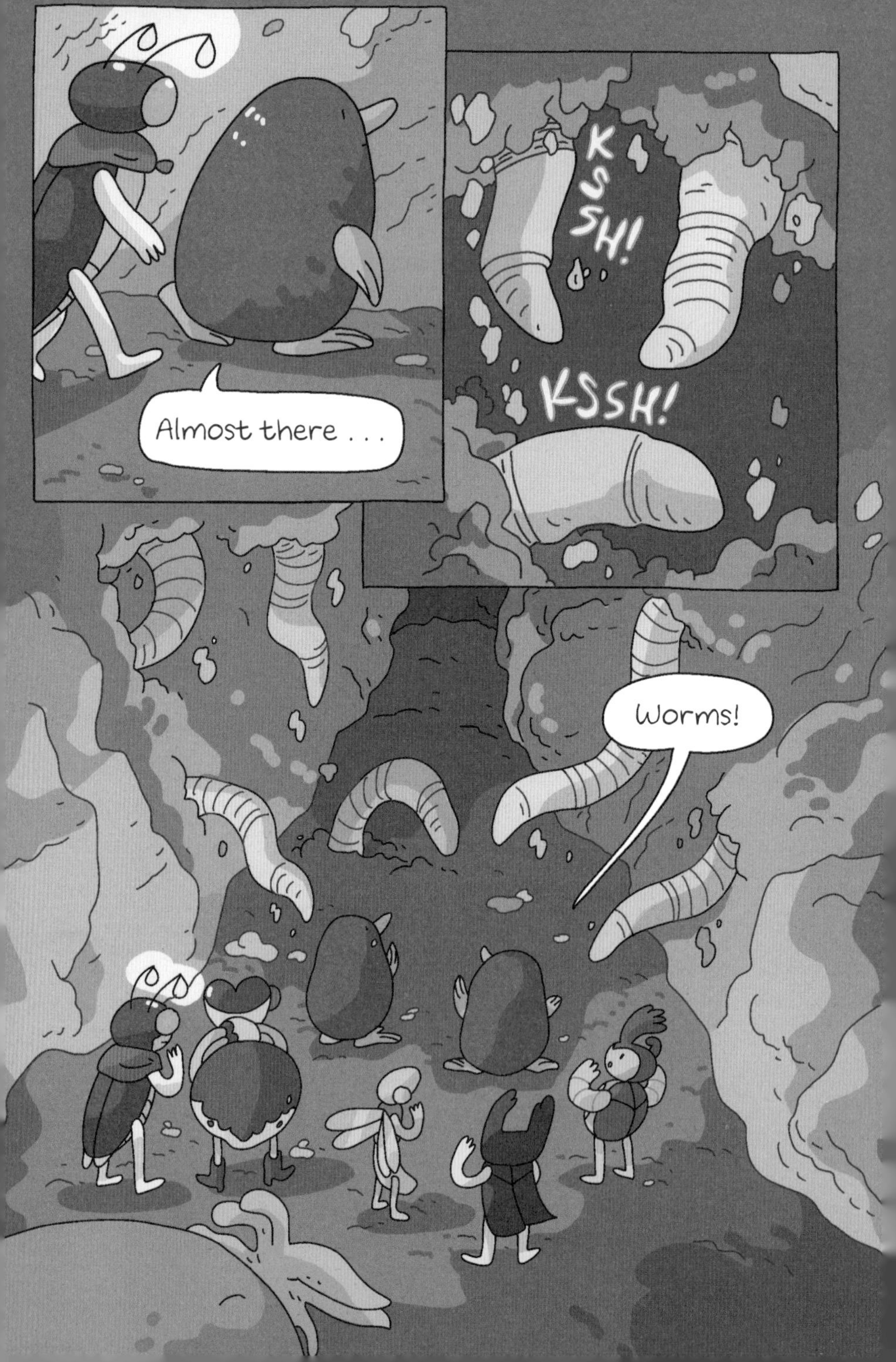
Almost there . . .
KSSH!
KSSH!
Worms!

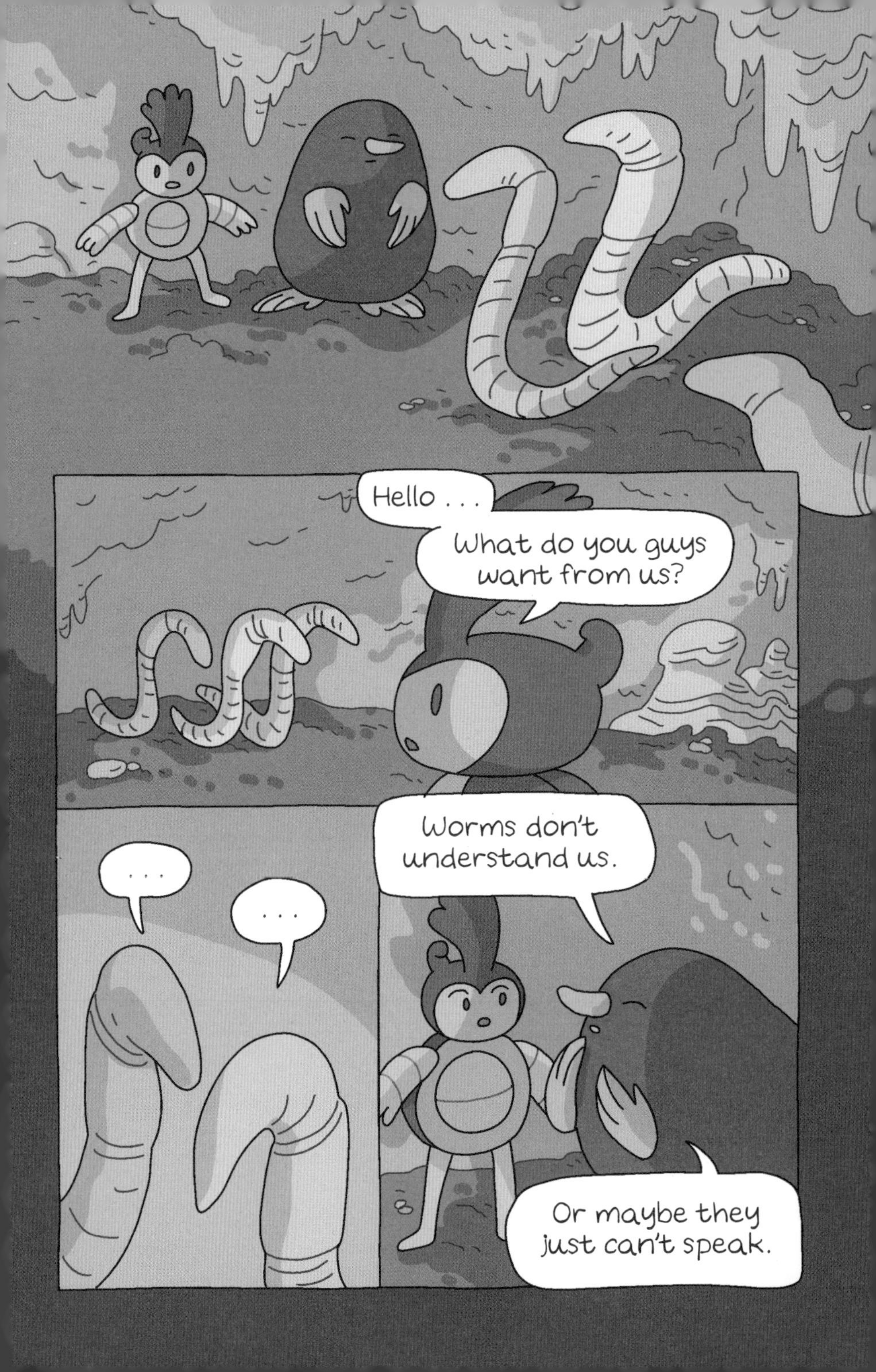
Hello . . .
What do you guys want from us?
. . .
. . .
Worms don't understand us.
Or maybe they just can't speak.

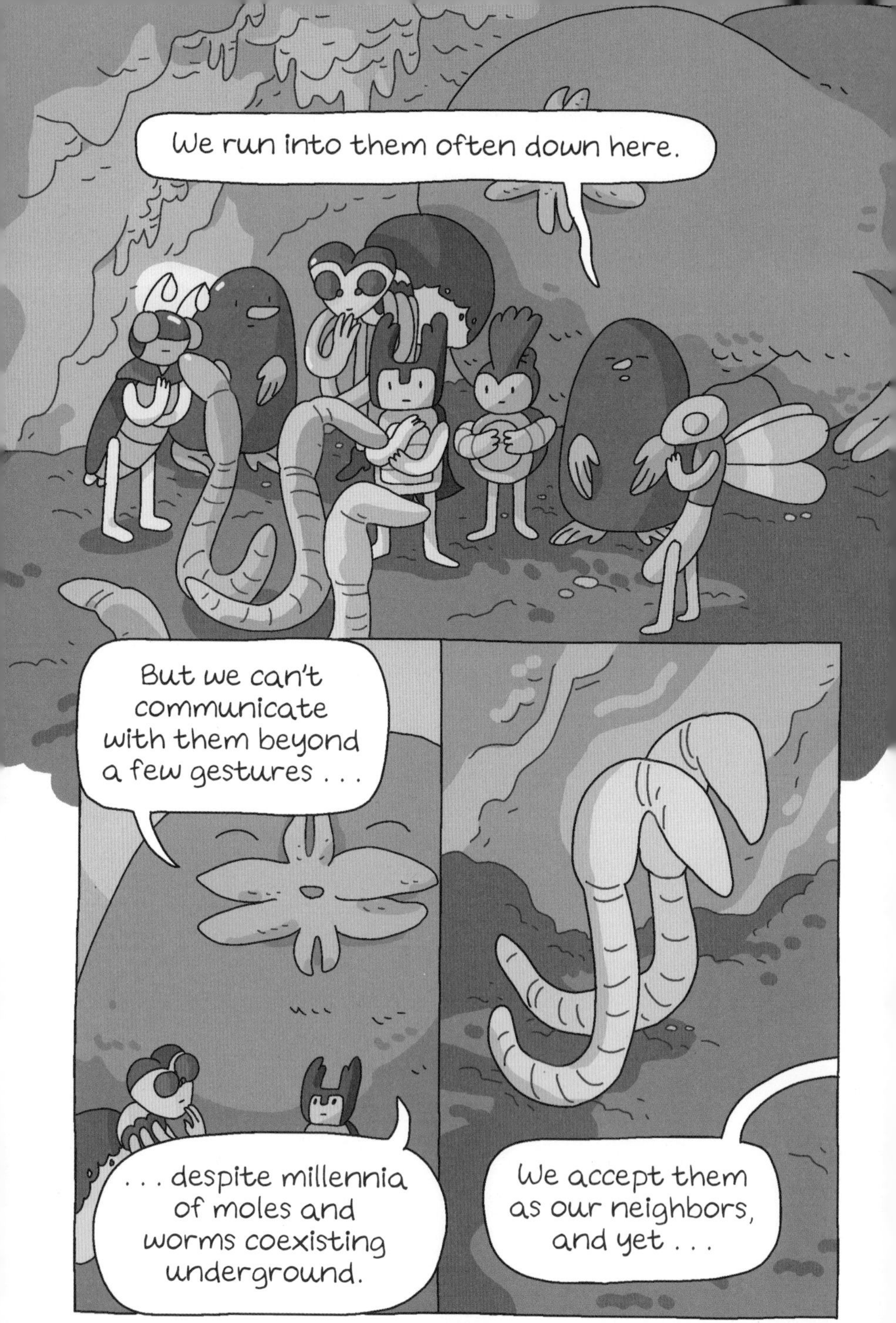
We run into them often down here.
But we can't communicate with them beyond a few gestures . . .
. . . despite millennia of moles and worms coexisting underground.
We accept them as our neighbors, and yet . . .

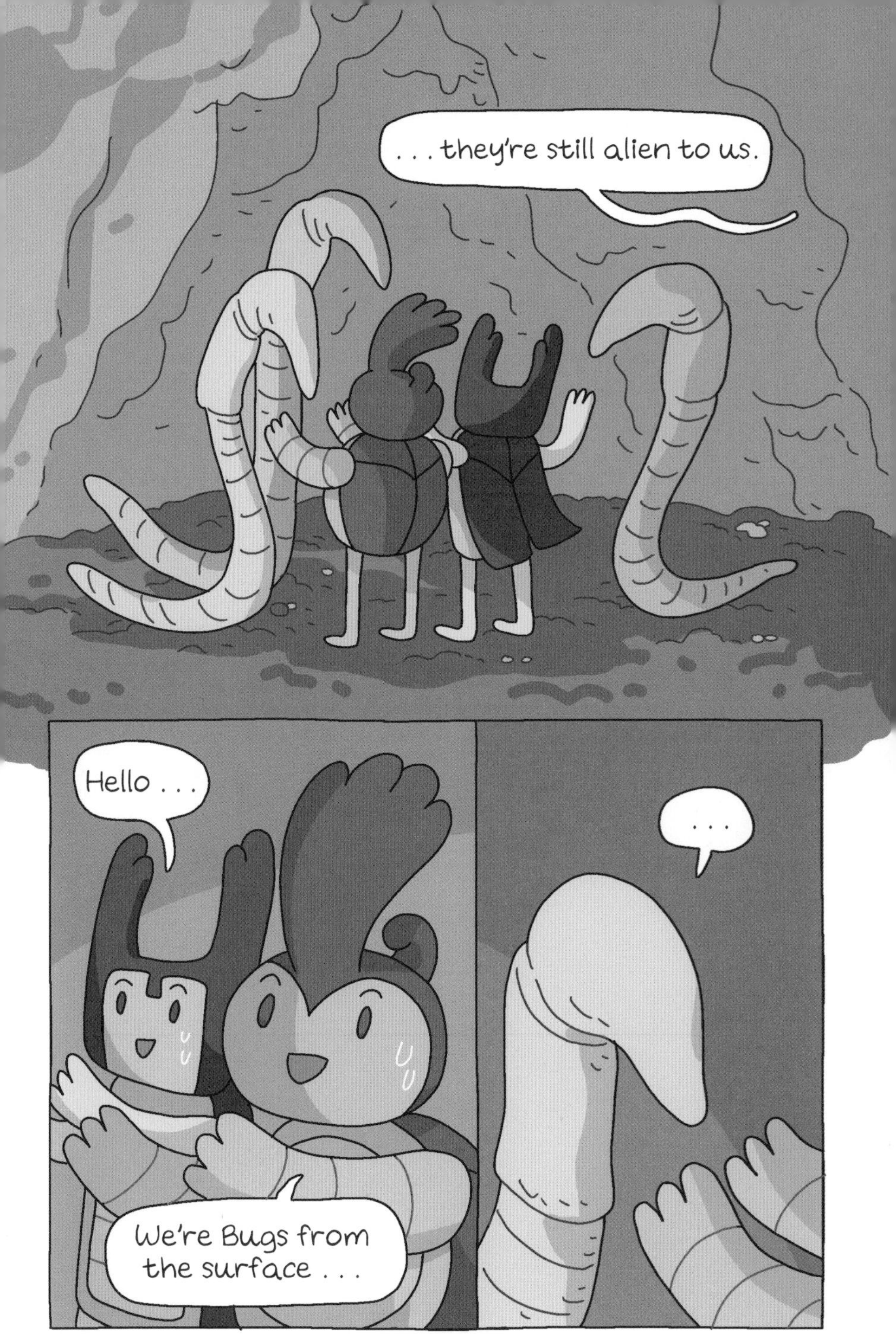
. . . they're still alien to us.
Hello . . .
We're Bugs from the surface . . .
. . .

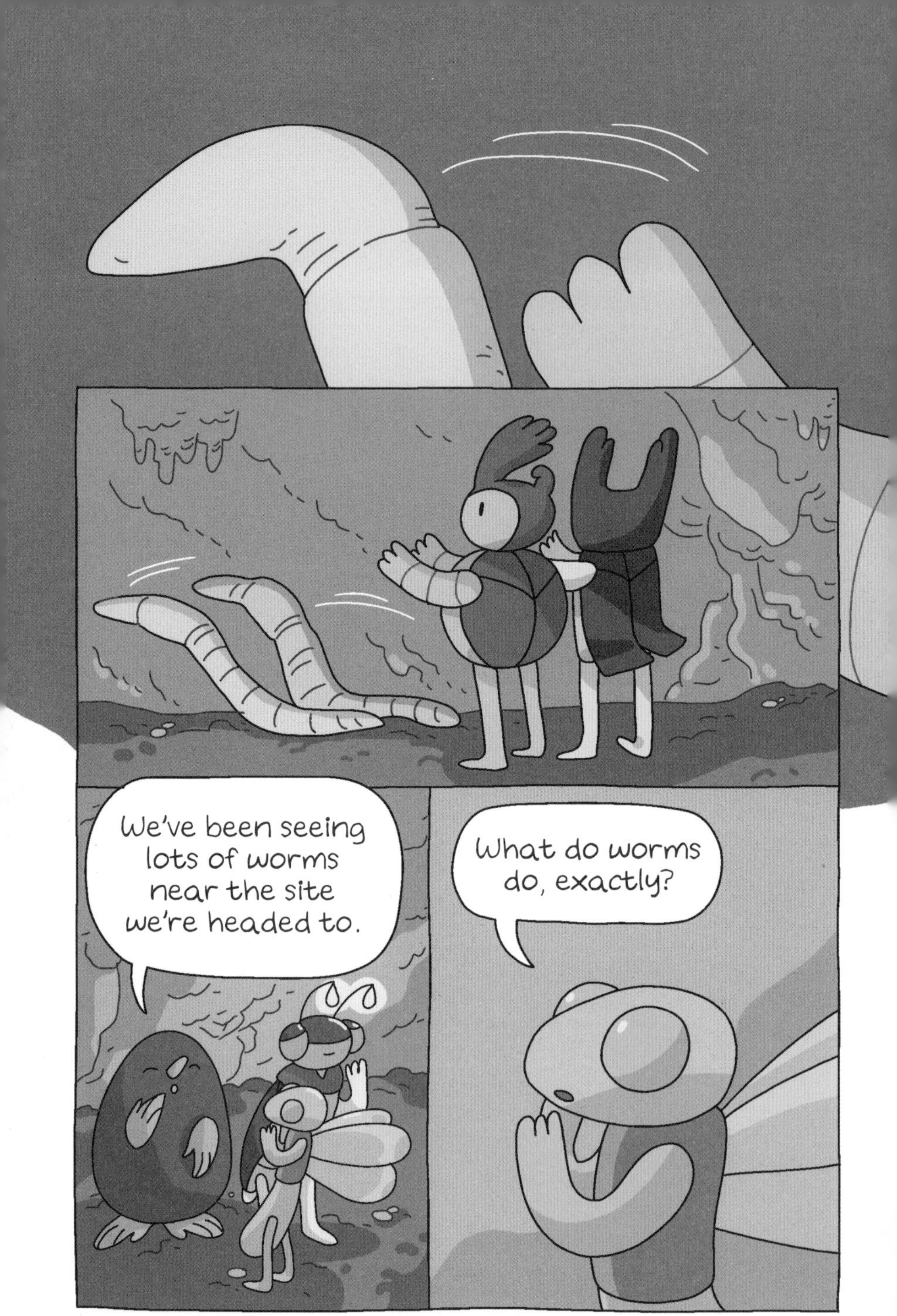
We've been seeing lots of worms near the site we're headed to.
What do worms do, exactly?

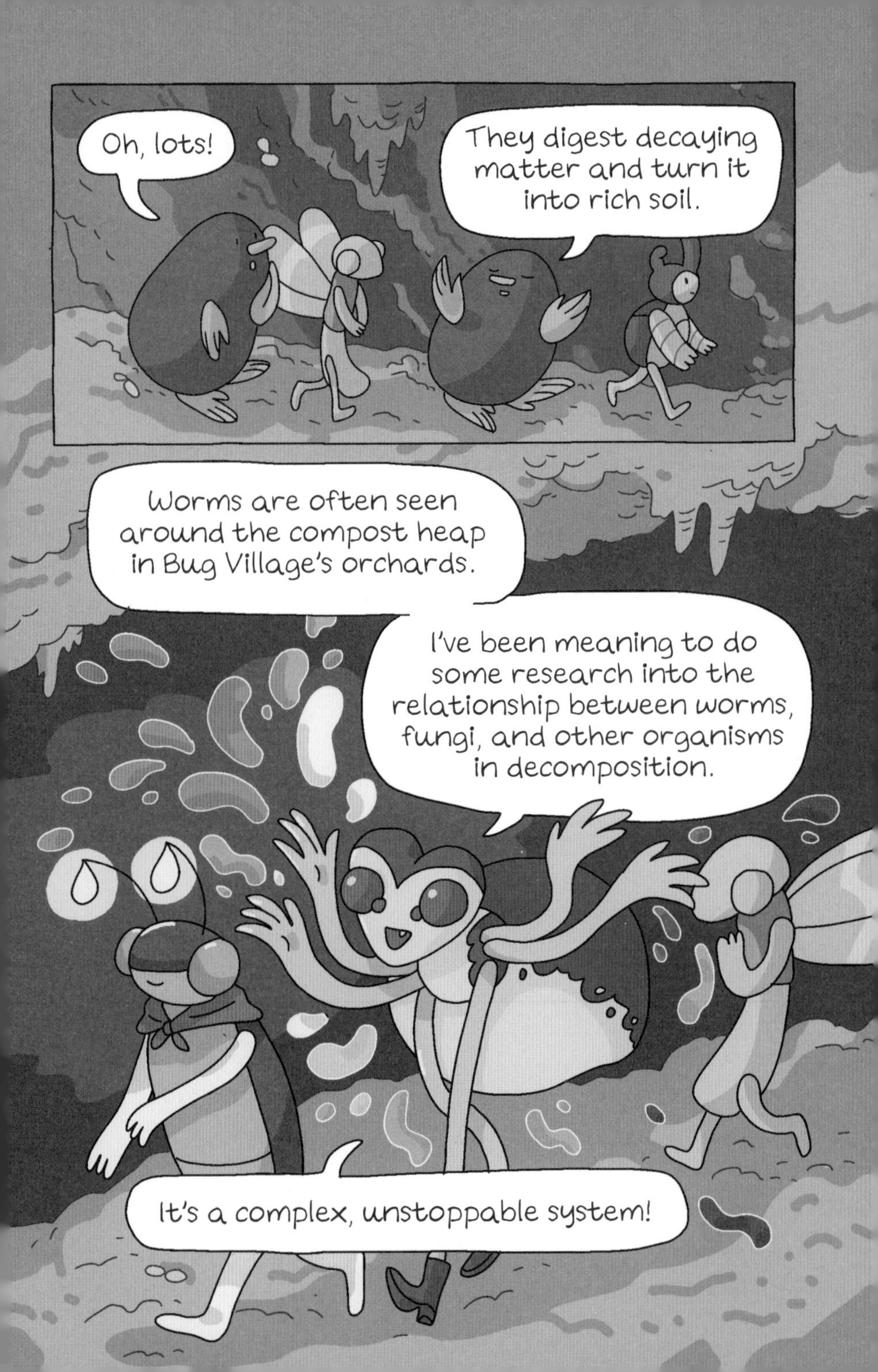
Oh, lots!
They digest decaying matter and turn it into rich soil.
Worms are often seen around the compost heap in Bug Village's orchards.
I've been meaning to do some research into the relationship between worms, fungi, and other organisms in decomposition.
It's a complex, unstoppable system!

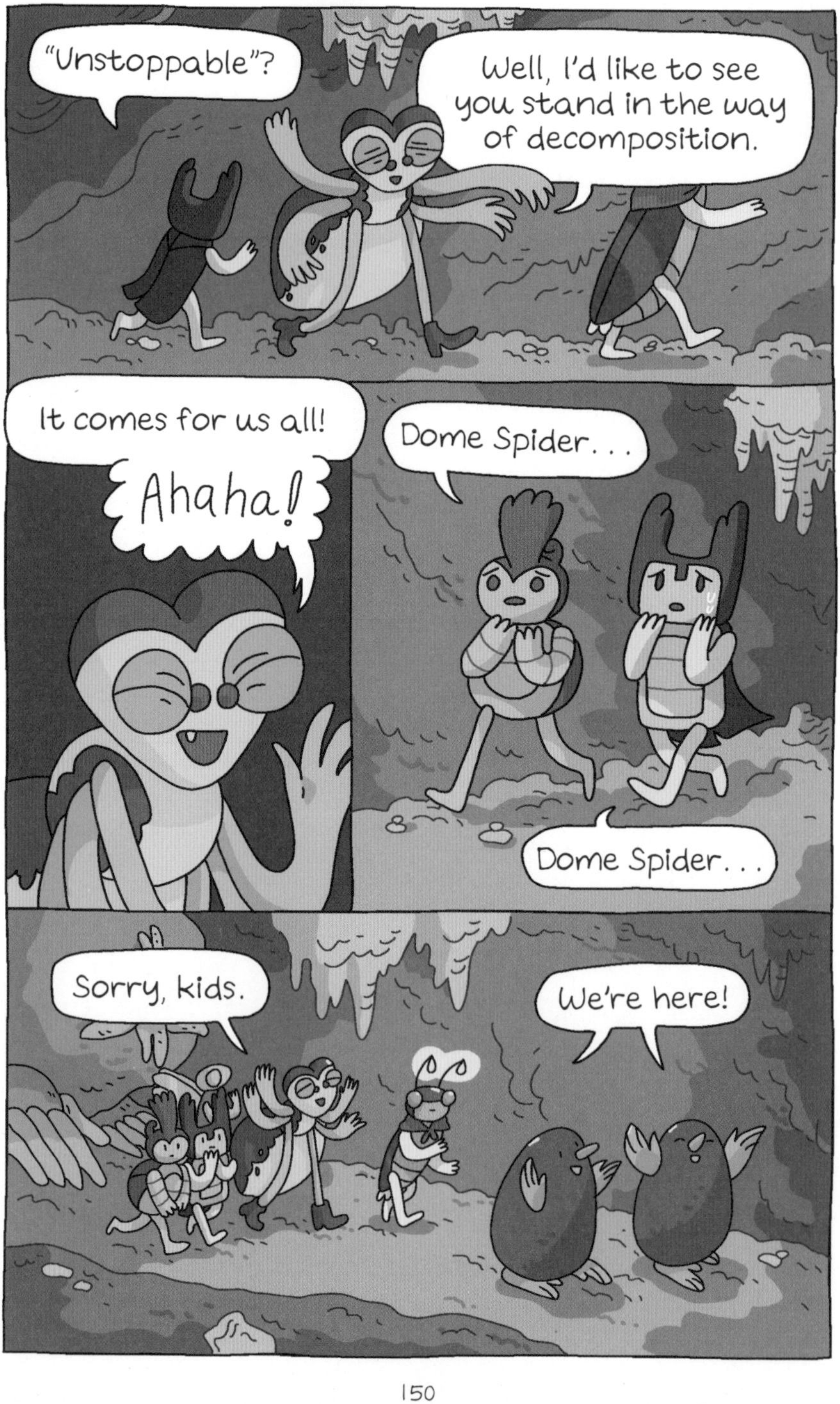
"Unstoppable"?
Well, I'd like to see you stand in the way of decomposition.
It comes for us all!
Ahaha!
Dome Spider. . .
Dome Spider. . .
Sorry, kids.
We're here!

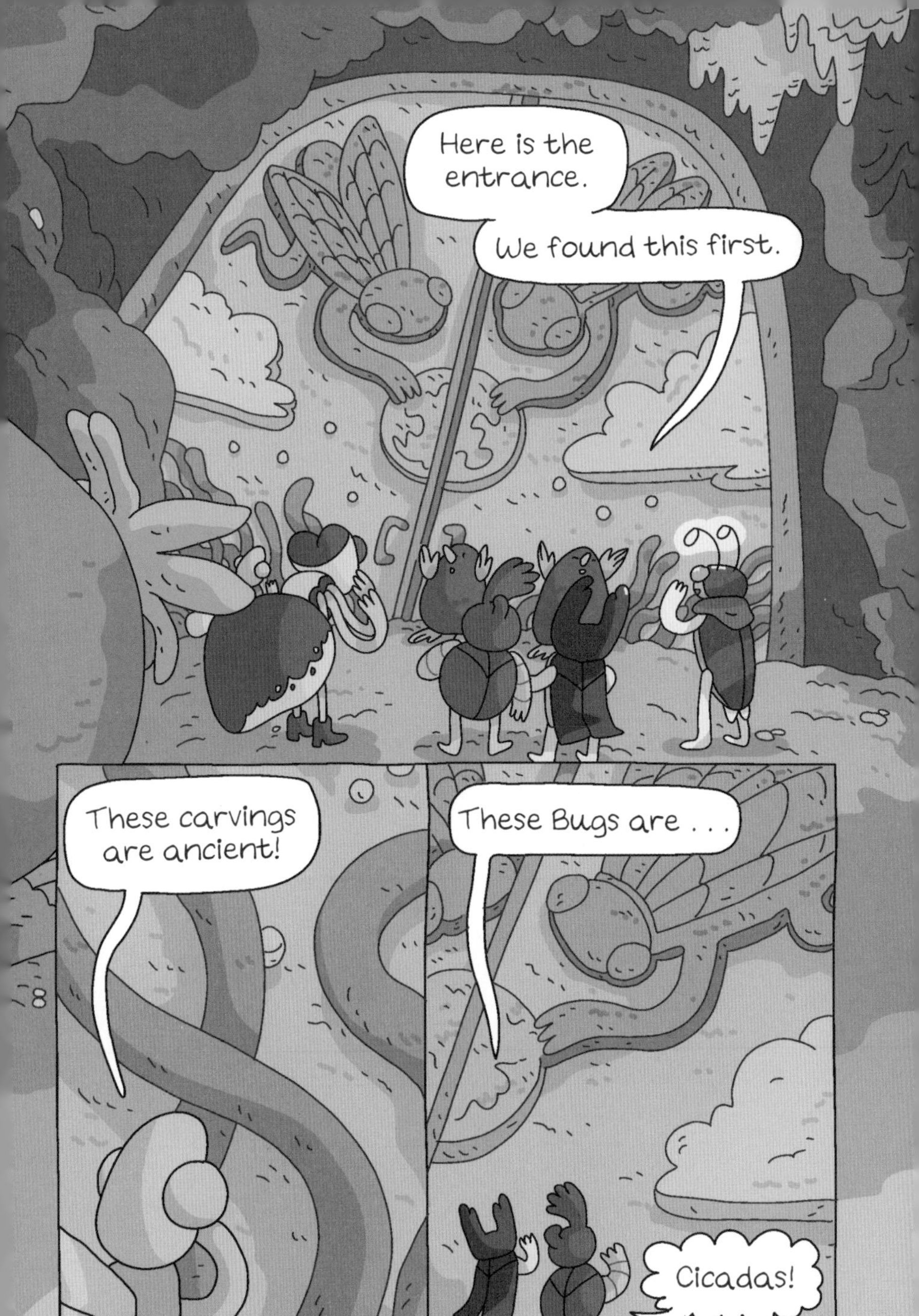
Here is the entrance.
We found this first.
These carvings are ancient!
These Bugs are . . .
Cicadas!

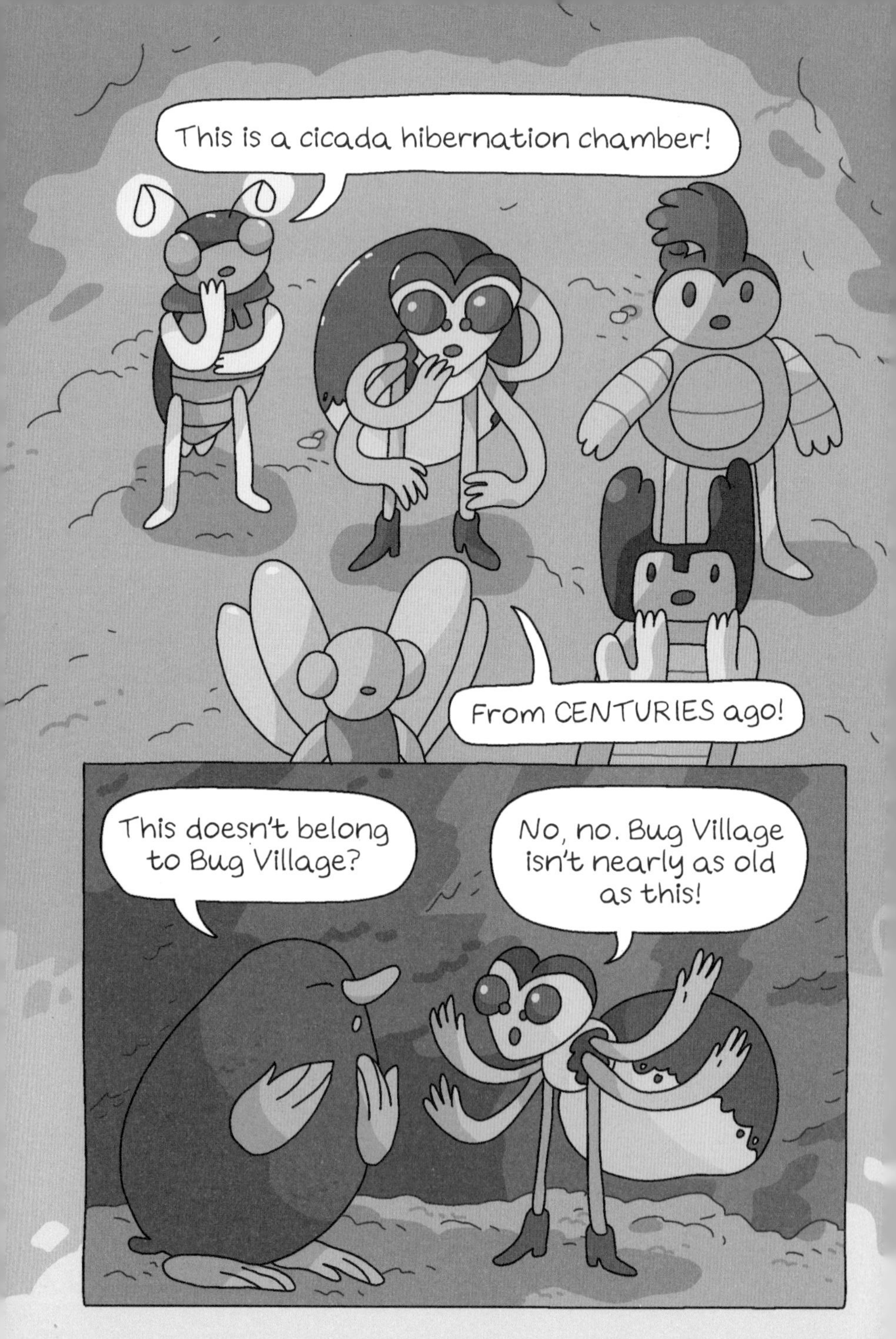
This is a cicada hibernation chamber!
From CENTURIES ago!
This doesn't belong to Bug Village?
No, no. Bug Village isn't nearly as old as this!

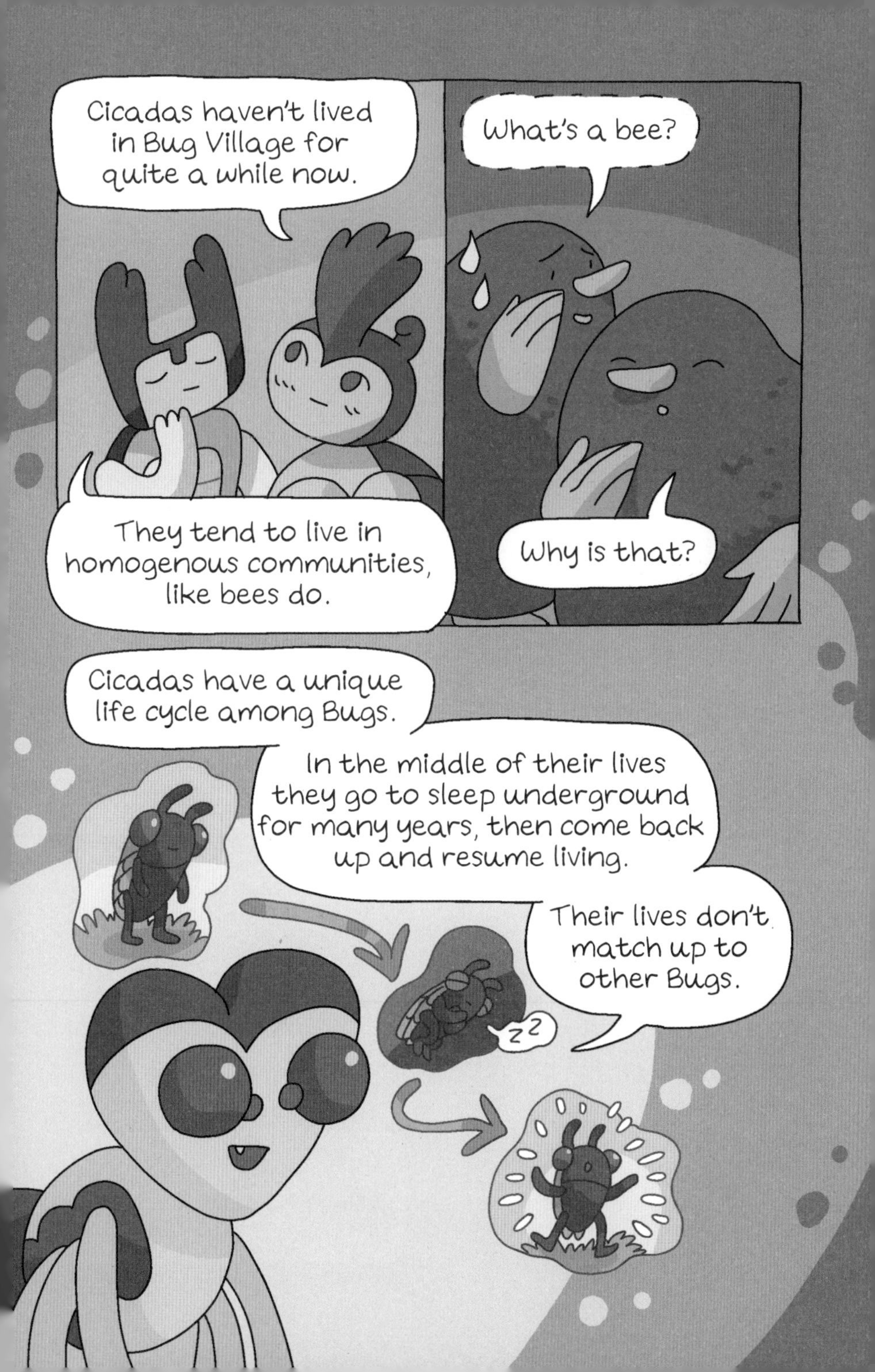
Cicadas haven't lived in Bug Village for quite a while now.
They tend to live in homogenous communities, like bees do.
What's a bee?
Why is that?
Cicadas have a unique life cycle among Bugs.
In the middle of their lives they go to sleep underground for many years, then come back up and resume living.
Their lives don't match up to other Bugs.
zz

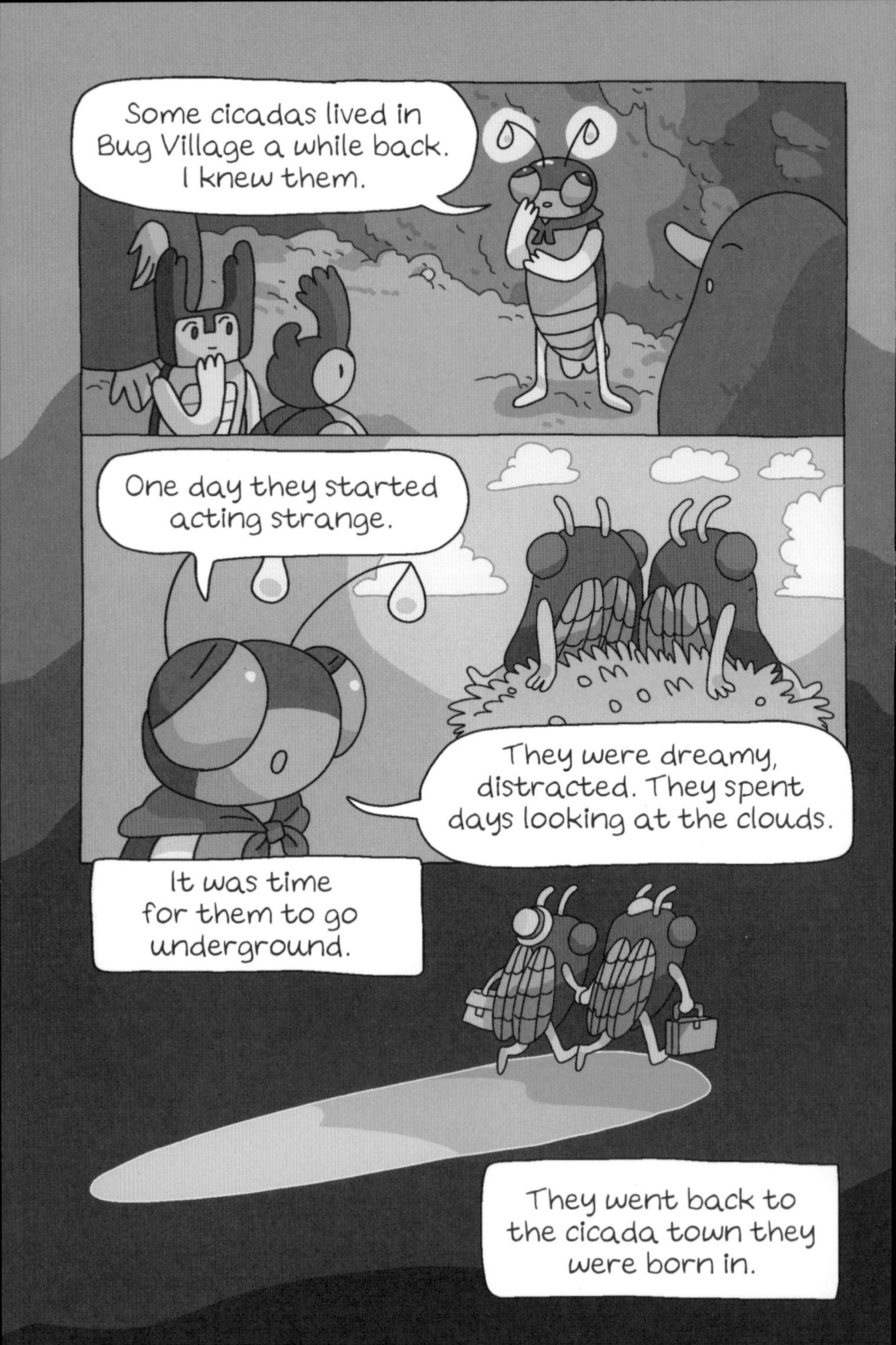
Some cicadas lived in Bug Village a while back. I knew them.
One day they started acting strange.
They were dreamy, distracted. They spent days looking at the clouds.
It was time for them to go underground.
They went back to the cicada town they were born in.

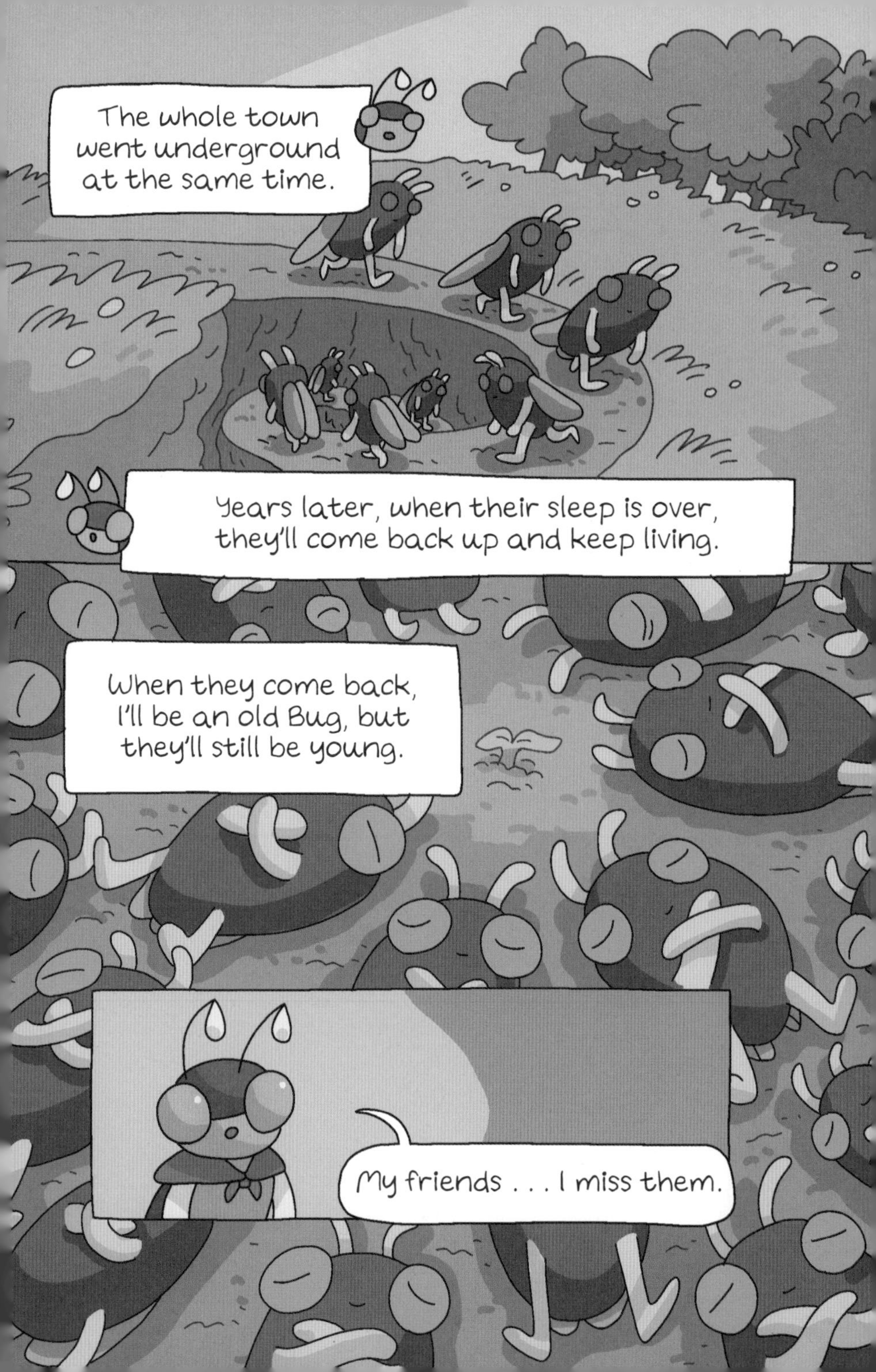
The whole town went underground at the same time.
Years later, when their sleep is over, they'll come back up and keep living.
When they come back, I'll be an old Bug, but they'll still be young.
My friends . . . I miss them.

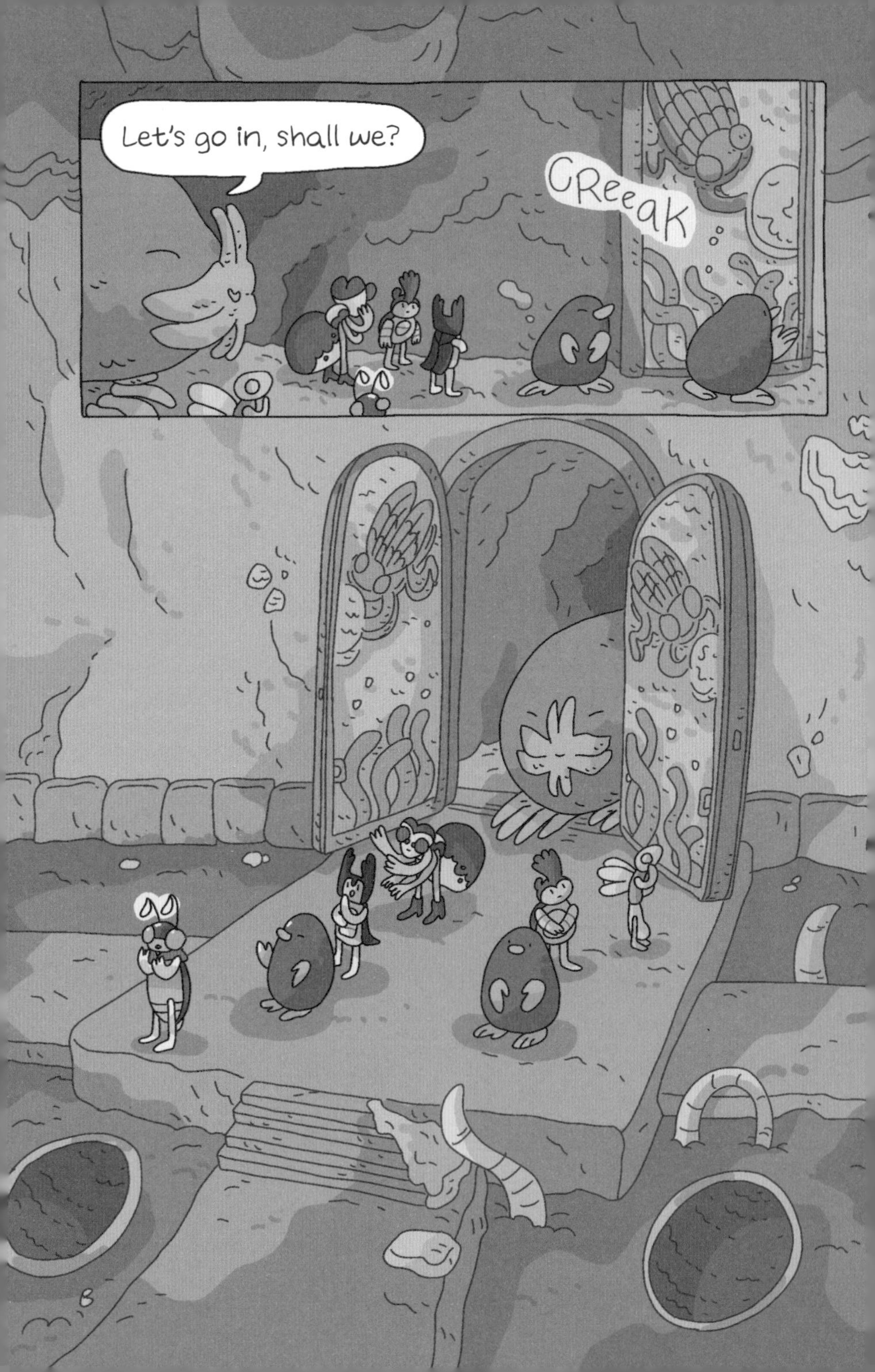
Let's go in, shall we?
CReeaK

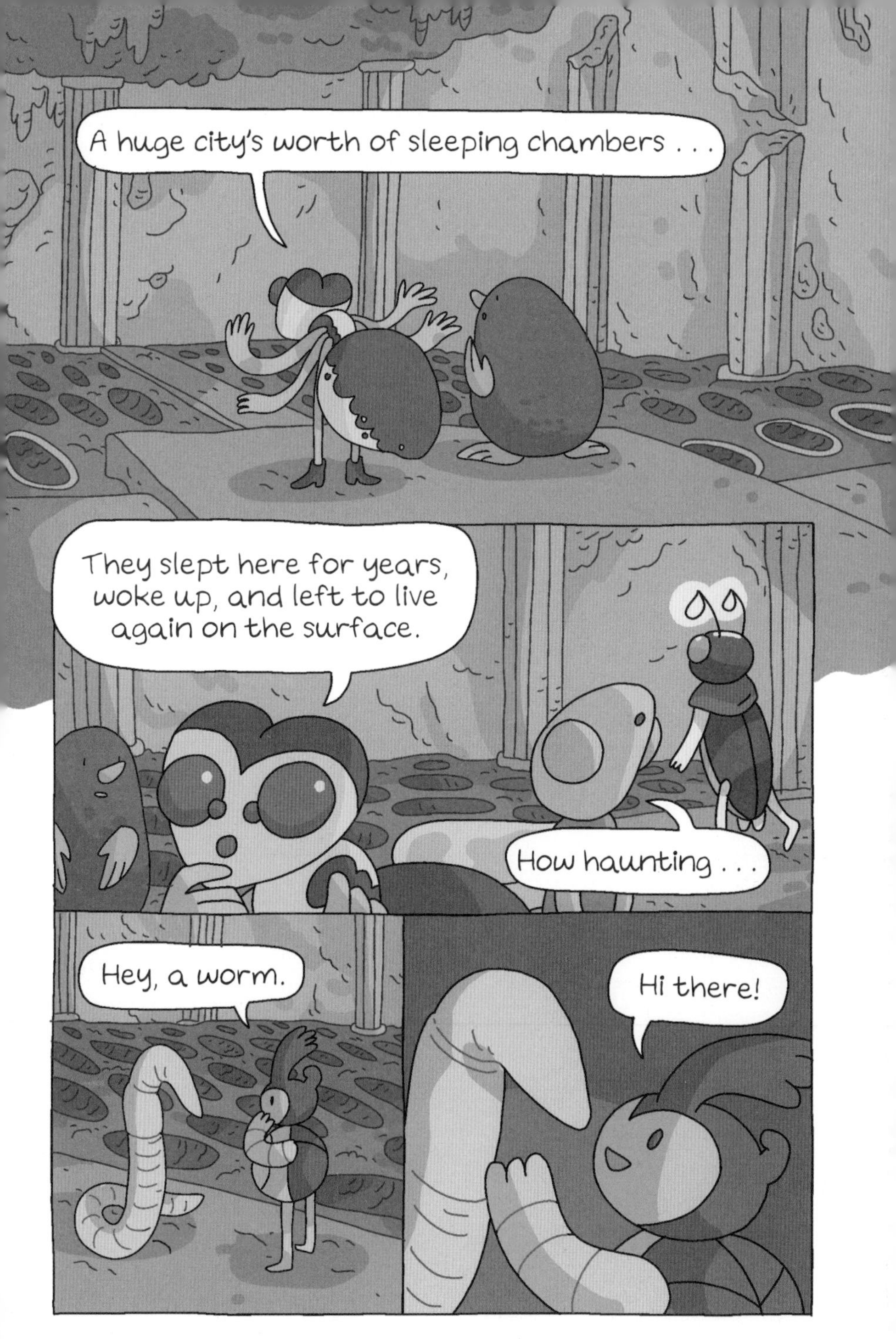
A huge city's worth of sleeping chambers . . .
They slept here for years, woke up, and left to live again on the surface.
How haunting . . .
Hey, a worm.
Hi there!

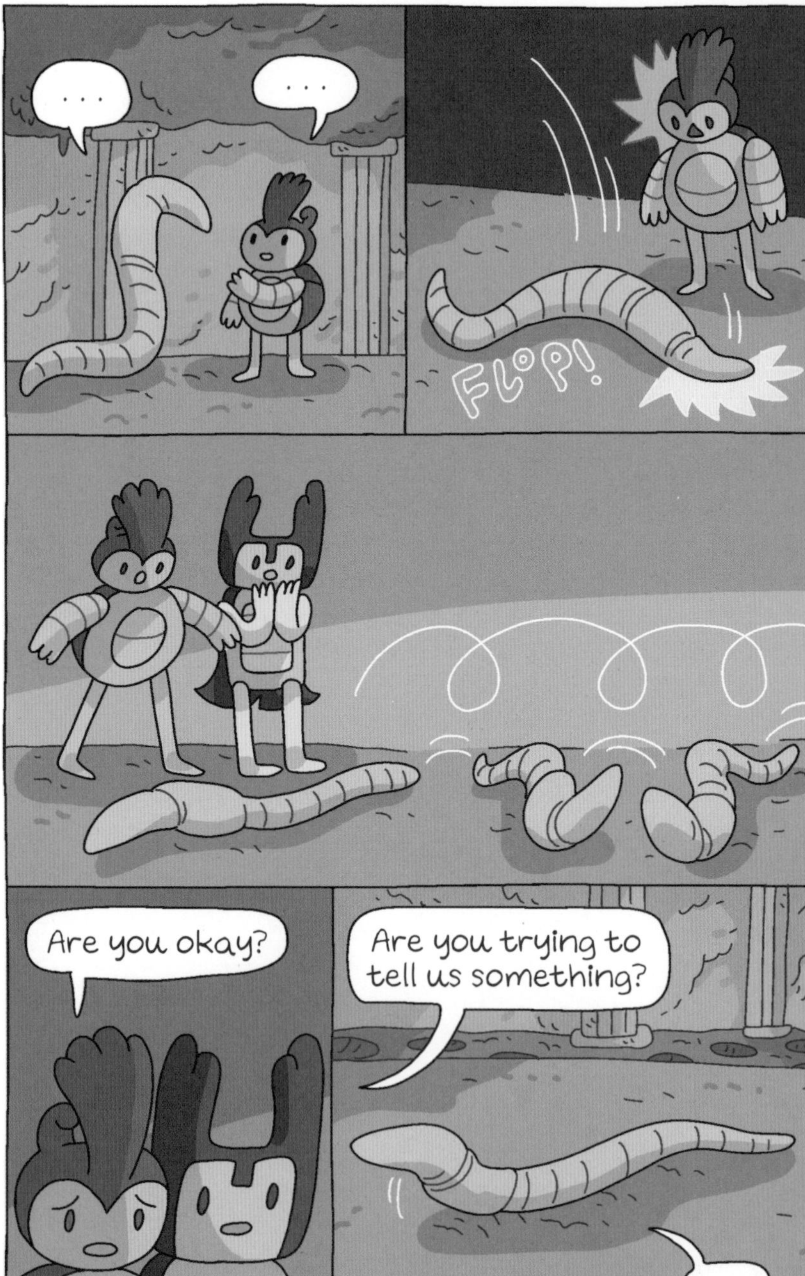
. . .
. . .
FLOP!
Are you okay?
Are you trying to tell us something?
. . .

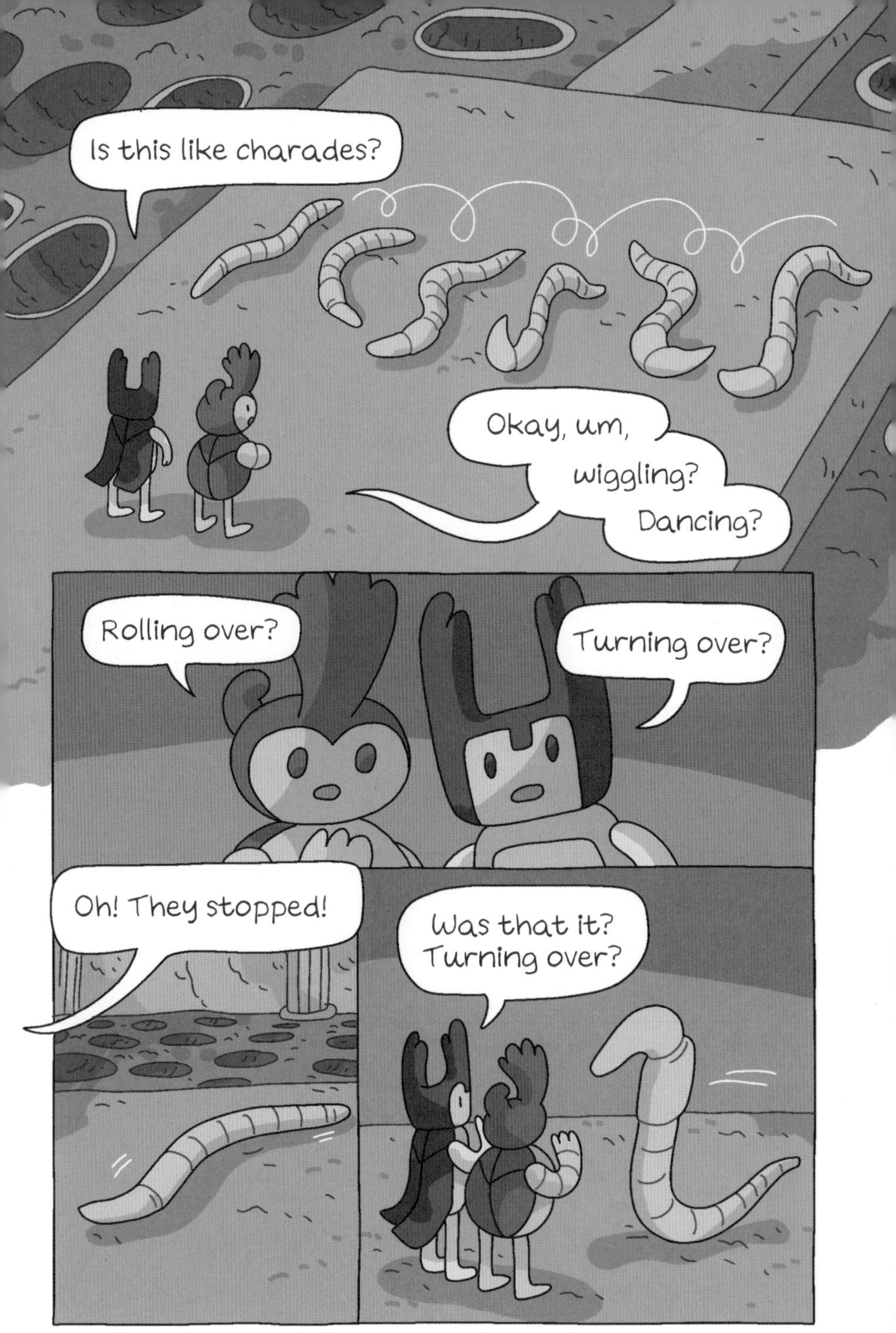
Is this like charades?
Okay, um, wiggling? Dancing?
Rolling over?
Turning over?
Oh! They stopped!
Was that it? Turning over?

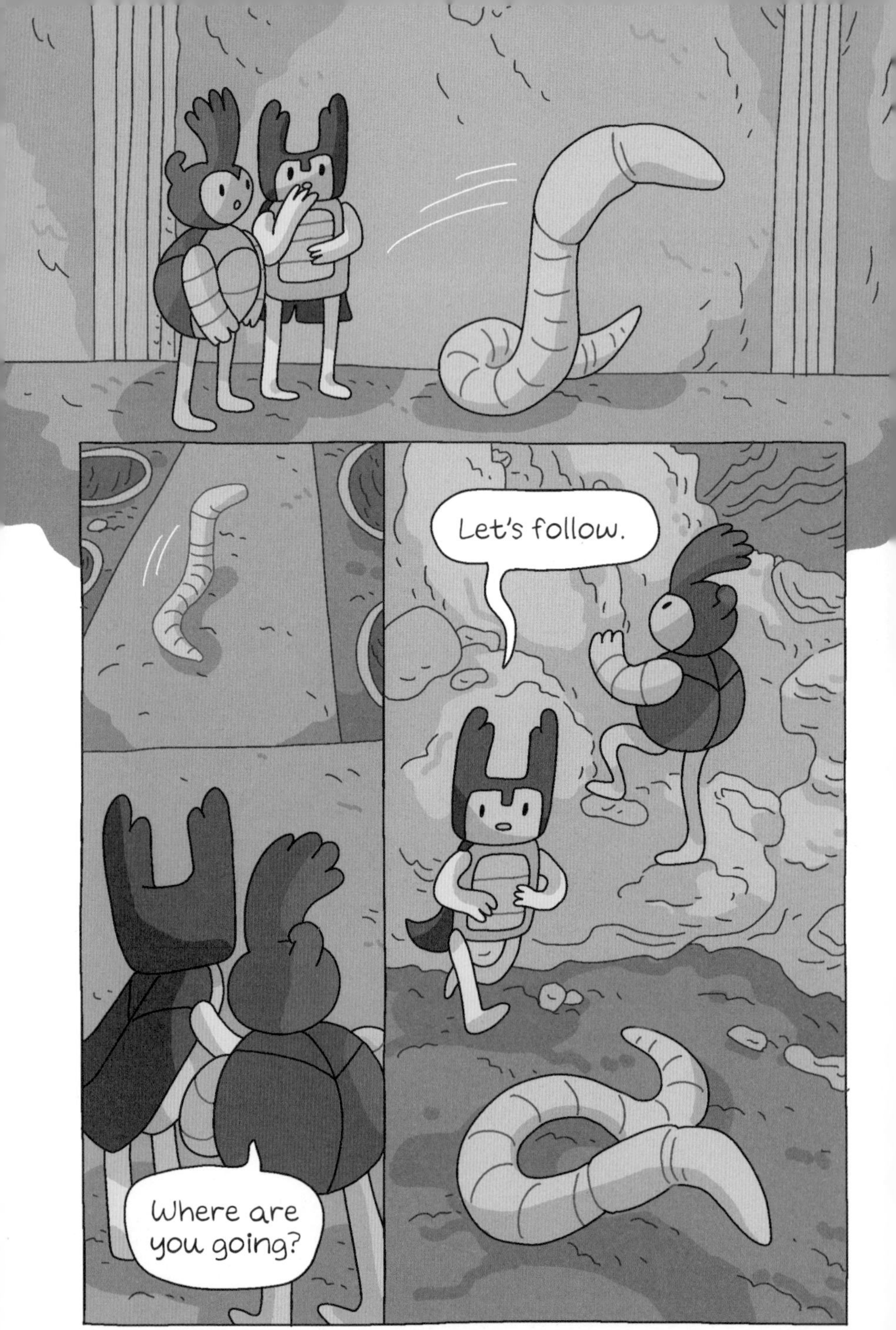
Where are you going?
Let's follow.

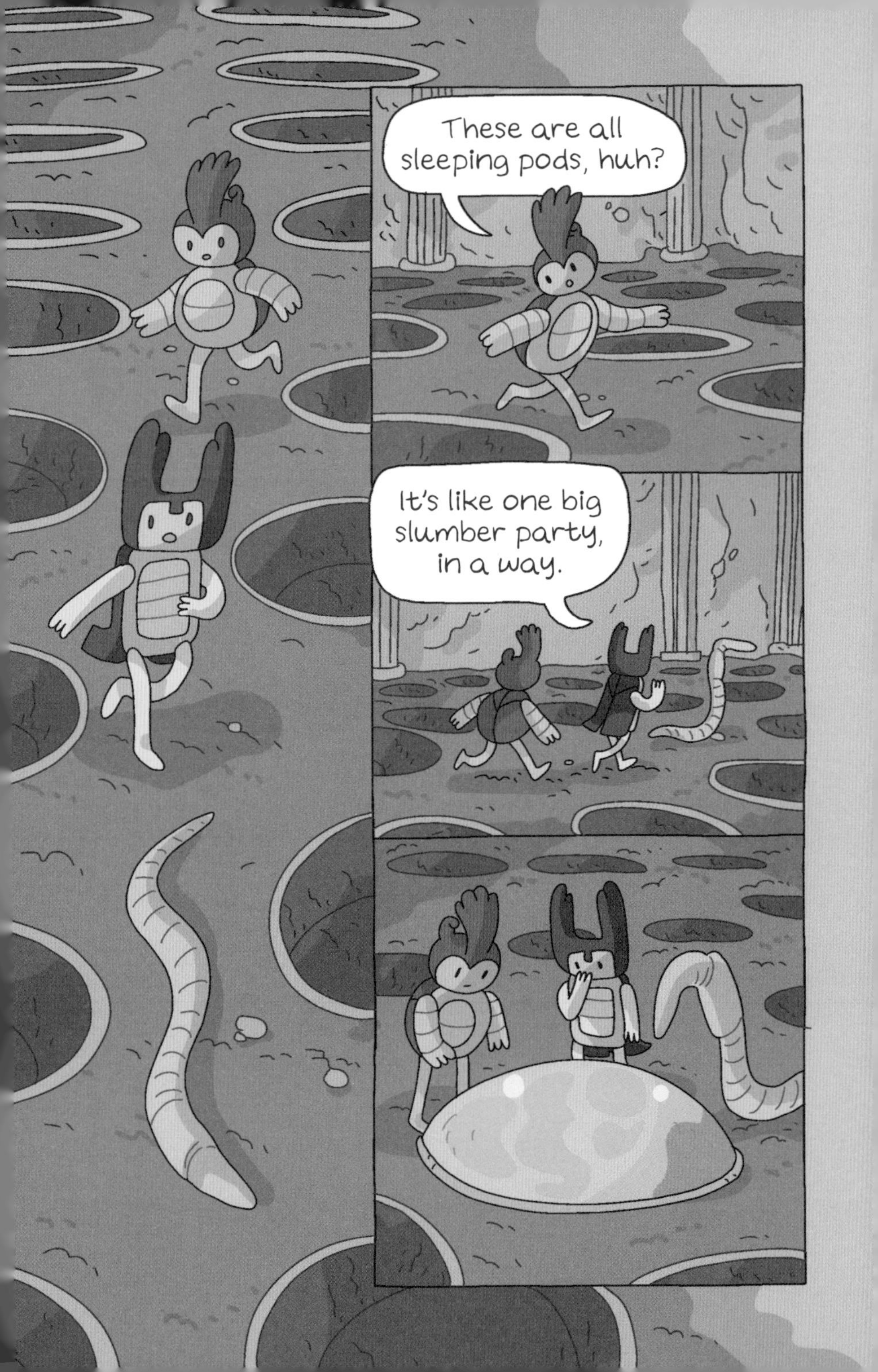
These are all sleeping pods, huh?
It's like one big slumber party, in a way.

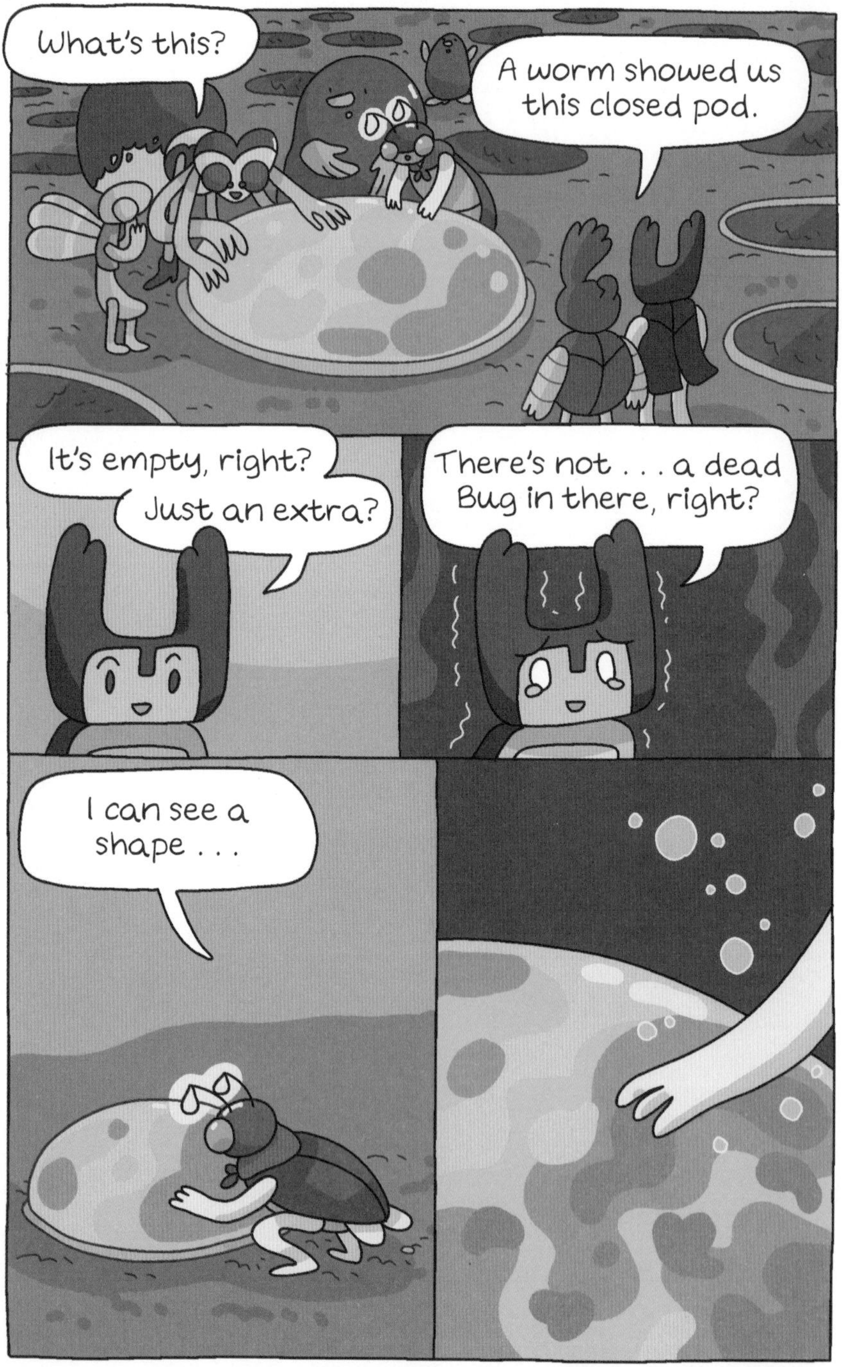
What's this?
A worm showed us this closed pod.
It's empty, right?
Just an extra?
There's not . . . a dead Bug in there, right?
I can see a shape . . .

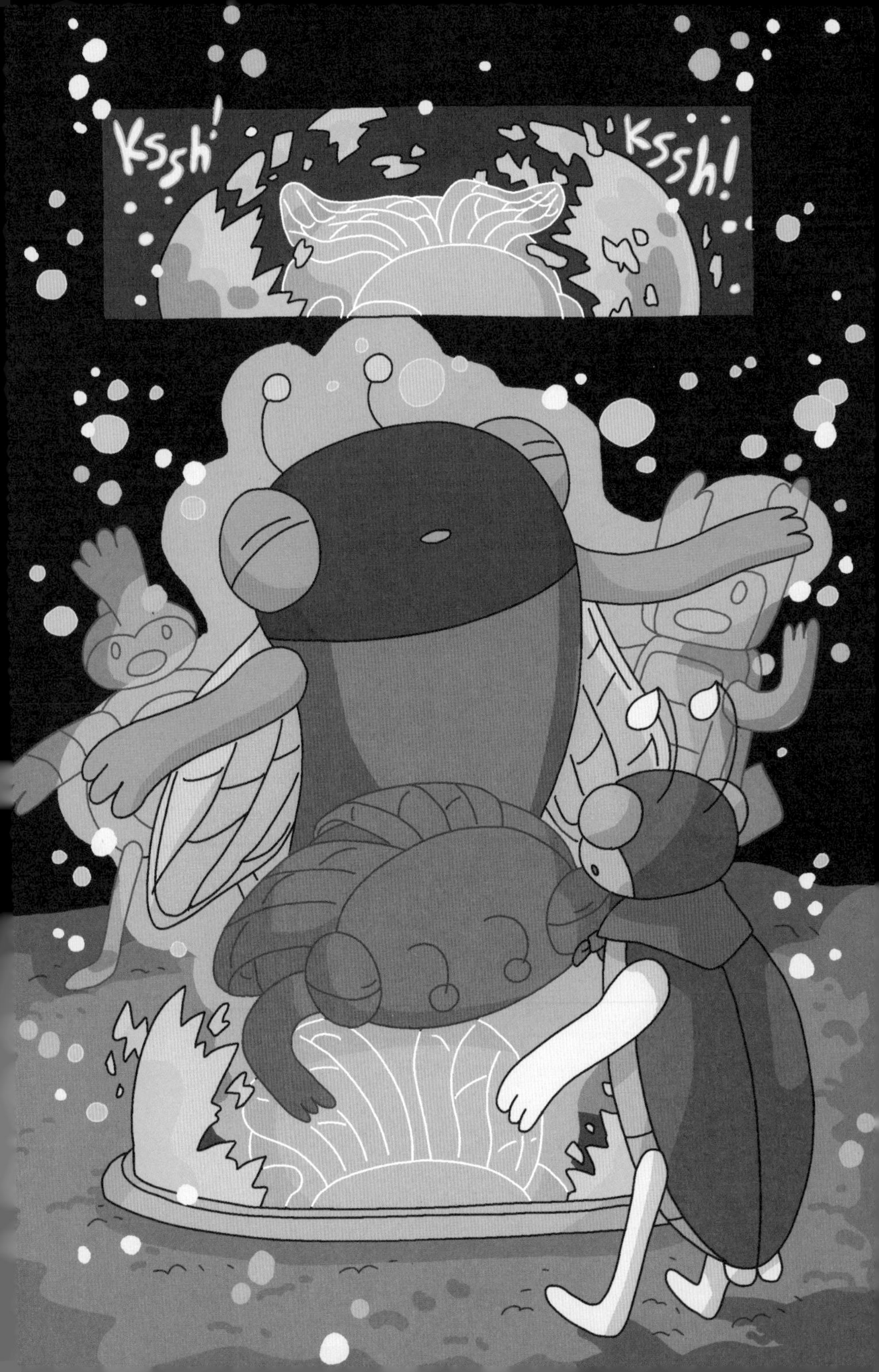
KSSH!
KSSH!

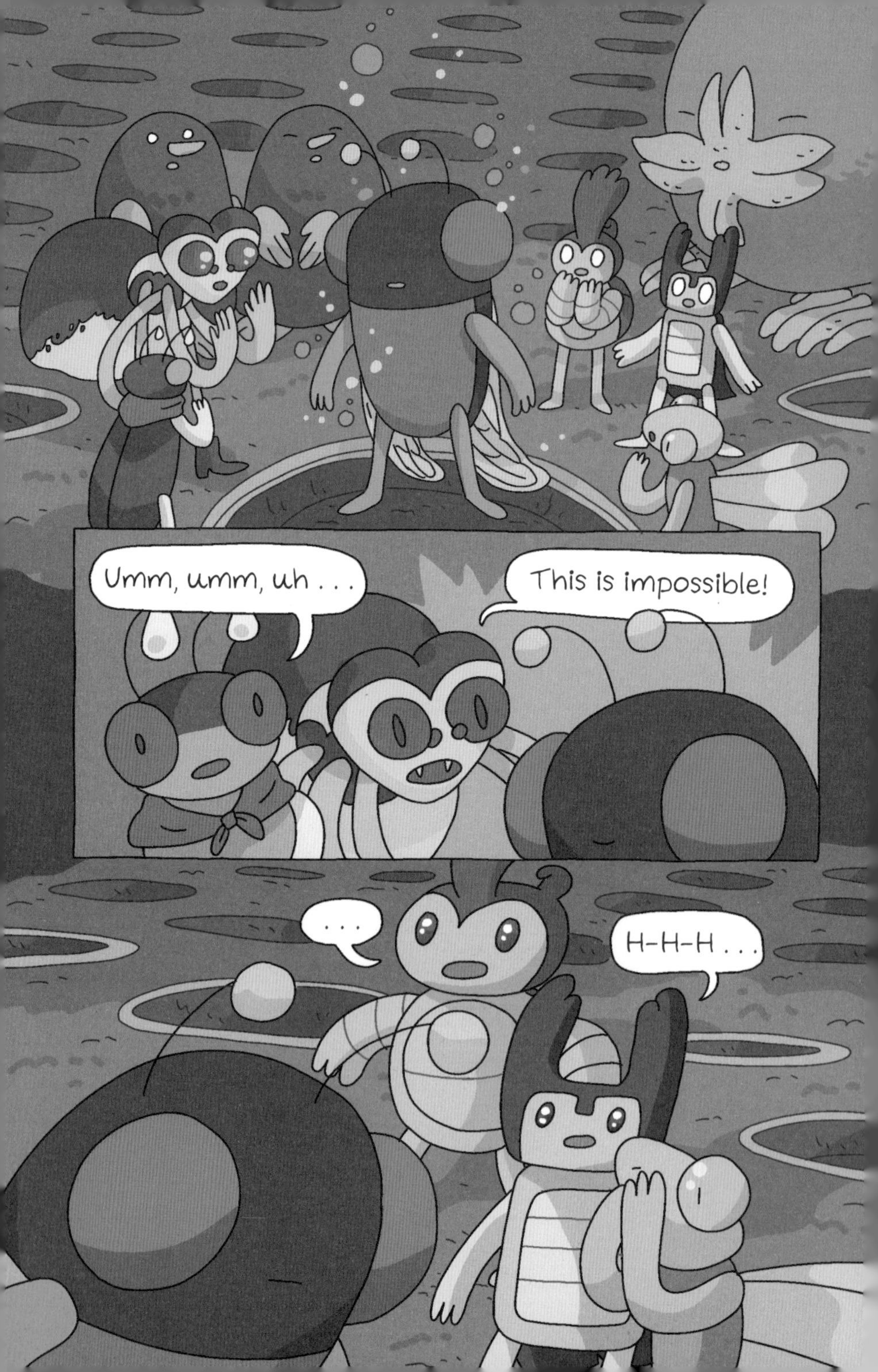

Umm, umm, uh . . .
This is impossible!
. . .
H-H-H . . .

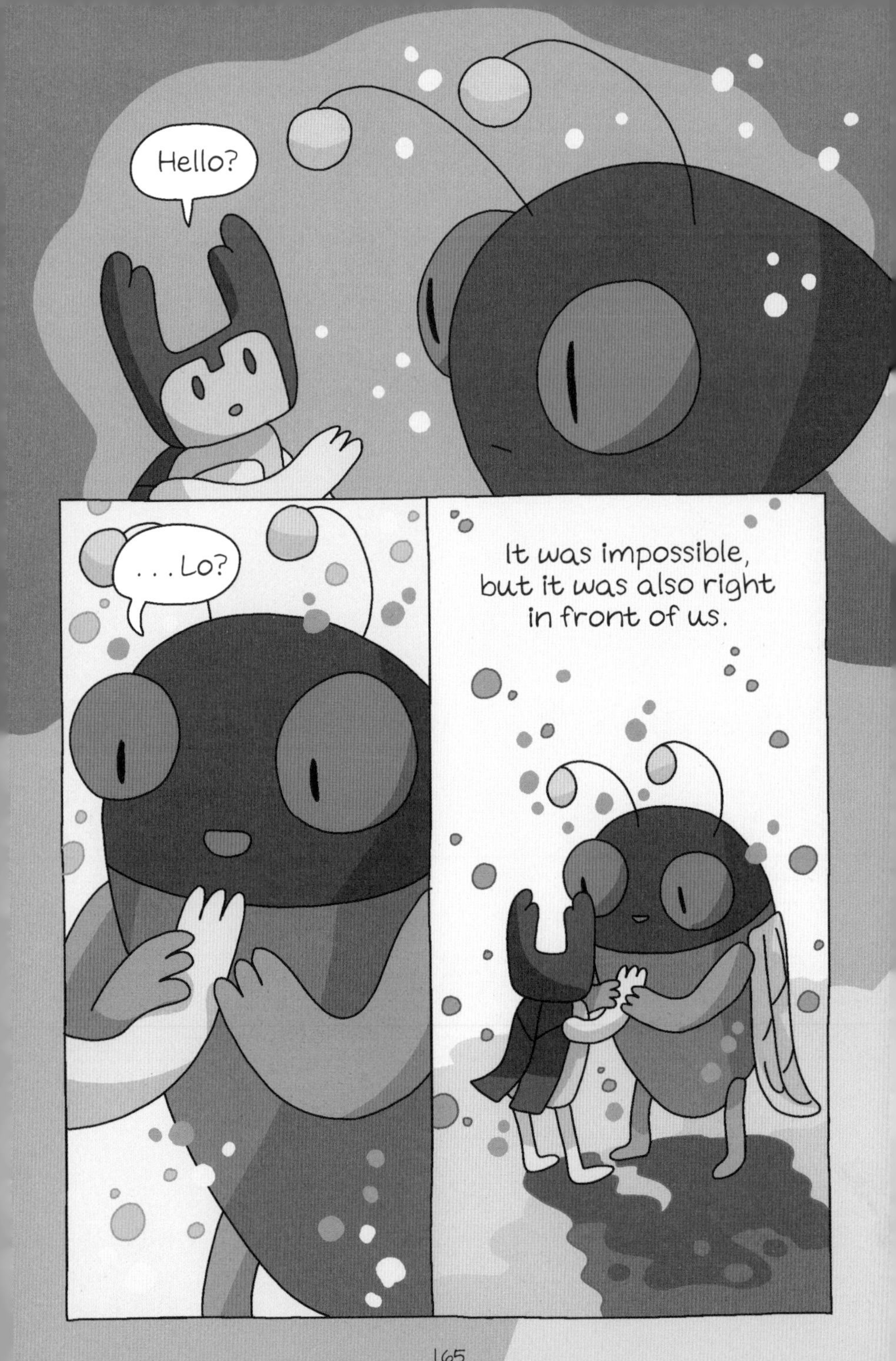
Hello?
. . . Lo?
It was impossible, but it was also right in front of us.

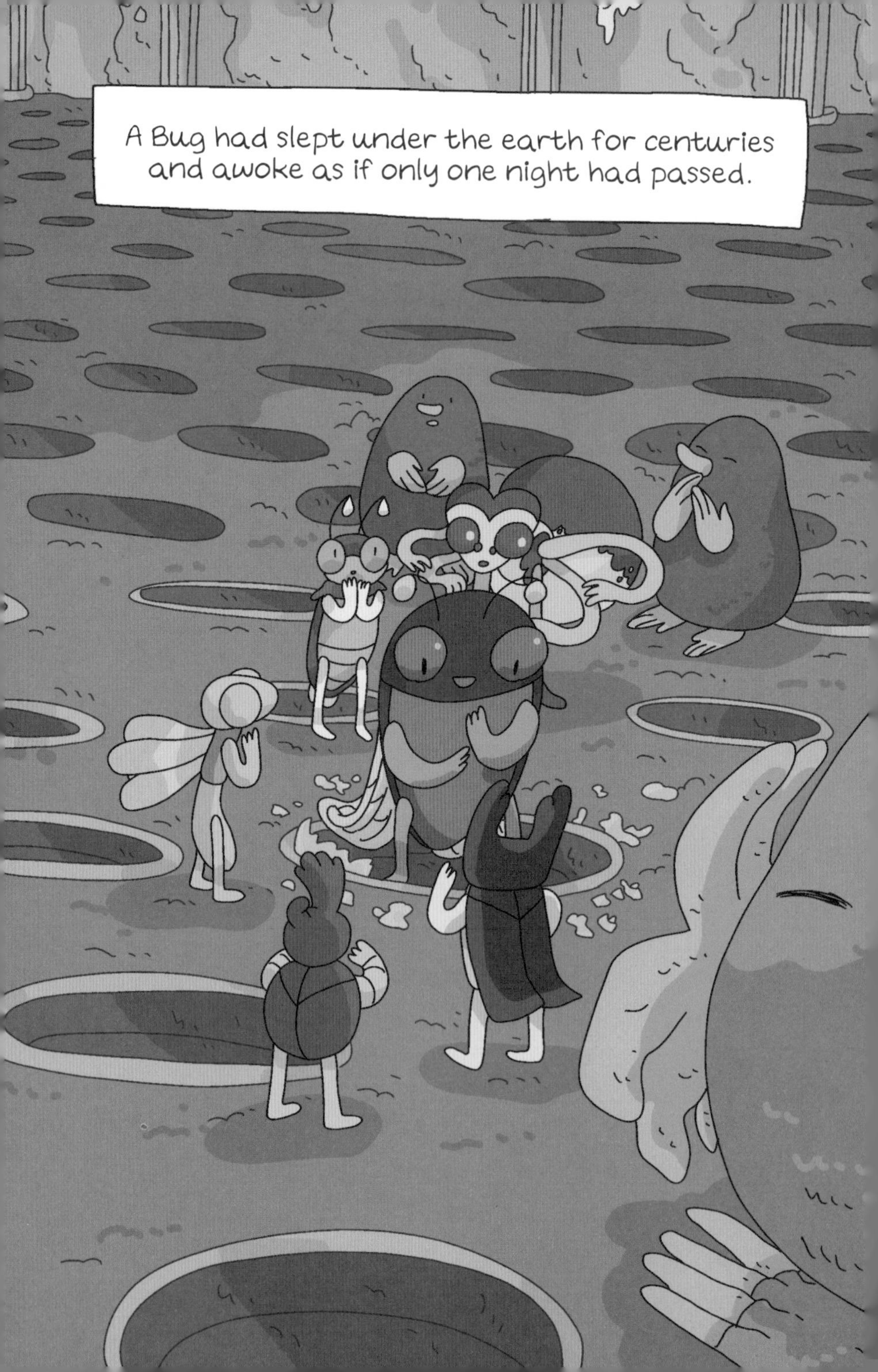
A Bug had slept under the earth for centuries and awoke as if only one night had passed.

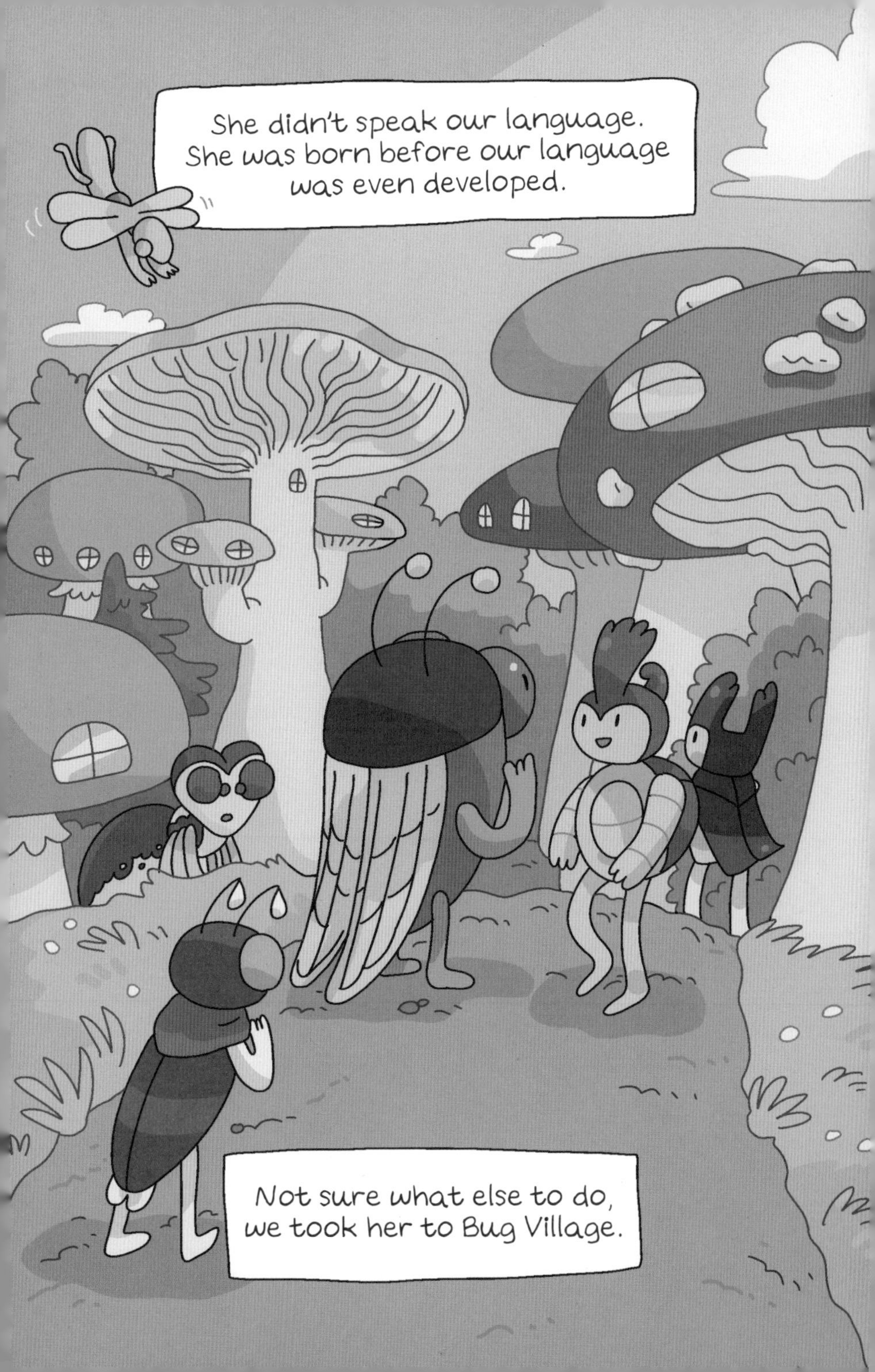
She didn't speak our language. She was born before our language was even developed.
Not sure what else to do, we took her to Bug Village.

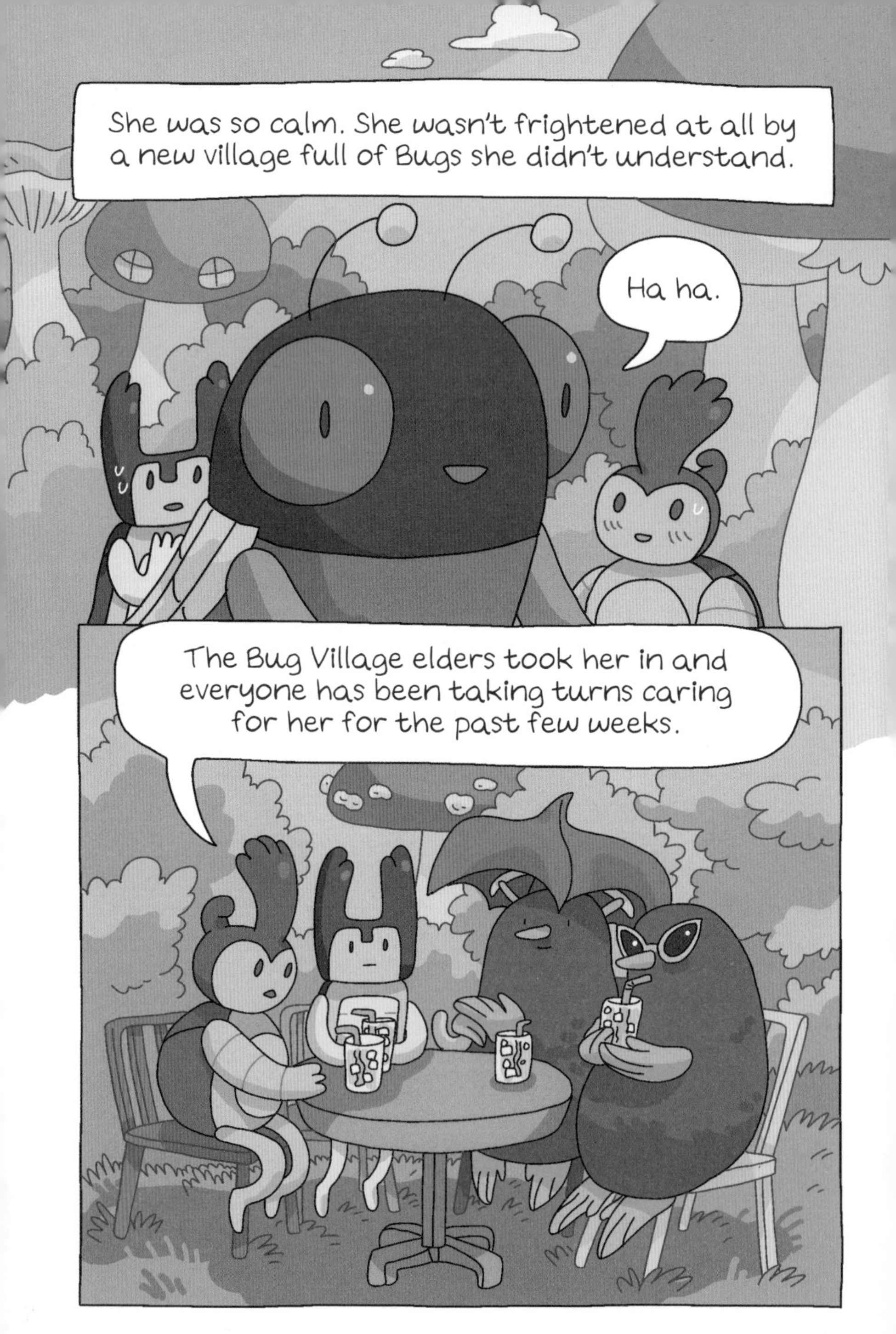

She was so calm. She wasn't frightened at all by a new village full of Bugs she didn't understand.
Ha ha.
The Bug Village elders took her in and everyone has been taking turns caring for her for the past few weeks.

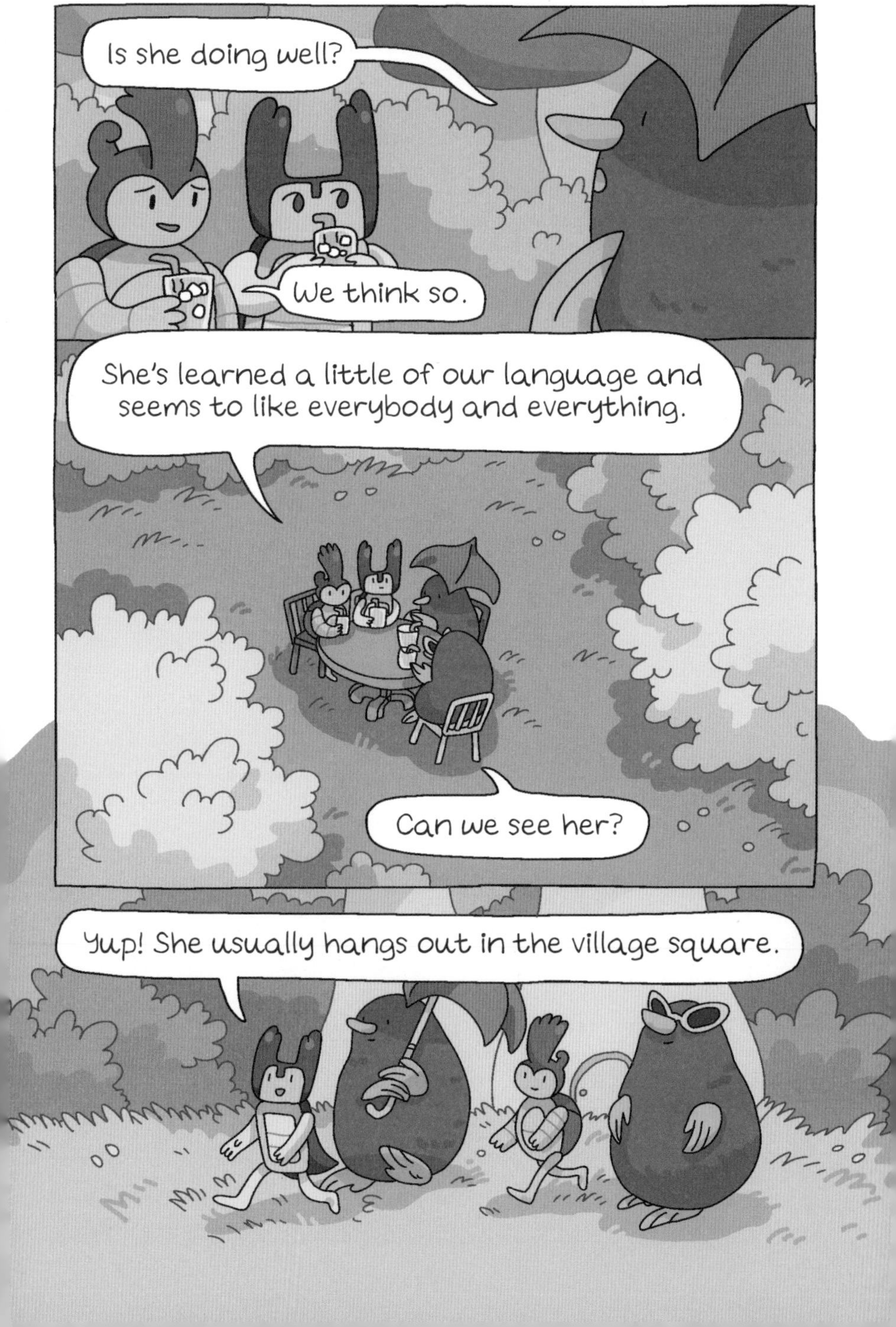
Is she doing well?
We think so.
She's learned a little of our language and seems to like everybody and everything.
Can we see her?
Yup! She usually hangs out in the village square.

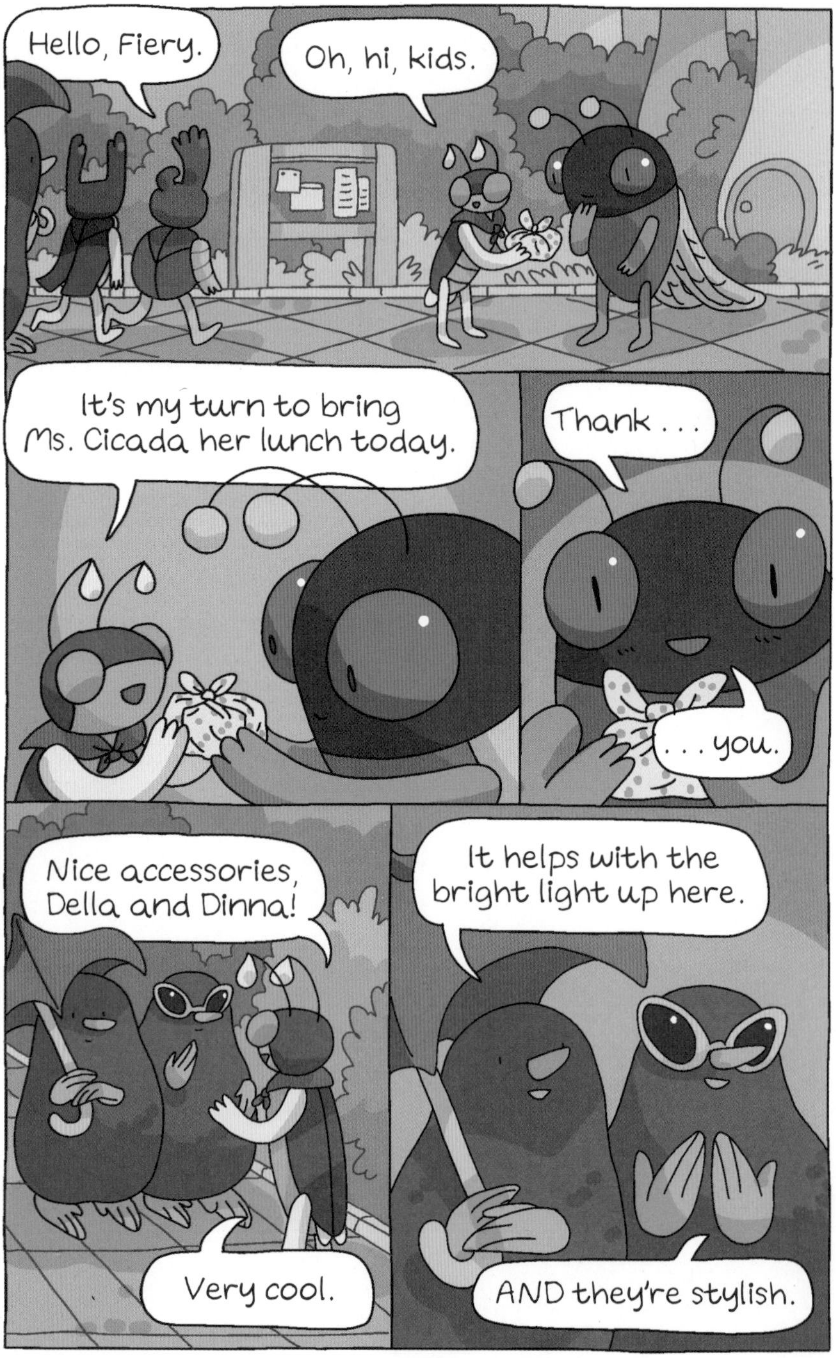
Hello, Fiery.
Oh, hi, kids.
It's my turn to bring Ms. Cicada her lunch today.
Thank . . .
. . . you.
Nice accessories, Della and Dinna!
Very cool.
It helps with the bright light up here.
AND they're stylish.

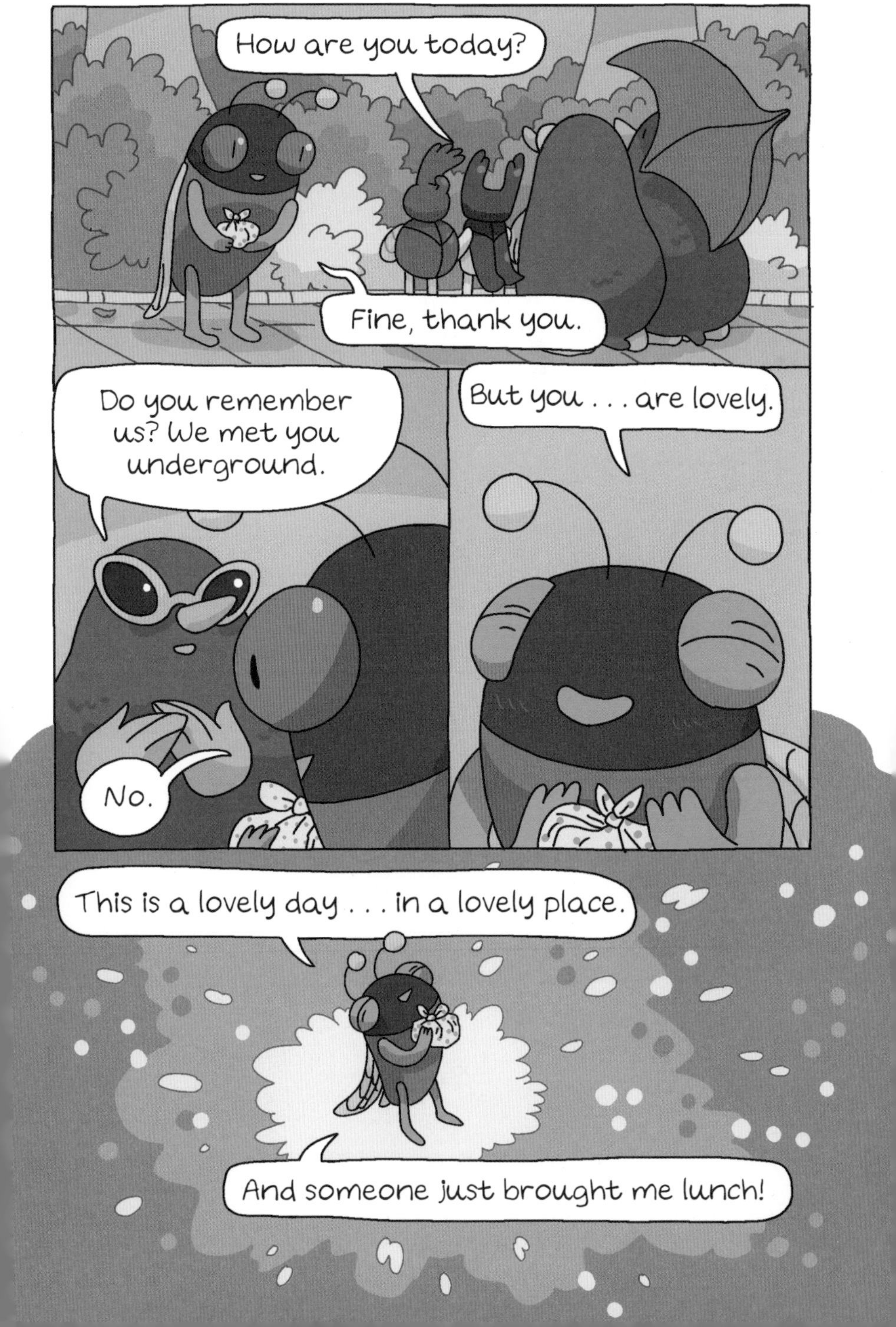
How are you today?
Fine, thank you.
Do you remember us? We met you underground.
No.
But you . . . are lovely.
This is a lovely day . . . in a lovely place.
And someone just brought me lunch!

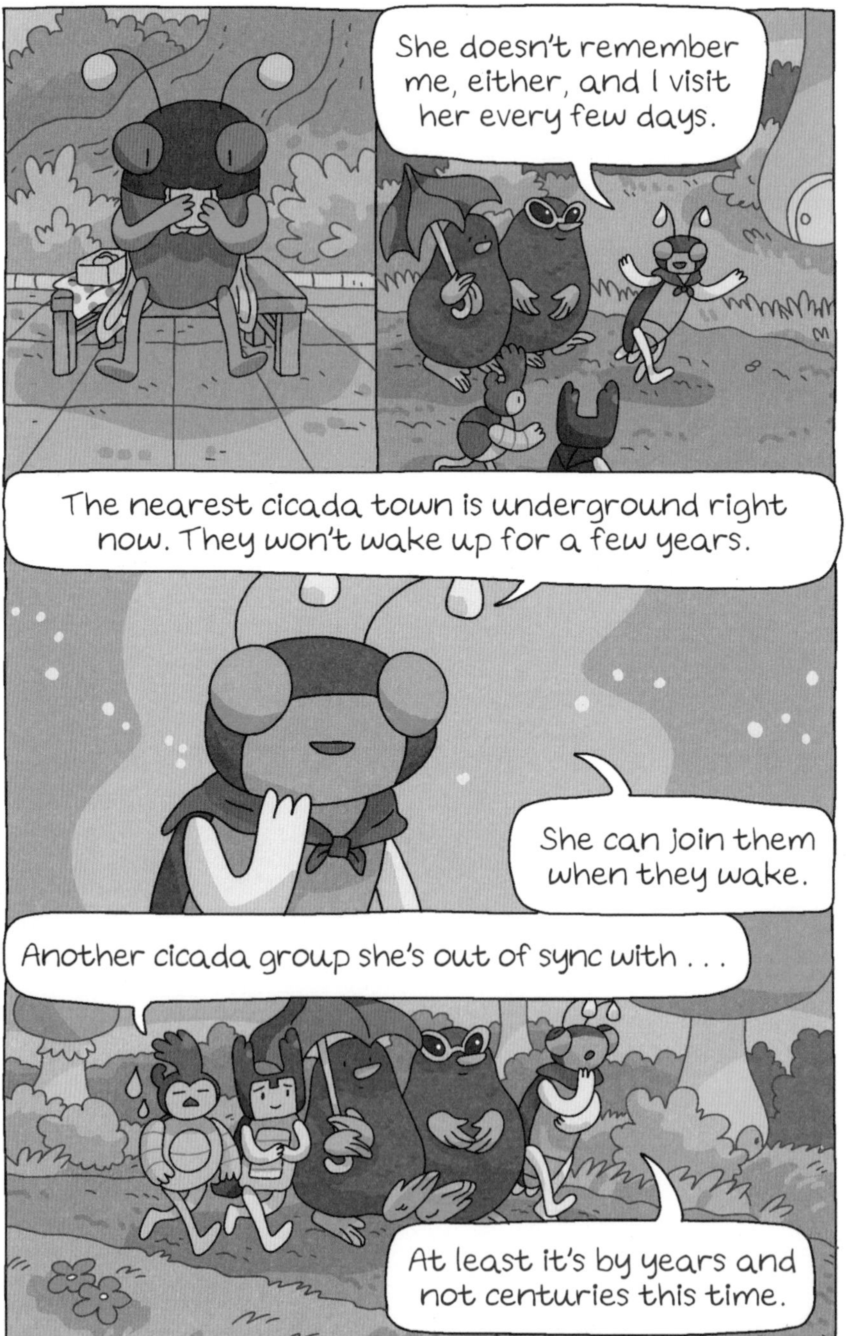
She doesn't remember me, either, and I visit her every few days.
The nearest cicada town is underground right now. They won't wake up for a few years.
She can join them when they wake.
Another cicada group she's out of sync with . . .
At least it's by years and not centuries this time.

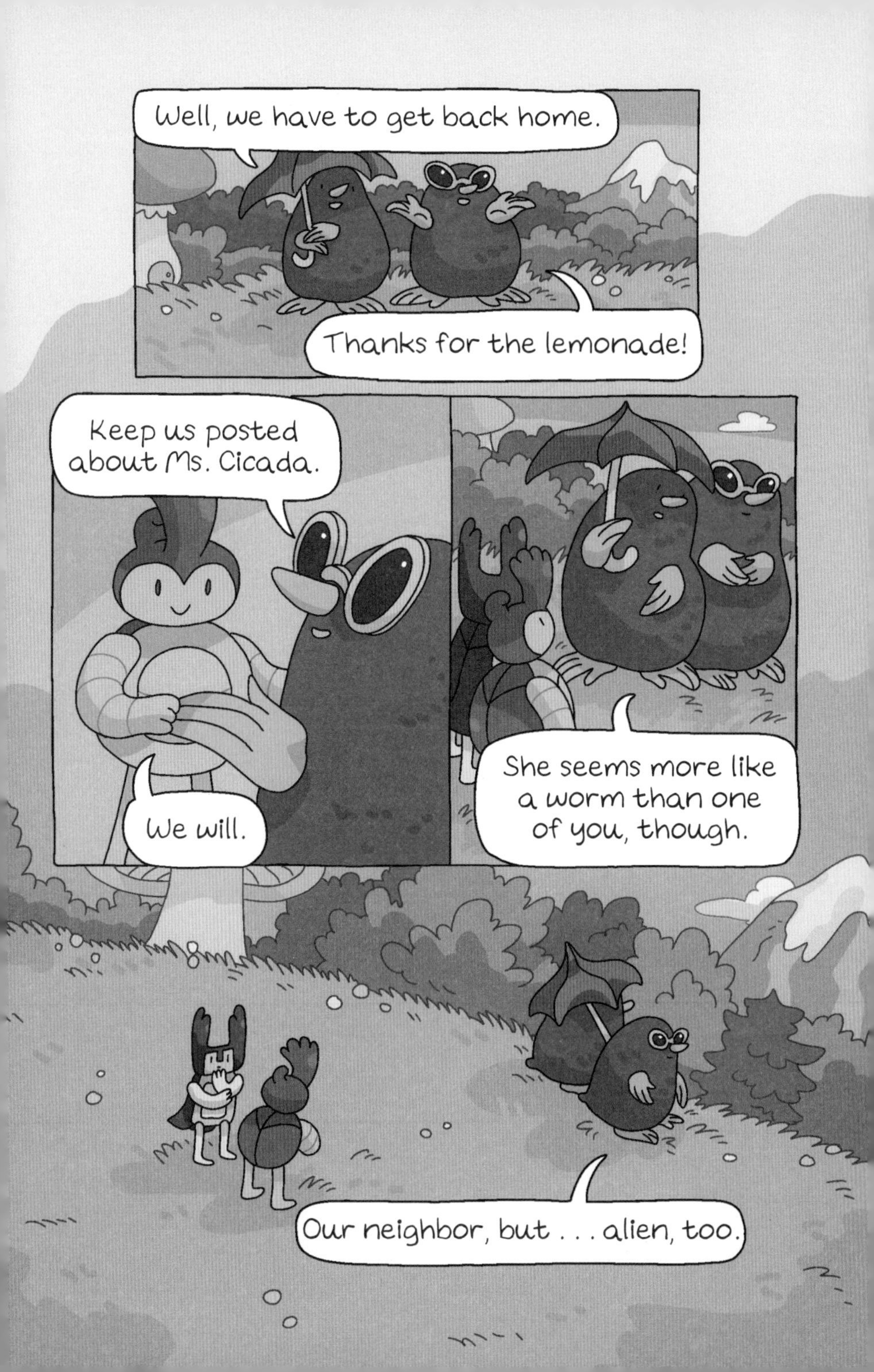

Well, we have to get back home.
Thanks for the lemonade!
Keep us posted about Ms. Cicada.
We will.
She seems more like a worm than one of you, though.
Our neighbor, but . . . alien, too.

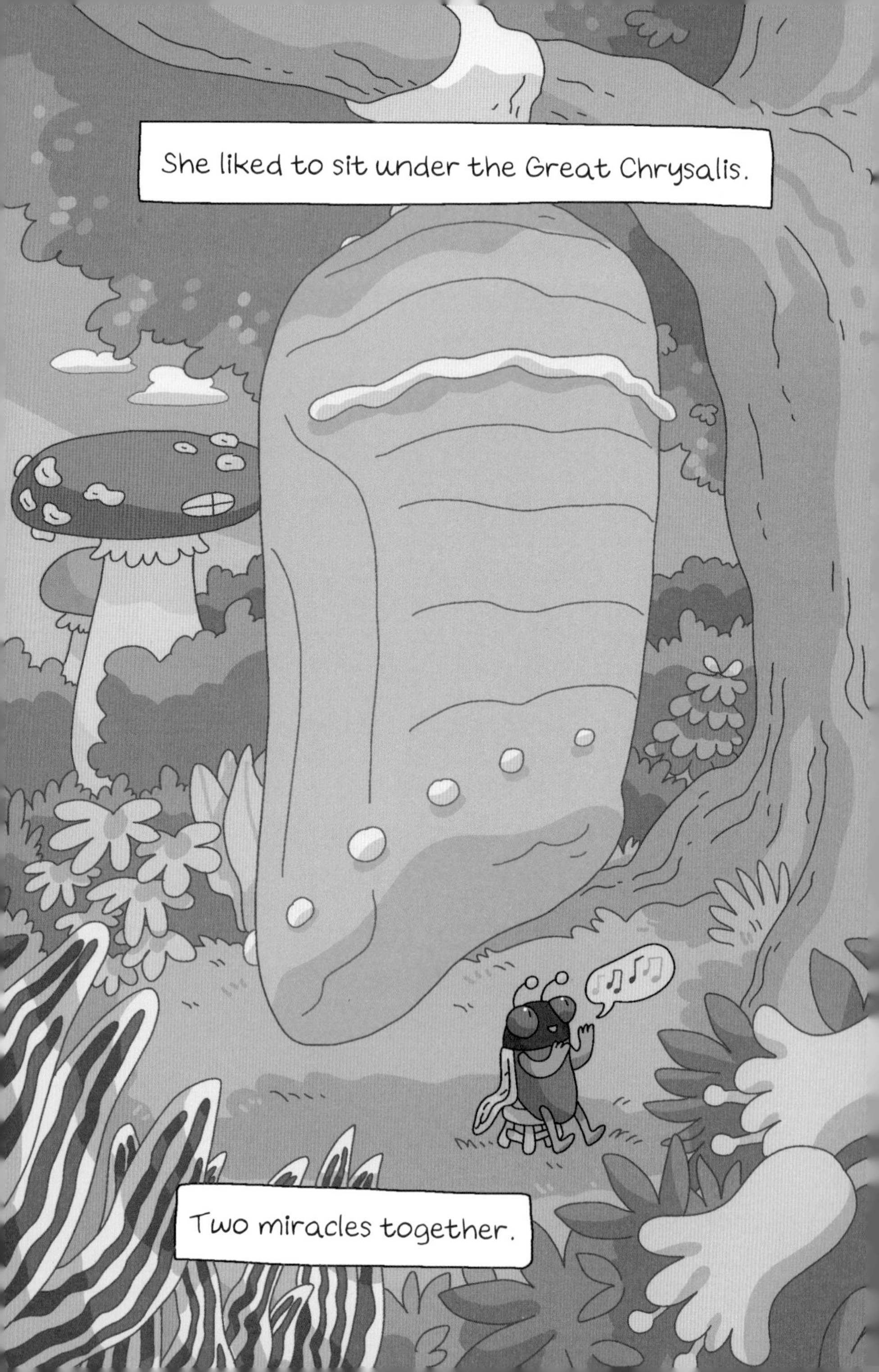
She liked to sit under the Great Chrysalis.
Two miracles together.

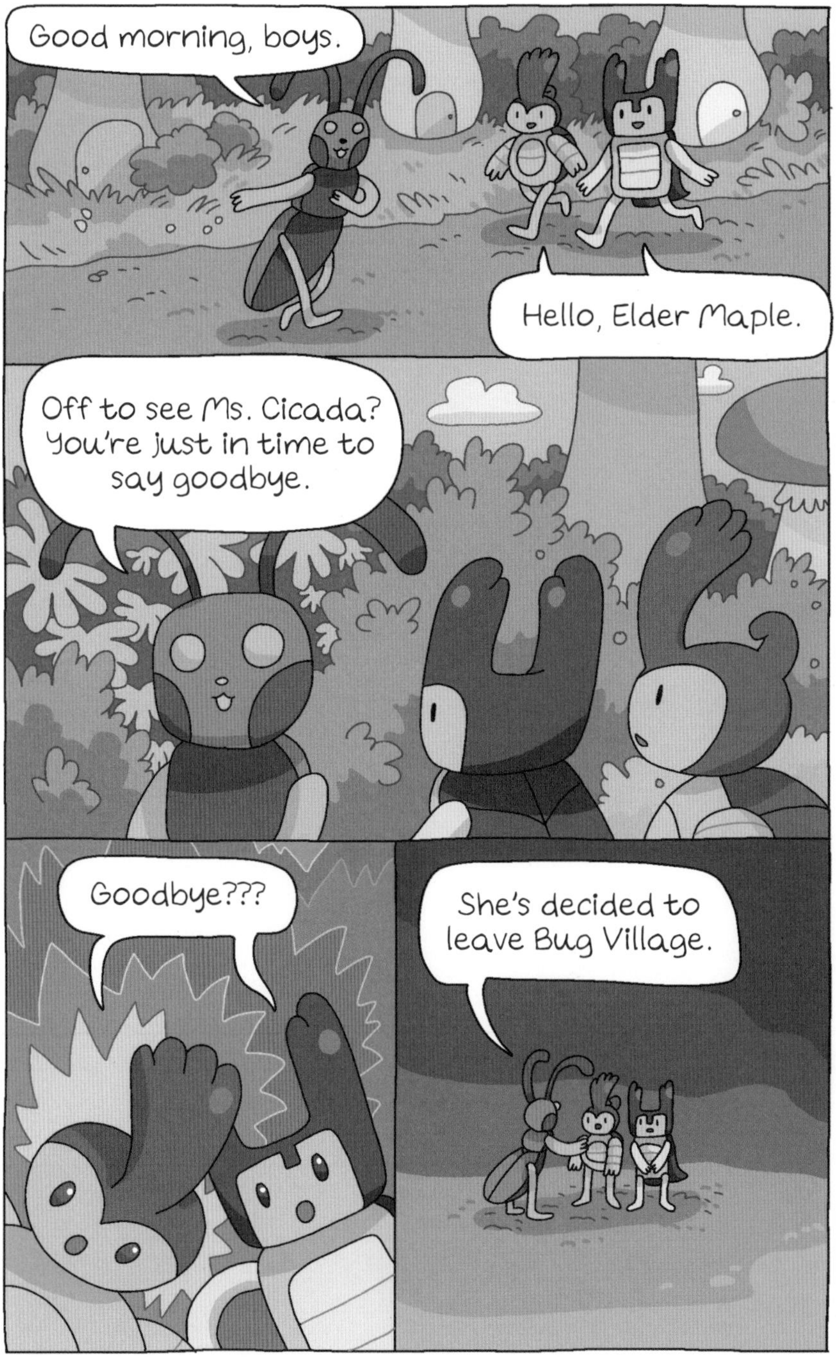
Good morning, boys.
Hello, Elder Maple.
Off to see Ms. Cicada? You're just in time to say goodbye.
Goodbye???
She's decided to leave Bug Village.

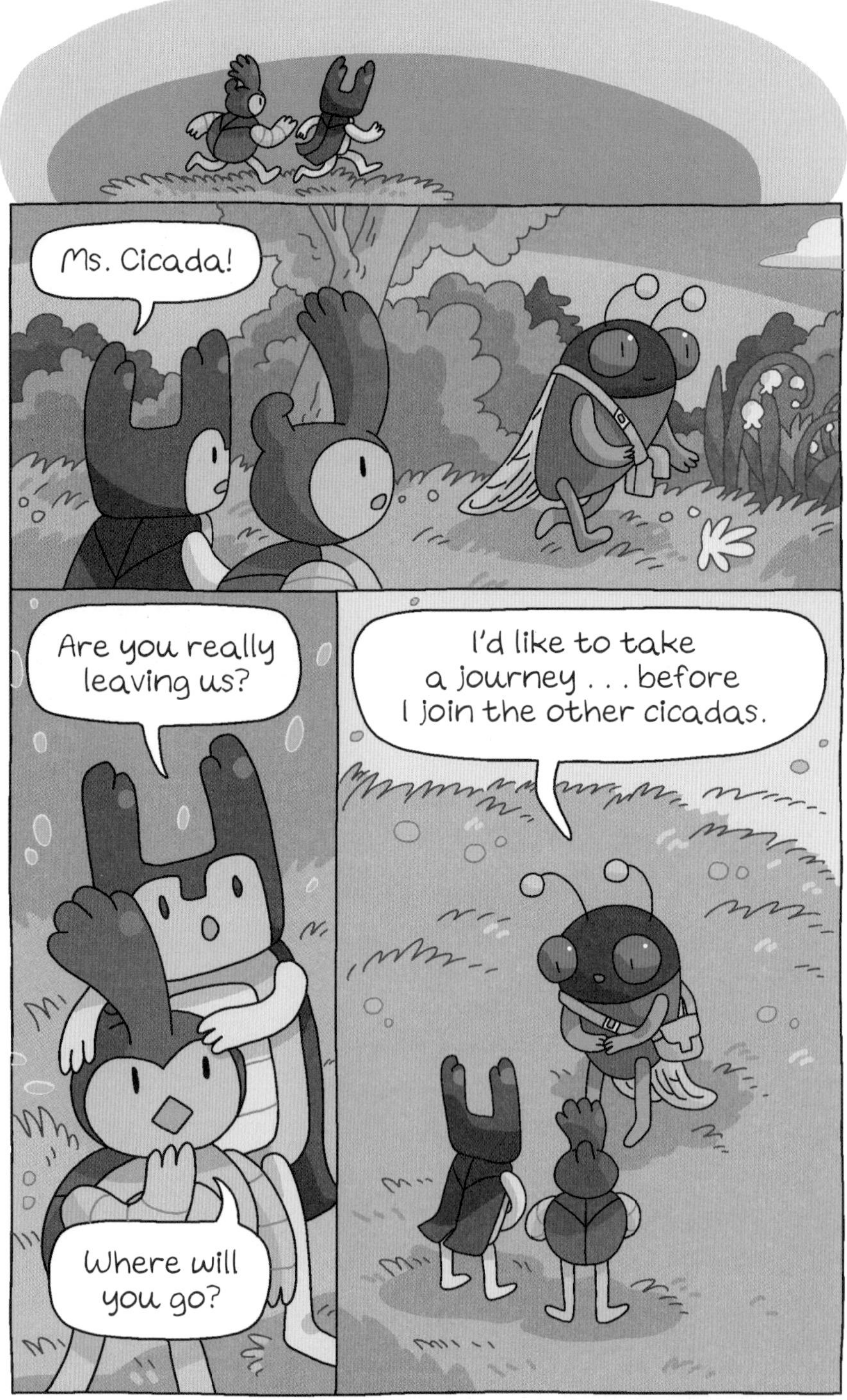
Ms. Cicada!
Are you really leaving us?
Where will you go?
I'd like to take a journey . . . before I join the other cicadas.

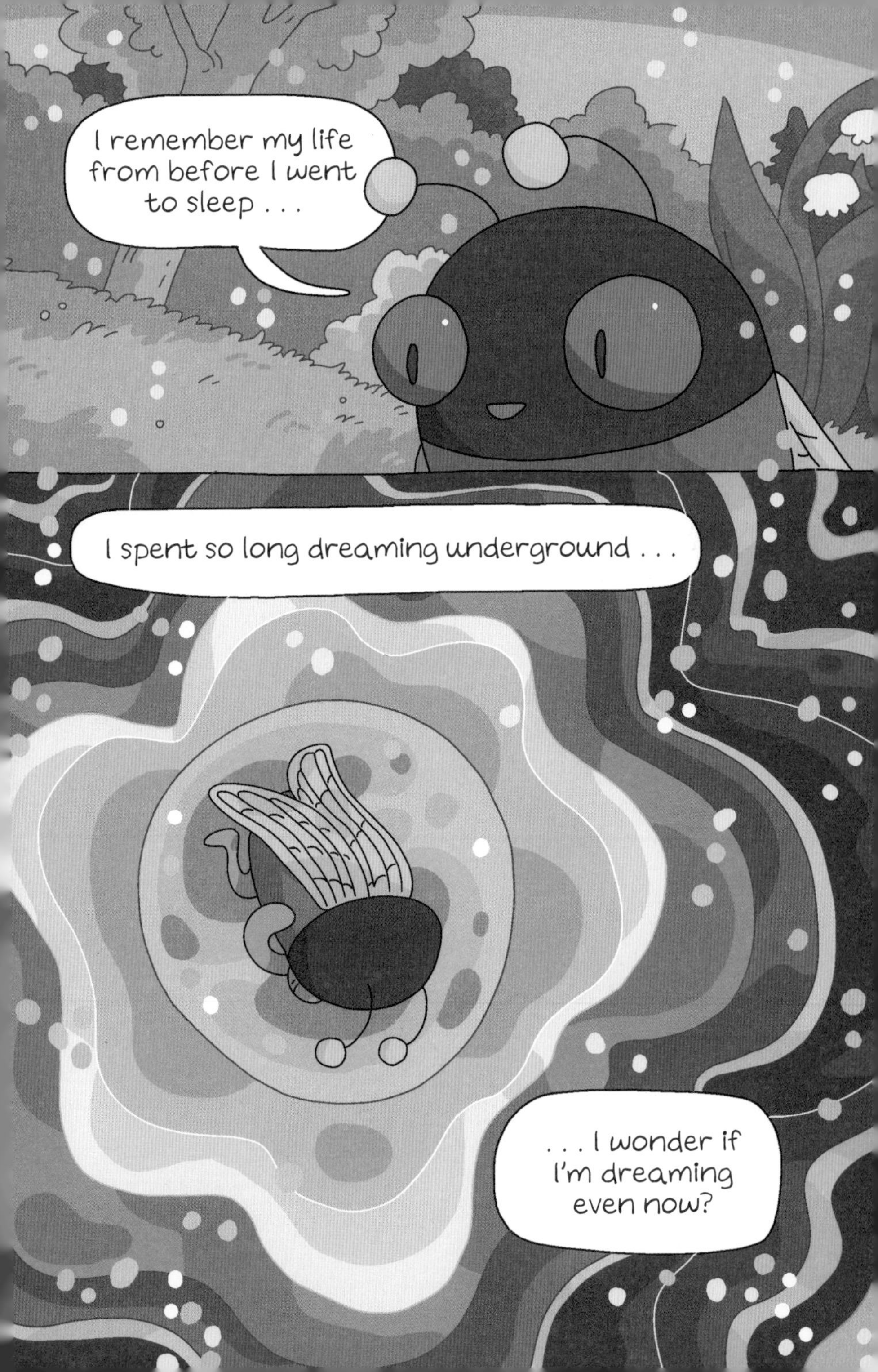
I remember my life from before I went to sleep . . .
I spent so long dreaming underground . . .
. . . I wonder if I'm dreaming even now?

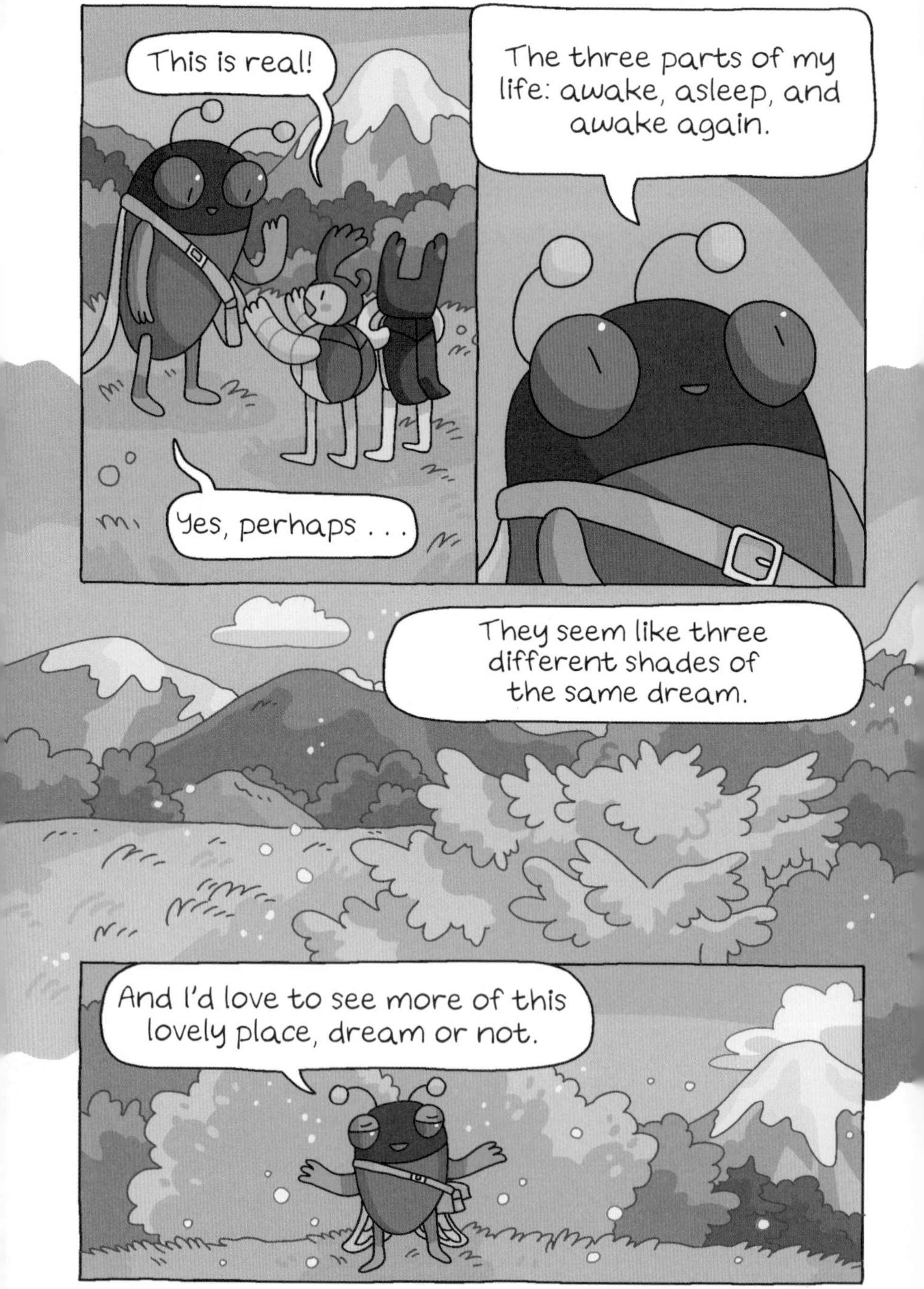
This is real!
Yes, perhaps . . .
The three parts of my life: awake, asleep, and awake again.
They seem like three different shades of the same dream.
And I'd love to see more of this lovely place, dream or not.

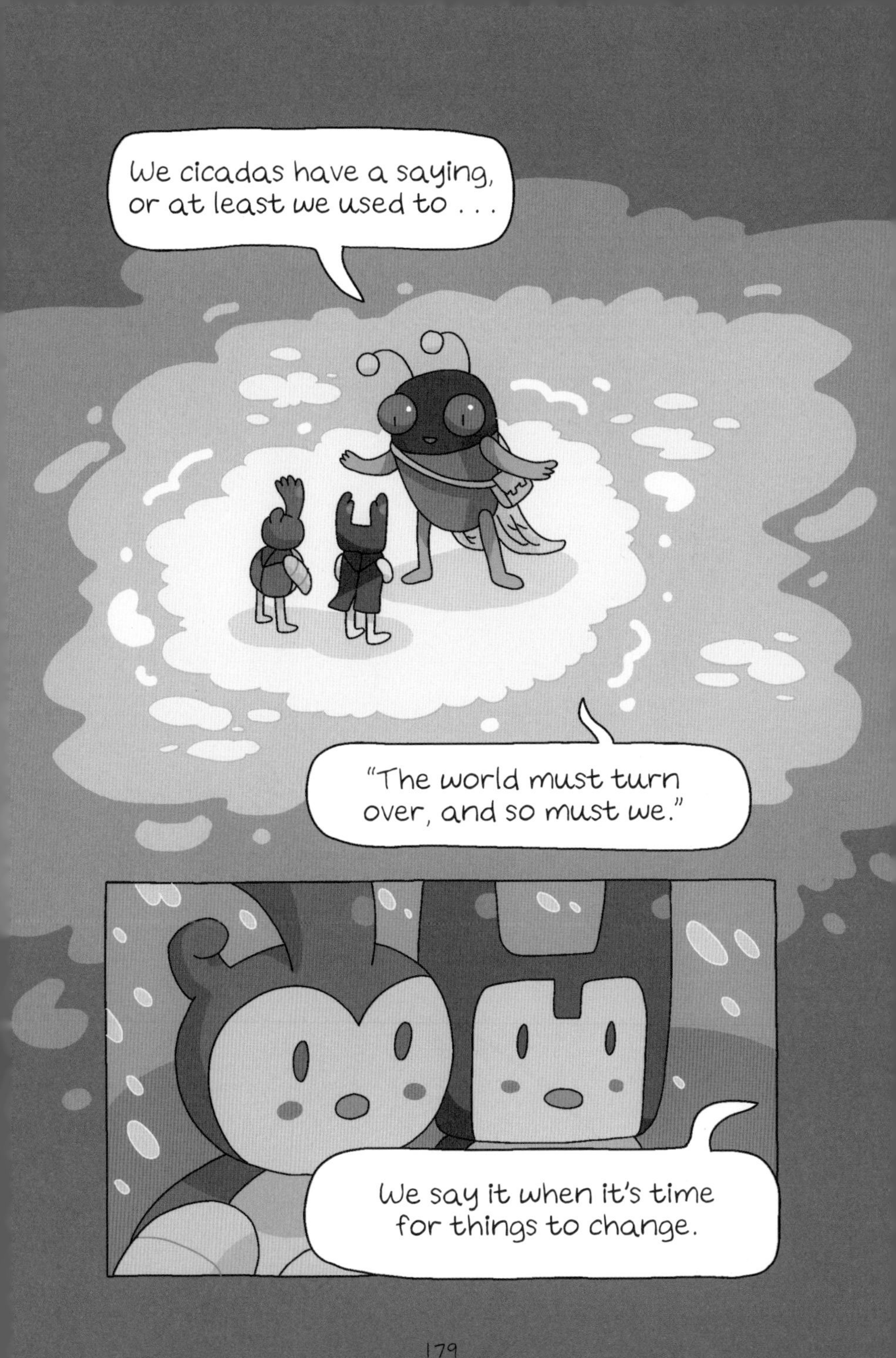
We cicadas have a saying, or at least we used to . . .
"The world must turn over, and so must we."
We say it when it's time for things to change.

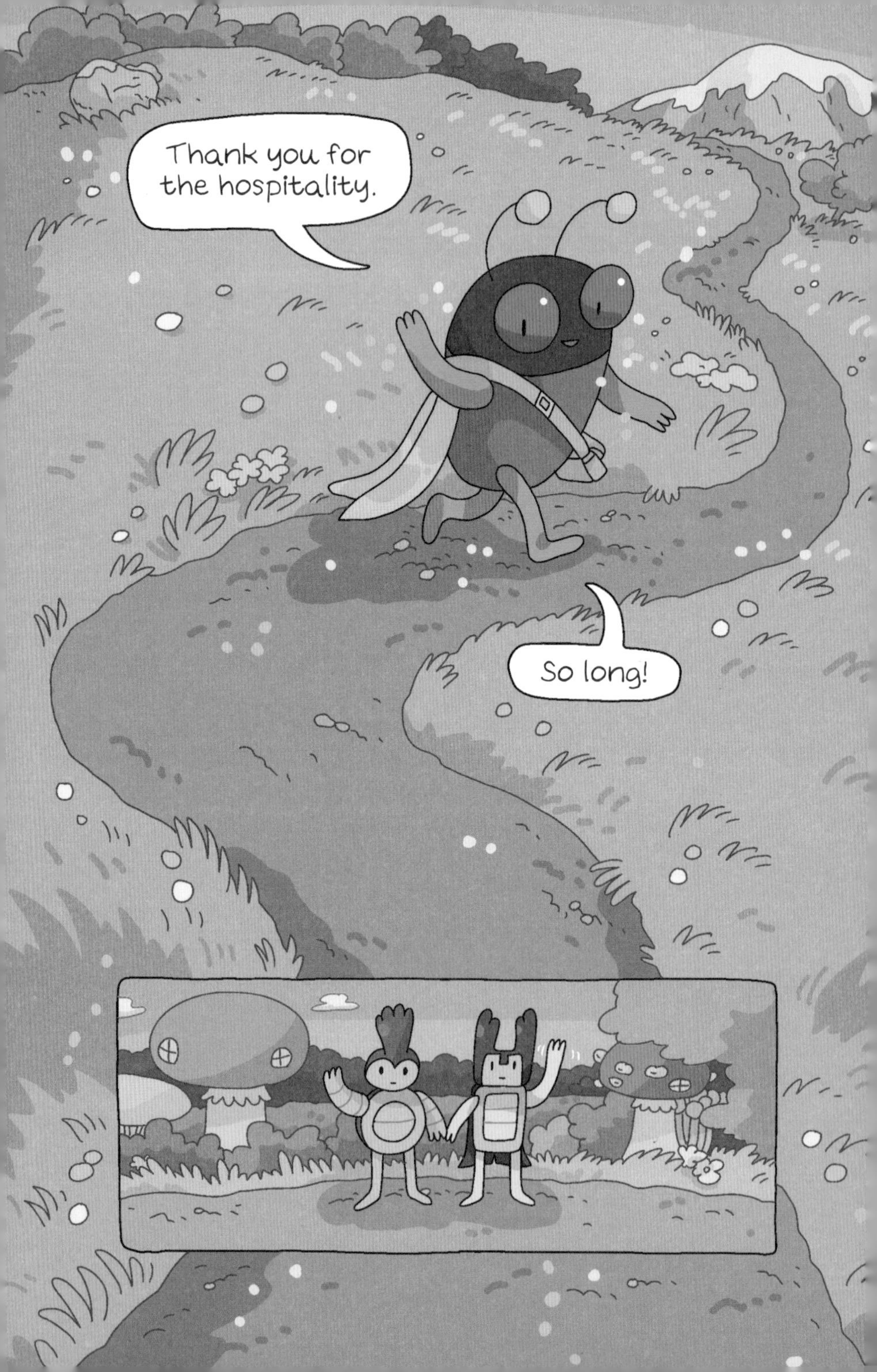
Thank you for the hospitality.
So long!

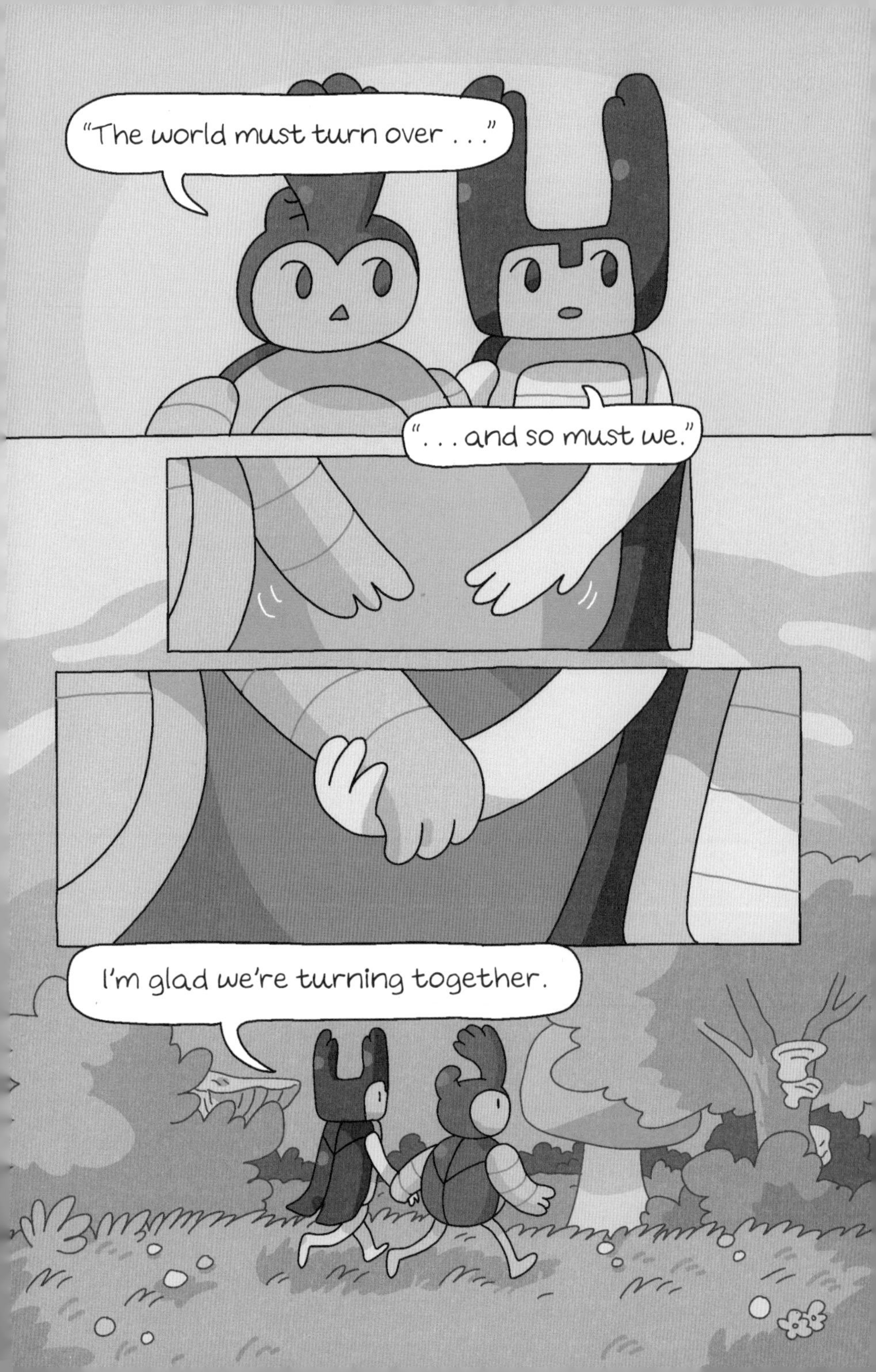
"The world must turn over . . ."
". . . and so must we."
I'm glad we're turning together.

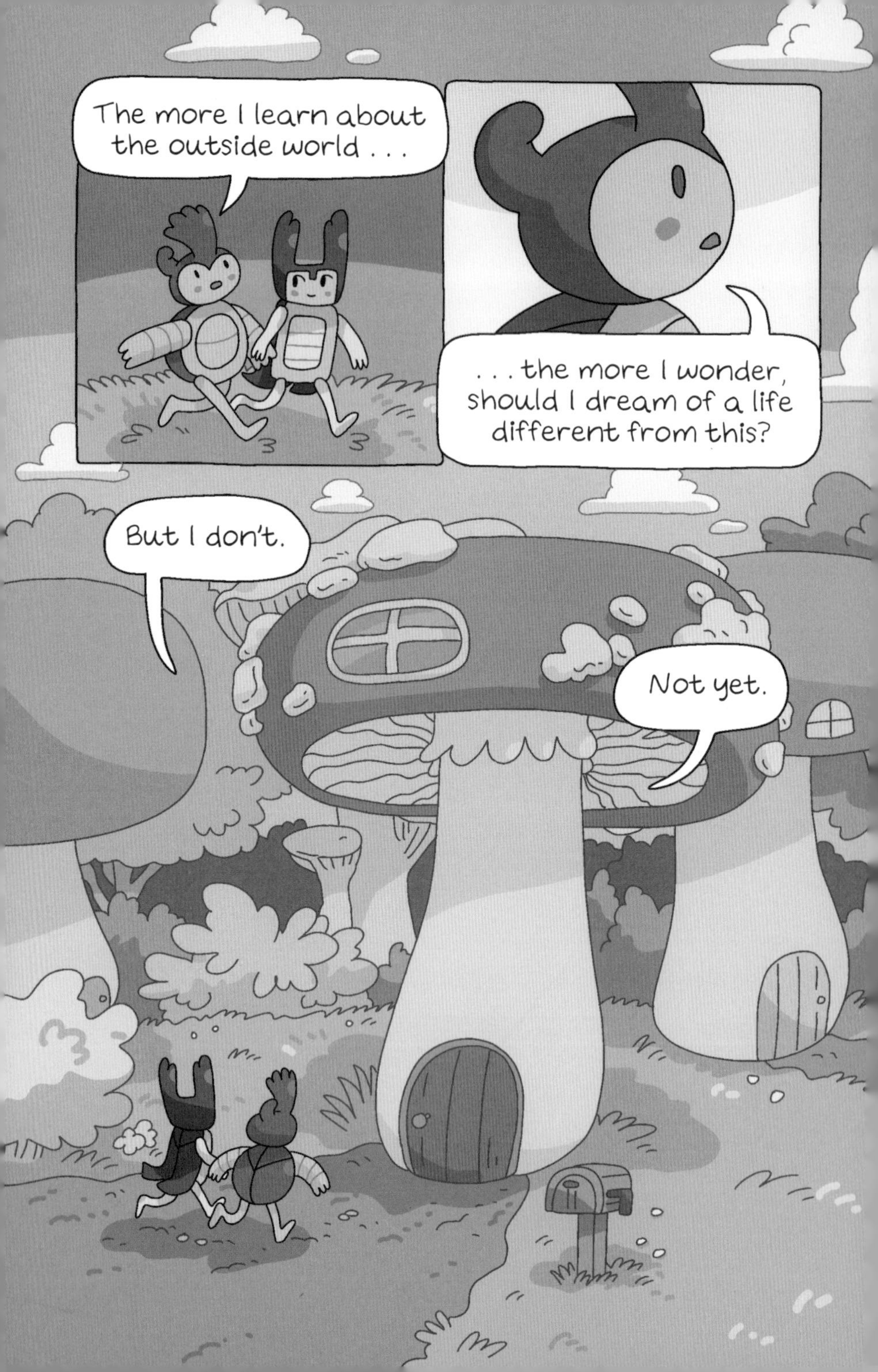
The more I learn about the outside world . . .
. . . the more I wonder, should I dream of a life different from this?
But I don't.
Not yet.

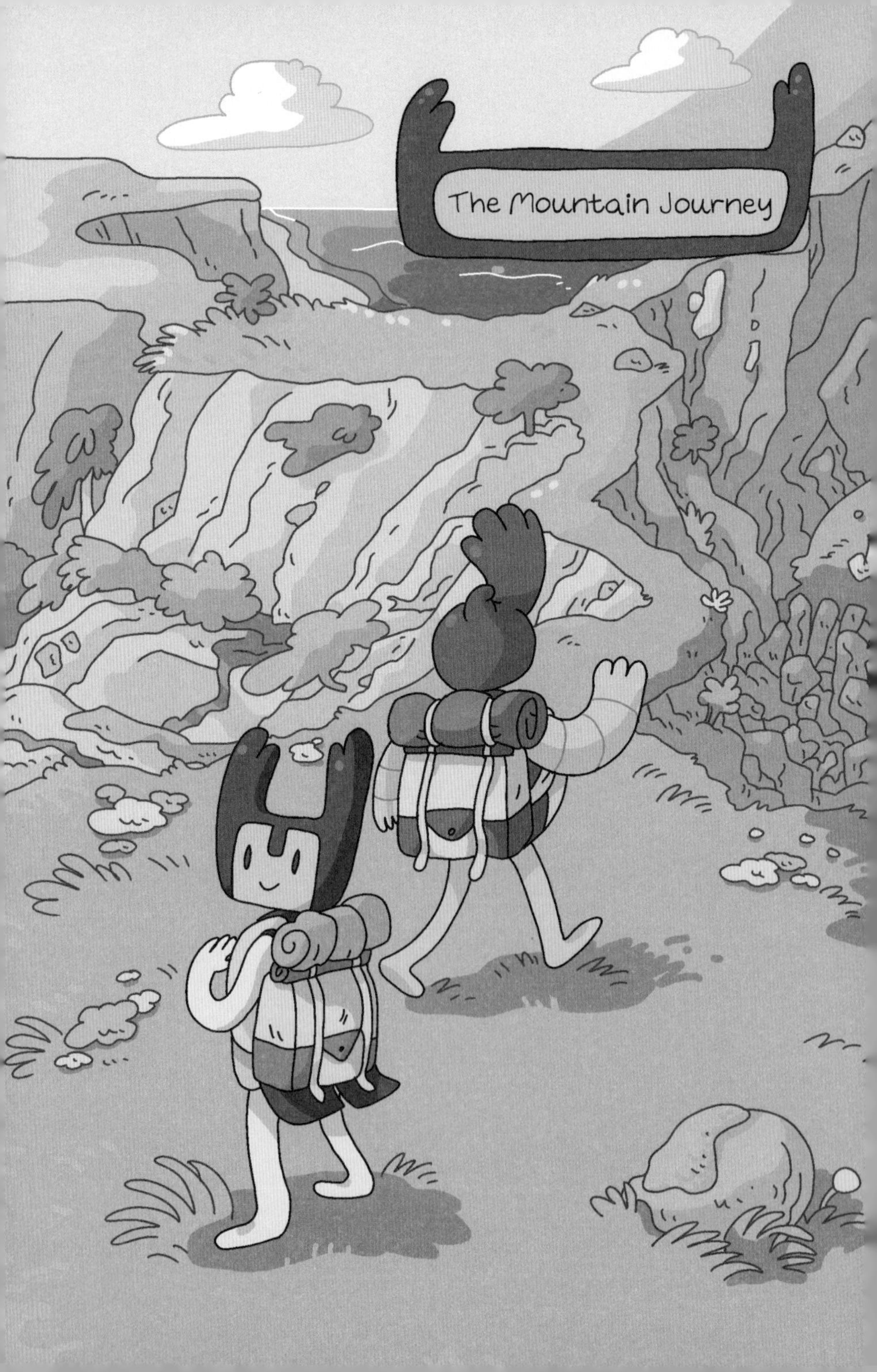
The Mountain Journey

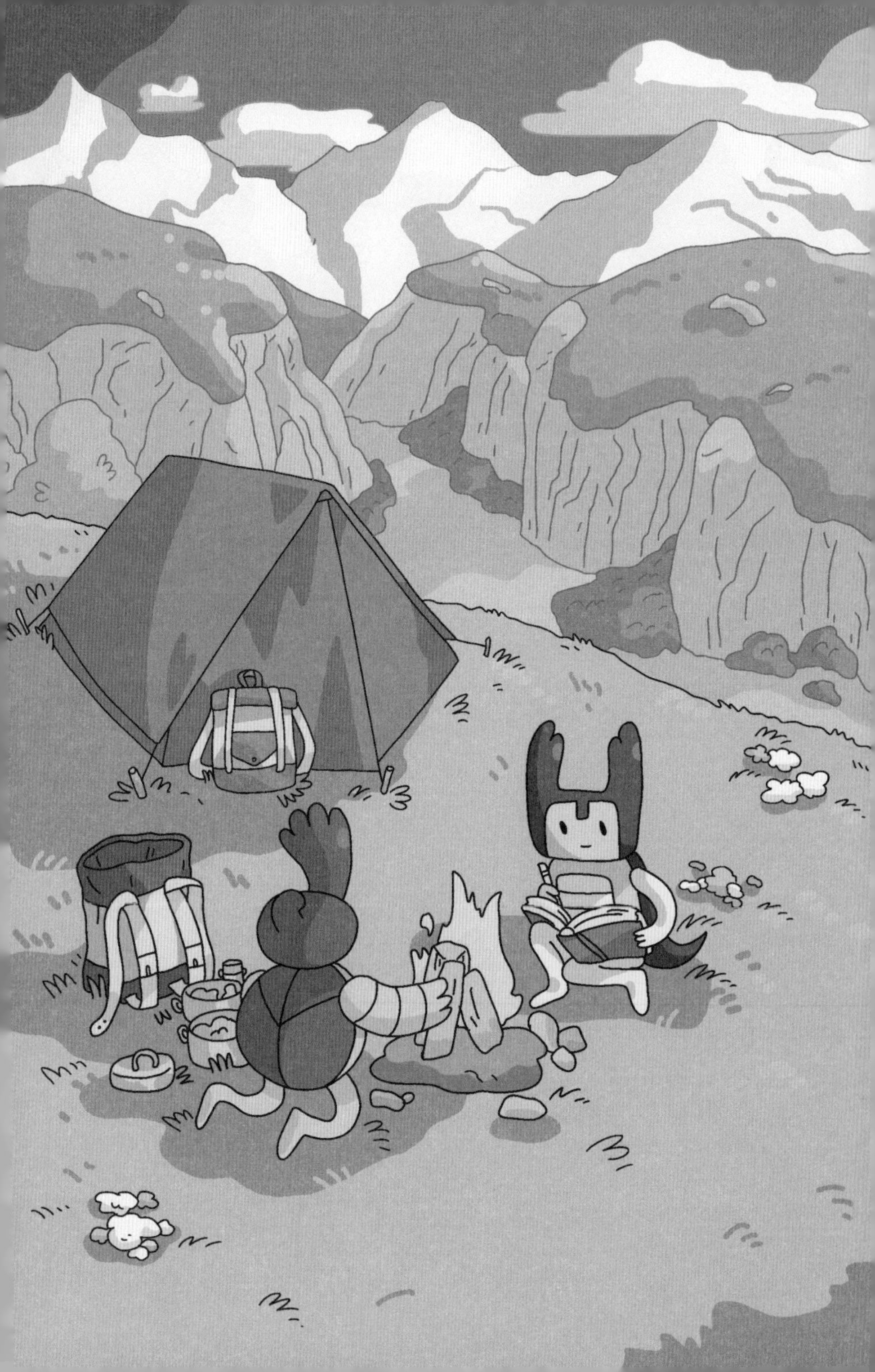

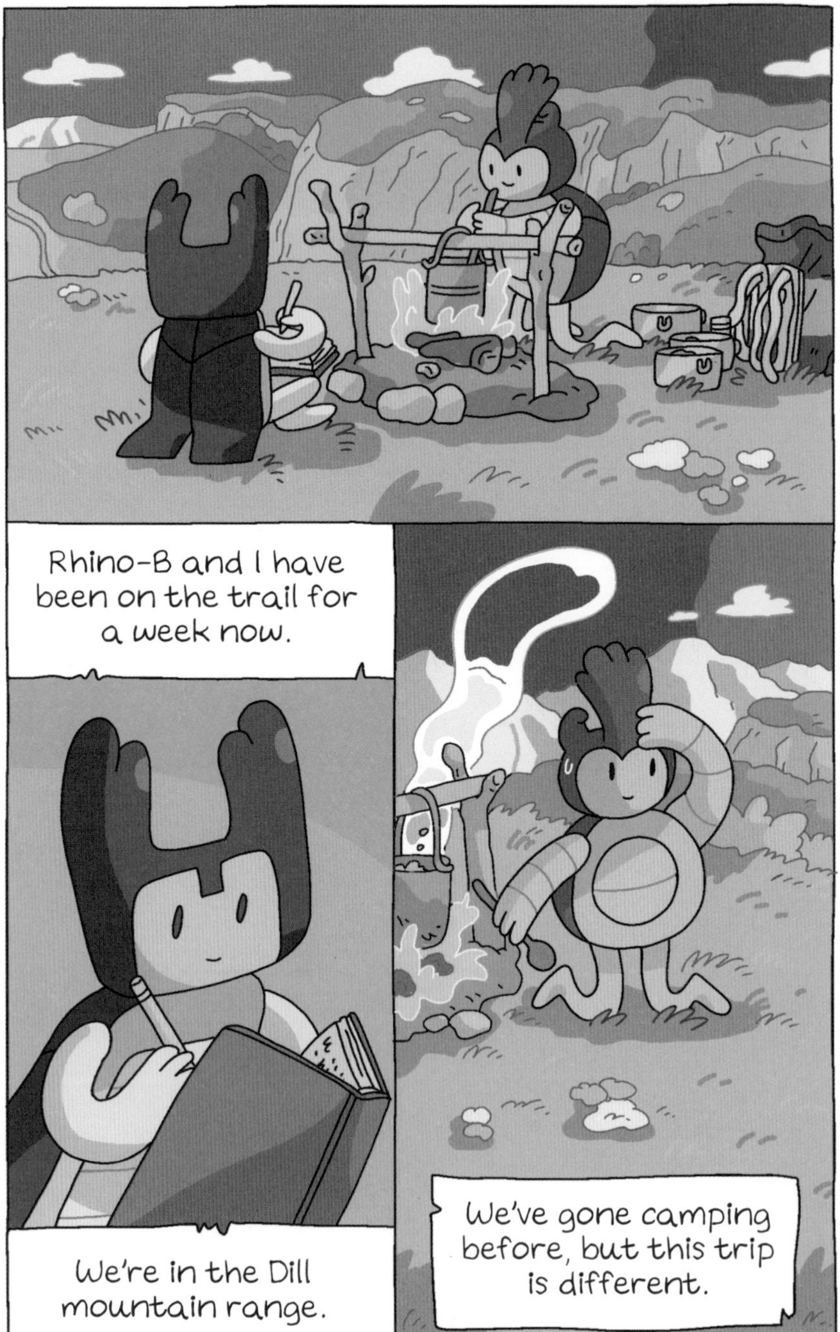
Rhino-B and I have been on the trail for a week now.
We're in the Dill mountain range.
We've gone camping before, but this trip is different.

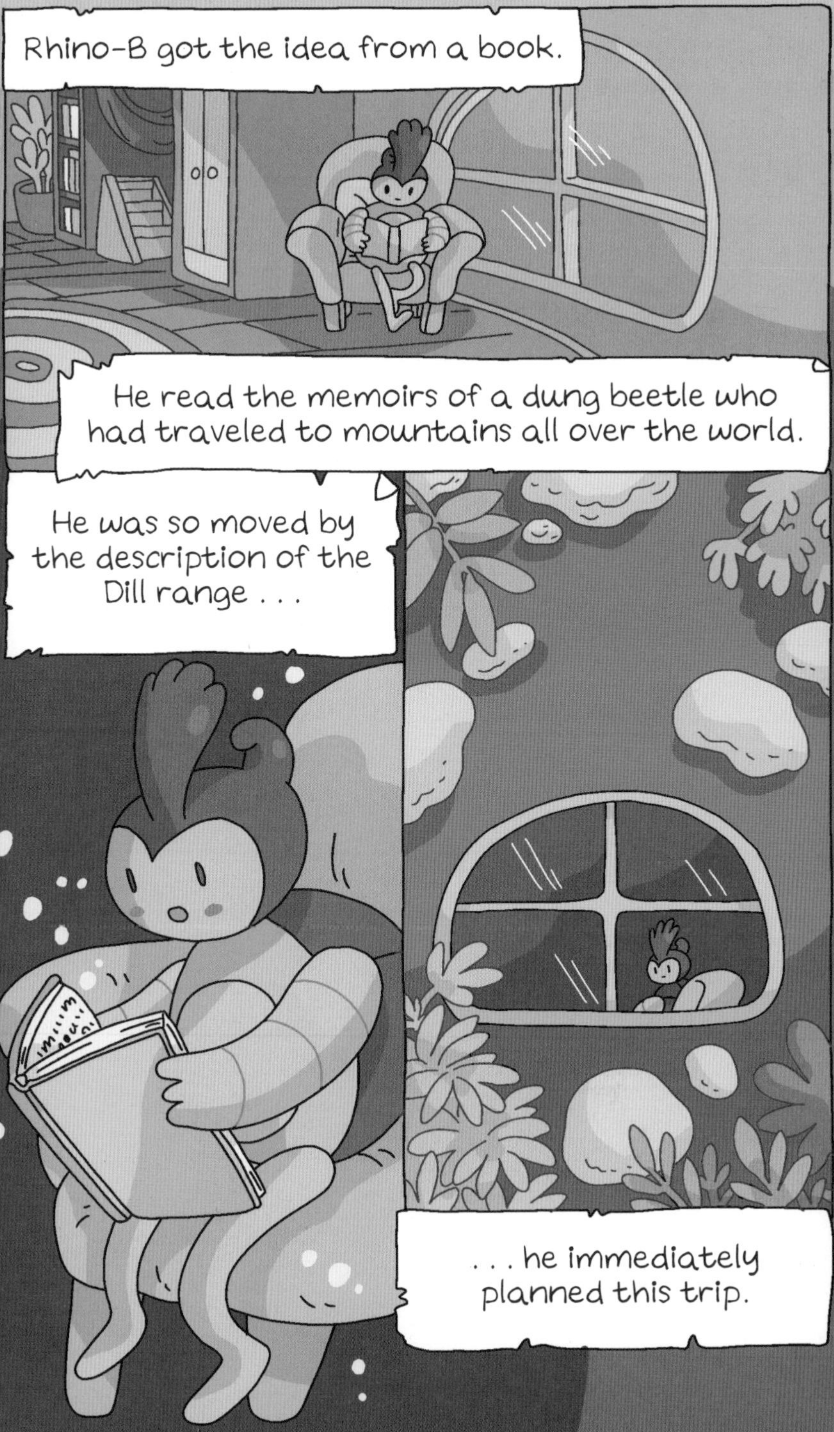
Rhino-B got the idea from a book.
He read the memoirs of a dung beetle who had traveled to mountains all over the world.
He was so moved by the description of the Dill range . . .
. . . he immediately planned this trip.

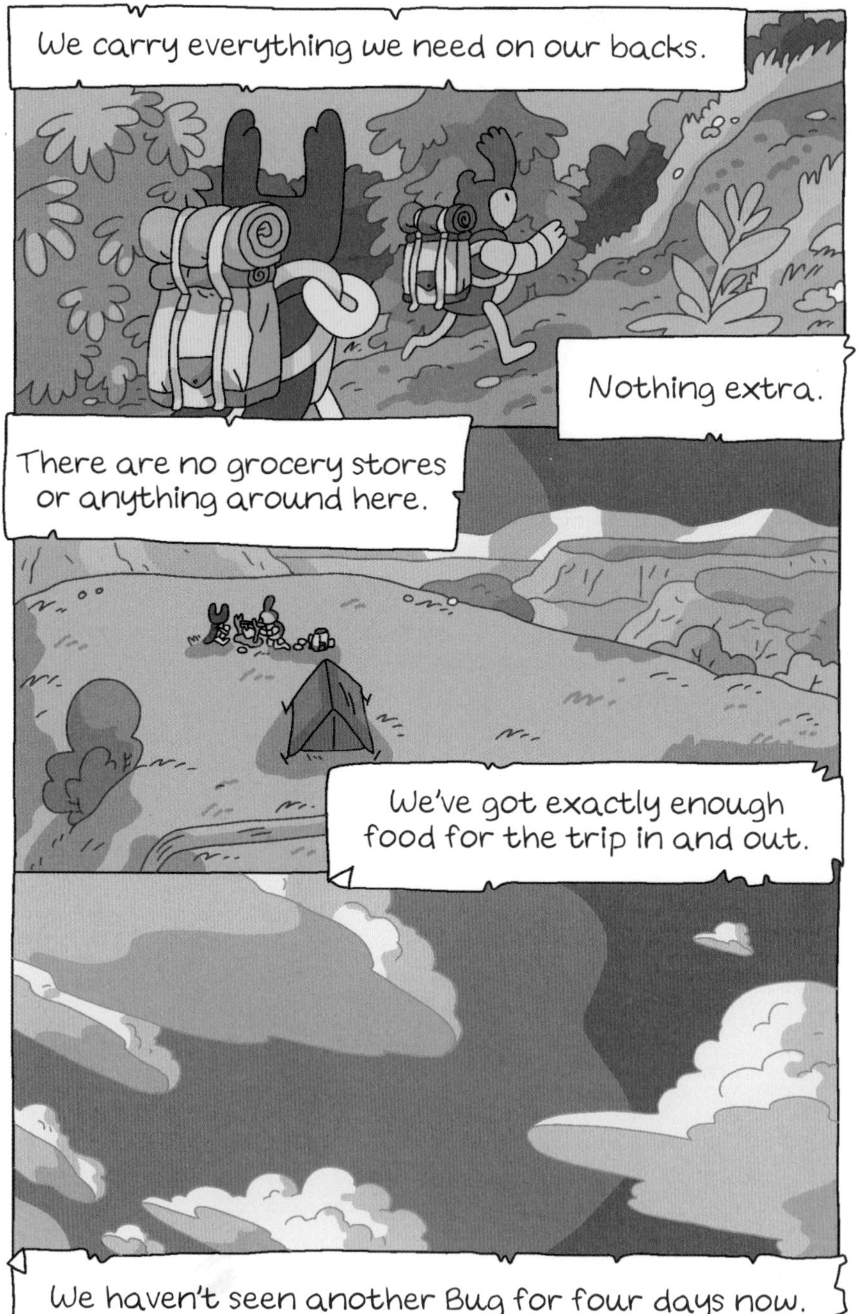
We carry everything we need on our backs.
Nothing extra.
There are no grocery stores or anything around here.
We've got exactly enough food for the trip in and out.
We haven't seen another Bug for four days now.

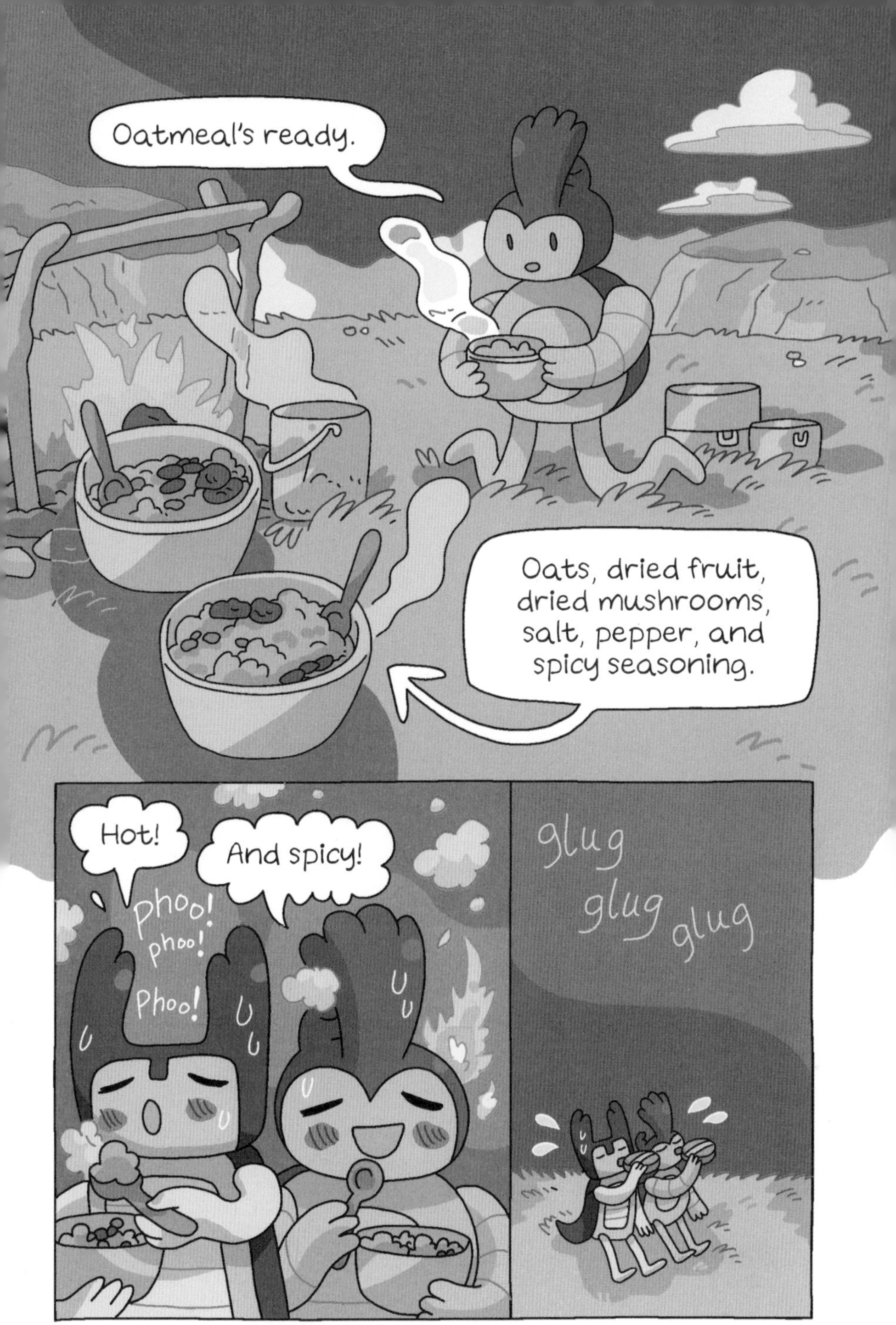
Oatmeal's ready.
Oats, dried fruit, dried mushrooms, salt, pepper, and spicy seasoning.
Hot!
And spicy!
phoo! phoo! Phoo!
glug glug glug

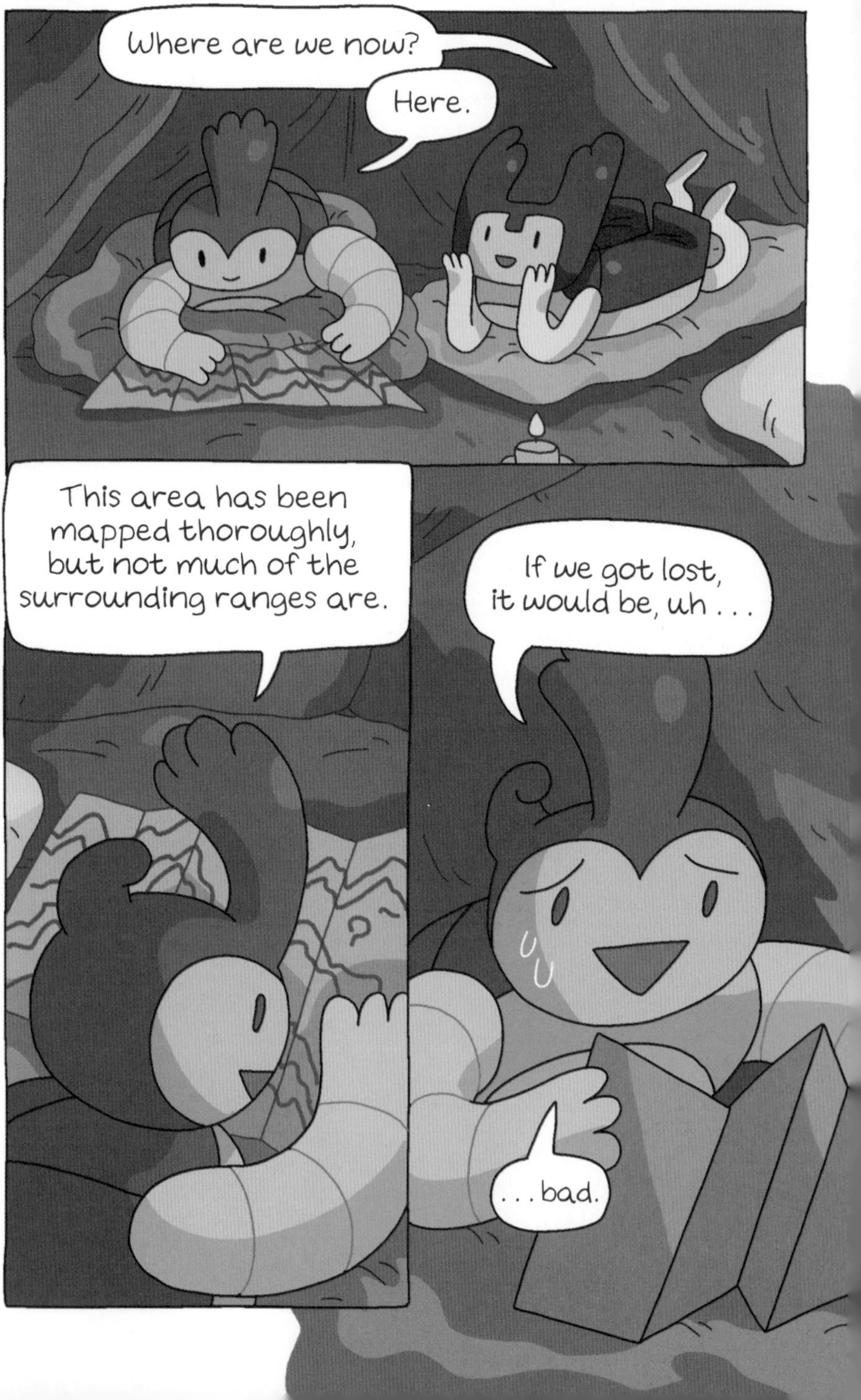
Where are we now?
Here.
This area has been mapped thoroughly, but not much of the surrounding ranges are.
If we got lost, it would be, uh . . .
. . . bad.

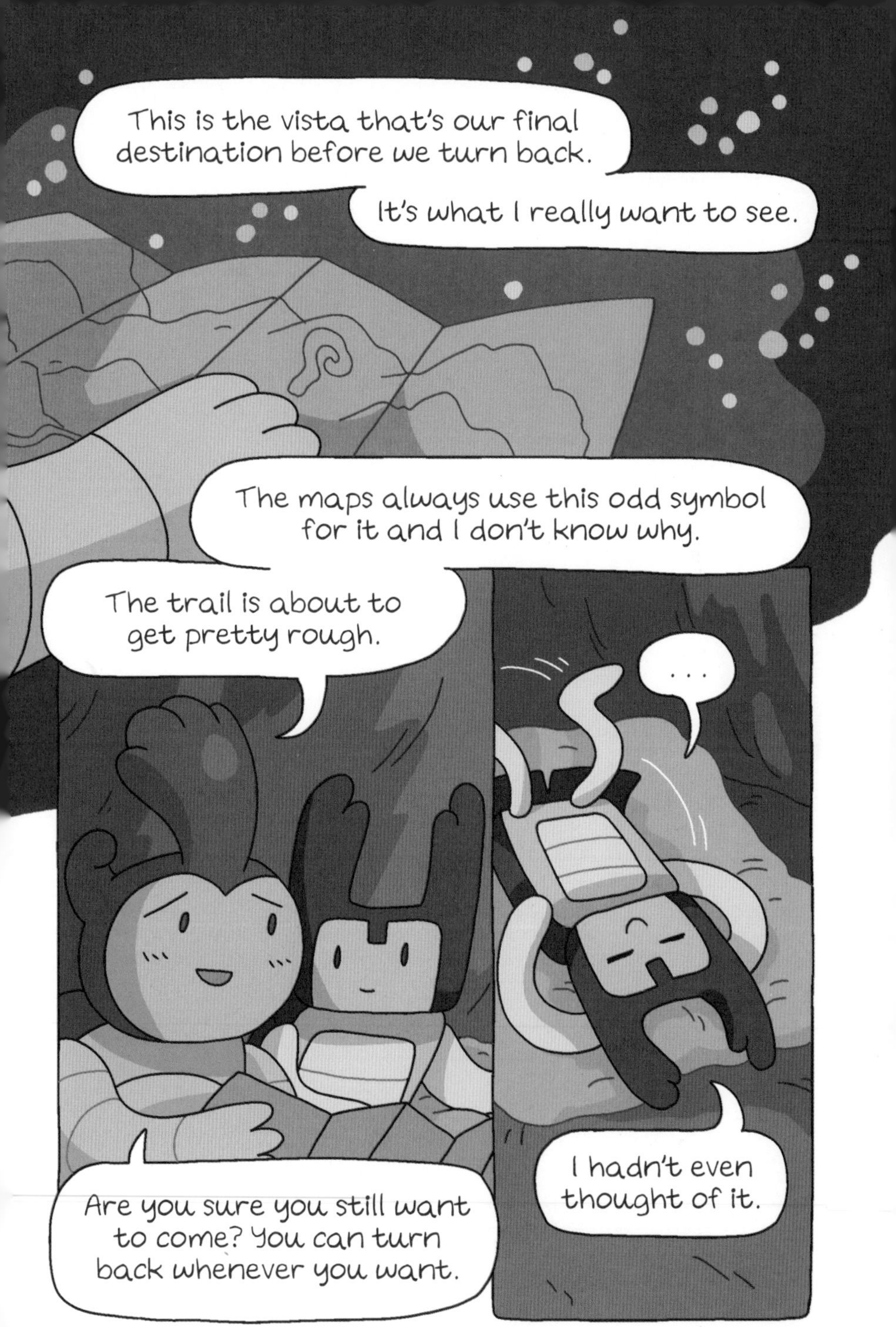

This is the vista that's our final destination before we turn back.
It's what I really want to see.
The maps always use this odd symbol for it and I don't know why.
The trail is about to get pretty rough.
. . .
Are you sure you still want to come? You can turn back whenever you want.
I hadn't even thought of it.

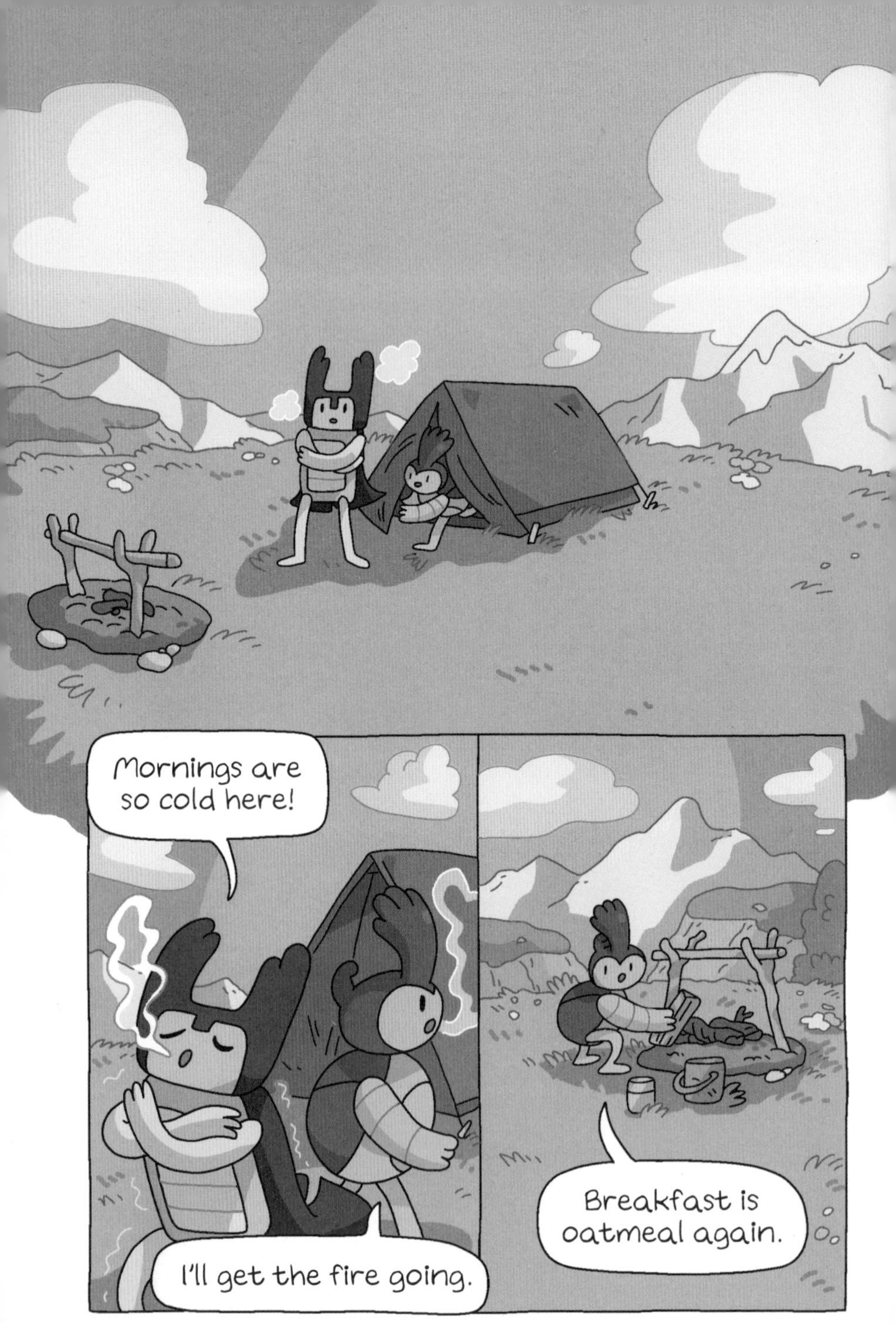
Mornings are so cold here!
I'll get the fire going.
Breakfast is oatmeal again.

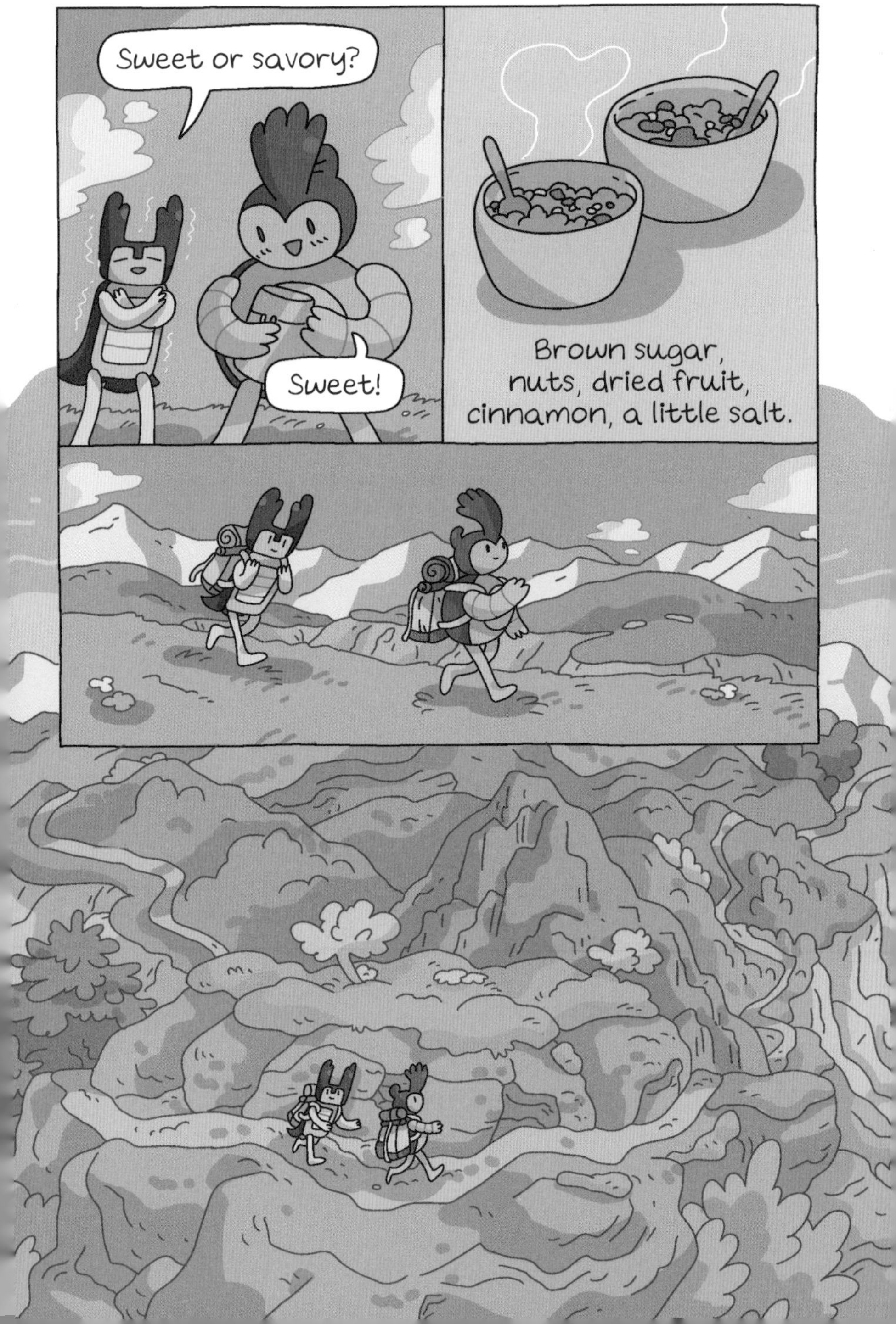
Sweet or savory?
Sweet!
Brown sugar, nuts, dried fruit, cinnamon, a little salt.

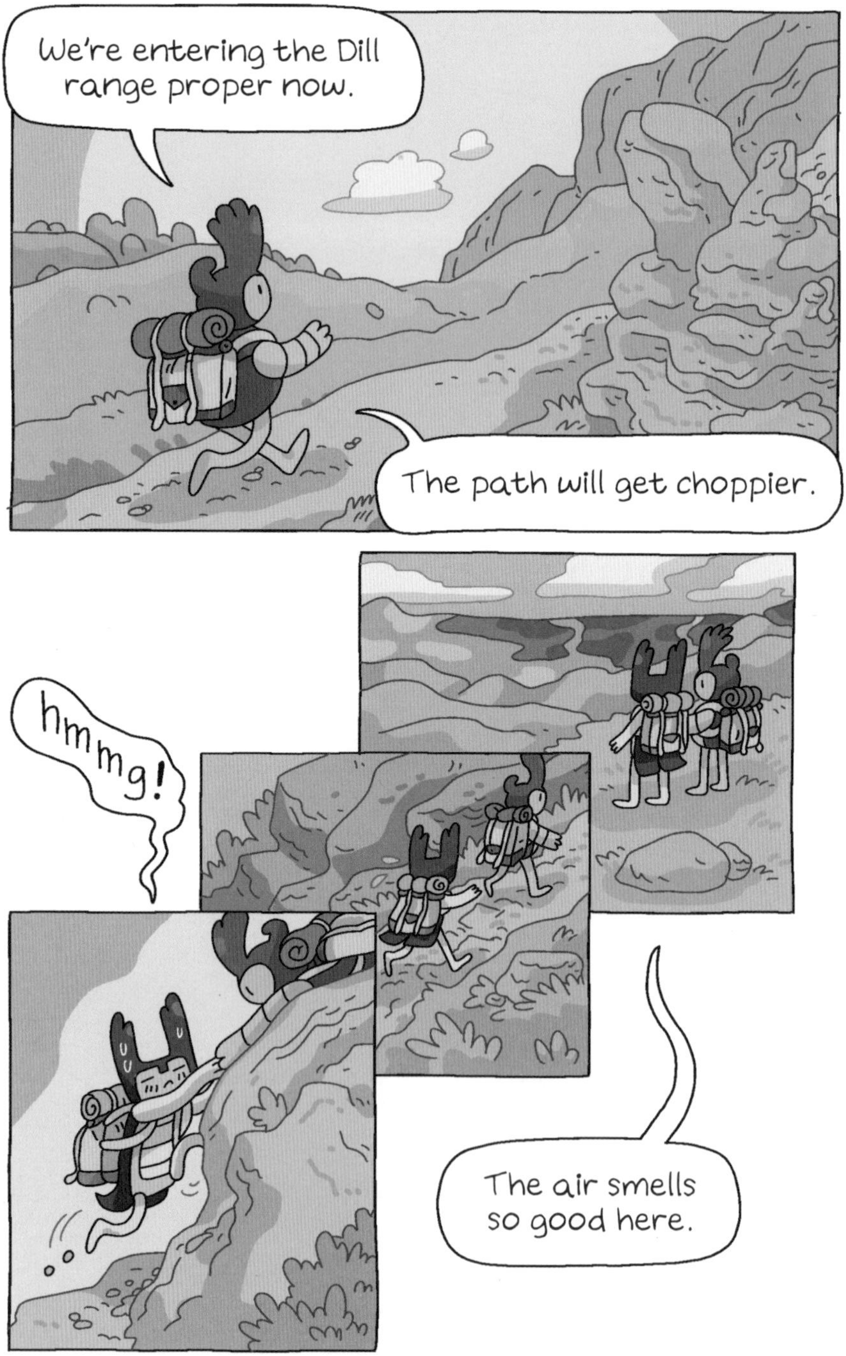
We're entering the Dill range proper now.
The path will get choppier.
hmmg!
The air smells so good here.

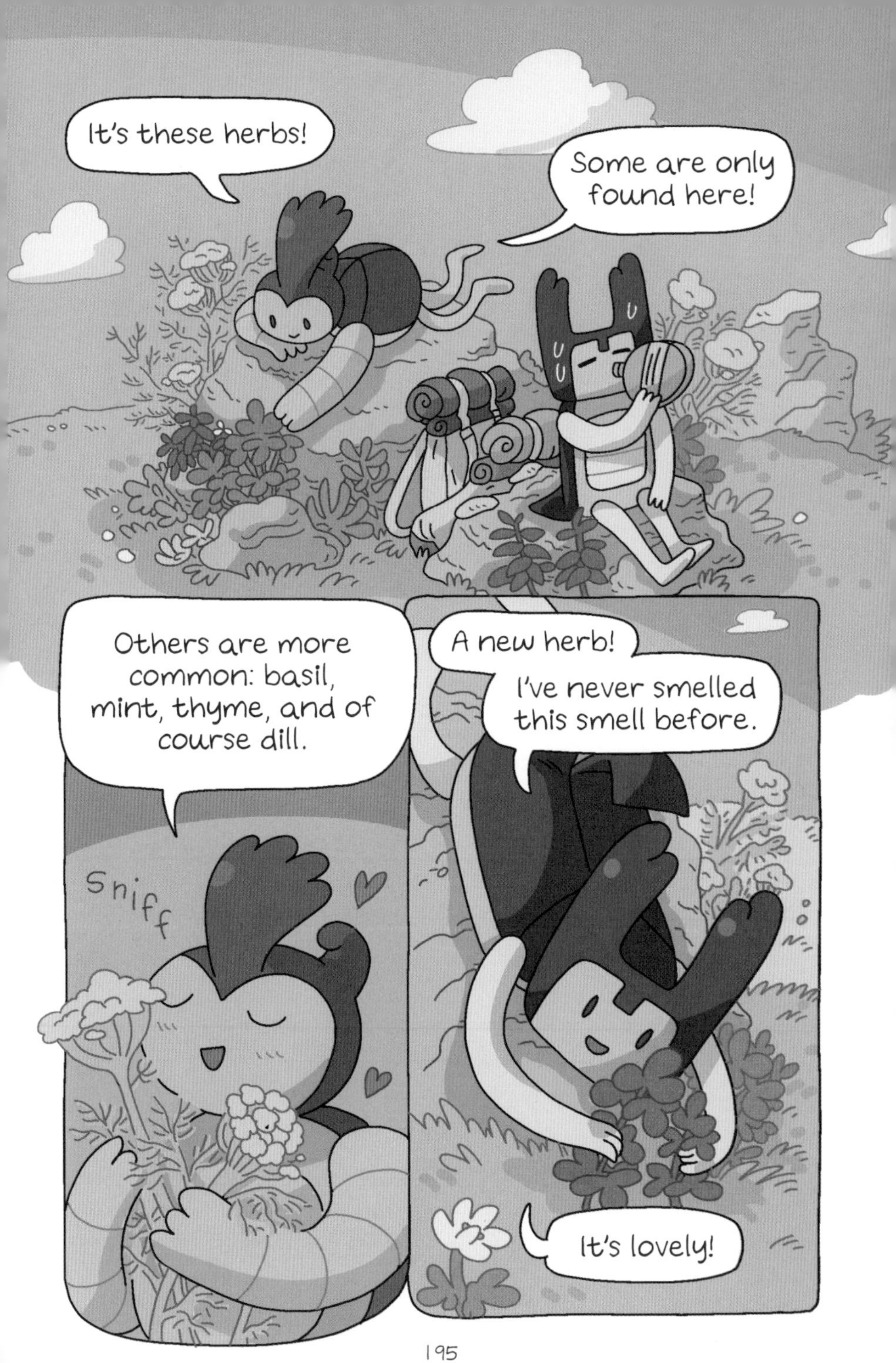
It's these herbs!
Some are only found here!
Others are more common: basil, mint, thyme, and of course dill.
Sniff
A new herb!
I've never smelled this smell before.
It's lovely!

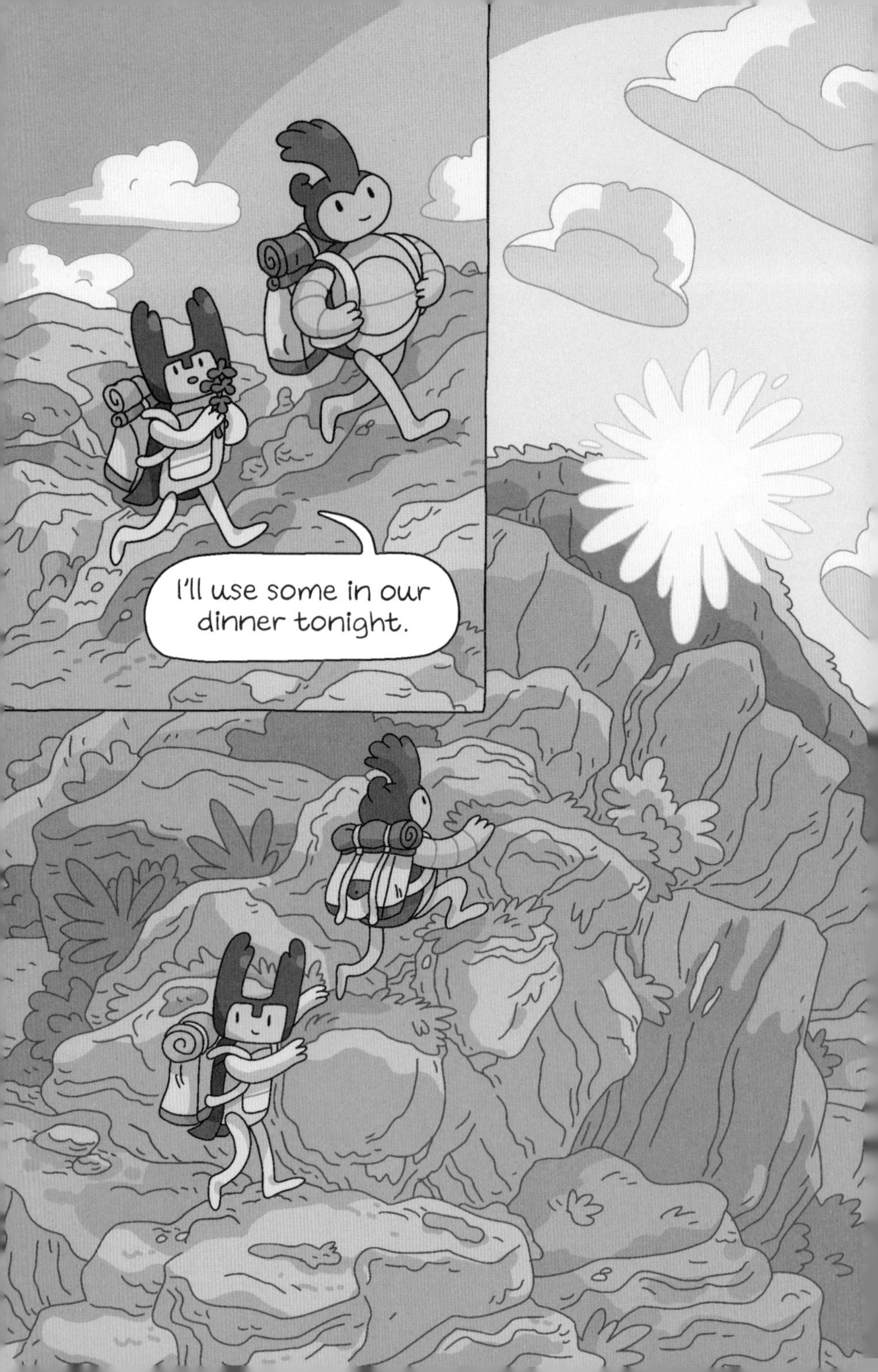
I'll use some in our dinner tonight.

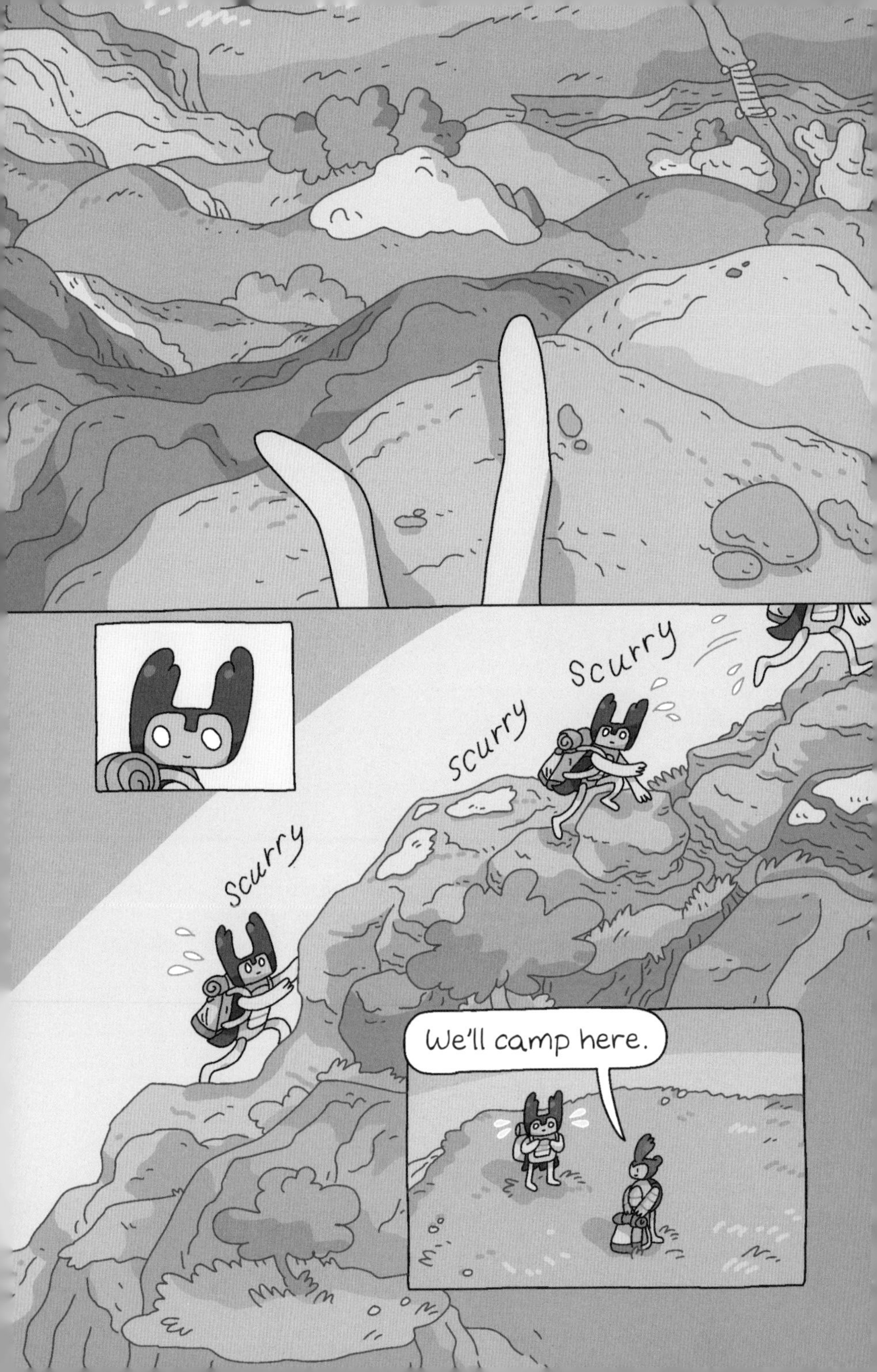
Scurry
scurry
Scurry
We'll camp here.

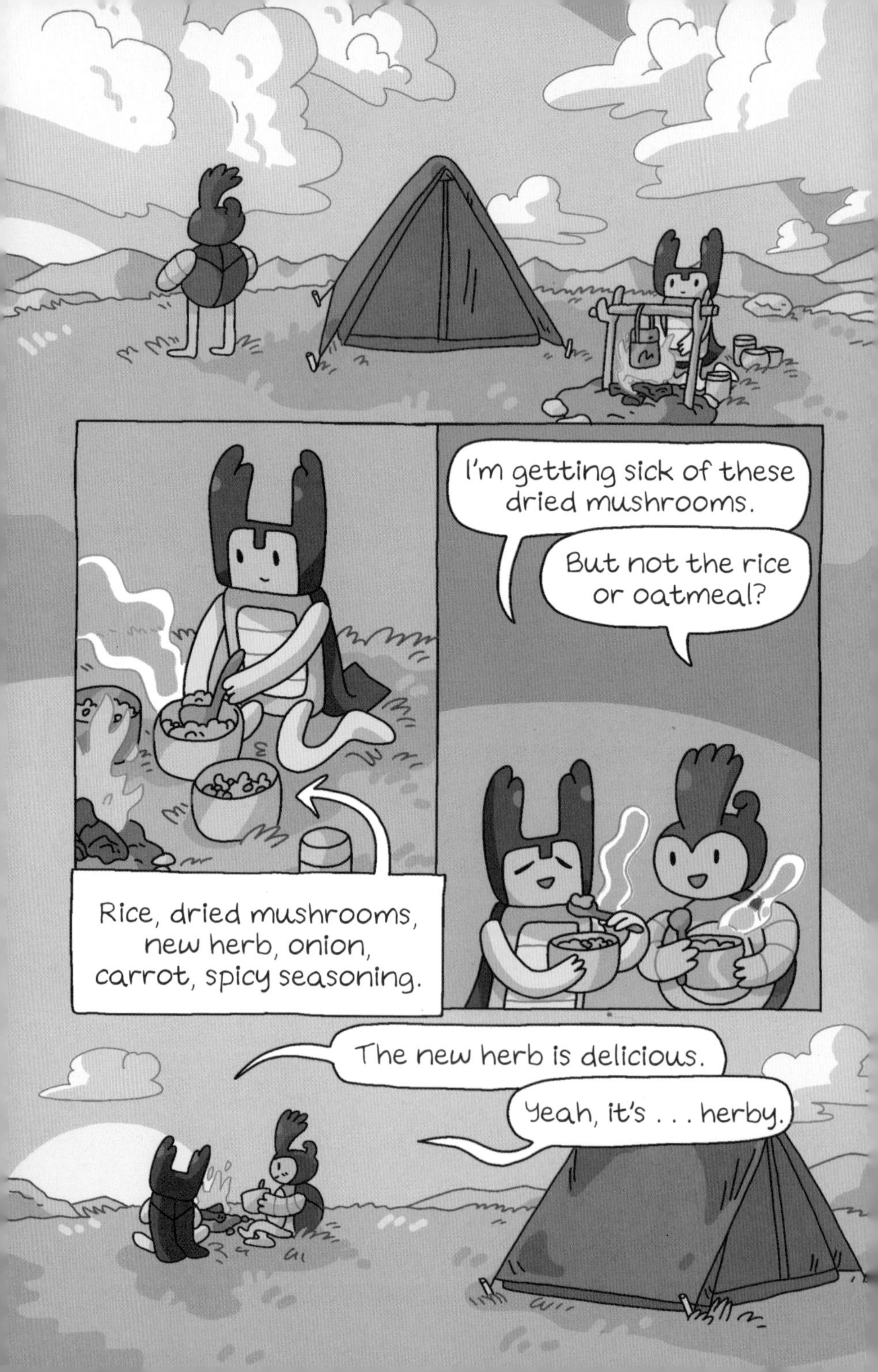

I'm getting sick of these dried mushrooms.
But not the rice or oatmeal?
Rice, dried mushrooms, new herb, onion, carrot, spicy seasoning.
The new herb is delicious.
Yeah, it's . . . herby.

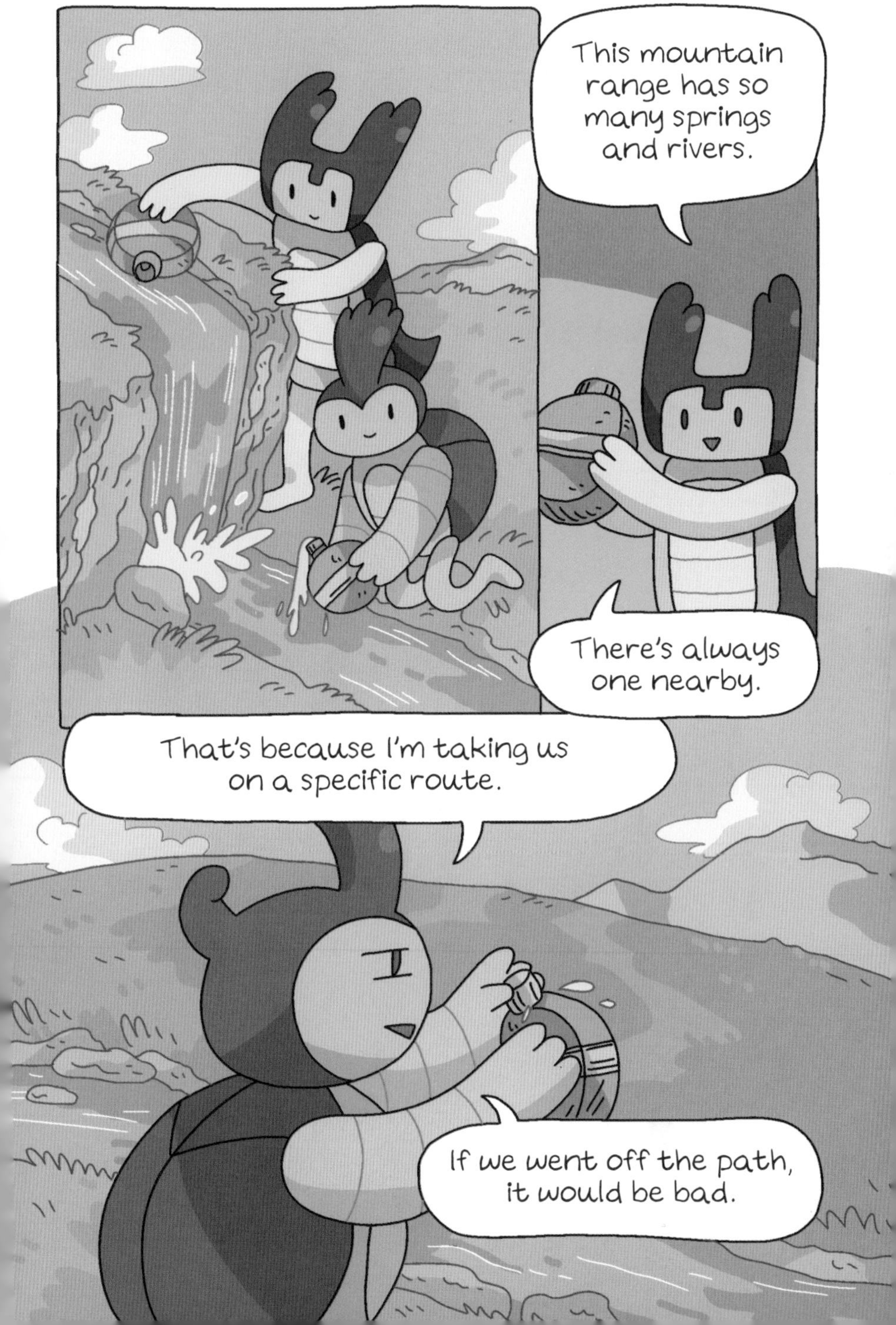
This mountain range has so many springs and rivers.
There's always one nearby.
That's because I'm taking us on a specific route.
If we went off the path, it would be bad.

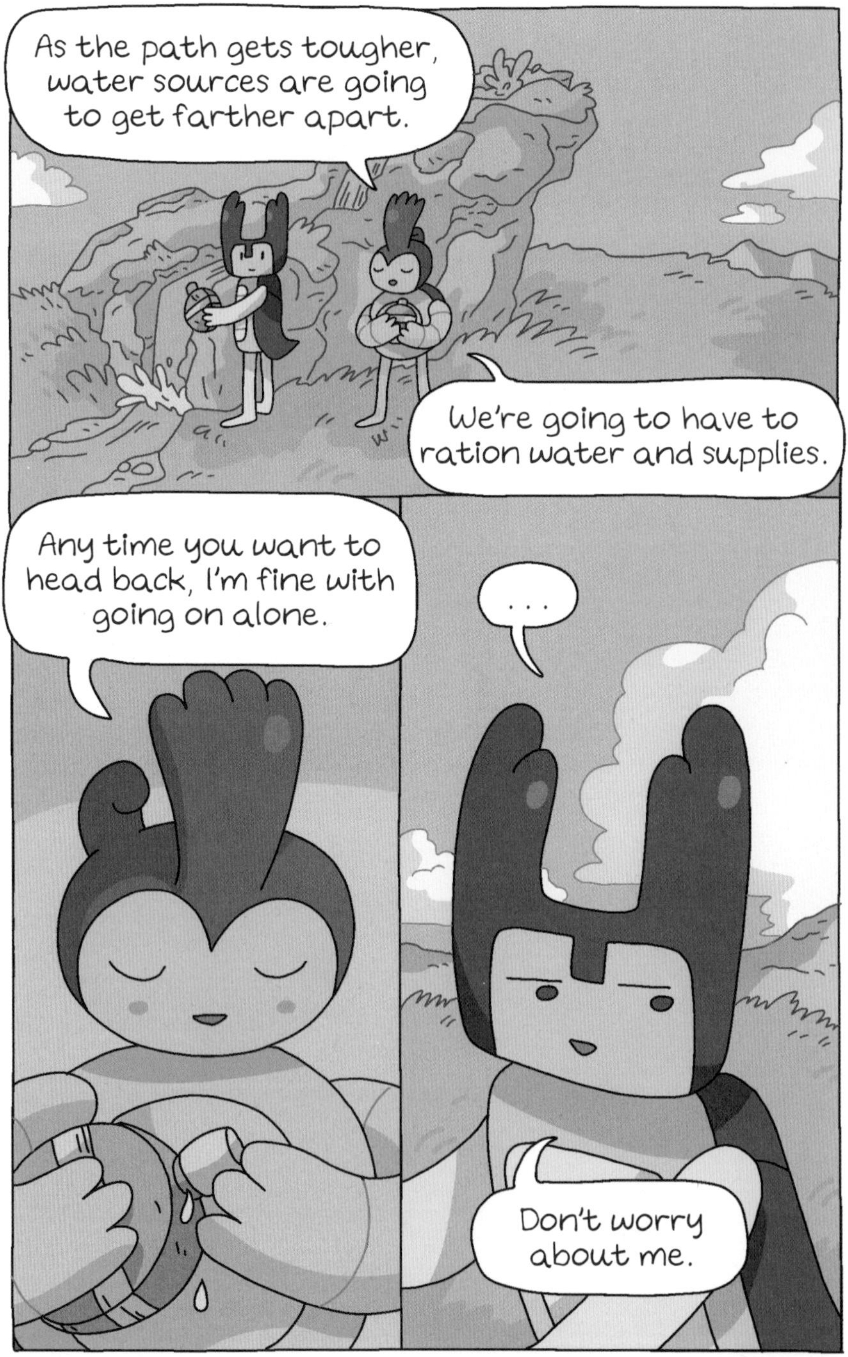
As the path gets tougher, water sources are going to get farther apart.
We're going to have to ration water and supplies.
Any time you want to head back, I'm fine with going on alone.
. . .
Don't worry about me.

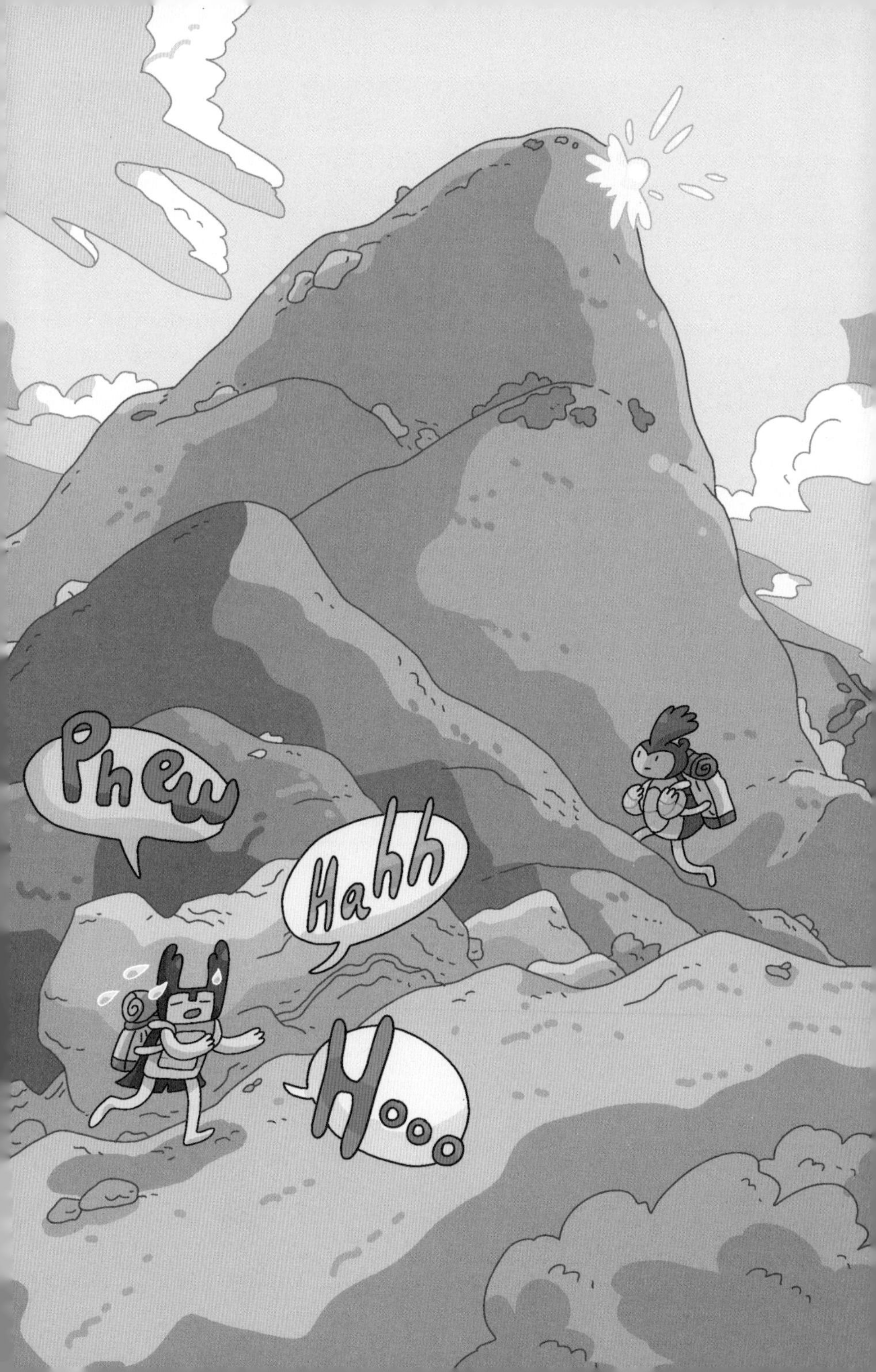
Phew
Hahh
Hooo

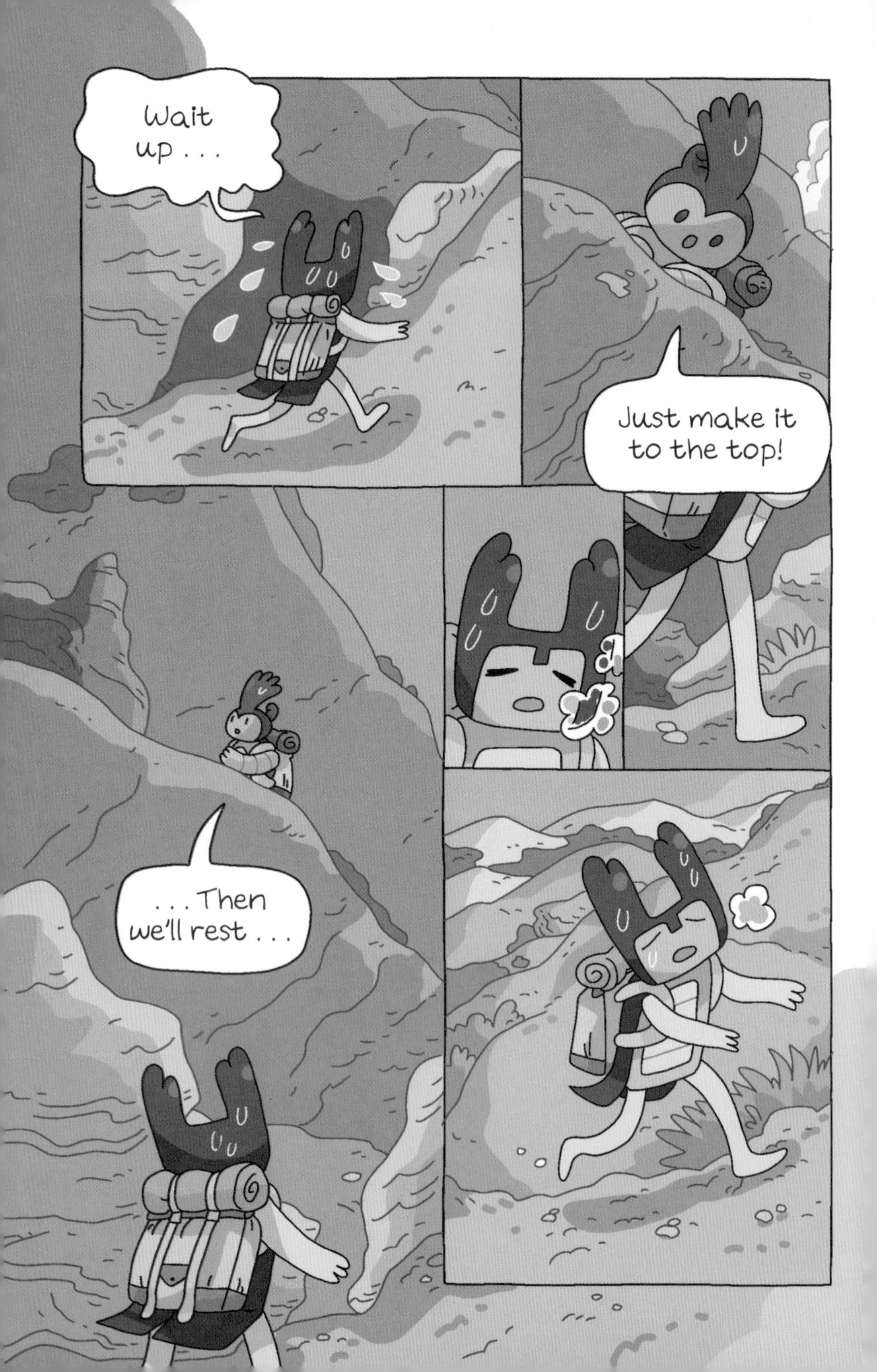
Wait up . . .
Just make it to the top!
. . . Then we'll rest . . .

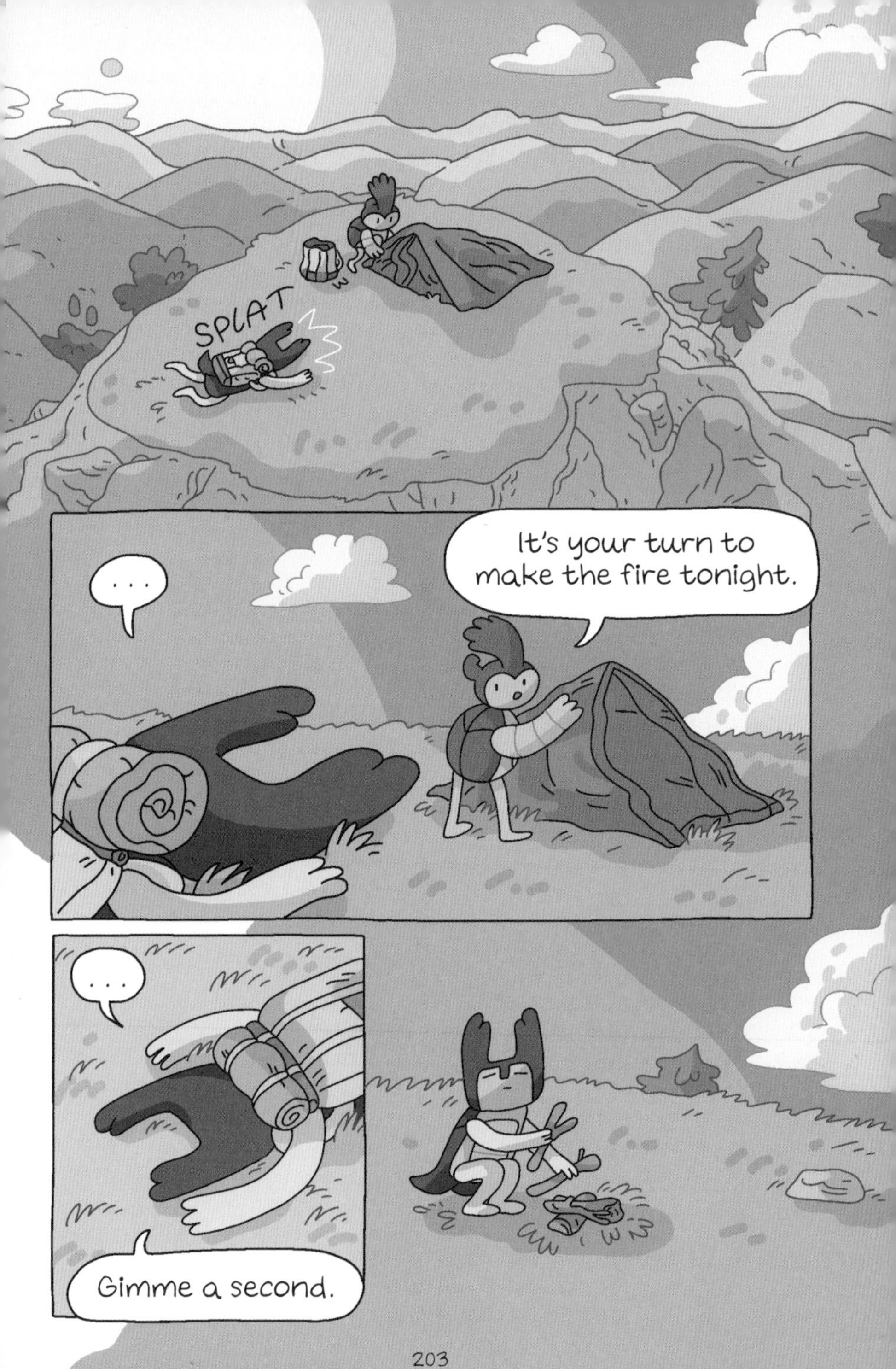
SPLAT
...
It's your turn to
make the fire tonight.
...
Gimme a second.

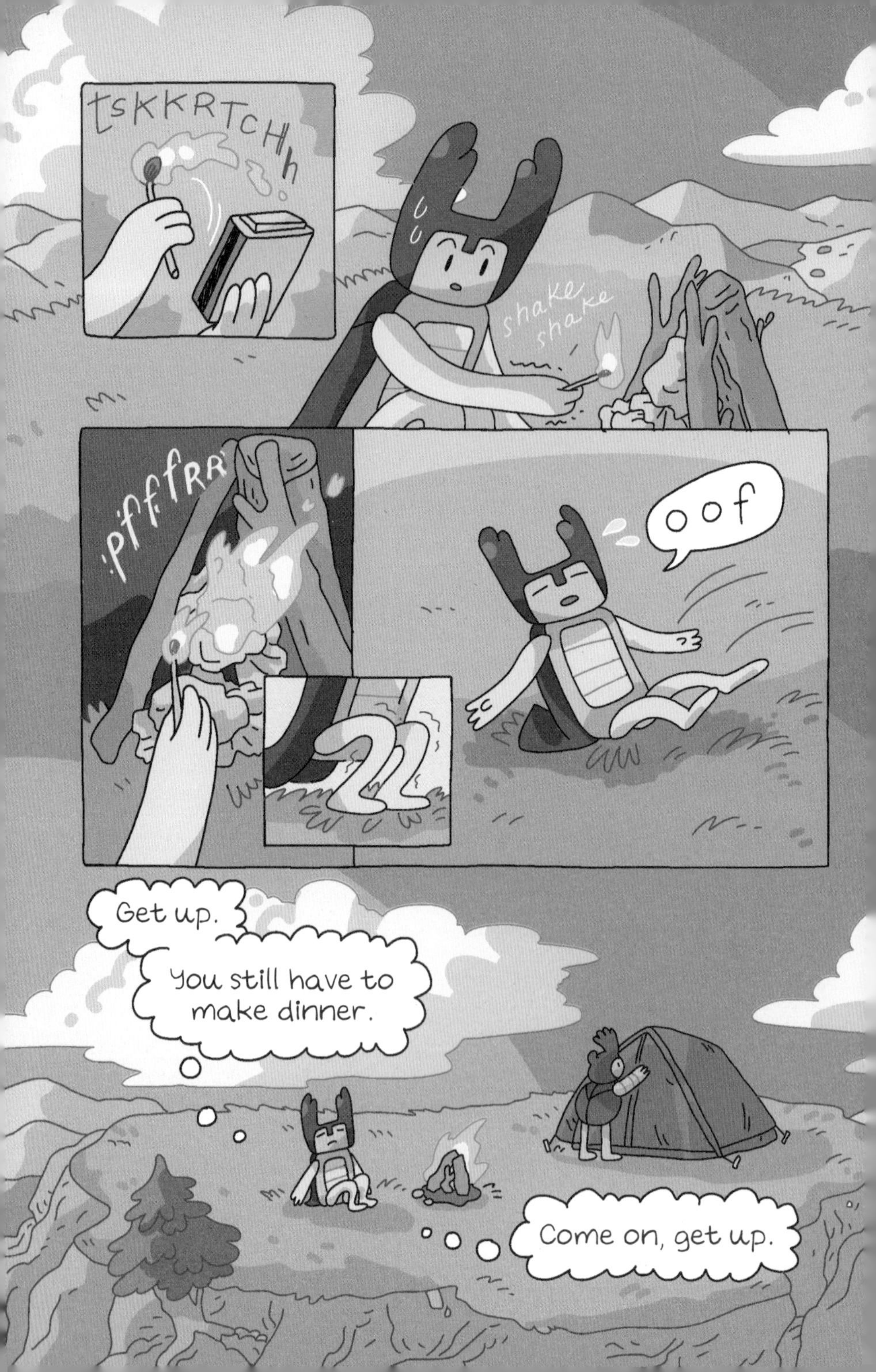

TSKKRTCHHh
shake shake
pffRR
oof
Get up.
You still have to make dinner.
Come on, get up.

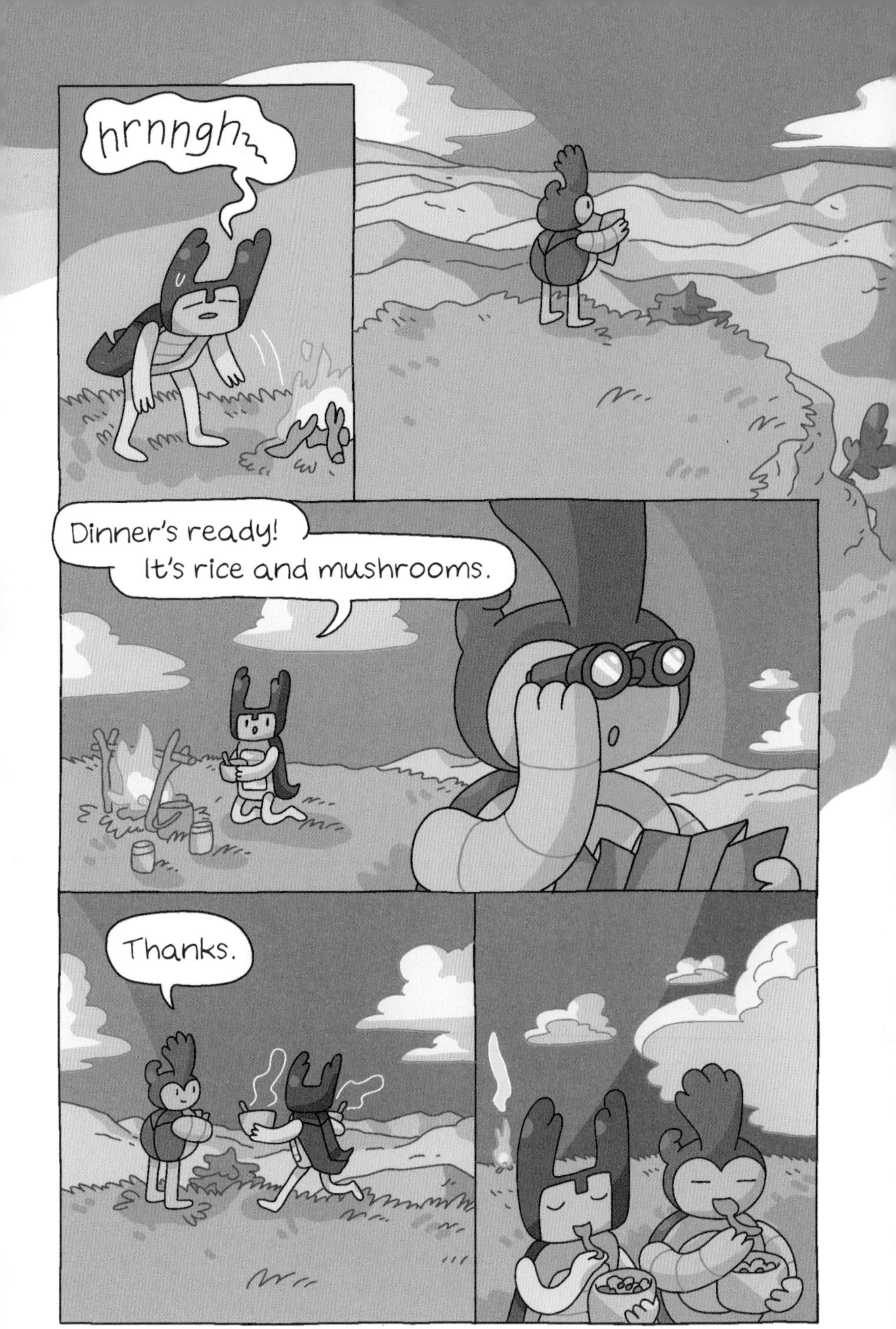
hrnngh
Dinner's ready! It's rice and mushrooms.
Thanks.

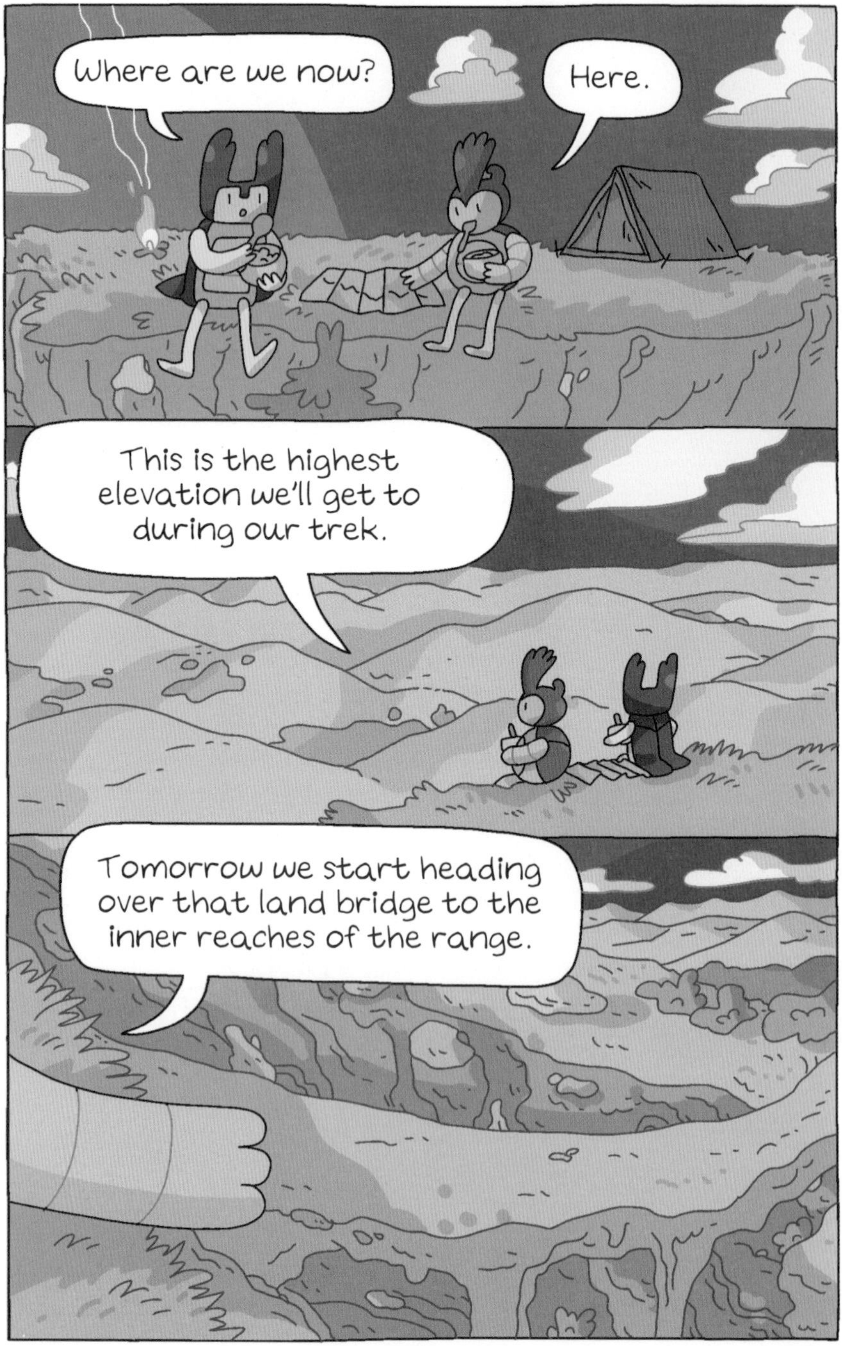
Where are we now?
Here.
This is the highest elevation we'll get to during our trek.
Tomorrow we start heading over that land bridge to the inner reaches of the range.

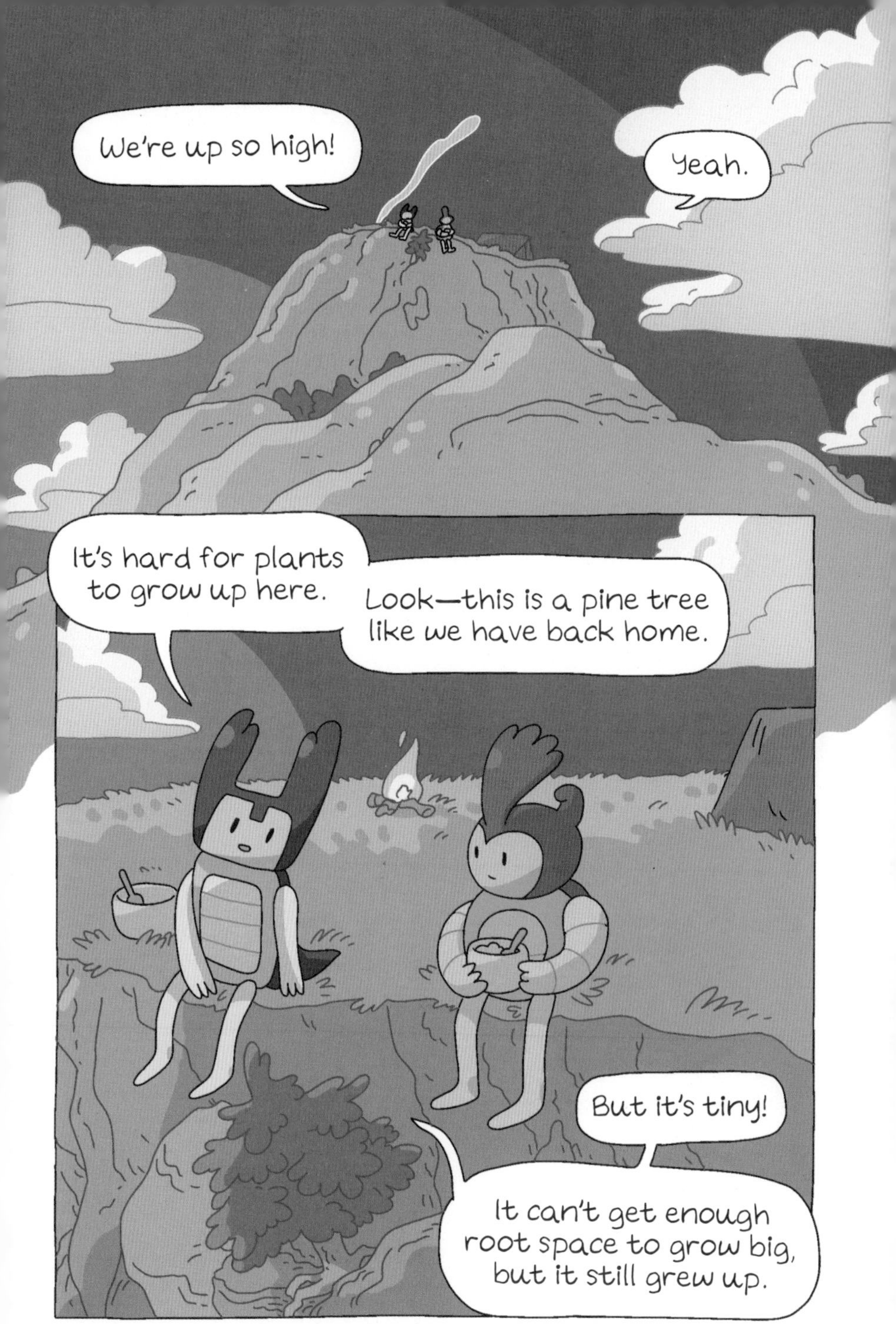
We're up so high!
Yeah.
It's hard for plants to grow up here.
Look—this is a pine tree like we have back home.
But it's tiny!
It can't get enough root space to grow big, but it still grew up.

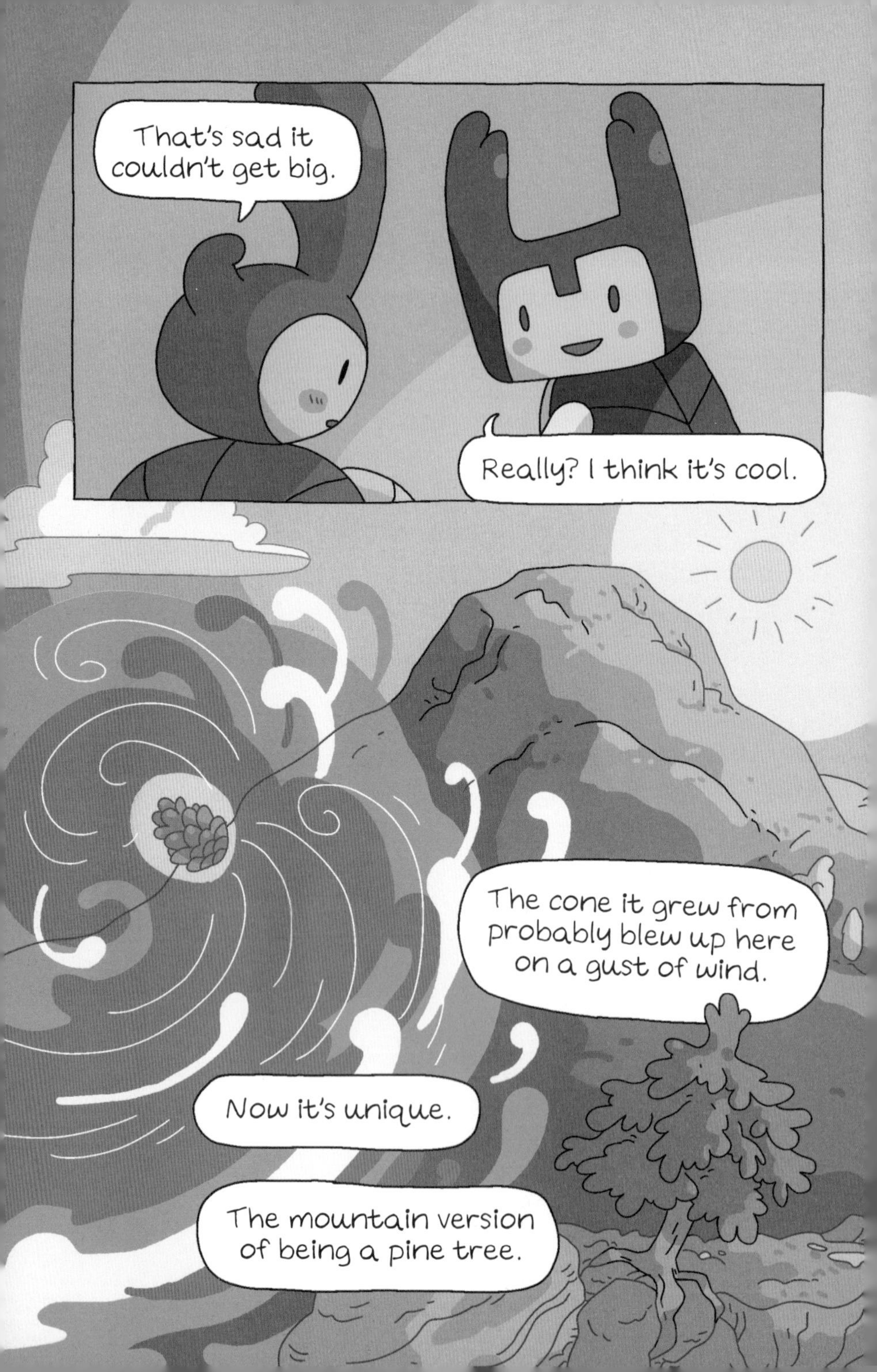
That's sad it couldn't get big.
Really? I think it's cool.
The cone it grew from probably blew up here on a gust of wind.
Now it's unique.
The mountain version of being a pine tree.

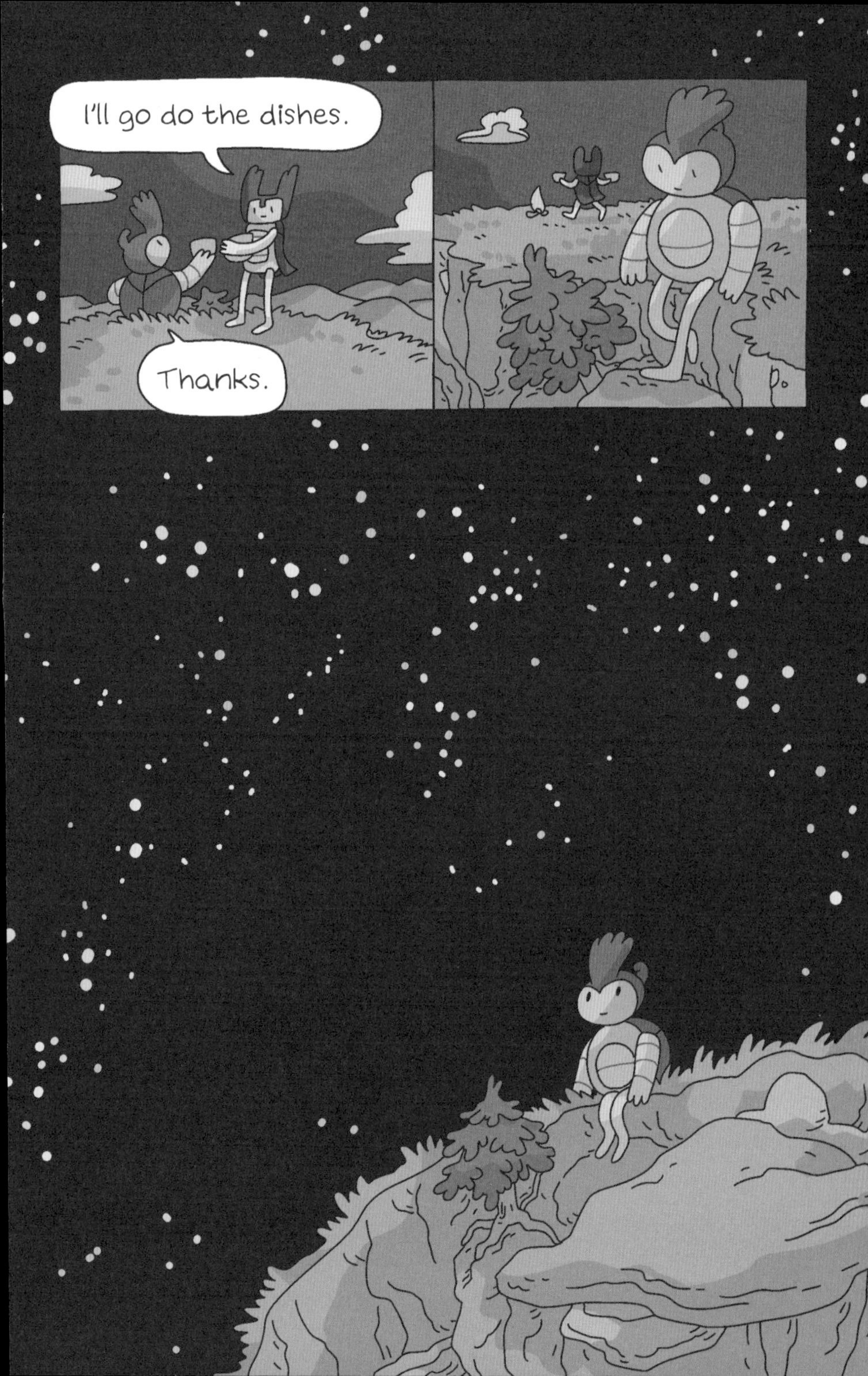
I'll go do the dishes.
Thanks.

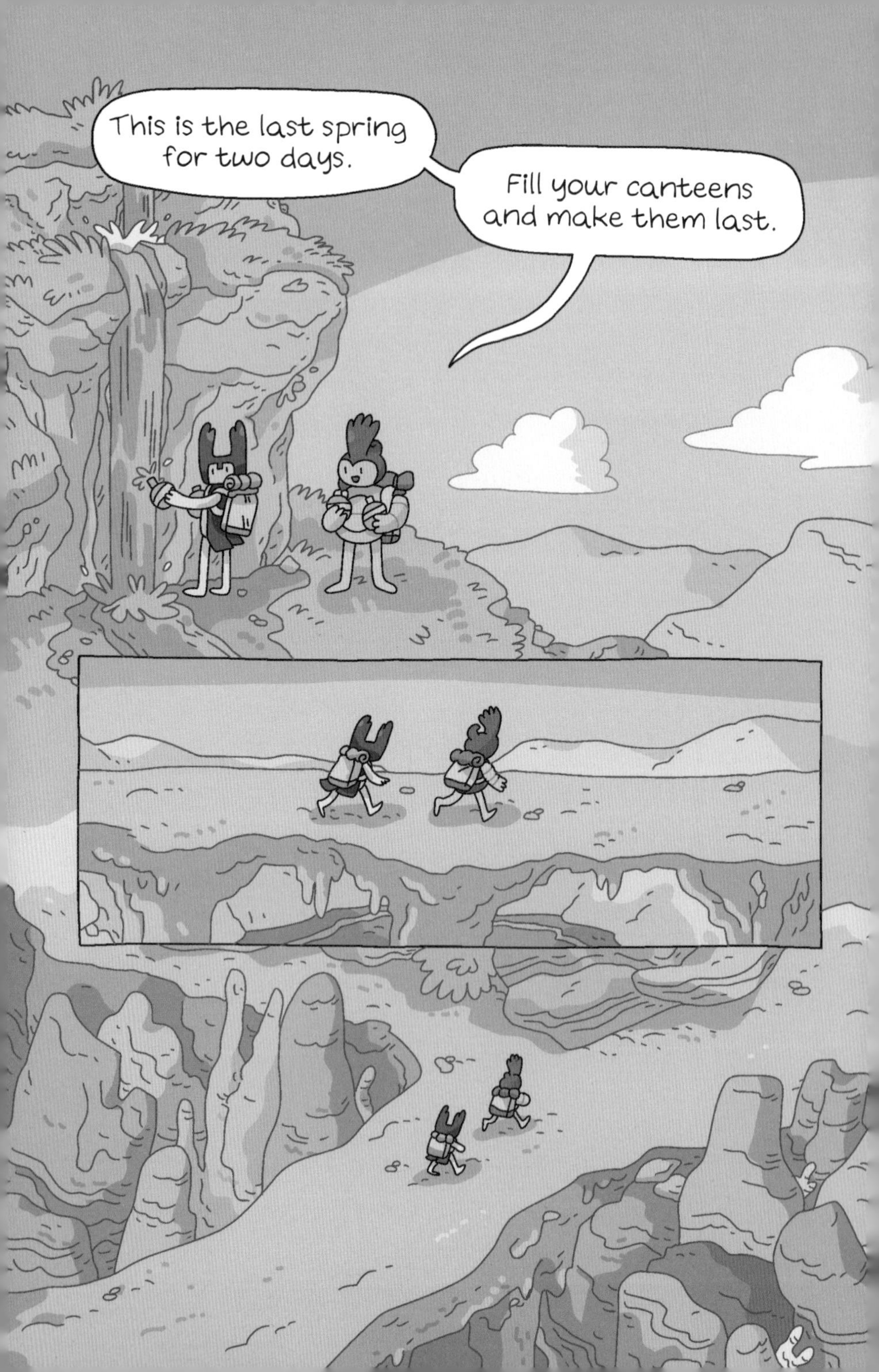
This is the last spring for two days.
Fill your canteens and make them last.

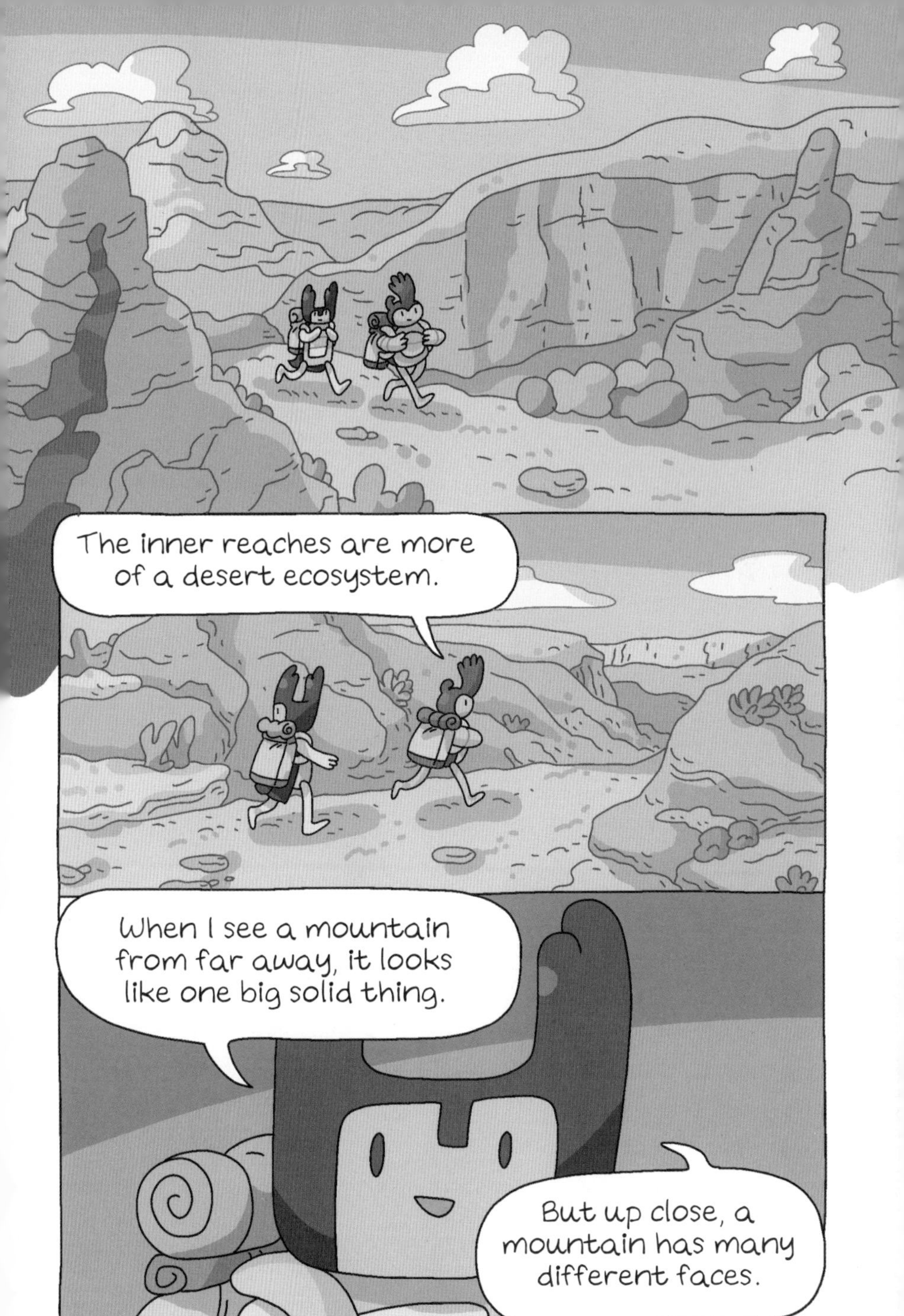
The inner reaches are more of a desert ecosystem.
When I see a mountain from far away, it looks like one big solid thing.
But up close, a mountain has many different faces.

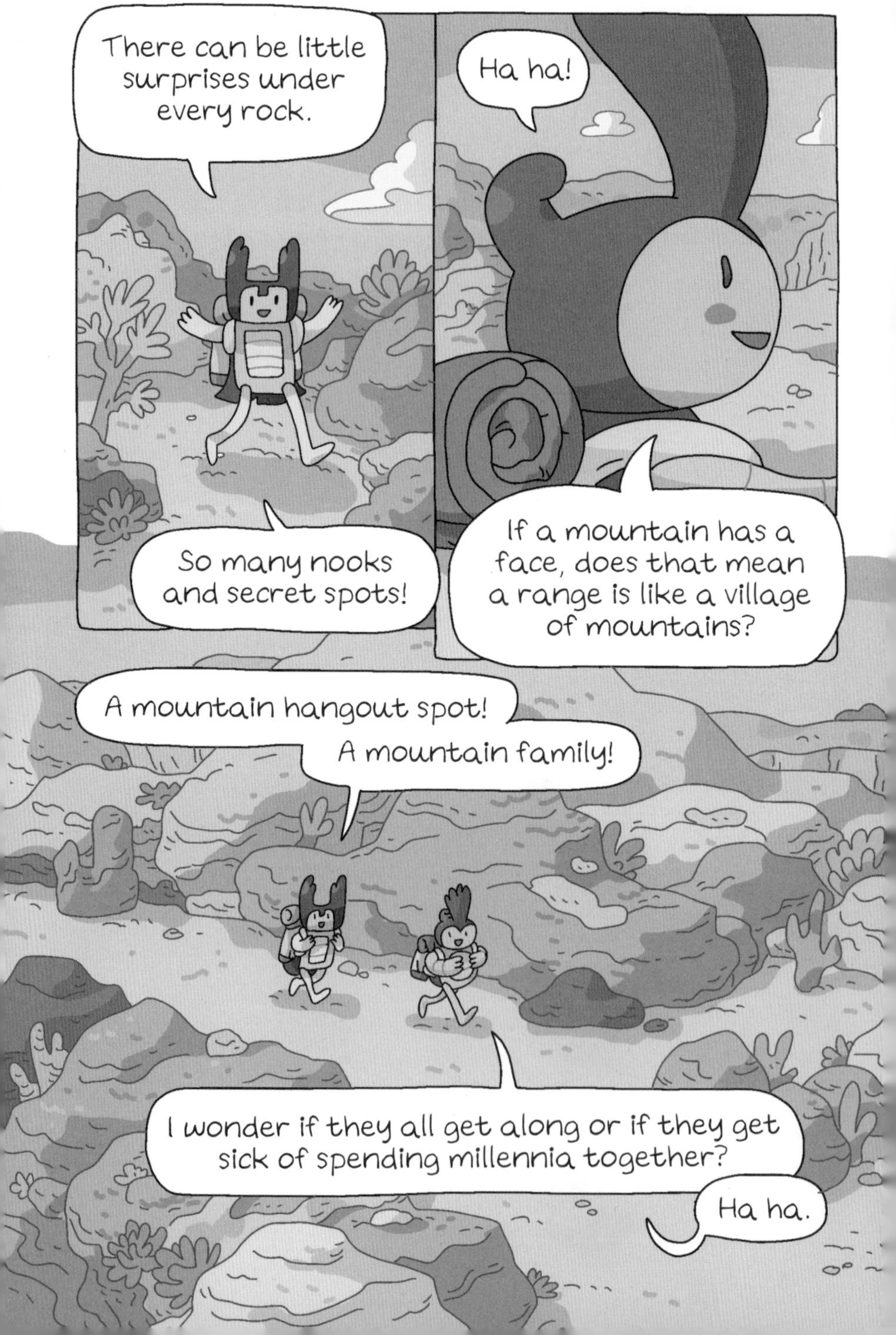
There can be little surprises under every rock.
So many nooks and secret spots!
Ha ha!
If a mountain has a face, does that mean a range is like a village of mountains?
A mountain hangout spot!
A mountain family!
I wonder if they all get along or if they get sick of spending millennia together?
Ha ha.

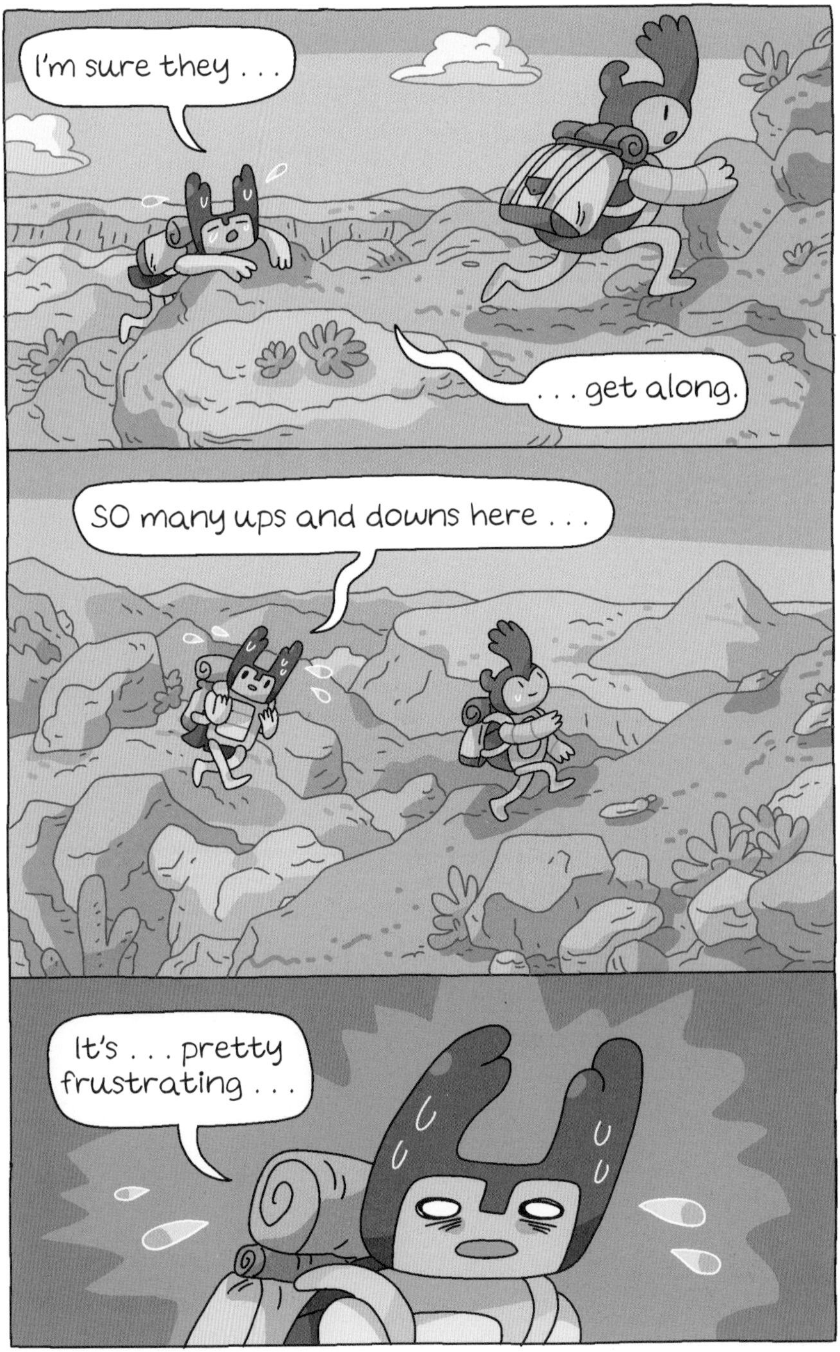
I'm sure they . . .
. . . get along.
SO many ups and downs here . . .
It's . . . pretty frustrating . . .

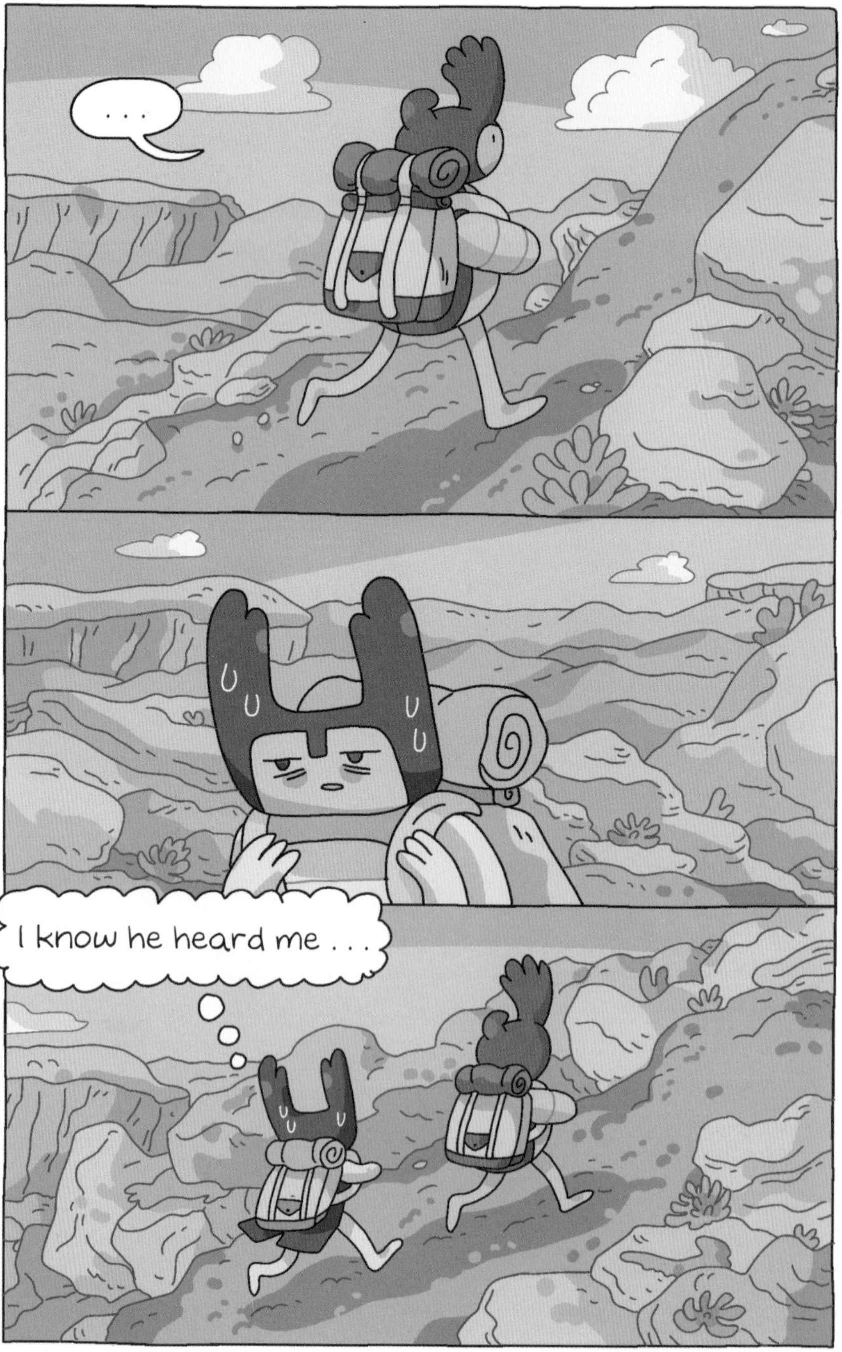
. . .
I know he heard me . . .

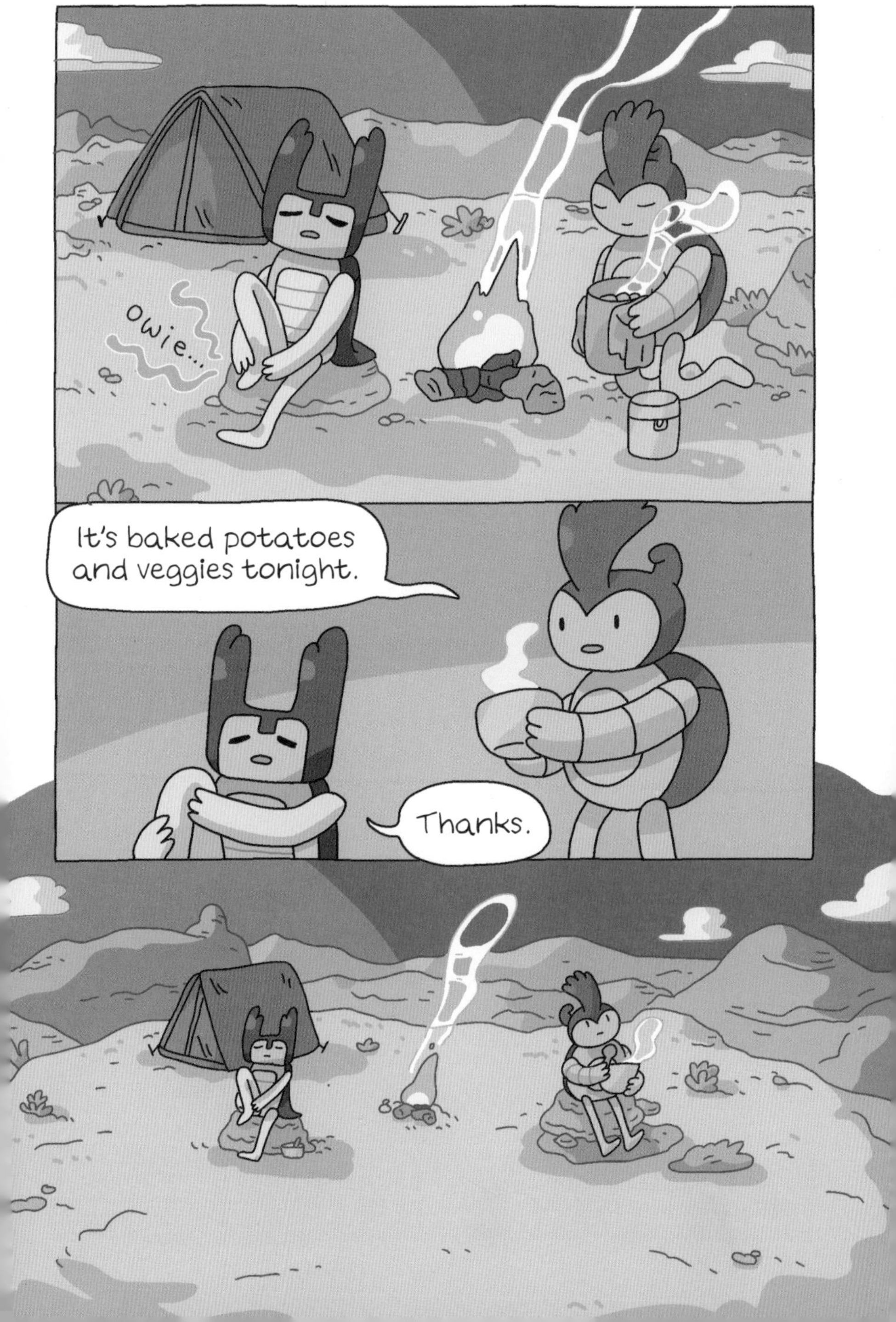
owie...
It's baked potatoes and veggies tonight.
Thanks.

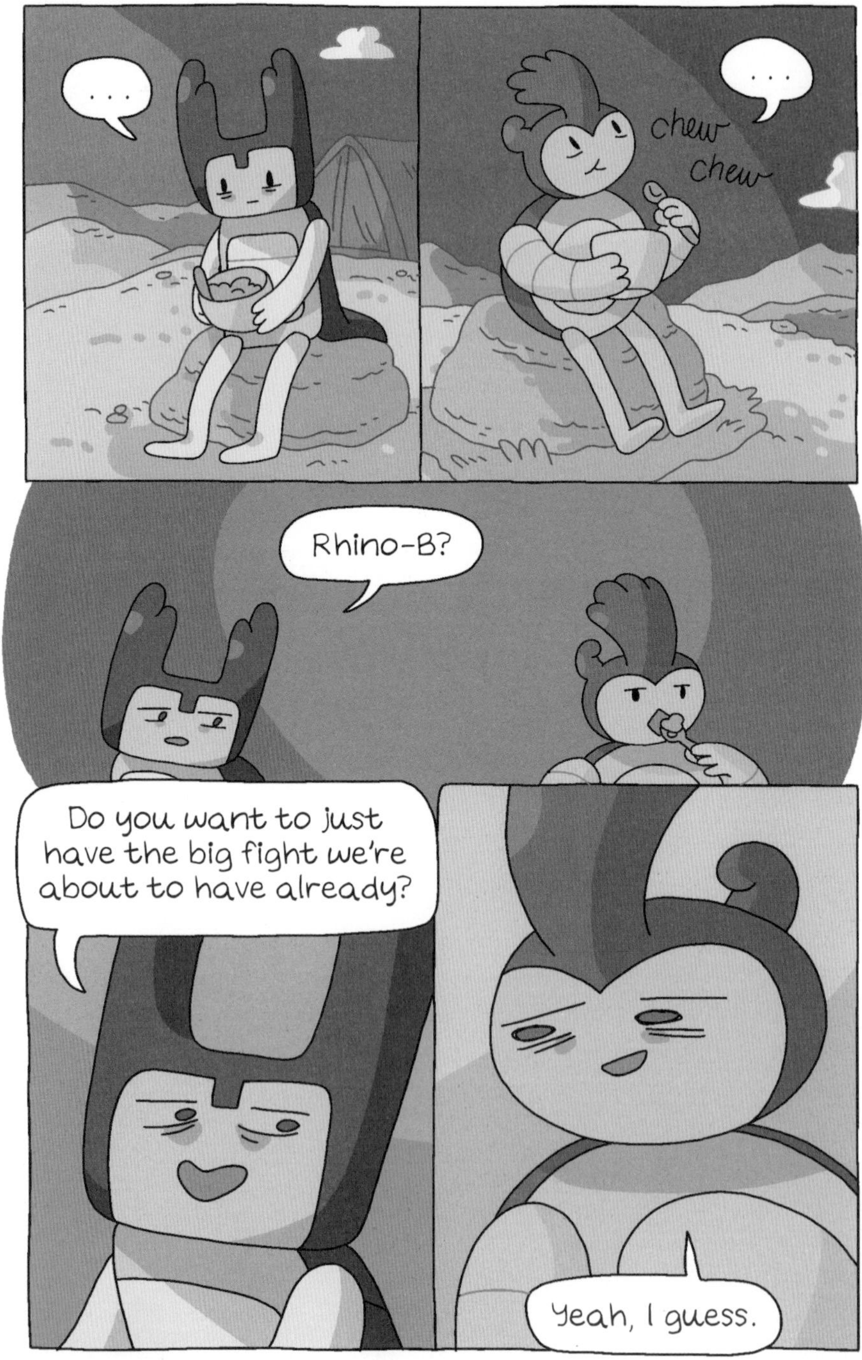
. . .
. . .
chew
chew
Rhino-B?
Do you want to just have the big fight we're about to have already?
Yeah, I guess.

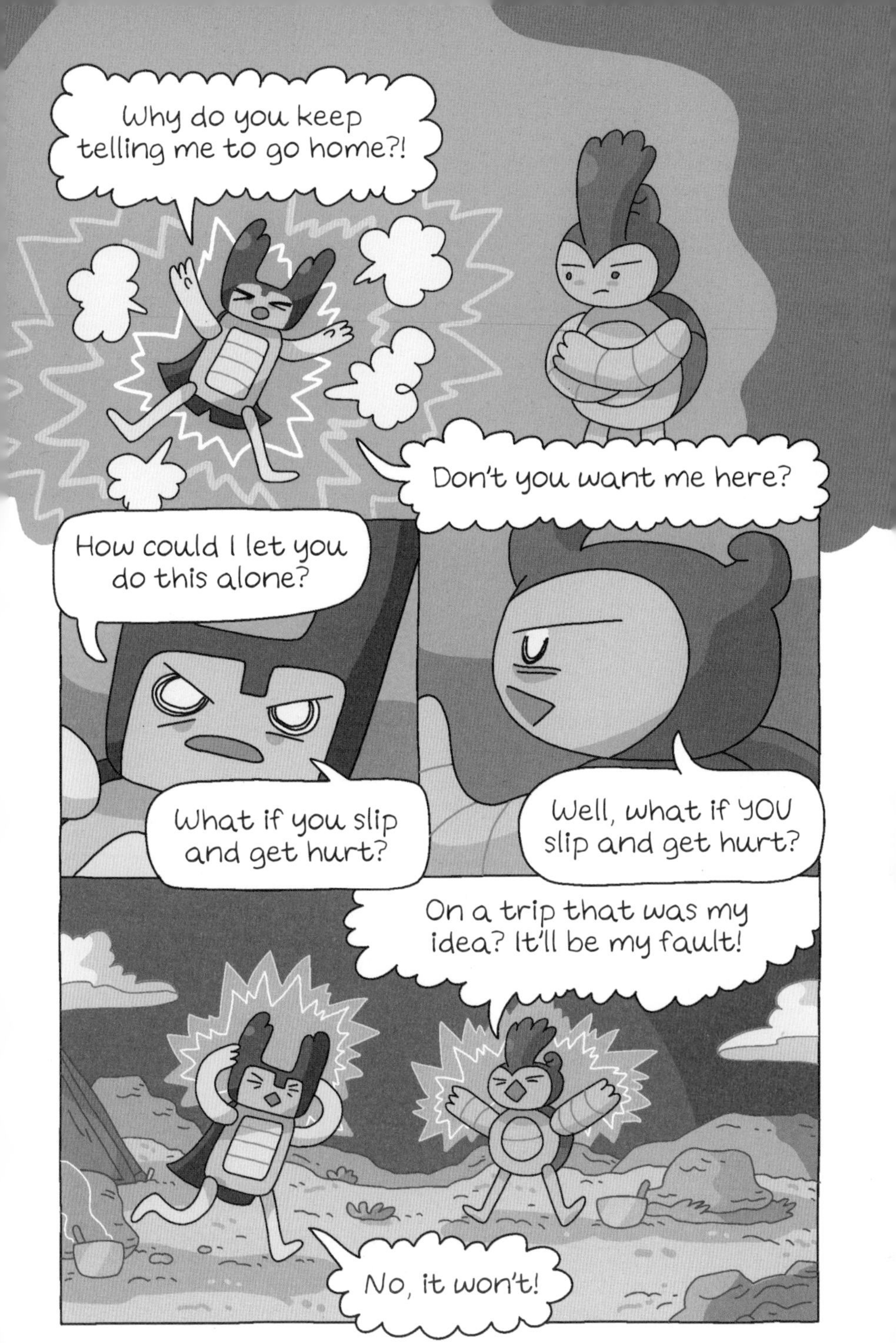
Why do you keep telling me to go home?!
Don't you want me here?
How could I let you do this alone?
What if you slip and get hurt?
Well, what if YOU slip and get hurt?
On a trip that was my idea? It'll be my fault!
No, it won't!

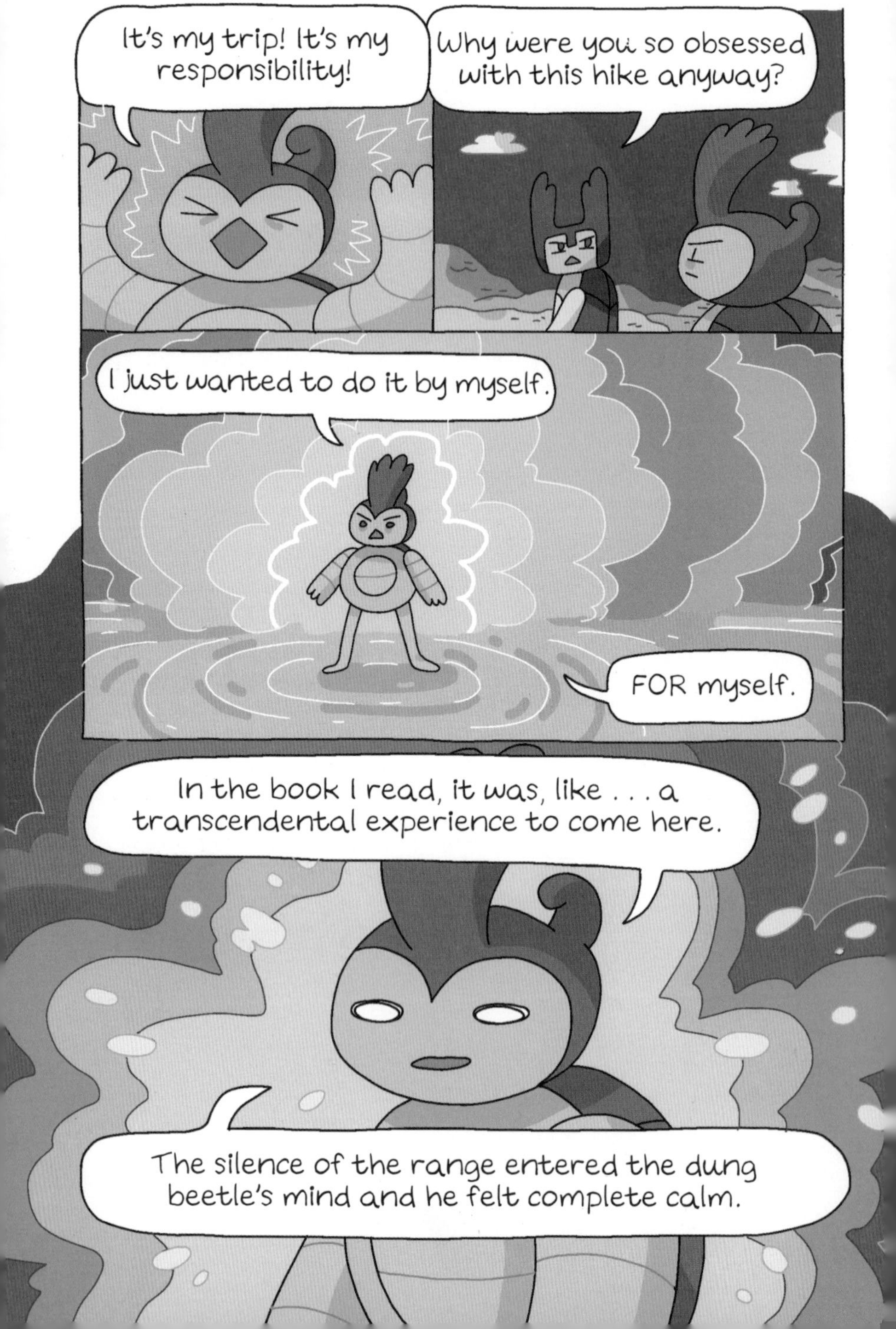
It's my trip! It's my responsibility!
Why were you so obsessed with this hike anyway?
I just wanted to do it by myself.
FOR myself.
In the book I read, it was, like . . . a transcendental experience to come here.
The silence of the range entered the dung beetle's mind and he felt complete calm.

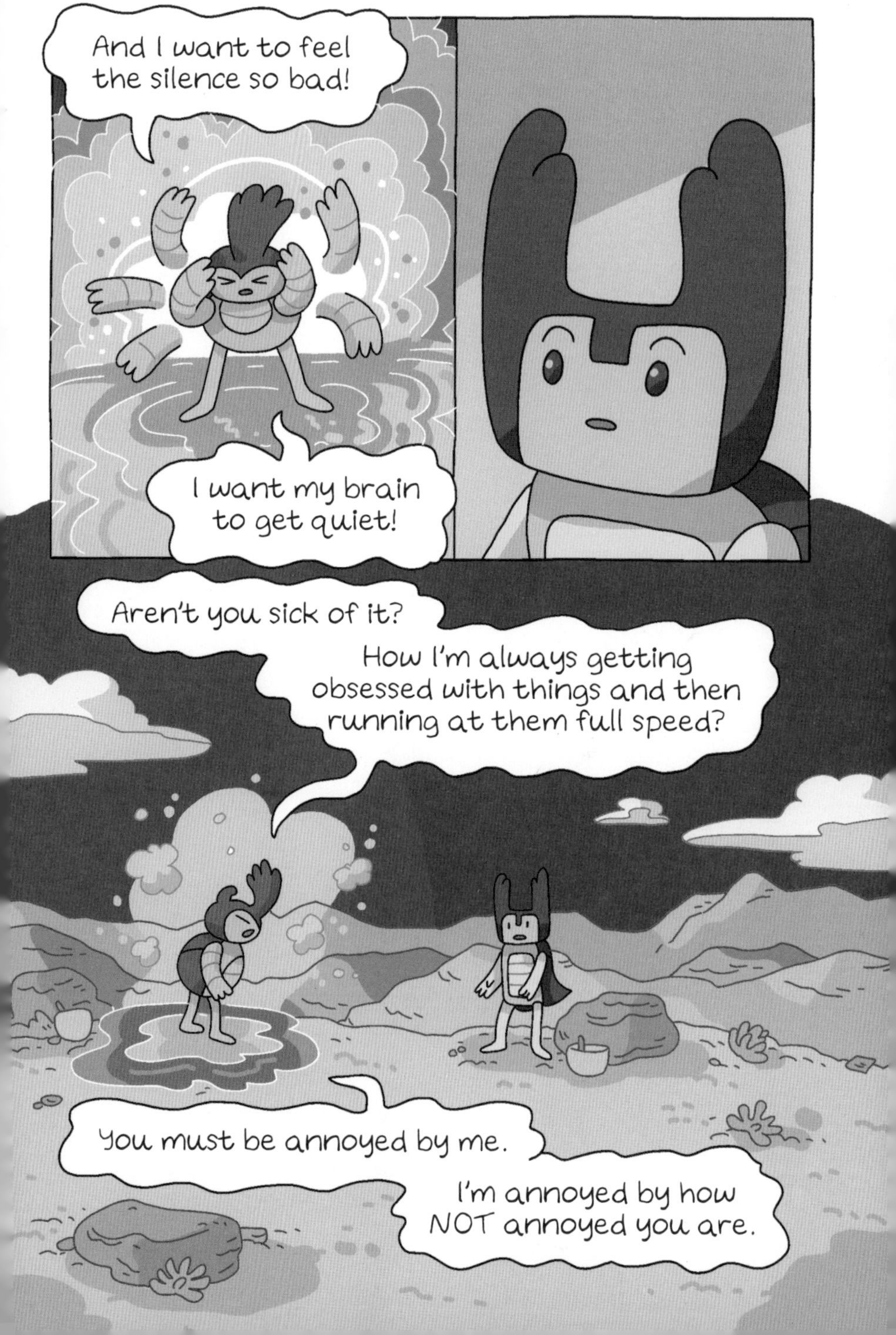
And I want to feel the silence so bad!
I want my brain to get quiet!
Aren't you sick of it?
How I'm always getting obsessed with things and then running at them full speed?
You must be annoyed by me.
I'm annoyed by how NOT annoyed you are.

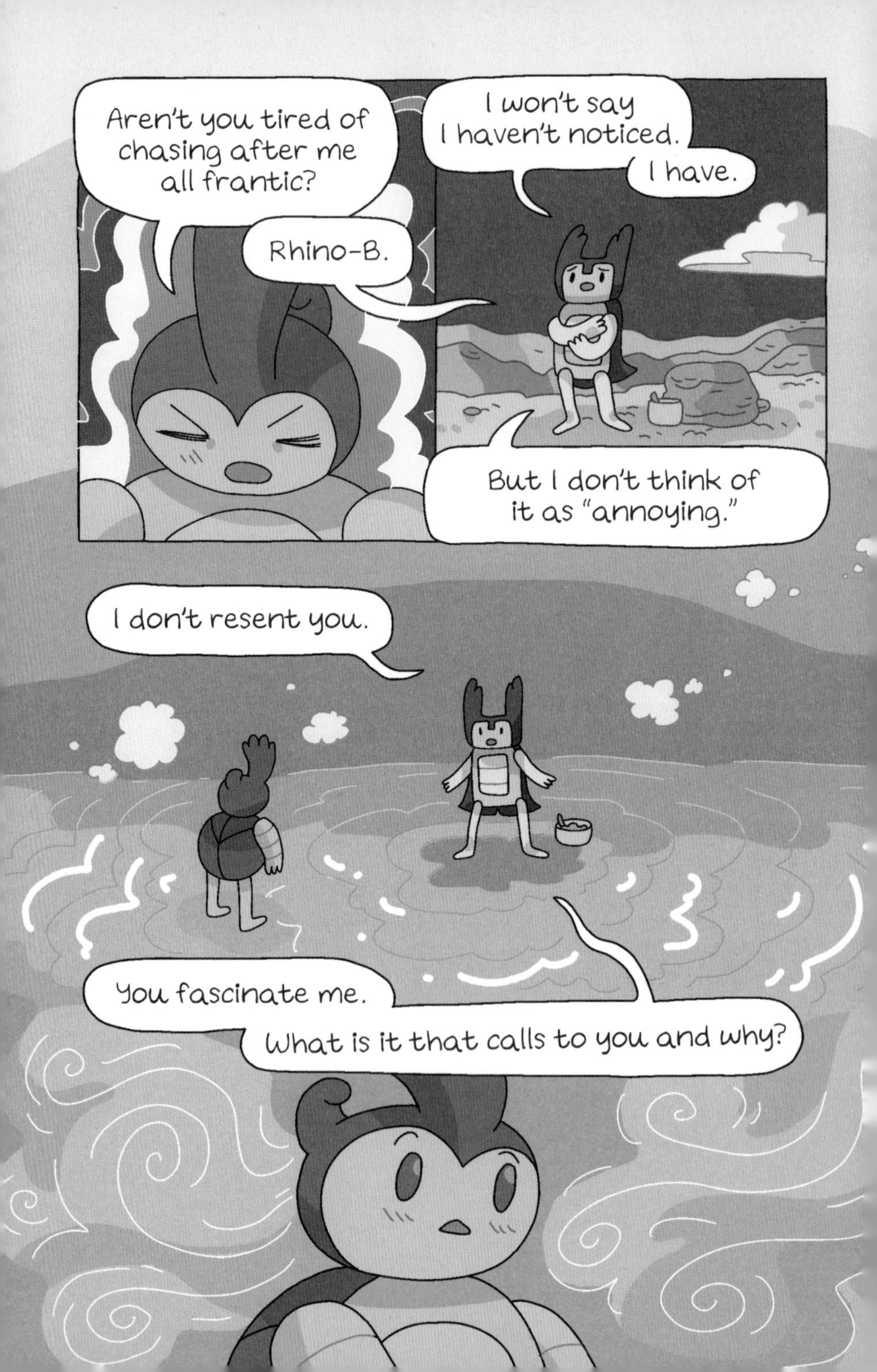

Aren't you tired of chasing after me all frantic?
Rhino-B.
I won't say I haven't noticed.
I have.
But I don't think of it as "annoying."
I don't resent you.
You fascinate me.
What is it that calls to you and why?

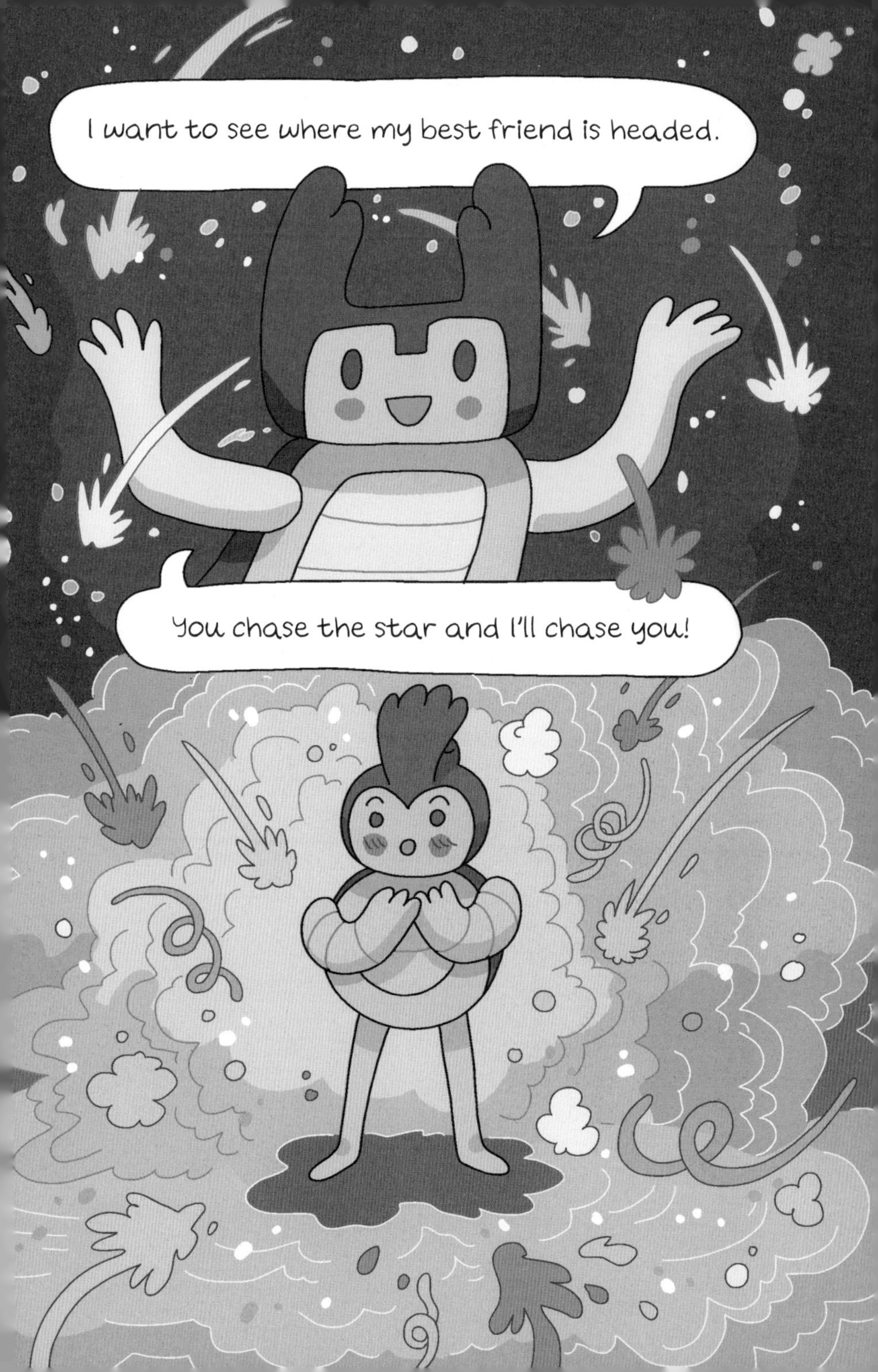
I want to see where my best friend is headed.
You chase the star and I'll chase you!

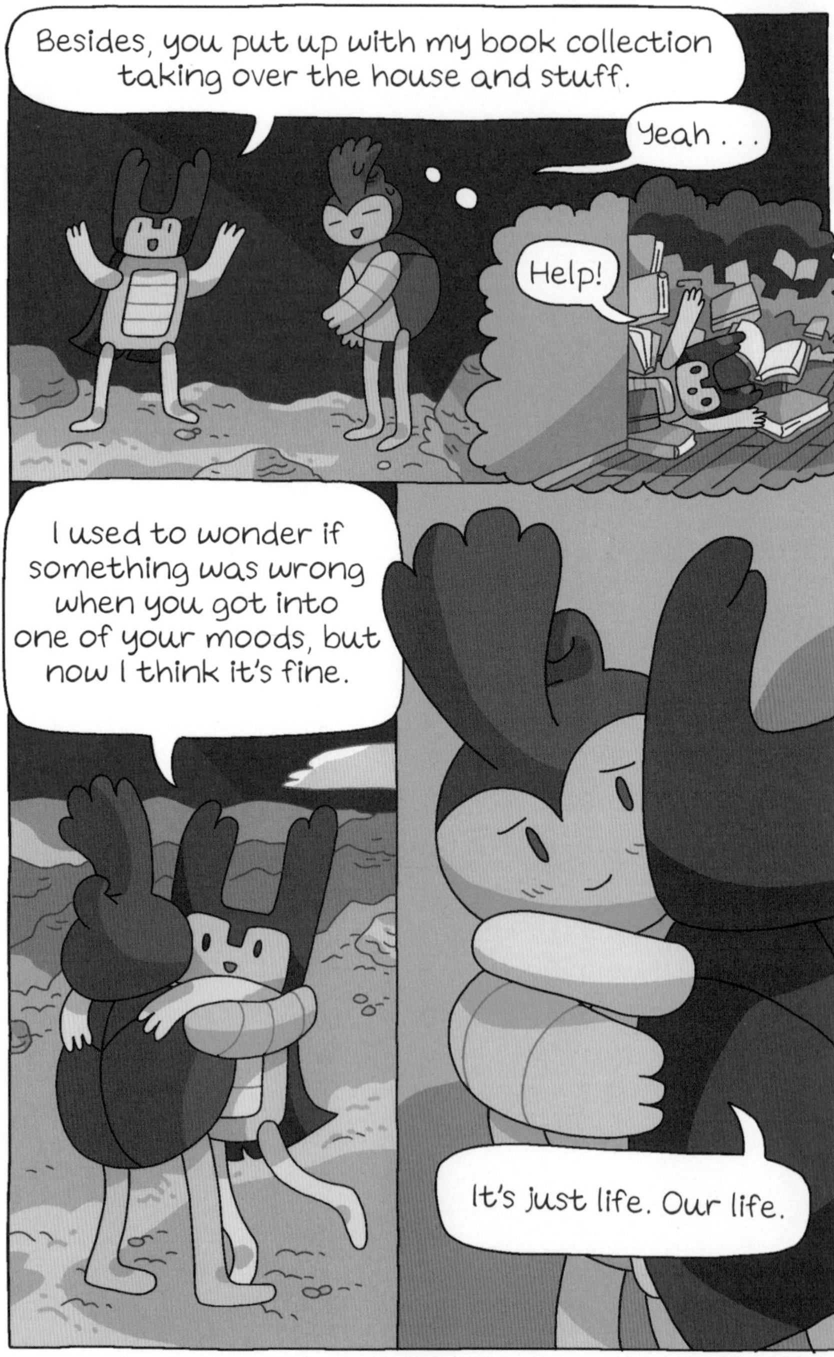
Besides, you put up with my book collection taking over the house and stuff.
Yeah . . .
Help!
I used to wonder if something was wrong when you got into one of your moods, but now I think it's fine.
It's just life. Our life.

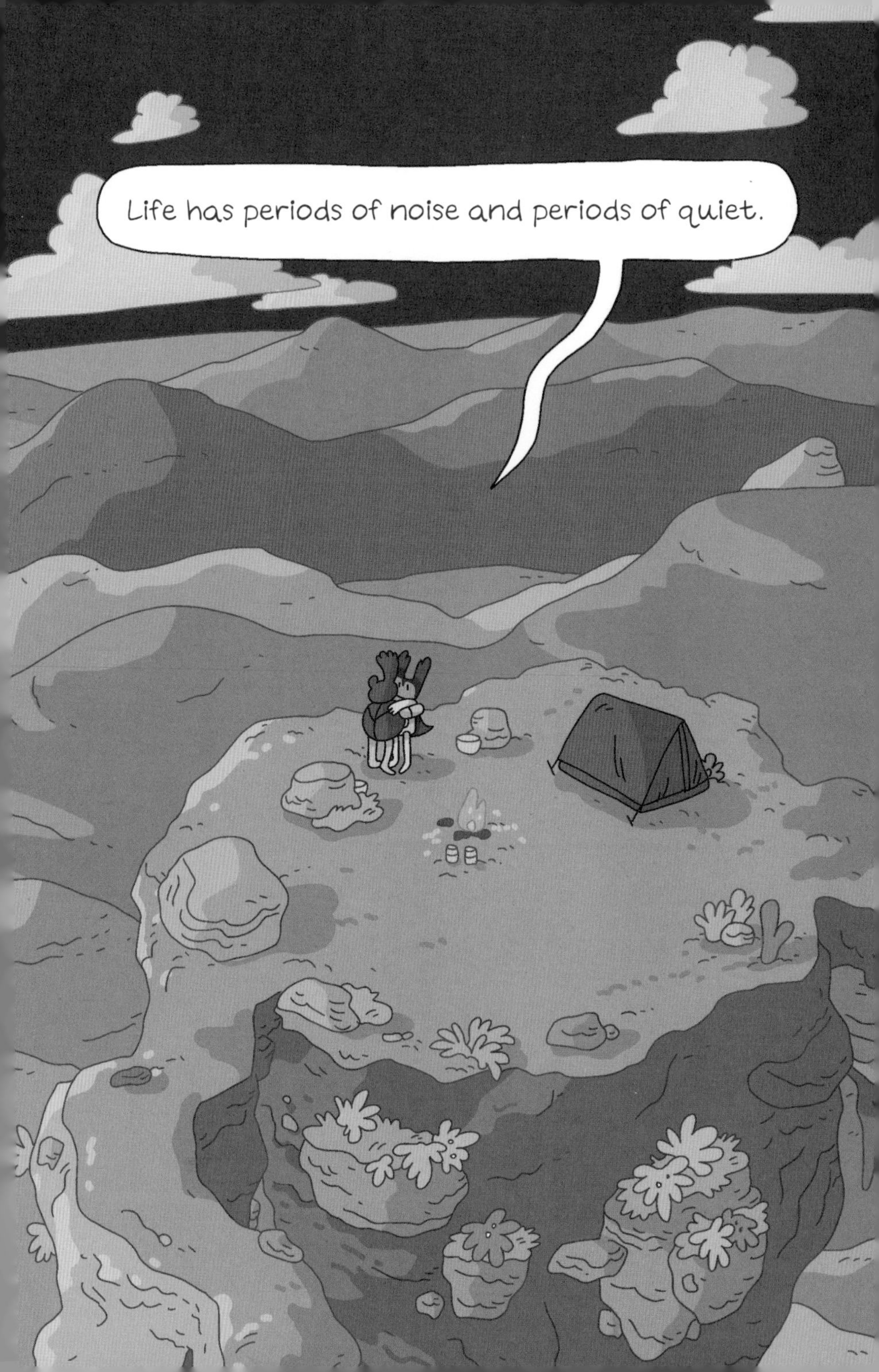
Life has periods of noise and periods of quiet.

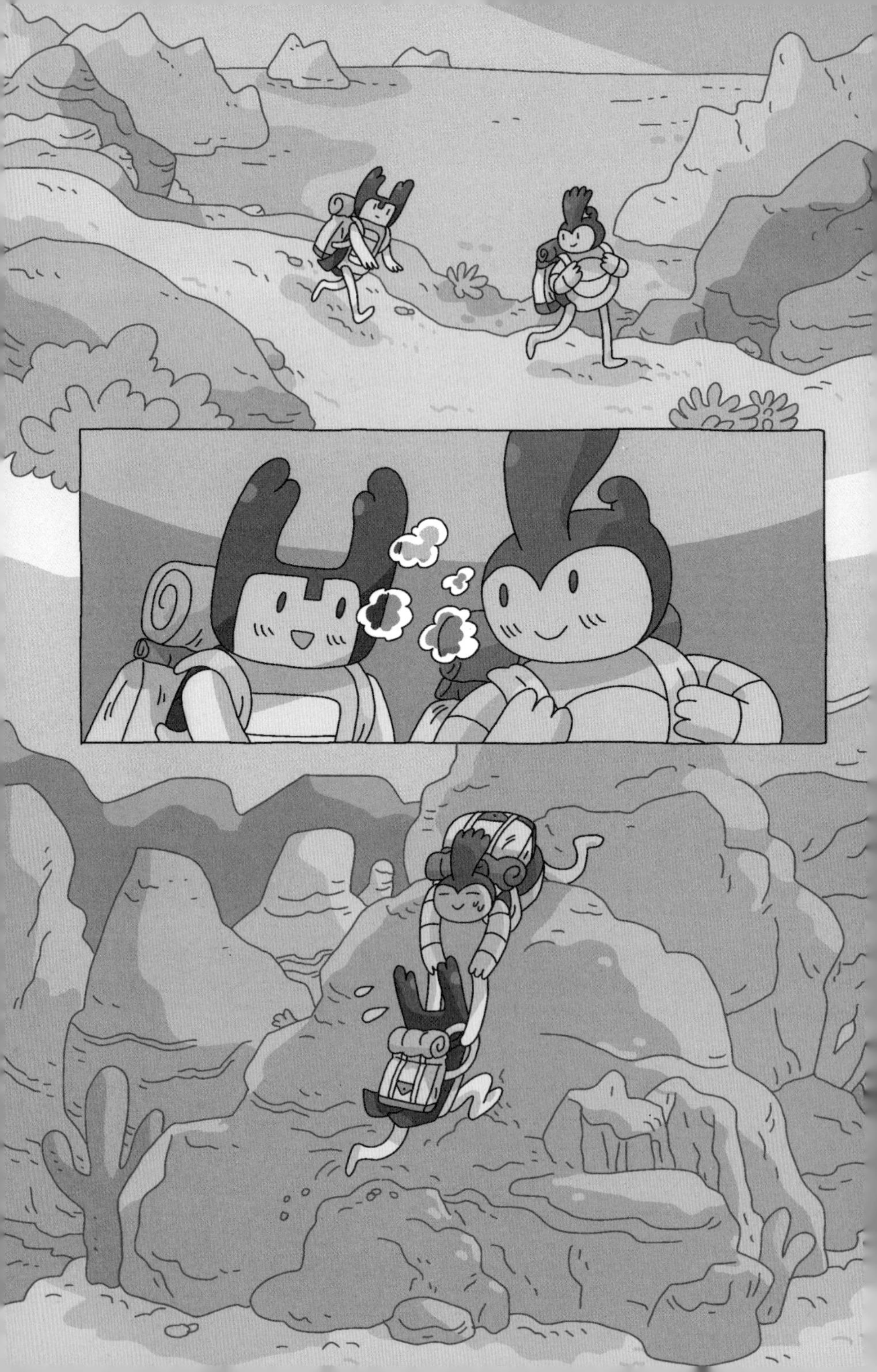

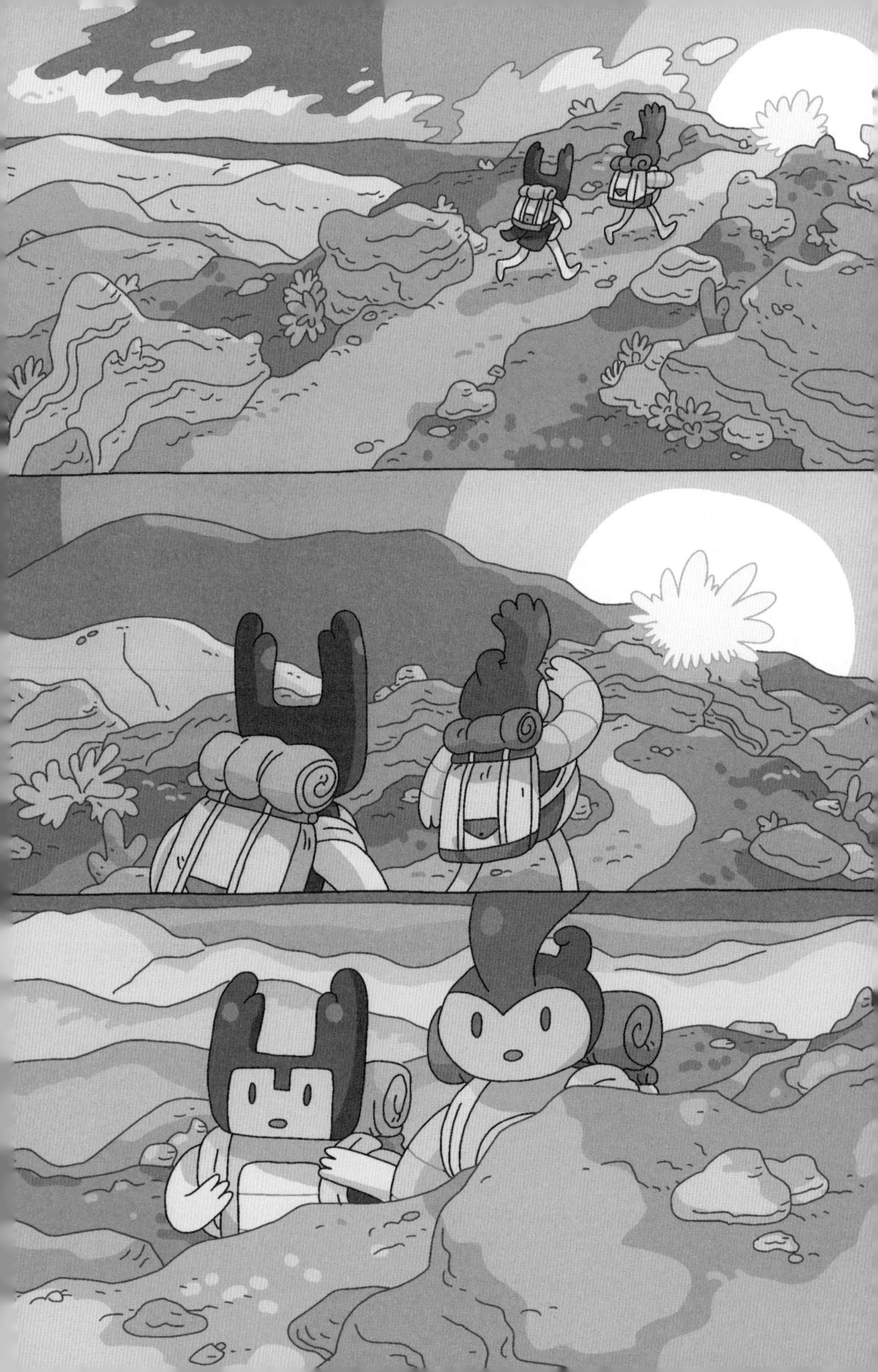

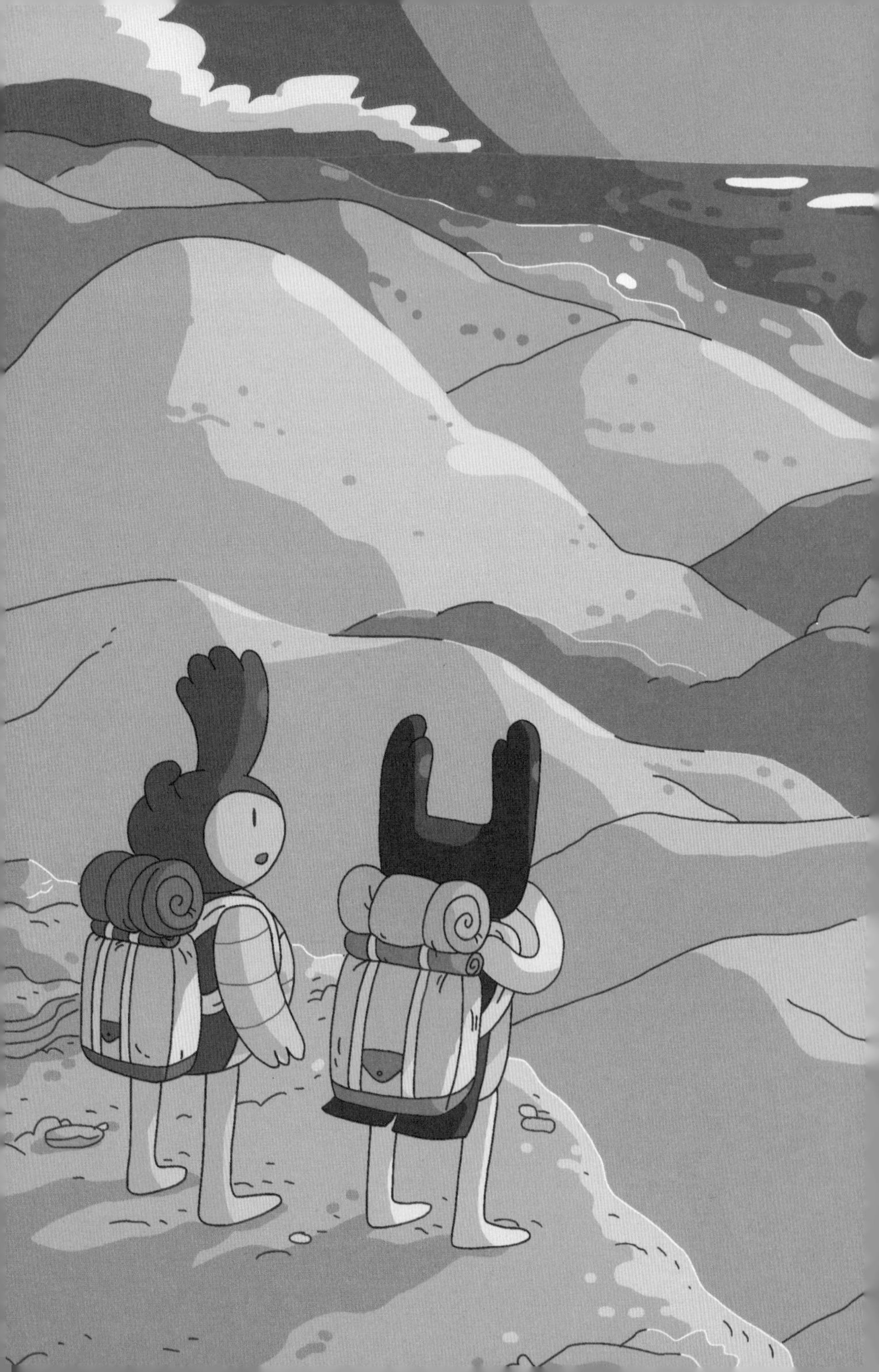

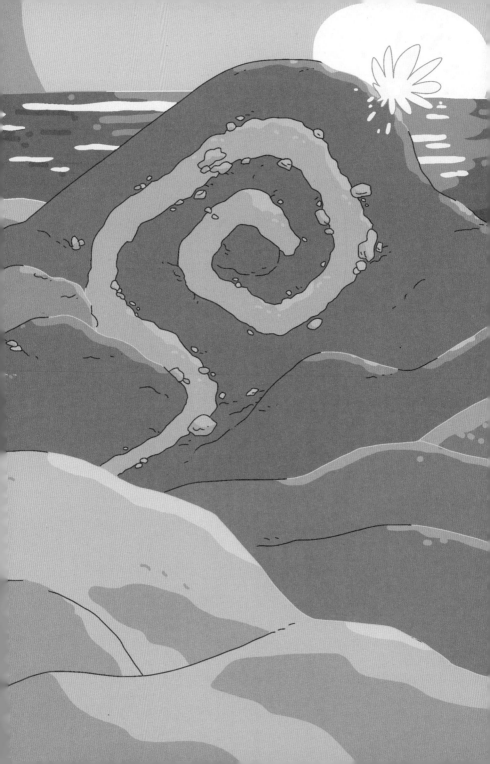

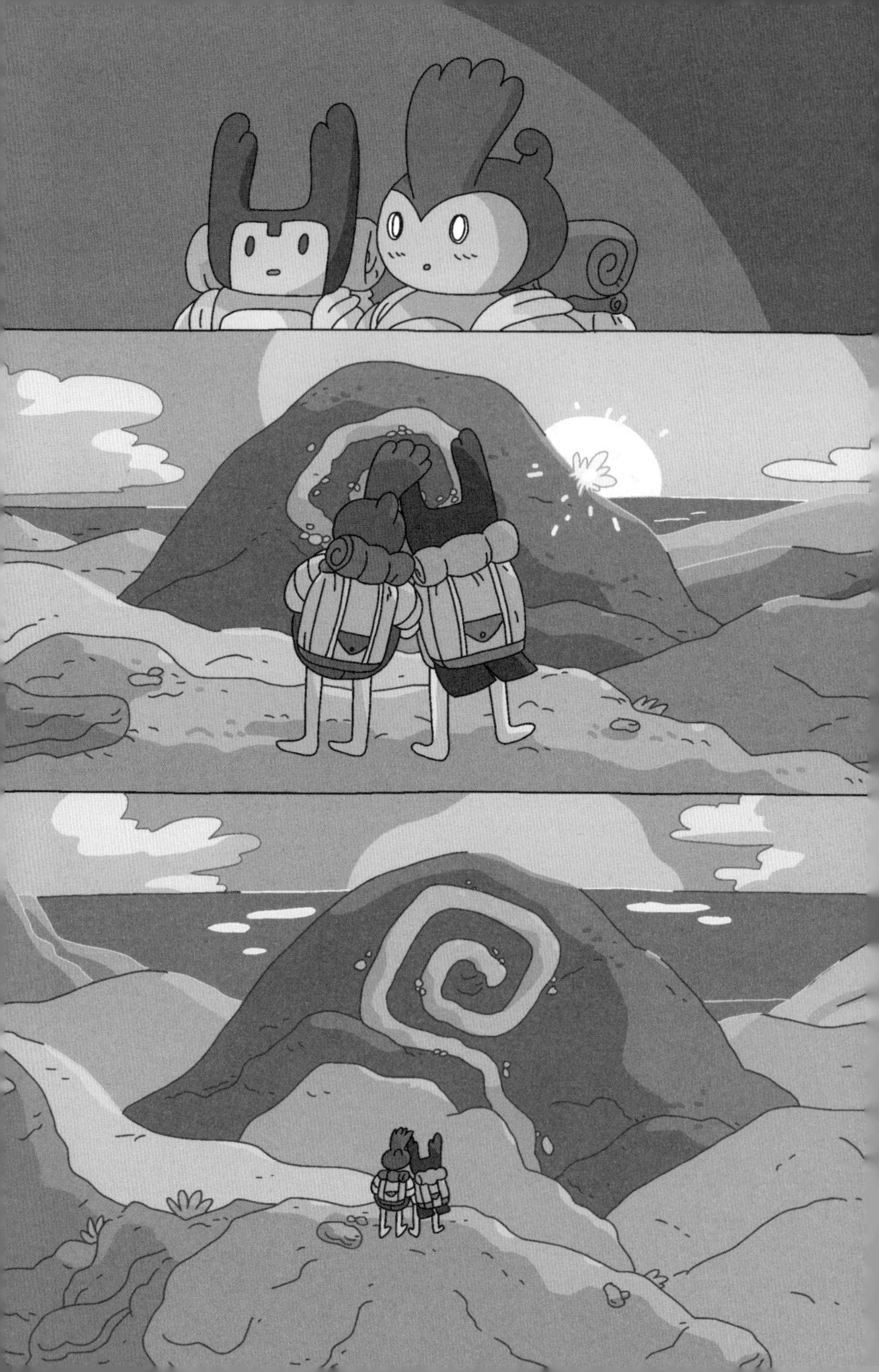

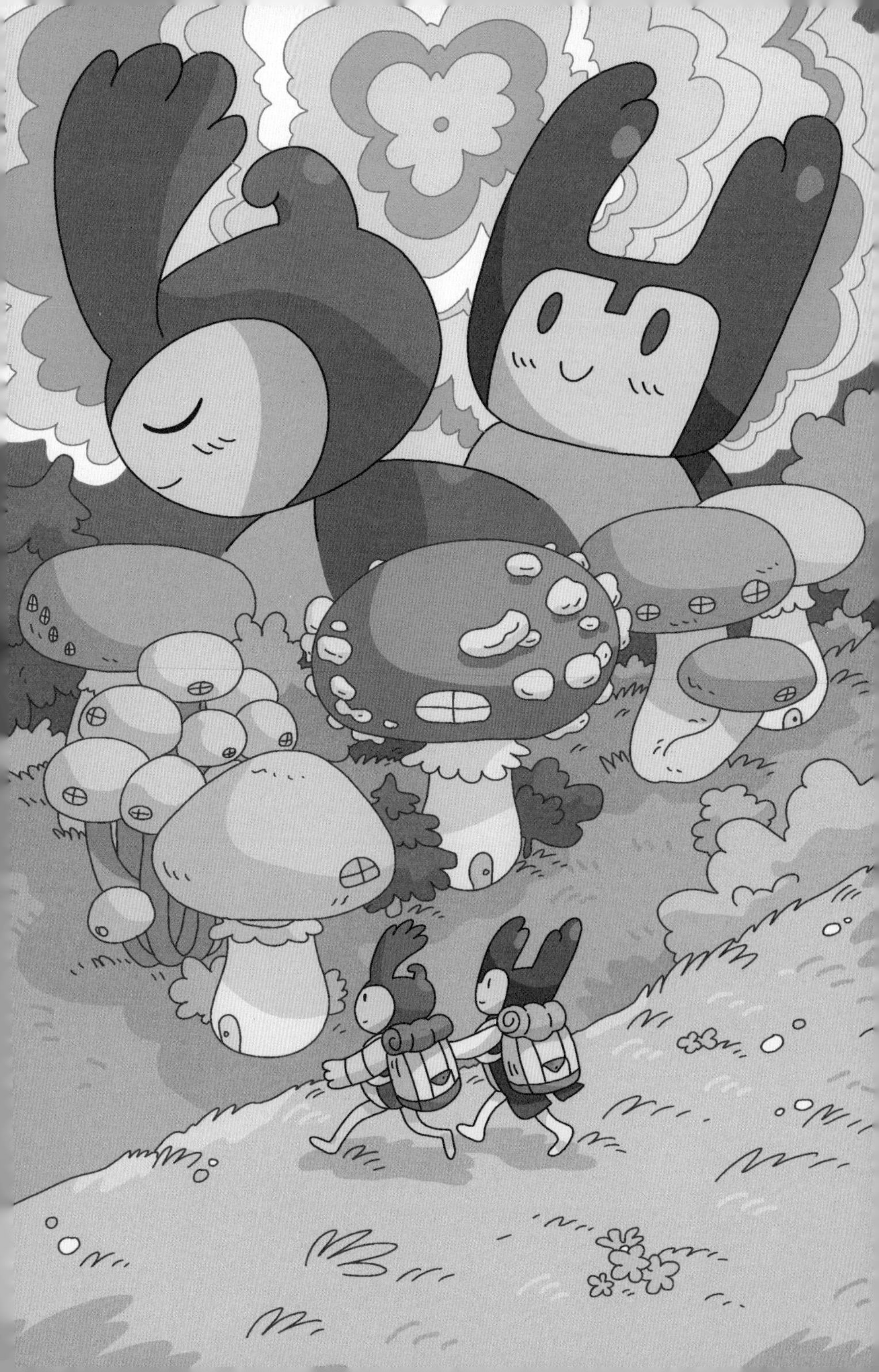

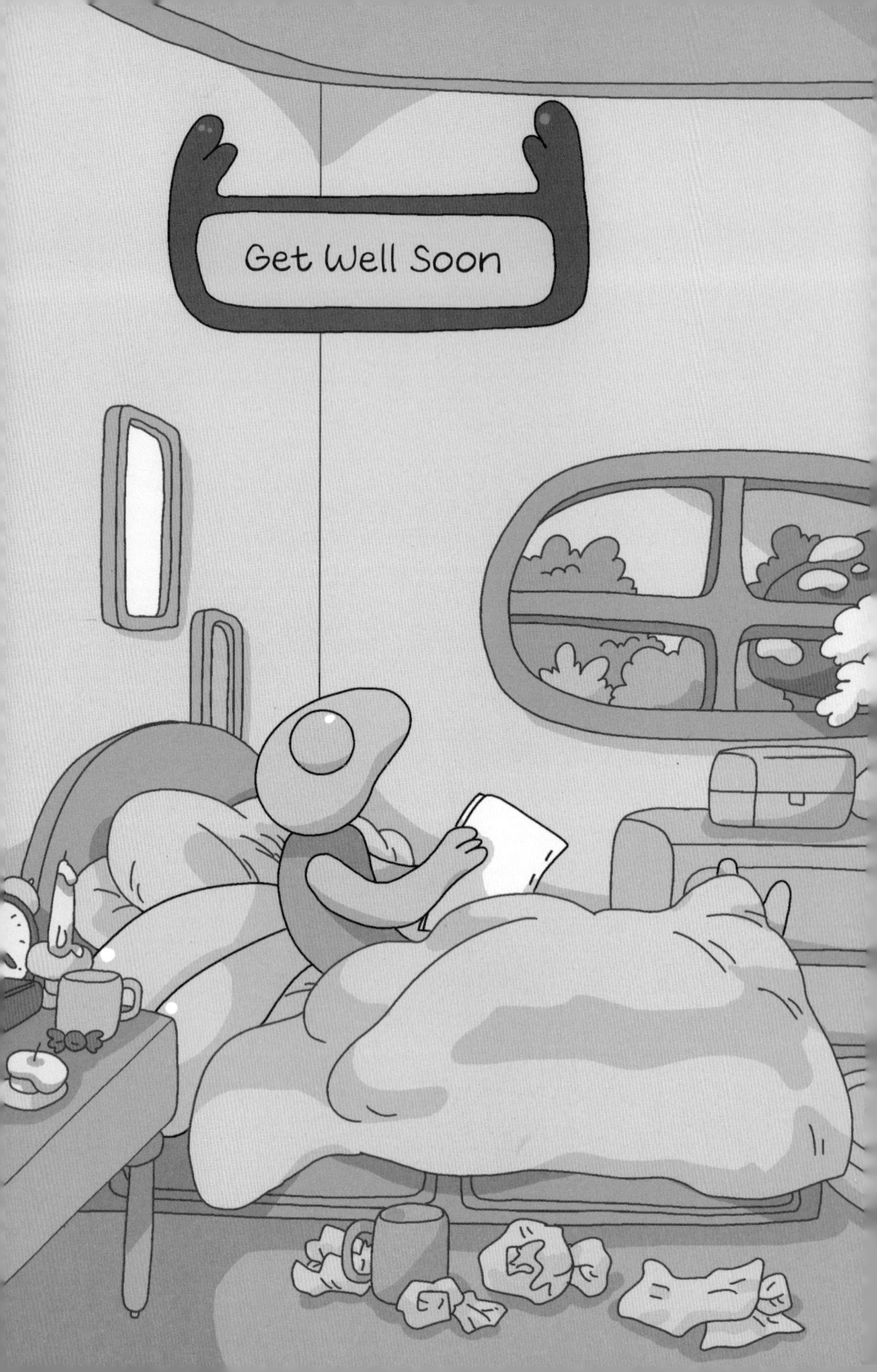
Get Well Soon

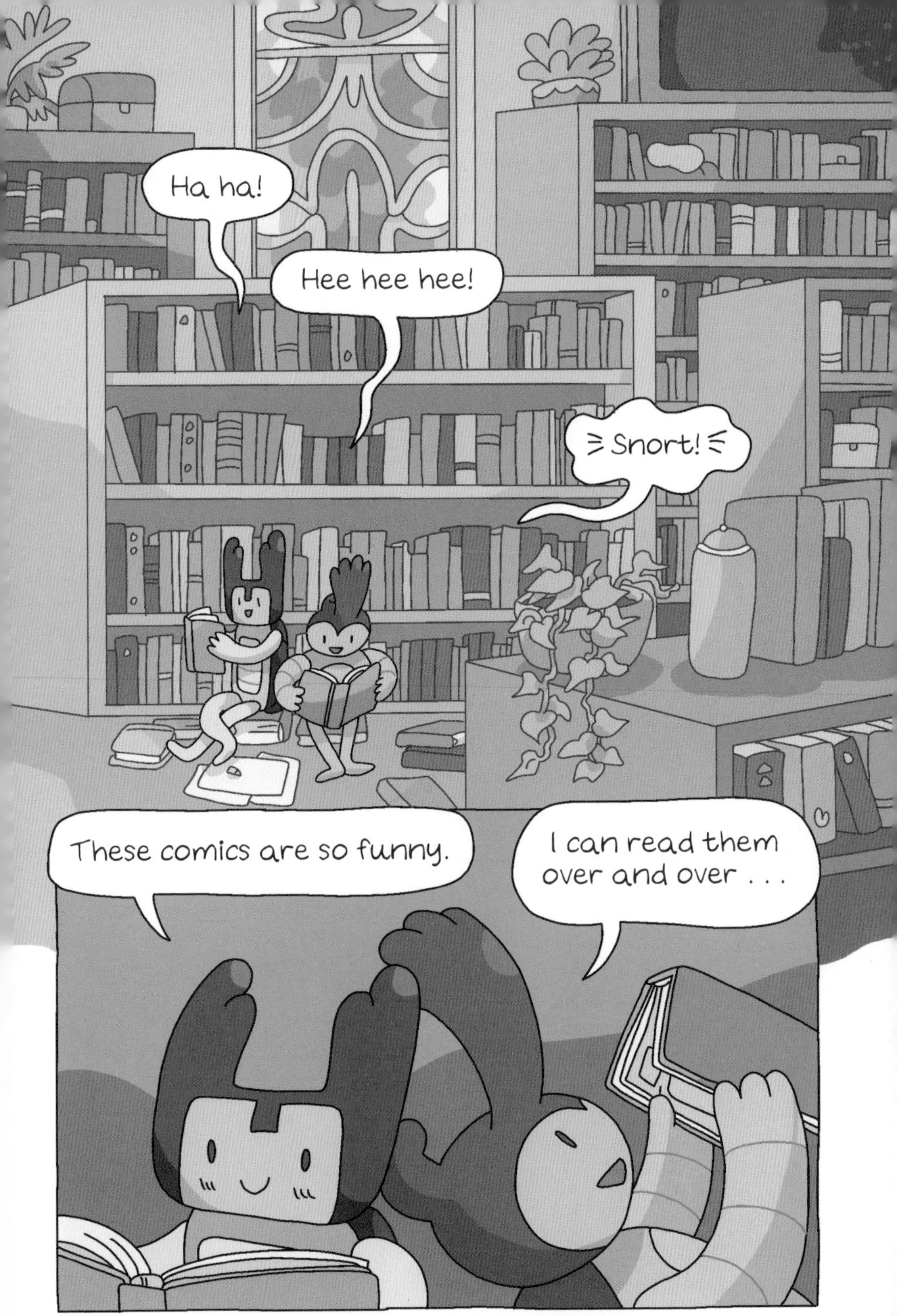
Ha ha!
Hee hee hee!
Snort!
These comics are so funny.
I can read them over and over . . .

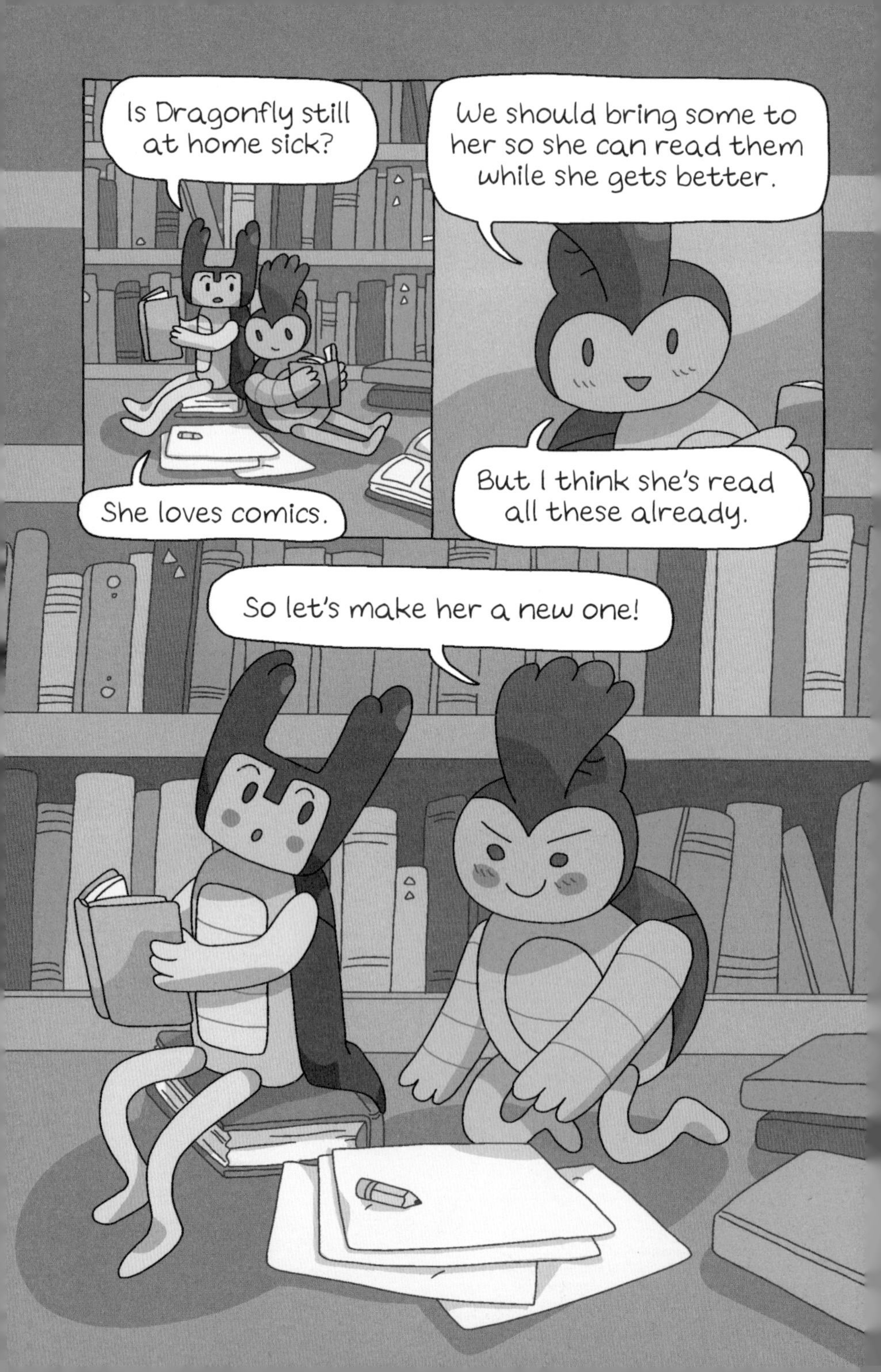
Is Dragonfly still at home sick?
She loves comics.
We should bring some to her so she can read them while she gets better.
But I think she's read all these already.
So let's make her a new one!

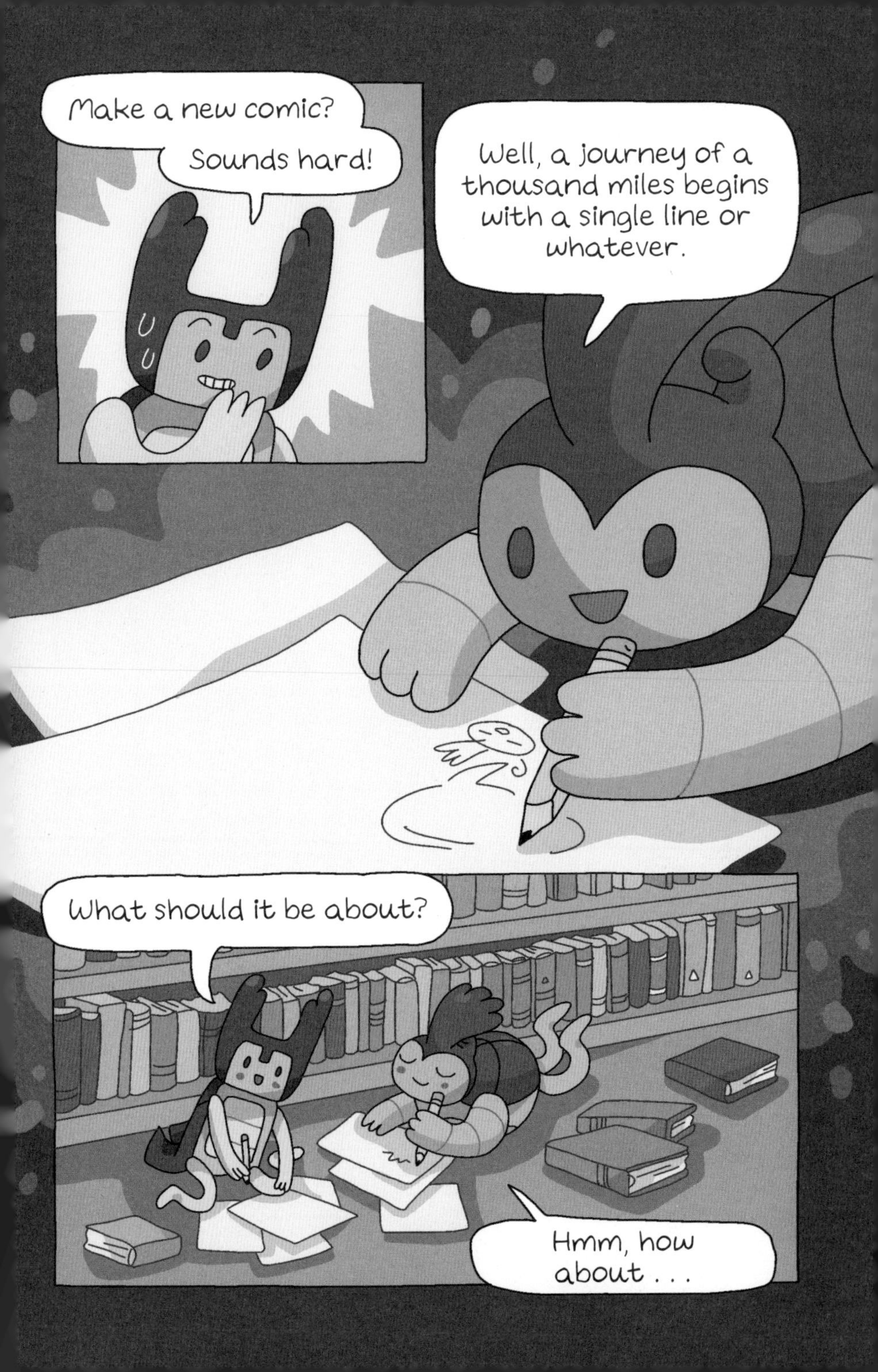
Make a new comic?
Sounds hard!
Well, a journey of a thousand miles begins with a single line or whatever.
What should it be about?
Hmm, how about . . .

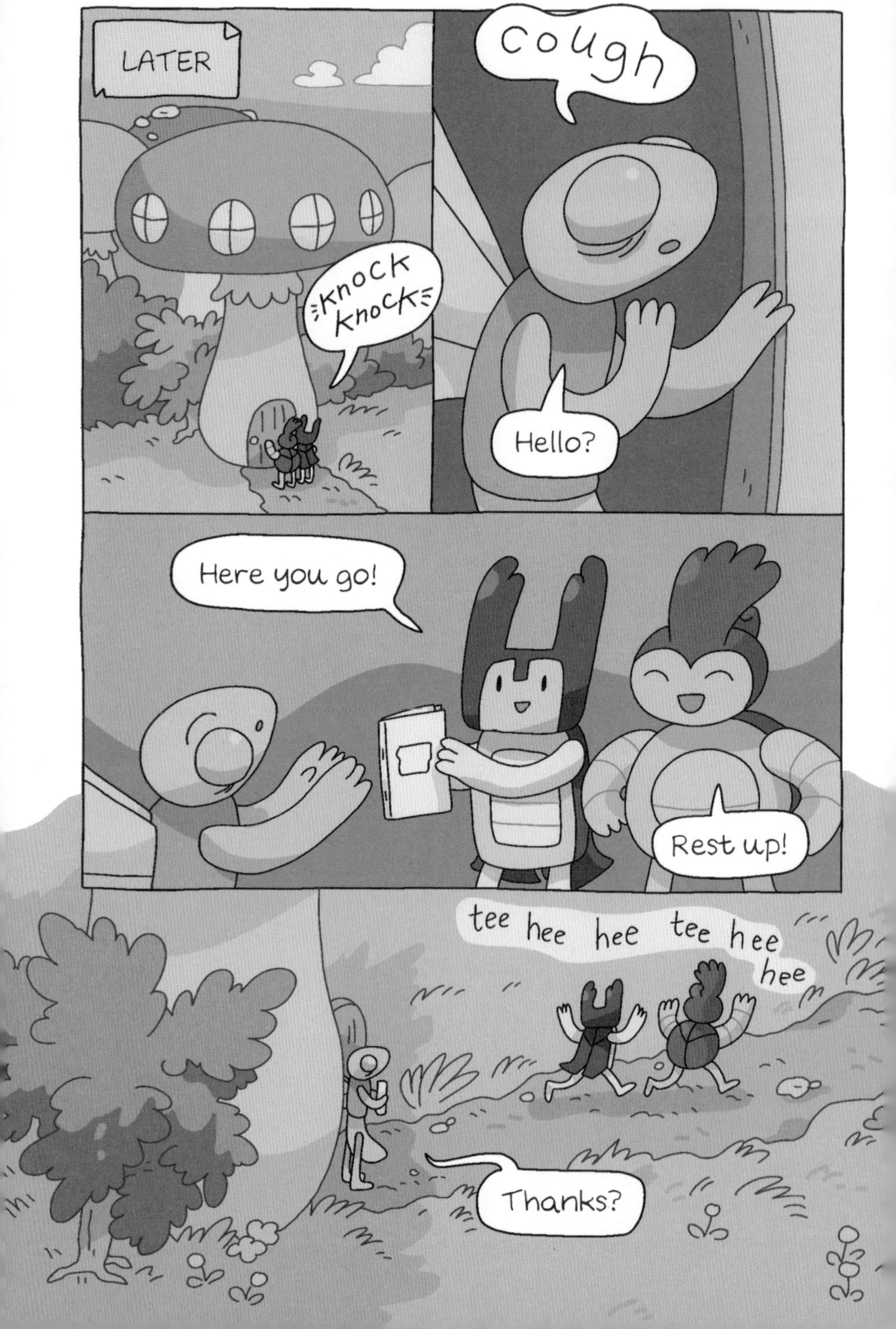
LATER
knock knock
cough
Hello?
Here you go!
Rest up!
tee hee hee tee hee hee
Thanks?

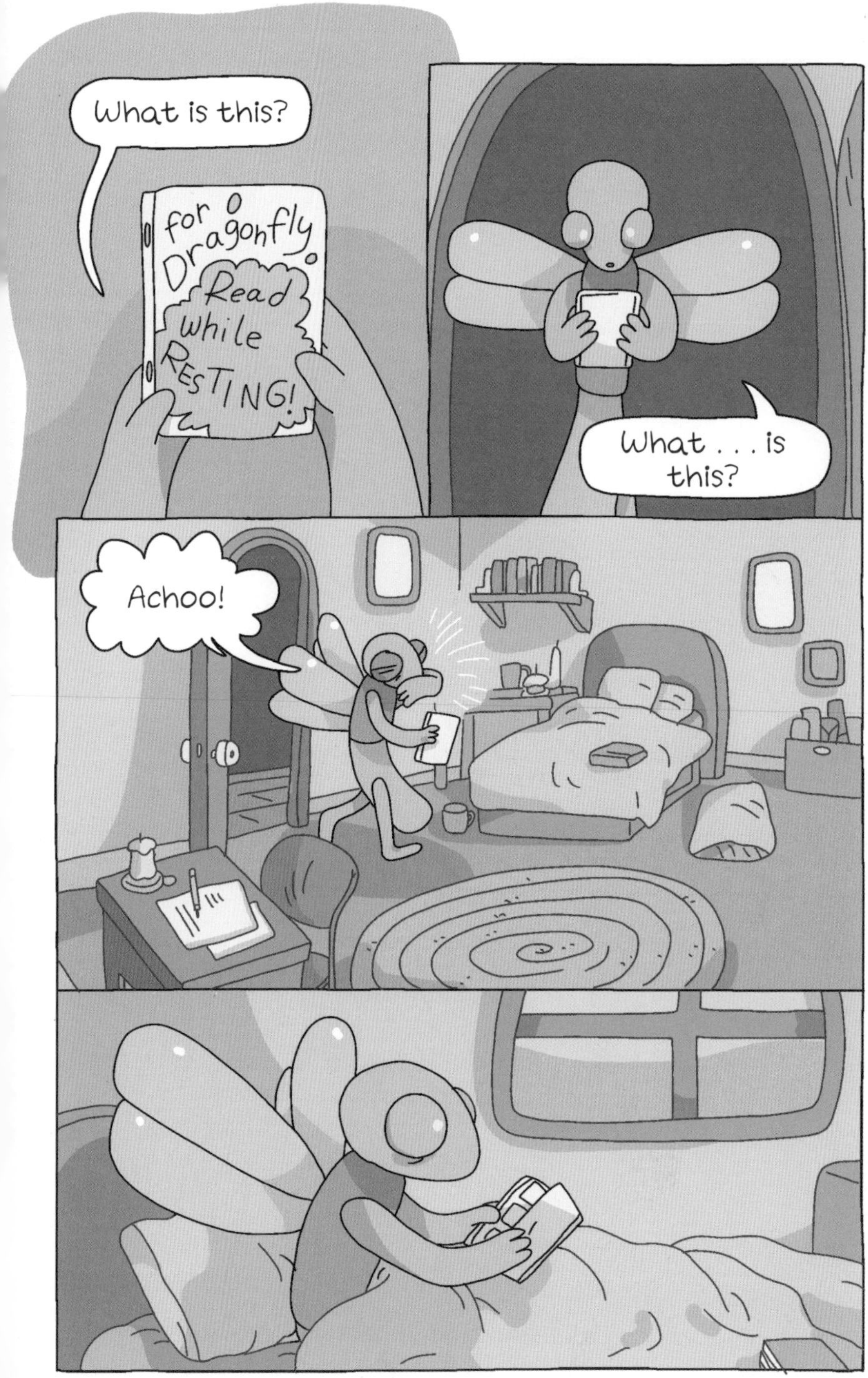
What is this?
for Dragonfly
Read while RESTING!
What . . . is this?
Achoo!

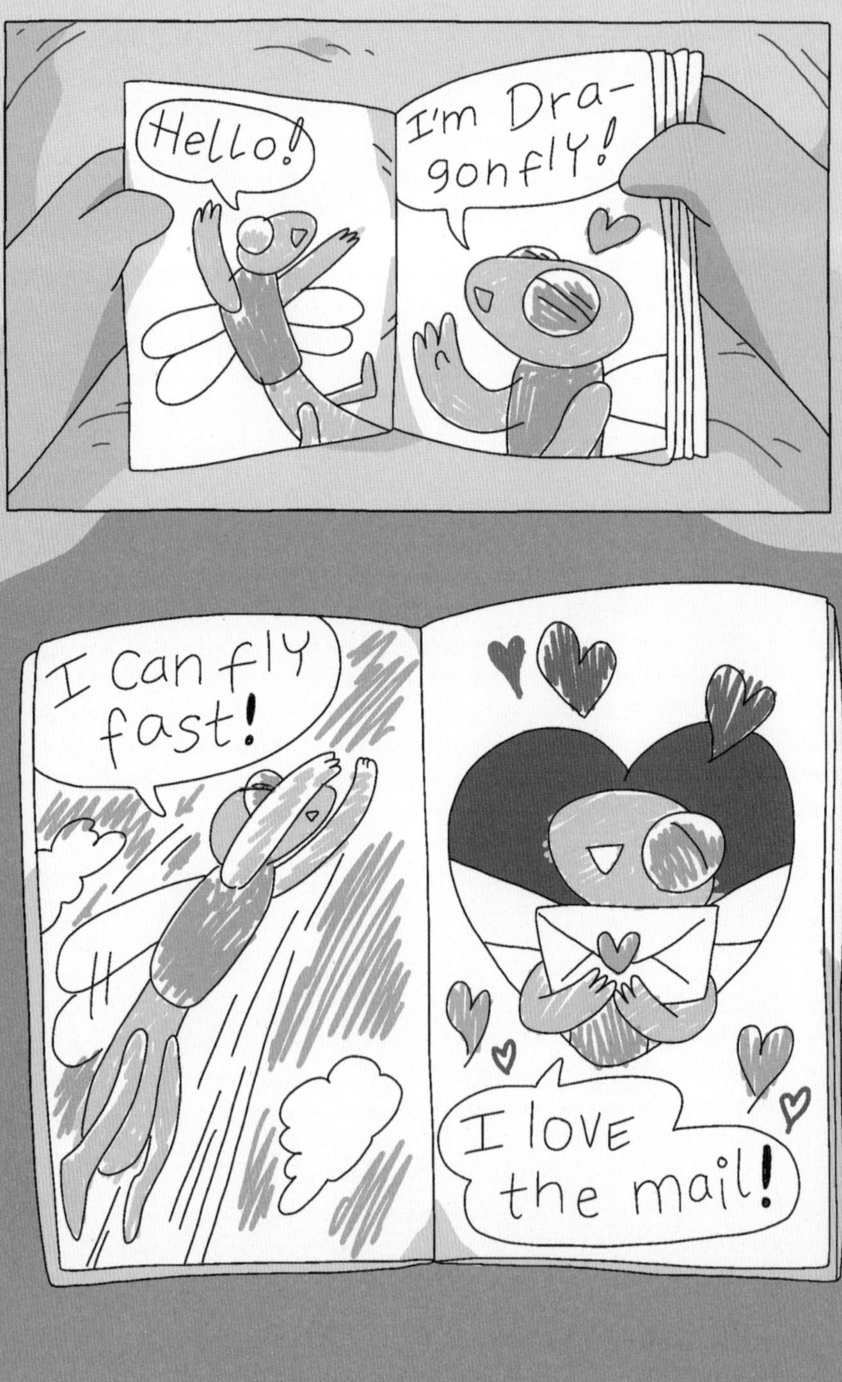
Hello!
I'm Dra-gonfly!
I can fly fast!
I love the mail!

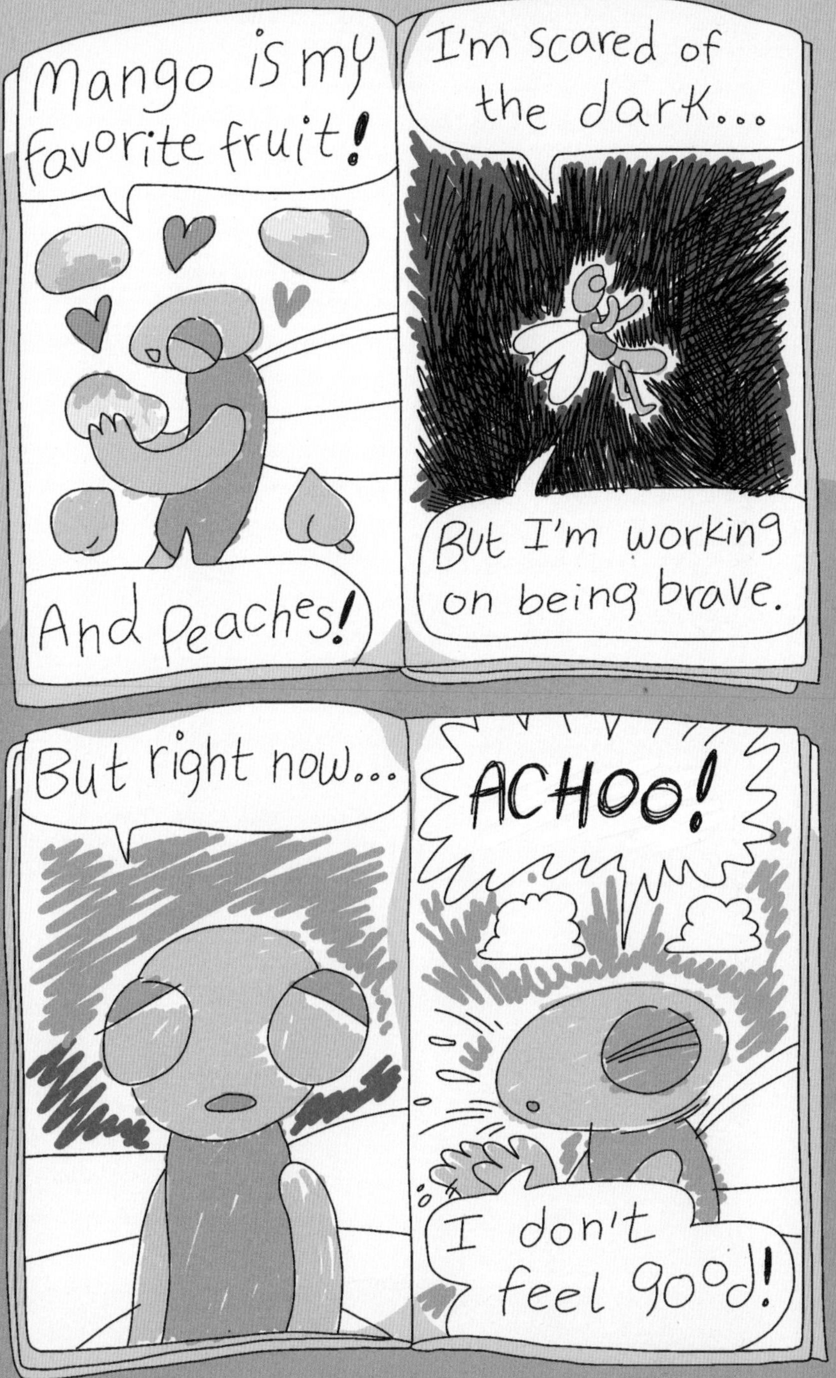
Mango is my favorite fruit!
And peaches!
I'm scared of the dark...
But I'm working on being brave.
But right now...
ACHOO!
I don't feel good!

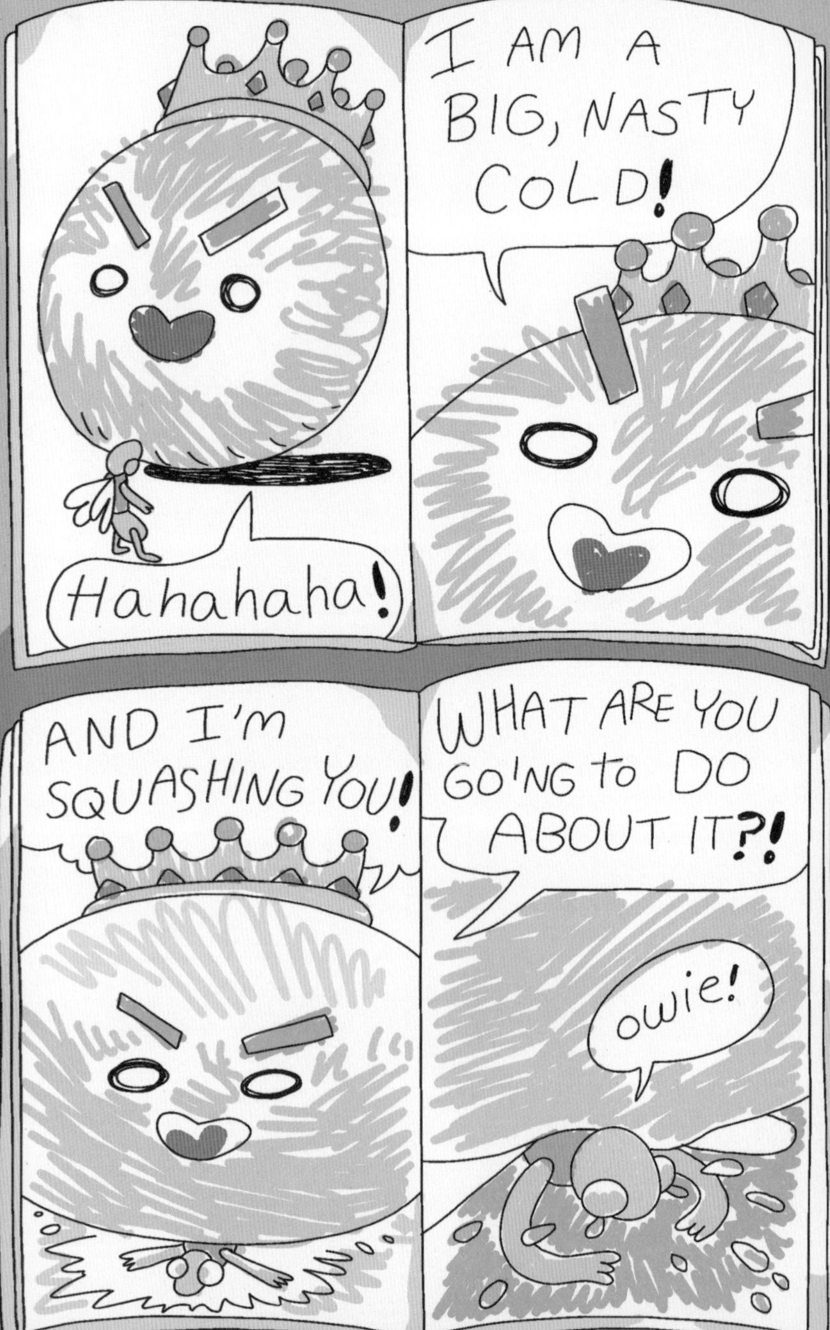
I AM A BIG, NASTY COLD!
Hahahaha!
AND I'M SQUASHING YOU!
WHAT ARE YOU GOING TO DO ABOUT IT?!
owie!

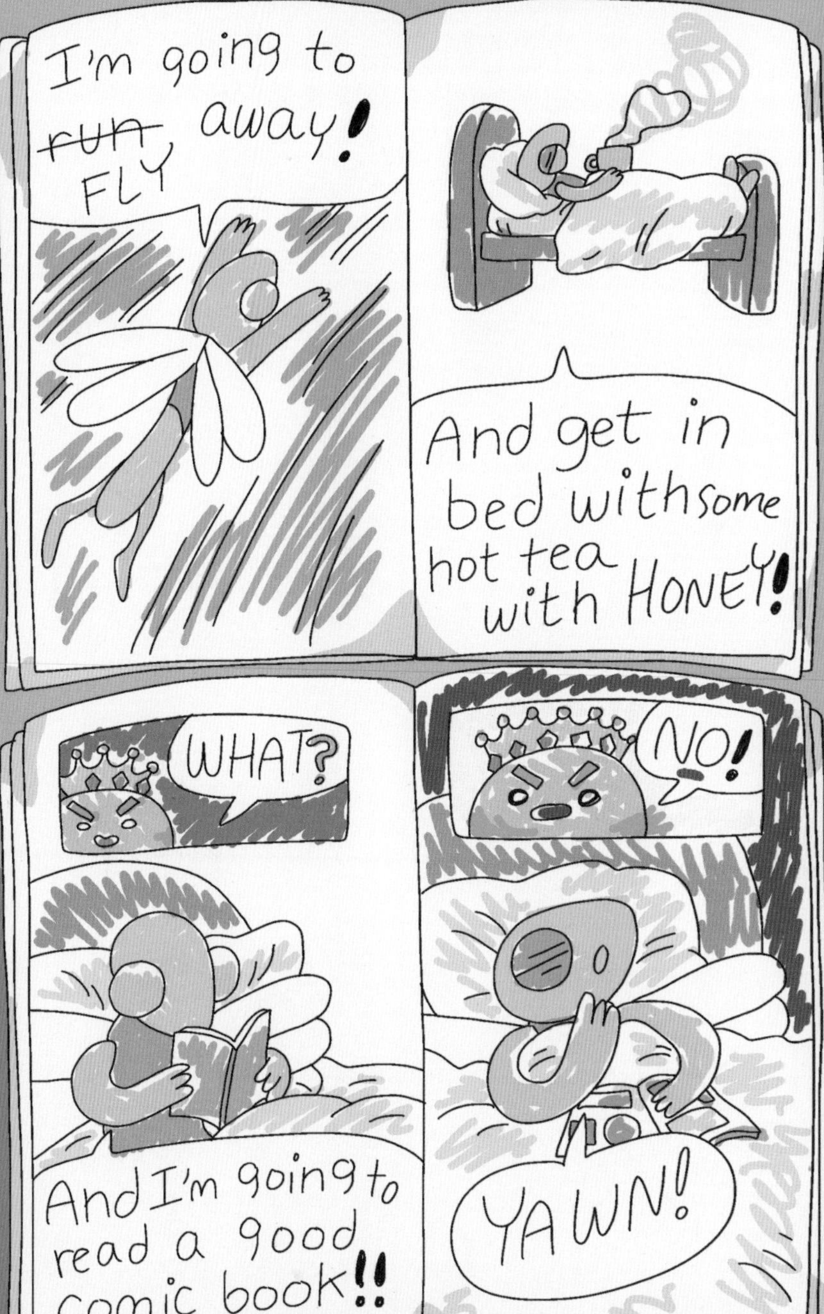
I'm going to run FLY away!
And get in bed with some hot tea with HONEY!
WHAT?
NO!
And I'm going to read a good comic book!!
YAWN!

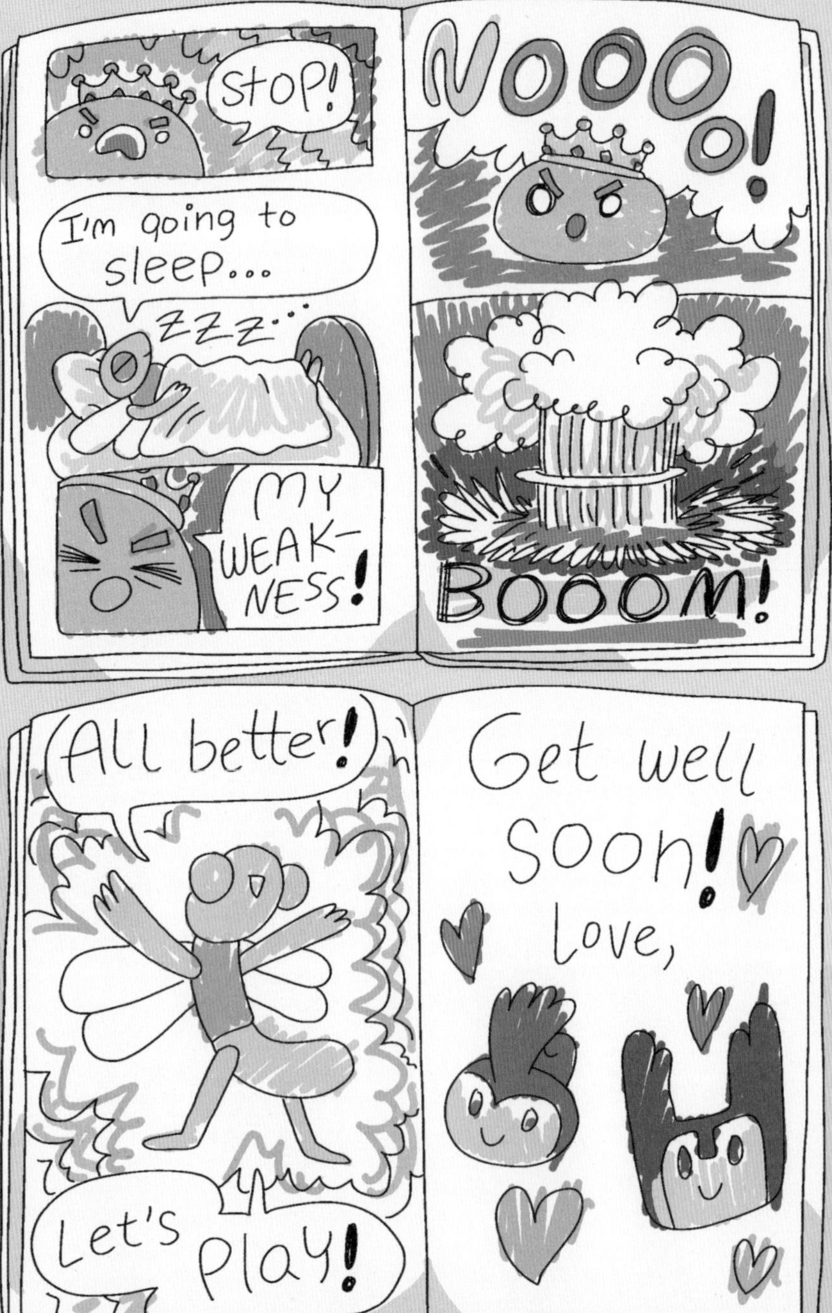
STOP!
I'm going to sleep...
ZZZ...
MY WEAKNESS!
NOOOO!
BOOOM!
All better!
Let's play!
Get well soon!
love,

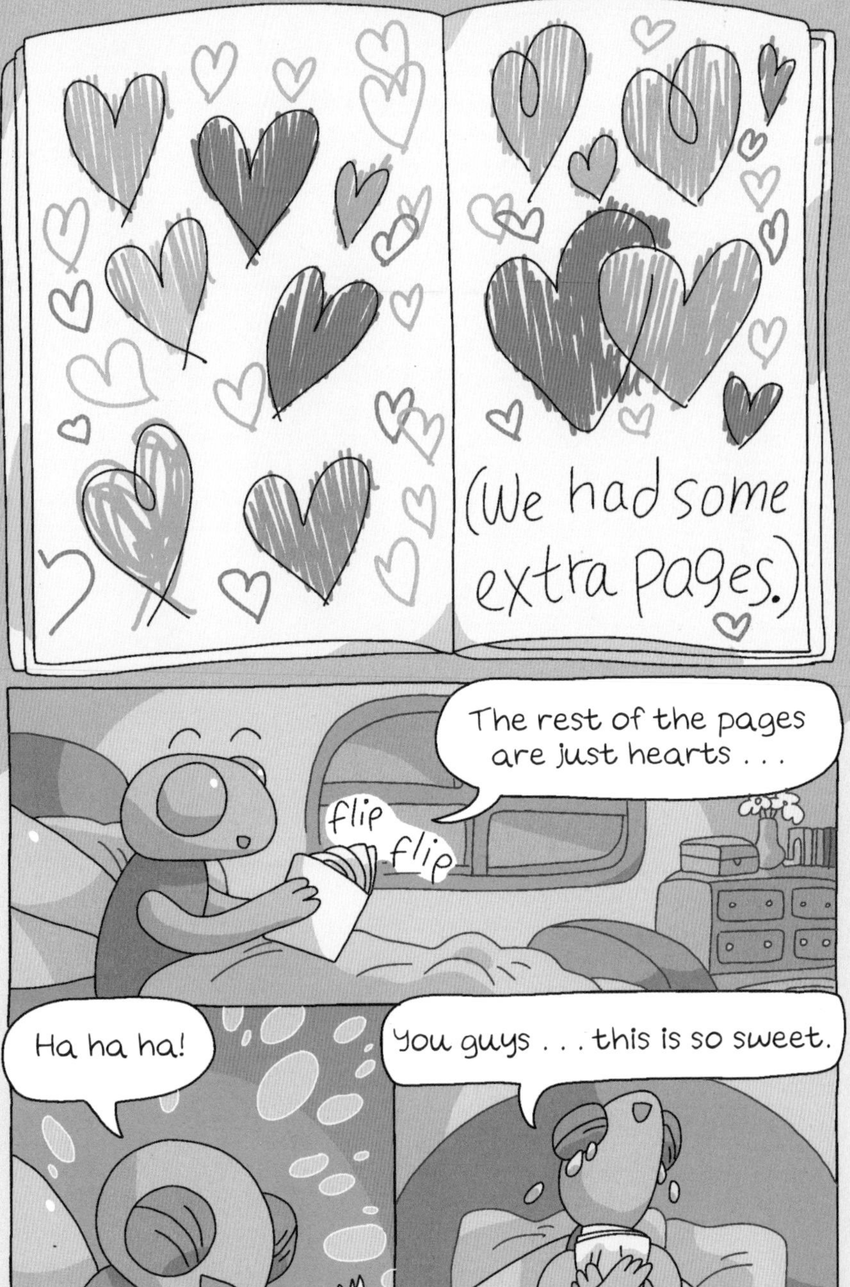
(We had some extra pages.)
The rest of the pages are just hearts . . .
flip
flip
Ha ha ha!
You guys . . . this is so sweet.

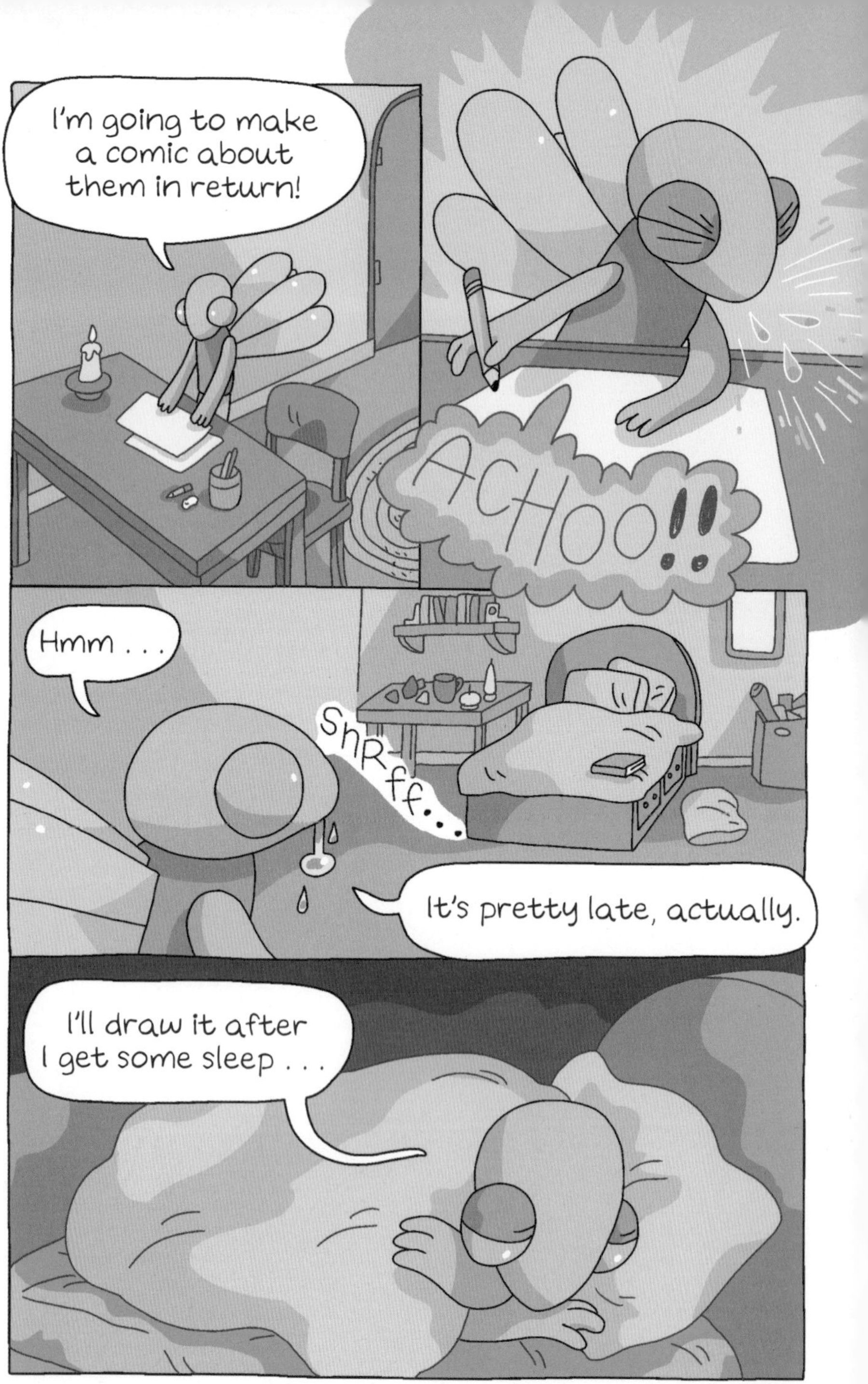
I'm going to make a comic about them in return!
ACHOO!!
Hmm . . .
SNR-ff. . .
It's pretty late, actually.
I'll draw it after I get some sleep . . .

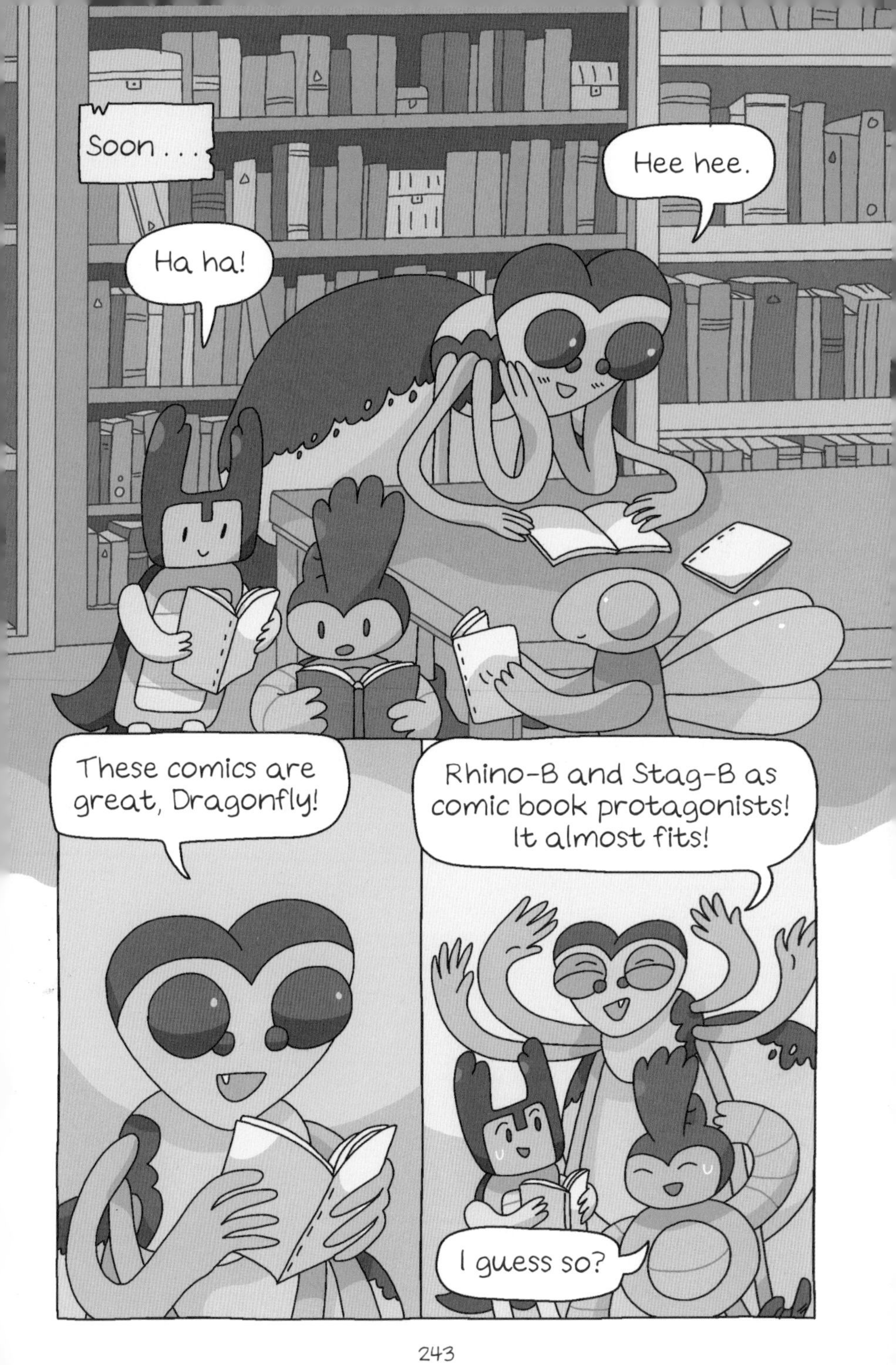
Soon . . .
Hee hee.
Ha ha!
These comics are great, Dragonfly!
Rhino-B and Stag-B as comic book protagonists! It almost fits!
I guess so?

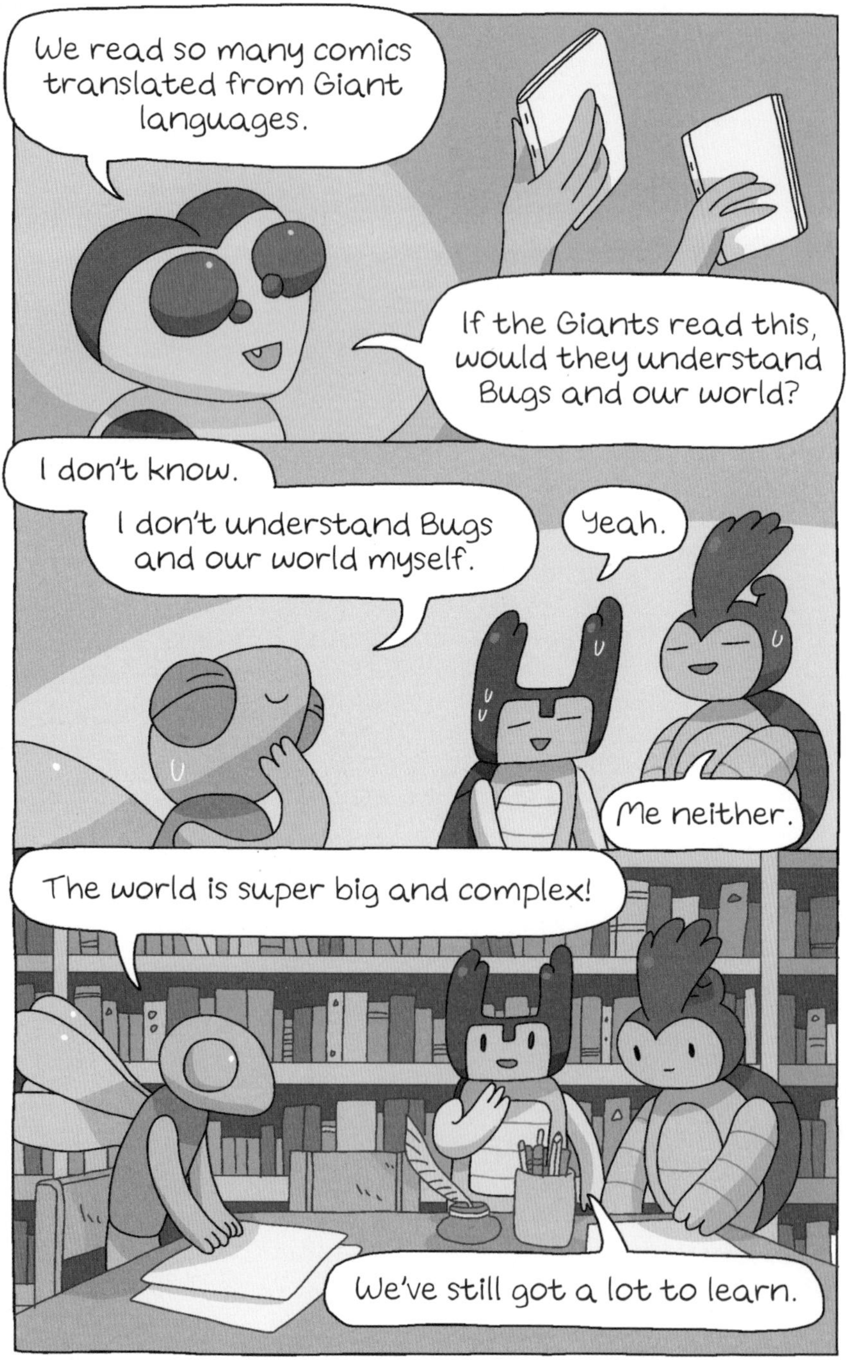
We read so many comics translated from Giant languages.
If the Giants read this, would they understand Bugs and our world?
I don't know.
I don't understand Bugs and our world myself.
Yeah.
Me neither.
The world is super big and complex!
We've still got a lot to learn.

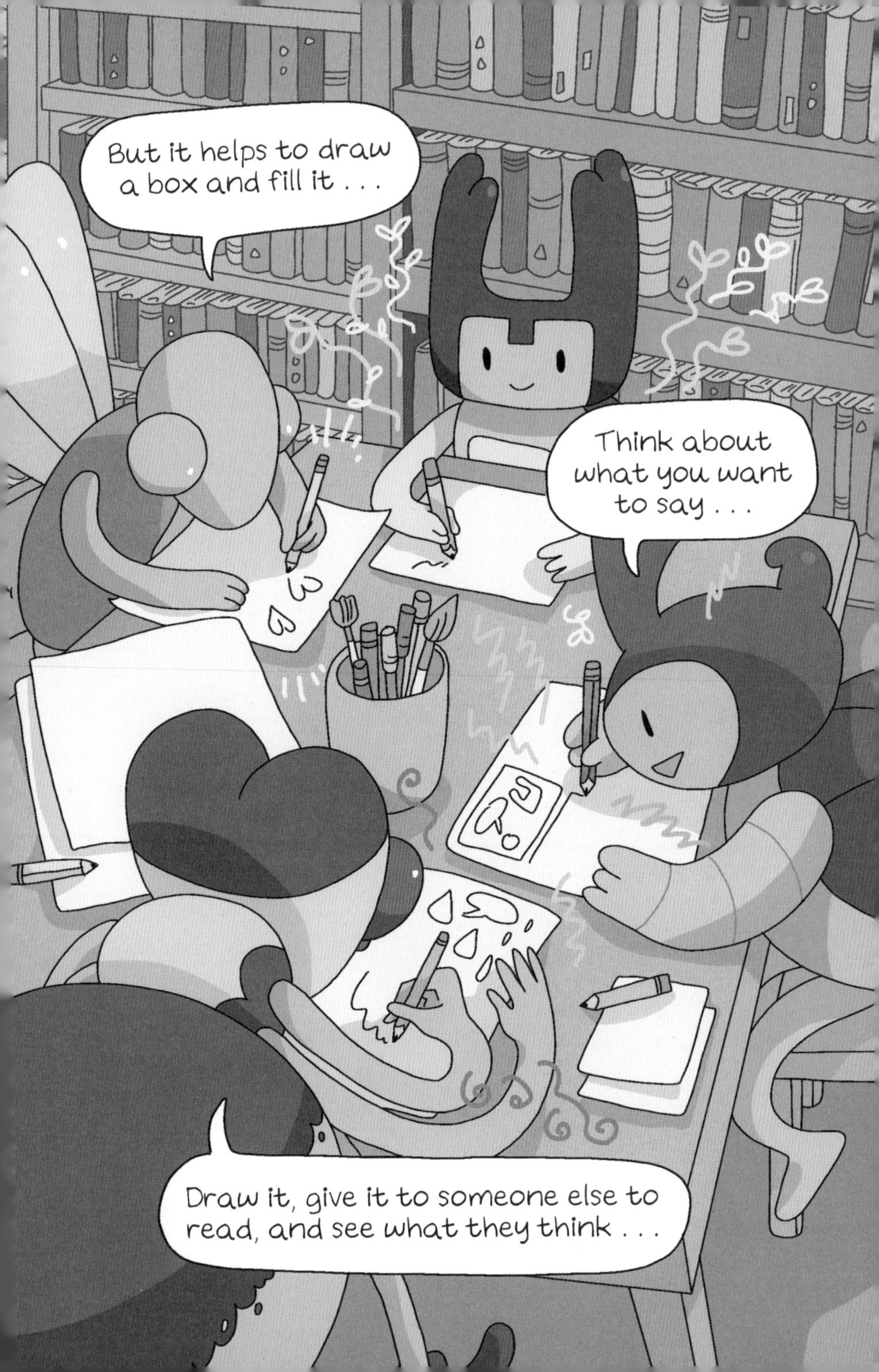
But it helps to draw a box and fill it . . .
Think about what you want to say . . .
Draw it, give it to someone else to read, and see what they think . . .

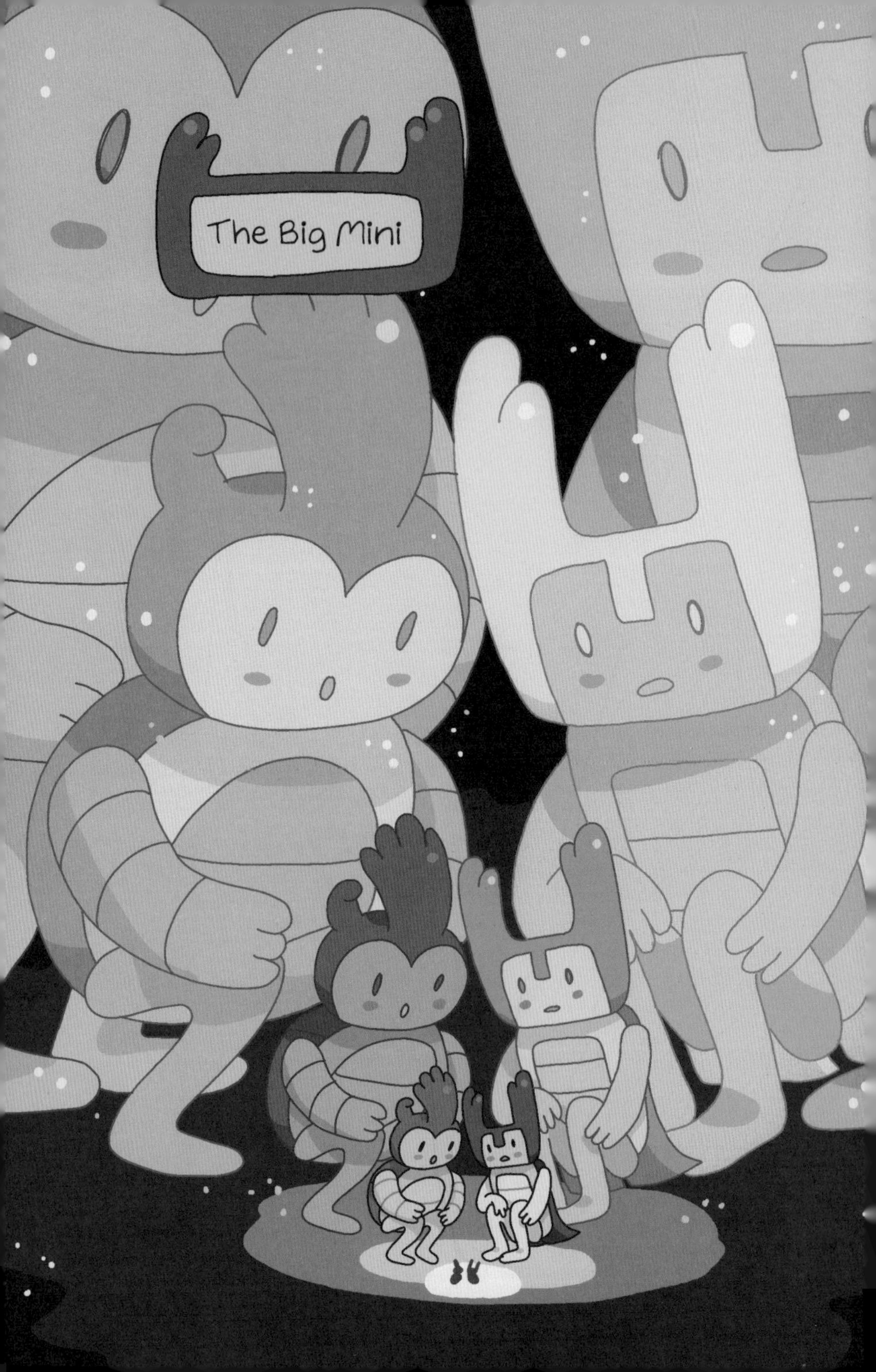
The Big Mini

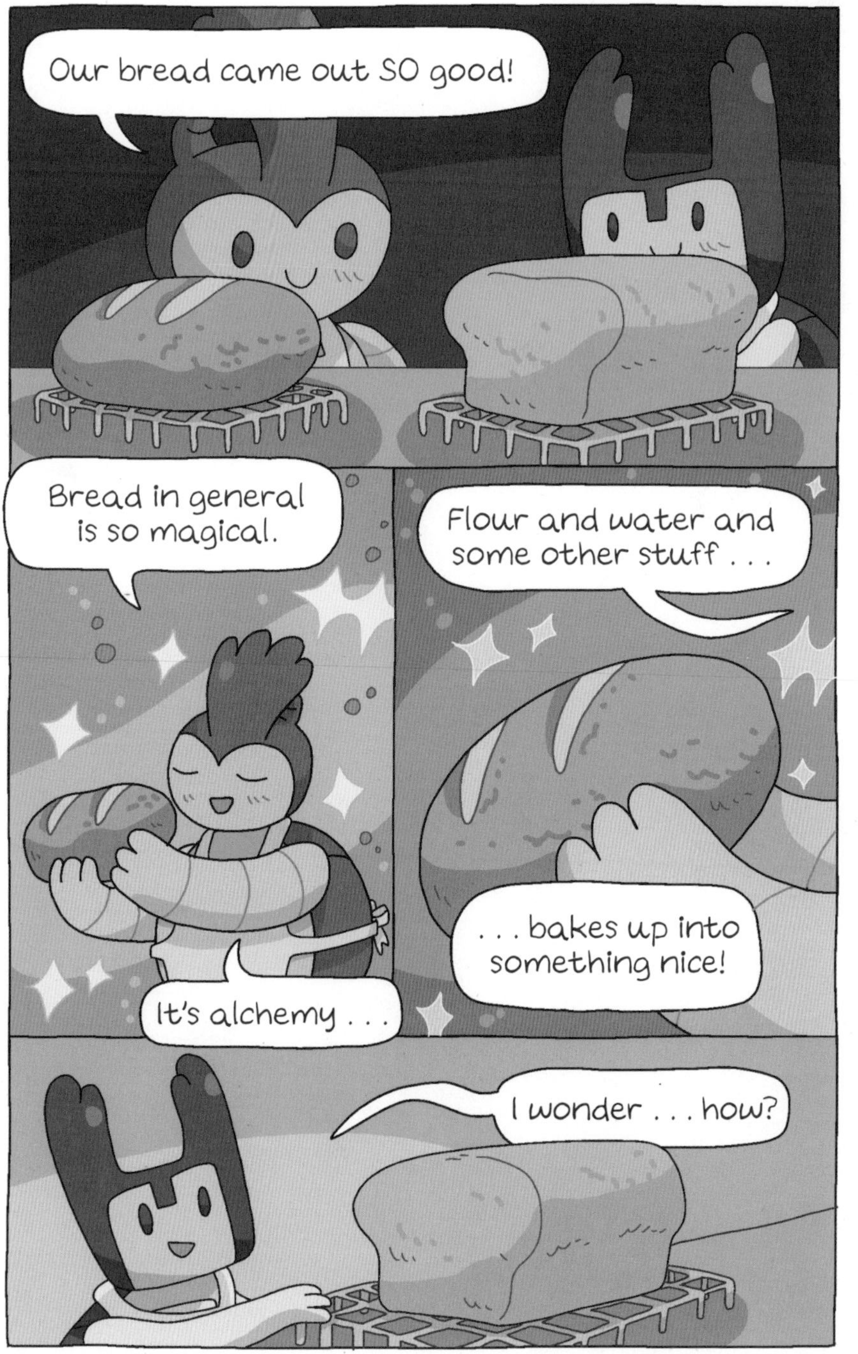
Our bread came out SO good!
Bread in general is so magical.
It's alchemy . . .
Flour and water and some other stuff . . .
. . . bakes up into something nice!
I wonder . . . how?

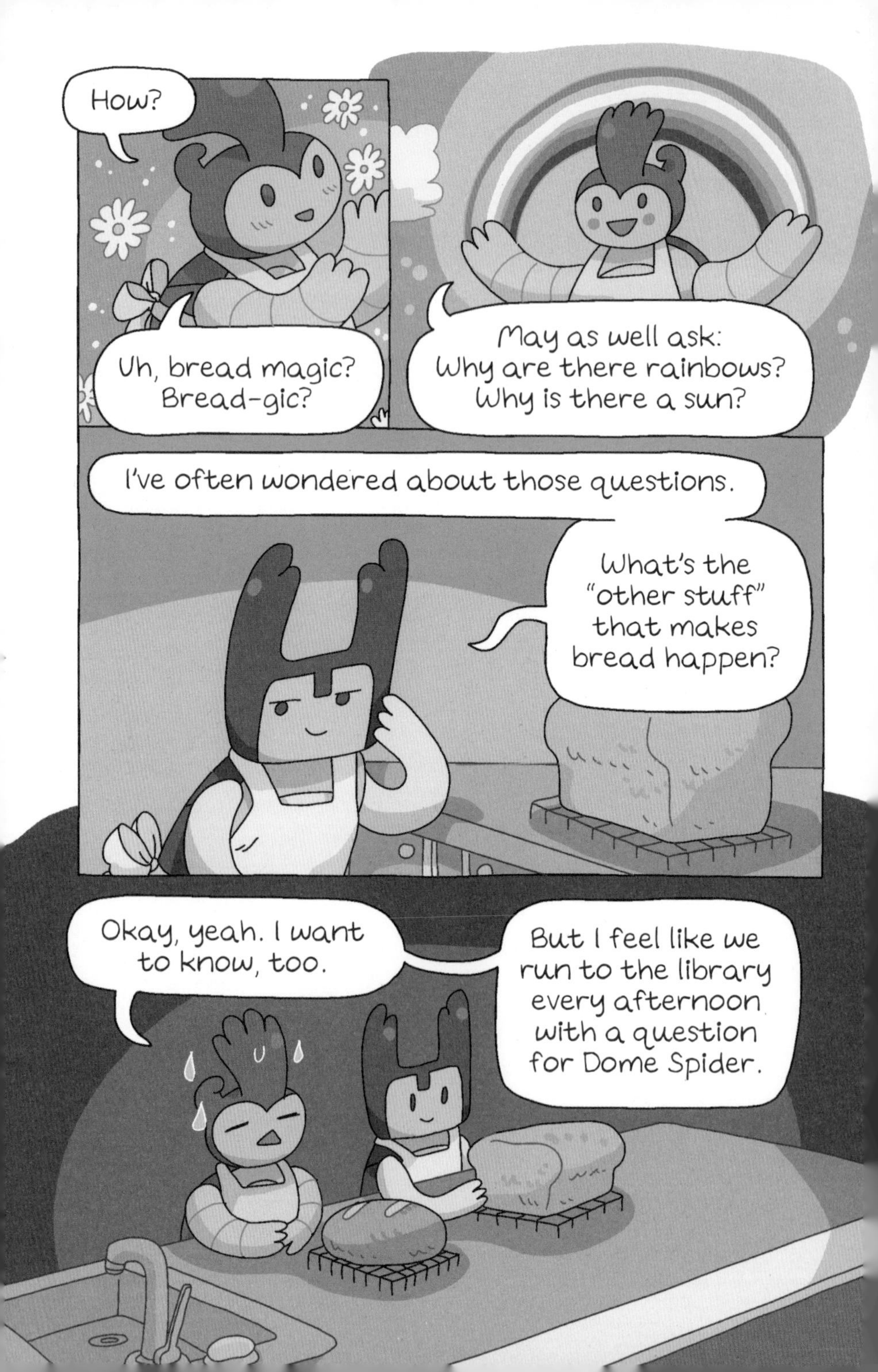
How?
Uh, bread magic? Bread-gic?
May as well ask: Why are there rainbows? Why is there a sun?
I've often wondered about those questions.
What's the "other stuff" that makes bread happen?
Okay, yeah. I want to know, too.
But I feel like we run to the library every afternoon with a question for Dome Spider.

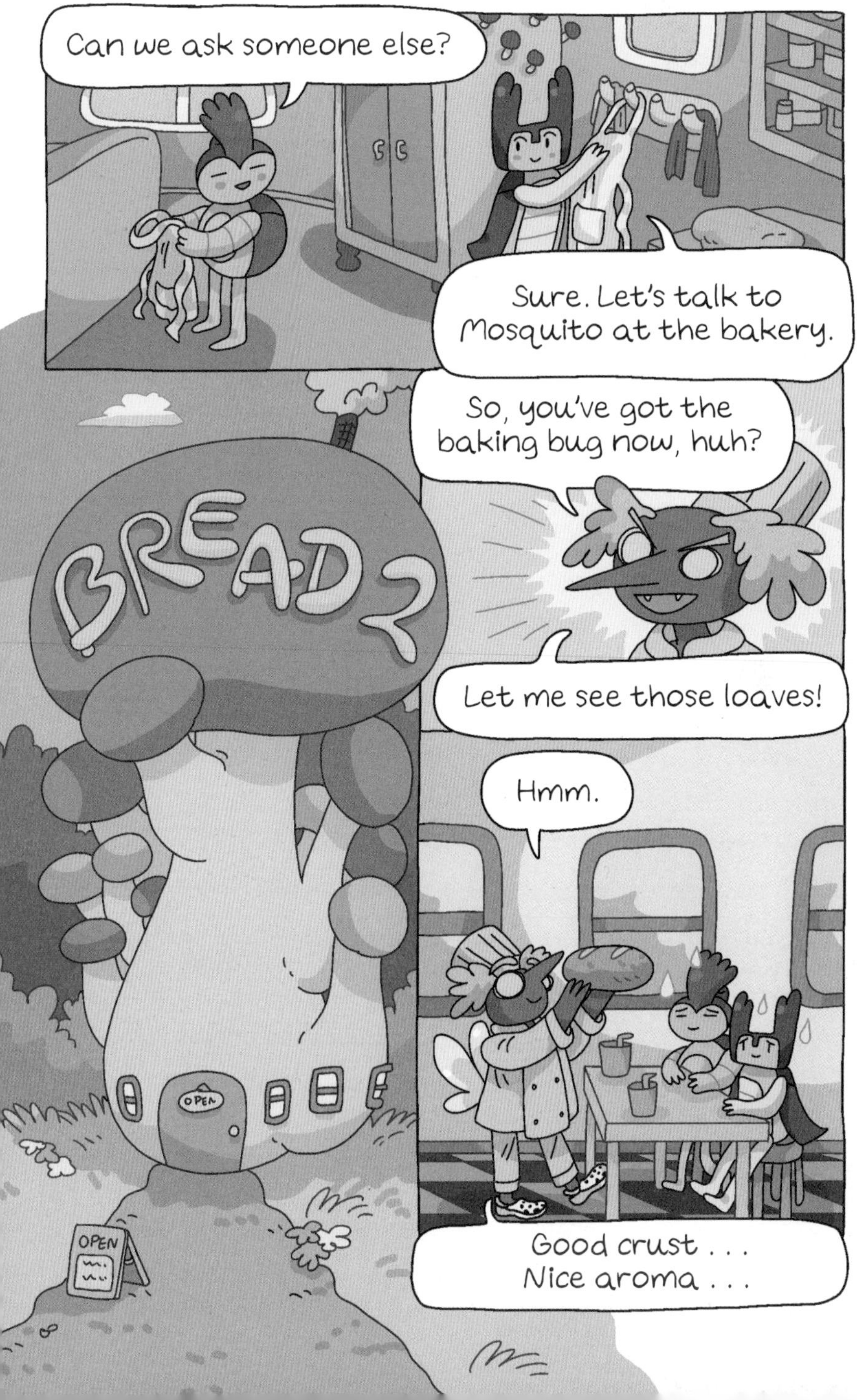

Can we ask someone else?
Sure. Let's talk to Mosquito at the bakery.
BREAD 2
OPEN
So, you've got the baking bug now, huh?
Let me see those loaves!
Hmm.
Good crust . . . Nice aroma . . .
OPEN

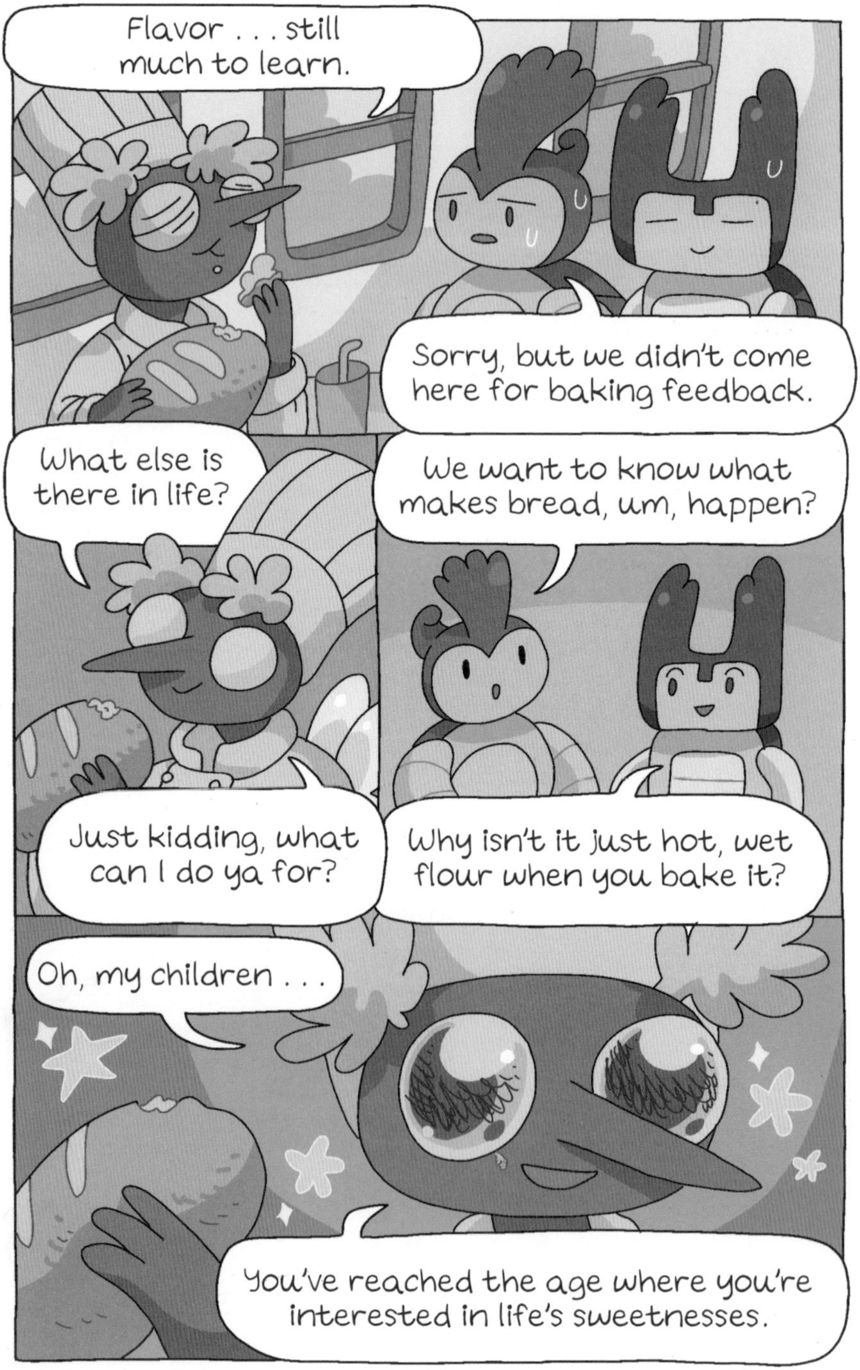
Flavor . . . still much to learn.
Sorry, but we didn't come here for baking feedback.
What else is there in life?
We want to know what makes bread, um, happen?
Just kidding, what can I do ya for?
Why isn't it just hot, wet flour when you bake it?
Oh, my children . . .
You've reached the age where you're interested in life's sweetnesses.

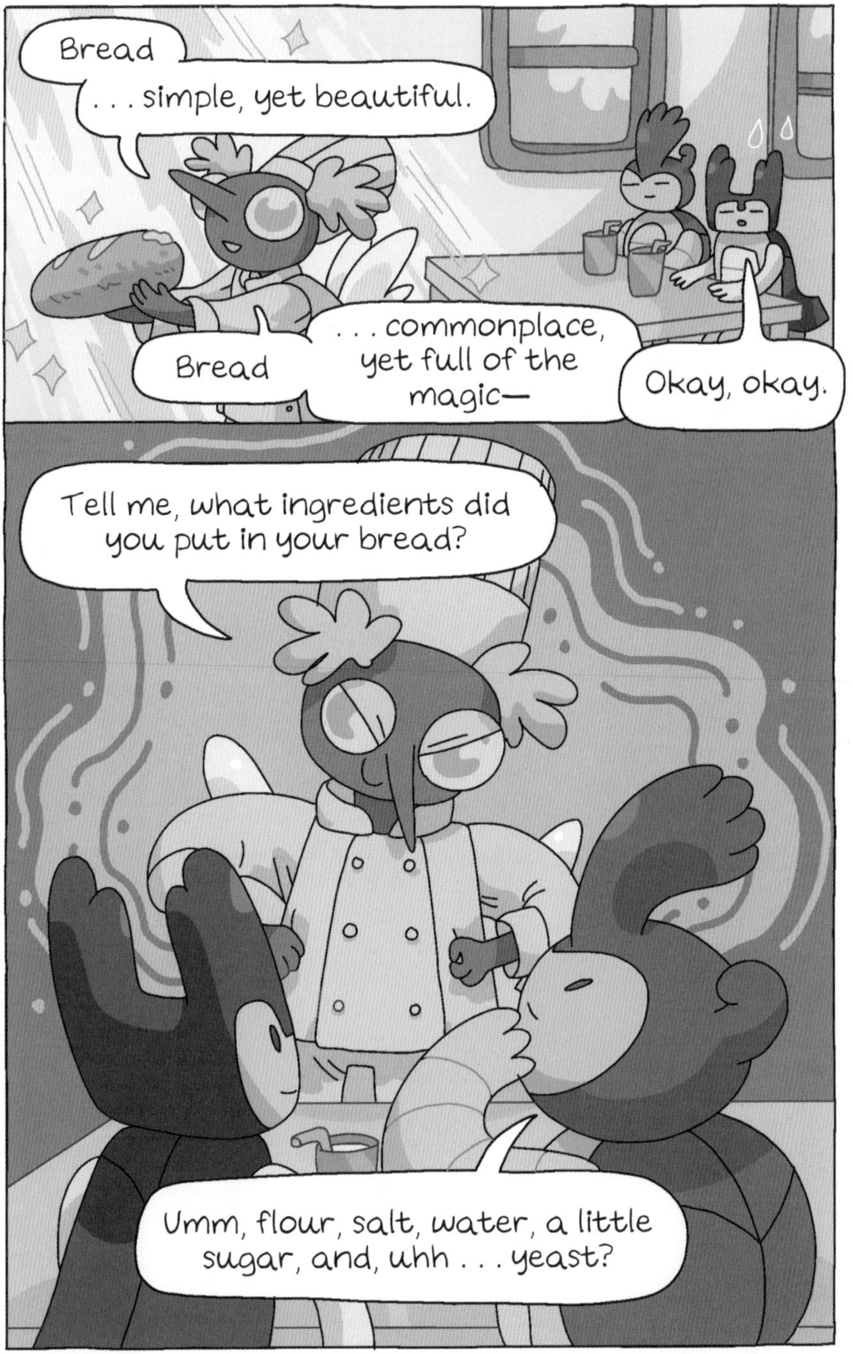
Bread
. . . simple, yet beautiful.
Bread
. . . commonplace, yet full of the magic—
Okay, okay.
Tell me, what ingredients did you put in your bread?
Umm, flour, salt, water, a little sugar, and, uhh . . . yeast?

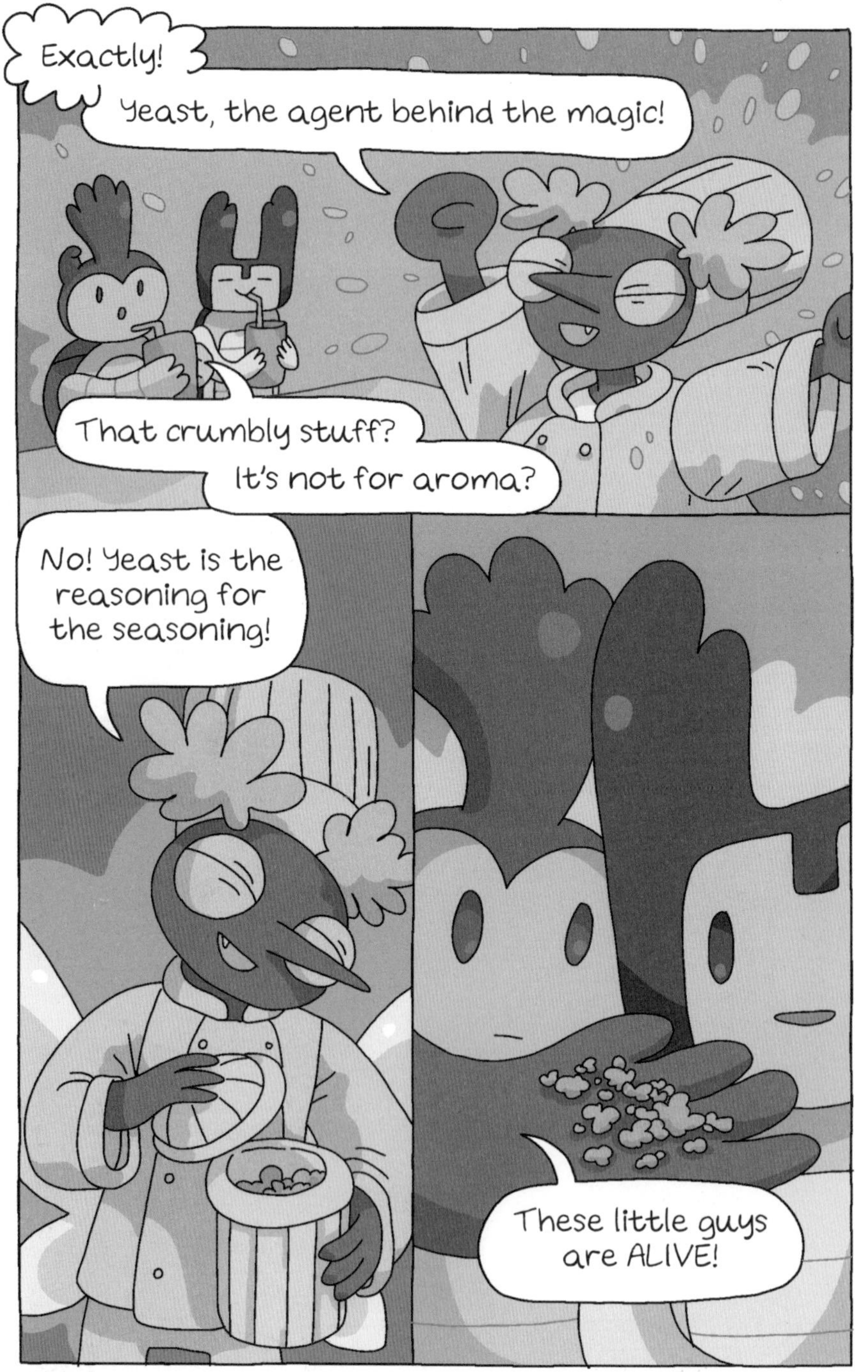
Exactly!
Yeast, the agent behind the magic!
That crumbly stuff?
It's not for aroma?
No! Yeast is the reasoning for the seasoning!
These little guys are ALIVE!

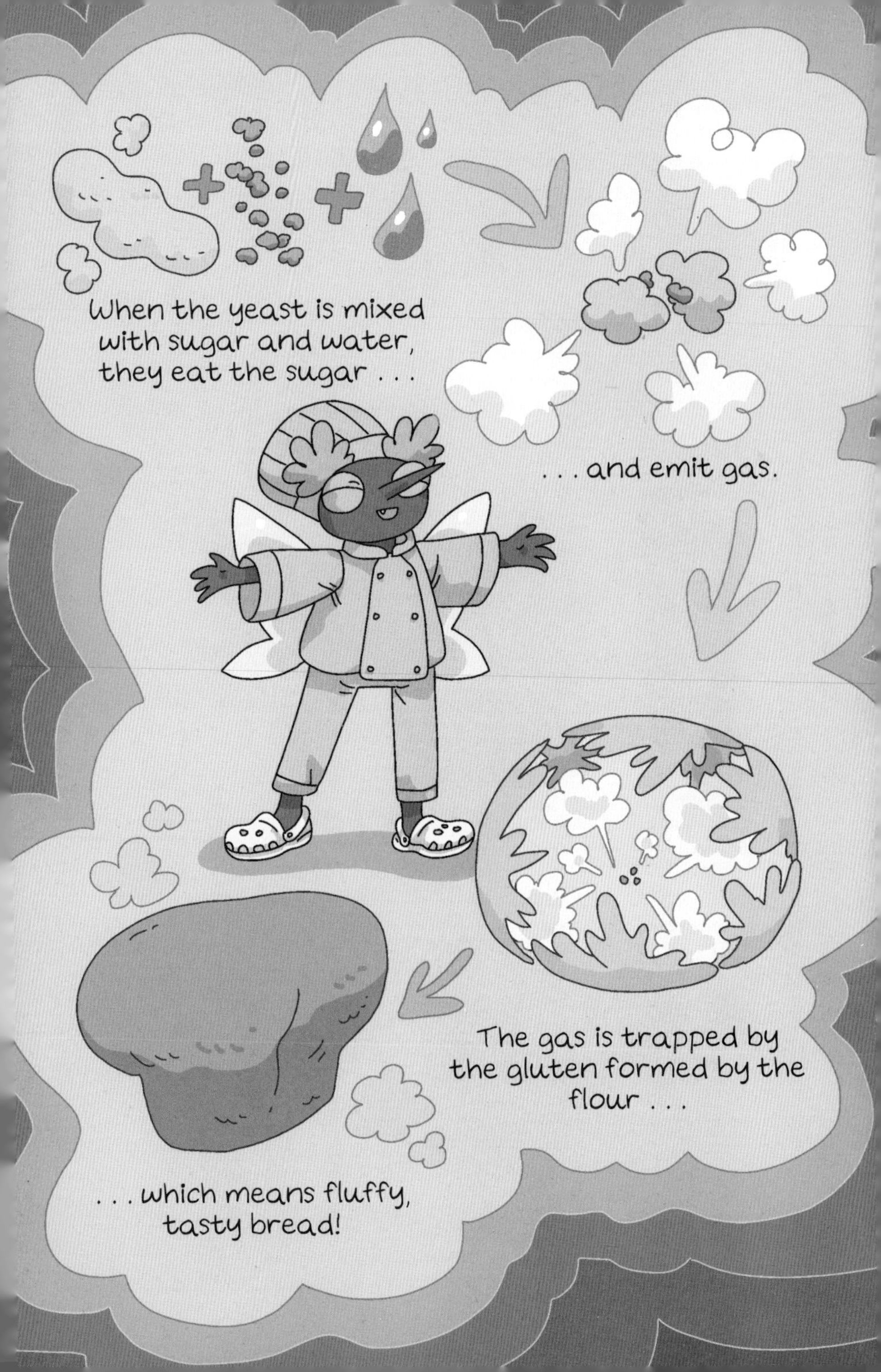
When the yeast is mixed with sugar and water, they eat the sugar . . .
. . . and emit gas.
The gas is trapped by the gluten formed by the flour . . .
. . . which means fluffy, tasty bread!

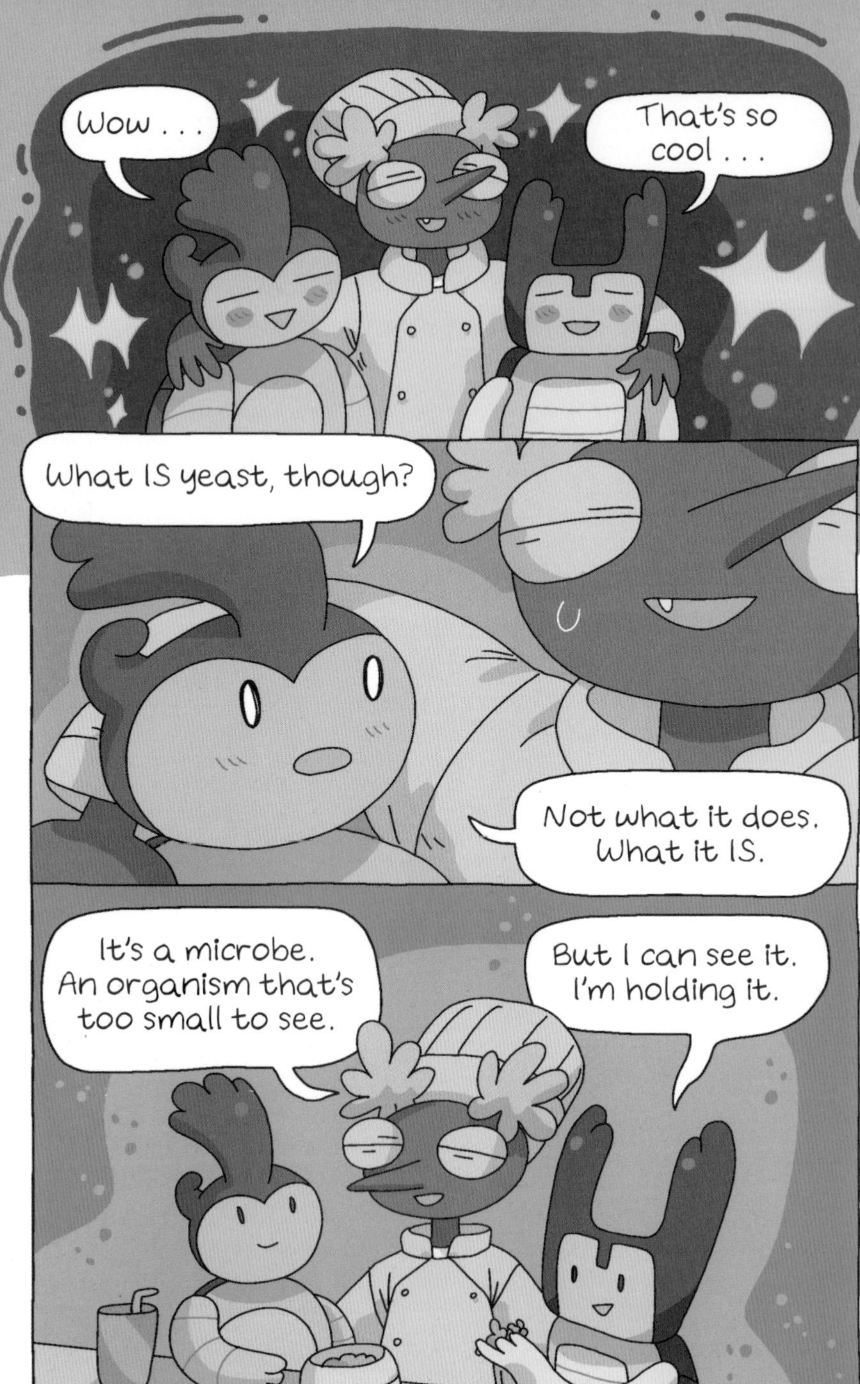
Wow . . .
That's so cool . . .
What IS yeast, though?
Not what it does. What it IS.
It's a microbe. An organism that's too small to see.
But I can see it. I'm holding it.

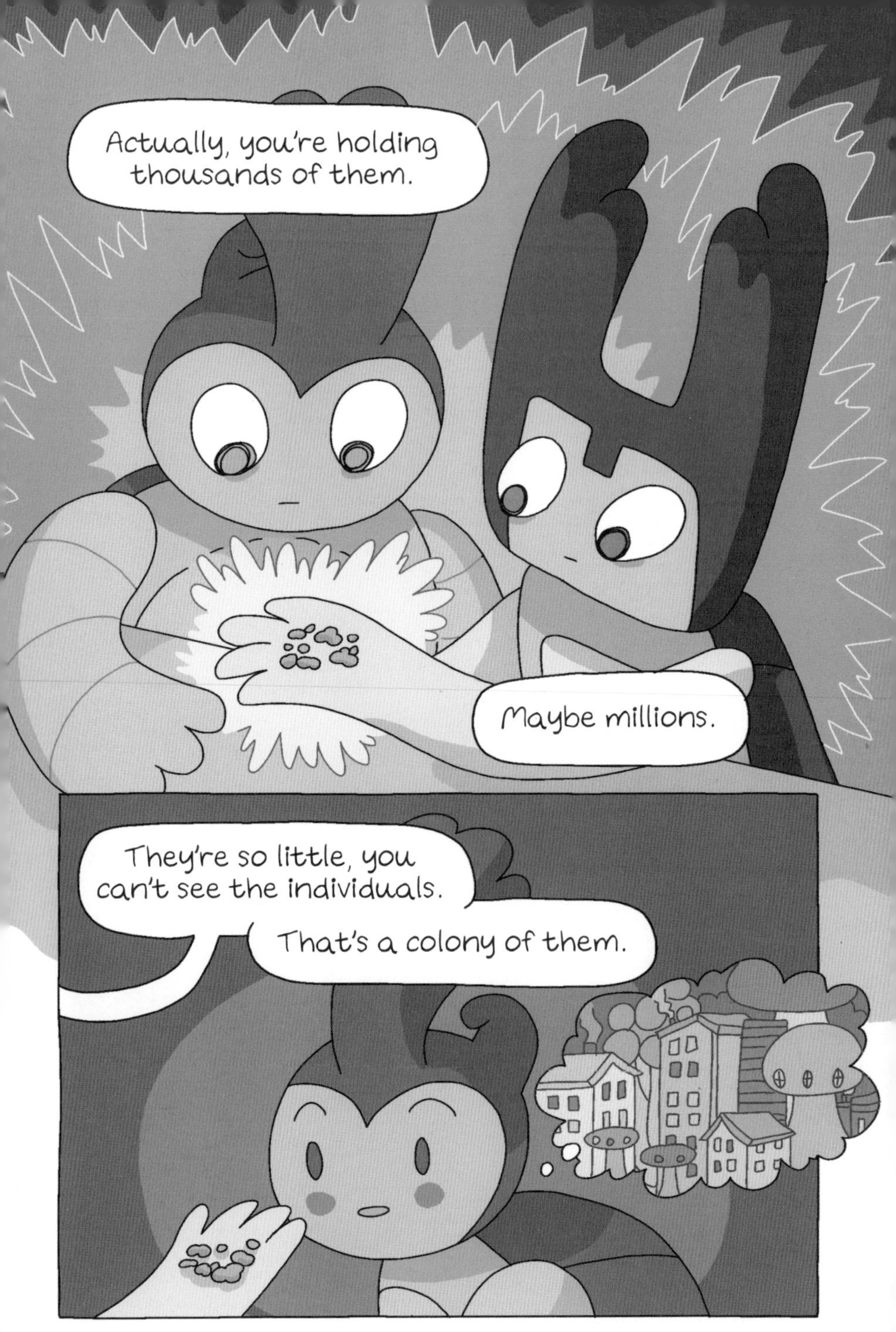
Actually, you're holding thousands of them.
Maybe millions.
They're so little, you can't see the individuals.
That's a colony of them.

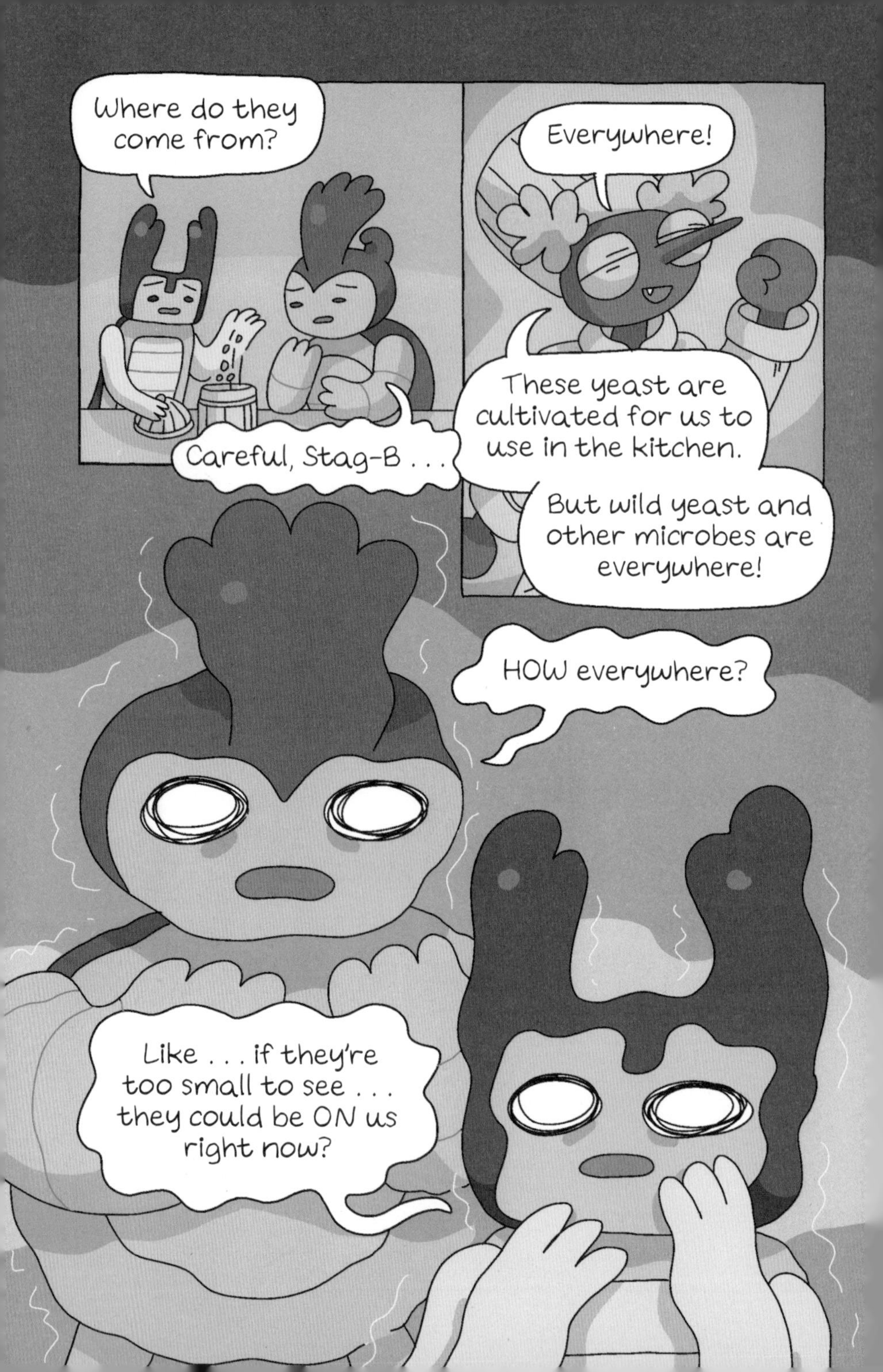
Where do they come from?
Everywhere!
Careful, Stag-B . . .
These yeast are cultivated for us to use in the kitchen.
But wild yeast and other microbes are everywhere!
HOW everywhere?
Like . . . if they're too small to see . . . they could be ON us right now?

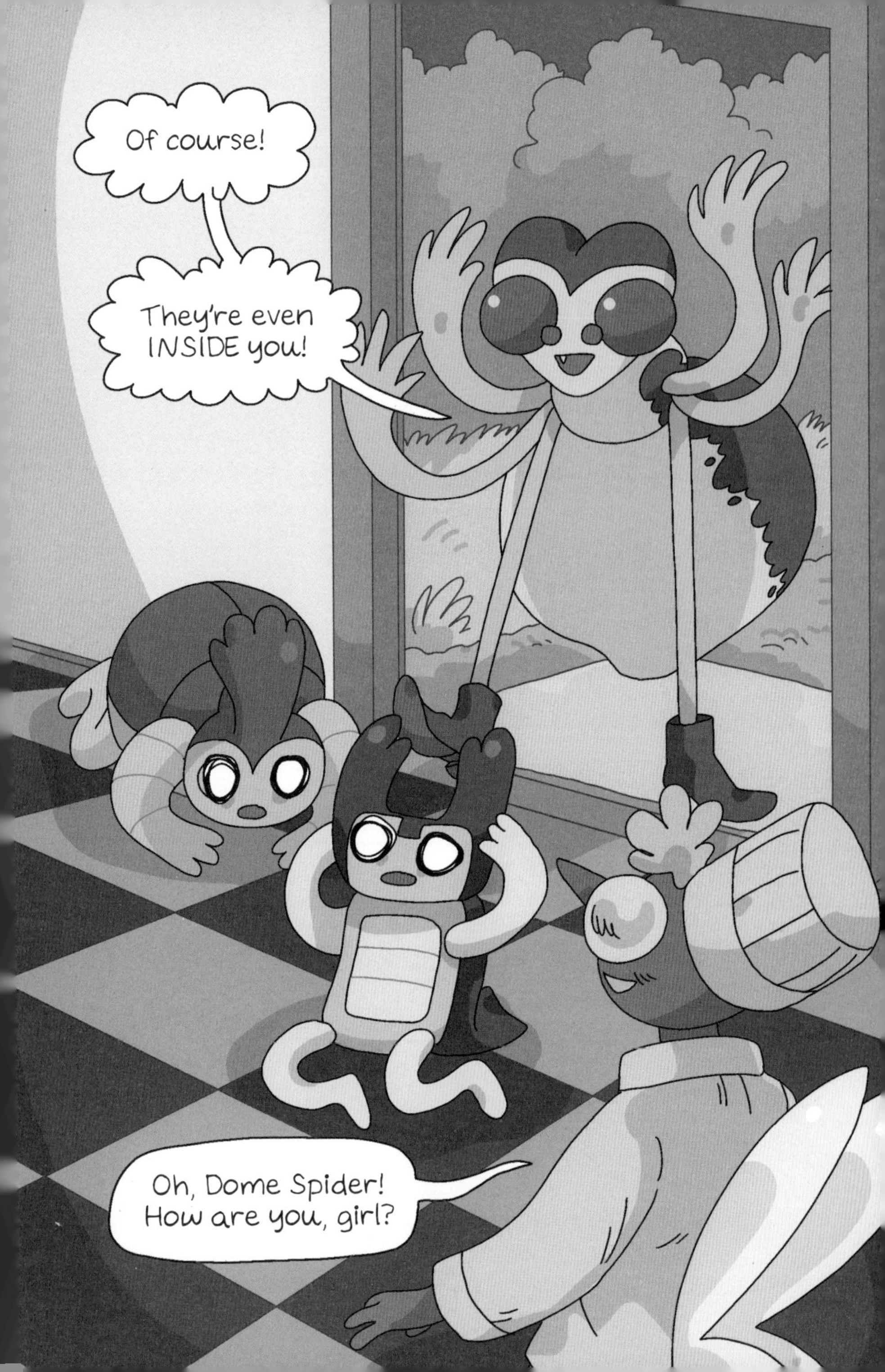
Of course!
They're even INSIDE you!
Oh, Dome Spider! How are you, girl?

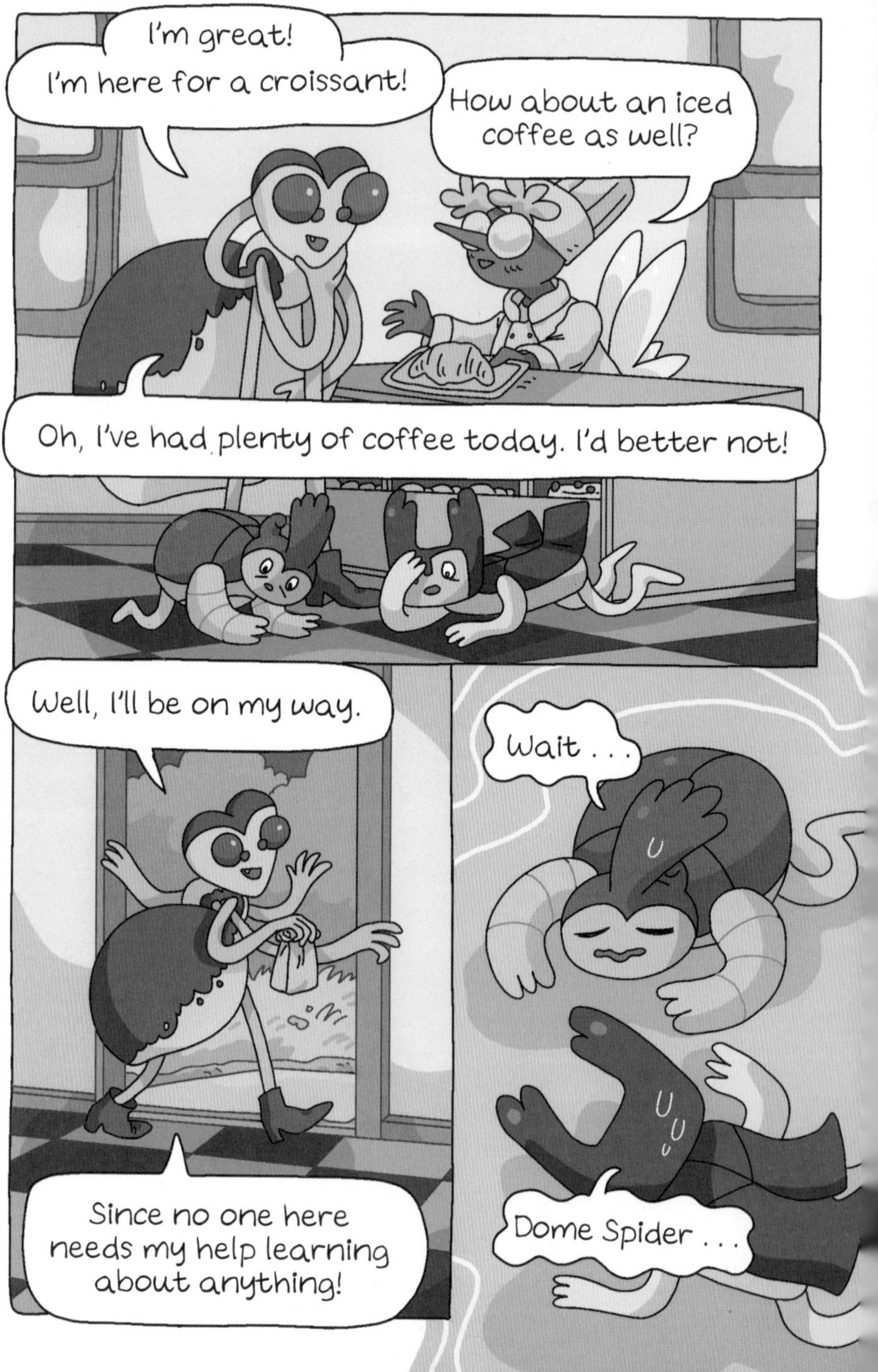
I'm great!
I'm here for a croissant!
How about an iced coffee as well?
Oh, I've had plenty of coffee today. I'd better not!
Well, I'll be on my way.
Since no one here needs my help learning about anything!
Wait . . .
Dome Spider . . .

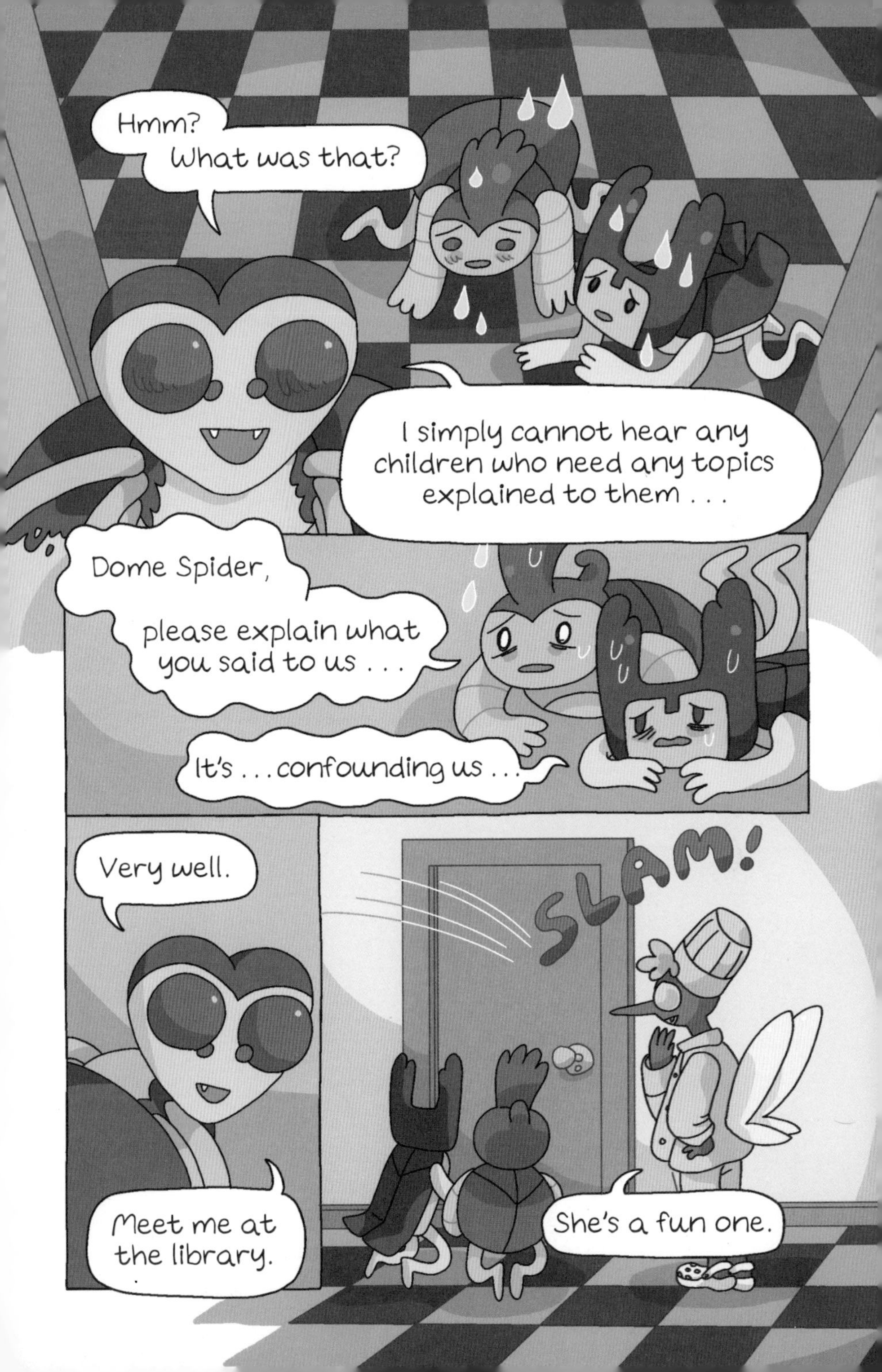

Hmm? What was that?
I simply cannot hear any children who need any topics explained to them . . .
Dome Spider,
please explain what you said to us . . .
It's . . . confounding us . . .
Very well.
Meet me at the library.
SLAM!
She's a fun one.

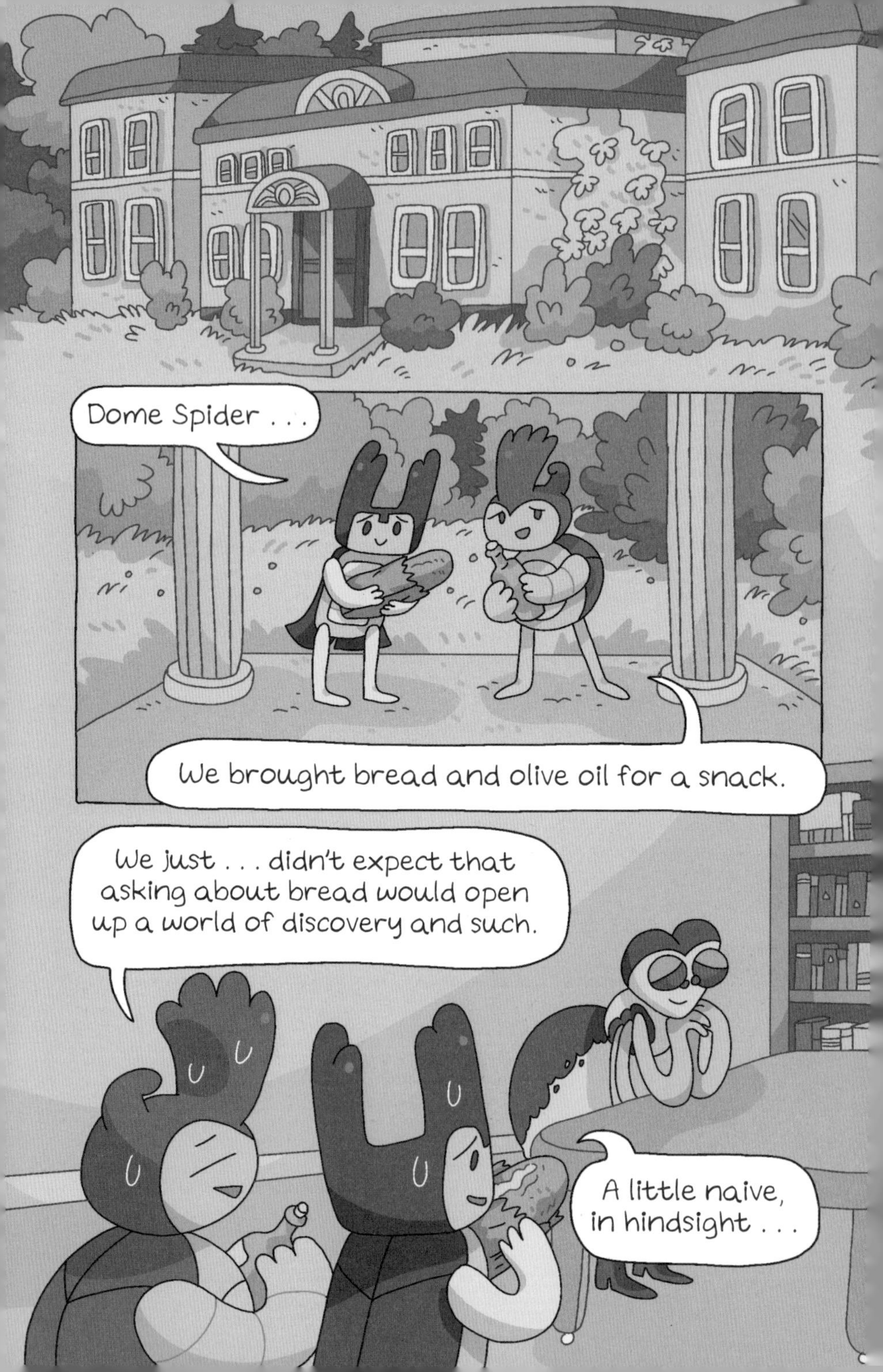
Dome Spider . . .
We brought bread and olive oil for a snack.
We just . . . didn't expect that asking about bread would open up a world of discovery and such.
A little naive, in hindsight . . .

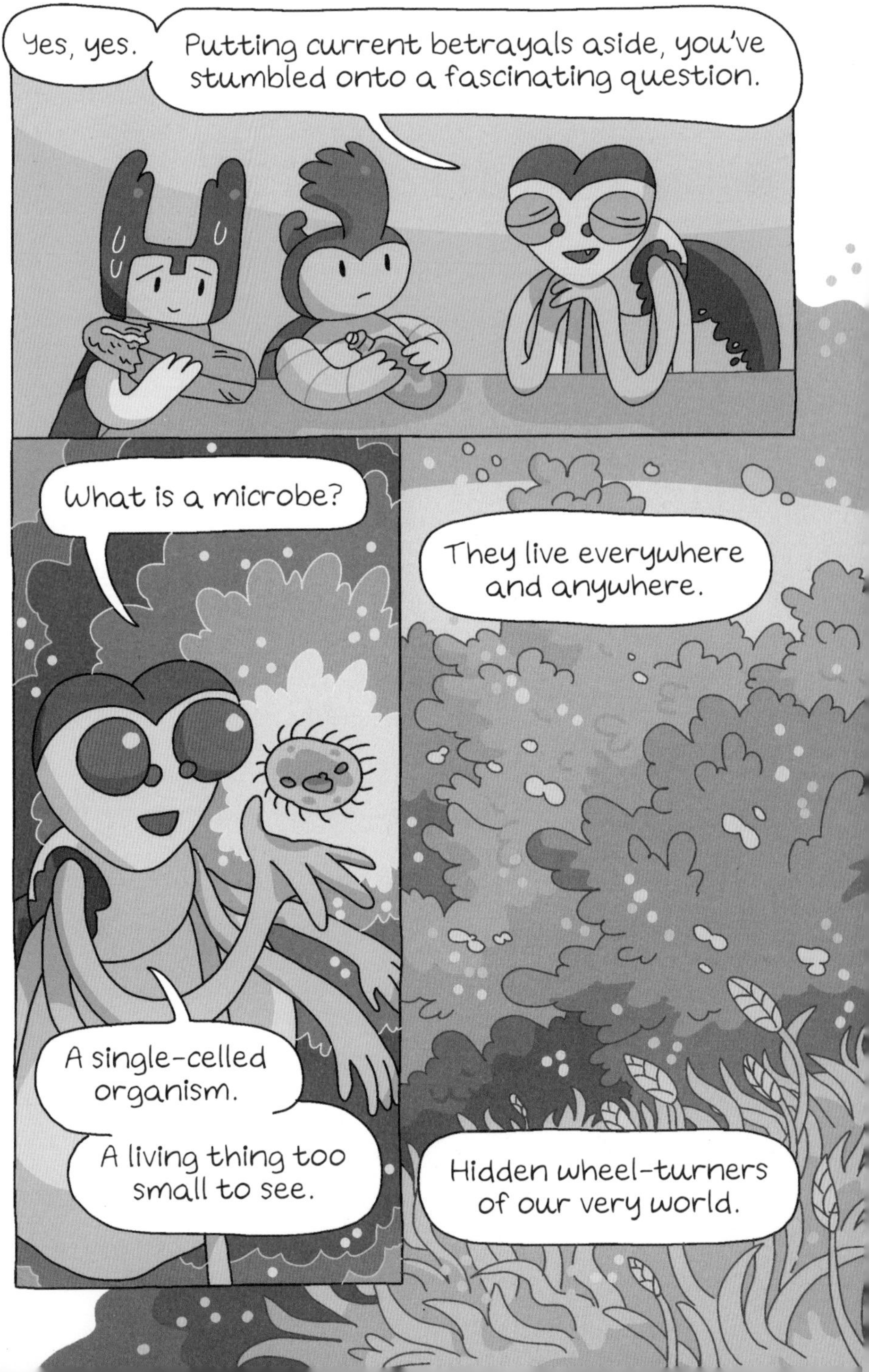
Yes, yes.
Putting current betrayals aside, you've stumbled onto a fascinating question.
What is a microbe?
A single-celled organism.
A living thing too small to see.
They live everywhere and anywhere.
Hidden wheel-turners of our very world.

Why do you wash your hands before you eat?
Because adults say so.
Yes, but WHY?
Uh . . . so you don't get in trouble?
How does a cold travel from one Bug to another?
Um . . . it just does?

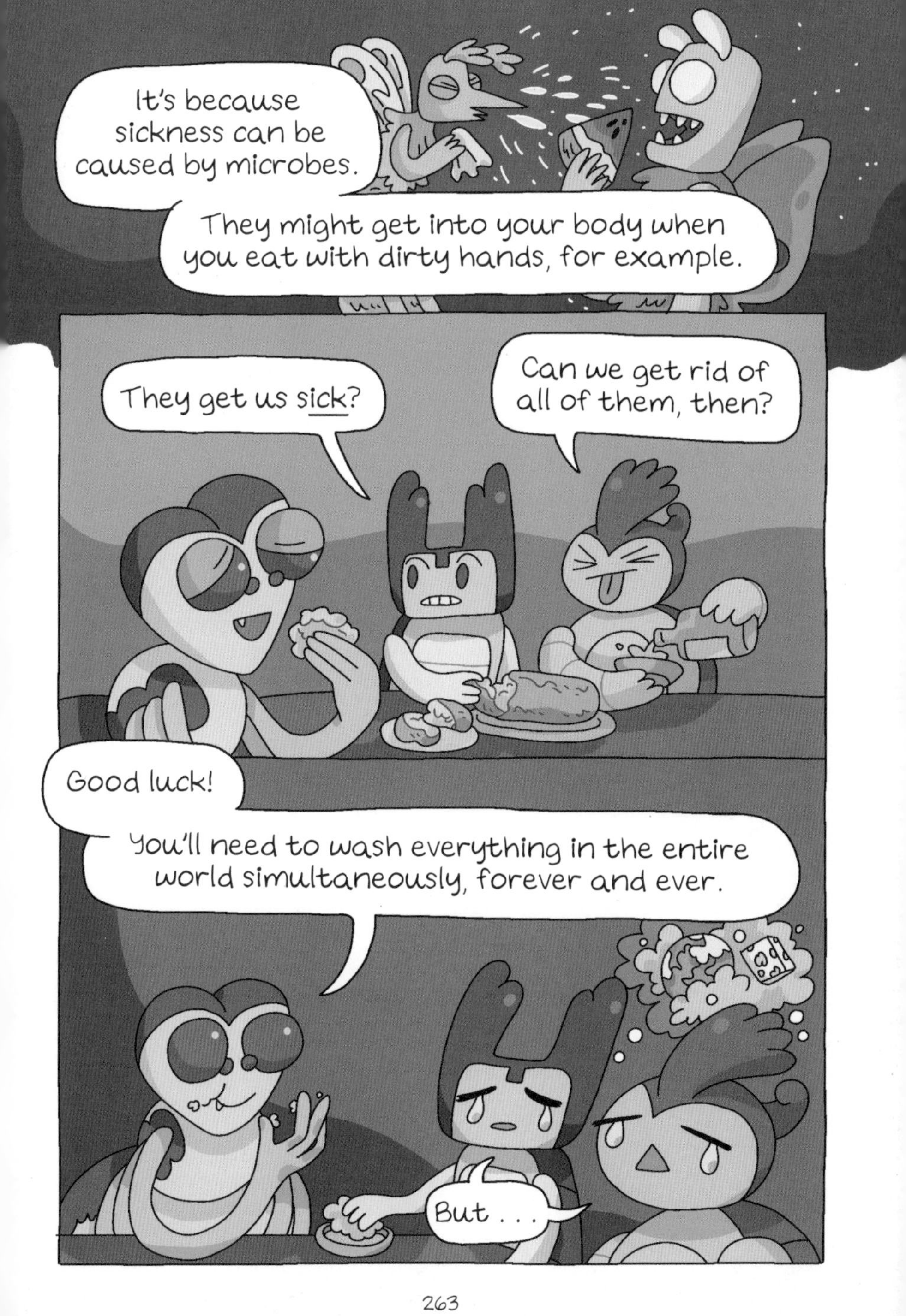
It's because sickness can be caused by microbes.
They might get into your body when you eat with dirty hands, for example.
They get us sick?
Can we get rid of all of them, then?
Good luck!
You'll need to wash everything in the entire world simultaneously, forever and ever.
But . . .

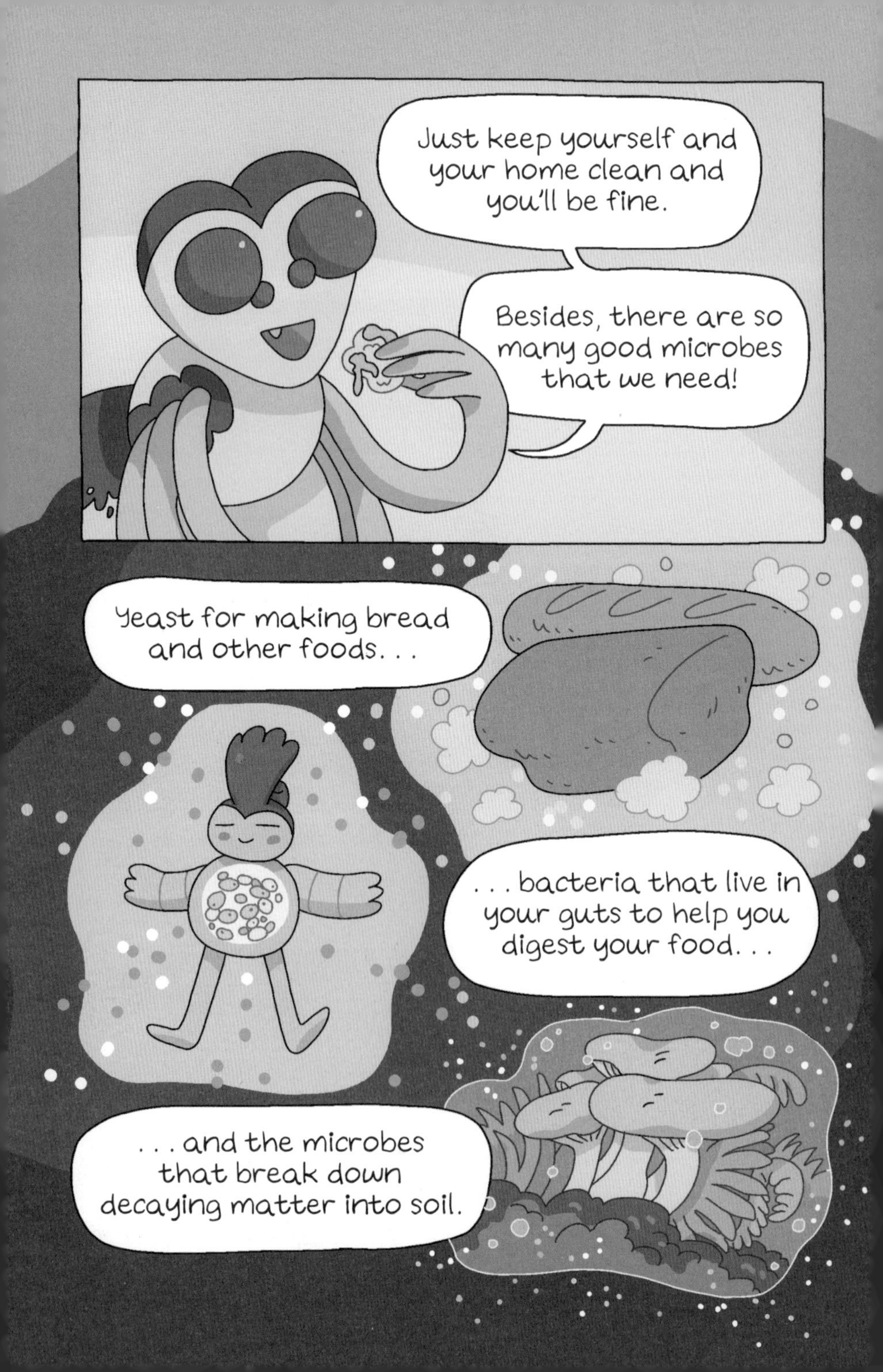
Just keep yourself and your home clean and you'll be fine.
Besides, there are so many good microbes that we need!
Yeast for making bread and other foods. . .
. . . bacteria that live in your guts to help you digest your food. . .
. . . and the microbes that break down decaying matter into soil.

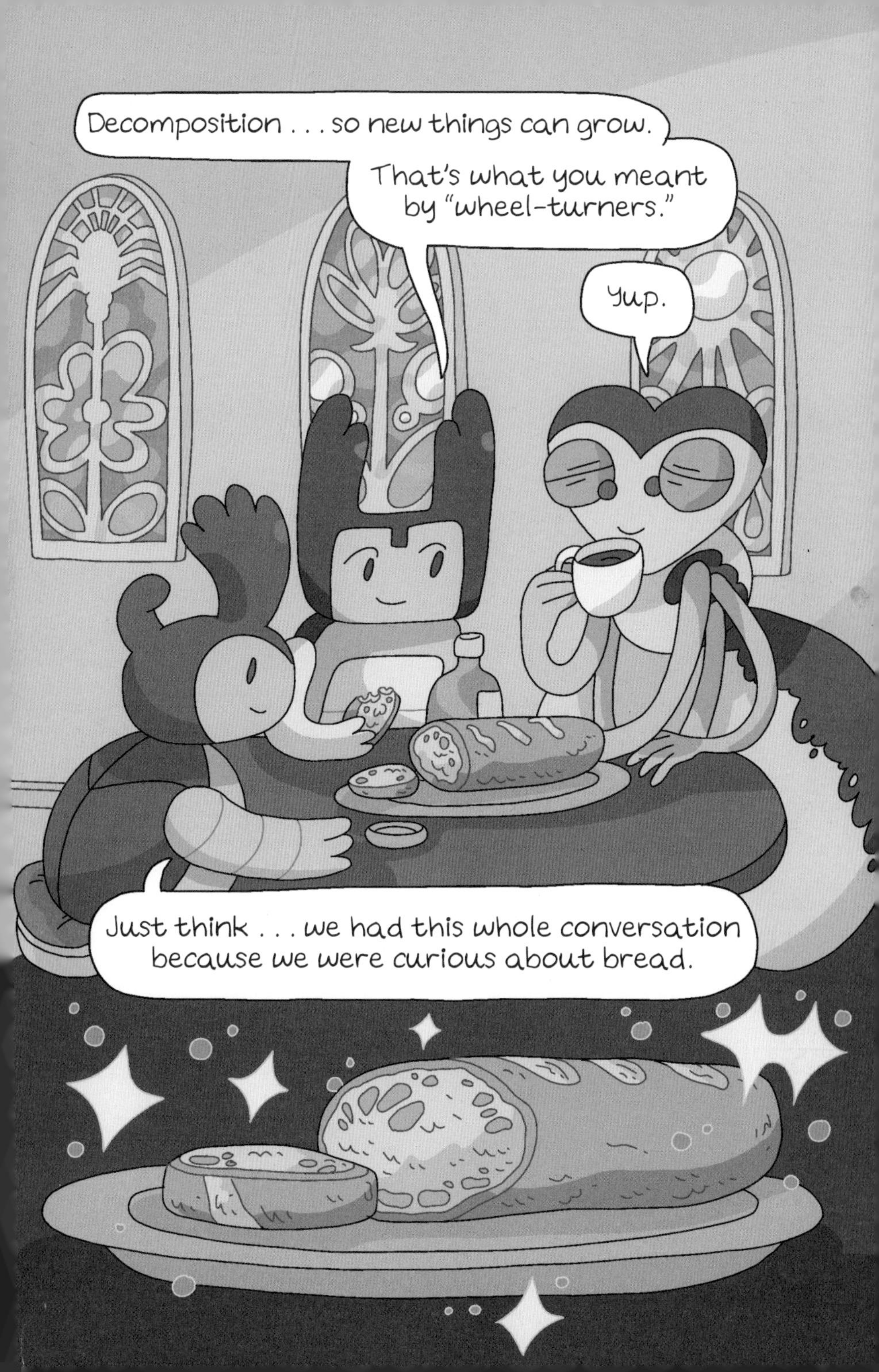
Decomposition . . . so new things can grow.
That's what you meant by "wheel-turners."
Yup.
Just think . . . we had this whole conversation because we were curious about bread.

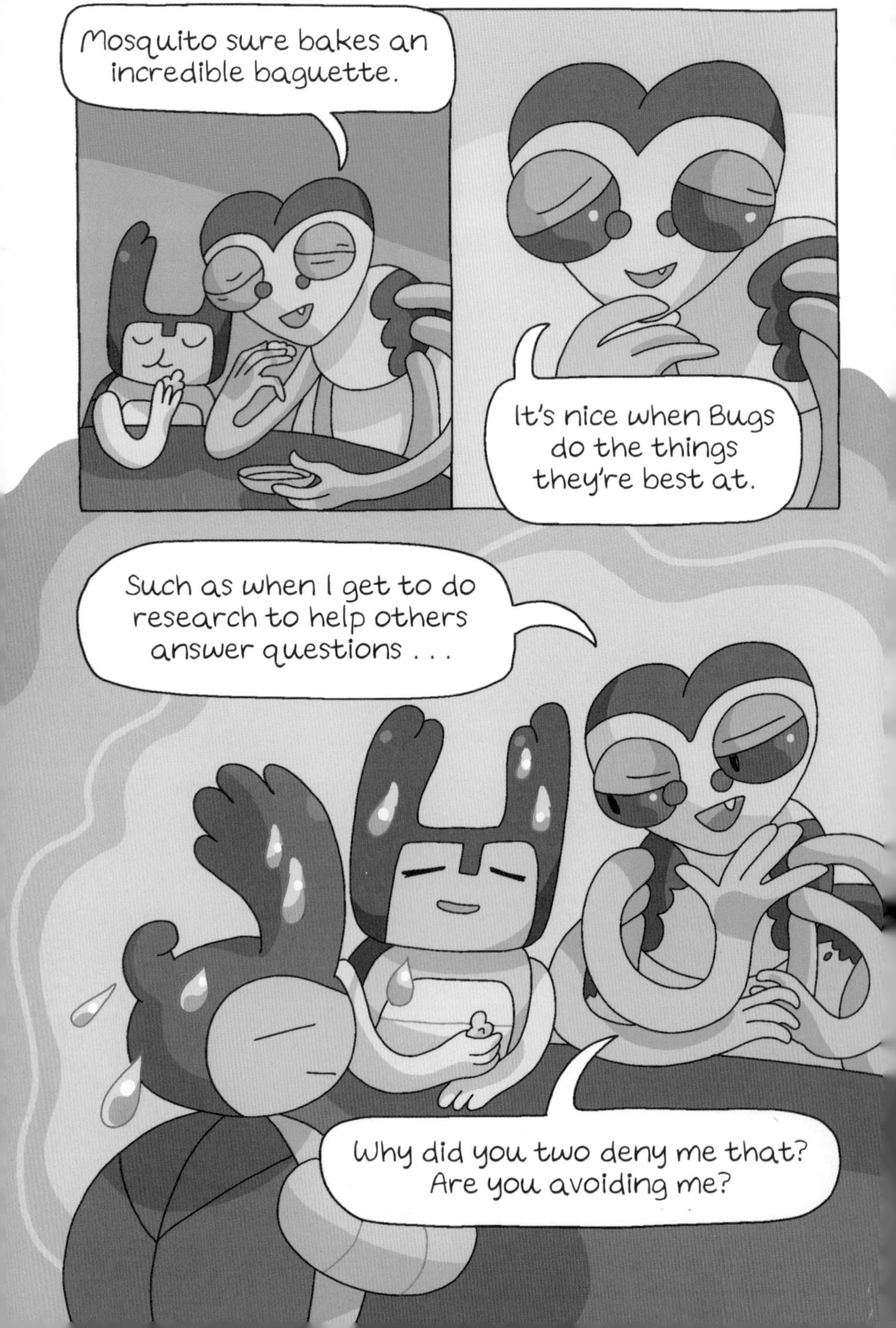
Mosquito sure bakes an incredible baguette.
It's nice when Bugs do the things they're best at.
Such as when I get to do research to help others answer questions . . .
Why did you two deny me that? Are you avoiding me?

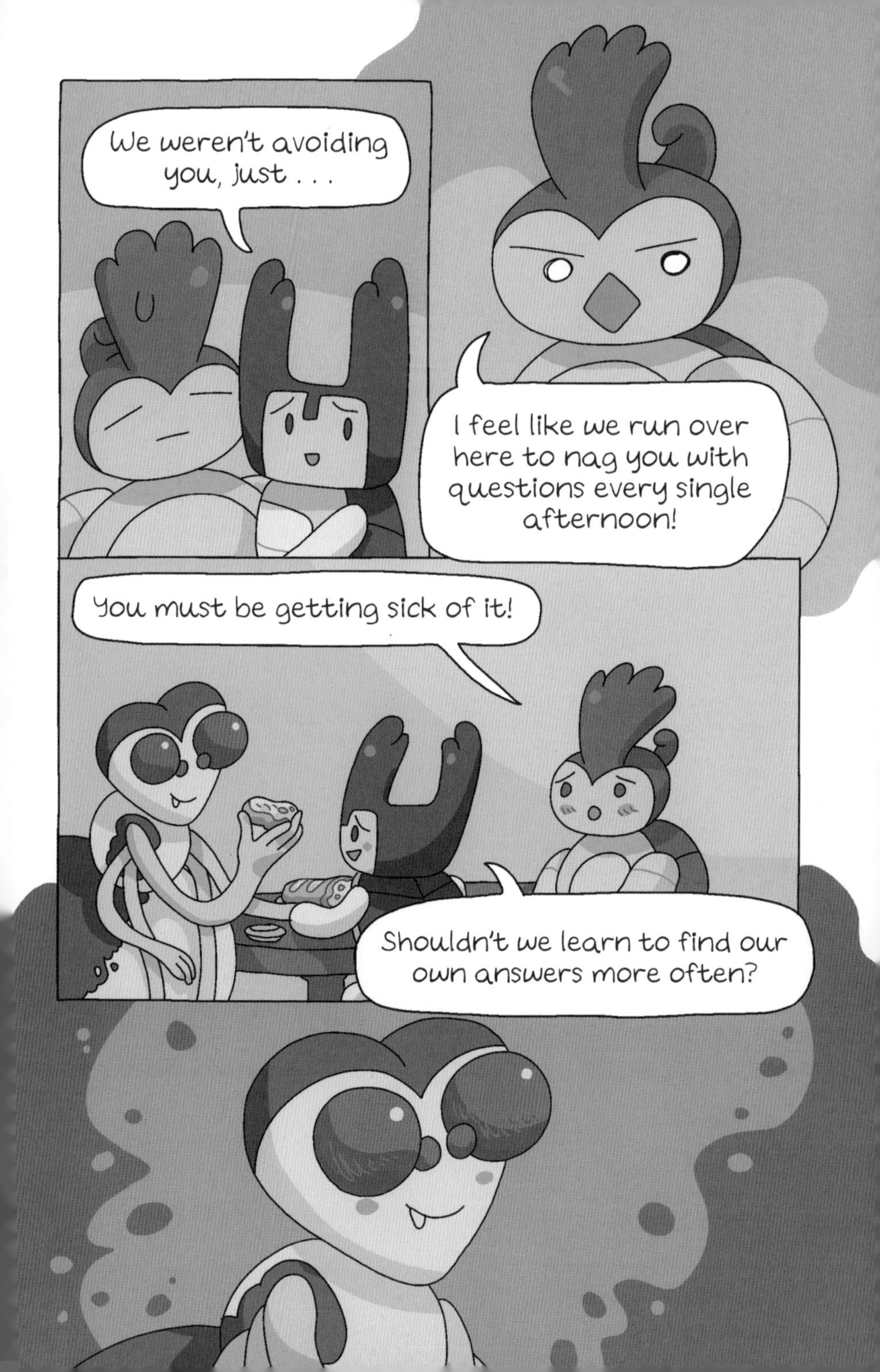
We weren't avoiding you, just . . .
I feel like we run over here to nag you with questions every single afternoon!
You must be getting sick of it!
Shouldn't we learn to find our own answers more often?

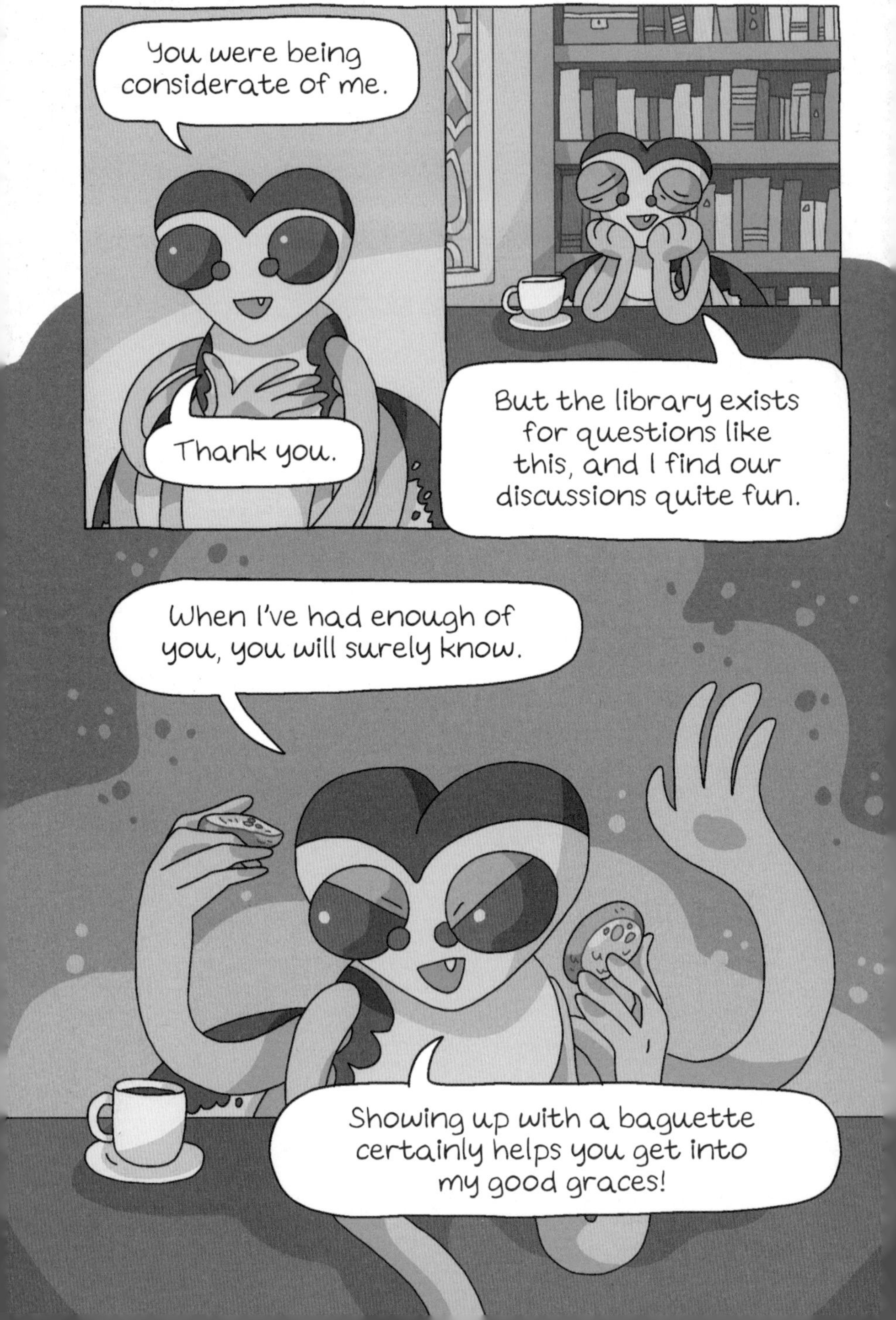
You were being considerate of me.
Thank you.
But the library exists for questions like this, and I find our discussions quite fun.
When I've had enough of you, you will surely know.
Showing up with a baguette certainly helps you get into my good graces!

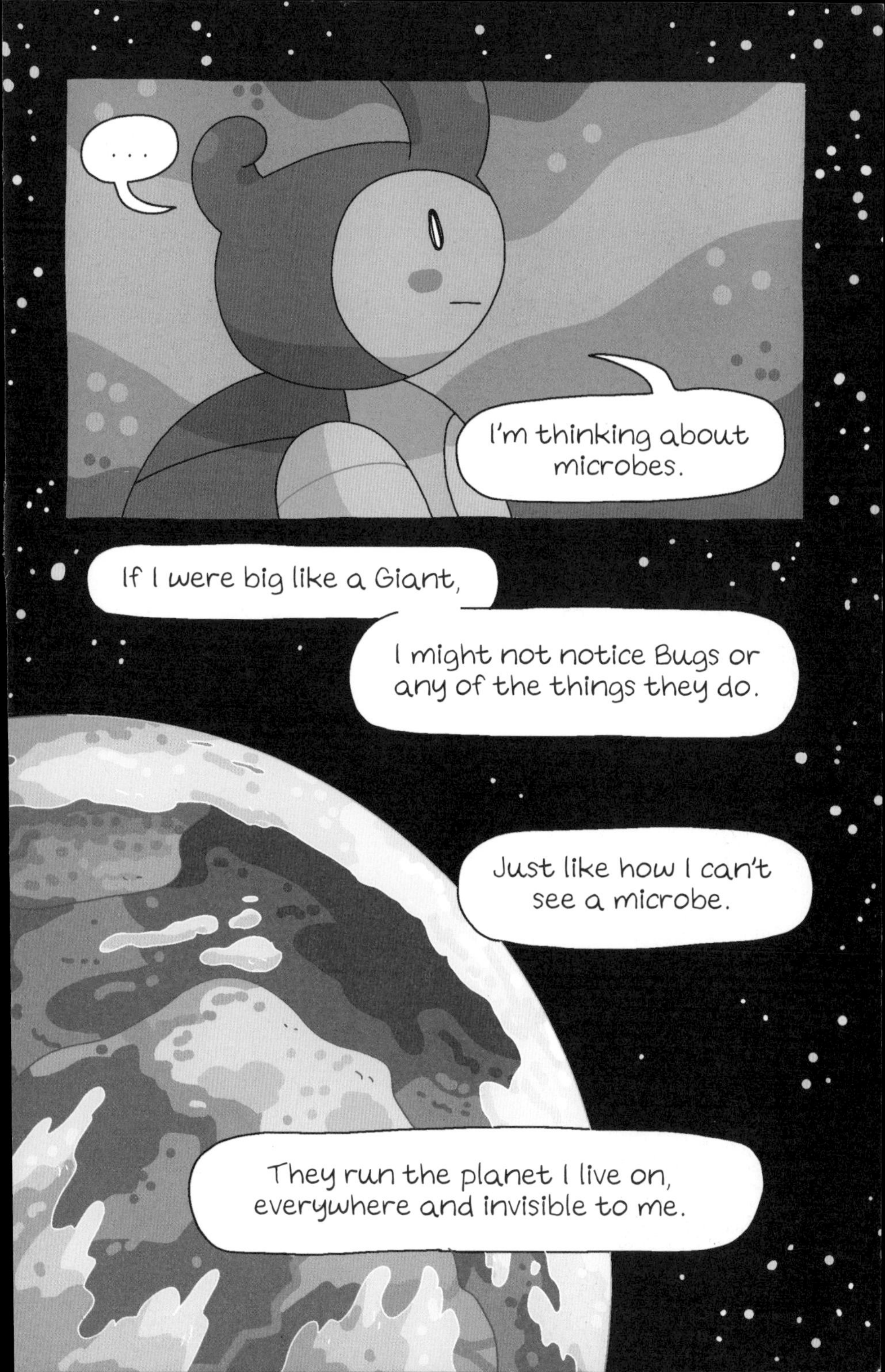
. . .
I'm thinking about microbes.
If I were big like a Giant,
I might not notice Bugs or any of the things they do.
Just like how I can't see a microbe.
They run the planet I live on, everywhere and invisible to me.

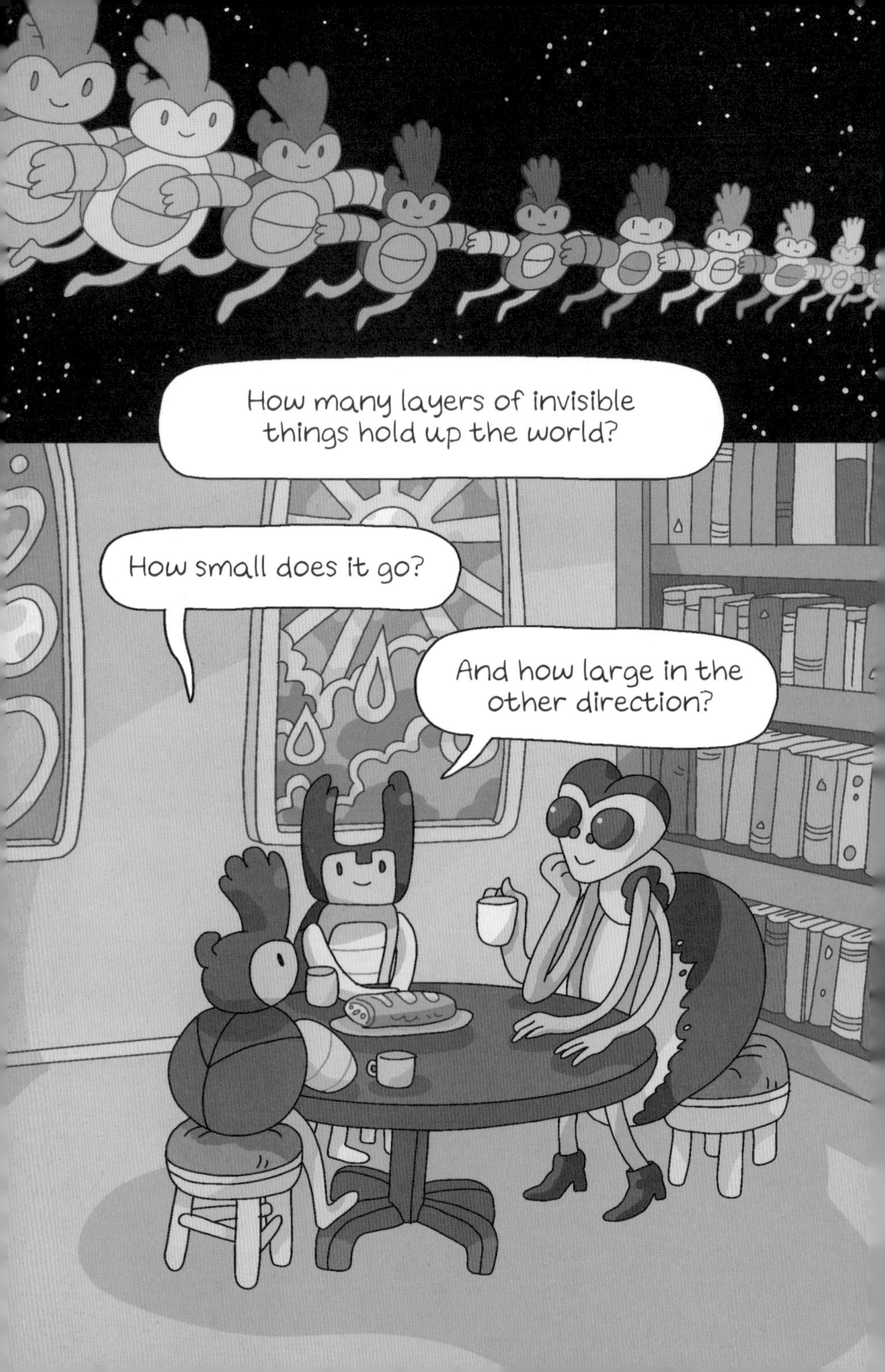
How many layers of invisible things hold up the world?
How small does it go?
And how large in the other direction?

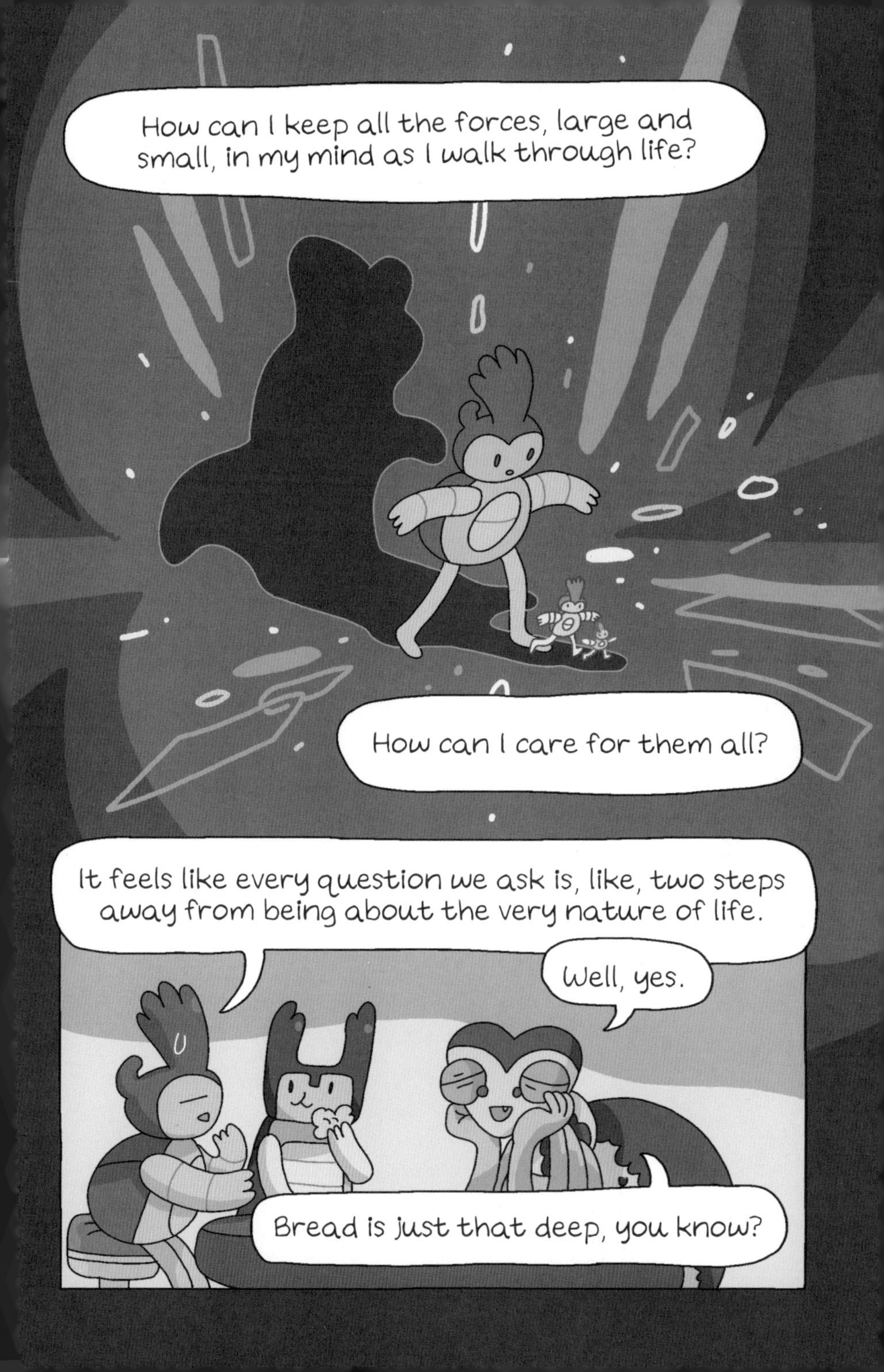
How can I keep all the forces, large and small, in my mind as I walk through life?
How can I care for them all?
It feels like every question we ask is, like, two steps away from being about the very nature of life.
Well, yes.
Bread is just that deep, you know?

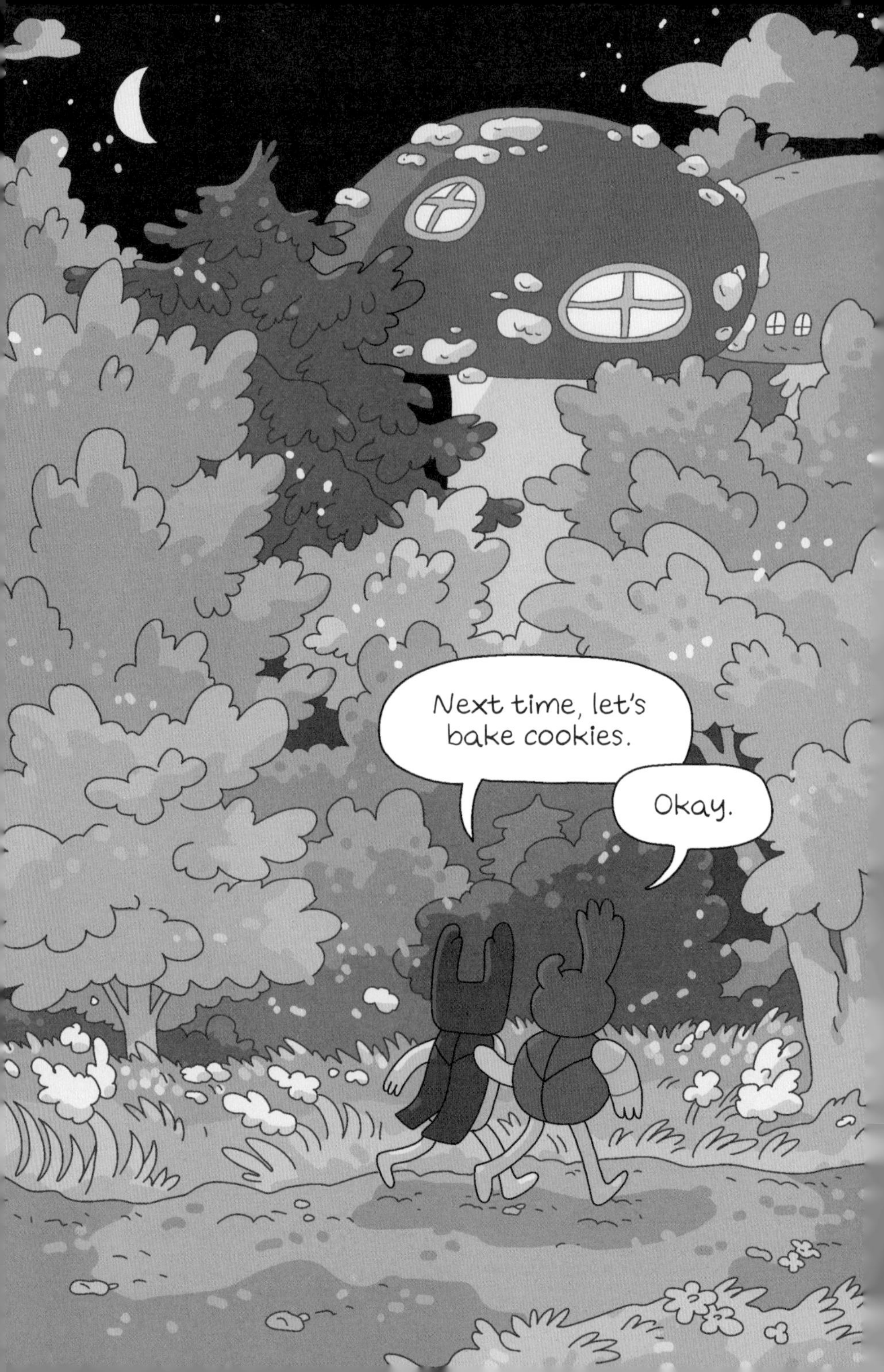
Next time, let's bake cookies.
Okay.

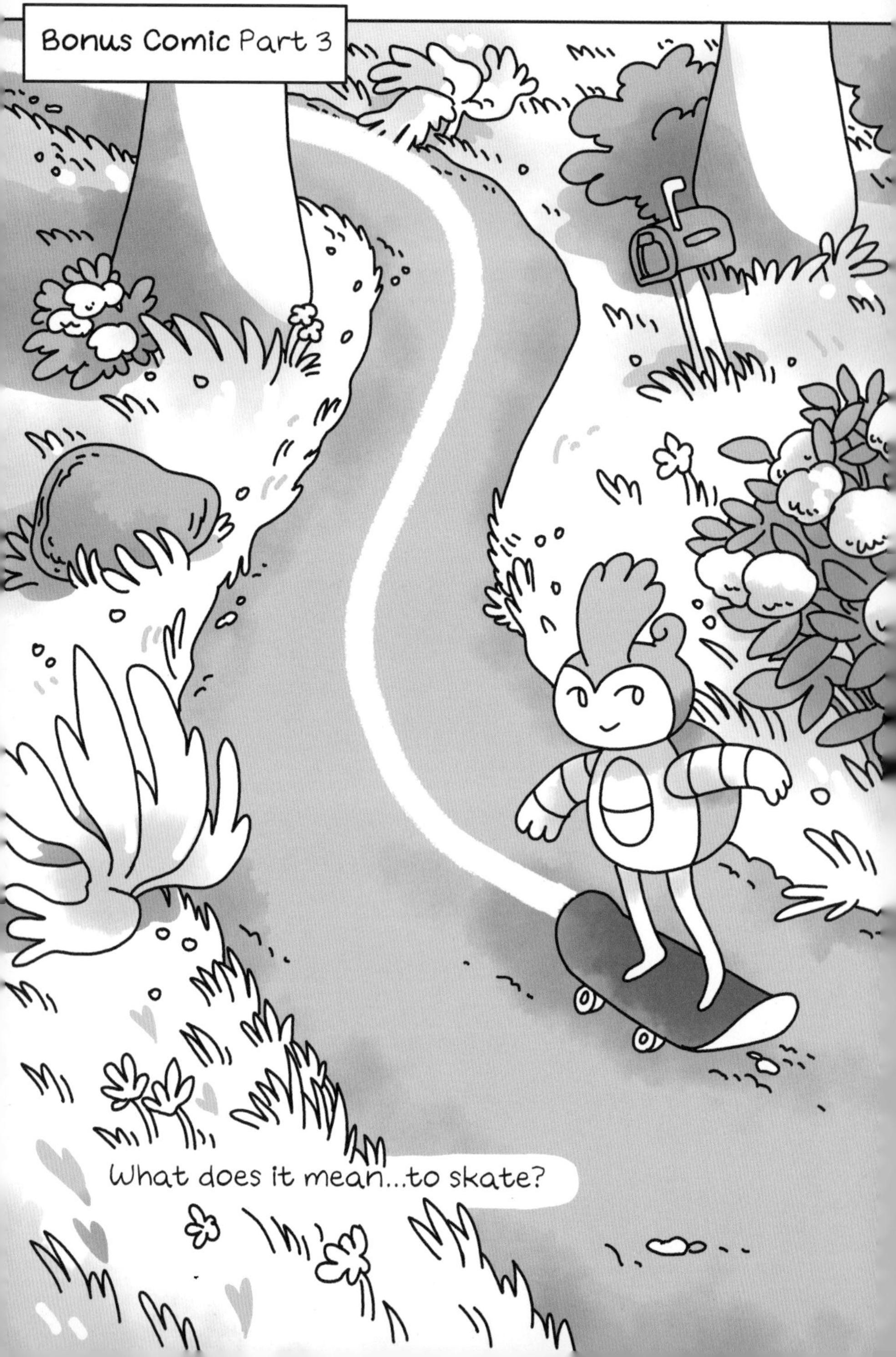
Bonus Comic Part 3
What does it mean...to skate?

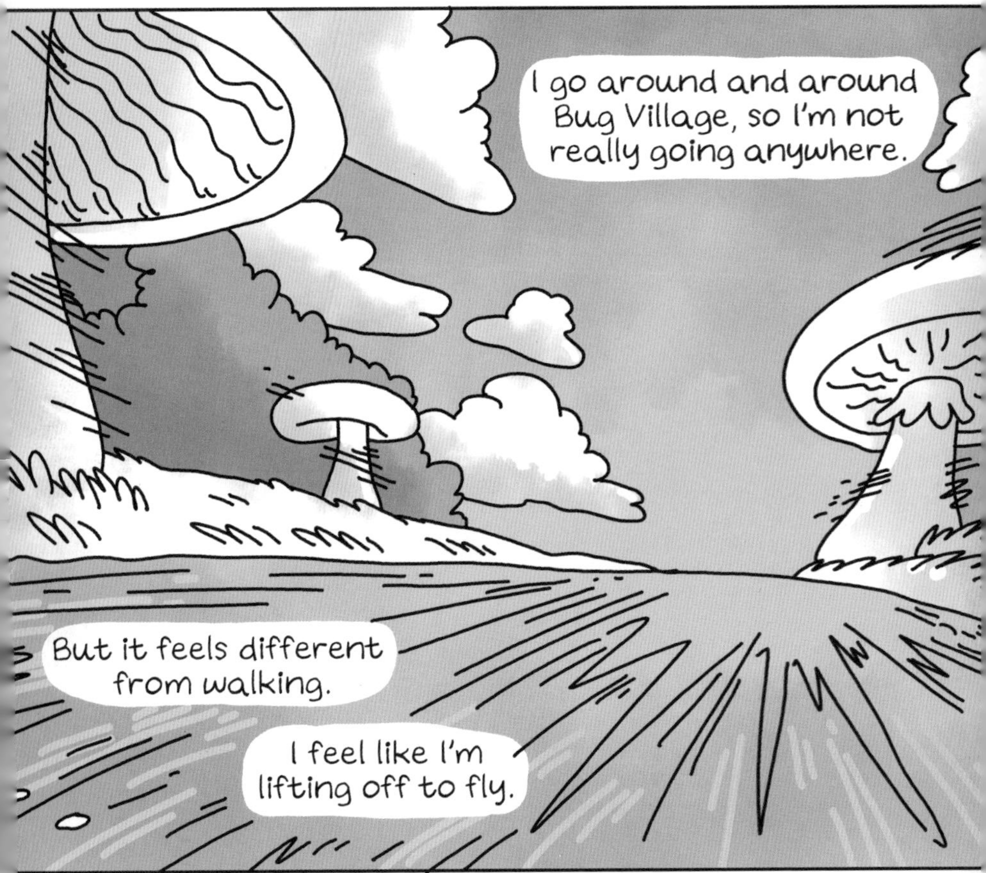
I go around and around Bug Village, so I'm not really going anywhere.
But it feels different from walking.
I feel like I'm lifting off to fly.

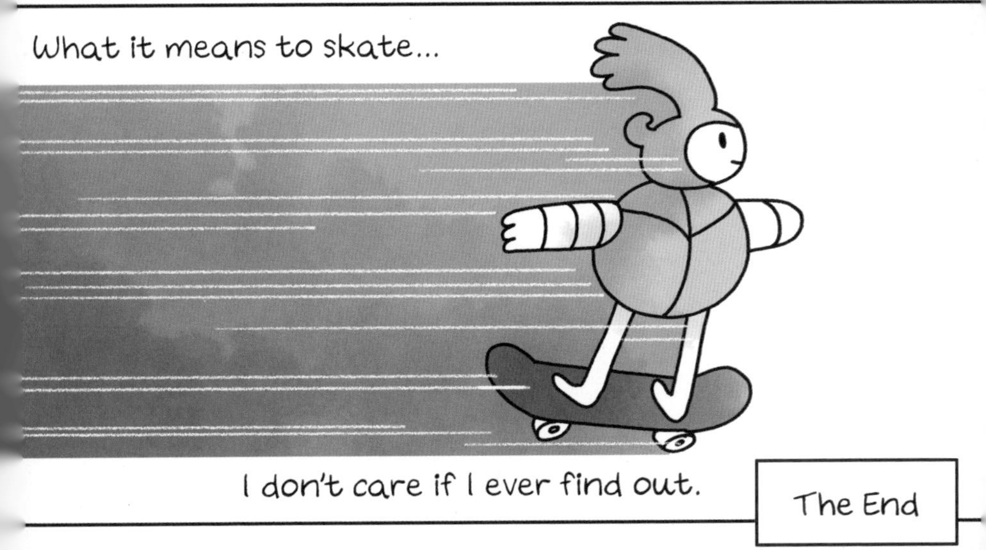
What it means to skate...
I don't care if I ever find out.
The End

Extra Art!

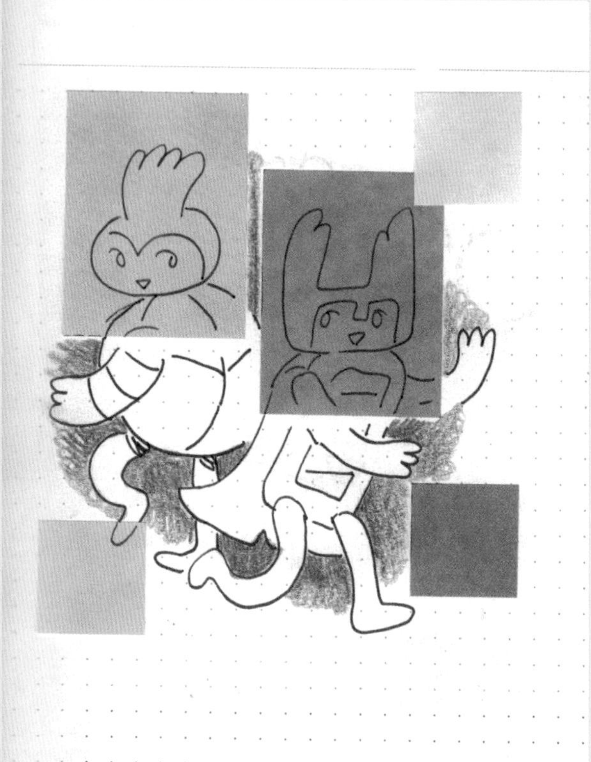

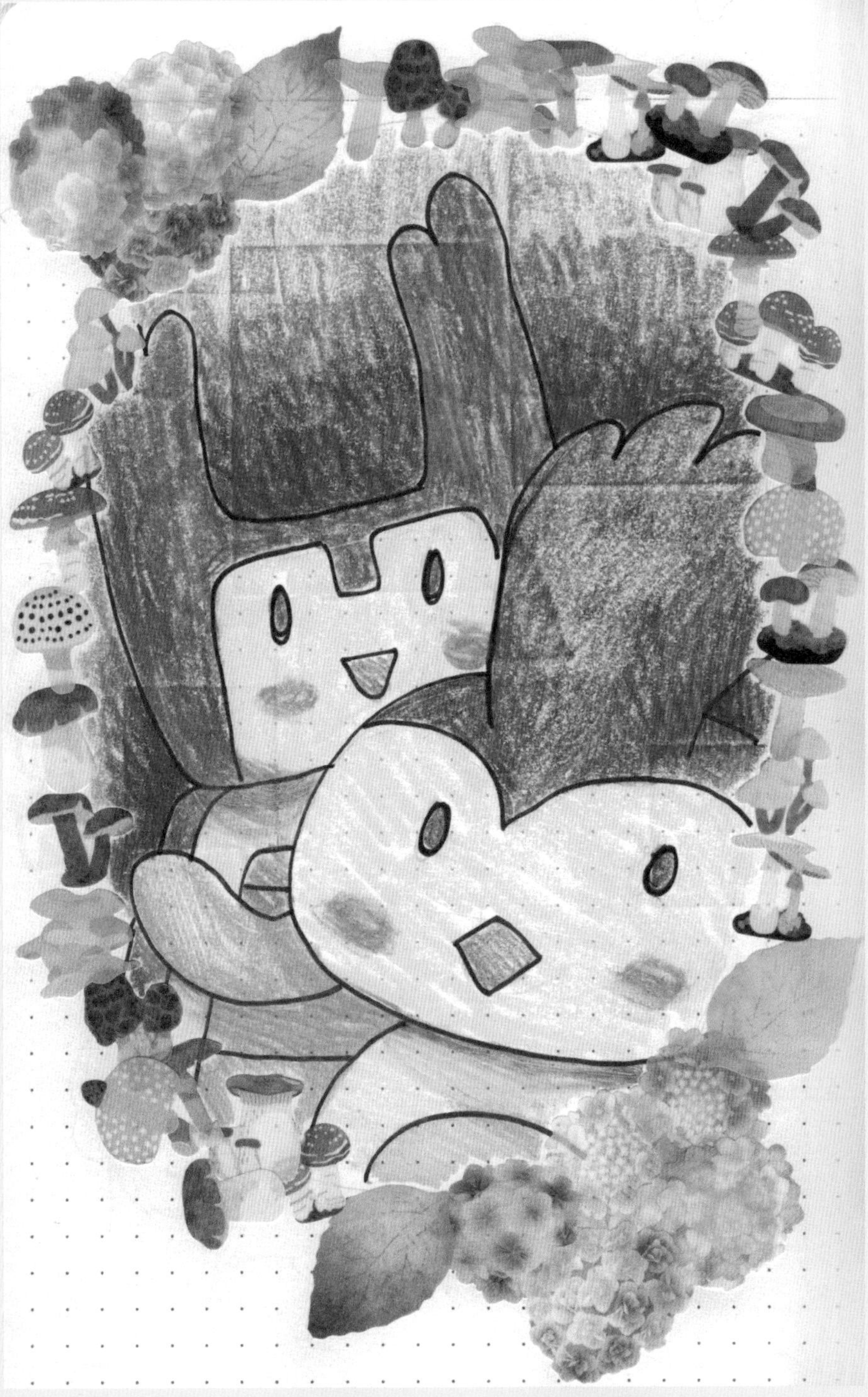

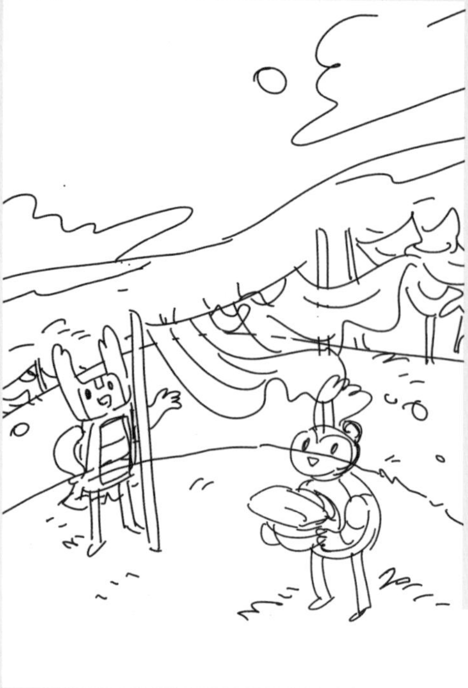

Early cover Sketches

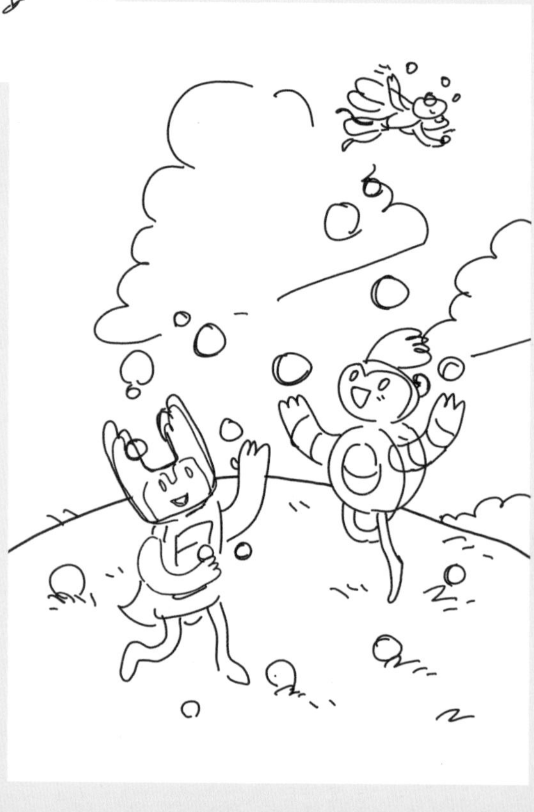

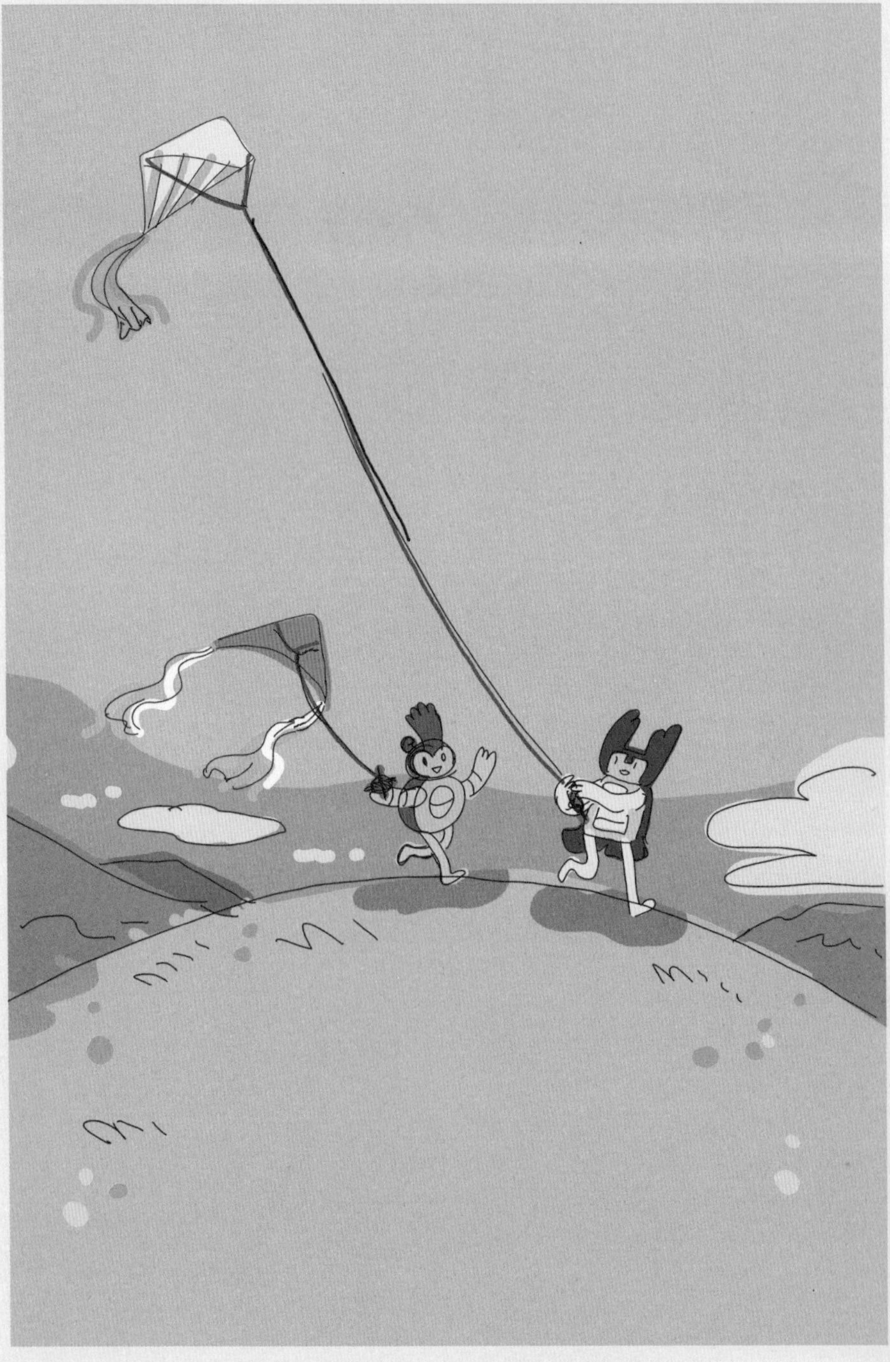

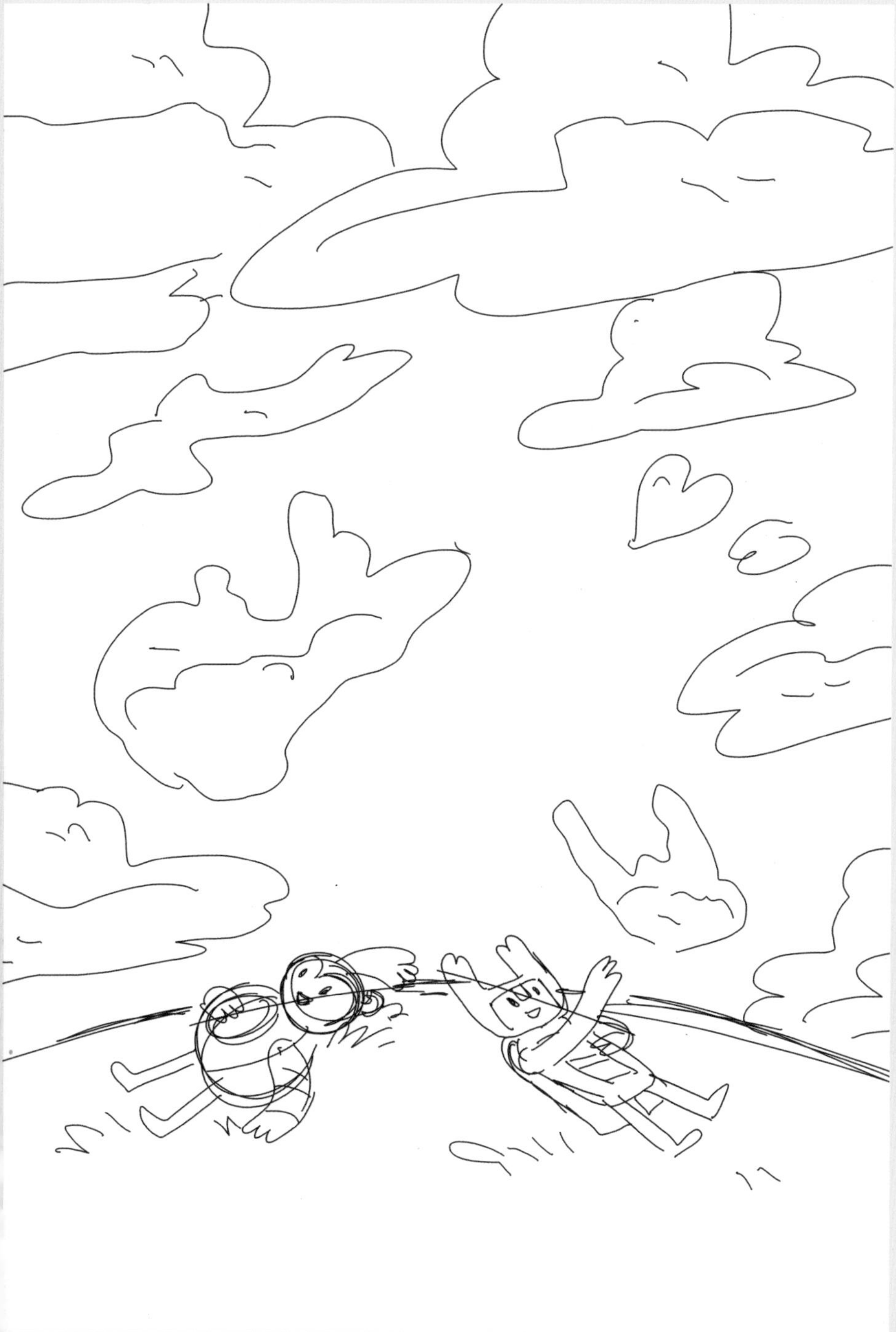

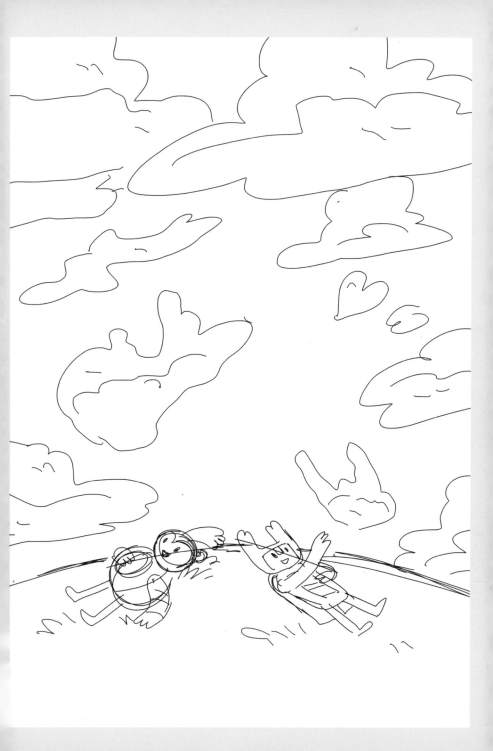

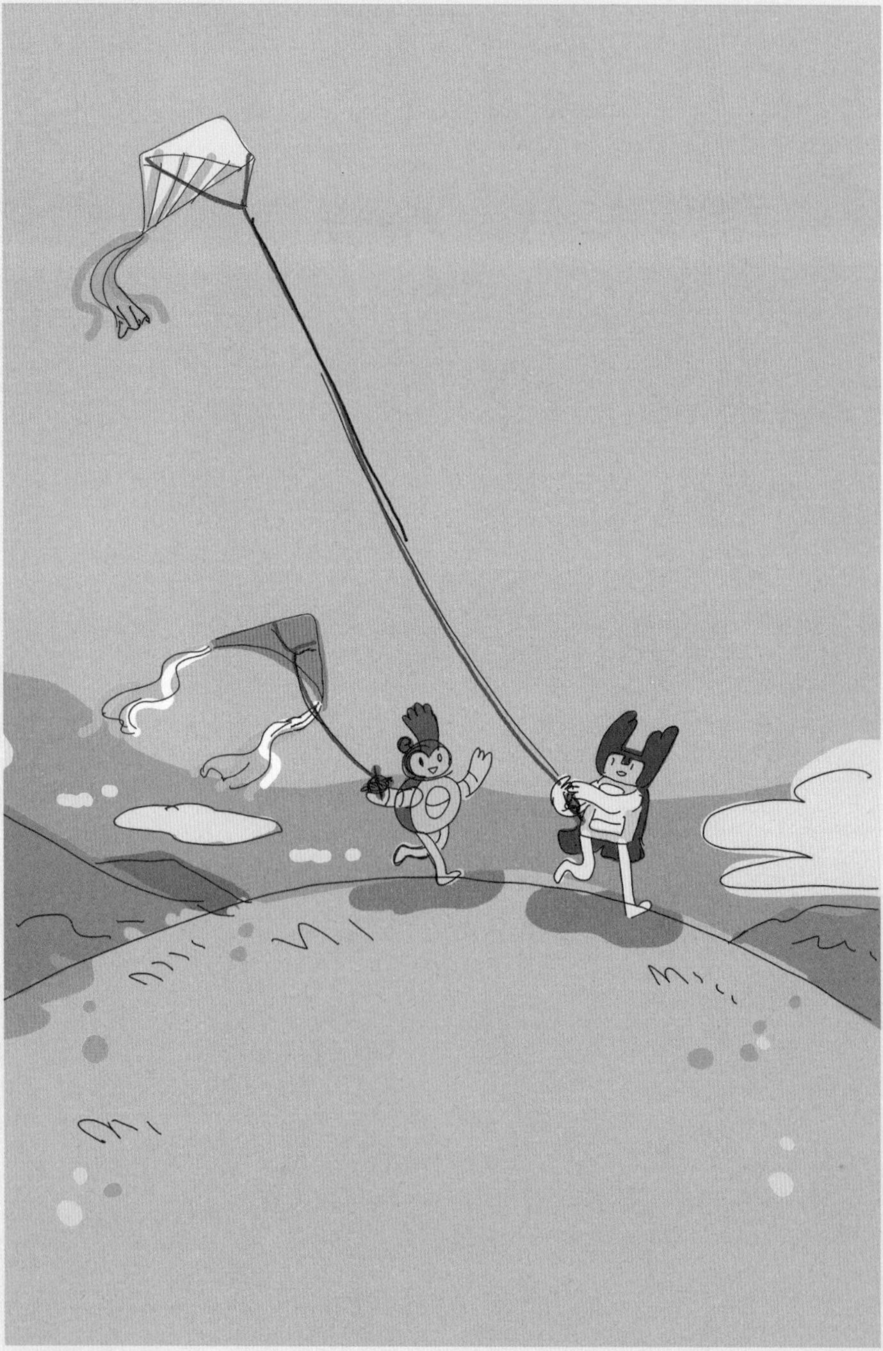

Laura Knetzger

grew up in Washington State, near Seattle. She wanted to be a cartoonist since she was eleven years old. She went to art college in New York City, and now she lives in Seattle.

She has a gray tuxedo cat named Chilly. Cats are definitely Laura's favorite animal.

Laura got the idea to make Bug Boys as she was watching a documentary about bug collecting called Beetle Queen Conquers Tokyo. She drew two cute cartoon bugs as she was watching the movie, then tried to make up stories about them.

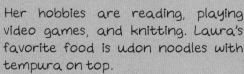

Her hobbies are reading, playing video games, and knitting. Laura's favorite food is udon noodles with tempura on top.